# MONUMENTS OF GRASS

~

## BOOK TWO – THE FUR POST

# MONUMENTS OF GRASS

*An American Romance*

~

## BOOK TWO – THE FUR POST

1760

* * *

# BRENDAN FRAIN

Monuments of Grass: The Fur Post
2$^{nd}$ (revised) edition © Brendan Frain 2025
Originally published in 2022 as 'Buffalo Rock'



ISBN: 978-1-7640051-1-1 (paperback)
ISBN: 978-1-7640051-8-0 (ebook)

Book design and typesetting by Typography Studio

Published by Brendan Frain

A catalogue record for this
book is available from the
National Library of Australia

*For Sat, in all her loveliness*

# *Introduction*

**18**TH CENTURY AMERICA WAS marked by two significant conflicts that profoundly reshaped the continent politically and militarily. The first of these conflicts broke out in 1754 when tensions between the major European powers culminated in the Seven Years War. The North American theatre of the global conflict is known as the French-Indian War (1754–1763). The war pitted the English colonies and their Native American allies against the French colonies and their allies.

After multiple early setbacks, the British forces gained the upper hand. A series of victories saw them capture several French forts culminating in victory on the Plains of Abraham in 1759. This victory secured Quebec and led to the capitulation of the French forces. The war ended with the Treaty of Paris in 1763.

Under the terms of the treaty, France ceded Quebec and the lands lying east of the Mississippi to Great Britain. (See map one, following). It ceded Louisiana to Spain in compensation for Spain's loss of Florida to the British. The war resulted in the expulsion of France as a colonial power in North America.

As has occurred often throughout history, the embers of one conflict ignited the sparks of another. In 1776, just over a decade on from the Treaty of Paris, the North American Colonies declared their independence from England. The resolution was prompted by growing popular resentment at British taxes and restraints on trade—in turn prompted by Great Britain's determination to recoup some of the massive financial expenditure incurred in the war against France. A contributory cause was unhappiness at the Royal Proclamation of 1763 which prohibited colonists from settling in the newly won French territories west of the Appalachian Mountains.

Following numerous battles and setbacks for both sides, the Americans under George Washington won a decisive victory at the battle of Yorktown (1781). The victory resulted in the surrender of the British forces under the command of General Cornwallis. In the 1783 Treaty of Paris Great Britain formally recognised its former colonies as the new and independent nation of the United States of America. (The 13 Colonies became states in 1776 upon agreeing to the Declaration of Independence.)

As a result of the war, Great Britain ceded much of its territory to the United States, including the land west of the Appalachian Mountains (see map two, following). The acquisition virtually doubled the size of the nascent United States which expanded from the Atlantic Ocean to the Mississippi River.

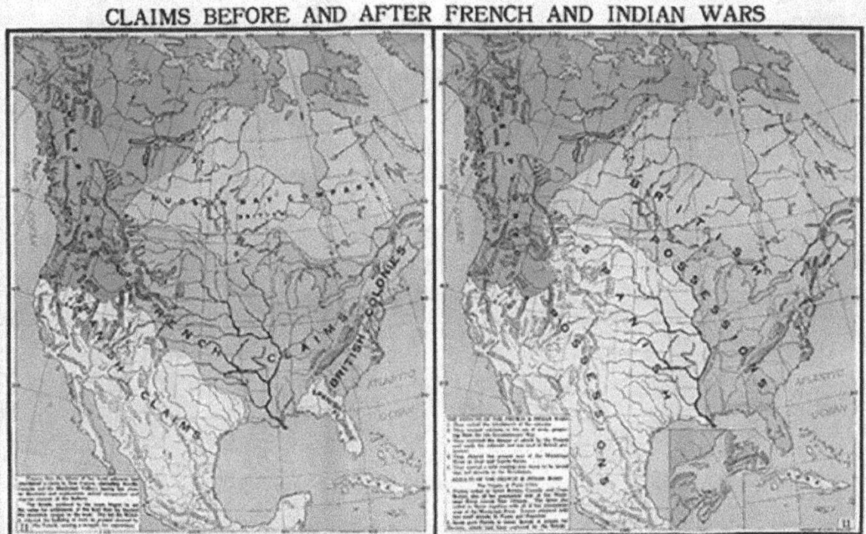


Map 1: North America before and after the French-Indian War (Library of Congress).

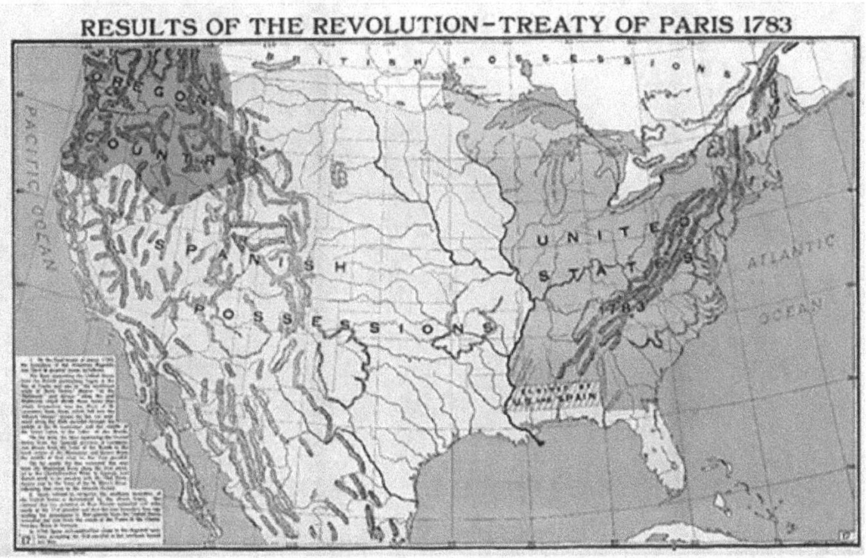


Map 2: North America following the Revolutionary War (Library of Congress).

# Contents

## T H E   F U R   P O S T

# THE FUR POST

*Thou shalt not make unto thee any graven image,*
*or any likeness of any thing that is in heaven above,*
*or that is in the earth beneath*

—EXODUS 20:4

## An Ocean of Grass

D OUBLY BURDENED—HIS SENSE OF loss magnified by the empty, wind-swept vastness—Boundless continued on through the undulating, mutable swells, uncertain of purpose or direction. The Missouri flowed through the wooded bluffs in a north-westerly direction, and he followed aimlessly along its course. He rested as the impulse took him, watered the horse and mule as they laboured in the heat, and made camp for the night when fatigued.

Three days after burying his companion, he forded a slow- moving creek, riding carelessly into the stream, and only remembering to look back for the mule once he had reached the other side.

Day after day, the landscape continued the same—the grasslands rolling in wind-blown waves to the horizon and seemingly devoid of life. As the mood took him, he abandoned the river to inspect the hinterland, scouring the slopes for signs of human habitation. But each scout revealed the same vista of cloud-checked uplands and overarching sky. 'I might be the last man on earth,' he despaired while stopped on a ridge to survey the distance. In every direction, he saw the same endless vistas of wind-tossed grass. He shivered, suddenly fearful of the rippling immensity. Cupping his hands to his mouth, he shouted a loud, 'Ahoy!'

He strained his ears but heard only the whinnying of the horse in reply, and the *whooshing* gusts of wind in the sere buffalo grass. Profoundly discouraged, he turned back to the Missouri, half persuaded that his journey had fetched him from the Maryland woods to the very edge of the world.

One afternoon, he made camp in a grove of trees and sat under a willow to rest. The day was hot and sultry and the copious mites a constant distraction. Towering white clouds drifted across the sky, and he worried about a thunderstorm as he sweated in the humid air. Prickly and disconsolate, he lit a fire, hoping the smoke would drive off the annoying mites. He ate a few mouthfuls of salted meat and sat with his back against the tree as the long afternoon began to wane. The warm air made him drowsy, and he dozed off, his head sinking to his chest.

When he awoke, it was dusk. He sat where he was, staring at the horizon. He felt he ought bestir himself to add wood to the smouldering fire, but a paralysing inertia held him in place. His ears registered the hoot of an owl, and he listened as the creatures of the night grass yelped and grunted in the darkness. The melancholy howl of a wolf floated on the air. The sharp, inquisitive face of the Patapsco preacher rose before him in the gloom. *'Perhaps, sir, you are in want of a calling?'*

'My calling is grass,' he mumbled. The night air was cool, a slight breeze blowing in from the west. Overhead, stars blazed through the branches. *'Rien, mon ami. Nothing.'* A fox barked and he drifted back into a fitful sleep.

He was woken by the whistling pops of a pair of foraging sage grouse. The sun was rising amidst a raft of pinkish cloud. He got to his feet, his limbs feeling stiff and heavy, and went to piss in the grass. Not fully awake, his attention was caught by a scurrying motion in the dark reeds. He stared at the spot, thinking he had disturbed a rabbit. Next moment, he glimpsed a small, squirrel-like creature as it darted through the stalks. A short time later, it appeared on a mound of earth where it stood upright on its hindquarters, head quivering as it surveyed its environs. A hawk screeched in the sky and the creature uttered a series of yips before van-ishing into a burrow.

Throughout the morning, he heard the creatures chirping and scurry-ing through the grass before the horse's hooves. *And they are aware of me,* he noted, as the inquisitive beasts popped up to observe his progress. As if playing a game, they waited until he was almost upon them before disap-pearing into one of the plentiful burrows dotting the grass. The burrows were so numerous that he climbed down and walked Buckshot, worried lest it step in one of the holes and break a leg. Prodigal followed in the bay's footsteps as if alert to the danger.

From that day onwards, the small darting creatures became a constant and abundant presence, their rustling movements in the reeds as pervasive as the wind itself.

His curiosity tweaked by the encounter, he grew cognisant of a constant and surprising aliveness in the tall prairie grass. Beetles, crickets, ants, spiders, and butterflies thrived amid the stalks—the insects providing sus-tenance for owls, grouse, meadowlarks, turkeys and magpies. He was mildly astonished to observe that the tiny owls lived in burrows in the ground, much like the prairie squirrel—as he came to name the latter. He shot one to taste its flesh but found the scant mouthfuls not worth the trouble.

Puzzled at the continuing absence of buffalo, he began to doubt the reports of their unparalleled abundance. The lack of any sign of Indians was another surprise, and he wondered if the rumours of cruel, bloodthirsty tribes inhabiting the plains were mere folk tales arising from a superstitious fear of the wind-haunted grasslands. 'Who knows but that any Indians might prove hospitable?' he told himself, pushing to the back of his mind the images of tortured and mutilated bodies lying back in the mountains.

One morning, he halted to observe movement in the distance. Using the spyglass, he picked out a herd of deer headed away from the river. Buoyed by the prospect of fresh venison, he tracked the deer through the grass, catching up with a group of does and fawns where they browsed on shoots along a creek. He stalked the herd by elbowing along a defile on his belly. When he was within forty yards, he brought down a fawn with a shot through the lungs.

As he roasted the ribs for supper, he became agitated by the presence of wolves howling and snarling in the gloom. Getting up, he added wood to the fire, and made certain that the horse and mule were securely tethered nearby. He slept close to the blazing fire, the pistol beneath his hand.

THE MISSOURI WAS HIS constant companion. A half-mile wide at this point, it flowed through the cloud-shadowed grasslands in a vast, unhindered stream. For long stretches, thick stands of timber lined its shores, the trees giving welcome relief from the relentless sun. At other times, the river was barely distinguishable amidst the long grass. The tantalising torment offered by the flowing water increased his suffering from the scorching heat. The oppressive air was made worse by the pestilential insects that sorely tried his temper and drove both horse and mule to distraction. Vexed to near madness, he lashed out at the swarming clouds. Chancing upon a bear, he shot the animal and liberally applied grease to his face and hands before rubbing some on the horse and mule. He continued at a slow walk while desperately hoping for a cool change in the weather. *I shall be basted ere I find a refuge.*

Following a sleepless night in which he was beset by mosquitoes, he was dozing in the saddle when he was startled to attention by a nicker from Buckshot. He glanced up to find himself halted in a stand of poplar trees. Before him stretched a wide creek. And across the creek stood an encampment of three dozen or more hide lodges. Now fully alert, he froze in place, fighting the urge to turn and flee.

On the far bank, a group of women crouched by the water washing clothes. The women laughed and gossiped among themselves as they wrung and twisted the garments. Behind them, the smoke from several small fires drifted through the encampment. A pack of dogs roamed between the lodges, snapping and snarling over scraps. A group of boys propelled willow hoops through the dirt with sticks. The peaceful domesticity of the scene caused him to linger in spite of his instinct to hasten from the spot.

Careful to stay within the protection afforded by the trees, he took out the glass and trained it on the village. His eye was caught by a group of young girls clustered around a companion whose hair they dressed with grease while fussing over her tunic. In an open space between the lodges, six or seven men smoked pipes around a fire. The men were dressed alike in simple breechclouts—their naked torsos burned dark by the sun.

Fearful of discovery, he was about to turn back when he was diverted by jubilant cries. The smoking men rose to their feet as a party of hunters emerged from the woods. Some carried deer carcasses across their shoulders; others were festooned with strips of bloody meat that hung from their necks. At the sight, the women abandoned the washing, shouting with glee as they hurried to greet the hunters and relieve them of the bounty.

The entire village gathered to watch as the women began to skin and butcher the catch—the task an occasion for much laughter. At that moment, one of the dogs began to bark furiously in his direction. Other dogs took up the cry, rushing to the riverbank to growl and snarl at where he was concealed. Several of the men turned to look. Alarmed, he turned the bay and hastily retreated, glancing back for signs of pursuit.

Over the next few days, he came upon several similar villages—the tipis strung out along the Missouri itself or along a tributary river or creek. The unwarlike appearance of the Indians—preoccupied with hunting or fishing—tempted him to reveal his presence and perhaps gain information about the way ahead. But a distrust of what he perceived as *aboriginal vicissitude* persuaded him that any such encounter would be foolhardy in the extreme. *Who knows, but that appearances may deceive?*

Brooding on this truth, he contented himself with observing the villages from a distance, his spyglass noting the complete absence of horses, as well as the flimsy, makeshift nature of the lodges. *Perhaps they are summer camps*, he surmised, having heard rumours of the nomadic ways of many of the grassland tribes.

He was surprised, therefore, to come upon a village comprised not of makeshift tipis, but earth houses, far sturdier in their design than the flimsy habitations he had observed previously. The village gave every appearance of a settled, agricultural community. Strips of cultivated land along the river were being tilled by women and small children. Through the glass, he watched other women fishing or mending nets by the river while a group of men were engaged in building a lodge. Bemused and enticed in equal parts by the air of agrarian tranquillity, he was sorely tempted to ride into the village and declare himself. But the same instinctive caution prompted him to shut the glass and ride away. *Surely, it must be only a matter of time before I come upon some post or fort.*

The Virginia hunters' assertion that only buffaloes, flies and savages inhabited the blowing grasslands came to mind even as he dismissed its veracity. *Have they, or any of their companions, ventured into this wilderness? And, if not, then what true knowledge may they claim?*

Tormented by the fierce sun, he made it a habit to abandon the river before noon each day to seek refuge in the surrounding hills. Sometimes, he found shade in a wooded recess or sheltered gully and rested there until the sun had traversed the zenith. At other times, finding no suitable nook— only the vast expanse of treeless plain—he returned to the river to soak his shirt in the slow, muddy water while grumbling at the suffocating heat.

One morning, shortly after fording a creek, he came across a sizeable buffalo trace. The trace led out from the Missouri towards a stand of cottonwoods atop a prominent ridge in the distance. He headed toward it, intending to seek relief in the shade.

By the time he reached the spot, the sun burned directly overhead. He discovered a small spring bubbling up through the trees and filled the canteens as the horse and mule slaked their thirst. The shade was so pleasant that he fell into a brief slumber. When he awoke, he took the spyglass and walked the short distance to the top of the ridge.

To his surprise, he found himself overlooking a great shallow depression in the plain. The broad basin stretched roughly three quarters of a mile across and ran east to west, flanked on both sides by a line of bluffs. A creek trickled its length, emptying into the Missouri in the distance. He took off his hat and fanned himself as he took in the grand prospect. A pair of hawks wheeled overhead, their cries clearly audible in the somnolent air. All around, the silent grasslands sweltered in the shimmering heat.

As he stood there, a strange noise came to his ears. The sound rolled and receded in waves, reverberating like the rumble of summer thunder. He glanced up at the cloudless blue sky, perplexed as to the source. Beyond the opposite bluffs, a plume of smoke rose up in the distance. 'The grass is afire!' he told himself, alarmed at the prospect. The thunder rumbled again, seeming to come from all directions at once. Suddenly the ground shook beneath his feet. *A fire and a quake!* He tensed, making ready to flee.

A brief, pregnant hush followed, the grasslands lying silent under the hard blue sky. He was still puzzling as to the cause when a noise of pounding hooves reached his ears. Moments later, a column of buffalo appeared from out of the dust cloud—for such it was, he realised. The beasts moved at a gallop, headed for the ridge directly opposite where he stood. Arriving at the ridge, they leapt over the rim, barely breaking stride as they rushed down the long slope to the fresh water and grass below.

More of the animals arrived, the trickling stream widening and deepening into a flood as the thunder of hooves reverberated in the air. The opposing bluffs were now boiling with buffalo, all frantic to reach the fresh water below. The deluge poured across the ridge in such uncountable numbers that he feared it must collapse beneath the prodigious waterfall of leaping, tumbling bodies.

Alarmed at the thick dust cloud he saw sweeping towards him, he beat a hasty retreat back to the trees. He had covered barely half the distance before he was engulfed in the stinging, choking haze.

Wheezing and gasping, his eyes sore and reddened with grit, he stumbled to reach the sanctuary of the grove. Half blinded, he fell to his knees by the spring, his throat parched and raw. Overhead, leaves shook loose as a fine, powdery dust rained down from the sky. He splashed water against his face, finally dunking his entire head in the spring. Flushed and feverish, he sank back against a cottonwood, his senses stupefied by the tremendous bellowing din that filled the air like the very noise of creation.

## 2

## A Finger of the Whole

HE AWOKE A SHORT time later, surprised to have dozed off. The grunts and roars of the great herd beset the air, bringing him back to alertness. Getting to his feet, he slapped a layer of dust from his shirt and trousers. The horse and mule were both coated with dirt, and he washed them down as best he could. Wetting his neckerchief in the spring and tying it around his neck, he retraced his steps to the top of the ridge. Once there, he exclaimed in astonishment. Below, the great basin rippled with a vast tide of buffalo, their numbers so swollen as to deceive his senses into thinking that he gazed upon the voluminous brown flood of the Mississippi itself. More buffalo arrived at every moment to try to force their way down the crowded slopes. He stared incredulously as Fesky's words echoed in his ears. *As many as the pigeon.*

The immense herd stretched all the way to the Missouri in the distance to create a living barrier to his westward path. *If I am to continue, I must pass through.* Perturbed at the thought, he lingered, wondering if he could ride around the flanks of the bellowing mass of animals. But he dismissed the notion even as it occurred. *Who knows, but it may take days?*

He returned to the cottonwood grove, undecided whether to try and navigate his way through the staggering multitudes to continue his journey. 'If I stay—or turn back—I may be discovered by hunting parties from the villages I saw.' Decided by this possibility, he saddled Buckshot. He was preparing to leave the grove when he was struck by an inspiration. Scouting the area for deadwood, he collected several armfuls which he tied into bundles and secured to the mule. He then refilled all six canteens to the brim. Satisfied with these precautions, he attached a rope bridle to Prodigal and slowly set off down the long slope towards the buffalo.

As he drew closer, the cacophonous fugue of snorts, grunts and roars grew to such a pitch that he feared his ears might crack. A potent, musky stench engulfed his senses, and he pressed the damp necktie to his mouth.

He halted on the flanks of the herd, hesitant to intrude upon the multitude. Cautiously, he passed the outliers, fearful lest they regard him as a threat. But the buffalo showed no curiosity or alarm, giving way before his advance like the parting of the seas. As he ventured deeper into the enormous herd, he felt a sensation of being absorbed into the panting mass as it closed ranks again behind him. In spite of the great congestion, there was space to move freely, small islands of cropped grass providing momentary refuge for the nervous stock.

Occasionally, a bull wandered up to sniff at Buckshot, spooking the bay. 'Get!' he cried. 'Skit!' He cocked the musket but was quick to realise the danger of sparking a general panic. Lowering the gun, he kicked the horse out of harm's way, the skittish mule following closely behind.

It took him the best part of two hours to make his way through the herd, his nerves on edge as the occasional bull snorted and flicked its tail at the intrusion. Reaching the base of the opposing bluffs, he dismounted and led the way upwards on foot, treading carefully in a vain attempt to avoid the piles of steaming dung that littered the grass. Arriving at the top of the ridge, he halted in shock.

Before him, as far as his stunned eyes could see, the rolling uplands were dotted with an immense assemblage of buffalo—their numbers so great as to blacken the hillsides. The buffalo in the valley were, he realised, *but a finger of the whole!* Incredulous, and scarce able to believe his eyes, he swept the surrounding ranges with the glass. At every turn, his gaze was filled with buffalo—the slopes so thickly populated that the landscape itself seemed in motion.

Shutting the glass, he sat back in the saddle, sharply doubtful as to the wisdom of proceeding. A picture of Mose came to mind, his erstwhile companion scoffing at his hesitation. *'D'ye wait for a magic carpet to fly over them?'* 'Have it your way, then,' he muttered. Soothing and cajoling the frightened horse, he rode into the prodigious herd.

After proceeding for four hours, he abandoned any hope of sighting an exit to the buffalo tide. Indeed, the astonishing plenitude seemed to increase rather than diminish the deeper he rode into the bellowing, resistless sea. Each bluff or ridge proved but window or vantage to a further, dizzying prospect—the buffalo as limitless as the grass itself. He continued on, unable to tell whether he rode on the flanks, or in the midst of or, indeed, at the head or tail of the staggering multitude.

As the sky reddened, he made camp on the top of a small crag—the prominence offering some protection from the snorting, grunting press of buffaloes. Pouring water into a pan, he watered the horse and mule before securely hobbling both. To guard against the prospect of being gored or trampled in his sleep, he built a roaring fire, adding sticks to the flames until the sparks leapt into the sky. *Should they break into a run for any reason, I am a dead man*, he cautioned himself before falling asleep.

THE SUN WAS ALREADY hot when he awoke—the pungent stink of buffalo assailing his groggy senses. He led off the horse on foot, unable to avoid stepping into the countless mounds of fresh shit that covered the grass. His eye was caught by something glinting in one pile of dung and he bent to see. A colony of beetles clambered through the mound, their hard black shells burrowing into the mass. As he continued, he observed each pile of freshly dropped shit was similarly populated by a blue-black swarm of flies and beetles.

Sliding his feet through the grass to rid his shoes of the omnipresent dung, he recalled something Mose had mentioned. That night, he experimented with adding the sun-dried waste to the fire. To his pleasure, the dried dung proved eminently combustible, burning with a steady, albeit odorous, flame that also seemed to ward off the irritating swarms of mosquitoes. From then on, he collected the dried matter each afternoon to supplement the dwindling supply of firewood.

The sun continued to burn with a fierce intensity, forcing him to constantly replenish the canteens from whichever muddy creek or stream he could find. The sweeping winds that seemed a permanent feature of the grasslands proved a blessing by dispersing the flies and midges that collected above the buffalo in thick swarms.

Early one afternoon, he halted, concerned that Prodigal was favouring his right foreleg. On investigation, he discovered a slight swelling just above the hoof. He pressed a poultice of dampened mud over the spot, worried lest the mule develop a sore. Deciding to make camp, he built a fire of sticks and dung and unwrapped the last of the salted venison. He ate half the portion, setting the remainder aside for the following day.

To his relief, the mule seemed to have recovered by morning, the animal moving freely as he walked it back and forth to test the leg. The incident was a sober reminder of his dependence on the livestock, and he carefully inspected the bay for bruises or cuts, perturbed at the thought of being abandoned on foot amidst the migratory host. He ate the remaining venison while in the saddle, cursing with vexation as the wind dropped away and flies buzzed the sweat on his nose and mouth.

He made camp in the late afternoon, building a small fire in a dry gulch bed—the only protective shelter he could find. He cleaned and loaded all three muskets. Avoiding the buffaloes nearest to the camp, he walked out to where a group stood feeding in the grass. Selecting a yearling cow, he sighted and fired. The surrounding buffalo moved away from the spot as the cow bleated piteously. Walking to within ten yards, he fired the second musket, striking the beast in the heart. A nearby bull issued a warning grunt, and he kept a wary eye on it as he hacked chunks of meat from the cow. He took only sufficient for his immediate needs. *Why salt, when I am camped inside such a plentiful larder?* he reasoned as he carried the bloody bounty back to the fire.

Day after day, his north-westerly passage took him against the tremendous south-easterly flow of buffalo, the herd offering little or no hindrance to his progress. Rather, the seemingly impregnable mass yielded dozens of porous avenues though which he proceeded with comparative ease. The only dangers were the numerous ruts that continued daily on all sides— the aggressive, bad-tempered bulls constantly butting heads for the rights to mount a cow. He gave a careful berth to all such disturbances, sharply aware that the unpredictable animals were as likely to turn and charge the horse and mule as each other.

As he soon discovered, the same ravines and hollows that enabled him to navigate the migratory flow also offered a haven to wolves—the numerous packs seemingly an organic part of the perambulatory herd. At times, he witnessed two dozen or more sprawled contentedly on a hillside as the buffalo passed by. Secure in their great numbers, the buffalo mostly ignored these interlopers, even the calves displaying little or no alarm at their presence. The wolves seemed content to lie in the sun, their bellies indolent with their last meal. But as the afternoon wore on, the packs gradually stirred into action, the older wolves scouting the nearest fringe of animals for sick, young or wounded buffalo. Acting in deadly concert, the wolves isolated and surrounded their prey, leaping and feinting to avoid the sharp horns of a frantic cow as they harried and tormented a calf before dragging it down with their sharp teeth.

Occasionally, a bull or enraged cow would turn table on the wolves, using their razor-sharp horns to lethal effect. Once, he saw a cow flip a wolf into the air. The wounded wolf rolled on its back, giving out high-pitched yelps as several buffalo surrounded it. Taking turns, the buffalo used their massive heads to try to crush the wolf while goring it with their curved horns. To his surprise, the battered wolf survived the assault, dragging itself off through the grass as the buffalo suddenly lost interest.

He had been part of the herd for three days when he witnessed a grizzly explode from out of a dry wash and pounce on a calf in a snarling ferocity of teeth and claws. Over the following days, he witnessed several more of these ambushes, the grizzly flattening itself to the ground in a gulch or draw before rushing out to seize an unwary calf. Despite his animosity, he nevertheless developed a grudging admiration for their boldness, the bears seemingly without fear of man or beast.

One morning, he halted the bay to watch through the glass as a charging bear brought down a weaning calf. The mother came immediately to the calf's defence, catching the grizzly broadside and sending it bowling over in the grass. The grizzly then turned on the cow, attaching itself to her neck and back as she struggled to dislodge it. The duel continued until the exhausted buffalo slumped to its knees, its belly eviscerated by the slashing claws of the bear. So spent was the grizzly from the struggle that it lay prostrate atop its mortally wounded prey, too exhausted to feed.

Nights brought a different menace as wild cats crept from gorges and buttes to scavenge the remains of wolf kills, their high-pitched screeches unnerving the horse and mule. The cats were often in competition with scavenging coyotes, the animals yelping and snarling as they fought over the remains of a kill. He saw four coyotes work together to drag down a spindly calf weakened through orphanage and the loss of its mother's milk. The nearest buffalo displayed bovine indifference to the calf's piteous cries—the incurious beasts giving berth as buzzards alighted to share the gruesome feast. He pondered the incident as he walked the horse. *Mayhap their staggering profusion renders them indifferent to such diminishments. They are like the pigeon—so infinite in number as to be imperishable.*

He was taken by surprise when, from the top of a bluff, he spied a distant band of Indians tracking the herd. Studying the band through the glass, he noted dog travois and tent poles as though the entire village had uprooted to follow the migratory beasts. The effect struck him as faintly humorous—as though the men and women were herding the animals rather than following after them. He watched through the spyglass until losing sight of the figures through the dust.

He came across pockets of elk, antelope and deer, the animals seemingly swept up in the massive suction of the migratory host. The interlopers promised a welcome change to his diet as he began to tire of the constant rounds of buffalo meat. But they proved far more wary than the buffalo and he soon abandoned his attempts to hunt one. *When I return to the river again, I shall eat nothing but fish*, he promised himself. It occurred to him that the sheer mass of buffalo had forced him away from the Missouri and further inland. The thought prompted a bout of anxiety as he tried to recall its proximate whereabouts relative to his position. *Surely, I am headed west,* he told himself, glancing up at the sun.

To divert himself during the hot, dusty hours in the saddle, he lapsed into dreamful speculation on the origins of the buffalo and its peculiar nature and physiognomy. Mulling on their preference for rolling vigorously in the dirt, he observed that oftentimes a buffalo would water in the depression before again wallowing in the mud and piss. *Perhaps the method is to ward off the flies*, he conjectured, trying to remember what he had been told about the habit—one so prevalent as to constitute, he deemed, a signal characteristic of the species. In dreaming fancy, he pictured himself standing in the Great Reading Room at Edinburgh University, lecturing on the exotic creature to an eagerly attentive audience. Pondering the reason that both male and females would battle fiercely over a choice shrub or sapling—the winner obsessively rubbing horns against the bark until the shrub was worn away—he conceded defeat. 'The cause for such single-mindedness over a mere shrub remains clouded in mystery,' he advised the unseen audience.

He felt himself on firmer ground when describing the struggle of rival bulls for the favour of a female. 'Such contests are mostly short and decisive, the victor bellowing in triumph as he chases the hapless rival from the field. But, on several occasions, the author has witnessed competing bulls engage in contests that lasted for an hour or more, the rivals still determinedly clashing horns even after the sun had set.'

As he became more adept at distinguishing between male and female, he noted that the latter often seemed the more dominant of the species—and not the least hesitant to violently chastise the younger males for breaching some buffalo etiquette or other. 'Perhaps,' he speculated, 'one witnesses among the buffalo an inversion of the primary instincts, which may, in some yet-to-be-understood measure, contribute to their astonishing profusion and may account for the largely peaceful concord between male and female of the species.'

Observing that the herd, despite its unimaginable size, seemed made up of small, individual groups travelling in concert, he mused on the existence of some invisible sympathy or instinct that linked the disparate parts into an organic whole. 'As men are linked by reason and collective interest—by morals, beliefs and habits—so, too, may the buffalo be adjudged to possess a not-dissimilar impulse for preservation of the species by means of a prolific and unprecedented rate of propagation.'

The fact that most cows seemed confined to a single birth calf flummoxed him for a time as he weighed fact against conjecture, evidence against speculation. Dwelling on the conundrum, he arrived at a not-altogether-satisfactory resolution by acknowledging what struck him as a profound paradox. *Nature, in her wisdom, has limited the number of offspring lest the buffalo in its fecundity overwhelm the earth.*

Pondering further the central fact of the buffalo—its inexhaustible number—he experimented with various means to calculate the size of the surrounding mass of animals. Quickly abandoning one fruitless attempt after another, he finally divided the plain into quadrants and, holding up his fingers and thumbs, subdivided each quadrant into squares. He then calculated the number of animals in a square, multiplying the answer by the number of days since entering the mass. By this whimsical method, he arrived at an estimation of between thirty and forty million of the beasts. Considering that number to lie midway between the improbable and the fantastical, he nevertheless made sober judgement that he was surrounded by a vast sea of twenty million or more animals, *or tenfold the reported human population of the English Colonies*, he hypothesised.

His speculations were brought to an end by a stumble from Buckshot as the horse caught its foot in a root. Annoyed at his inattention, he roundly cursed the obstruction as he dismounted to examine the limb.

As another fiercely hot day dawned, he uncorked the last of the water bottles and sipped carefully on the contents, worried that his supply was almost exhausted. Weary of the noise and the pervasive stink, and fatigued from the scorching sun, he sought an egress from the herd. Raising himself in the stirrups, he shaded his eyes to scan the horizon but could discern no end to the staggering abundance. A sudden, violent rainstorm caused him to seek hasty shelter in the lee of a sandstone bluff. As he watched the rain churn the dry earth, he observed that the buffalo stood motionless—their shaggy heads turned into the downpour as though frozen in the moment. Struck by the sight, he took advantage of the shelter to sketch the nearest animal, adding the legend: *Buffalo standing in rainstorm*. The rain soon diminished, and he climbed into the wet saddle to continue his passage.

The storm filled to overflowing the numerous dry creeks and gullies that bisected the grass. But the air remained heavy and humid as the flies and mosquitoes returned with a vengeance. The damp air released even more potently the pungent odour of the herd, the overpowering stench filling his nose and mouth. He stopped at a creek, roundly cursing the plague of insects. The water was muddy and littered with clumps of floating wool from the actions of buffalo wallowing further upstream. Worried that the stock might take sick as a consequence of the befouled water, he led them away to a smaller streamlet. Unpacking the shovel, he dug a small trench alongside the trickling water. After some minutes of digging, he uncovered a spring of clear water and refilled the water bottles. Taking off his shirt, he splashed water over his chest and arms before smearing a layer of wet mud to his face and hands as a defence against flies.

The landscape became hillier, the way impeded by frequent bluffs and ravines. The buffalo adroitly navigated the steeper obstacles while squeezing through the gullies and washes. Stopping at the foot of one particularly high bluff, he tethered the bay, intending to climb the bluff and survey the country ahead. Taking the spyglass, he climbed to the summit and glassed the surrounding ranges, sighting the dotted mass of buffalo at every turn. 'They are like the droplets of the ocean,' he muttered, putting aside the glass. He descended the bluff, preoccupied with an image of the buffalo undulating before the wind like stalks of grain bending in the breeze.

Two weeks after entering the stupendous herd, he discerned a thinning in its ranks. The following day, he spied a hillside empty of buffalo and steered in that direction. As he reached the elevation, he turned to look back. In the distance, the populous mass continued its migration, a fine dust haze hanging over the great diaspora. Flocks of sparrows, meadowlarks and magpies swooped the freshly churned earth in its wake, darting for insects thrown up by the countless hooves. Even as he watched, the last of the buffalo disappeared into the hills until the rolling prairie lay empty once again. As the sound of hooves rumbled into the distance, he urged Buckshot forward, his senses slowly adjusting to the hot, vaporous stillness and shimmering grass.

## 3

# *The Rock*

THE NEXT MORNING, HE reconnected with the Missouri where it looped across the plain. He breathed a sigh of relief as he reached the shore—thankful at the prospect of fresh water and glad to be free of the enormous herd. He wrinkled his nose, smelling the creature on his hands, shirt and skin. *I stink of buffalo.* He made early camp, intending to bathe in the stream and wash away the stench. The river was wide at that point, the water a muddy-brown flow interspersed with frequent sand banks. After immersing himself in the stream, he washed the buckskin shirt and leggings and hung both on a branch to dry. He took the spare shirt from among the cargo and dried himself with it before putting it on.

Eager to catch fish after the unrelieved diet of meat, he attached a length of twine to a branch and baited the hook with a worm. Within minutes, the line jerked, and the branch almost pulled from his grip. To his irritation, the twine snapped and whatever fishy creature had taken the lure swam away. He tried again, successfully snaring a fish with a long, flat snout, which he hauled ashore and brained on the bank. After filleting the fish, he held it over the flames, greedily shoving the roasted flesh into his mouth as each portion was cooked.

He lay down beside the embers of the fire, pondering his progress. By his reckoning, he had crossed at least six major rivers and countless streams and creeks since Mose's death, and still he appeared no closer to finding some end or resolution to his journey. *Surely these grasslands cannot go on forever.* Haunted by the prospect, he fell asleep.

The morning dawned cool and fresh. The buckskin shirt was almost dry. He pressed his nose into the soft cloth, smelling the musk of buffalo. *'Tis as good dyed into the skin.* He stuffed the washed shirt into the saddle bag. Feeling refreshed from the bath and the meal of fish, he set out, a gusting wind keeping the mites at bay. The river was thickly wooded at this point, and he followed a trace between the trees.

In the afternoon, he shot an antelope and butchered it in the protective shade of a large elm. As he cooked the ham over a fire, he felt a cool breeze against his cheek. He glanced up to where a luminous mass of dark cloud obscured the sun. In the time it took to roast the meat, the sky had darkened to a purplish hue, making it seem like dusk. Hastily swallowing a handful of the hot meat, he abandoned the meal to lead the horse and mule into the thickest part of the grove where he left them securely tethered.

He collected a number of long branches and dug the ends into the earth to form a tipi. As drops of rain began to fall, he cast around for moss and leaves to cover the structure. Finally he draped the deerskin cape over the branch roof and secured the shelter as best he could with loops of twine. He went back to the meat and took the remaining ham into the shelter with him.

The sky was now almost black and the air moist with rain. A flash of lightning lit up the gloom as he bit off a chunk of meat. A tremendous blast of thunder shook the sky. Within seconds, the rain turned into a lashing downpour, the trees shaking wildly in the gale as a rumbling thunder beset the air.

Huddled in the buffalo robe, he endured an hour of misery as lightning flashed and immense crashes of thunder burst overhead. He cradled his arms around his knees and pulled the hat low over his eyes as rivulets ran around his feet and blasts of wind rattled the branch shelter. Before long, a steady stream of water trickled through the grove, causing him to fear that he would be forced into abandoning the position in the midst of the storm.

The rain was now so intense that he could see barely a yard outside the flimsy shelter. He heard a loud crack as a branch split off from a tree. *I am in danger*, he worried, peering up through the sheeting rain at the branches above his head. As torrential downpour continued to lash the grass, he huddled beneath the soaked robe, his wretchedness complete.

As suddenly as it had begun, the savage storm blew itself out. In a matter of minutes, patches of fresh blue sky shone through the cloud. He crawled out of the shelter, his first thought for the animals. He found them trembling and bedraggled—their coats sodden with rain, but none the worse for wear. 'Good Buck,' he said, stroking the bay's neck. 'And you too, Prodigal, have earned your spurs this day.'

Electing not to stay in the flooded grove, he led the horse away from the river, walking it through the soaked grass. Around him, the landscape was bathed in brilliant light, rainbow hues illuminating the plains. Struck by the sombre beauty of the drenched hills, he mounted the bay and set off at a walk. *Poor Mose would have hated getting wet.* He grimaced as he pictured the trapper's irascibility.

The following day, the hot weather returned, the sun burning away the morning mist as it vaulted into the sky. He drizzled water over his neck in an attempt to keep cool. The mites had returned, buzzing and droning around his face in a black cloud that drove him half-mad with annoyance. He was navigating through a series of small bluffs when, to his surprise, he heard a dog bark from somewhere up ahead. He pulled rein, confounded to see a party of Indians emerge from a stand of trees not two hundred yards distant. The Indians stopped in their tracks, as shocked as himself by the unexpected encounter. For a moment, the two parties stared at each other. Then the barking dog raced forwards, yelping and snapping at Buckshot. The bay reared and he fought to control it. He heard a yelp as the dog was sent flying by a kick from the mule. The Indians stood stock still as though thunderstruck.

He held up a hand. *'Bonjour!'*

One of the Indians notched an arrow to his bow. Turning the horse, he kicked it into a canter. As he glanced backwards, he saw another of the Indians extend an arm, seemingly to restrain the archer.

'Skit!' He whipped the bay into a gallop as the mule followed after. Looking back, he saw the Indians stood in place, looking after him as he fled. After a safe distance, he pulled up and continued at a walk with occasional glances behind. *Mayhap they intended no harm.* On reflection, he wondered if they were not as equally spooked by the sight of the horse and mule as they were by himself. *I have seen no sign of horses in the country.*

His flight had taken him back to the river, and he dismounted to rest the winded bay. The area was heavily wooded, but through the screen of trees he spotted a birch-bark floating in the middle of the stream, the occupants intently watching the water as they fished. Proceeding cautiously, he soon came upon what appeared to be a veritable fleet of bullboats and birch-barks. Some sat motionless as their occupants fished, while others moved back and forth across the river. Tethering the animals, he stole through the trees, ears alert for any untoward sound.

He had not gone far when he observed a sandstone bluff rising high above the river. It was crowned by a wood palisade. A path ran down the bluff to the muddy river shore. Dozens of men and women climbed or descended the path, many of the women carrying baskets or cradleboards across their backs. At the foot of the bluff, numerous shrieking children splashed and played in the river. He judged the village to be a sizeable one, larger than any he had so far encountered. *They look peaceful. Perhaps they would welcome a stranger.*

He heard a shout and turned to see one of the birch-barks headed for the shore near to where he had left the horse and mule. Quickly, he retraced his steps. Walking the horse through the trees, he was relieved to find open grass again. The bay whinnied and turned his head as though reluctant to leave the river and the shade of the cottonwoods.

After riding for an hour, he drew rein on the shore of a wide river that crossed his path. The water was shallow and slow-moving, and he guessed the distance across at around a thousand yards. Taking off his hat, he wiped an arm across his forehead as he contemplated the water and yet another crossing. 'A good day for a swim, Buck,' he said, nudging the horse forward. *I am become like Mose—talking to my horse. This is what too much solitude does to a man.*

Soaked from the river crossing, he made camp and chewed on the remains of a doe he had shot and salted two days earlier. He rescued the log from the saddlebags, relieved to find it securely dry within its oilcloth wrapping. Making himself comfortable under a cottonwood, he wrote a few, desultory observations of the Indian village. He had, he realised, forgotten the date entirely, and pondered whether the month was June or July or, indeed, August. *I am indeed in buffalo time*, he thought, recalling a remark of his late companion. The remembrance set him into a melancholic mood, which he attempted to dispel by getting up to check on the damp supplies.

Next morning, he continued in the same direction, doubly eager to come upon some sign of civilisation. The sun was fiercely hot and he covered his neck as he rode, wondering if there were any end to the sprawling amphitheatre of grass and hills. *Surely, I must soon reach some boundary or inhabited region.* Dimly, he pictured Mose's hide map while recalling the French captain's claim that the lands east and west of the Missouri were in the possession of France. 'Then where the devil are the forts?' he muttered, the oppressive solitude weighing more heavily upon him than usual.

The heat was relentless, and he worried for the horse. It was panting heavily, its neck glossy with sweat. He looked around for some shade where he might rest the animal. Sighting none, only hillocks and grass on all sides, he continued, suffering greatly in the heat.

Shortly after noon, he spotted a dark shape rising up in the distance. Shading his eyes, he identified the object as a massive rock—the edifice rising to a considerable height above the plain. The smooth sides tapered upwards to a curving spine that rose at one end to form a pinnacle—the massive, blunt precipice of which he fancied to stare out over the plain. He headed directly for the object, drawn by the prospect of shade. Overhead, the sun had crossed a few degrees west of the zenith, its angle emphasising the solidity and permanence of the rock as it absorbed the heat and light of noonday.

As he drew nearer, he puzzled at the imposing rock's singular presence on the level plain—idly conjecturing whether some divine hand, bored at the endless wastes, had not scooped up a distant mountain and set it down amidst the prairie grass to startle and amaze passers-by.

He rode up almost to the base before entering the rock's shadow. In the shade, it towered above him, veins of ancient sediment gleaming in the greyish, iridescent stone. Dismounting, he turned the horse and mule loose to graze while he inspected the object. Beneath his hand, the smooth, weathered stone—cool even in the burning air—felt hard and unyielding. Stepping back, he gazed up at the summit—his vision briefly dazzled by a flash of sunlight along the rim. Turning, he surveyed the deserted plain. Nothing moved, even the scavenging birds fled to shade in the smothering heat. He drank from the water bottle, electing to remain in the shade until the heat of noonday had passed. He sat down, his back against the rock. Overcome by the stifling air, he soon fell asleep, his head lolling to one side.

HE AWOKE WITH A start, scrambling to his feet in search of the horse. He found it further along the rock, grazing in the shade alongside the mule. He hobbled both animals, deciding to make camp in the shelter of the giant crag. He built a small fire from twigs without lighting it. He emptied a canteen into the pan and held it up for the bay to drink. 'Tomorrow, mayhap we shall find a creek or meet back up with the river and you can drink to your heart's content,' he promised. He refilled the pan and offered it to the thirsty mule.

He unpacked the cargo and unwrapped a portion of salted antelope rib. He chewed slowly on the meat while gazing into the distance. The air was suffocatingly warm, and he wondered that any creatures could thrive in the scorching heat. He dozed off for a second time. When he awoke, the sun had shifted further to the west and the shadow of the rock projected twenty or thirty feet into the grass. It had grown surprisingly cool in the shade, and he walked out into the sunlight for warmth.

He spent the remainder of the day mending a rip in his breeches and rummaging through the diminishing quantities of supplies. To his regret, he had no more than a handful of tea leaves remaining, and he set them aside. 'For some other time,' he told himself.

The light was now diminishing, and he lit the fire, confident of the protection offered by the massive rock. Lying down in the cool grass, he rested his head on a folded-up blanket and stared up at the darkening sky. When he opened his eyes again, the fire had flickered to embers and the sky was ablaze with stars. Feeling a slight chill in the air, he got up and fetched the buffalo robe. He added the last of the sticks to the fire before lying down again beneath the robe. Next to him, the massive rock flowed upwards toward the stars, its solid mass compounding the darkness of the night.

He lay on his back listening to the crackling of the fire, the snuffling of the mule and the sighing breaths of the horse. A fiery streak amidst the vast, glittering firmament caught his eye and he pondered the transient spark. *Were there worlds out there—as philosophers had speculated?* As he dwelt on the tantalising notion, he fell fast asleep.

He awoke sometime after dawn, a cool breeze against his face. Fading stars glimmered in the sky. Rising above him, the rock seemed to soar upwards to the heavens. The whistling call of a meadowlark sounded from somewhere in the grass. Snug under the heavy robe, he lay on his back, lazy to get up and resume the long, tiresome journey. *What is there but more of this confounded grass?* Something had bitten him and he itched the bite, suddenly resentful. *It was his ambition to see these damnable plains, not mine.* In the shade, the bay snuffled and shook its neck.

It was full light before he roused himself sufficiently to water the animals and slake his own thirst. To his surprise, the rock seemed to have changed colour, emitting a pinkish hue in the bright morning sunlight. He examined the stone closely with fresh, morning eyes. His inspection detected small grains in the stone interspersed with lighter coloured specks, almost milky in colour. *It may change colour according to the degrees of light,* he speculated, recollecting the iridescent colours of the dolphin caught at sea. Turning his attention to the day ahead, he saddled the bay and secured the wicker baskets to the mule. Shortly afterwards, he rode out from under the shadow of the great rock.

To his relief, the day was less fiercely hot than the previous one, a layer of cloud obscuring the sun. The landscape continued unchanged, the rolling grassy plain interrupted by the occasional gully, wash, or creek. He had ridden in a north-east direction towards the rock, and he now adjusted his course to the north-west. He was, he hoped, within a day's ride of the Missouri. Glancing back over his shoulder, he fixed the position of the rock. 'Thou shalt be my mark,' he said.

He came across a stream and watered the animals. The landscape was rich in shrubs and trees, and he sighted numerous buffalo as well as antelope and a herd of mule deer. He had ridden around ten miles when he stiffened at the sharp, unmistakable crack of a musket. He pulled up the bay, his head cocked to the sound. A second shot rang out, the noise echoing on the air. *It could be French—or Indians.* He debated with himself for a few moments before cautiously continuing towards a thicket from where the shots seemed to have emanated.

Reaching the trees, he dismounted. Leading Buckshot by the bridle, he proceeded stealthily past the shadowy trunks in the direction of the shots. He stopped again at the sound of voices, his hand cupping the muzzle of the horse. Leaving it behind, he advanced, musket at the ready. He heard a dog yelp. Beyond the last few trees, he saw two men bent over a deer. A pair of dogs, attached to a travois, were lying in the grass nearby. The men wore linen shirts and knee-length breeches. One was bare headed, the other wore a well-worn cocked hat. He heard French being spoken as the men conversed amiably over the carcass. As he debated whether or not to reveal himself, he heard, to his astonishment, one of the men exclaim aloud at some obduracy of the carcass.

'Perish the bone sack!'

Astonished and gratified to hear an English voice, he called out in French, careful to stay hidden behind a thick oak. '*Bonjour! Un ami!*'

'*Au nom de Dieu!*' The men straightened up in shock. Snatching up their muskets, they realised that they had forgotten to reload. In a panic, they poured powder while staring at the thicket. '*Qui êtes-vous?* Show yourself!'

'*Un ami!*' He called out. 'A friend. I mean no harm!'

A short silence followed as the alarmed hunters raked the trees for any sight of him. 'Be you French or English?' one demanded.

'Neither! Scottish!'

'You are alone?'

'Yes.'

'Step forward, then! Let us see you.'

Holding up his hands to show no ill intent, he cautiously stepped out from the cover of the trees.

'What in blazes?' The speaker, the one wearing the hat, eyed him with sharp suspicion. 'From which rock, gully or godforsaken nook do you present?'

'From the eastern mountains. I rode west—'

'From which mountains? Where?'

'The Alleghenies.'

'The Ally-who?'

'The Alleghenies. To the east of here. On the border of the English colonies.'

'You say you rode?'

'I did.' Without turning his head, he called for Buckshot to join him. Prodigal followed. The hunters' eyes widened with astonishment at sight of the animals.

'Queerer and yet queerer!' The speaker turned and said something in French to his companion. The other man, a stout, bearded fellow, grunted a reply as he regarded Boundless through narrowed eyes.

'Louis here wants to know which company you work for. The truth, now!'

'I do not work for any company. I came here to hunt buffalo and catch beaver.'

'Who for?' The man's tone was challenging.

'For none but myself. My companion was killed by a bear. We rode out here to explore and hunt.'

'You rode across the prairies—from the east?'

'I came here along the Missouri.'

'By boat?'

'No. On horseback.'

'Then you came down the Ohio?'

'I assure you, friend, I came overland—from the Alleghenies.'

The dogs were snarling and growling at Boundless, their hackles raised. The speaker turned and roundly cursed them in a mix of English and French.

He spoke again to his companion. The latter replied, a suspicious edge to his voice as he regarded Boundless.

'Louis says you are an English spy!'

'Not so! I am a hunter, like yourselves.'

'Then not like us at all, friend. We are employed in the fur trade. Beaver is our preferred fare—Merciful Jesus, what now?' Frowning, the speaker cocked an ear to his companion. '*Autres*? Louis asks if you have seen other white men.'

'You are the first living souls—apart from savages—I've seen since God knows when.'

'Then must we make a winsome sight!' The speaker set down his musket. 'Meekus Pinch, citizen of Boston, Massachusetts. This comely fellow be Louis Reneau.'

'Boundless McLennan. Late of Maryland, by way of Pennsylvania.'

'Then step closer, Boundless McLennan.'

Boundless did so, holding out his hand. The two exchanged handshakes. He then extended his hand to the Frenchman, who, with a trace of hesitation, accepted, his eyes mistrustful.

'Ha! Pay him no heed. The tribe are snickerty everywhere on account of the war.'

'You are English, Mr Pinch?'

'Just Pinch, if ye please. Aye. Born and bred. But now aboriginal to the wilderness that has teated me these past two years.'

'And your companion?'

'In spite of his long face, an honest-born Frenchie from the Quebec.'

'You have a cabin nearby?'

'We have a post nearby.' Pinch waved to indicate the direction.

'Just the two of you?'

'The two ignoble critters afore you, and a half-dozen more ungodly specimens back at the post. But come, see for yourself. 'Tis but a mile yonder.'

## 4

## A Veritable Town

THE POST WAS A formidably large stockade situated a short distance from the banks of the Missouri. Cottonwood logs sunk into the earth formed a palisade that stood sixteen feet high and stretched over four hundred feet on the facing side. Two protruding bastions sat on diagonal corners, their position giving defensive cover to all four sides of the stockade. The *fleur-de-lis* fluttered from a pole within the log walls. 'You have a well-defended post,' he remarked to Pinch as they approached, surprised at the extent and solidity of the fortifications.

'Aye. It was a military fort until three year ago—before Monsieur Thibault and his partners seized possession.'

'Monsieur Thibault?'

'The bourgeois—that be "gentleman" in English. A shrewd fellow but hampered by an excess of industry. He has us tend, uproot and replace the logs as if it were still a fort.'

'But a wise precaution, is it not—in such a wild country?'

'Ha! He almost lost his hair to the Iroquois as a young man and has been overfond of it ever since.'

As they walked up to a large gate set into the palisade, the dogs began to whine and howl. An answering chorus rose from within the log walls. A voice sounded over the yelps, the unseen speaker remonstrating with the dogs. '*Chut, mes beautés!*'

Striding up to the gate, Pinch banged on the logs. '*Ouvrir!*'

'*Qui est-ce?*' demanded the same, querulous voice from within.

'Who the blazes do you think, you slack-mouthed toothpick!' Pinch kicked the gate. 'Open up, you witless imbecile!'

A moment later came the sound of the heavy gate being unbarred. It dragged open to reveal the most grotesque creature Boundless had yet laid eyes upon. An overlarge, misshapen skull bobbed atop a spindly neck—the fellow's head wobbling all the while like a spinning top. His eyes bulged, imparting a permanently astonished expression to the sallow features. The impression of gaping idiocy was heightened as the brute gawked at Boundless and, behind him, the horse and mule. '*Mère de Dieu! Au nom des Saints bénis, qu'est-ce que c'est?*'

'King George, come to pay a visit!' Pinch shoved past the astounded gatekeep.

Boundless followed Pinch into the stockade, unable to keep his eyes from the gawking patchwork that hobbled alongside. The fellow's dirty linen shirt hung loosely from a bent, stick-thin body. A pair of soiled, homespun breeches covered the skinny legs as the creature alternately hopped and hobbled to keep pace.

A pack of dogs, confined to a fenced enclosure, caught sight of the horse and mule and leapt and howled in a frenzy of excitement. '*Chut, mes jolis! Silence!*' The creature hurried off to calm the agitated pack—the thin legs carrying him in a shuffling, sidelong gait. Bending over the fence, the fellow lavished kisses and caresses on the agitated hounds, all the while mumbling praise and endearments.

'What is his name?' Boundless asked, as the oddity chanted and cooed over the frantically yelping dogs.

'I call him Jack, Jubilation, Odd bod, or such as the weather brings to mind. He answers mostly to the name of Quoi. That's Frenchy for "what in blazes?", as he greets every remark the same. Although, in truth, he is much put upon. He is here on Monsieur Thibault's favour.'

Pinch threw out an arm as they followed a track around a disused barn. 'Behold! Our little home.'

Boundless was taken aback at what appeared, on first impression, to be a small village. Two dozen or more log buildings—several with stone chimneys projecting above the pitched, shingled roofs—lined a dirt street. There appeared to be a barracks, and a line of domiciles resembling row houses. A number of assorted sheds and huts were grouped together. His observation took in a blacksmith's forge, a powder magazine, a smokehouse and chicken coop. The largest building resembled a double-story ware-house, a flight of steps leading to the raised door. An open space in front of the buildings might once have been a parade ground. In a corner of the stockade stretched a sizeable vegetable garden. The buildings, and indeed the entire stockade, appeared deserted in the summer heat.

''Tis a veritable town, is it not?' Pinch seemed pleased at his look of surprise. 'The blame again falls to Monsieur Thibault—a most particular fellow. He insists on maintaining each and every plank as though the soldiers were expected back at any hour.'

At that moment, a man emerged from the doorway of a large log build-ing with smoke issuing from the chimney. He stood stock-still in surprise as he took in Boundless together with the horse and mule.

Pinch raised a hand in greeting. '*Monsieur Thibault! J'amène un invité pour à diner!* That be the bourgeois,' he explained in an aside to Boundless. 'He speaks nary a lick of English—any more than Louis here.'

Thibault descended the steps and approached them, his eyes fixed on Boundless. '*Qui est-ce?*' His voice was sharp and authoritative.

'Oh, him! This here be Mr Boundless McLennan. Boundless, I present Monsieur Thibault, manager and chief of this here post.'

Boundless nodded. '*Bonjour, monsieur.*'

The bourgeois stood over six feet tall, his bony frame clad in a striped linen shirt with an open collar, a russet waistcoat, brown knee breeches and leather boots. His inquisitive features were framed by a short, neatly trimmed goatee, clean-shaven upper lip and bushy sideburns.

'*Qu'est-ce qu'il fait ici?*' Thibault addressed the question to Pinch while his eyes, piercing and intelligent, remained fastened on Boundless.

'*Il est un chasseur anglais. De l'Ohio.*' Pinch gestured to beyond the stockade walls. '*The Ally—quelque chose ou autre.* My own French ain't so peerless,' he confessed to Boundless as Thibault looked to Louis for more information. Louis shrugged and shook his head.

'*Est-il ici pour commercer avec les Indiens?*' Thibault's gaze took in the pistol stuck into Boundless' belt.

'*Non. Un chasseur. De l'Ohio.*'

'What does he say?'

'He suspects you to be an English spy.'

Quoi had re-joined them, his mouth gaped open as he hung on to every word—hovering so close that Boundless could feel the fellow's hot breath.

Boundless pointed to himself. '*Un ami, monsieur—*' He glanced at Pinch. 'What is French for "I assure you"?'

'Deuced if I know.' Pinch motioned to Thibault. '*Un chasseur. Comme il le dit.*'

'*Ainsi vous dites. Mais pourquoi est-il ici, si loin de l'Ohio?*'

'He wants to know why you are here.'

Boundless returned the Frenchman's gaze, growing exasperated at the interrogation. 'Tell him I came to explore the plains and to hunt buffalo.'

Pinch relayed this, listening as the bourgeois fired another question. 'He wants to know where you are headed.'

'Tell him I do not know—and to blazes with all the questions!'

At that moment, another man appeared from one of the buildings, a look of surprise on his face as he saw Boundless.

'Meet Monsieur Lapointe,' said Pinch as the man approached. 'He is one of the clerks that assist Monsieur Thibault with the men and the books. He has a fair grasp of English. 'Monsieur Lapointe! Meet Mr Boundless McLennan.'

The newcomer was of average height with freckled skin and a thick brown moustache. In spite of the heat, he was wearing a soiled brown frockcoat. ''Ello, Monsieur.' He extended a hand to Boundless, his face creased with curiosity.

'Pleased to meet you,' said Boundless, shaking hands. He turned his attention back to the bourgeois, half-expecting another question.

Monsieur Thibault considered him a moment longer, his gaze frank and appraising. He then turned and headed back to the large cabin, beckoning for Boundless to follow. '*Venez, monsieur. Mangez avec nous.*'

'Hooray!' Pinch slapped him on the shoulder. 'He gets it! The plain gist of it, anyways.'

'What the devil was all that business about being a spy?'

'I will explain. But first, let us eat. I could chew a rat's arse!'

The cool interior of the log building resembled a spacious hall. A large stone hearth, enclosing a brick oven and a chimney, was set against the end wall. The smell of smoke and cooking drifted from the fireplace. The middle of the room was occupied by two long tables, each capable of seating twenty or more people. Everything, from the plank floor and chinked walls to the sturdy tables and chairs, looked solidly constructed. Parchment stretched across the two small windows filtered afternoon light into the room.

A door opened from a room set on the left side of the hearth and a girl with dark, smooth skin and dressed in a deerskin tunic stepped out. She appeared to be no more than fifteen years of age. She halted in surprise at seeing Boundless before continuing to the fireplace. She knelt and tended to a large pot suspended above the flames by an iron tripod.

Thibault sat down at the nearest table, motioning for Boundless to do the same. Several wooden bowls were stacked on the table and Louis began to pass these around. Spoons and pewter mugs followed.

The girl approached Thibault and began ladling the contents of a pot onto his plate.

'Who is she?' Boundless whispered, his eyes on the girl as she moved on to Louis.

'That be White Deer,' said Pinch, 'wife of Guillaume. A Hidatsa, if you please. Her father is a big man in the tribe. She is a great prize and invaluable to maintaining good relations with the Indians.'

With averted gaze, the girl ladled a mess of stew into Boundless' bowl before retiring back to the hearth where she sat on a stool.

'*Manger!*' Thibault spooned into the meal without ceremony. Scarcely had they begun to eat when a commotion arose from outside, highlighted by howling dogs. Stuffing a spoonful of stew into his mouth, Quoi hastened from the table.

'Now you be in for a treat,' said Pinch.

After a few minutes, the door opened and a lean, dark-skinned individual with long black hair tied in a tail stepped inside. A scar running from jaw to temple gave him a fierce, forbidding aspect. He growled something to Quoi, which resulted in the gatekeep's bobbing head shrinking into his body like a turtle's into its shell.

'That be Askook, the very devil!' Pinch wiped a hand across his mouth before hailing the other man. 'Askook, *je vous présente,* Monsieur Boundless McLennan.'

'*Bonjour,*' said Boundless.

The other man did not answer but gave a hard stare before sitting down. The girl hurried to bring him food.

Boundless muttered to Pinch. 'Does everyone suspect me of being a spy?'

Pinch laughed. 'These be fraught times, friend. And folk in the fur trade hold each other in more mistrust than they do Lucifer himself.'

The rest of the meal continued in silence. Boundless ate slowly, aware of the many curious looks cast in his direction. Pinch supped noisily, stopping only to smack his lips and praise 'the very exact fist of salt' as he consumed a second bowl of stew. As Boundless finished his own bowl and set down the spoon, Thibault, who had eaten sparingly, raised a hand. The girl at once got to her feet and began to clear the table. The Frenchmen took out pipes. Louis offered Boundless a pouch and he shook his head. '*Non. Merci.*'

'You do not enjoy a pipe?' Pinch raised an eyebrow.

'I have never acquired the habit.'

The Bostonian sat back, savouring the draw. 'And I have never been without. Why, my mammy claimed I sucked the stem in preference to the teat!' He reflected on this notion through a puff of smoke. 'A habit I have since corrected through long and arduous practice.'

Thibault set his elbows on the table, his eyes on Boundless. '*Et maintenant, dis-nous l'histoire de comment tu es venu ici.*'

'What does he say?'

'He wishes to hear how you made your way here—alone, and on horseback. Chant the tale. I will parcel it out in the French.'

Boundless began a slow and halting account of his adventures since crossing the mountains, pausing frequently to allow Pinch to interpret. Quoi listened with open mouth, his eyes turning from Boundless to Pinch as the latter passed on the account with what seemed to Boundless suspicious gusto. Thibault toyed with a spoon, nodding at points in the tale. Lapointe sat with sober face, attentive to the details. Louis leaned forward, eyes fixed on Boundless. Askook listened with an air of contemptuous indifference, his eyes narrowing at Boundless' account of the fight with the Shawnee.

Suddenly Quoi gasped—shooting Boundless a look of mingled horror and astonishment. Thibault smiled while Louis laughed out loud. Having said nothing so remarkable as to warrant such a response, Boundless stared accusingly at Pinch.

'What did you say?'

'Your history—upon my soul!'

'As I have said it?'

'What? A little salt ain't permitted?' Pinch snorted. 'The bones were bare, skinned of colour and particularity. I merely added a tinge of powder, as would any self-respecting man.'

'You would oblige me by sticking to my words.'

'And so I do—spite of their paucity!'

When the account concluded—with that morning's chance encounter— Thibault, who had observed Boundless closely throughout, cleared his throat. '*Vous êtes un chasseur compétent?*'

'He wishes to know if you be a capable hunter?'

'Yes. *Oui.*'

Thibault spoke again—the question drawing a surprised exclamation from Pinch. 'Well, friend,' he said, turning to Boundless. 'You appear to have won favour with our noble prince. He asks if you wish to join the company?'

'He wishes to offer me employment?'

'And why not? A skilled hunter is of great value in this godforsaken spot. What say you?'

'But do you not have hunters already? You yourself—'

'Fie!' Pinch scoffed. 'Only through dire necessity. It was purely by chance that we brought down that specimen you saw this morning.'

'On what terms?' he asked as Thibault watched and listened.

'In truth, a pittance. But it will offer you a roof for the winter—which is fearsome—not to mention the exclusive society of yon nuzzlewit. If you agree, he will draw up a contract specifying wages and conditions. Do you accept?'

Boundless hesitated but a moment. 'I do. *Oui*.' He extended a hand to Thibault who shook it across the table.

'*Bien*.' Rising from the table, the bourgeois signalled for Lapointe to accompany him. The two walked outside, engaged in conversation.

Askook noisily scraped back his chair. Quoi stared fearfully, as though beholding an object of mixed dread and fascination. With a bellicose glance at Boundless, the Indian headed for the door.

'What offends the fellow?'

'Pfft! Pay him no heed. Offence be as natural to him as drawing air. 'Tis his very constitution.'

'But what was the offence?'

'The villain fancies himself a hunter—though in truth, he is handier, they say, with a knife. He is jealous lest you usurp his position.'

'And do I?'

''Twere better the scoundrel was usurped all the way back to the foul belly that gave him birth.'

Boundless raised an eyebrow. 'Strong words.'

'But fitting. You shall see for yourself the character of the man. But come, our noble master wishes me to escort you around the post.'

They emerged from the cabin to a fresh chorus of howls and yelps. Pinch let loose a string of curses. 'Those cursed hounds be a bane.'

'Why so many?'

'There are no horses here—apart from your own—so we must depend on the dogs. Your horse will no doubt prove a tremendous novelty to the heathen.'

'They have no horses at all?'

'Very few. 'Tis rumoured the Mandan have a small herd. The Arikara, also, are said to own some, but I have not seen any.'

They strolled along a dirt street, Pinch pointing out the various buildings. 'The icehouse … the forge … Our last blacksmith drowned in the river, and the brigade must bring back a replacement. The carpentry shop … the chapel—now a canoe shed.'

'Pardon? The brigade?'

'Aye, the remainder of our merry band.'

Curious, he was about to ask another question when Pinch waved him off. 'You shall meet them all in good time.'

Pinch pulled open the door of the canoe shed. Inside, wooden frames supported six birch-bark canoes. Pinch laid a hand on one. 'A norther,' he said. 'Strong enough to withstand rapids yet light enough for two men to porter between them.'

Closing the door, Pinch led the way to the next building. The interior was occupied by a large wooden frame. A heavy beam extended from the frame, the end suspended above a wooden crib.

Pinch sat on the beam and dangled his feet. 'The fur press. We use it to squeeze the bales we send back east.'

The voice of Thibault sounded from nearby and Pinch stood up. 'Ne'er a moment,' he grumbled. Outside, he pointed to a conical building. 'The smokehouse … You will be expected to keep it full.'

Continuing, he led the way to a large building that resembled a barracks. 'The bunkhouse. It used to be where the soldiers slept.' Pinch opened the door to reveal two rows of twenty beds each, positioned along the walls. Some of the beds had small stools beside them. A stone fireplace stood at one end of the room. In front of it was a table with two chairs. 'Choose one closest the fire.' advised Pinch 'In winter, you will thank me for it.'

'Where does Monsieur Thibault sleep?'

Pinch stepped outside and pointed to a house with a garden in front. 'Over there—in his own little house along with White Deer.'

Nearby were three smaller houses, the furthermost of which stood a hundred paces from the single-storey row houses he had glimpsed earlier.

'The junior clerks, two of them, sleep in the houses,' explained Pinch. They used to quarter the army officers. Lapointe, the senior clerk, lives in that one.' He pointed to the largest of the three. 'He has a Mandan wife—Scattered Corn Woman. She is back visiting her family at the moment. And there is where the married men sleep.' He pointed to the row houses.

'Married? You mean they bring their wives with them?'

Pinch hooted with mirth. 'Do you think any Christian woman could survive a journey across so much wilderness? No, I mean what the French call "country wives", women or *mihe* from the nearby villages who live with the men during the winter. They turn up in late summer, when the brigade returns, and depart again for their villages in the spring.'

'And Monsieur Thibault allows this?'

'Why would he not, since he leads by example? Such alliances are invaluable. We live here on the permission of the Mandan, who own this land. The more we marry into the local tribes, the safer we be.'

'And does he also have a wife—a Christian wife—back east?'

'In Montreal? Yes.'

Boundless thought about this. 'And you, yourself—if you will pardon my asking?'

'Married? Once. A fine woman.'

'And no longer?' he asked, curiosity getting the better of him.

Pinch grimaced. 'The tribe moved, and she went with them. Where, I do not know. Come.' He led off along the small street.

Boundless quickened his step to catch up. 'The brigade?' he asked.

'What?'

'You said "when the brigade returns". Did you mean the soldiers?'

Pinch laughed. 'Monsieur Thibault would not thank you for that. By *brigade* I mean the fleet of canoes that convey the furs east in the spring and return in late summer with supplies and trade goods.'

'What is the present month?'

Pinch seemed unsurprised by the question. 'August. The men should be back in two or three weeks. Although it depends on the weather, the Indians, the lakes, and God knows what.'

'How many canoes—in the brigade?'

'Five. Up from four the year before last and three the year before that. Each canoe carries up to six paddlers—*voyageurs*, in the French. Take my advice. If Thibault ever offers you to join with it, protest as though your life depended upon it.' Pinch swatted a fly. 'I am still scarce recovered from my own exertions of three years past. 'Tis carrying and paddling until your arms be ready to fall off. It is slavish work and therefore to be avoided at all costs. Come, we are almost finished.'

Pinch paused outside another building. 'Tack and implements. Formerly a powder magazine.' He pulled at the door, surprised to find it open. 'It is usually locked. Look for yourself.'

In the dim light, Boundless made out a great variety of axes, saws, hammers, hoes, trenching tools, chisels, files, bits of wood, coils of ropes, lengths of chain, ladders, and sundry other implements, including a small vice. Boxes of nails sat on a shelf, and lengths of cut timber leaned against one wall.

'I have seen trading posts not half so well-stocked.'

'Brought here, and left, by the soldiers. And all necessary for the maintenance of the post. Each year, we must cut fresh logs to replace those that are cracked or rotted. 'Tis a never-ending chore.' Pinch kicked at a log lying on the dirt floor. 'Thibault insisted on acquiring the lot when he took over the fort. The fellow could sell fish to a fisherman.'

They continued along the street. 'There must indeed be considerable upkeep,' Boundless said, gazing around the many buildings.

Pinch spat into the grass. 'Guillaume—his Christian name, although never use it—has a horror of idle hands. In spring and autumn, as the weather allows, it is hammer, nail, bang, saw, fill, chink, and all to dizzy the brain. It is a rare moment when a man might enjoy a pipe in peace. This calmness you see now'—Pinch gestured around them—'will last only until such time as the brigade returns. Then 'tis hurry this and hurry that and the devil take the hindmost!' Grumbling, he shook his head, as though much put upon.

The day was fine and warm. Through the buildings, Boundless saw Quoi hobble to the dog pen with a bucket of scraps. The gatekeep walked with a shuffling gait, as if each leg was as mismatched as the rest of him. Pinch followed his gaze. 'A rare specimen,' he said.

He led them back towards the main cabin, stopping before the double-storey building, the largest in the stockade. A flight of three broad steps led up to the door. 'The trading house—where we store trade goods and barter with the Indians.'

Pinch ascended the steps and pulled open the door. 'I half expected to see Askook,' he said, peering into the shadowy interior. 'The fellow skulks here as if it were his private lair.'

The room was a considerable size, the walls lined with shelves containing an assortment of clothes and utensils. A table and standing desk stood near the front beside a woodstove.

'That is where Guillaume maintains his ledgers and oversees the trades. He marks every pelt and pot that crosses back and forth.' Pinch pointed to a flight of steps. 'Upstairs, we store dried goods, such as powder, flour, sugar and tea.' He placed a hand on the nearest shelf. 'These will be full to overflowing once the brigade returns. In season, we be as well stocked as a New York emporium.'

'See the treasure that brings us to such a hellish place!' Pinch gestured to where a number of pelts lay piled on the plank floor. Bending over, he selected a pelt and handed it to Boundless. 'This be brown gold.'

Boundless squeezed the greyish-brown fur between his hands. It felt thick and oily, as though coated with wax.

'That specimen was formerly part of a coat. See the sides?' Pinch folded to demonstrate. 'It has been cut and trimmed for the purpose. The sweat has turned it yellow. Greasy fur. The finest. It no doubt fetched the owner a wool blanket or twenty fishhooks.'

'Why greasy? Is it the wax?'

'Aye. The French call it *castor gras* or fat beaver. It is considered of finer quality as it has been taken in spring when it still has its winter fat. The Indians sew the pelts into a robe and wear it next to the skin until the long hairs are worked off. The English call such worn pelts coat beaver.'

Pinch picked up another pelt, holding it out for Boundless to examine. 'This is *castor sec*—parchment beaver. It is dry, like parchment. It still has the long hairs. Sun-dried on a willow hoop instead of worn.'

Boundless ran his hand through the layers of fur, his fingers discriminating the long, outer hairs from the short, inner ones. Unlike the first, the pelt was a silvery-grey colour. 'And both sorts are of equal value?'

'The coat is worth more. Some merchants claim the difference is now moot, at best. Why, I cannot say. But the Indians, the older ones in particular, will insist on the distinction.' Pinch bent down and selected another pelt, handing it without comment to Boundless.

'It feels different. The underfur is … shorter?'

'Absent, more like. That is summer beaver. Not worth the trouble of catching. The other'—Pinch nodded at the coat beaver—'was caught in early spring—after the underfur had grown all winter. That be prime beaver. The Indians demand more in trade for such. In truth, it is all Guillaume is interested in.'

Boundless studied the glossy pelt in his hand. 'It is worth much—compared to a buffalo robe, I mean?'

'Buffalo?' Pinch snorted with derision. 'Pound for pound, prime beaver will fetch three times your buffalo.'

'The trade is of such worth?'

'Worth?' Pinch's eyes widened. 'Why, the entire world doth wag upon its tail! Why else do the French and English armies fight each other? A pelt speared by a simple savage in the forest brings ten shillings in Montreal, and five more in London or Paris.'

'Then I am eager to catch one of these wondrous creatures for myself.'

Pinch shook his head. 'Guillaume forbids it—for fear of upsetting the Indians. The Mandan are peaceful and care neither one way or the other. Which is as well, since we abide here at their sufferance. But the Arikara are prickly and claim sole rights to the animal.'

'Arikara?'

'An irksome bunch. They have several villages nearby.'

'Then you do not snare the beaver yourself?'

'For what good reason? The Indians are masters at it, and much depends on our good relations with them. Which is why Thibault took a Hidatsa woman to wife. He is an almighty fusspot at times, but straight as an arrow with the Indians. They know and trust him. But he will get his money's worth in all things, down to the last brass *sou*.'

Boundless placed the pelt back on the floor. 'I have much to learn.'

Finishing the tour, they headed back to the main cabin which, Pinch informed him, was known variously as 'the big house', 'the hall', or, in French, *la grande salle*.

'It is where we eat all our meals and play cards in the evenings. It will soon be as familiar to you as the house in which you were born.'

Across the way, a door opened and Askook stepped out, an axe across his shoulder. They watched as he made his way across to a small grass enclosure that housed a huge pile of cut logs. The half-breed walked with a peculiar strutting gait as though arrogant of the world.

'He looks an ill-tempered sort.'

'A truer word rarely spoken. He would as soon sink a knife into your ribs as say hello. Indeed, 'tis rumoured he has done so on more than one occasion. The fiend takes especial delight in tormenting Quoi, although never in Guillaume's presence. He is notoriously quick to take offence but dare not break the peace lest he be kicked from the post—which knowledge does little to mend his temper.'

'Earlier, you called him a half-breed?'

'Aye. His father was French. His mother Cree. Or the reverse, I can never think. Although some say the devil himself had a hand in the birth. 'Tis Guillaume to blame.'

'How so?'

'He hired the villain from a village along the Frost River, thinking his knowledge of Cree would prove useful. Ever since, he has been a thorn in our side. I suspect Guillaume would willingly discharge him, but the fellow is cunning enough to stay on his good side—just! Although his mistreatment of Quoi will surely get him the boot one day.—Speak of the devil!'

Boundless glanced up to see Quoi limping towards them.

'The creature looks as if he would babble. Come, let us away!'

Pinch completed the inspection by showing off the stout defensive wall. 'Strong enough to keep out Pharaoh's army,' he boasted. 'You will not see a stronger fort this side of the Mississippi.'

A flight of steps beside the main gate led up to a plank walkway secured to the inside of the wall. The walkway was positioned approximately four feet from the top so that defenders could fire down upon any enemy.

Pinch nodded at Boundless' impressed look. 'The expedition had its own engineers, and a plan based upon military forts along the Ohio.'

'Expedition?'

'A story for later. Part of Guillaume's good fortune.'

'Do tell.'

Pinch held up a hand. 'A tale for the pipe, friend. I feel in need of a lie-down. In some darksome cranny where Guillaume will not think to look.'

The following morning, Boundless sat across from the bourgeois in the 'hall', as he had come to think of it. Pinch sat alongside, the Bostonian explaining the document lying on the table before him.

'In sum, and in total, the contracted duties—as an *engagé* of *La Société des fourrures des Grands Lacs*—the Great Lakes Fur Company, in plain sense—include the following:' Pinch cleared his throat. 'First and foremost—'

'You do not read from the contract?'

'Save for the hunting, it is the same as for myself. I have it to memory. Shall I proceed?'

At his nod, Pinch ticked off the duties on his fingers. 'Provisioning the post with meat and fish—that be the prime obligation. Cutting wood, tending the garden—as hunting allows, and general upkeep of the post. Other labour or tasks as required. The conduct of all to be virtuous and upright and so on and so forth.'

'That is all?' Boundless glanced at the listening Thibault.

'It is—except for defence of the post, if necessary.'

Thibault was studying his reaction to Pinch's recital. '*Vous approuvez?*'

'He asks—'

'*Oui!*' he said, guessing the question from Thibault's expression.

'*Très bien!*' Thibault dipped a quill in a bottle of ink and passed the pen, indicating where he should make his mark. An approving look crossed his face as he watched Boundless sign his name. Getting to his feet, he extended his hand. '*Bienvenue à notre petit poste.*'

'*Merci*, Monsieur Thibault.'

'You be a signed man!' Pinch clapped him on the shoulder.

Boundless halted, struck by an afterthought. 'I forgot. For how long am I bound?'

'Until the heavens dissolve and the earth doth crack! Fear not. It is but a year, no more. Guillaume is the most cautious of men, as you shall discover.'

'And do all the men sign such contracts?'

'Sign, no. Place their mark, yes. In any case, 'tis but a scrap of paper.'

Boundless grimaced. ''Twas but a scrap of paper that fetched me here.'

'How so?' Pinched gave him a curious look.

'A tale for another day.'

Pinch cogitated, a sagacious look on his face. ''Tis true then—what they say?'

'What is?'
'That a scrap may lead to a scrape? Is that the essence?'
'Aye. The very soul.'
'Then let us find some rum—to mark all such scraps as scraped us!'

## 5

## A Tale of Good Fortune

NEXT MORNING, PINCH VOLUNTEERED to accompany Boundless as he prepared to scout the surrounding country in preparation for his first hunt. 'Unless you mean to ride the horse,' he added.

'I have had enough riding to last me the end of my days,' assured Boundless. 'Are you set?'

The air was warm and humid as they walked out through the gates. Pinch had exchanged the tricorn for an equally frayed straw hat. His spare, wiry frame was clothed in a soiled linen shirt and canvas pants.

Boundless carried Mose's musket with his own slung across his back. 'Which way?' he asked.

'All roads be the same. Generally, we head away from the river towards the parts where you first found us. The open grass has the most game.'

'Let us see the river, first.'

They headed the short distance to the Missouri, which was lined with thick stands of cottonwood. 'How wide is it?' asked Boundless, gazing out over the river.

'Half a mile, mostly, although it floods to three-quarters.'

The fort was situated on a natural bend or 'bow', the river visible for a good distance upstream before disappearing around a bend. Downstream, its course was visible for less than a half-mile before it vanished around the bottom of the curve. The water flowed strongly past where they stood, logs and branches carried along in its sweep.

'The brigade comes from up there.' Pinch pointed upstream. 'When it leaves, it must battle the current before turning off to an inlet about a mile and a half upriver.'

'And from there?'

'A question upon which much hangs.'

The teasing evasiveness in his normally garrulous companion intrigued and perplexed Boundless in equal measure. *There is some mystery here*, he speculated, determined to draw it out of the fellow.

'We get fish from here,' said Pinch. 'Even through the winter ice.'

'It gets so cold?'

'Cold?' Pinch stared in astonishment. 'A prairie winter is a thing to behold. Enjoy the summer, for it will turn colder by degrees until you think Old Jack himself has you by the throat!'

'I am used to cold. The Highlands were fierce in winter.'

'I cannot say, as I have never travelled there. But winter on these prairies be a tale unto itself. On certain days, no one—not even the Indians—dare venture forth.'

They walked back past the fort and headed inland, walking in reverse of the north-easterly direction they had followed the previous day. The country was marked by rolling shrub-covered hills and rich stands of timber.

'Spend as much time outside the post as possible while the weather allows,' said Pinch. 'Louis slips off on the slightest pretext—and will not thank you for filching him of the excuse of hunting.'

'Yet more offence! And yourself?'

Pinch removed his hat to scratch his head. 'In truth, I flee the arduous monotony of the post—abandoning Simon-o'-the-Gate to tend to the chores, feed the dogs and generally mumble and presuppose in between duties.'

'Is the fellow truly a half-wit?'

'Poised at equidistant points between feeble-mindedness and lunacy and inclining by degrees to the latter.'

'It is a wonder that he finds himself out here—so far from the care of his family.'

'Ha! Not so wonderful—the family themselves being solely responsible for his exile. They reasoned the heathen could make better sense of his prattle. Guillaume took him here as a kindness to the father and, indeed, clucks over him like a mother hen.'

'I wonder that you do not hunt for yourselves,' said Boundless, eyeing a group of mule deer. 'The game is so abundant.'

'We are paddlers and fetchers rather than hunters. Hardly any of us are tolerable shots with a musket. That deer you caught us with was the first we brought down in four days of trying. We depend on the Indians to supply us with meat, smoked fish, pemmican and rice. Nevertheless, Guillaume wishes to ensure we can feed ourselves if necessary. The Indians be contrary at times, and game grows exceedingly scarce in the winter.'

'Contrary?'

'Betimes. Often, they hold a grudge if they feel they have not secured the true value for their furs. Then they avoid us and seek other means of trade.'

'There are other traders in the area?'

'None, apart from the few French trappers who live among the Indians and share their lives. To my knowledge, we are the only company this far west of the Mississippi. But the Indians are not loath to trade the pelts on to other tribes—all the way to the Lakes if need be. There be an invisible thread linking Indians, traders, middlemen, supply posts and depots from here to Montreal.'

'Invisible thread?'

''Tis a figure. A *fur road*, say. The pelt be valuable enough to bury or suspend differences between otherwise warring parties along the way. Each tribe is jealously courted by the merchants through their agents with the aim of monopolising the supply. 'Course, they be abetted by those thieves in Quebec.'

'Thieves?'

'The French government. They seek to control the profits by choking the supply through licensing.'

'And we—the company, I mean—are licensed?'

Pinch nodded. 'Rascals, all!'

Enjoying the day and the gentle stroll, they walked several miles to a small creek where Pinch insisted on stopping for a pipe. The great rock could be seen rising in the distance.

'Seat yourself. Time here passes an hour slower than elsewhere.' Pinch sat down in the grass, sprawling out his legs to make himself comfortable while taking out his pipe and tinderbox.

'There are a dozen buffalo not a half-mile distant,' observed Boundless.

Pinch grimaced while taking out the char cloth. ''Tis a heavy taste. I prefer your venison or rabbit. Besides which, we lack the skill or wherewithal to kill the creature. I have seen a half-dozen shots poured into the beast, and it merely shakes his head as if to say, "how d'ye do". The only buffalo meat we get is from the Indians. The bow and arrow will bring the creature down quicker than a musket ball.'

Boundless chose a spot on the grass and lounged on his elbows, feeling languid in the sultry air. Above, huge white clouds towered in the blueness of the sky. They sat companionably for a few minutes, Pinch content to puff on his pipe in silence.

'Pinch, I have been wondering. Why was everyone so put out by my arrival? Did they really think me a spy for the English army?'

'The army?' Pinch looked bemused. 'It is not the army that troubles them. The war is far away from here. There is a tale to tell that will explain the alarm at your sudden appearance.'

'That mysterious tale again!'

Pinch made a rumbling sound and hawked into the grass. 'You say you know nothing of the fur business?'

'Apart from what I have learned from you this morning.'

'Then let me tell you, it is a cutthroat affair, with rivalries and jealousies on all sides.' Pinch put the pipe back into his mouth and pondered for a while as if savouring the suspense. 'You need hold that in mind while I tell the tale.'

'While summer yet holds!'

Pinch acknowledged the impatience with a lift of the pipe. 'I call it—the tale—"Guillaume's Good Fortune" and came by it in bits and pieces.'

Staring into the distance, Pinch puffed on the pipe as he assembled the parts. 'It begins ten year ago, in Montreal. Guillaume was, by all accounts, an industrious fellow who had tried, and failed, at several enterprises. In an attempt to change his luck, he quit his birthplace and headed to New Orleans to try his hand at a hardware business. Alas, the business failed ere it had hardly begun. That was his first stroke of fortune.'

Pinch plucked his chin, relishing the quizzical frown on Boundless' face.

'He was about to return to Montreal a bankrupt failure when, by chance, he heard of plans by the French government to send an expedition up the Missouri. The purpose was to explore the country, contact the Indians, and build a fort to secure the territory for France. Guillaume, having nothing better in mind, applied to join the expedition as a negotiator with the Indians—he had picked up some of the lingo—and was accepted. That was his second stroke of fortune.'

Lifting the water bottle to his mouth, Pinch took a long swallow. 'Did I say "second"?' He pushed the cork back in the bottle.

'You did.'

'The expedition was made up of soldiers, mapmakers, botanists, missionaries, and what have you. They proceeded up the river from New Orleans in a dozen keel boats. They went further north than any man before them, excepting a handful of trappers. After two months of arduous travel, they made contact with the Mandan far up along the Missouri. They wintered here and built that fine fort you now call home. It was intended as the grand headquarters of the French empire west of the Mississippi. While visiting the Indian tribes in his capacity as trade emissary, Guillaume happened to meet a French trapper who had married into the Hidatsa.'

'His third stroke of luck?'

Pinch chuckled. 'Hit squarely on the nail! The trapper introduced him to a Hidatsa hunter named Road Maker—so named for his skill at finding new pathways to the best hunting grounds. And that was the greatest fortune of all. For Road Maker claimed to know of a secret water route clear across the prairies to the great lakes in the east.' He cocked an eyebrow. 'D'ye understand the import?'

'Not yet, excepting the fellow has found a new way to the east. What of it?'

'What of it?' Pinch took the pipe from his mouth to stare.

'I am but a novice to this trade and these parts,' Boundless protested, chagrined that he had perhaps missed the point of the tale.

'In which case, I must step back to the beginning.' Pinch ruminated on the extinguished pipe as he sought a fresh starting point for his tale. 'Know that—up until a few years ago—beaver trapping was confined to the east or to the far north-west. A few adventurous souls had journeyed up the Great Lakes and onto the prairies. But no one knew of a route—a passable route joining the St. Lawrence in the east to the Mississippi Valley in the west. Do you understand?'

'I am as unfamiliar with the geography as I am the history.'

'And yet further back …' Breaking off the tale, Pinch took out his knife. He used it to gouge a horizontal 'V' shape in the grass.

'Lake Superior, here,' he said, pointing to the right tip of the V. 'The post, here.' He pointed to the left tip. 'The distance in-between be formidable—especially as the rivers do not oblige us by flowing in straight lines, or from east to west. The way from Montreal to Lake Superior is well mapped. And there are various waters that lead from the lake to the Mississippi. But from thence, so the reckoning went, 'twas easier to drift south to where the Mississippi runs into the Missouri.' He traced a finger down one arm of the V to the apex.

'I have seen it—the joining of the waters.'

'Aye. And from your account, you followed the Missouri north to here'—Pinch moved the knife blade up the other arm of the V—'so you will appreciate the distance involved. That was the route of Guillaume's original expedition. The way is long and arduous and takes you away from where you wish to be.' He glanced at Boundless. 'Do you see the problem?'

'A great distance, I suppose?'

'A fearsome distance. Well over a thousand miles—and that just from here to the lake head. Add another thousand from the lake to Montreal and you will appreciate the difficulty of maintaining men and supplies in such a distant outpost, notwithstanding the quality of beaver.'

'So, Monsieur Thibault, or this Road Maker, knew of this other route, a shorter one?'

For answer, Pinch scraped a rut connecting both arms of the 'V' well above the forks. 'D'ye see the value? Shorter and quicker and, above all, *secret*. A water road that takes one from the tip of Lake Superior acrost the whole of Louisiana to the Mandan country. But it is not all smooth paddling. There is much portaging betwixt river, stream, and creek.'

'Portaging?'

'Aye. *Carrying*. Canoes, furs, stores, everything, between lake and stream.'

'So, what did Guill—Monsieur Thibault do with this knowledge?'

'Do? First of all, he had to prove it—demonstrate that the Indian wasn't a liar. So, with the major's permission, he quit the expedition in order to make his way back to Montreal, west to east. Of course, he had to convince the Hidatsa to guide him—which the fellow agreed to upon being given a musket and powder, and the promise of much more to come.'

'Being another stroke of luck—that the Indian agreed to be his guide?'

'The fifth in my tally. The two made the perilous journey and arrived safely at the north shore of Lake Superior, true to the Indian's word. Guillaume now knew he had a tremendous commercial secret, one of enormous value. But being Guillaume, he bided his time. Then came another stroke of luck—the present war.'

'The war?'

Pinch grinned. 'Mischief for most, opportunity for Guillaume. You see, the French recalled their outlying garrisons to strengthen the forts along the Ohio. Upon learning of this, Guillaume promptly looked up his old friend, the major. And, with the latter's intercession, struck a bargain with the authorities to take possession of this fort and all its supplies. The sole condition was that he maintain it—and the French presence in the territory—until the war should conclude. Armed with this mandate, he approached a group of Montreal fur merchants with the promise not only of a new and secret route to the west, but also a fort or outpost waiting to house the expedition. Impressed—by his person, 'tis said, as much as his information—they raised the capital to send him back with the army when it sent a fleet of keel boats to evacuate the garrison. Only this time, he took with him thirty men plus six canoes. He took possession of the fort and re-established contact with Road Maker, rewarding him with handsome gifts. The latter agreed to join the company as a guide.' Pinch paused, his eyes twinkling. 'And lo and behold, the Indian had a sister. A comely lass that had already caught Guillaume's eye.'

'White Deer!'

Pinch slapped his knee. 'To seal the compact! And then—a year after arriving, Guillaume sent back three tons of finest prime beaver to Montreal. The shareholders were so toothsome they voted him an instant partner—on condition that he remain out west as bourgeois to oversee the business and maintain their interests, which he does to this day.'

'And the route yet remains a secret?'

'It does. And to further illustrate Guillaume's cunning, he insisted they call the venture "The Great Lakes Fur Company", to deceive any spies from rival outfits into thinking the source of the furs was the country northwest of the lakes.' Pinch paused, awaiting a reaction.

'A most clever fellow,' agreed Boundless, his admiration genuine. 'So that explains the suspicion at my arrival? He thought I had stumbled upon the great secret?'

Pinch nodded. 'Stumbled upon or fitted to expose. It was *your* luck that the horse and mule convinced Guillaume of the veracity of your tale.'

'But surely it will only be a matter of time before the route becomes known?'

'Each and every *voyageur* must take a solemn Catholic oath to protect it. And even then, all the men are handpicked for their honesty and trustworthiness—the mad dog Askook excepted. Mind, even if they should forfeit their oath, it is hard to see them picking their way through the thousand swamps and marshes betwixt here and Lake Superior without an experienced and knowledgeable guide.'

Boundless stared at the crushed grass, trying to picture the liquid road. 'And each year the canoes make the journey to Montreal and back?'

Pinch stared in amazement. 'Are you mad? 'Tis a journey halfway round the earth! The men leave here as soon as the ice on the river allows—April or sometimes May—and paddle east for two months. At the same time, another brigade sets out from Montreal. The two meet midway, at an *entrepôt*—supply depot—that Guillaume established at the head of Lake Superior.' Pinch gouged a point in the grass. 'There, the men from the west, the *hivernants,* or winterers, meet with the so-called *pork eaters* from the east. The two exchange cargoes—goods and supplies in one direction, fur bales in the other. The brigade then rests up for two weeks or so before starting the arduous journey back, weighted down with the supplies. In late August, or sometimes September, they arrive back at the post, as you shall see.'

'A dangerous journey, I hazard?'

'Aye. The men risk daily death from rapids, weather, injury, drowning or attack by hostile Indians. It is hard to say which is more murderous to the back—the paddling or the carrying. It is the reason why I stay on in the summer.'

Boundless sat for a few minutes, absorbing all that he had heard while Pinch smoked another pipe.

'Well? What say you?' Pinch eyed him speculatively. 'Now that you know our great secret?'

'I say again that there is a great deal for me to learn. And also, that Monsieur Thibault is, most assuredly as you say, an enterprising man.'

'He is that. Albeit an overly industrious one. A grievous flaw in otherwise so sterling a character.'

They sat in silence for a while, each lost in his own thoughts. As they got up to continue, Boundless indicated the great rock in the distance. 'That is a most peculiar shape,' he said. 'Does it resemble anything to you?'

'Resemble?'

'The likeness, I mean, to some animal?'

Pinch stared, brow furrowed, as he considered the question. 'A lion, mayhap?' He glanced at Boundless. 'A lion?'

'Something else. With that big protuberance as the head.'

'A horse?'

'Does it not most resemble a buffalo?'

Pinch squinted for a moment. 'I confess I never gave it a thought. But now that you raise the matter, I suppose one might fancy it as such—at a stretch.'

They were interrupted by a jovial hail. A party of Indians appeared from out of a nearby gulch and advanced towards them. Without thinking, Boundless cocked his musket, halting in surprise when Pinch laid a restraining hand on his arm.

'Do not be afeared. They are Hidatsa. We do much trade with them.' Pinch held up a hand. *'Ma'kahpitami!'* he called out as the Indians approached.

'You speak their tongue?'

'A mite. Sufficient to say "hello", although not so much as to dispute taxation rights.'

In spite of Pinch's assurance, Boundless remained vigilant as the Indians drew nearer, scanning the party for any sign of hostile intent. The Indians were clad in simple breechclouts, their naked torsos gleaming with grease in the warm sun. He caught a potent whiff of sweat as they approached.

Each Indian carried a bow in one hand and a fistful of arrows or a hatchet in the other. He felt for the knife in the sash around his waist, his instincts primed for danger in spite of his companion's relaxed demeanour.

'Iakash.' Pinch greeted the men. The Indians stopped a few feet away, their eyes on Boundless.

'Iakash,' the nearer savage replied. He stood a head shorter than Boundless. His greased hair was arranged in tufts and threaded with feathers, bone ornaments and strips of calico. Dye markings and healed scars covered his chest. He said something to Pinch as his companions stared curiously at Boundless.

Pinch uttered a reply and gestured to the sky.

To Boundless' amazement, the stony-faced Indians broke into uproarious laughter—their fierce demeanour dissolving in merriment as they turned to one another to embroider the joke.

'What the devil did you say?'

'They wished to know where you had come from. I told them you had dropped from the sky. Leastways, I *think* I did. The language is devilish hard to figure.'

One of the Indians pointed and said something to his companions, the remark drawing more laughter.

Pinch joined in, adding to the humour in a show of fellowship. 'Do not be concerned,' he said in an aside. 'They mean no disrespect. They are extremely fond of a jest and, by this means, show acceptance.' He pointed to a group of deer where they grazed in the distance. 'Go! Get fat on the critters. *Manger!*' he said, rubbing his stomach to emphasise the point.

The Indians started off—with good-humoured looks at Boundless.

He let slip a sigh of relief as he watched them go. 'You do not fear them?'

Pinch stared in surprise. 'Fear them? Why would I? They are fine fellows and true to their word. They are our partners in the trade and give us permission to hunt on their land. If I had the choice, I would live with them year upon year. You think I jest? But indeed, I would. Aye. And mayhap marry a pretty young *mihe* and raise my own tribe!'

Boundless gazed after the departing Indians. 'What name did you give them?'

'Hidatsa. There are also Mandan and Arikara in the area. We trade with all equally and without favour. The Mandan and Hidatsa are much alike—old allies. The Arikara are fiercer and less friendly. They are the ones that forbid the taking of beaver.'

'And you have visited their villages?'

'Many times. The Mandan—who are the real overlords—lodge along the river, ten miles from the post.'

'I should like to visit for myself.'

'And you shall, if Guillaume approves. He is a stickler for each thing in its place. You are now the post hunter, so he will expect you to bring in game, first and foremost. But if you do that well, then perhaps he will allow you to join a trading party as a reward.'

Later, back at the post, Boundless retired to bed early. Lying on the bunk, his hands crossed behind his head, he reflected on the day's events. The air in the barracks was warm, the long summer twilight splendid through the half-open door. Feeling sleepy, he yawned. As he closed his eyes, he pictured the Indians—their fierce demeanour made civil by laughter. And behind them the great rock—rising immensely in the distance.

## 6

## The Brigade

H E AND PINCH WERE taking turns to chop firewood when a musket shot sounded in the distance. Hardly had the sound died away before Quoi hobbled through the open gate, his reedy voice trembling with excitement. '*La brigade, Monsieur Bourgeois! La brigade!*'

A second shot echoed on the air. Thibault, half-dressed in shirt and breeches, appeared in the doorway of his house. '*Dépêchezvous, Monsieur! Dépêcheztoi!*' Quoi scurried back through the gate.

Pinch set down the axe. 'The brigade has returned. Come, meet your new comrades.'

They made their way to the river where Louis, Lapointe and Askook already waited. Five birch-bark canoes proceeded towards them from upstream. Sunlight flashed on the wet paddles as the heavily weighted vessels drove through the water in a line. Shading his eyes, Boundless counted five or six men in each canoe.

'*Salut! Salut!*' Quoi hopped from foot to foot, arms flailing, his face alight with enthusiasm.

Pinch shook his head. 'Last year the dunce tipped himself into the water.'

Driven by powerful strokes, the canoes forged towards the shore. Hails and shouts sounded from the vessels as Quoi, now giddy with joy, jigged and hooted on the grass.

'*Arretz!*' A man, sitting in the bow of the lead canoe, roared out the command and the crew lifted their paddles from the water as the heavily laden canoe glided in toward the shore.

'That be Gaston Theroux, or Red Beard, the *pilote* or lead man in the brigade,' said Pinch. 'He oversees the water as Guillaume oversees the land. A most capable fellow. As to his sobriquet—look no further than the ginger tuft that sits 'aneath his jaw.'

As the canoe was about to drive up onto the bank, Askook splashed into the water and gripped the bow, swinging the vessel parallel to the shore. Theroux, his face blistered from sun and wind, was the first over the side. Unlike the paddlers, who wore woollen caps on their heads, and striped, muslin or calico shirts, he was dressed in a felt beaver hat and wore a waistcoat over his linen shirt. He greeted Pinch cheerfully in French. 'You old rascal!'

Pinch threw up his hands in pretended horror. 'I heard the Indians had scalped you and chopped off your balls!'

Theroux chuckled. 'To hell with the Indians! It was the fucking river that almost killed us!' He glanced curiously at Boundless before turning in response to a hail from Lapointe.

The other canoes drove into the shore, and laughter filled the air as the paddlers, clad in knee-length pantaloons fastened by garters, splashed to the grassy bank, their voices showing relief that the long voyage was safely concluded.

Quoi squealed with excitement as a stocky, tow-haired man swept him up into the air. 'Hello, darling! Did you miss me?'

A grinning man pumped Pinch's hand. 'I told you I'd be back—you lazy bastard!'

To Boundless' eyes, the men all seemed cut from the same cloth—their bodies wiry and their faces weathered by wind and spray. He noticed how their bonhomie excluded Askook as the half-breed dragged the heavy canoes up onto the bank.

Pinch nudged him and steered his gaze to where a slightly built man dressed in deerskin stood apart from the others, his arms hanging loosely by his sides. The man's long hair was tied into plaits and looped up around his waist, his dark features unmistakably Indian.

'That be the famous Road Maker,' said Pinch. 'He is the one that pilots them through the thousand-and-one swamps and rapids between here and the lake head.'

Boundless stared curiously at the Indian and was about to approach and introduce himself when he was interrupted by a shout from Theroux. 'Let's get on with it! Unload the cargo!'

'Boundless! Over here!' Pinch called him over to where he stood conversing with a solidly built youth with a head of thick black hair. 'Come, meet a fellow Scot.'

The youth thrust out a hand. 'Thomas Bannock, friend. Pleased to make your acquaintance.'

'Boundless McLennan. And I the same, I assure you. Did you say "Scot"? By your speech, I place you as native to the Colonies.'

'Meaning I lack the proper Highland tone?' Bannock grinned, his face flushed from the paddle. 'The truth is I am more Montrealer than Scot, and half as much French as English.'

'French?'

'Aye. Blessed with three years of Jesuit schooling. 'Twill drive the presbyter out of any man!—Pardon!' Seeing Theroux glare in his direction, Bannock hastily abandoned the conversation to help with the unloading.

Planting his hands on his hips, Theroux called out instructions as the men began to unload the cargo. Several cast curious looks in Boundless' direction as they formed in a line and passed the freight from hand to hand under Theroux's shouted orders. 'Hurry up! We don't have all day!'

When the cargo was stacked on the grassy shore, Theroux bid the men wait while he conversed with Lapointe. Pinch took advantage of the brief respite to introduce Boundless to the members of the brigade.

'Boys! Meet Boundless McLennan. The newest member of our tribe.'

The men took it in turns to clasp his hand in a firm shake and introduce themselves as Robert, Pierre, Norman, Andre, Edouard, and so forth until Boundless lost all track.

'They are not all French,' he said, having shaken hands with an Enok and an Abel—the last a powerfully built fellow with a handshake that made him wince.

'That is the new blacksmith,' said Pinch, 'to replace the one drowned in the river.'

Two young men, dressed like the *pilote* in waistcoats and beaver felt hats, directed the men as they gathered around the dozens of bales and kegs assembled on the shore.

'Who are they?' Boundless asked.

'They are the new junior clerks. They will manage the goods and assist the bourgeois and Monsieur Lapointe.'

Theroux clapped his hands. 'Come on boys! Move your bony arses! The bales won't carry themselves.'

Boundless watched as the men hoisted the heavy bales onto their backs, securing the load with a sash tied around the forehead. Then, bending and straining under the weight, they set off up the grassy bank.

When he attempted to lift a bale, he was stopped by Pinch, who laid a restraining hand on his arm. 'Careful, or your guts will pop out! Leave it to them as are used to it.'

Following the brigade members back to the post, Boundless was surprised to see a throng of Indians—men, women and children—gathered outside the open gate of the stockade. A festive air ensued as several of the returning brigade set down their bales before running to embrace a willing female. Others happily lifted infants in their arms to bestow kisses as the mothers laughed. One female, an infant in her arms, went from Frenchman to Frenchman, interrogating each one. She plucked the sleeve of Theroux, who shook his head and shrugged. 'Romain didn't come back with us,' he said in French.

Turning his attention to the men consorting with the women, he berated them in a loud voice. 'Hurry up, you motherless bastards. Save your stiff cocks for later!'

The ribald words were met with laughter as the men disentangled themselves and returned to the task at hand. Within the hour, a great number of bales, kegs and boxes sat in the dirt outside the storehouse, the clerks conversing with Lapointe as he checked the bills of lading. Thibault oversaw the whole, pointing and shouting as he commanded the men.

'Those to the storehouse!' He pointed to a crate with his name written on the side. 'And those boxes to my quarters.'

The stockade rang with noise and activity as more and more Indians arrived to witness the return. The men were content to squat on the ground and smoke pipes as the naked children ran back and forth without hindrance, chasing after each other with shrieks of excitement.

'From now until next spring it be nothing short of bedlam,' said Pinch into Boundless' ear.

Standing among the bales were numerous tubs marked as *farine, beurre, sel, sucre, boeuf, porc,* and *pois.*

'What is in those?' Boundless pointed to a pile of small kegs.

Pinch smacked his lips. 'Rum, wine, and brandy. Thank God!'

'Who for?'

'For our own throats—as you shall soon see. Guillaume is very strict on not trading wine or spirits to the Indians.'

'That is a considerable weight of goods,' said Boundless, impressed by the quantity of cargo.

'Each bark will haul a ton or more.'

'Each?' He glanced at the dripping birch-barks where they had been carried up from the river and positioned in a line. 'But they cannot be longer than twenty-five feet,' he said, dubious at the claim.

'Thomas!' Pinch hailed Bannock as the latter walked past carrying a spruce paddle under his arm. 'How much weight to each norther?'

Bannock placed the tip of the paddle on the ground, using it as a post to stretch his back. 'Near to three thousand pounds.'

'Including the crew?'

Bannock shook his head. 'Crew extra.'

Astonished by the figures, Boundless did a quick sum. 'That be fifteen thousand pounds of pure cargo!'

'And each pound felt in the bones!'

Marvelling at the weight, Boundless compared it with that carried by the shallops and barges on the Patapsco River back in Maryland, concluding that the comparison favoured the canoe. 'It is a great wonder that they do not capsize in the rapids,' he said.

Bannock laughed. 'Often, they do! We almost tipped twice on the lake, the waves were so fierce. Coming, sir!' Responding to a summons from Lapointe, he tucked the paddle under his arm and hurried off.

'He is an experienced man, for all his tender years,' observed Pinch, looking after the Montrealer.

'This is his first winter at the post?'

'Aye. I have not seen him before.'

Inside the storehouse, a great variety of goods were unpacked onto the plank floor. Boxes of soap, sacks of lead shot, and quantities of tobacco sat alongside iron cooking pots and kettles made of brass and tinplate. Dozens of blankets, shirts and shoes were gathered together in neat piles amidst straw hats, rolled yards of cloth and yarn, and a great profusion of ribbons, lace, buttons and handkerchiefs. Open boxes contained fishhooks, awls, knives, flints, iron arrowheads, files, saws, clay pipes, powder horns and numerous small pots of paint.

Seeing Boundless bend to inspect a pot of paint, a man grinned and motioned to his face. *'Pour le visage!'*

'Don't allow them inside!' snapped Lapointe as a group of eager women tried to force their way into the storehouse.

'They are mad for first pickings,' remarked Pinch.

After the cargo had been unpacked and stored, and the canoes placed in storage, the men briefly retired to their quarters—the bachelors to the bunkhouse, and the married men to the row houses with their 'wives' and children.

Making his way to the bunkhouse, Boundless sat on his usual bed nearest the fire, establishing ownership as the *voyageurs* squabbled over the remaining beds. To his surprise, no one queried his claim.

Pinch, who had staked ownership of the bed opposite, reassured him on the point. 'As year-round men, we get preference,' he said.

Boundless noticed three volumes sitting on the table near the fire. He squinted at the French titles, wishing he had brought books of his own. 'Place your order for when the brigade returns,' said Pinch. 'But it will be the following year before you receive them.'

He saw one man claim a bed near the door. Pinch chuckled at the sight. 'A first timer. He thinks only of the summer breeze. Next year, he will be wiser in his choice.'

Late in the afternoon, the entire company gathered in the main hall for a celebratory supper. The room reeked of sweat, tobacco and the smell of roast venison. The long tables were filled to overflowing, the familiar peace shattered by roars of laughter, animated gossip, and the ale of good fellowship. On the hearth, White Deer , assisted by several of the native wives, chopped vegetables, peeled potatoes, and tended to the single large pot and several roasts basting above the fire. Jugs of beer, wine and punch sat on the tables alongside the trenchers and knives.

'Did I not say it would resemble a Boston tavern on a feast day?' Pinch blew out a cloud of tobacco smoke, a satisfied look on his face.

Boundless took his place, squeezing into a space between Pinch and Bannock. The noise and laughter briefly subsided as White Deer and the other wives went around handing out thick slices of venison. The meal was accompanied by pea soup, fried bread, wild rice, squash, potatoes, sweetcakes and mince pies.

''Tis the last supper—afore the sermon,' chewed Pinch in Boundless' ear, the remark puzzling him. Thibault was seated at the next table, the bourgeois seeming to enjoy the banquet and the boisterous festivity.

'What news of the war?' Boundless asked Bannock, raising his voice to make himself heard above the noise.

Bannock swallowed a mouthful of bread. 'It appears the English are winning. 'Tis said they now control the western frontier.'

Boundless absorbed this for a moment. 'You have no particular sympathies?'

'The war is bad for trade—for both sides.'

Pinch leaned across Boundless to stare at a blond-haired, broad-faced young man with a wisp of beard sitting at the second of the two tables. The youth ate heartily while seeming to block out the noise all around him. 'I hear there is a tale to yon shovel-face.'

Bannock glanced in the direction. 'Bjornson?'

'Aye, the Swede. What gossip?'

'You have sharp ears. 'Tis rumoured that he was a Lutheran preacher, expelled for enamouring one of his flock.'

'You say!' Pinch listened agog, his eyes on Bjornson.

'He is reputed to have got a married woman with child—a great scandal in the Pietist community. He was chased out in fear of his life, and can never return, 'tis said, so hard was the disgrace. The jest among the men is that he was defrocked for defrocking.'

Pinch gave out a loud guffaw, ejecting crumbs and spittle in the process. 'The poor gluepot is a preacher *sans* church, and a clergyman *sans* collar.'

They watched curiously as Bjornson swallowed the contents of his cup at a gulp.

'The church has no prohibition against strong drink, I see,' said Pinch.

''Tis his only comfort and solace. Whatever his sins, the man be a fellow worshipper.'

'He is new, then, to the brigade?' asked Boundless.

'As new as myself. The fellow is not one for a yarn. He keeps to himself and drools and mumbles over the good book every chance he gets.'

'Where is he from?'

'Delaware, I believe. There are many Swedes there.'

'And you say he can never return?'

''Tis the rumour. But who knows?'

As the talk switched to another topic Boundless regarded the Swede with a pang of fellow feeling. *If the rumours are true, then we both are exiles.*

THE PLATES WERE CLEARED, and pipes produced as a fresh cask of rum was breached. Thibault's habitual air of sober caution seemed set aside for the evening, his eyes bright as he listened to the man beside him. The room was warm and stuffy. Boundless briefly considered getting up to leave the door ajar when Thibault called for silence. He leaned back to address Theroux, seated a few chairs down from him.

Bannock whispered in his ear. 'Now you shall have the epic tale!'

Theroux wet his lips to narrate the events of the arduous journey, beginning from the *entrepôt* at Lake Superior. Boundless did his best to follow as Theroux recounted the events of the passage. He picked up the word 'Iroquois'—the name drawing muttered exclamations. When his narration was completed, Theroux looked to Thibault, who lifted his cup in salutation. '*La Brigade!*'

'*La Brigade!*'

'*Et St Joseph!*' Pinch thrust out his cup, drawing laughter.

Bannock nudged Boundless. 'He is religious to inspire a fresh cask!'

To his consternation, Thibault now glanced in his direction, a twinkle in his eye. '*C'est à votre tour.*'

'He wishes you to relate your adventures,' said Bannock as all eyes turned to Boundless.

'Again?' he groaned.

'If you wish, I can interpret.'

The offer brought an immediate protest from Pinch. 'Nay! I have the tale to heart!'

'Boundless?'

'It is true, he has related it before.' Boundless hesitated. 'But I will trouble you to relate the facts as I describe them.'

'And I will trouble you to respect the occasion.'

'Occasion?'

'A convivial dinner—attended by stout men and true, all accustomed to the brag of the bark, and expecting the same. Now, pray, begin. Your audience sits all agape. Dish up the ham and I shall dash the sauce.'

'Then let it be plain and wholesome!'

For the second time, Boundless described, in sparing detail, his trip across the prairies, omitting as superfluous any incident that hampered the thrust of his account. The Frenchmen listened with puzzled incomprehension. Several times he looked to Pinch for a sign that the latter would take up the tale in French, only to receive an irritable 'Whist!' each time.

Reaching the end, Boundless trailed off into awkward silence. He hissed at Pinch. 'Are you awake! Do you begin, at least?'

'An instant!' Pinch took a judicious belch—holding up his forefinger as if to test for wind direction. The gesture drew a burst of laughter.

Boundless groaned, fearing the worst. 'Pinch! Do not—'

'*Messieurs … et mesdames*!' Pinch shaded his eyes to peer around the table as if seeking out the latter. 'You are now about to hear the epic tale of how the Englishman came to be here. A tale full of drama and sights strange to behold!' The words were greeted with chuckles.

With this brief prologue, Pinch launched into the account, slipping into a stentorian voice complete with pantomime gestures and comical asides that drew laughter.

In spite of assistance from Bannock, Boundless quickly lost track of the account—his amanuensis giving way to chuckles as he tried to keep pace with Pinch's dips and swerves. As the windy, blustery rendition shook out yet more yards, the avid listeners erupted into loud guffaws.

'Observe how he authors the tale!' Boundless groaned with dismay as delighted laughter greeted some new, outlandish concoction from the animated Pinch. He saw Thibault smiling broadly as he followed along. 'What does he say now?'

'He claims—' Bannock shook with mirth as Pinch staggered up from the chair to aim an imaginary musket at the hearth.

'*Pouf!*' Pinch swung the musket in another direction and fired again. '*Pouf!*'

'*Pouf!*' cried the audience.

Florid and breathless, the raconteur collapsed back into the chair. Draining the cup of punch with a single swallow, he held it out for a refill. 'Where the devil was I?' he demanded, imbibed in his own loquaciousness.

'Up the buffalo's arse!' A voice yelled, to roars of laughter.

As Pinch concluded—with yet another windy flourish—mugs were raised in a toast as beaming looks were directed at Boundless. To add to his chagrin, the man sitting across stretched over to grasp his hand, a huge grin on his face.

'Nay. Be not cross,' Bannock shouted into his ear. 'As Pinch has said, 'tis merely the boast of the paddle. The country be so grotesque and fantastical that the tale must eclipse the scenery or else be lost in the telling.'

As the noise and laughter died away Theroux rapped his mug on the table. 'Your attention!'

A respectful silence fell as the bourgeois pushed back his chair. Standing up, he took a sip of punch and cleared his throat. Hooking both thumbs in his waistcoat pockets he cast a solemn glance around the tables. 'Gentlemen. I give thanks to God that you have all returned safe and sound.'

Boundless saw several faces exchange sly, knowing glances as Thibault addressed the brigade in firm tones. 'What does he say?' he whispered to Bannock.

'He talks about the year ahead. Observe his stance—much like a parson! 'Twill be much ado about honest hard work and sober diligence! It is said he gives the same sermon each year. The men have it by heart. I had every word on my passage here.'

Bannock shared a grin with another of the men as if to confirm the joke.

After the speech, which featured the words '*diligence*' and '*honnêteté*' several times, Thibault concluded to enthusiastic applause. He sat down, nodding in acknowledgement as the men raised their cups in a toast.

A short noise-filled interlude followed after which a fiddle, a flute and a tambourine were produced.

'Now the festivities begin!' Pinch swallowed another draught of punch, his manner gleeful.

'Hark. And ye shall hear the angels sing!' confirmed Bannock. At the other table, a bushy-haired youth rose to his feet with a toothsome smile.

'Who is he?'

'The *chanteur*. Listen, and you shall hear the stroke of the paddle!' Bannock raised his mug. '*C'est L'aviron!*'

The *chanteur* obliged, launching into the song with gusto while slapping his thigh to the shake of the tambourine. Reaching the refrain, he paused, his head cocked in anticipation. At once the entire brigade joined in, their voices reverberating around the hall:

> *'Ç'est l'aviron qui nous mène, qui nous mène.*
> *Ç'est l'aviron qui nous mène en haut!'*

As the song ended to cheers and applause, Theroux loudly called for another: '*À la claire!*'

The singer grinned at Theroux and without ado launched into the tune:

> *À la claire fontaine*
> *M'en allant promener*
> *J'ai trouvé l'eau si belle*
> *Que je m'y suis baigné*

Struck by the plaintive melody, Boundless found himself nodding along as the brigade joined in the chorus:

> *Il y a longtemps que je t'aime,*
> *Jamais je ne t'oublierai!*

Hardly had the chanteur sat down—to back-slaps and more cheers—than another singer stood up to take his place. At his signal, the fiddler scraped a slow, trembling air that provoked a hush in the festive mood.

Bannock grimaced. 'Now you shall hear such a mournful to-do! The tune is a favourite and brings forth floods of tears. It is a tale of the ghosts of former *voyageurs* that haunt the rivers and trails. I scarce know whether to laugh or cry at each rendition.'

At a glance from the fiddle player, the singer began, his rough, untutored voice strangely affecting. The song continued for several verses, the singer at one point extending an arm to point to the distance, an anguished look on his face. Heads turned in the direction as if the ghostly wraiths might be present in the room. The fiddle died away and the singer held the last throbbing note as tears rolled down the faces of the listeners. Wiping his eyes, he sat down as if overcome with emotion while his companions fêted him with thunderous acclaim.

Thinking the festivities were ended on that tragic note, Boundless was surprised when the fiddler struck up a rousing jig, quickly restoring the festive mood as two men jumped up to step a reel while the others clapped in time. Another man whirled Quoi in his arms, the latter hooting like an Indian. Set down on his feet again, the simpleton hopped and jigged to the fiddle, his frenzied efforts drawing hoots of laughter, which inspired further, manic shuffles. The half-wit shambled himself into such a state that he tripped over his own feet, tumbling in a heap. Sitting up, he joined in the laughter, braying with glee at being the cause of such mirth.

Pinch sighed. 'The poor devil be as witless as a trout.'

A Frenchman produced two metal spoons and began to play them against every part of his body, drawing cheers for his dexterity. Pinch roared with laughter at some jest. The door opened and Boundless felt a gust of cool air. He turned to see Askook—absent during the feast—enter. The half-breed stood just inside the door, a taciturn look on his face as he surveyed the revels. As he turned to leave, he halted, one hand on the door, directing an aggressive stare at Boundless. Boundless felt Pinch poke his ribs to draw attention to some new source of gusto. When he turned to look again, the half-breed had gone.

## A Theft and a Fight

OVERNIGHT, THE STOCKADE WAS transformed into a thriving village—the burgeoning population swollen daily by the arrival of trading parties from the Indian camps. Boundless quickly accustomed to the sight of women walking between the buildings and the squeals of children playing hoops. Whether at the behest of their consorts or not, the Indian wives dressed modestly in deerskin tunics and leggings—one or two wearing dresses their 'husbands' had fetched back from the east. The children, for the most part, ran naked, their exuberant energy unrestrained by any words of reproach from either their doting mothers or genial fathers.

The women lit cooking fires on the open ground and generally behaved as if the stockade were no different from an Indian village. Boundless was struck by the air of proprietorial confidence as they went about their chores. *Pinch is right. We are the tenants, not they*, he acknowledged, observing the careless independence of a Hidatsa wife as she walked past carrying an armful of wood. Although generally preferring the company of their own clan, the women otherwise displayed little concern for tribal allegiances—whether Mandan, Hidatsa, Arikara or Cree—communicating peacefully among themselves in a hodgepodge of Indian, French and sign.

In addition to preparing game and dressing hides, the women tended the vegetable gardens and, so Pinch informed him, kept the men supplied with moccasins in summer and snowshoes in winter. 'The post could scarcely run without them,' said Pinch. 'I give six months before you find yourself a willing wife.'

'Will you wager on it?'

Pinch affected an expansive air. 'The truth be my stake,' he declared grandly.

The married men occasionally accompanied their wives to the nearby villages to visit their in-laws. They returned laden with smoked fish, vegetables, wild rice and sweet syrup drawn from the maple trees that lined the numerous creeks.

'See again the value of the Indian alliance,' remarked Pinch as a Frenchman returned bearing sacks of fresh corn and a smoked ham. 'It is why

Guillaume is so keen to encourage such liaisons. The more bonds between the Indians and ourselves, the safer we be and the better the trade.'

In spite of these contributions, the pressure on food stocks with so many mouths to feed was considerable. Buffalo were still plentiful in small groups, along with antelope, deer and elk. Boundless made two or three kills a day, using the mule to carry the carcasses back to the post. The horse and mule continued to garner admiring attention, the Indians, both adults and children alike, seemingly fascinated by the animals. Each morning when he turned them loose to graze, the event occasioned intense curiosity.

'Trade them or save them for food,' advised Pinch as he watched Boundless navigate the horse through an admiring throng. 'Meat gets mighty scarce around January.'

'Food? They carried me all the way from Maryland!'

'Aye and did their duty. Would you have them starve or freeze to death?'

One afternoon, the search for game led him to a region of rolling hills several miles north-east of the fort, which, he had learned from the Indians, was a favourite gathering spot for elk. To his surprise, he came upon a ring of earth mounds similar to those he had discovered east of the Mississippi. The mounds blended so seamlessly with the surrounding bluffs that it took a while for him to recognise them for what they were. The earthworks were smaller but more numerous than the earlier finds, and he counted over two dozen, easily riding over the smaller ones. From a distance, he glassed the landscape but was unable to determine any pattern to the hillocks. Intrigued by the discovery he questioned Pinch on his return to the post.

'I have seen them. What of them?'

'Did they not strike you as unusual?'

'Piles of earth? What is there to concern a man?'

'Who built them?'

Pinch frowned as he studied the playing cards he had laid out in a row on the table. 'Indians,' he said. 'Who else?'

'Which ones?'

'How the devil should I know?'

'Would you ask Monsieur Thibault to ask White Deer?'

Pinch pursed his lips, intent on the cards. 'They were built long ago, as you say. Hundreds of years or more. She would not know, any more than I.'

'Perhaps someone in her tribe has knowledge. Perhaps there are stories, or legends, passed down.'

'Perhaps, perhaps, perhaps.' Pinch muttered at a card and sat back in the chair. 'Whoever built them is long dead and gone. Why dig up their bones?'

'Are you not the least curious? You, who have the sharpest nose for news and gossip of every kind?'

Pinch hunched forward over the cards. 'I concern myself with the scandals of the living, not the bones of the dead!'

THROUGHOUT THE WANING SUMMER days and into autumn, the men were kept busy with repairs to the stockade. A stand of trees along the river was felled and hauled back to the post to replace a rotted section of the log palisade. Other logs were squared, mortised and tenoned to replace split timbers in the walls of the storehouse. When not hunting or butchering, Boundless joined in to assist with the repairs—enjoying the robust good humour of the Frenchmen and their tendency to turn the most routine chore into a contest. Construction continued until darkness set in and all outside work ceased for the day. Following supper, the men sat around the hall to take part in keenly contested games of dice or piquet, on which they often gambled a week's wages.

Thibault or his deputy, Lapointe, kept a sharp eye on the men throughout the day, chivvying them to remain busy. In particular, both men maintained a keen watch on Pinch, the Bostonian demonstrating an unending relish for cards, dice and rum, and little else. In exasperation, the bourgeois often shooed him out of the cabin and onto some task or other.

'He accuses me of neglecting my duties,' grumbled Pinch. 'And would have me hammer, dig and fetch all the live-long day.'

One afternoon, Boundless went to collect the horse and mule from the riverbank where he had left them to forage while he briefly returned to the fort. Upon his return, he could not find them. He followed their tracks for a half mile through the woods, increasingly concerned as he discovered moccasin prints alongside the hoof prints. The combined prints led him back into the prairie grass where the tracks vanished amidst the waving stalks.

He stood and surveyed the grass in every direction but saw no sign of the missing animals.

Alarmed, he returned to the fort, hoping to find they had returned on their own. Dismayed to find them nowhere in sight, he returned to the river and scoured the trees and bushes in a further, fruitless search. As the sun began to sink in the sky he made his way back to the post, angry and suspicious and convinced that the animals had been stolen. His wrathful denunciation of the unknown thieves drew little sympathy from Pinch.

'It was only a matter of time. You should have sold or exchanged them both, as I advised.'

'How do you know they are taken?' asked Bannock, coming over to join in. 'They may turn up tomorrow morning.'

'They know to return at dusk. And I found moccasin prints alongside their tracks.'

As word spread about the missing animals, one of the Frenchmen came up to speak to Bannock. 'Jules claims he saw an Arikara buck eyeing the pair yesterday,' the latter reported to Boundless. 'He said the fellow had a covetous gleam in his eye.'

'Is he here at the post? Can he point him out?'

'Ha!' said Pinch. 'The scoundrel will be far away by now along with his prize. Besides, Guillaume would not thank you for disturbing the peace.'

The bourgeois, learning of the incident from Theroux, summoned several visiting Arikara—the main suspects—to the trading room, where he interrogated them for a quarter-hour, Pinch relaying the outcome.

'They blame it on that party of Cree that visited two days ago. They claim Askook met up with the Cree at the Hidatsa village and the horse was discussed. Of course, the villain fiercely denied any knowledge of the matter when questioned and blamed the Arikara themselves. We may never discover the truth. That he is somehow involved would not surprise me in the least. The fellow is a villain through and through and would certainly be aware of the great value of the animals. But mayhap the Cree stumbled upon the horse while passing and thought it an opportunity too great to pass up. Whatever the cause, 'tis certain they are taken.'

With the news, Boundless was forced to bitterly concede that the animals were lost forever. 'You deserved better, both of you,' he muttered, distressed at the loss of the bay in particular. He thought back on his first acquaintance with the creature in the pasture behind Jacob Gottschalk's trading post. The knowledge that his last link with Mose and the Maryland woods had been lost added to his simmering anger over the theft.

The next day he passed Askook in the street. He gave the half-breed a hard stare, certain of his involvement. The Indian returned the stare with an air of smirking knowledge that brought his suspicions instantly to the boil.

'What do you know of my missing horse?' he demanded. In his agitation, he laid hold of the Indian's arm.

Snarling, Askook threw off his grip. *'Chien anglais!'*

'My horse?' Boundless repeated, his blood up in spite of the other man's hostile demeanour.

Spitting in the dirt, Askook let loose with a string of insults.

His temper boiling over, Boundless lashed out, shoving the Indian hard in the chest. 'Go hang!'

With a look of astonished rage, Askook stood stock still for a moment before launching himself at Boundless. Next moment, the two were rolling in the dirt, punching and gouging. Cries of alarm went up as others gathered to witness the fight.

The half-breed was a strong and skilled fighter, using his head, elbows and teeth. But Boundless had both hands on the Indian's throat and squeezed relentlessly as Askook rained blows on his head and neck. Askook tried to drive a thumb into his eye and Boundless clamped his teeth on the digit, drawing a gasp and a violent curse.

'*Ça suffit!* The Indian was abruptly hauled off Boundless. Two Frenchmen held the enraged half-breed in their grasp as he fought madly to escape, all the while showering Boundless with curses and threats. Boundless got to his feet, his head sore from the repeated blows.

'*Au nom du Christ que se passe-t-il?*' Theroux pushed his way through the spectators. '*Assez, j'ai dit!*' he snapped as the incensed Askook struggled to free himself from the restraining hands.

"*Fils de pute!*' Throwing off the men holding him, Askook lunged at Boundless.

Before the furious half-breed could reach his target, Theroux had seized him by the shirt and flung him to the ground. The Indian jumped nimbly to his feet, hissing with rage, and pulled a knife from the sash around his waist. The action drew gasps and cries of alarm from those watching.

'*Vous osez?*' Theroux squared up to the maddened Indian, his hand on his own knife, his voice dangerous. '*Retournez à l'entrepôt et restez-y jusqu'à ce que je vous envoie chercher. Allez-y!*'

For a moment, it seemed as if the incensed Askook would defy the command. Then, slowly, with a furious stare at Boundless, he turned away as the crowd parted to allow him passage. Theroux turned to Boundless, his face angry. '*Toi aussi! Retournez au dortoir et restez-y.*'

STILL BREATHING HEAVILY FROM the savage fight, Boundless sat down on the bunk, his thoughts in turmoil. A short time later, he was unsurprised to be summoned to Thibault's private room at the front of the main hall.

Bracing himself, he opened the door. Bannock was waiting to interpret. Theroux was there also, eyeing him as he entered.

'*Quelle absurdité est-ce! Je ne permettrai pas de me battre sur le poste!*' Thibault confronted Boundless, a look of angry disapproval on his face.

'He is much put out,' said Bannock, a note of amusement in his voice. 'Tell him I was defend—'

'*Ç'est interdit!*' Thibault interrupted, his voice sharp.

'He is sorely disappointed in you.'

'*Pardon, Monsieur Bourgeois.*' Boundless addressed Thibault directly, his voice apologetic. 'Tell him it will not happen again. He has my word.'

Thibault's stern look softened at the apology. Folding his arms, he stroked his chin with one hand before addressing Boundless again.

'He understands your distress at the loss of your animals. He is certain, too, that Askook had a hand in the matter. He says that the scoundrel has exhausted his patience. He will be discharged and sent back with the brigade in spring. He asks that, until then, you steer clear of him as much as possible. Do you understand?'

Boundless heaved a sigh of relief. 'Yes, Monsieur. I am sorry.'

'*Aller!*' Thibault waved a hand in dismissal.

BY SUPPER, THE INCIDENT was the talk of the post. To his surprise, Boundless found himself fêted for his role. Several of the Frenchmen came up to clap him on the shoulder, uttering imprecations against 'The violent madman!'

A veteran voyageur named Edouard shook his hand in front of the entire table. 'Well done!' he said loudly as Bannock translated. 'You would have performed a service if you had plunged a knife into his black heart!'

The comment drew a chorus of approval.

'You see now the contempt they hold for the villain?' said Pinch as they waited for supper to be served. 'No one would miss the fiend should he disappear.'

'Where is he?' Boundless looked around the hall.

'The dog has been banished from the supper table for a week as additional punishment. The entire brigade will be relieved that he is to be booted from the post.'

''Tis a pity Monsieur Thibault ever hired the villain in the first place,' agreed Bannock.

'Count yourself lucky the rascal didn't go for you with a knife or hatchet,' said Pinch. 'But be alert,' he warned, his voice sober. 'The fellow nurses a grudge like the devil himself and will do you harm if he gets the least chance.'

'In particular as he is to be booted from the post,' added Bannock. 'No doubt, the scoundrel will hold you to blame for that.'

In the days following the incident, he saw little of Askook. Whenever he sighted him, the half-breed flashed murderous glances in his direction. But, perhaps mindful of his parlous position within the company, the Indian contented himself with deadly looks and a silent yet menacing aggression.

'The fellow is determined to have it out,' Boundless remarked to Bannock on being subjected to yet another venomous stare.

'Endure him for the winter. With luck, he will fall—or be pushed—into the river and drown in the rapids.'

A week later, Boundless was returning from the tool hut, a leather harness slung over his shoulder, when he unexpectedly found himself face to face with the half-breed. He stiffened in the narrow street, tensed for a fight. Askook stood stock still, one hand on the handle of his knife, a look of burning hatred in his eyes. For a moment, neither man moved. And then, his expression full of malice, the half-breed swept a hand across his throat, the inference unmistakable.

## 8

## The Mandan Village

OCTOBER SWEPT IN ON brisk north winds, snow flurries, and cold nights. The fire was lit in the bunkhouse—to remain lighted until spring. Keenly aware of his responsibility to keep the smoke-house filled, Boundless went on extended hunts, taking a dog travois to haul the meat. Each travois was pulled by two dogs and consisted of two cottonwood drag poles reinforced with two short cross-poles and laced together with sinew. 'How much can they haul?' he asked Pinch, dubious of the arrangement as he calculated the weight of a whitetail.

'Fifty to sixty pounds. And as much again over snow and ice.'

'That is not much,' he reflected, once again keenly regretting the loss of the horse and mule.

'When the snow comes, you can take the sledge and haul as much meat as you are able.'

Thibault introduced him to a Mandan hunter named Shining Hair on account of his glossy, flowing locks, of which the man was inordinately proud. In return for a pound of tobacco, the Indian, who spoke rudimentary French supplemented by extensive signs and gestures, showed him several spots along the forested river where the buffalo liked to shelter from winter storms. At first awkward and cautious in the Indian's presence, he was soon won over by the man's cheerful, relaxed demeanour and obvious goodwill.

'The Mandan are fine folk. Peaceful and good-natured,' said Pinch when Boundless raised the matter. 'They are not as prickly as the Arikara—and entirely different from the pestiferous Sioux.'

'*Votre travail est de nourrir nos ventres,*' answered Thibault when Boundless sought permission to accompany one of the trading parties on their visits to the Mandan, his meaning requiring no translation.

Sobered by the reminder, he expanded his daily hunts, travelling several miles to a spot said by Shining Hair to be a favoured haunt of mule deer. On four successive days, he made kills, enlisting the help of the Frenchmen and an additional travois to haul the meat back to the post. In spite of his success, the food stocks diminished at an alarming rate. Pinch's many warnings about winter shortages caused him no little anxiety as he con-templated the number of mouths to feed and recalled the scarcity of the

Maryland woods in winter. *'Mayhap it is your gun that stands between us and starvation.'* Pinch's words came back to haunt him as he traversed the bluffs in search of ever-diminishing game.

AS OCTOBER DREW TO a close, he learned of a planned trade visit to the Mandan villages along the Heart River. 'It is the headquarters of the tribe,' said Bannock, already selected to go. 'The village is reputedly the largest in the entire territory, and I am keen to see it for myself.'

Envious of Bannock's opportunity, Boundless determined to approach Thibault a second time, brushing aside Pinch's objection. 'Did he not turn you down only three weeks since? The man is most particular in the matter of tasks. And yours is to hunt, as mine is to scurry hither and thither at his every pleasure.'

'Who knows, but he may be in better mood?'

Thibault, peering at a ledger, listened as Pinch made the request on Boundless' behalf. For a long moment, the bourgeois stared at the column in front of him, immersed in the figures. Finally, without looking up, he motioned with the quill. *'Aller! Visitez votre Indiens! Et vous, aussi, Pinch!'* he added as they left.

'See how my helpfulness doth convict me!' Grumbling, Pinch kicked a chair.

'Perhaps it is a reward for overflowing the smokehouse,' joked Boundless.

'Or mayhap he discovered a lost fortune in one of his deuced columns!' moaned an exasperated Pinch.

On the day of departure, Boundless sat alongside Bannock at breakfast wearing the cape he and Mose had fashioned back in Maryland plus a beaver fur hat. Outside, it was still dark. 'It will be my first time sitting a canoe,' he said to Bannock. 'What is it like to paddle one?'

'You sit and you stroke, and you chafe your hands,' answered Bannock, biting off a chunk of fried biscuit. 'Take my word for it, a half-day of paddling like a dervish, and you cannot feel them anymore.' Deliberating whether or not to eat a pair of hard-boiled eggs, Bannock tucked them in his pocket for later consumption.

'And our sole purpose is to trade?'

''Tis not beaver he seeks so much as to strengthen our alliance with the Indians. We bring gifts and goods for exchange, the purpose being to keep the Indians agreeable.'

'You know this?' he asked, impressed with Bannock's understanding of the workings of the post.

'I clerked three years in Montreal and read dozens of reports from posts like this one.'

'Like this one?'

Bannock hesitated, an enigmatic look on his face. 'In truth, not like this one. Most of the posts were just west of the lakes or further north, towards the Hudson Bay. A post this far west is … unusual.'

'Unusual?'

Bannock gave a short laugh. 'You have me! *Unheard of!* A great many fur houses would give considerable sums to learn of the route across from the lakes. Never fear'—Bannock raised a hand in mock surrender—'I, too, have taken an oath to protect it.' He pinched his chin. 'All the same, a most lucrative secret,' he teased, as if to test Boundless' own resolve.

'Bonjour!' Pinch sat down, yawning, a steaming mug of tea in hand. He sipped from the mug in silence, his obvious distaste for the venture drawing an exchange of looks from his companions.

While waiting for Pinch to finish his tea, Boundless and Bannock stood outside, stamping their feet to keep warm. The morning was wan and overcast with a light breeze that carried flakes of snow. Quoi approached, carrying a bucket of slops to feed the dogs. The fellow's shuffling gait was made more lopsided by the heavy bucket. He unlatched the gate to the pen, all the while cooing endearments to the eager pack. Snapping and growling, the dogs swarmed around, leaping and lunging for the bucket. Several were almost pure white—their coats standing out against the blue and grey hues of their pack mates. All shared the same sharp features and inquisitive look of the wolf.

Quoi tossed the scraps while clucking in a caressing singsong. 'Eat, my darlings! You, Grey Eyes, leave him alone! Stiff-Cock, you've had your share! Don't be greedy, my sweetlings! There is enough for all.'

'See all of nature gathered there,' remarked Bannock. 'One day, the poor fool will slip, and the hounds will have his throat.'

A work party came outside carrying a sledge and axes to cut firewood. Setting down the sledge, they talked among themselves. The sledge was fashioned of birch-wood, the boards lashed together with deerskin thongs. Curled up at one end, it measured over ten feet from nose to tail and stood less than sixteen inches wide.

They heard a cry from Quoi as he attempted to round up four of the pack for the sledge. The dogs made sport of his clumsy attempts at capture, slipping and wriggling from his grasp as he admonished the culprits with a mix of shrill denunciation and fervid praise.

'We shall arrive at the Judgement ere the half-wit has done,' said Pinch, joining Boundless and Bannock.

'He has one!'

Quoi dragged one of the dogs by the scruff—crooning words of encouragement in between offering the occasional kick with his puny legs. The work party helped secure the fractious dogs, dishing up plentiful blows and curses as they did so. The howls and yips from the dogs drew distressed pleas from Quoi. 'He has a tender nose!' he cried, cradling a dog in his arms to protect him from an exasperated woodcutter.

The door opened, and Emile, the junior clerk emerged, drinking tea from a mug. He nodded to Boundless, his face pale and serious in the cold morning light.

The door opened again, and Theroux emerged, laughing with Henri, a wiry Frenchman with a ready grin and a penchant for practical jokes. 'Are we ready?' Theroux looked around, his face flushed in the cool breeze. 'Then let's go!'

Dragging a *canot du nord* from the shed, they carried it to the shore and set it down in the water. To Boundless, the birch-bark frame looked as if one might easily put a shoe through it. Henri took a paddle from a bundle lying in the canoe and handed it to Boundless. 'Your mistress! Be gentle with her.' The paddle was painted red and was as long as a musket, reaching up to Boundless' chin.

In the morning light, the river looked cold and forbidding, sticks and logs from further upstream sweeping along in its flow. Henri and Bannock held the craft while Boundless stepped in, treading gingerly on the thwarts. Henri directed him to a seat in the middle of the vessel. Pinch sat next to him, while Henri and Bannock took the seat in front. Emile sat in the bow and Theroux in the stern.

'Let's go!'

They set off, sweeping the paddles to move out into the stream. Boundless copied the method of his companions, timing his stroke to theirs. Once they were underway, his companions 'dug' into the water with short, choppy strokes, holding the paddles almost upright. Waves rocked the craft as they held within twenty yards of the bank. Sand blew into their faces as the wind gusted from the shore. Boundless found the birch-bark alarmingly unstable, the least movement seeming to tilt it dangerously to one side.

The canoe bounced and dipped through the waves as he compared the experience of paddling to that of rowing. *The shoulders must serve as oarlocks. The effort is all in the arms.*

As they built up a rhythm, the stroking became easier, and they took the opportunity to rest when a stretch of rapid water pushed them along without much effort. 'How far?' he asked Pinch.

'The Heart? Ten miles or so. We should be there in under the hour.'

Four miles downriver, they passed a village of earth lodges. A group of women knelt by the water's edge, washing clothes. The women called out as they passed, urging them into the shore.

Henri bellowed a response through cupped hands. *'Une autre fois!'*

Adjacent to the village were stretches of cultivated land. Women moved about the fields, hoeing and weeding, some carrying infants on their backs. The sight brought to Boundless' mind Pinch's description of the Mandan as farmers of great skill and industry. As they paddled past a field of winter squash, he had a dizzying sensation of sailing past the farms and plantations along the Patapsco.

He was tiring from the exertion when he spotted a prominent bluff rising above the river in the distance. A number of lodges were visible on top. A small fleet of bullboats fished the river below the bluff. He recognised the village as the same one he had previously been at pains to avoid on his solitary journey. Just below the bluff, another river spilled into the main channel.

'The Heart River!' called out Henri.

As they approached the conflux, the size of the village became clearer, its imposing vantage seeming to proclaim the Mandan's status as suzerain over the vast swathes of land extending east and west of the Missouri.

'Look!' Bannock pointed to the shallows.

Boundless followed the pointed finger—exclaiming as he caught his first sight of an Indian mounted on a horse. The man sat at the water's edge to stare, looking for all the world like a native *conquistador* with his long hair and feathered lance.

'Lord above,' breathed Pinch. 'What new thing is this?'

They turned into the Heart, battling the current and returning hails to the fleet of bullboats. Safely within the reaches of the tributary river, Boundless saw another village on the opposite shore. The occupants had noticed their arrival and gathered on the bank to watch. As it became clear that their destination was the west-shore village, a dozen bullboats put out and stroked vigorously in an attempt to precede them across the river.

Bannock turned, a grin on his face. 'They do not wish to miss out on the spoils!'

A crowd of men, women and children awaited their arrival at the foot of the bluff. Boundless observed several ponies foraging the marsh grass along the mud-bank shore. Bannock had also noticed them and said something to Henri.

''Tis rumoured they purchased a small herd from the Arikara,' he relayed to Boundless. 'The elders protested, but the young braves are mad for horses and will not be denied.'

They were now less than twenty yards from the waiting Indians.

'Lay paddles!' called out Theroux, and Boundless copied the others in stowing his paddle. Their momentum took them into the shore, where willing hands reached out to grasp the bow.

'I told you I'd be back!' Henri scrambled out of the canoe as a shriek sounded and a young child ran forth from the crowd. Laughing, Henri hoisted him into the air.

'Another one!' said Pinch to a shake of the head from Theroux.

Showing no fear of strangers, the children flocked around, pulling and tugging at their coats. Most of the children were naked, and seemingly immune to the cold. To Boundless' shock, many of the adult men were naked as well. He glanced at Pinch, who shrugged. 'They are not overly fond of clothes.'

A few of the men wore buffalo robes, the robes seeming as natural as skin to their bodies.

The bales were lifted out of the canoe and set down on the dry mud. With a glance, Theroux led off up the steep slope. 'Let's do it!'

Hoisting a bale onto his back, Boundless followed, conscious of the stares of the Mandan as they parted to allow him passage. They were surrounded by a mob of curious, laughing children as they ascended the bluff. He sighted Shining Hair among the onlookers and called out a greeting. The Indian raised a hand in welcome. Absurdly proud at this recognition in front of his comrades, he continued up the path.

At the top of the bluff, they entered the village through a stout palisade. He looked around, impressed at the number of lodges within the fortifications. The inhabitants, attracted by the commotion, stepped out to watch their arrival. They struck him as confident and prosperous looking. Theroux led the way deeper into the village, passing the outer lodges before arriving at a large clearing that formed the heart of the village. At its centre stood a red painted post surrounded by a fence. Numerous small fires burned in the clearing. Women knelt around drying frames and cooking pots, gossiping as they worked. Men sat around the fires, talking and smoking pipes. Groups of shouting youths chased after a hoop while others flung sticks at a stone rolled through the grass.

On the far side of the clearing, some older youths fired arrows at a target sunk into the earth. Dogs and small children wandered freely between the fires.

Stopping outside a lodge larger than the others, Theroux motioned for them to set down the bales. Catching his breath, Boundless stared at the busy scenes in the clearing, bemused to be reminded of his first impressions of Philadelphia. 'This is the largest Indian village I have yet seen,' he said to Pinch.

'Aye. 'Tis Philadelphia to the rest.'

Startled at hearing his own comparison voiced back to him, Boundless gestured to the lodges.

'How many houses do you suppose?'

'Henri has mentioned a figure of a hundred,' answered Bannock. 'Suppose twelve or thirteen to a lodge. Then one thousand or more inhabitants in this one village.'

'So many?'

'From here, the Mandan rule the country in every direction as far as the crow flies,' said Pinch. He frowned at Bannock. 'Twelve to a lodge? More like twenty!'

'Then that would double the figure—to two thousand.' Bannock shook his head.

'Look at the size of the houses,' argued Pinch, 'and judge for yourself.'

The lodges themselves seemed to rise up out of the earth, their domed roofs covered with willow branches, dried grass and sod. The outer 'skin' of earth and grass gave the houses a resemblance to a creature of some kind. Smoke issued from holes cut into the roofs. Stout cottonwood porticos hung with hide curtains protected the interior from wind or rain.

The crowd swelled as their presence in the village became more widely known. Boundless observed with curiosity the great variety of skin colour—from complexions as pale as his own to the coppery darkness of the Chesapeake Indians. So singular were the complexions that he fancied he might be gazing on the inhabitants of any town in Europe. The majority of the men seemed of his height or taller, the women shorter and generally stouter. Once again, he was struck by the inordinately long hair favoured by the Mandan, many of whom trailed dark locks that reached almost to the ground. The men were heavily inked with coloured dyes that decorated their faces and torsos.

'What are we waiting for?' asked Bannock, his voice revealing his impatience.

'The headman, Buffalo Hawk,' answered Pinch. 'He knows we are here and will plan his appearance to impress the others with his importance.'

'My God, what a stench!' A bareheaded man emerged from the crowd, holding his nose in comical fashion. He wore a breechclout and was naked from the waist up. He appeared little different from the Mandan save for the long, grey hair that flowed freely down his shoulders and an equally grey beard.

With a shout of delight, Theroux embraced the man. 'Jacques! How are you, you old scoundrel?'

'Still alive—in spite of all!' His eyes twinkling, the man thrust out a hand to Pinch. 'Pinch, you rascal!'

'How is the har-reem, you old sinner?' Pinch vigorously pumped the other man's hand. 'Boundless, Thomas. Come meet Jacques Bonnet. He has three wives!'

'Four!' The Frenchman held up four fingers.

At that moment, an elderly man, attended by two women, stepped from the doorway of the lodge. He was wrapped from head to toe in a buffalo robe. His dark face was pitted with tiny marks—whether through disease or art was hard to tell. Although stooped in appearance, he gave forth an unmistakable air of command. A hush fell over the assembled crowd as the Indians drew back to allow the man respectful passage.

'*Bonjour, mon ami!*' Theroux raised a hand in greeting.

'*Bonjour!*' The Indian grimaced in the wintry sunlight. Boundless glimpsed the figure of a swooping bird dotted on one side of his neck and a buffalo head on the other.

At a raised eyebrow from Theroux, the clerk dug into his haversack and took out a large object wrapped in cloth, which he handed to the man— evidently a chieftain. 'For you, my friend.'

Murmurs arose from the watching Indians as the chieftain unwrapped the cloth to reveal a heavy Dragoon pistol. The polished brass lock gleamed against the dark wood stock and burnished barrel. The Indian examined the gift with scrupulous attention, cocking the weapon and holding it up as if to fire at a target. The action drew cries of admiration. The chieftain nodded and gave a contented grunt, clearly pleased with the gift and the impression it created. Gathering the robe around him, he turned back to the lodge, beckoning them to follow.

'The villain was tickled pink by the cannon,' whispered Pinch. 'It made him a big man in front of the tribe.'

'Villain?'

'Aye. He is smooth as water for the nonce, but the devil himself if crossed.'

Boundless hesitated before entering the lodge, glancing at the unattended bales. 'The goods are safe?'

'As your mother's milk!'

He followed Pinch through the framed entrance. As his eyes adjusted to the dim interior, he found himself in a large, warm space. A grouping of four strong pillars overlaid with crossbeams supported the log roof. The floor was compacted with clay. In the centre, a circular fireplace, curbed with stone, was sunk into the earth. A bubbling pot hung suspended over the flames. A hole cut into the roof allowed light to enter and smoke to escape. To the left of the entrance, a small platform supported an assortment of shields and pots and a painted buffalo skull. Decorated animal hides hung from the walls. Beds raised on platforms lined one wall.

As Boundless was adjusting to the gloom, Pinch pushed him towards the fireplace. He felt hot and sweaty inside the cape and took it off. So warm was the interior that two Indians lounging beside the fire were entirely naked. A heavy stink of grease, sweat and wood-smoke permeated the air. The elderly chieftain groaned as he sat down on a reed mat. He motioned for them to do the same. More men joined them, coming in from outside to sit beside and behind the chieftain. Two young women approached bearing clay jugs from which they poured a beverage into cups.

Boundless recognised the oblique lines decorating the rim of the grey-coloured cup as identical to some of those at the post. He nudged Pinch and pointed to the pattern.

Pinch nodded. 'Aye, we traded for the dishes.'

'What is it?' he asked, lifting the liquid to his nose.

'I've always been afeared to ask. But it drinks as smooth as punch.'

Boundless sipped the cool liquid, tasting faint odours of blood, milk and berry on his tongue.

Another woman approached bearing a dish of sweetmeats, which she laid on the floor before him.

'They are a most hospitable people,' Pinch said into his ear. 'Eat!'

Boundless took a strip of dried buffalo tongue, eating it under the approving gaze of his hosts. The tongue was seasoned with nuts, berries and seeds, each portion with its own distinct flavour. He selected another morsel, rounded into a ball. His tongue detected sunflower seeds in a mix of baked meal, similar to pemmican. He glanced at Bannock, who ate with hearty appreciation, his face signifying his approval as he chewed vigorously on a strip of jerky.

The Indians sat in contemplative silence as they waited with what struck Boundless as exceeding courtesy for their visitors to finish eating. Beside him, Pinch mumbled appreciation as he ate with gusto. 'By Harry, but it eats good!'

Boundless looked around the lodge, struck by its size and the soundness of its construction. Storage holders hung from the roof and what looked like a shrine was decorated with buffalo heads and painted shields.

'*Huka!*' The headman turned and grunted to the onlookers behind him. A young woman came forward and knelt at his side, her hands on her knees.

'His daughter,' said Pinch, swallowing a mouthful of jerky. '*Manger, messieurs,*' said the girl as she signalled for more food.

Pinch chuckled at Boundless' surprised gasp. 'Her father sent her back east to the Jesuits to learn the language and customs. He is a cunning old fox and realises the value of playing the French and English off against each other.'

Boundless stared at the girl, noting the satisfied look on her father's face at his curiosity. 'Tell me about this Jacques,' he said, looking around for the Frenchman.

'Are you not eating that?' Pinch took the last morsel of buffalo tongue. 'Jacques? He was here when we first arrived. He was a *coureur des bois*—an explorer and trader, who took to Mandan ways and married into the tribe.'

'How long has he been here?'

Pinch swallowed and smacked his lips. 'A dozen years or more. He has proved useful in passing on knowledge of the tribe. Guillaume holds him in esteem, since it was Jacques who introduced him to Road Maker.'

They finished eating, and Theroux took out a tobacco pouch, which he handed to the headman. The Indian took out a twist of tobacco and passed it on to the next man, who did the same. Boundless flexed his back, feeling stiff from the unaccustomed position. The girl's father spoke again, and she listened attentively before repeating the words in French to Theroux. The guide said something in reply and opened a hide-wrapped bundle at his feet, drawing out several gifts, which he presented to the headman as a prelude to trading. The chieftain nodded, grunting with approval as he examined in turn a hatchet, a knife with a handle of decorated bone, and a necklace of tinkling copper cones, which seemed to hold his interest. After further inspection, he laid down his pipe and began to speak in the querulous voice of the Indian as his daughter leaned in to catch the words.

The seated Indians listened with solemn faces, as though attending something of great moment. The older men sat nearest the fire, the younger ones to the rear. Beyond the firelight, a group of women and children listened with the same attentiveness. A toddler stumbled into the circle around the fire, the men treating the child with chuckles and fond indulgence. Boundless saw few signs of weapons apart from a knife thrust into a deerskin sheath at the waist of the man opposite.

A long wooden pipe inlaid with bone and fringed with a hank of dyed buffalo hair was produced and handed to the chieftain. He pressed tobacco into the bowl, taking his time as though performing a ritual. The man beside him took a smouldering stick from the fire and handed it to him. Placing the stick to the bowl, the old man sucked deeply, releasing a cloud of tobacco smoke into the air. He took the pipe in both hands and handed it to Theroux, who accepted it the same way. Taking a deep inhale, he passed it along to Henri, who did the same before passing it on to Emile, who in turn passed it on to Bannock.

When Boundless' turn came, he inhaled lightly, suppressing the urge to cough as the smoke sucked into his lungs. He emitted the smoke in a soft breath, pausing to indicate—so he hoped—his savouring of the tobacco, in spite of his intense dislike of the substance.

The pipe was returned to the headman who motioned to the seated women. A young woman got up and disappeared into the shadows. She returned bearing an armful of pelts, which she laid on the ground before the visitors.

Pinch picked up a pelt, signalling Boundless to do the same. He selected a small, dun-coloured fur which he identified as martin. The young woman returned bearing another armful.

'Ha! The very business!' Pinch passed a beaver pelt for examination. 'A fine specimen. A winter catch.'

The pelt felt soft and cool in Boundless' hands. The dark hairs held a glossy sheen. For an instant, his mind reeled, and he was back in Mose' hovel, fingering his first buffalo robe.

Bannock passed a luxuriant pelt for his attention. ''Twill fetch a half-guinea when felted and shaped.'

Theroux set down the fur he was inspecting and nodded to the headman.

'Now we filch the devils—lest, indeed, it be the other way round,' whispered Pinch.

Following his companions back out into the cold air, he helped Bannock and Pinch lay out the trade goods on a square of canvas. Bolts of serge, stroud, molton, and flannel were arranged for inspection along with quantities of twine, threads and worsted yarn. Tin kettles, knives, scissors and nails were laid out along with buttons, flints, hatchets, jars of paint, fishhooks, beads and boxes of flints.

The clerk now took charge, examining furs and making entries in a journal. The air was filled with gossip as the Indians picked over the heaped goods. Boundless glanced at Bannock where the latter held up items for inspection. The Montrealer urged an undecided *mihe* to trade, using hand gestures and imprecations in French.

'He has the merchant tone,' said Pinch, following Boundless' gaze.

Conscious of his deficiencies in the art of bartering, Boundless picked up a roll of fustian, which he presented for the inspection of an elderly woman.

'A fine cloth,' he said, feeling awkward in the role. The woman briefly examined the material before brushing it aside with a muttered insult.

Pinch laughed. 'She has cloth enough! Here. Try the glass!' He picked out a small looking glass, holding it up so that the woman could see her reflection. 'O beauteous maiden!'

With a brief pause to inspect her image, the woman grunted and brushed it, too, aside. Complaining in an exasperated voice, she turned to tussle with another woman for a heavy fry pan. 'Three beaver!' said Pinch, holding up his fingers as the women vigorously contested the pan.

Boundless felt a tug on his sleeve and turned to see a *nakhó* with her head wrapped in a blanket demanding his attention. She held up a clasp knife while speaking with considerable animation.

'Two pelts!' He held up two fingers. '*Deux!*' Without more ado, the woman turned to a companion and took two draped pelts from her arms. She thrust the pelts into his hand and quickly retreated with her prize, her expression gleeful.

Pinch bent to inspect the pelts. 'The second is muskrat. She has fleeced you. But no matter. We shall have them all afore we leave.'

'Surely they do not yet have sufficient pelts for all of these?' Boundless motioned to the goods.

'Much of it is in the form of credit. Observe Emile. He keeps account of everything. Guillaume will demand the exact particulars for his ledgers.'

'They will not try to cheat?'

'Some, mayhap. But Indians are mostly honest to a fault. Where we lose track of the goods, they remember.'

With the supply of pelts seemingly exhausted, the women came forward with quantities of pemmican, grease, dried fish, meat, and sacks of the food portions they had enjoyed in the lodge, tendering the same in return for goods.

Four hours after their arrival, they set back for the post, the canoe laden with furs, skins, robes and hides. The sky was already darkening, and a freezing wind tore at them as they paddled against the current. Boundless shivered as he gazed at the murky water, wondering how difficult it would be to reach the bank should they capsize.

'The water sucks you down,' huffed Pinch, as if reading his mind.

Back at the stockade, he carried the pelts into the storehouse, his mind still digesting the details of the visit. 'They mind me of Scottish fishwives,' he ruminated, recalling the noisy press of women around the fish stall on market day.

As they laid the traded goods on the table for entry by the clerk, his mind turned again to the dark, watchful gaze of the headman's daughter. Closing the storehouse door behind him, he headed for the hall, tugging the cape around his throat.

He had barely sat down to eat when the door burst open, the blast of cold air drawing shouts of protest. An animated Quoi hovered on the threshold, his thin face quivering with excitement. *'C'est ici, messieurs, c'est ici!'*

A group of Frenchmen stood up to investigate the cause of his agitation. Spooning a mouthful of corn and gravy, Boundless followed them to the door. Outside, a blizzard of white flakes streamed through the darkness. His arms outspread, Quoi stomped and whirled in a frenzied dance, a rapturous look on his face as he tried to catch a flake on his tongue.

The Frenchmen laughed while shouting encouragement. *'Là. Non, là-bas!'*

No stars could be seen as snow fell from the darkness. Beside him, Pinch shivered and drew the coat tighter around his body. 'Now you shall see such a *grip* as will turn your hair. Mark, we shall not see the grass again these five months or more.'

## 9

# *An Almighty Grip*

A MONTH OF WINTER HAD utterly transformed the world beyond the post—the frozen plain hardly recognisable from the wind-rippled ocean of summer. The bluffs and hillsides were blanketed with snow, the prairie grass buried beneath a smooth, crystalline powder.

He had been out all morning on a fruitless hunt. Around him, nothing moved in the white silence. Panting for breath, he leaned on the cottonwood poles, undecided whether to continue or to turn back and hunt the woods along the river. Ice droplets clung to his face, and his breath wreathed like smoke in the freezing air. He stretched to relieve his aching back, exhausted from slushing through the deep powder.

To ward off the biting winds, he had adopted the *hivernant* habit of wrapping a blanket around his body beneath the capote—the bulky dress doubling the effort of moving about in the snow. Beneath the blanket moccasins, he wore thick wool socks. His hands were sheathed in gloves lined with rabbit fur.

Thus wrapped and shod, he set off each day, every step a laboured exertion inside the muffled warmth of the capote. But in spite of his best efforts and long hours scouring the frozen woods and fields, he returned with game only one hunt in three.

Since the first heavy snowfall, he had assiduously practised the art of wearing the 'Indian shoe', the hooped willow frames indispensable for traversing the snowfields surrounding the fort.

'Hoist the foot! Like so!' Pinch had demonstrated as he struggled to master the cumbersome footwear.

'I waddle like a duck!'

'You would drown without them. The drifts are deep enough to swallow a man. I have seen a corpse fished out of a bank twelve feet deep.'

Boundless cocked a disbelieving eyebrow. 'You jest?'

'Not a bit of it.' Pinch shook his head. 'It happened in my first year at the post. The poor fellow—a Dutchman, I believe, from New York—went out walking merely for the sake of it. He was blue, and stiff as a board when found—his eyes staring out of his head. This cold will kill quick as fire.'

The warning sounded in his mind as he surveyed the white, barren plain. The reflected glare from the bright sun stung his eyes and the wind seemed to have increased in strength. *There will be no fresh meat today*. He turned in his tracks, glad to be within sight of the stockade.

The drain on the food stocks lightened in December as the married men and their families retired to the security of the Indian villages.

'They will not be back until spring,' said Pinch, professing envy of their lot. 'They will be warm and well-fed while we freeze and starve on scraps.'

Potential shortages were eased by the continuing arrival of Indian trade parties. Mandan, Hidatsa, Arikara and Cree were frequent visitors, each delegation bringing fish, pemmican and jerky, as well as pelts, in exchange for goods. These supplies, together with his own contributions of winter hare, deer and elk, helped the icehouse remain sufficiently stocked. However, he remained deeply conscious that, as Pinch often remarked, the prospect of starvation was but a 'hair lick' away.

''Tis the same every year. We rely on the Indians for pemmican and dried fish, and vegetables and such game as they are willing to trade. So long as the Indians are fed, then so are we.'

As the snow hardened and compacted, he exchanged the travois for the full dog sled, Pinch claiming that a team of six could drag a moose carcass across the snow.

'The stick is the common tongue,' he said, teaching Boundless the commands for driving the traineau. '*Mush* them to start,' he said. 'And *whoa* to stop.'

'They respond to the English words?'

''Tis not the words they respond to but the tone. Carry a stout branch or knotted rope and beat them until they know your hand, else will they fight and scrap every step of the way.'

He discovered the worth of the advice the first time he secured the dogs to the harness. The creatures rounded on each other, growling and biting. He whipped them until his arm was sore. Pinch raised an arm to hold back Quoi who cringed and whimpered in concert with the stinging lash. The half-wit followed the sledge out the gate, warbling anxiously in the chill air. '*Au revoir, Yeux Gris! Adieu, Queue Anneau!*'

In spite of his complaints that they scared away the game, Boundless developed a grudging appreciation for the sturdy, wolfish dogs. On the coldest days, they hauled the sledge without complaint, waiting patiently, curled up like cats, noses tucked under their tails, as he scouted the landscape. But just as often, they proved fractious and ill-tempered, snapping and snarling as he laid about them with the knotted rope, frustrated at their noisy yelps and howls.

Often, he came across wolf prints in the snow, their ghostly presence a constant, unseen companion to the hunt. As he bent over a kill, he was aware of their hungry eyes watching and waiting. At moonrise, their plaintive howls echoed through the wintry landscape, the wails evoking an answering chorus from the dogs that spooked him the first time he heard it. Sometimes he abandoned the pursuit of a buffalo or elk as the tracks became mixed with the prints of pursuing wolves.

Once he chanced upon a moose, stranded in a drift. The exhausted bull stood passively in place as he brought it down. He stood for a moment, listening for the sounds of the pack. Satisfied that he was unobserved, he cut away chunks of meat from one side of the carcass. He covered the remains with snow, heaping the powdery whiteness over the crimson bloodstains. Finding a branch, he attached a length of red sash to one end and planted it in the snow. By the time he was finished, the light was fading. Slowly, he retraced his footsteps across the frozen landscape. After a half-mile, he turned to spy the sash where it fluttered in the distance.

When he returned the following morning, the moose had been dug up and consumed, only the horns, bones and hooves remaining.

DESPITE THE SEVERE WEATHER, the voyageurs maintained an easy camaraderie, their rough good humour and informality of station greatly adding to the peace and harmony of the post. He felt a growing admiration for their jovial spirits and uncomplaining manner. One evening, he witnessed an impromptu dance contest in the snow—the men laughing and clapping as the contestants tumbled and slipped in a bid to outdo each other. '*They are as independent and resolute a group of men as I ever saw*', he confided to his journal.

Most evenings, the men played cards or dice in the main hall while filling the air with pipe smoke. The occasional quarrel—usually over a turn of the cards, quickly resulted in a handshake—enforced, if need be, by the senior men. Quoi hobbled to fetch or refill cups, stopping to chortle at each diversion of the moment. Amused at his feverish excitement over a game whose strategies he so thoroughly failed to grasp, several of the Frenchmen tried to teach him the rules of piquet, only to abandon the task one by one to the good-natured jibes of their comrades.

'The fool thinks each card a thing unto itself, bearing no relation to the trick,' commented Bannock, observing the simpleton's befuddled expression on being told to exchange a card. ''Tis useless to try and teach him otherwise.'

'You mean, to teach an old dog new tricks?' suggested Pinch.

'Do you mean to trump me?'

'He steals a suit. What say, Boundless?'

'He is thinking of his buffaloes. Boundless!' Pinch gave the chair leg a kick.

The sole irritant to disturb the peaceable air of the hall remained the fiercely taciturn Askook. The half-breed kept mostly to himself, his simmering temper and reputation for violence creating an invisible space around him. He spent much of his time shut up in the cold solitude of the storehouse—'communing with devils' speculated Pinch. At mealtimes, he sat hunched over his trencher spooning food into his mouth, his surly countenance a bar to conversation. Once finished, he rose immediately and repaired back to his 'lair', as Pinch termed it, in the storehouse.

'There strides a grievance unto himself,' observed Bannock, eyeing the half-breed as the latter exited the hall one night following supper.

'Never a truer word,' agreed Pinch. 'Thank God we only have to put up with his stink for a few more months.' He glanced at Boundless. 'The two of you do well to avoid each other.'

Boundless shrugged as if unconcerned. But oft times, he felt the Indian's eyes boring into the back of his head, the half-breed making no attempt to hide his hatred.

HE WAS SAT AT the table one evening, half-listening to Pinch and Bannock as they smoked and yarned to pass the hours until bedtime. A north wind rattled the door and cold draughts seeped in through chinks in the logs. A roaring fire blazed in the hearth—the continued replenishing and preservation of the blaze being considered no less than a sacred duty. They were seated at their customary end, nearest the fire, an unvoiced agreement among the company, establishing, so Pinch pronounced, the separate principalities of St Joseph and St George. Further along the table, a group of Frenchmen played a noisy game of piquet.

'What the blazes does he do out there?' asked Bannock as the door slammed shut behind the half-breed.

'Plot revenge upon the world,' opined Pinch, puffing out a stream of tobacco smoke.

'Does he not freeze?'

'He lights a fire in the brazier. It keeps him warm enough.'

'Louis claims he lies with a bitch. For the cold or his health, I know not.'

'It would not amaze. No doubt he seethes over his banishment.'

'Is it true,' asked Boundless, 'that he has murdered a man?'

'So 'tis rumoured, and I do believe it. 'Tis said he fell into a dispute with a trader on the Lachine River. He is reported to have beaten the wretch to death with his bare hands. Aye, and smiled while doing so.'

'And you believe such cabin tales?' scoffed Bannock.

'Ask poor Nod, whom the devil delights in tormenting.' Pinch glanced to where Quoi sat perched on a stool, his head trembling above a sock he was darning.

'Himself a rare creature,' agreed Bannock, turning to gaze.

Pinch studied Boundless over the pipe. 'How like you now our pleasant clime? Did I not speak truly?'

'So far, it is not so very different from a Highland winter.'

'Pshaw! This is for naught. A mere fandango. One winter, we were shut up inside for nigh on a month, so terrible was the weather.'

'What did you eat?' Bannock winked at Boundless.

'Eat? Why, our bellies were too froze to permit such fripperies!'

'I heard you ate your shoes.'

''Tis true—in part,' agreed Pinch, mulling on the pipe.

'In part?'

'The soles were awful hard on the teeth. It is why I keep a leather belt— to chaw upon if need be.'

As his companions bantered, Boundless glanced around the room, his gaze falling upon Bjornson. The Swede sat against the wall, reading scripture by the light of a lantern, his lips moving as he traced a line with his finger.

Bannock, following his gaze, nudged him. 'See how the good pastor mumbles his verse?'

'"For thou art a stranger, and also an exile," quoted Pinch.

'You are familiar with scripture?' teased Bannock. 'I thought you a misplaced Turk!'

'Learned to heart—by the stroke of the birch. I still feel the sting in every word.'

'And you, yourself, Boundless, are undoubtedly a member of the Kirk?'

'Indeed, I am not.'

'A freethinker, then?' Bannock raised an eyebrow.

'Brother Boundless be a heathen—like the savage. He prays to the buffalo and chants in tongues.'

'Be such the case?'

Boundless gave a snort. 'He talks through his hat, as usual.'

'Through his shoe, more like—being both possessed of a tongue.'

'A trump!' Pinch raised his pipe to acknowledge the quip.

They fell silent for a few moments, the only sound being the occasional exclamation from a Frenchman as a card turned his way. Boundless was deliberating whether or not to retire to the bunkhouse when Pinch gave a deep sigh.

'What is the matter?' asked Boundless.

'There be no respite.'

'From what?'

Pinch shook his head for answer. Absently scratching his cheek, he regarded Bannock, who sat with his eyes on the card game. 'Come, Thomas. Tell us the tale of how you landed here, in this godforsaken wilderness.'

'You pan for mischief,' said Bannock, his eyes still on the game.

'Not so! You have not told us what misbegotten purpose fetched you to these savage parts.'

'What purpose could there be other than to make your acquaintance?'

'Ha! The truth now.'

Bannock turned back to the table. 'Truth? Then I say truly—'twas, and is, ambition.'

Pinch hummed judiciously as he considered this. 'But to what end— since ambition itself be an affliction the majority of men suffer? Although not I—and I say so with no false claims to modesty—having thrown off the caul while yet a babe in arms.'

'Brother Pinch, your aversion to ambition be well enough remarked upon.'

'Even so. Your ambition—to advance yourself in the trade, I suspect?'

'It is. Fur being the only business for a man with hopes to better his station. It is what fetched my father to Montreal and me from thence to here—to better grasp the mechanics of the trade.'

'Surely it is more safely grasped, in all its mechanics, at a Montreal desk?' objected Pinch.

'True, friend—insofar as principles are concerned. But an understand-ing of the practicals requires a presence here, on the field of battle.'

'Hold fire. Which is it to be—practicals or mechanics?'

'One and the same, in the instance.'

'Not so. The one refers to the methods, the other to the doing—the doing of said method. Does it not?' Pinch looked to Boundless for confirmation.

'I know not.' Boundless yawned, still contemplating whether to retire to the bunkhouse.

'By *practicals* I refer to the basic operations of the trade—the getting of the beaver by one man—your heathen—and from thence, its passage from the one hand to the other until it ends up a hat on the head of a duke in Cadogan Square.'

'From savage to duke?' Beguiled by the figure, Pinch smoked on it.

'For a man to get ahead in the fur trade he must first understand the business in all its parts. You, Boundless, take my meaning?'

'And am I a block that do not take it equally?' demanded Pinch.

'I meant only to draw agreement.'

'Perhaps you try for bourgeois—to reign over us like Guillaume?'

Bannock laughed. 'You shall not bait me, Pinch. I know your tricks.'

Confounded, Pinch turned his attention to Bjornson. The Swede was hunched over the Bible on his lap, frowning with concentration as he pored over the lines.

'Mark how the priest attends his rites.'

'He is a priest?'

'An expression only. The Lutherans, I believe, are governed by a tribe of elders. Come! Join us, O gladsome Swede!'

Startled out of his study, Bjornson looked up. His frown deepened on seeing Pinch. Shaking his head, he returned to the page.

'Perdition to the tribe!' Exasperated at the failure of his plot, Pinch picked at a thread from his sleeve. 'And I am sick to death of this foul weather! My sacred oath if I do not return with the brigade in spring—and never come back.' He pulled the thread.

'You are too fond of this barbarous country to deny yourself, friend Pinch.'

'Indeed, I confess, I am. Here be none of your noisome stink of the city. And the Indians be more civil than your sour-faced grasp of a merchant. And speak to me not of shrunken bellies. A few months hardship in winter is small price to pay for salubrious air and good company.'

The conversation fell silent. The door to Thibaut's private retreat opened and White Deer stepped out. Walking to the hearth, she knelt to tend the fire.

Boundless watched as the girl—for she seemed hardly a woman— poked the logs. 'Does she not miss her family?'

'No doubt. But Guillaume is greatly fond of her—and she spends part of the winter with her parents at the Hidatsa camp, the one by the lake. She will depart any day now.'

'She is pretty enough, for an Indian,' observed Bannock.

'With skills as both cook and seamstress. Witness!' Pinch tugged at the collar of his shirt to show a sewed patch.

Boundless watched as the girl rose to her feet and returned to the room. 'And when Guillaume returns to his family in Montreal, what happens to her?'

'Cast aside, no doubt,' offered Bannock.

'Not so—at least "not so" in the way you would have it,' objected Pinch. 'The truth be,' he said, reflecting on the pipe, 'that the Indians measure such things differently from you or me.'

'From Christian folk, you mean?' rejoined Bannock.

Pinch sucked on the pipe. 'The Indians are not joined, as is your Christian. According to Jacques, who has taken more than his share of Indian maidens, your heathen treats each day as a bale, to be taken up each morning and set aside again each night. Hence, each new day be a thing unto itself. Hence, the glue that binds each thing to another is weak and easily discarded for a fresh bind. And hence and so forth.' He puffed on the observation.

'A sage philosophy,' opined Boundless.

'A Catholicism for the wilderness,' agreed Bannock. 'Of which—do many convert, to the Christian faith?'

'The Jesuits would like nothing better,' said Pinch. 'But the Iroquois, in particular, resist fiercely. Even so, some whole clans, so it is reputed, have taken up the cross.'

'You do not approve?' asked Boundless, seeing the frown on Bannock's face.

'I do not.' Bannock's voice was blunt. 'The Iroquois claim—with truth, I do believe—that it—conversion—is but a prelude to abandoning the woods for the cabin and the plough.'

'Is such a thing even possible?'

'Both true and possible,' confirmed Bannock. 'I myself have seen several families domesticated to the field—even to the raising of chickens and cows. At one settlement, it is said, they even attend their own church.'

'I have heard it said, too,' put in Pinch, unwilling to cede the discourse, 'the conversion, I mean. As to the attending church …?' He glanced doubtfully at Bannock.

'On my oath! I had it from a Black Robe himself.'

'See how he mumbles his script!' Pinch returned his attention to where Bjornson squinted in the firelight.

'I have found him a sociable enough fellow when he chooses,' remarked Boundless.

'Then you more than me. Between himself and the half-breed, not a word of a yarn.'

'But surely, they are as chalk to cheese?'

'One whistles up the devil, the other, Luther. Come, friend! Join the merriment!' Pinch kicked out a chair. 'Come, sir! Your throne awaits!'

'Join us, Bjorn,' chimed in Bannock.

With a pained expression, Bjornson tucked the Bible in his pocket and got to his feet.

'How now!' whispered Pinch.

'He is not yours to make sport with,' Boundless warned as the Swede approached.

'You do wrong me,' said Pinch, professing a wounded tone. 'Come, Brother Bjornson! Come, sit thy bones.'

'A cold evening, gentlemen.' Bjornson's blue eyes were wary as he sat down. His angular face, made paler by the lack of sun, was topped by an unruly thatch of blond hair. Around his neck he wore a large crucifix on a leather tie.

'We talk of future hopes. Whether to stay and endure this wild country or return to the comforts of the city? What say you?'

Bjornson noisily cleared his throat. 'I am necessary to stay here for three years—by the terms of my hire.' The English was leavened with his native Swedish.

'Ha! Then are we all necessary men.'

'You will not return with the brigade?' Bannock looked surprised at the news.

The Swede shook his head and glanced along the table to where Louis sat. 'Louis has expired his contract and wishes to return to his family. I am to stay in his place.'

'Is this your first time in Indian country?'

'*Ja*. First time.'

'You have family—back east?'

The Swede mumbled a reply.

'Are we to understand that as a 'no'?' frowned Pinch.

'What drew you here—to this wild spot?' asked Bannock.

Bjornson shifted in the chair. 'For work. To feed myself.'

Bannock chuckled, 'A choice summation!'

'As clear as pudding! Would that all truths were so wondrously bright.'

'Nay, Pinch, be friendly.'

Bannock leaned into the Swede. 'If you needed to feed yourself, as you say, then why not do so in Delaware?'

'It is as God wishes.' Bjornson gazed around the hall as if wishing to be elsewhere.

'Does He, indeed?' Pinch exchanged glances with Bannock. 'Then perhaps he also wishes that you find yourself an Indian maid to take to wife.'

Bjornson appeared shocked at the notion. 'A true Christian would never do such a thing!'

'Why not? 'Tis said the Indians believe in a soul, the same as us.'

'Never!'

'Yet they revere a Creator—the same as us.'

'If God be a thing of sticks and bones!' Bjornson's pale face flushed with the reply.

'The Indian be true to his own beliefs. And who knows but that those beliefs be as worthy as our own?' insisted Pinch.

'*Abscheulichkeiten der Kanaaniter!*' Bjornson spat the words.

Pinch snorted. 'I have a better ear for the Mandan!'

'English, prithee, good fellow,' said Bannock.

'What do Swedes believe? What branch, I mean, of the faith?' Boundless asked, interceding in an effort to rein in Pinch, who had the quarrelsome bit between his teeth.

Pinch jumped in again before the Swede could answer. ''Tis said they hold to salvation by grace alone—perish the works.'

Bannock laughed. 'Then, Pinch, you be a true Lutheran!'

'In his barbarous way, the savage be as religious as you or me,' asserted Pinch, his dander up in the face of Bjornson's affronted expression.

'As yourself, perhaps,' said Bannock, 'but there may be other, stouter Christians among us.'

'Your Indian be the best Christian I know,' argued Pinch. 'He remains true to his word, loyal to his neighbour, and faithful to his gods—of which he has plenty, being exceedingly devout in that respect.'

Bjornson muttered angrily, taking the bible from his pocket and clasping it in his hand.

'What is it? Speak if you have a mind,' challenged Pinch.

In spite of a warning glance from Boundless, Pinch maintained his polemic—whether to further bait the agitated Swede or out of true belief, Boundless could not guess. 'I say only that the savage be as authentic in his belief as the Baptist or the Turk. Jacques, who claims authority in such matters, swears that the Mandan have their own priests. And that they do observe worshipful ceremonies of their own. Jacques opines that they believe everything, including animals, has a soul.'

'I will not listen to such blasphemy!' Bjornson scraped back the chair with a force that startled the card players. 'I bid you all goodnight!' The Swede stomped off, his face like thunder.

'Did I offend him—by the mention of souls?' Pinch stared after the upset Swede. 'I was but baiting him. The oaf has no humour.'

'You do tease him too much.' Boundless watched as Bjornson slammed shut the door behind him.

'I do but pierce his glumness. 'Tis winter outside, why endure it within?'

'Between his conscience and the great scandal with the congregation, the fellow is half-lunatic,' suggested Bannock.

Pinch stood up. 'Gentlemen, I must boil the snow.'

They watched their companion make his way to the door. 'A little Pinch seasons a large pot,' opined Bannock.

'A strong pepper, no doubt.'

'You are close with him?'

'I have known him only a few weeks longer than yourself.'

Bannock flexed his fingers. 'The truth is, friend, that your average *engagé* be no better than a daily man. He dreams only of a full belly at night, with no thought to partake in the greater spoils of the trade. You, however, hold the cards closer to your vest. Do I speak truly?' He studied Boundless with shrewd anticipation.

'Do you fish for some purpose or ambition of my own? Speak plainly.'

'As you wish.' Bannock sat back, an air of breezy confidence in his manner. 'For example, I see by your curiosity to visit the Indian villages that you, like myself, are anxious to master the trade. And why not? It is a lucrative business. I see, also'—he glanced up as the door opened and Pinch stepped back into the hall—'that, unlike Pinch, you have a lively interest in the commerce end of the trade. We are alike, in seeking to make more of ourselves—are we not?'

'You come at things in roundabout fashion.'

'I mean no offence, Boundless, and would not have us at odds with one another.'

'And none intended on my part. I am employed as a simple hunter. No more and no less. I do but state the truth of my situation.'

'And were that situation to change—through necessity or the offer of some other, more lucrative prospect?'

'Then would I consider the same on its merits.'

'Well spoke! When opportunity presents itself, a man must grasp it with both hands. Do you not agree?' Bannock halted as Pinch rejoined them.

'A day's wages lost!' Pinch sank back into his seat. 'I lingered to wage on the dammed trick.' He gouged spent tobacco from the pipe with his thumb, a peevish look on his face as he regarded the card players.

Bannock stood up. 'I must also to boil.'

'What is your opinion of the fellow?' Boundless asked, watching as Bannock made his way to the door.

'Bannock? A shrewd one. Keen to make a mark—much like yourself.'

'Me?' Boundless stared in surprise.

'Aye. 'Tis the sickness I mentioned. It doth infect the very air.'

'You think I have ambitions, like Bannock—to advance in the trade?'

Pinch took the pipe from his mouth, his gaze suddenly thoughtful as it rested on Boundless. 'No. I fear your contagion runs far deeper.'

'Do you bait me, like the Swede?'

'Ah ha!' Pinch jumped up from the chair as one of the card players got up to leave. 'Another hand, friends?' he said cheerfully, taking the vacated chair.

Boundless left the cabin, peevish at being lumped in with Bannock. He pondered the remark as he lay in the bunk. *It is wrong of Pinch to mistake curiosity for ambition—or to consign such ambition to the fur trade.* His irritation was overtaken by a picture of bloodthirsty Iroquois dressed in wool breeches and lace gowns while taking fellowship. He fell asleep contemplating the image as a Frenchman snored mightily in a nearby bunk.

## 10

## *Heavenly Fire*

THROUGH HABIT AND GEOGRAPHY, his hunting forays invariably led him towards the rock—the massive object offering the sole shelter from the blasting gales that swept the plain. One morning, he halted the sledge a short distance from the monolith. Normally stark and forbidding in appearance, it was transformed under the clear skies, the bright, winter sunlight endowing it with a pristine beauty that recalled his first encounter with the prominence in the slumberous heat of summer. The dogs lay panting in the traces, pink tongues hanging out, and breath steaming into the chill air.

He spotted something moving in the snow at the base of the rock. Through the glass, he spied a solitary buffalo, its black, shaggy robe a blot against the gleaming whiteness. 'Something has spooked it,' he thought, willing it to remain in place. The buffalo stood in suspense for some moments—its frozen vigilance resembling a carved figure in the chill air. As if sensing danger, it dropped its head and ploughed through the snow to disappear around the rock.

Disappointed, he roused the dogs. *'Mush!'*

Returning to the post, he unharnessed the dogs and sat down on the hall steps. It was late afternoon and already dark. A full moon hung low in the eastern sky, the orb seemingly frozen against the distant stars. The door opened behind him, and Pinch stepped out, a blanket over his head.

'By Christ! We shall all freeze afore this blasted winter ends! Hold this!' Handing the blanket to Boundless, Pinch went to piss in the snow, steam rising from the jet of water.

'My ends are froze! Damn me if I don't hear my own teeth achatter!' With a violent shiver, Pinch took back the blanket and headed back inside. He paused, his hand on the door.

'Are you not coming?'

'In a minute.'

'Beware lest you freeze to the step, and we find you a gargoyle by morning!'

*A gargoyle?* Boundless mulled the image, seeing himself fixed in ice, a plume of frozen water issuing from his mouth as the Frenchmen stood around in shock.

He heard a noise and saw Quoi limping and lurching toward him, conversing with himself, the slops bucket in hand. He stopped in surprise as he noticed Boundless. '*Que fais-tu, anglais?*'

'I am looking at the moon.' Boundless motioned to the brilliant, yellow orb.

'Eh?' Quoi craned his neck to gawk up at the sphere. '*La lune?*'

Exclaiming at '*les manières bizarres et les curiosités des Anglais,*' Quoi continued towards the dog pen. Passing the canoe shed, he turned and cackled. '*Dors bien, anglais! Rêve de la lune!*'

Boundless stood up, slapping the snow from his breeches. *Now am I well and truly dammed—judged a lunatic by Quoi!*

He was seated in the bunkhouse, darning a pair of socks, when he heard raised voices from outside, the noise highly unusual at such a late hour. Suddenly, the door flew open, and Bannock stuck his head in. 'Boundless! Come see!'

He hurried to the door as the voices grew louder. A group of men were gathered in the street, staring up at the sky.

'God in heaven!' The shocked exclamation sprang from his lips as he looked up. The night sky shimmered with brilliantly coloured lights that trembled and shook as though the heavens themselves were on fire. His mouth fell open at the dazzling tapestry.

Bannock laughed with delight. ''Tis the northern fire! I have seen it often, but never like this!'

Boundless stared, wonder-struck, at the coruscating flashes of purple, green and crimson. The dancing lights filled the sky, zooming and blazing like sheet lightning. Around him, voices were hushed in awe. And, in truth, he confessed to himself, he felt a little afraid—the blazing flares threatening to consume the earth and all it held, like a spark to powder.

In spite of the chill air, he watched, mesmerised, for a quarter hour before retreating back to the warmth of the fire. He made a quick note in the journal as others around him talked about the spectacle in amazed voices while preparing for bed. After a brief description of the 'heavenly fire,' he concluded:

*The country hovers between ice and fire, a land of such astonishing extremi-
ties as to defy belief. A person beholds one breathless spectacle after another
until the mind becomes exhausted with the effort of trying to hold, nay,
contain, such diverse and wondrous phenomena. The miracles of grass,
buffalo, fish and other abundances of nature are replicated in the skies and*

*continue to unfold until the mind staggers at the glories of Creation in all its resplendent and manifold guises.*

It took him some time to fall asleep. And when he did succumb, it was in awed, fitful consciousness of the flashing drama shaking the heavens just above the roof where he slept.

AS DECEMBER GAVE WAY to the new year, a skin of ice covered all but the mid-channel of the Missouri. One morning in late January, he tested the thickness by cautiously venturing out twenty yards from the shore—retreating quickly as he saw water bubbling up through the ice. He returned to the post, hoping that the next day might prove more amenable for hunting.

To his disappointment, the morning dawned grey and windy, a thick bank of cloud blocking out the sun. Determined to hunt, in spite of the weather, he took the dog sledge and set out across the white plain. He had gone less than a mile, however, when 'powder devils' whipped up so much snow that he could see barely ten yards ahead. Shielding his eyes against the wind, he turned back, thankful for the homing instinct of the dogs.

By nightfall, the winds had strengthened to a raging gale that shook the walls of the bunkhouse. He lay in the bunk, appalled at the fury of the howling winds as the fire leapt and flickered in the draughts. *I must endure three more months of this,* he told himself as the pervasive cold and darkness began to take a toll on his mood.

To escape the noisy, smoke-filled hall, he took nightly walks around the stockade. He devised a route that took him through the street, past the tool hut, the forge, the smokehouse, and around the former parade ground—avoiding the log wall and the drifted snow piled up at its base. He had barely traced this route one evening when he noticed another figure, huddled against the cold, trudging towards him. As the two drew closer, he recognised the other man as Bjornson. He coughed to alert the Swede, who appeared sunk in thought. Startled, the Swede mumbled a greeting and hurried past. Boundless continued on his way, ruminating on the fellow and his rumoured scandalous past.

He saw the door to the storehouse open and someone step out. He tensed as he recognised Askook. At that moment, Quoi emerged from a shed with a bucket of scraps. Askook made as if to dash at the startled gatekeep. With a yelp of fright, Quoi scurried away, spilling the slops in his haste. Taking a pipe from his pocket, Askook called sneeringly after the fearful creature. As he leaned back against the storehouse doorway to smoke, his gaze wandered to where Boundless stood watching. An oath leapt from his lips. Pipe in mouth, he advanced a few feet into the yard where he stood with legs spread, thumbs hooked into his belt. He stared tauntingly at Boundless, as if daring him to issue a challenge. When Boundless made no move to do so, the half-breed ostentatiously cleared his throat and hawked in the snow. With a challenging jut of his chin, he turned slowly on his heel and made his way back into the storehouse.

The next evening, Boundless encountered Bjornson again, in spite of varying the time of his walk—as did the Swede! The fact amused him. On impulse, he turned as they drew abreast of each other. 'Bjorn, shall we walk together?'

Thereafter, they made it a practice to walk together for a half-hour following supper. Neither man spoke much on these nightly perambulations. Bjornson seemed forever preoccupied, sometimes mumbling and sighing to himself, while Boundless, in spite of his curiosity about the Swede, welcomed the companionable silence after the noisy hall.

The nightly rambles did not take long to catch the attention of Pinch and Bannock, who at once pressed him for details.

'What confidences have you dragged out of our gloomy pastor?' Pinch fixed him a probing stare as though to mentally extract the answer.

'Has he revealed the secret of his dalliances?' put in Bannock.

'None, and no, is the answer. And now, if you will excuse me, gentlemen, I must depart—with sorrow, 'tis true, yet must.'

A SPELL OF FINE, cloudless weather saw him spending long hours traversing the snowfields in pursuit of game. To avoid the blinding glare of the reflected sunlight, he cut holes in the wool toque, pulling it down over his eyes and staring out through the slits.

One morning, to his surprise, White Deer approached as he was about to set forth on another hunt. Shyly, she proffered a dish containing a paste of soot and grease.

'*Comme ça.*' Dipping fingers in the paste, she made as if to smear it under her eyes.

'*Merci, Madame.*' He followed suit, blackening his eyes.

'*Que fais-tu?*' Quoi, who was passing by, pounced on the bowl. Hooking fingers into the paste, the half-wit streaked his face. Putting a hand to his mouth, he screeched like a savage while chopping the air with an imaginary hatchet. White Deer quickly retreated, an expression of mingled pity and fright on her face. Still uttering the occasional whoop, Quoi dragged open the gate, the black streaks against his white face and bulging eyes enhancing the impression of idiocy. '*Au revoir anglais! Ne te noie pas dans la mer blanche!*'

INCREASINGLY BORED AND RESTLESS as winter ground on, he cast about for some project or diversion to see him through the long nights. On a day of blowing snow—so thick he had to check his passage from the cabin to the bunkhouse—he took out the log and sat down at the small table. Idly, he turned the pages, his eyes tracing the entries back to the Maryland woods. He paused over the list of supplies deemed necessary by Mose for the journey to the plains. He lingered over a sketch of the giant bones discovered back at the Ohio, shaking his head at the recollection. In his mind's eye, he saw Mose fret and fuss over the wood raft that would float them across the mile-wide waters. He pictured his former comrade sipping whiskey, pipe in hand while yarning with Pinch and the amiable Frenchmen as snow fell outside. *You would be at home here, old friend.*

He turned a page, mulling over several sketches of buffalo. One, in particular, caught his eye—the figure of a bull standing ramrod-stiff while caught in a rainstorm. He tugged his chin, recalling the moment of the sketch.

The door opened, followed by a blast of cold air. Abel, the blacksmith, walked in. '*Good evening,*' he said cheerfully, bending to retrieve something from beneath his bed. '*Supper is being served.*'

'*I'm coming,*' he answered, still caught up in the buffalo. As the door closed, it struck him that he had unthinkingly understood the blacksmith's words and, moreover, answered in French. Pleased with the fact, he put the quill case into his pocket and followed Abel back to the hall. Over supper, he gave scant attention to Pinch and Bannock, giving ear instead to the conversations around him. As the men split into groups to play piquet or dice, he found a spot at the end of the table nearest the fire. On a scrap of wrapping paper, he made a list of all the French words he knew.

A passing Bannock peered over his shoulder. 'Do you write your testament?'

'The most common words I hear around me.' He pushed the paper forward.

Bannock peered at the list. '*Castor. Peau. Builoire. Froid. Couverture.* You have spelt *bouilloire* wrongly. You must add a naught and double the l.'

'Do I at least pronounce it aright—*bouill-oire?*'

'Close enough—like a Mandan!' Bannock yawned. 'Bed for me.' He got up and left.

Pondering the remark, he sought out Pinch, interrupting the latter at cards. 'Say a word—in Mandan.'

Pinch frowned at the cards. 'Bother the Mandan.'

'Forbear. A single word.'

Pinch grunted in annoyance. 'Which one?'

'Any. It doesn't matter which.'

'*Tashkasha!*'

'What does it mean?'

'Hello. You are a fine fellow.'

'Can you write it down?'

'Are you mad?' Pinch fixed him an exasperated stare. 'Indian is meant for the tongue only. It is not intended to be writ.'

'I try only to capture the sound, for my own purposes. What is the word for buffalo?'

'Too devilish to say. And—do you forget, I am as unlettered as a savage?'

'The word, then?'

Pinch rumbled in annoyance. '*Mideegaadi.*'

'*Mid-ee-gaddy.*' He wrote down the sounds. '*Mid-ee-gaddy,*' he repeated. 'What about the word for hunt?'

'For God's sake! Leave me be with your blessed words!'

By questioning Henri and several other of the Frenchmen, he managed to compile a list of two dozen Indian words, in either the Mandan or the Hidatsa, approximating the sounds as best he was able.

'*Mid-yap-ha,*' he said, hailing Louis as the latter entered the cabin. Louis stared, perplexed.

'*Mid-yap-ha! Beaver.*'

Louis scratched his head. '*Beaver? Míd-apă.*'

Boundless frowned. 'Did I not—Never mind!'

Frustrated at the intractability of the Indian tongue, he turned his efforts back to the French. He was trying to compose a simple sentence, intending to show it to Bannock for correction, when he became aware of someone looking over his shoulder.

He glanced up, startled to see Thibault—the bourgeois normally retiring to his quarters in the afternoon, and not seen again until the next morning.

'*Vous étudiez le français?*'

'*Oui, monsieur. J'essaie.*'

Thibault nodded, a thoughtful look on his face. '*Bien,*' he said, and walked away.

The next morning, he surprised Boundless by handing him a small leather-bound book. '*Pour vos études.*' Smiling, he waved away Boundless' attempt at thanks.

'I know the book,' said Bannock with a glance at the title when Boundless showed him the volume. 'I studied it under the Jesuits. It is a book of familiar tales. Would you like me to write one out in English?'

'I would indeed.'

Grateful for the diversion, he studied the volume an hour each evening, glancing from the page to Bannock's translation and back again as he attempted to understand the tale in the original French. Under Bannock's guidance, he read the words aloud, seeking to master the pronunciation as he made use of the long winter evenings to teach himself French.

Seeing him poring over the book, Thibault stopped to check on his progress. 'What did he say?' Boundless asked Bannock as the bourgeois left.

'He said that each of your companions resembles a creature from the tales. Try to guess each one.'

Monsieur Lapointe, learning of his endeavour, assisted by loaning him a French-English dictionary and offering to help with grammar and syntax. He accepted gratefully, determined to learn the language so that he might join in the speech of his companions.

One night, he came across the brief list of putative Indian words tucked inside the pages of Guillaume's book. He screwed up the scrap of paper and tossed it into the fire. *This is truly a land of tongues. There be as many speeches as the buffalo!*

## 11

## Buffalo Dance

I N THE MIDDLE OF February, an invitation arrived to attend a buffalo dance at the Mandan village. To his surprise, he was selected to attend, drawing envious groans from Bannock. 'I offered Gaston a week's wages, but Henri offered him two!'

'Tell me about the dance—what is the purpose?'

''Tis said to bring back the buffalo—when the miracle would be to keep them away!'

They set out the following day in a party of eight. The wind was cold and sharp, causing Boundless to bury his nose in the capote. They travelled along the shores of the Missouri, carrying with them gifts of tobacco and blankets as well as the fiddle and tambourine.

'*Pour la danse*' said Louis when he queried the instruments. The Frenchman smiled mysteriously, his lips white with frost. '*La danse verticale et horizontale!*'

Uncertain he had caught the Frenchman's meaning, he was reminded of Pinch's salacious claims as to the nature of the ceremony.

They arrived to find the village in a state of great excitement. Logs and branches had been stacked in the plaza for a huge bonfire. The men had gone to elaborate lengths to dress their hair for the occasion. An Indian he recognised as Turtle Shell walked past, his long, flowing locks entwined with shells and dyed porcupine quills. Others had fashioned sticks into their hair and coiffured it into a stiff crest on top of their heads. A few had fastened eagle feathers into the quiff, the tips ornamented with horsehair and coloured with yellow dye.

Not to be outdone, the women had dressed in their finest deerskin tunics, the skirts ornamented with elk teeth, and the bodices sewn with buttons, shells and feathers. Their hair shone with freshly applied grease. Many had adorned their faces with white, red and yellow paint.

With the Mandan's usual courtesy towards guests, they were shown to a lodge and offered food and drink. Louis ate sparingly and advised Boundless to do the same. '*Garde ton ventre pour le festin,*' he said, and patted his stomach.

As the sun began to sink towards the horizon, they joined a crowd of several hundred Indians gathered in the plaza. Six women dressed in beige-coloured tunics and with white buffalo robes around their shoulders approached, each carrying a drum decorated with feathers and hanks of buffalo hair. The women passed through the dense gathering, the assembly standing aside to allow reverent passage.

The mood of eager anticipation grew as the huge bonfire was lit. A row of men began to beat drums as women began to chant. It was now dark, the roaring flames from the fire offering the only illumination.

A collective gasp sounded as a group of warriors entered the fire-light—their appearance evoking cries of admiration. In spite of the cold, the dancers were naked apart from breechclouts, their bodies painted with red, black and white concentric circles. In one hand, they carried a rattle, which they shook in time to the drumbeats; in the other hand, they held a long wooden rod. On their heads, they wore bundles of willow boughs, the sticks flopping as they began to shake and twirl. The fire continued to burn fiercely in the cold night air, the flames leaping skywards as the dancers whirled and gyrated to the pounding drums.

Above the repetitive chants and drumming, Boundless heard the incongruous sounds of the fiddle and the tambourine. Two Frenchmen had joined the dancers, shouting and calling as they jigged and stepped to the scraping fiddle.

Hands seized Boundless and pulled him towards the revelry. He tripped a few awkward steps, self-conscious in the capote and hat. Beside him, a fellow *engagé* danced with unabashed fervour, his face flushed as he roared out songs in his native Breton. The coldness of the wintry night, the ululating cries, and the shuffling dancers proved intoxicating. Swept up in the fervour, he flung his arms above his head and whooped a Scottish war cry, hopping and springing with abandon. The Breton caught his arm and the two of them skipped a reel until out of breath.

Exhausted, and sweating profusely in spite of the cold, he returned to the lodge for a rest. He spied Louis seated with Jacques Bonnet amidst a group of old men to one side of the fire. Beckoning him over, Louis moved to allow him room to sit.

'*La véritable danse va commencer!*' The Frenchman's eyes were bright with anticipation.

A man entered the lodge and led a young woman clad in a buffalo robe into the firelight. To Boundless' astonishment, she shrugged off the robe to reveal her nakedness underneath. Unashamedly presenting herself before the seated men, she displayed her charms as her husband exhorted the old men with pleas and gestures. A man climbed to his feet and reached for the young woman, her husband ushering them out of the lodge together. No sooner had they departed than another young woman entered, led also by her husband. To Boundless' consternation, the man propelled the woman towards him—holding out her hand and beseeching him to take it. Profoundly shocked, he turned away from her nakedness.

Jacques chuckled and dug him in the ribs. 'The husband recognises you as a famous 'unter. He wants you to take his wife in the hope that some of your skill will rub off on him.' He made an obscene gesture and pushed Boundless to his feet. 'Go! Fuck her for the buffalo!' The young woman uttered a supplication and took his hand as he protested. He turned to Jacques in confusion, only for the Frenchman to urge him on. 'Go! To refuse is a great insult. You must take her!'

The woman led him out into the snow and to a nearby lodge. He followed, torn between shame and lust. In the firelit shadows of the lodge, she pulled back the hide curtain to one of the bed chambers around the wall. The chamber contained a square wooden case overlaid with furs. Leading him inside, she dropped the robe to reveal her nakedness. Embarrassed, he tried to look away. She said something, and gently guided him onto the bed. Tugging off his moccasins, she lay down next to him, appearing not the least bit shy. With murmurs of encouragement, she took his hand and placed it on her warm belly. Her eyes were dark pools in the firelight, her voice importuning as she tugged at his breeches. Her urgency communicated itself to him and he struggled to pull down the buckskin trousers. She lifted her thighs, guiding him inside her as he thrust in a fever of excitement. He was dimly aware of another woman leading Louis to the adjoining chamber. He felt the woman murmur beneath him as he spent himself inside her.

To his amazement, the husband seemed grateful for his participation, thanking him when he returned to the lodge. He sought out another Frenchman for explanation, only for the man to brush aside his questions. *Amuse-toi. C'est la danse!*

Still reeling from what had transpired, he made his way back to the chanting Indians in the plaza. The pounding drums, monotonous chants, and sinuous shuffle of feet quickly banished any lingering sense of doubt or decorum. He drank freely from the many cups pressed into his hand, thirstily imbibing the fermented beverages. The frantic scenes around him took on an increasingly dreamlike quality until he scarcely could tell whether he watched or danced.

As more logs were thrown onto the fire, two men draped in grizzly skins manifested from the darkness—their actions unmistakably bear-like as they growled and clawed the air. The apparitions aroused the spectators to a fever pitch as the ravenous beasts fell upon the dancers, roaring and snarling with horrible intent. The onlookers cried out in supplication and threw morsels of food at the beasts—some of the younger males darting forwards to count coup. The shadowy, bear-clad forms leapt and growled with fearsome savagery as the onlookers wailed and tore at their hair. Abruptly, the beasts took flight to shrieks of triumph—to his shock, he recognised his own voice loud among them.

A hush fell over the crowd as a heavily disguised figure appeared in the firelight—his arrival greeted with cries of horror. Clad in loose skins and daubed with dye so as to resemble some terrible spectre, the intruder howled and swooped with terrifying menace. Spreading his arms wide, he wailed and threatened, darting towards the crowd and drawing cries of terror in response. He was driven off with frenzied shouts and the casting of sticks. No sooner had the ghostly presence fled than a dozen men wearing buffalo heads rushed before the ecstatic spectators. Dipping their horns and making mock charges, the buffalo dancers snorted and whirled as a mood of ecstatic jubilation seized hold of the onlookers.

Chanting and ululating, the Mandan revellers coalesced in rapturous triumph. Bodies pressed upon bodies as men and women swayed and moaned to some ancient, incantatory rhythm that rose into the night along with the soaring sparks of the fire. Boundless cried out and joined in the chants, the primitive sounds leaping natively to his lips. In the cold, clear night he moaned and crooned himself hoarse, jigging and stomping to the point of exhaustion. As dawn paled the sky, he stumbled back to the lodge where he scarcely had time to stretch out on the buffalo robe before he sank into the most profound slumber of his life.

IT SEEMED HE HAD barely closed his eyes before Louis was shaking him by the shoulder. *'Réveille-toi ! Nous devons partir avant que le temps ne se gâte!'*

Blinking and yawning, he stumbled out into the open. The sharp wind stung his senses, and he longed to crawl back under the warm robe. The village was deserted except for a few female slaves and a group of small boys chasing a dog with a stick tied to its tail.

Louis had finished hitching the traineau in between glancing up at the grey sky, evidently concerned at the prospect of snow.

'*Aller!*' The Frenchman cracked the whip and the sledge started off, the sleepy revellers stumbling alongside. Pulling the hood of the capote over his face, Boundless trudged after the sledge, yawning and shivering against the cold. Blowing powder had obliterated their former tracks, and the plain lay smooth and untrodden before them. No one spoke. He blinked against the blinding whiteness, his breath a vapour on the freezing air.

**12**

***Le Québec est tombé!***

S LOWLY, WITH INFINITE GRADATION, the days began to grow longer and the skies milder. Flocks of ducks passed overhead as the biting gales of winter shifted to warmer westerly breezes. One day, the ice cracked on the river—the sound carrying as far as the stockade.

''Tis the noise of spring,' said Pinch as a general mood of cheerfulness infiltrated the company.

'I was never so glad to hear it,' said Boundless, heartfelt in his relief.

The melting snow left lakes of water on the prairie grass, the cold, soggy mire unpleasant to walk on. 'I shall need a canoe to hunt!' he exclaimed, his shirt and breeches splattered with mud. But hunting became less necessary as Indian parties resumed their trade visits, bringing with them meat, fish and pemmican.

In preparation for spring baling, the country husbands returned from the Indian villages, their families in tow. Once again, the post echoed to the cries of children as they tore around the compound.

Boundless was seated on the storehouse steps, cleaning the musket, when he heard a commotion outside the stockade. He stood up to look as a handful of Frenchmen started towards the open gate to investigate.

'It's the trade party back from the Hidatsa,' said Pinch, coming to join him. 'Something is amiss.'

'*Le Québec est tombé! La guerre est finie!*' The returning men shouted the news, their voices hoarse. '*La France a capitulé!*'

'Did ye hear?' Pinch turned to Boundless, a look of surprise on his face. 'The war is over!'

The news caused consternation as men hurried from all quarters of the post to hear the details. The sledge, piled with pelts, lay forgotten as a crowd gathered to fire questions at Edouard, leader of the party.

'How did the Indians know—before us?' asked Boundless as Bannock joined the incredulous throng around the returned men.

'How do they know anything? 'Tis passed along, from mouth to mouth.'

Bannock listened again as more information was dragged from the breathless Edouard. 'It happened last year, shortly after the brigade had left the lakes,' Bannock relayed to Boundless.

'*Calmez-vous!*' The voice of Theroux cut through the noise as the *pilote* pushed through the crowd surrounding the returned party. ,

'*De quoi toute cette agitation à propos de la guerre?*' He demanded. The onlookers fell silent, hanging on every word as he closely questioned Edouard.

'What does he say?' Boundless pressed Bannock as the interrogation continued, the answers drawing gasps of dismay from the men crowded around.

'The Indians claim both the French and English commanders were killed in the battle. They heard the news from a French trapper. And—' Bannock listened again to the harried Edouard. 'They described Jean Delac. Edouard knows of him. He insists the reports are true.'

The news dominated conversation for the remainder of the day—the surrender and the fortunes of France the sole subject of conversation, as the men expressed shock and disbelief at the report. Rumours and hearsay flew back and forth as opinions were traded regarding the defeat, each new assertion igniting further speculation and debate.

'It was hardly unexpected,' said a sanguine Pinch when Boundless found him leaning against the storehouse, smoking his pipe and observing a group of Frenchmen in heated argument with each other. 'We knew the Frenchies were in retreat.'

'According to Bannock, the men are claiming the post will be shut down—that this will be the last brigade.'

'Pfff!' Pinch waved the pipe. 'Who wears the crown does not matter—so long as the victor keeps his hands in his own pockets.'

The fervid gossip continued until supper when the men gathered early in expectation of an announcement from Thibault. An expectant hush fell over the hall as the bourgeois, a strained look on his face, emerged from his private room accompanied by Theroux.

'*Silence!*' commanded the latter as Thibault took up position in front of the hearth, facing the men.

The bourgeois looked around the tables, his expression grave as Bannock interpreted for Boundless' benefit.

'My friends. What you have heard is true. The war is lost. It is only a matter of time before France formally surrenders.'

The stark confirmation had a sobering effect, the pronouncement hanging in the air like smoke from a fired musket.

'We were betrayed!'

The anguished cry was greeted with shouts of agreement. Everyone began talking at once as heated arguments broke out—voices blaming the government in Paris, the lack of troops, the Indians, or the French generals for the defeat.

Thibault waited for the angry recriminations to die down before speaking again, his voice full of feeling. 'The reed bends in the wind but is not broken. France may be defeated, but her spirit remains indestructible!'

The rousing declaration was greeted with loud applause and shouts of 'Vive la France!' Someone passed a glass of rum to Thibault.

Boundless turned to Bannock. 'What did he say? I only understood a tenth of it.'

'He said France is defeated but unbowed.'

As Thibault began speaking again. Bannock obligingly continued to interpret for Boundless.

'He bids us have patience and counsels that a prosperous future lies ahead.'

Thibault paused and, with a glance toward Pinch and Boundless, continued.

'He says that here there is no discord, only brotherhood and friendship.'

Edouard, sitting opposite, reached across the table, a solemn look on his face. Boundless grasped the proffered hand, moved by the display of comradeship.

'Sir, what will it mean for us?'

The question brought the entire hall to attention as the men hushed each other to hear the response.

Thibault nodded at the question and took a sip from his glass before replying.

'What does he say?' asked Boundless.

'He must return east to discuss the future with his partners. But profit is profit, regardless of which rooster runs the coop.'

Boundless glanced at Pinch who gave a smug look in return.

Thibault raised the glass of wine and spoke again, his voice hoarse with emotion. 'Gentlemen. Eternal France!'

In a burst of patriotic emotion, the men cheered and pounded the tables. A tousled youth, the favourite *chanteur* of the company, was urged to his feet. He began to sing in a trembling, plaintive voice, unaccompanied by the fiddle. The men fell silent, the song inducing sighs and free-flowing tears. As one, they joined in the refrain, voices rising in a fervent, yet tender and heartfelt chorus, *'I have loved you for a long time. I will never forget you!'*

IN SPITE OF THIBAULT'S attempts to keep the men occupied with work, gossip continued to sweep the post about the future of the company, each day bringing fresh rumours.

'I hear that the post will soon be abandoned,' declared Denis, a *milieu* from Trois-Rivières, to everyone within earshot.

'Nonsense!' objected Bannock. 'How can that be so when Monsieur Thibault has yet to confer with the partners?'

The Frenchman looked nonplussed and shrugged. 'I say only what I hear.'

Amidst the endless conjecture, Pinch remained sanguine, blithely dismissing each new rumour as it arose. 'As Guillaume said, the post brings in profits, does it not?' he asked as his companions sat around drinking tea. 'What matter who pays the piper—England or France?'

'The licensing restrictions may change to favour English companies,' Bannock pointed out. 'There will be increased competition for furs—from New York and Albany. And the Indians may seek new alliances with the English.'

'Enough with the deuced war!' Pinch pulled a pack of cards from his pocket. 'A hand, gentlemen,' he said, laying out the deck. 'Harry must have his supper and Ned his new shoes.'

Taking advantage of the opportunity when he found himself alone with Pinch, Boundless brought up a matter that had been on his mind. 'Remember when you told me the tale of Guillaume's good fortune?' He glanced around to check that no one was listening. 'May this not be another twist to add to the tale?'

'How so?' asked Pinch giving Boundless a puzzled glance.

'This fort—it belonged to the French government, did it not?'

'Aye.' Pinch nodded.

'Now that there is no government, and no army, who does the post belong to but he who occupies it?'

Pinch burst into a delighted guffaw. 'By Saint George, but you are right!' Beaming, he slapped Boundless on the shoulder. 'The tale yet continues!'

THE RUMOURS AND GOSSIP continued as the weather grew warmer, hushed only by Thibault's impatience as he sought to dampen speculation and turn attention back to matters at hand. A busy series of trades brought in a late abundance of pelts—the furs stacked to the height of a man on the storehouse floor. In addition to the prized beaver, the Indians traded the pelts of buffalo, bear, otter, fisher, wolverine, elk, moose and a variety of other animals, including wolf, raccoon, lynx, muskrat, antelope, and squirrel. Thibault seemed delighted with the quantity and quality, declaring the harvest equal to the best he had seen.

All energies now turned to baling as the entire company joined in to sort and press the pelts for transport. Boundless worked alongside Bannock, following the more experienced man's instructions to place the less valuable pelts of moose or summer beaver on top of each pile. 'Lay them hide to hide,' explained Bannock. 'It will preserve the fur.'

'You have baled before?'

'No, but I have untied a great many.'

A balance scale was used to ensure each pile came as close as possible to the uniform weight of ninety pounds, the weight of sixty to seventy pelts. As each pile was finished, it was transferred to a wooden crib beneath the fur press. Four or five men then pushed on the heavy wooden beam balanced atop the crib. The weight of the beam squeezed the furs into bundles small enough to be carried by one person. As a final step, each *pièce* was wrapped in deerskin and secured with ropes.

Groaning and stretching his back, Pinch kicked a bale from the growing pile. 'Fancy hoisting that—and mayhap one other—over miles of slippery rock and trails so thick with roots as to cripple a fox. And then repeat the task until you've shifted all of the brutes!' He shook his head in disgust. 'Not for me!'

A sudden rain shower sent the men scurrying for shelter. Boundless ducked inside the storehouse to find Bannock seated on the floor, eyes closed, and his back against the wall. The storehouse smelled of damp fur, the burgeoning trade goods that had once filled its space now almost gone.

Boundless brushed the rain from his shoulders and peered out at the grey sky. 'Fifty bales so far, and more to come,' he said.

Bannock nodded without opening his eyes. 'I expect the tally to be eighty or more afore we are done.'

Boundless marvelled at the figure. 'I spent a year hunting and trapping the Maryland woods with a companion—an experienced man. Yet, in that time, we collected scarcely the equal of two bales.'

'Aye. But we have the tribes of nations collecting on our behalf.' Bannock adjusted himself against the wall. 'The method is very efficient. Eighty bales will produce ...' He scratched his jaw, 'Five thousand furs, and more.'

'And the value?'

'It will depend on the pelt and the market. Suffice to say, a single beaver will double or triple in value as it makes its way east and then double again once landed in France or England.'

They heard shouts from the yard. 'The rain has stopped,' said Boundless, getting to his feet.

THE WEATHER RAPIDLY TURNED warmer, drying the stockade and soaking up the lakes of meltwater in the grass. Wildflowers began to bloom, adding colour to the landscape so that soon the bleak greys and whites of winter were no more than a memory. The irruption of good spirits ushered in by the warm weather continued as the canoes were carried out from shelter and inspected to see that they had wintered without harm. Extra paddles were cut from trees along the river as preparations began for the departure of the brigade. The Missouri was now mostly free of floating ice, while snow lingered only in nooks and crannies along the bank.

'No more than a week,' hazarded Pinch as he gazed up at the clear blue sky.

Two days before departure, the company sat down to give thanks for the year just passed. Boundless entered the hall to find the bourgeois and Lapointe conferring behind the stand-up desk, which had been carried from the storehouse for the occasion. The smells of roasting meat came from the hearth where White Deer and the Indian women were preparing the feast. He took a chair held out for him by Bannock. 'A meeting of the stockholders,' the Montrealer whispered as he sat down. 'He tells us our tally for the year.'

The hall began to fill as the men took their places at the two long tables. Amidst the noise and chatter, Thibault and Lapointe talked at the front of the hall as they waited for everyone to be seated. Pinch arrived and joined them.

'Do you still stroll with our friend?' asked Bannock, eyeing Bjornson as the Swede took his place at the adjoining table.

'I do,' affirmed Boundless. 'He is a decent fellow, with a sharp eye for pretence.'

Pinch frowned at the description. 'And where would he find pretence here?'

'I meant semblance—as in the speaking of one thing and the doing of another.'

'Hypocrisy, you mean?' Bannock raised an eyebrow.

'Yes and no. I mean—'

'The airs we give ourselves?'

Boundless blew out his cheeks in defeat. 'I know not what I mean, except that he is a sharp fellow.'

'And expert at sharpening,' said Pinch. He waited for a moment. 'Did ye not take the meaning?'

'We did, Pinch. We did.' Bannock slapped the older man on the shoulder. 'Pestle to the bowl. Needle to the thread. Bottle to the glass—'

'Needle to the thread? Surely, thread to the needle?'

'Aye, Pinch. Thread to the needle.'

'*Messieurs!*' The chatter died away as Thibault cleared his throat and began to speak.

The account continued for a quarter-hour, Bannock interpreting where he could for the benefit of Boundless.

'"Twas a fine year,' he summarised at one point as the men clapped and turned to congratulate one another.

'He carefully avoided mention of the war,' noted Pinch.

'He is sick of it, as is everyone else.'

A hush fell over the hall as Thibault finished. After a word with Lapointe, he crooked a finger at Boundless, a faint smile on his lips.

'What now?' Boundless asked as heads turned in his direction.

Bannock pushed him to his feet. 'Go! God summons you.'

Perplexed and self-conscious, Boundless made his way past the crowded tables to where the bourgeois awaited him on the hearth.

Motioning him to stand to one side, Thibault produced a red worsted cap, which he placed on Boundless' head. Holding out a hand to his deputy, he took possession of a new wool capote, which he held up for Boundless.

'He wants you to try it on for size,' said Lapointe.

Feeling faintly embarrassed in front of the watching faces, Boundless nevertheless thrust his arms into the roomy sleeves.

Thibault belted a red wool sash around his waist to complete the transformation. Smiling, he turned Boundless to face the grinning voyageurs. '*Messieurs, je vous présente un compatriote hivernant!*'

'*Bienvenue dans notre tribu!*' came the chorus.

BOUNDLESS WAS STILL RECEIVING congratulations from the jovial Frenchmen when he received a summons to join Thibault in his private room at the front of the hall. He knocked on the door, accompanied by Bannock as interpreter. Thibault welcomed them in and bade them sit as he uncorked a bottle of wine. As he did so, he spoke to Boundless, allowing time for Bannock to relay the message.

'He must return with the brigade to consult with his partners. The

English victories and the French surrender will have caused much uncertainty. In his absence, he wishes you to supervise the post.'

'Me?' Boundless looked at the bourgeois in surprise. 'But Monsieur Lapointe, surely, is the head clerk?'

'He will be returning with Scattered Corn Woman to her village for the summer.'

'Then Pinch?'

Thibault chuckled at mention of the name, his lean features creased with humour.

Grinning, Bannock turned to explain. 'He says that were he to leave Pinch in charge, the post would fall down about his ears. Do you accept the responsibility?'

'Yes, sir. I do! And thank you!'

Thibault nodded. '*Bien. Et maintenant …*' He poured a glass of wine for each of them. '*Messieurs, à votre santé!*'

That night, Boundless wrote a brief letter requesting necessities from Montreal, the expenses to be deducted from his wages:

*Any reliable account of the upper Missouri Indians, their history, manners and speech. The Essays, Moral and Political, of Mr Hume. All volumes to be in English. Two blank journals, amply stitched in fine leather. A good quality linen shirt. A dozen quill pens. 8oz of ink powder. Three yards of checked flannel. Six pair woollen socks. Three yards of sewing thread. A small skinning knife with leather sheath. A metal sharpening file with a stout wood handle.*

He considered the list for a moment before adding, 'The essays of Montaigne, in the original French.'

He looked up as Pinch came in. To his annoyance, the Bostonian peered over his shoulder.

'Add a pound of boiled sweets and a linen shirt for me.'

'Why not make your own list?'

'I have. I forgot to include the shirt and sweets.'

'They will not know to calculate the separate charges to you.'

'They will supply a list of items, and costs.'

'But they must deduct the costs from our wages.'

'Then I shall hand you the coins—when the supplies arrive.'

Frowning, Boundless included the items, adding in parentheses, '*To be charged to Monsieur Pinch!*'

## 13

### *God's Instrument*

THE DAY BEFORE DEPARTURE, the men gathered in the yard to toast the event with rum punch, and brandy saved for the occasion. It was a fine afternoon with only a light breeze. The bourgeois relaxed in a chair placed outside the hall door, a glass of wine in hand. The festivities soon evolved into a sporting contest, the men challenging each other to various games. The ungainly figure of Quoi happily joined in the diversions. Clad in an overlarge beaver hat that slipped about his ears, he warbled with excitement as two of the men hoisted him up on their shoulders and challenged another team to a footrace. Urging on his 'little horse' with shrieks of encouragement, he chortled with glee as the other team staggered and slipped.

Bannock laughed as he watched the frolics. 'The poor fool is beyond man or angel.'

'What will happen to him—when Thibault returns to Montreal?'

'He will take him—or leave him to the next bourgeois. What else can he do? God must bear his own mistakes.'

Someone nailed a scrap of cloth to the stockade fence, and the men took turns to throw hatchets at the target, wagering sums of their hard-earned wages on the outcome of each throw. Boundless relaxed against the press, enjoying the good-natured ribbing as the men lined up to aim at the mark. A hatchet sailed through the air and thudded into the logs a foot above the target.

'Wash your eyes out! You missed by a mile!'

'Another inch and it was over the stockade!'

'You throw like a duck!'

Hooting with derision, Quoi hobbled forward to free the hatchet.

As the men laid wagers on the next throw, the storehouse door opened and Askook emerged. The Indian, strictly forbidden from drinking by Thibault on account of his temper, nevertheless appeared drunk. He staggered and almost fell down the steps, putting out a hand to steady himself.

Boundless watched the half-breed wipe his mouth as his attention was seized by the noisy Frenchmen as they laughed and joked while contesting the game.

'Give me a turn!' Stumbling forwards, Askook snatched the hatchet from the next thrower—a bearded veteran of over twelve brigades.

The man protested, attempting to wrest back the hatchet as others joined in to remonstrate.

'I have a right!' Askook clung to the hatchet, resisting all attempts to pry it from his grasp.

'Let him throw!' a voice taunted. 'With luck, it will bounce back and split his skull!'

The men drew back as Askook stood unsteadily behind the line scratched in the dirt. Drawing back his arm, he breathed heavily and then lowered his arm. Scowling at jeers from the mocking Frenchmen, he drew back his arm again. With an explosion of breath, he sent the hatchet looping through the air towards the mark. *'Voila!'*

*'Manqué!'* A gleeful Quoi shuffled forwards to tug the hatchet from the logs. *'Manqué!'* he cackled, oblivious to the enraged Askook. Brandishing the hatchet and slapping his lips, he hopped from foot to foot. 'Whoo! Whoo!'

'Imbecile! I hit the mark! You pulled it out too soon.' Askook lunged at the jigging Quoi and clutched him by the throat. Quoi shrieked in terror as others rushed to intervene. A struggle ensued as the men dragged the cursing Indian away from the gatekeep. In the confusion, Askook fell—or was knocked—to the dirt.

'Go back to hell, devil!' The veteran voyageur whose turn he had usurped aimed a kick at Askook's head as the Indian picked himself up. The half-breed retreated across the yard, spewing dire threats and curses.

Thibault stood up to investigate the disturbance at the same time that Bjornson emerged from the storehouse in response to the commotion.

'What is all the fuss?' the Swede asked as Askook passed.

'Mind your own business, dogshit!'

The affronted Bjornson responded. 'There is no cause to be rude. I was simply asking—'

'Shut your mouth, you son of a whore!' Askook turned and lashed out, knocking the shocked Bjornson to the ground.

The incensed half-breed proceeded to rain kicks on the dazed Swede. Bjornson threw up his hands in a desperate attempt to defend himself while crying out for help. The savage assault continued as the petrified Swede attempted to scramble beneath the steps of the storehouse. Askook dragged him back out, venting his fury in an explosion of curses amid a barrage of kicks and blows.

Boundless rushed forward to pull the enraged Indian away. 'Enough!'

'I will teach you to mind your business!' Eyes blazing, Askook attempted to stomp Bjornson's head.

'Stop, damn you!' Boundless shoved the drunken Indian. Caught off-balance, Askook stumbled backwards and fell to the ground, striking his head against the storehouse steps.

Several men hurried forwards to haul the dazed Bjornson to his feet.

Ashen-faced and trembling, the Swede could barely stand. '*Guds Moder! Guds Moder!*' He repeated the words over and over as his legs began to shake. He would have fallen but for the supporting arms.

'Make way!' Thibault pushed through the knot of men followed by Theroux, who knelt beside the insensible Indian and felt for a pulse.

'Is he dead?' asked Thibault.

'He is still breathing.' Theroux shook his head as though regretful of the fact.

At that moment, Askook groaned. Thibault turned to the watching men. 'Take him to the canoe shed and lock him in!'

Motioning for Theroux to follow, Thibault walked apart a few paces. The two engaged in earnest conversation as the stricken Askook was hauled away.

Bannock clapped Boundless on the shoulder. 'Well struck! You saved the pastor.'

'*Genom dig har Gud räddat mig från vildaren!*' Bjornson seized his hand, the Swede's eyes glistening with gratitude. The men pressed in to listen as the shaken Swede stuttered grateful thanks in a mix of French and his native speech.

Pinch shook his head. 'The fellow babbles in tongues. He has lost his wits through the beating.'

'Not so.' Bannock cocked an ear, his face keen as he listened to the words pouring from Bjornson's mouth. 'It is French. He says that God has … delivered him. Through you, Boundless. He says that … through you—his instrument—God has delivered him from the heathen.'

Boundless muttered in embarrassment as the Swede continued to voice tearful thanks while pressing his hand between his own. 'It was nothing. *Rien.*'

The following morning, he stood on the banks of the river to watch the brigade depart. Although swollen with the spring run-off, the river ran free of ice. The weather was fine and sunny. A balmy breeze ruffled the grass. The canoes, heavily laden with bales and ballast, sat low in the water. Thibault was perched in the second craft, the parfleche pouch containing bills, letters, orders, and a ledger in his lap. The men sat patiently in place, waiting for the return of three of their members—despatched to fetch Askook.

'Will they restrain him—in the canoe?' Bjornson asked, his face cut and bruised from the beating.

'They will bind him hand and foot,' said Pinch. 'If he proves a nuisance, they will not hesitate to throw him over the side.'

They heard a shout as a breathless Frenchman appeared on the rise above them. The man shouted again while pointing to the distance.

Boundless heard Pinch mutter in disgust.

'What does he say?'

'The dog has escaped! And taken a musket with him!'

## 14

## A Death in the Grass

**F**EARS THAT ASKOOK MIGHT return to claim vengeance kept nerves on edge as the few remaining men maintained a watchful alertness following the departure of the brigade. But as the days passed without incident, an air of cautious yet relaxed vigilance descended on the post. This relaxed air was reinforced by frequent goodwill visits from Mandan or Hidatsa hunting parties.

Lapointe departed with his wife for the Mandan village, as did Abel—the blacksmith having formed a liaison with an Arikara woman. The blacksmith was accompanied by Jacques, the post carpenter, the latter hopeful of emulating his companion's success. With White Deer also returned to her village, the duties of cooking fell to Boundless and Bjornson—both men adamant that neither Quoi nor Pinch be allowed anywhere near the pot. Instead, Boundless assigned both men to gardening duties, reckoning that between them the two might produce a tolerable crop of vegetables. He and Bjornson busied themselves with making minor repairs to the storehouse, chinking gaps where required, and replacing hinges.

As May passed into June, more and more buffalo arrived. Their darkbrown winter coats had fallen away, revealing the tan colour beneath. Wisps of fine wool clung to the grass—blown from stalk to stalk or entangled in the reeds. At times, the buffalo were so numerous he was forced to close the stockade gates lest they wander inside. Indeed, on more than one occasion he turned back from a scouting venture, defeated by the sheer mass of buffalo blackening the prairie in every direction.

He was walking to the storehouse when he saw Pinch by the stockade gate. The Bostonian was laughing at Quoi, who was stood outside the gate. Going to investigate, he saw over Pinch's shoulder a group of buffalo feeding in the grass. Quoi was taunting the creatures while preparing to flee back inside the stockade should they take offence.

'*Monsieur Buffle!*' Quoi made a loud honking noise, causing a bull to turn and look in his direction. After teasing the animal for some minutes, the chortling Quoi turned back to his duties. 'Honk!' he called out, setting the dogs to bark. 'Honk!' he yelled at Bjornson, causing the unwary Swede to jump.

As uncropped grass became harder to find on the surrounding plain, it became a regular occurrence that small groups of cows with calves ventured nearer the post to feed. Boundless had only to walk outside the gate to shoot the first of six he killed over the course of two days. Filling the smokehouse with the choicest cuts of hump rib, loin and tenderloin, he abandoned the rest to the wolves.

To appease Pinch and supplement the diet, he made regular trips to the river to fish, the transparent water yielding an abundance of the sturgeon whose taste he had come to enjoy. The visits of several groups of Indian women to pick over the few remaining goods in the storehouse brought in in fresh supplies of wild rice, maple syrup and pemmican flavoured with juneberries, nuts and wild onion.

In the endless search for fresh shoots, the buffalo soon moved on, leaving the plain littered with piles of dung. The days became hotter and longer. Summer thunderstorms drenched the grass and rattled the sides of the cabins before the sky cleared and the sun emerged again, hotter than before. In the evenings, when the air had cooled, Boundless and Bjornson went for walks in the grass outside the stockade.

Sidestepping a pile of fresh dung, Bjornson complained sourly at the 'lake of shit' the buffalo had left in their wake. 'The devils shit everywhere,' he grumbled, stopping to scrape his shoe in the grass, 'like brown snow.'

'It is part of the prairie, like the grass,' said Boundless, waiting for Bjornson to resume walking.

Bjornson conceded the point, regaining his equanimity. 'True. One must accept what God has created.' He heaved a sigh. 'Even so, I am no admirer of the beast. It is ugly, flea-ridden, and foul in its stench.'

'No more so than the wolf or the bear, surely?'

Bjornson made a humming sound as he considered the point. 'But so much!' said the Swede, sidestepping another pile of dung. Moisture and sweat streaked his brow. He carried a musket he had borrowed from the storehouse.

'Can you fire that weapon?' Boundless swapped his own musket from his left to his right hand.

'Fire? Yes. Hit something?' Bjornson shrugged.

'You have hunted?'

'A little—as a boy.'

The post-prandial jaunts outside the stockade soon became a habit— the rolling bluffs an ideal background for their rambling conversations. They took two or three of the dogs with them, making desultory talk as the animals bounded through the grass in chase of butterflies or meadow larks.

Throughout the hot days of July, the pair wore a path in the long grass, slowly coming to confide in each other while trading observations on the events of the day. Somewhat to his surprise, Boundless discovered that beneath his companion's Lutheran gloom lurked a robust intelligence and a mordant eye for the foibles of their comrades that yet fell short of humour. Steeped in the religious doctrines of his church, Bjornson was nevertheless ready to offer an opinion on subjects ranging from astronomy to the causes of the concluded war—albeit all viewed through the same perspectival lens.

'There are other reckonings, surely,' protested Boundless one day in response to the Swede's solemn assertion that the value of a life was measured in its degree of servitude to God. The two were inspecting the stockade fence, marking logs for replacement. 'Mark that one,' he said, tapping a log.

Bjornson stepped forward and blazed a scar into the wood.

'By your measure, you would condemn whole races who know nothing of the Christian God,' resumed Boundless. 'Take the Mandan, as instance. They observe the obligations of family and tribe and are honest in their dealings with us.'

'Then the greater pity that they do not accept the true Redeemer.'

'They have their own gods.'

Bjornson snorted. 'Idols of clay!'

'And what of good, sensible men such as Theroux, who reject dogma and clergy, both?'

'They serve unknowingly. There are many paths to God.'

'Rather, many paths to knowledge, God being but one.'

'Then which path led you to here—through the desolate wilderness?'

'Mischance, misfortune, and a thousand other errors. Do not say it was predetermined.'

'Predetermined, no. Guided, yes.'

'Then my Guide led me into some rough places!'

'And led you out again!' chuckled Bjornson, his expression leavened with rare humour.

In spite of their growing friendship, Bjornson resisted all Boundless' attempts to satisfy his curiosity regarding the Swede's enigmatic past, Bjornson remaining evasive whenever Boundless alluded to the subject.

'Do you miss your family?' Boundless asked one morning. They were working side by side to repair a broken step to the storehouse. The air was fresh and mild after several days of scorching heat.

Bjornson said nothing as he struggled with a resistant nail. He continued to work in silence for some time before setting down the pry bar to wipe his brow. 'Before ... I was a man of standing within the congregation. I erred,' he said awkwardly. He paused, staring into the distance. 'And so, here I am.'

Boundless nodded, wondering what Pinch would make of the "And so." 'We have all made mistakes,' he pointed out. 'Doubtless half the company is here through circumstances not of their choosing.'

Bjornson said nothing, focusing his attention on the bent nail.

Boundless considered pursuing the question but gave up. *If Pinch cannot pry it out of him, then who am I to try?*

One fine afternoon, deep in a discussion of navigational charts, they walked to within sight of the rock monolith before stopping to drink water and rest. The day was warm and humid, the lush grass loud with the buzzing of insects. Boundless drained half the canteen while idly observing a group of buffalo as they foraged in the distance. 'What impression do you form of that rock?' he asked, turning to his companion.

Bjornson spat out water and wiped his lips with the back of his hand. 'The rock?'

'Yes. When you look, what do you see?'

Bjornson squinted, a puzzled look on his face. 'I see a big rock. What else is there to see?'

'Does it mind you of anything—a shape, perhaps?' Boundless waved a hand at some buffalo feeding near the object. 'Take a look there. Now look up at the rock again. What do you see?'

Bjornson took off his hat and scratched his head, perplexed at the game. 'I see the buffaloes and the rock, as before.'

'Do you not see a figure to the rock?'

'Figure?' Bjornson grimaced as he shaded his eyes to better observe.

'See there—the front piece.' Boundless pointed to the lofty pinnacle. 'Does it not suggest something?'

Bjornson stared, bafflement etched on his face. 'What?' he asked finally.

'A creature. Do you not see it?'

'I see only what is to see—a rock.'

Boundless sighed and picked up the musket from the grass. 'Let us head back.'

Bjornson followed, stopping once to stare back at the rock. 'I see only what is there,' he insisted.

THROUGHOUT AUGUST, SO MANY Indian delegations visited the post that Boundless was scarcely able to keep count of the pelts and food they brought in exchange for goods. The visitors willingly accepted that the shelves were bare pending the return of the brigade and were content to be given credit in the form of a slip of paper signed with his name. He kept scrupulous accounts of the transactions, knowing that Thibault would insist upon such on his return.

'I did not realise there was so much work to do,' he grumbled to Pinch one afternoon as he bade farewell to a band of Arikara.

'You are acting bourgeois now. You must keep the books as would Guillaume himself.'

'And what about Lapointe? Will he spend the entire summer with the Mandan? He is supposed to be the clerk, not I.' Boundless sighed, feeling restless. 'I feel like going on a hunt.'

'Fie on the hunt!' Pinch waved a hand at the distance. 'We have so much fish, pemmican, rice and meat that you need not stir outside the gate until the brigade returns. Savour the respite.'

In spite of the advice, the next morning, Boundless handed the care of the trades ledger to Bjornson, anxious to enjoy the summer prairie before the brigade returned. He set out accompanied by his favourite dog, intent on a leisurely ramble. He had progressed no more than a mile when he came upon a group of Mandan armed with lances and bows. Six Indian dogs, each dragging an empty travois, accompanied the party.

'*Bonjour!*' he called out, recognising Wolf Tail and Spotted Eagle.

Curious to observe the Mandan method of hunting, he joined the party as they headed for a small herd of buffalo that fed in the grass not far distant. The buffalo appeared unperturbed by their approach, the wind being favourable to the hunters. At a signal from Spotted Eagle, the Indians spread out in a line, notching arrows to bows. As they approached the animals, one eager youth, who appeared to be barely of an age to hunt, advanced ahead of the others, drawing a hissed reprimand from another hunter. Chastened, the youth retreated.

Crouching low in the grass, the Indians closed to within twenty yards, the stench of buffalo strong upon the wind. A solitary bull lifted its head to stare. Suddenly rising up out of the grass, Wolf Tail loosed an arrow at the beast. His companions immediately followed, discharging a volley of arrows to the accompaniment of whoops and yells. As the buffalo milled in confusion, the hunters discharged more arrows. A spike bull toppled to the grass, a dozen feathered shafts sticking from its side. The other buffalo set off at a lumbering run to escape the hunters. A wounded calf lay in the grass, calling out piteously as it struggled to rise.

'Watch out!' Boundless shouted a warning as a cow wheeled, realising that the calf was not at her side. Snorting with fury, she charged the hunters. The Mandan scattered in their bid to avoid the danger. The eager boy he had noticed earlier stumbled and slipped in his haste. As he tried to rise and flee, the enraged cow impaled him on her horns, tossing him effortlessly into the air. Before his shocked companions could intervene, the infuriated beast stomped and trampled the stricken youth. Careless of danger, his companions rushed in to distract the animal. Spotted Eagle risked life and limb to dash forward and drag the motionless youth from beneath the stomping hooves.

As abruptly as it had begun, the contest was over. Abandoning her calf, the cow wheeled and trotted off to rejoin the scattered herd. A glance was sufficient to show that the boy was dead, the intestines ripped from the belly by the sharp horns. The skull was shattered, one eye hanging from its socket. The Indians seemed stunned at the loss, moaning in consternation as they stood over the body. One started a chant, the ragged song rising on the air as the others joined in. With a grim face, Spotted Eagle motioned to Boundless as if to say, *'The hunt is over. Leave us to care for our dead.'*

Boundless recounted the incident to Pinch and Bjornson back at the post, drawing scant sympathy from either man, Pinch intent on cleaning his pipe, and the Swede preoccupied with cutting his meat.

'It happens,' said Pinch, looking up. 'Your buffalo be docile as a lamb one moment, fierce as a lion, the next.'

THE INCIDENT WAS STILL on his mind following supper as he and Bjornson took their nightly 'digestive', strolling up and down in the grass before retiring. The air was still, a chorus of yellow warblers twittering in the reeds. A pale full moon was rising in the north-east quadrant. The scene looked vaguely familiar as he stopped to observe the faint glitter of stars through the dusk.

Neither man spoke beyond a word or two as they trudged through the dry grass. The sun had almost disappeared as they turned back towards the post—a crimson flush along the horizon heightening the prairie gloom.

Boundless pushed open the stockade gate when he noticed Bjornson hanging back, his gaze on the darkening plain.

'Do you see something?'

Bjornson uttered a sigh. 'Surely, God was found in a place like this.' His voice was sombre in the dusk.

'In the grass?'

'In the wilderness.'

'Then, mayhap, God is a buffalo.'

Boundless heard a sharp intake of breath from his companion. 'Come,' he said, slapping the Swede on the back and ignoring his disapproval. 'I am for bed.'

The remark came back to him later as he lay in the bunk pondering the day just passed and seeing the sprawled body lying pierced and broken beneath the punishing hooves.

## 15

## A Business of Murder

T HE WEATHER GREW EVEN hotter, a plague of flies and mosquitoes pestering men and dogs alike to the point of insanity. Quoi wrapped a neckerchief around his head so that only his bulbous eyes showed. Boundless shot a bear and used the grease to coat his face and neck. Pinch and Bjornson soon followed suit.

A northerly gale blew up one afternoon offering some respite from the dense, black swarms and Bjornson insisted on joining Boundless as he set off on a scout. They walked for two hours, enjoying the relief afforded by the gusting wind. As they returned within sight of the stockade, they heard a gunshot, soon followed by a second.

'The brigade?' questioned Bjornson.

Boundless shook his head. 'Too soon.' He shaded his eyes, wishing he had brought the spyglass. 'It's Pinch,' he said. Their companion stood in front of the open gate, waving an arm in agitated summons.

Alarmed, Boundless began to walk faster—a niggling, unspoken fear hurrying his steps. Alongside, Bjornson panted as he endeavoured to keep pace.

As they approached, Pinch advanced to meet them, his face wild with shock. 'What is it?' Boundless demanded, his eyes searching the stockade behind Pinch.

'See,' said Pinch, his voice strained. He gestured to the stockade, its gate wide open.

With the musket held in readiness, Boundless entered the fort. He stopped short with an exclamation as he beheld the stockade fence. Quoi was staked to the timber by a lance driven clean through his thin body. His head was pinned back against the wood, the wispy hair wound around a protruding nail. Boundless stepped closer, his gorge rising at the sight. Behind him, Bjornson moaned in horror. Quoi's face was unrecognisable. Both eyes had been gouged from their sockets and the nose and ears hacked off. The tongue had been torn from the bloody mouth. A swarm of flies buzzed around the wounds. Two dogs lay at his feet, their throats gruesomely slashed.

'I was down at the river. When I returned, I found the poor soul like this.' Pinch's voice was distressed, his face ashen.

'How long were you gone?' Boundless was unable to tear his eyes away from the black, gaping sockets.

'No more than a half-hour.'

'And you did not leave the gate locked?'

'I did, but the poor fool would have opened it at a knock.'

'The houses?' Boundless looked around the stockade, his grip tightening on the musket.

'Empty. And all intact. This was purely a business of murder.'

'Who?' asked Boundless, already knowing the answer.

'He has returned.'

'Christ preserve us!' Bjornson crossed himself.

'Help me get him down.'

Pinch tugged the lance free of the wood and flesh while Boundless braced the body. He looked at Bjornson. 'Lend a hand!' he admonished. Pale with revulsion, the Swede helped lower the corpse to the dirt.

'He was always a mean and vicious devil!' Pinch trembled with anger as he contemplated the mutilated remains. 'The poor fool was innocent. He didn't deserve such baseness.' Reaching out a hand, he shooed away the flies as they resettled on the badly swollen face.

'We will bury him behind the stockade. Thibault will want to know where the body is laid.' Boundless crouched to inspect the dirt. 'By the prints he has found a confederate. Perhaps two.'

'If so, why not wait inside and murder us all as we returned?' asked Pinch.

'Some game is afoot. No doubt he intends this to unnerve us.' Boundless stood, forcing himself to think. 'Pinch, fetch two shovels. Bjorn, climb up onto the ramparts and keep sharp watch. Take the musket. And shout if you see anything.'

THE FOLLOWING DAYS PASSED in suspenseful vigilance. Boundless kept the gate permanently locked and forbade his companions from venturing outside. One man was posted as sentry at all times. As the days passed without further incident, they slowly began to relax their watchfulness, reasoning that perhaps Askook had fled in fear of retribution.

'Or mayhap his new companions have discovered his wolfish nature and dispatched him,' suggested Pinch.

One morning, a week after the murder, Boundless announced his intention to go on a scouting expedition. 'I will not go far,' he said in response to his alarmed companions, who entreated him to remain within the safety of the fort. 'I shall be careful, never fear.'

Holding the musket, he slipped through the gate, waiting until he heard Bjornson bar it behind him. 'Keep close watch,' he warned, before setting off through the grass.

The day was hot and cloudless, and he headed in the direction of the rock, intending to scout the area for signs of the attackers. As he walked, he kept a vigilant eye on the surrounding hillocks. The musket was set at half-cock and the spare was slung over his shoulder. The pistol was thrust into the belt around his waist.

Beneath the hot sun, the wind-blown pastures swelled, desolate and cloud-shadowed, to the horizon. But in spite of the emptiness, an acute feeling of danger prickled the back of his neck, the torpid air pregnant with threat. As the post fell behind, he scoured the grass for signs of ambush, every nerve primed.

Stopping for water, he took out the eyeglass and carefully surveyed the blowing grass. He was aware of his own breath and the beating of his heart in the noon hush. He heard a rustle in the grass and turned sharply in that direction—breathing with relief as a pheasant flew up from the reeds. He continued, eyes scanning the grass.

He had made up his mind to turn back when he noticed the stalks broken in one spot a few yards from a narrow creek. *Someone has passed by here.* He glanced around but could see nothing other than the tall, waving grass. Crouching, he searched the dry earth, finding footprints. He remained in place, silently observing the plain. Turning slightly to his left, he froze as he glimpsed a patch of dark-brown skin almost hidden amidst the reeds. Every nerve on edge, he took out the pistol and spare musket and cocked each while keeping an eye on the danger. He perspired freely in the heat, sweat running down his face.

He had no sooner readied the weapons than the concealed savage—no doubt suspecting he had been discovered—leapt to his feet and rushed through the grass towards him, a hatchet clutched in his hand. Boundless jerked up the musket, firing from the hip. The Indian gave a hoarse cry and tumbled face forward into the grass. The gunshot sounded in his ears as he spun to the rear, his hand reaching for the other musket.

He remained frozen in place, eyes straining for any movement. In the fraught silence, Askook's taunting voice sounded from the reeds. '*I will kill you slowly, Englishman. I will cut out your heart and eat it while you watch.*'

A puff of white smoke rose up from the grass and a ball flew by him. He returned fire, aiming just below the wisp of smoke.

Another shot came from his right as the unseen Askook moved position. Boundless fired again, drawing another taunt from the concealed voice. *'Did you see what I did to the imbecile? He was crying and begging for mercy even as I sliced out his tongue.'*

The cat and mouse game continued for several tense minutes, both men exchanging fire before quickly moving position.

*'Soon I will have my revenge!'*

The voice sounded to his rear. He moved several yards to his left, crawling through the grass on his belly. A musket fired again, the ball ripping through the stalks. He remained in place, nerves strained, each man waiting for the other to give away his position.

A plan formed in his mind, and he laid the cocked pistol at his feet in the dirt. The half-breed fired again, the shot ripping through the grass to his right. He fired in return and deliberately exposed himself to reload the musket. The stratagem brought instant results. With a piercing yell, Askook leapt up from concealment and raced towards him, knife in hand. Snatching up the cocked pistol, he fired as the Indian closed the distance. To his horror, he heard a click as the weapon misfired. Next instant, Askook was upon him—the half-breed launching himself through the air and knocking Boundless to the grass with the impact.

A desperate struggle ensued, neither man having the advantage as they twisted and rolled in the grass. The Indian jabbed the knife at Boundless' eye, missing the mark but scoring his cheek. He brought his knee up into the Indian's groin, eliciting a sharp hiss. Askook had him by the throat with one hand, the other scrabbling in the grass for the dropped knife. He jammed his fingers into the half-breed's mouth and dragged down on his jaw. He yelled in pain as the Indian bit down on his fingers, the teeth cutting through to the bone. He felt the discarded pistol under his back and twisted his body as he reached for the weapon. Seizing it by the barrel, he swung it against the side of the half-breed's head. He felt the bone jar under the impact. Stunned, Askook relaxed his choking grip. Boundless squirreled out from under the half-breed and struck him full on the crown with the pistol stock. The skull gave a sharp, cracking noise, like the sound of a musket shot. The Indian uttered a strangled gasp and slumped onto his side, his eyes wide with shock. Shifting his grip, Boundless hammered the heavy pistol against Askook's face. He struck again and again in a maddened fury, shattering bones with each blow. Spotting the dropped knife, he grabbed it and slit the half-breed's throat.

Utterly spent, he sat back in the grass, trembling and gasping for air. Beside him, Askook lay on his back, his shattered face swollen and distorted. Suddenly plagued by thirst, he lifted the canteen and gulped down the contents. He held up his fingers, grimacing at where the bone showed through the severed flesh. He stood up to examine the other body lying in the grass. The confederate looked nondescript, his naked torso burned almost black by the sun. The wound above the rib cage was alive with buzzing flies.

Picking up the muskets, he took a last look around, still heaving for breath. The surrounding pastures were empty, the wind rustling through the reeds. Slowly, he began to retrace his steps back to the post, his dazed senses barely able to register the brutal fight. Behind him, the plain sweltered in the heat, the bodies lost to sight amidst the omnipresent grass.

**16**

# *Some Vague Purpose*

ON A WARM SEPTEMBER morning, three years after his arrival at the post, Boundless hitched up the dog travois, eager to take full advantage of the lingering summer. The day was fine and clear, not a single cloud blemishing the sky. As he led the dogs through the gate, he came across Pinch standing in the grass outside, his eyes fixed on the horizon.

'What is it?'

'There.' Pinch pointed to where a party of Indians rode slowly through the grass in the distance. 'It is something I cannot get used to. They say the Arikara have a herd of three hundred already—stolen mostly or traded from the Blackfoot.'

'I saw a party of Mandan two days ago, all mounted,' agreed Boundless, himself surprised at the rapid spread of the horse among the sedentary tribes. Indeed, so quickly had the animal become a feature of Indian life that it was increasingly rare for him to encounter a hunting party on foot—the Indians riding up to the buffalo and then dismounting to hunt. 'Perhaps we ought to acquire some for the post.'

'No fear! I prefer my own two shanks. Besides, what would they eat?'

'What do the Indian horses eat? Grass. And there are plenty of cotton-woods along the river to sustain them through winter.'

'Hush!' said Pinch, his voice comically irritable. 'Lest Guillaume have us shoeing horses from now to doomsday.'

Boundless laughed, feeling jubilant in the bright day. 'I will bring back a fine catch,' he promised, releasing the dogs.

Pinch called after him as he set off through the grass.

'Venison, remember! None of your godforsaken buffalo!'

He allowed the dogs to run ahead through the dry reeds, the travois skittering in their wake. Every few minutes, they stopped and turned to look back to make certain he was following. He walked at a leisurely pace, enjoying the unseasonable warmth—the air of such piquant transparency as to banish all thoughts of the coming winter and the continuing uncertainty over the future of the post. A cloud-shadow raced over the grass, the stalks bending as if in obeisance to the wind. His footsteps took him towards the rock, the object a lodestone for his hunts and rambles. Stopping for a drink, he uncorked the water bottle, while staring absently at the horizon.

In the two years since Thibault's return from Montreal, the fate of the post remained undecided. 'My partners wish to suspend judgement until the details of the peace treaty are known,' the bourgeois had announced to the company on his return. 'So let us be patient and see what Fortune—or England, dictates.'

Boundless smiled to himself at the memory, proud that he had understood the words.

'We shall make a Frenchman of you yet,' Thibault had remarked when Boundless mentioned the fact. 'And as for the post, do not be in a hurry to pack up your muskets. "Patience is bitter, but its fruits are sweet," he quoted, an enigmatic look on his face as Boundless turned to leave.

'Nevertheless, mayhap it is time to consider my future,' Boundless pondered, swilling the water in his mouth. But standing there, in the midst of the blowing grass, he felt neither the desire nor the urgency to make plans. He poured water into a pan and fed it to the thirsty dogs.

'*Out on the plains, there is only buffalo time.*' Mose's words echoed in his mind as he corked the bottle and surveyed the billowing pastures. He pictured the bones of his former comrade lying somewhere in that blanched, mutable sea, a twinge of regret shadowing his pleasure in the day.

The dogs whimpered and snuffled, eager to continue. He reached down to scratch the ruff of the nearest—a favourite he often chose to walk with him. He spotted a movement in the distance and shaded his eyes. A group of whitetails fed in the grass, tails twitching as they grazed. Calling out to direct the dogs, he started forward in the direction of the deer.

The ruminative mood returned as he stood over the warm remains of a doe. He slowly and methodically gutted the carcass, lingering over the task in the mild air. '*Careful of the udder! Turn the deuced blade!*'

'I hear you, Mose,' he said, and turned to the dogs for witness.

HE WAS SITTING IN the empty bunkhouse cleaning the musket before supper, when the door opened and Bannock entered.

'There you are! I have been looking for you.' Bannock pulled up a chair near to where Boundless sat at the table unscrewing the musket lock. 'I would speak with you, Boundless,' he said, his voice unusually solemn.

'What is on your mind?'

Bannock stroked his chin as if casting about for where to begin.

'What are your thoughts on what Thibault has said?'

'About waiting on the details of the peace treaty?'

Bannock nodded.

'Pinch may be right. The post is surely too lucrative to abandon, whatever the surrender terms.'

'Even if it is abandoned, you would have no trouble finding another company to take you on—if that be your wish?' Bannock raised an eyebrow indicating the words were a question.

'Mayhap. If it comes to that.'

'Good hunters are of considerable worth,' Bannock continued, 'especially experienced men who have already wintered in these parts and are familiar with the ways of the Indians.' He glanced around before lowering his voice. 'You are a capable man, Boundless. Can I trust you—as a fellow Scot—with a grave confidence?'

'You can,' answered Boundless, curious as to the other man's intention.

'This is to be my last winter at the post. When I leave in spring, I shall not return.'

The news caught Boundless off-guard. 'You would abandon me to the charms of Pinch?'

Bannock smiled. 'Aye, and the festive Swede also.'

'I shall miss you. Are you sick of the wilderness so soon?'

'Hardly.' Bannock glanced at the door. 'In truth, I am … *associated* with a new company, set up in Albany. We intend to claim a stake in the fur trade by opening up a post in the north-west.'

Boundless set aside the lock, a frown on his face. 'Does Thibault know of this?'

'He does not.' Bannock's voice was flat. 'And were he to learn of it, I would risk my person. Rivalries in the trade are cutthroat.'

'So that is your mission here—to spy out Thibault's road to the Lakes?'

Bannock held up a conciliatory hand. 'Not to spy—but to scout. My— our, interest lies above Rupert's Land, in the far north-west. We have no interest in setting up an outpost to rival this one, I swear. I am here merely to observe how to set up and provision a post. I shall be made head clerk of my own post in return.'

As Boundless made no reply, Bannock continued. 'North-west of Rupert's Land lies an inexhaustible supply of furs. Why should the Indians—or the Hudson's Bay—have it all to themselves?' He paused, studying Boundless. 'What is it you wish for—for yourself?'

Before he could think to reply, Bannock answered his own question. 'I will tell you—a fair return for your labours, the same as any man. Do I speak truly? Then, if so, you must value that labour and invest it wisely, as with any capital. There are fortunes to be made—the least of which goes to the hands that collect and bale the bounty. Ownership—of both labour and goods—offers the only sure return.'

Boundless looked up, a wry smile on his face.

'What is it?' asked Bannock.

'I have heard such words before. And yet I sit here, penniless!'

'Because you are a hired man only, not a shareholder in the enterprise, as is Thibault.' Bannock leaned forward, his face intent. 'I have the authority to offer the right man a stake in the company—the same as my own—to grow, in time, into a full and equal share. Ownership, Boundless. You could be a stakeholder—all in return for your assistance in setting up and maintaining a post, similar to this one, in the north-west. And, unlike your situation here, your interest will extend all the way from the outpost to the buyers in Albany and London itself. As the profit accumulates on each pelt so, too, does the return. "The incremental chain of supply."' Bannock grinned. 'I had that nugget from an Albany merchant.' His face grew serious again. 'This is a rare opportunity, Boundless. And when opportunity presents, one must strike. What say you?'

Using a strip of linen to remove fouling from the lock, Boundless considered the offer. In his mind's eye, he saw Mose—eyes bright with enticement, laying forth the same promise of beaver riches. His thoughts turned to the stack of baled furs, contrasting their bulk with the paltry tally harvested by himself and his former companion. *Five thousand pelts!* The figure seemed scarcely credible. Participation in such a venture would, he admitted to himself, be a guaranteed path to prosperity. Even as he acknowledged the fact, however, a small, faint voice summoned him back from the alluring bait—the admonitory voice pressing a vague yet persistent claim to he knew not what. Bannock sat waiting for a reply, an expectant look on his face.

'I am sorry—and glad for the offer, but I must refuse. I have interests of my own to pursue.'

'Oh.' Bannock's face dropped.

'But have no fears. Your confidences are safe with me.'

'As you say.' Bannock leaned back against the chair, his manner betraying his disappointment. A shower of rain began to fall, the drops audible on the roof. 'It is a blow. We should have made sterling partners.' He sat forward suddenly, his eyes scrutinizing Boundless. 'You made mention of some interest of your own: to do with the trade?'

'A project whose particulars yet elude me.' Boundless shrugged, perplexed himself as to his meaning.

'But it involves a commercial venture?'

'I am uncertain.' He felt Bannock's stare, the other man now doubly curious.

'An uncertain project—with uncertain benefits? Do I say fairly?' persisted Bannock.

Boundless made no response, other than to shrug again.

The rain grew heavier. Bannock closed his eyes as though deep in thought.

Boundless rubbed the ramrod with a greased rag. 'The terms of the treaty may influence your plans, might they not?' he asked. 'England may extend the Hudson's Bay monopoly to the entire north-west and forbid all competition?'

For a moment, he thought Bannock had abandoned the conversation, but after a ruminative silence, Bannock responded, his voice low, as if confiding a private thought. 'You neglect another interested party.'

'The Indians?'

'The colonies themselves. Why should they not claim the chief share of their own bounty?'

'I hardly take your meaning. Do you refer to the English merchants?'

'I do not. I refer to the colonies as a separate entity, with interests bound to neither those of England nor France.'

Boundless frowned to comprehend. 'You mean independence?'

'I do. And why not? France is defeated, and there are influential voices that argue now is the time to rise up and throw off the yoke of England as well. Why should we be beholden to a crown that takes much and offers little—save tax upon tax, in return?'

Boundless set aside the musket, his interest piqued. 'There is talk of this?'

'There is—among the Boston merchants in particular. Some advocate limited self-government under the king; others agitate for independence altogether, from both king and parliament.'

'To what end?'

'A free republic—of the united colonies. So far, it is talk only, and God knows that the colonies squabble endlessly among themselves. But in the future?' Bannock looked at Boundless. 'The New World is tethered to the Old as a buffalo to a doe. It is an unnatural leash that binds the stronger and more vigorous to the smaller and weaker. Do you not agree?'

They heard voices as the rain stopped and the door opened.

Bannock stood up. 'Remember—not a word,' he cautioned.

At supper, Boundless barely listened as Pinch complained about his back. When he did speak it was to excuse himself and retire early to the bunkhouse. Bannock looked at him with puckered brow as he passed. He nodded reassuringly, interpreting the look as saying, *'Did I do wrong to impart my trust?'*

Over the following days, neither man mentioned the conversation, Bannock seemingly resigned to his refusal while Boundless himself scarcely gave the proposal another thought, puzzling instead on his own refusal to accept—nay, even consider, the offer. *For what reason?* he asked himself, mulling on the conversation. *I cannot say—except it be for some vague purpose of my own.* The specific nature of that purpose eluded him, the notion so confounding that he banished it to the back of his mind.

AS WINTER CLOSED IN, he sought diversion in the books he had ordered from the east. Picking up the volume of Montaigne, he turned the pages, peering at the dense text in the dull light of the bunkhouse lantern and translating with the aid of a comprehensive French–English dictionary he had ordered from Montreal to replace the one Lapointe had provided.

'What is that word?' He pointed out a French word to Bjornson who sat nearby reading the Bible.

Bjornson squinted at the page. 'I am not familiar with it … "windy" perhaps, from the context.'

'Like Pinch?'

Bjornson chuckled. 'Very like!'

He repeated the word to himself, memorising it for future reference.

Bjornson smoothed his fingers over the page, murmuring the verse. After some moments, he raised his head. 'We could find work among one of the fur companies that operate nearer the lakes.

'Pardon?'

'If it is true that the post is to be abandoned, we could find work with another company, could we not?'

'Hang fire. Who said the post is to be abandoned?'

'There is talk among the men … that is the reason the bourgeois returns to Montreal a second time.'

'He goes only to find out about the treaty provisions and the decision of his partners.'

*'Ja,'* said Bjornson. 'But if it is to be abandoned, then I say we could find work for another company.'

'Perhaps.' Boundless returned to the page, musing on the companionable 'we.'

The one notable event of the early winter was Pinch's liaison with an Arikara woman. The Bostonian failed to return from a trade visit, only to reappear several days later with a sackful of dried fish tied to his back and the Indian wife in tow. The Frenchmen treated his return as casually as they had greeted his departure—Thibault's only interest in the liaison concerning trade opportunities, about which he questioned Pinch at length.

'What is her name?' asked Boundless as Pinch prepared to move his few belongings out of the bunkhouse and into the married men's quarters. The woman waited on the steps outside, a shawl around her shoulders and a pipe in her mouth. She was squat and middle-aged, her wrinkled features blackened by the sun.

'Buffalo Bird Woman.' Pinch gazed at his *amour* with considerable satisfaction.

'What made you choose her?'

Pinch looked up in surprise. 'She picked me!'

Boundless suppressed a smile. 'And her family?'

Pinch shrugged. 'Her husband was killed long ago. Since then, she has lived as a widow.'

'Does she speak English—or French, at least?'

'A few words of the latter, only.' The admission seemed a cause of satisfaction to Pinch.

'Your ... liaison may be short-lived, depending on Thibault's meeting with his fellow owners.'

'That to the owners!' Aiming a kick at the bunk, Pinch exited the cabin.

## 17

## A Fearful Encounter

THE WEATHER WORSENED AS a series of blizzards dumped a half-foot of snow on the grass. Along the Missouri shore, ice formed in ridges, like small, frozen waves. By early December, the river had frozen over—the 'ice road' now used as a path for the sledges.

In the middle of the month, the married men and their families retired to the warmth of the Indian villages, offering Boundless some relief due to the reduced number of mouths to feed. In defiance of the freezing cold, the remaining *hivernants* organised sledge races in front of the stockade. Divided into teams, they harnessed themselves to the sledges before battling through the snow in a race to the finish line. The contests were attended with much laughter and good humour in spite of the harsh weather.

'They are a hardy bunch,' he remarked to Pinch, standing on the store-house steps to watch.

'Aye, while their bellies are still fed. But the winter will be long and hard.'

The words came back to him as he searched for game without success, the frozen prairie seemingly devoid of life. Many times, he came across fresh elk sign, which he tracked for miles before the cold and fading light forced his return to the stockade. He came to suspect that a wolf pack was shadowing him to scavenge any kills. Several times, he endeavoured to lure the wily animals into an ambush, only to abandon the plan as he caught them watching from a distance.

Unable to find elk or buffalo, he set numerous snares for mink, muskrat, fisher, winter hare and beaver, Thibault relaxing his prohibition against taking the latter. Beaver tail, whether turned into soup or eaten fried, boiled or stewed, was especially prized by the hungry men. He found the taste tolerable but preferred the flavour of buffalo and longed for their return. Indeed, in their absence, the wintry plains struck him as doubly forlorn haunted as much by the absence of buffalo as by the rippling summer grass.

He turned to ice fishing, hoping to net some of the fleshy surgeon he had formed a taste for. Kneeling in the middle of the frozen river, he contemplated the slate-grey clouds and the bare trees along the shore. A gust of wind ruffled his cheeks. Pinch's tale of the frozen Dutchman came to mind as he chipped away at the ice. After a frozen half-hour huddled over the hole, he gave up and returned to the post, his face blue with cold.

He was sitting with Pinch, remarking on the weather, when the door to Thibault's private room opened and White Deer emerged. Kneeling before a small wooden tub, she proceeded to scour the cooking pot. Sitting on his customary stool by the hearth, Bjornson gave a covert glance in her direction before returning to his Bible. A moment later, he looked up again, the page seemingly forgot. Pinch muttered disparagingly as he observed. 'Our poor Luther pines for his prairie chick. Doubtless he will stare until his eyes do pop or his tongue catches fire.'

'Are you mad?'

'Do you not see it?'

'See what? That which is only in your fevered thoughts?'

'Do you not see the way his eyes caress her?'

'Hush!' Boundless looked around to see if anyone overheard.

'Or the way she feeds him a second ladle from the pot each time?'

'Hold your tongue—if such a thing be possible!'

'I say only what my eyes do see.'

'And your tongue must repeat?'

'No harm. Guillaume, too, has eyes. Calm yourself. He cannot fetch her back to Montreal with him and must dispose of her here when the time comes.'

'You are privy to his thoughts, no doubt?'

'It is the custom. Or would you have him introduce her to his wife?'

'I would have us not speak of it!'

'As you wish.' Pinch brooded on the pipe, his eyes half-closed.

White Deer had finished scrubbing the pot and stood up to return it to its place. He saw Bjornson look up, his eyes following her as she added a log to the fire. *Surely not?* Bemused by the notion, he returned to the bunkhouse.

IN JANUARY, AN INTENSE, biting chill settled over the landscape. When it was Boundless' turn to dash to the woodshed for a fresh supply of logs, the air was so cold he feared his teeth might crack. The mercury dropped to minus forty-four degrees on Thibault's barometer. The frozen plain was subject to sudden, violent windstorms, during which the snow drove into exposed skin like lead pellets.

Returning from a hazardous and fruitless hunt, he stopped, struck by the sky along the horizon. The sun was setting in a layer of cloud, the pale luminance shot through with wan yellow streaks. The sight put him in mind of the unusual sunset before the storm at sea. The reminder sent a shiver down his spine that had nothing to do with the cold.

Food stocks began to deplete at an alarming rate as the Indians remained in their snowbound villages. The smokehouse sat empty of meat, the men subsisting on the last supplies of pemmican supplemented by rubaboo and jerky. As the weather allowed, Thibault despatched several missions to the Indian villages to trade for food. Each one returned empty-handed, the Indians reserving what scant resources they possessed for their own mouths.

In the trying conditions, the stoic good humour of the voyageurs began to fray, quarrels breaking out over trifles. Thibault opened a keg of rum and allowed each man a daily glass, exhorting them to keep up their spirits while reminding them that spring was no more than two months away.

'Nothing,' Boundless reported to Bannock as the latter dragged open the stockade gate following yet another futile hunt. 'The plain is as barren as the moon.'

He blew on his chilled hands before attempting to unhitch the dogs. *They are as lean as ourselves,* he thought, feeling the ribs of his favourite through its bristly coat.

That same day, Thibault took him to one side. 'We must hope for the miracle of the fishes,' he said, his grave expression belying the jest.

'Does he intend to starve us?' complained Pinch over supper. The stocks of dried peas and corn were almost exhausted, and Thibault had ordered rationing, much to the disgruntlement of the famished company.

'He wishes to convert us to the Hindoo—who live on air,' ran the macabre jest as the men stared at the meagre portions served up on each trencher.

The sub-zero cold continued as the winds gusted at gale force. *La mort blanche,* as the Frenchman termed the dense, swirling blizzards that swept the plain, made it too dangerous to venture outside the post. The men were reduced to subsisting on corn soaked in lye and a thin soup flavoured with root vegetables.

The men went about with haggard faces, their usual robust humour absent. The previous night, the starving dogs had rounded on one of their own and consumed it, hide and all, leaving nothing but the gnawed bones as evidence. At Thibault's behest, Boundless selected four of the older and weaker animals and shot them for the pot. Only the stern intercession of the bourgeois prevented the ravenous men from taking muskets to the entire pack.

A tub of tobacco was placed in the cabin, and all were invited to take freely, the constant smoking doing little to take the minds of the men from the ravages of famine. Increasingly alarmed at their perilous situation, Thibault despatched Boundless along with a sledge full of trade goods to the closest Hidatsa village, six miles north along a creek.

'Never mind the cost,' he urged. 'Bring back food, even if you hand over the sledge itself.'

Accompanied by two of the younger and fitter Frenchmen, he set out mid-morning for the village. The biting winds had dropped, and the sky was a thin, watery blue. They reached the encampment shortly after noon. Smoke rose from several of the lodges, although the village appeared deserted. A sense of unease dogged him as they approached the houses. A hundred yards from the nearest lodge, he held up a hand for his companions to halt.

'What is it?' asked Bernard, a youthful adventurer not two years arrived from Paris.

'Where are the dogs?'

'My God!' The youth's eyes widened as he took in the silent, snowbound lodges.

'Keep your eyes open!' With a warning glance at his companions, Boundless led the way into the hushed village.

The first lodge they tried was deserted, the hide screen flapping in the wind. Snow had drifted inside, and the cooking pot lay on its side in the cold fire pit. Now convinced that something was deeply amiss, Boundless continued on to the next lodge, the unnerved Frenchmen cocking their muskets. They passed the stripped carcass of a horse lying frozen in the snow. Only the bones and patches of horsehide remained.

The Frenchmen exclaimed in shock as they came across a body. All four limbs had been hacked off. The naked torso had been gouged and torn, the missing entrails leaving a reddish stain in the snow. A few yards further on, they came across a second body, that of a woman, similarly butchered. His companions crossed themselves, muttering in revulsion at the grisly sight.

'Hush!' Boundless held a warning finger to his lips.

Holding the musket at the ready, he stepped cautiously into a lodge. The overpowering stench of cooked flesh caused his eyes to water. As his eyes adjusted to the dim light, he saw between sixteen and twenty Indians—men, women and children—huddled inside. They glanced up as they saw Boundless but made no move to either welcome or discourage his presence. Their eyes were sunken as they regarded him without emotion, seemingly listless to the point of apathy.

'Remain vigilant,' he ordered, deeply disturbed by the profound lethargy of the occupants.

'Look!' The younger of the two Frenchmen pointed to where a child gnawed on what appeared to be a piece of rib bone. The child's mother gripped him in a protective embrace and shrank back, her eyes unnaturally bright as the Frenchman approached. The youth hastily crossed himself, his voice fearful as he recognised the meat as a hand, the bones blackened by fire. 'Christ protect us!'

Boundless gestured to his unnerved companions. 'Let us go,' he said quietly. 'There is nothing here.'

Thibault listened with barely disguised horror as he reported the gruesome scenes. That evening, the bourgeois stationed an armed man at the door of the hut containing the last few handfuls of corn and dried beans. Dark rumours of cannibalism—sparked by the revelations of the young Frenchmen—circulated through the company, heightening their fears. Concerned at the prospect of an attack, Thibault posted two sentries above the gates. 'Who knows, but the poor devils might imagine we have food,' he said, urging vigilance.

Just as they prepared to shoot the remaining dogs, a party arrived from the Mandan bringing a supply of pemmican made of horse meat as well as several sacks of dried vegetables. The bounty drew hoarse cheers from the desperate men. After what seemed a feast to the starving company, Thibault drew Boundless aside.

'Jacques has sent word that the Mandan are barely surviving but that matters are much worse in the surrounding villages.' The bourgeois shook his head, a resigned look on his face. 'We are in God's hands.'

THE WORDS PLAYED ON Boundless' mind as he readied the sledge the following day, determined to bring back game though he perish in the attempt. The morning was bitterly cold, washes of pale-blue sky peeking between stretches of grey cloud. To his surprise, Pinch joined him, the Bostonian professing himself sick to death of the odorous hall.

'If not famine, I shall perish from the stink and boredom,' he said, blowing on his hands.

'And this has nothing to do with the need to cut firewood?' Boundless gestured towards a work party readying another sledge.

Pinch pulled a sour face. 'For the love of God, let us go ere Guillaume ropes me to yonder dogs!'

Boundless set out in a south-easterly direction, intending to traverse as wide an area as possible in the hope of finding tracks. The sky had cleared to a frosty blueness, the air transparently chill. Much to his annoyance, Pinch leaned heavily on the sledge rail as the dogs panted and huffed in the traces. 'Do not overtire the dogs,' he warned.

As they progressed, he stopped the traineau several times to scan the horizon for signs of game.

'You would be better off to lay snares along the river,' said Pinch, keen to return to the warmth of the cabin now that the work party had departed. 'There is too much snow for deer or antelope.'

'There!' Boundless pointed to the distance.

Pinch shaded his eyes. 'What is it?'

'Buffalo tracks,' answered Boundless without hesitation. 'A dozen at least. They are headed for the rock. Mush!' He urged the dogs onwards.

They pursued the herd for a mile, passing fresh droppings in the snow as they drew nearer. The weather changed again, a thin skein of cloud obscuring the sky. The rock loomed in the distance, its black sides gleaming with ice. The buffalo stood huddled beneath it. In the dull, greyish light, their shaggy winter coats gave them the appearance of mythical beasts.

Boundless called a halt to consider the best way to come up on the herd. 'They are probably all bulls,' he said.

Closing to within two hundred yards, he left Pinch with the dogs and advanced alone, downwind of the herd. The buffalo grunted suspiciously as he approached. Breath poured out from their nostrils, frosting in the air. Selecting the largest, he advanced to within twenty yards. The bull raised its head, velvet nostrils glistening as it expelled a gout of warm breath. The wiry black curls on its forehead were dusted with snow. It gave a snort and regarded him with a baleful eye. After a suspenseful pause, it dropped its massive head to sweep aside the snow. Dropping to one knee, Boundless aimed the musket, targeting the lung behind the front elbow.

The crack of the musket shattered the silence—the shot echoing in the air. The buffalo crumpled onto its side, breath expiring from its nostrils in a dense cloud. As he switched muskets, something caught his eye. He glanced up in time to see a large chunk of snow dislodge from the summit. It fell to the ground in a soundless explosion of white powder. The buffalo shied away from the impact, their movements slow and ponderous in the thick snow. The stricken bull lay unmoving, a pool of crimson seeping out from under the woolly coat. He heard a whoop as Pinch started the dogs forward.

Quickly stepping towards the remaining buffalo as they milled about in the snow, he selected another and fired, striking it in the shoulder. The bull ploughed through the powder in an attempt to escape, trailing a line of blood across the snow. Reloading, he fired again, the shot stranding the animal in a drift. It stood bewildered for a moment, bellowing after its companions as they lumbered off in fright. Hastening forward, he fired a third shot, striking the distressed animal in the heart. It dropped to the snow and lay still, its hot breath still pouring into the air.

Behind him, Pinch dragged the dogs to a halt.

'By the bones, but we shall dine well this night!'

The starving dogs growled and strained to reach the shot bull as it gave a last, spasmodic kick and lay still.

'Hold tongue!' Grabbing the lead dog, Pinch forced it, yelping, to the snow.

Boundless fetched the butchering instruments from the sledge. The knives were wrapped in deer hide, the metal blades cold as ice to the touch.

'Shall we take a pipe afore we carve?'

Boundless gaped at the bald impudence. 'While you smoke, your companions starve!'

They started with the first bull, taking meat from the top side only. They paused frequently to rest, chests heaving with exertion, hands and sleeves coated in blood and grease. The dogs watched from where they lay on their bellies, eyes bright as they followed every cut and thrust of the knives. 'Do not throw them any scraps,' warned Boundless as Pinch made ready to do just that. 'You will set them into such a frenzy as will summon the dead.'

'And who is there but the dead to hear?'

After two hours, they were but halfway through the butchery—their heavy clothes and the powdery snow rendering the task arduous in the extreme. When they had taken about two hundred pounds of meat from the first buffalo, they took a moment to rest before moving onto the next. Feeling over-warm from the exertion, Boundless started to take off the capote when he heard a warning growl from the dogs.

He glanced up, alarmed to see a party of Indians appear from around the rock. They were unlike any savages he had seen before, their appearance strange and disturbing in a way that prickled the hairs on his neck. He glanced towards the musket where it stood propped in the snow against the sledge.

Pinch looked up. 'Christ save us!'

The intruders appeared to be as surprised as themselves at the encounter. Standing stock-still less than twenty yards away, they made no motion to advance or exchange greetings. A grim and terrible air in their aspect made Boundless wish he had the loaded musket in hand. Their dark faces were streaked with scars and pierced with bits of bone, the effect chilling to behold. Shrunken skulls and paws were sewn into the buffalo robes that wrapped their bodies.

'*Háu!*' Pinch called out, his voice hoarse.

The strangers made no response, their stance rigid in the frozen silence. The foremost among them—a terrifying figure with a menacing, hawkish face—stared out from under a bear skull head-dress. The unblinking gaze was black and pitiless, the skull imparting a primal savagery to the forbidding countenance. A flint knife was tucked into a hide sheath around the man's waist. In his hand he held a lance tipped with stone. His companions held similar weapons, the tips raised to point at the two companions. In the hushed air, their sinister silence was pregnant with threat.

'*Háu. Nitéwesha!*' said Pinch, trying to draw a response. 'Speak, thou painted fiend!'

'Tread softly!'

'*Nitéwesha!*' Pinch held up a palm.

The Indians gave no sign of acknowledgement. Boundless held his breath, wondering if he dare make a move towards the musket. One of the savages stepped forward. He wore a buffalo skull head-dress and, in his hand, carried a small gourd attached to a stick. He shook the gourd at Boundless while uttering some barbarous chant. As he advanced a step, rattling the gourd, his companions tensed as though for attack.

'The devils mean us harm,' hissed Pinch. 'Prepare yourself!'

'*Manger!*' In the fraught moment, Boundless pointed to the fresh buffalo carcass. '*Manger!*' He repeated and made as if to scoop food into his mouth. The headman made a motion with his hand and the other savage stopped his chant. Extending the gourd, he stared at Boundless with piercing savagery, his face conveying an expression of mingled horror and anger. Placing a hand over his eyes as though to shield them, he spat into the snow and slowly stepped back.

'*Manger!* Eat!' Boundless backed away from the kill, motioning to Pinch to do the same. Slowly, the two retreated, stepping back awkwardly in the wooden hoops. The Indians maintained a terrifying silence—their glittering menace a hair's breadth from violence.

'Har!' Pinch shook the sledge. The dogs were already on their feet, hackles raised as they snarled at the savages. '*Mush! Aller!*' The sledge jerked forwards, its load of secured meat swaying dangerously.

Boundless followed, stepping as quickly as possible in the snowshoes. The savages stood motionless, as though frozen in place like some grotesque gargoyles. A chunk of meat bounced from the sledge, and he bent to retrieve it.

'Leave it, for pity's sake!'

Pinch whipped the dogs without mercy as they hurried to put distance between themselves and the unknown Indians. Glancing back, Boundless saw that the Indians had fallen upon the abandoned bulls like a pack of ravenous wolves. Ripping pieces of raw flesh from the carcasses, they stuffed the bloody chunks into their mouths while tearing off more.

For a quarter-hour, they continued at a hurried pace, putting more distance between themselves and the savages. When the rock was almost vanished from sight, he called on Pinch to bring the sledge to a halt. 'The meat!' He pointed to the loose cargo.

'Whoa, you devils!' Pinch dragged the panting dogs to a stop.

Working quickly, and with anxious glances over their shoulders, they re-secured the meat under the deerskin hide.

''Tis a great pity we must abandon the rest. We have taken scarce a quarter.' Boundless scanned the snow to their rear. 'Have you ever seen the like?'

'Never! They had bones through their flesh!' Pinch shivered, the shock of the encounter still fresh in his voice.

'And their weapons—the knives were of crude stone. Did you see? Who or what in God's name are they?'

'They looked thirsty for blood. Upon my soul, I feared that heathen with the shake-stick was about to pronounce the last rites. Merciful Jesus!'

Back at the post, the Frenchmen crowded around as Pinch—fortified by a glass of rum—regaled the listeners with lurid accounts of the intruders.

'Savage?' he cried, lapsing into English in his horrified retelling. 'So terrible-seeming as to freeze the blood of a Turk!'

Thibault listened carefully as Pinch elaborated on his fervent account. Using Bannock as interpreter, he questioned Boundless for confirmation, asking for specific details of the Indians' appearance and mode of dress. '*Attendez une minute*,' he said, and summoned White Deer from his private room. As Thibault imparted the details, the girl paled and trembled. Thibault laid a hand on her arm and murmured reassuringly. She spoke in a soft, frightened voice, her eyes large as she glanced at Boundless.

He turned to Bannock. 'What does she say?'

'They—the savages you describe—are known to her people as ...' Bannock paused to listen. '*Pardon, monsieur?*' he asked of Thibault. At the latter's nod, he put a question directly to the shaken girl while interpreting for Boundless' benefit.

'The ones you encountered are known as "bone-eaters". Cannibals, I suspect. They were the original occupiers of the land, before the Mandan even. They—the Hidatsa—tell of a great battle many years ago, long before she was born. The Hidatsa and their allies, the Mandan, defeated the … bone-people and killed them all, or chased them from the land. She claims that the ones you saw were ghosts. You were undoubtedly the first white men they have seen, to which fact you may owe your lives.'

'Tell her they were of flesh and blood.'

'Nay! The girl speaks the truth.' Agitated from the account, Pinch held out the glass for more rum. 'They were surely apparitions from hell.' He shuddered. 'I pray never to encounter such fearsome spectres again so long as I do live!'

WITH AGONISING SLOWNESS, WINTER released its deadly grip. The heavy grey clouds gave way to a pale-blue sky as spring's light drove back the winter darkness. Flocks of ducks winged overhead and trade with the Indians resumed, bringing in much-needed supplies of meat and fish. The famished men slowly regained their colour and vigour as they feasted on dishes of corn, squash and venison. Now that they had survived the harsh winter, their humour and good spirits returned as they made light of their recent travails and made teasing reference to the shrunken figure of Theroux, formerly the stoutest of the company. 'He fasts willingly that he may weigh less on the paddlers,' they praised, lauding such saint-like generosity.

The married men returned with their families bearing tales of the great deprivations endured in the Indian villages. 'The Mandan slaughtered half their horse herd,' reported Bannock. 'Most of the remainder perished from the cold or starved. Their headman claimed it was the worst winter in memory.'

Henri added to the grim news, repeating the tale brought by a headman that several villages had starved to death in the extreme cold. "Tis rumoured that the inhabitants of one village slaughtered and ate their slaves to survive.'

Boundless listened soberly to the report, reminded of the Hidatsa village and the listless faces of the inhabitants.

'Another month of that cold and who knows what might have become of us?' said Bannock.

'Bjornson carries a fine flank steak,' said Pinch, the jest falling flat.

The severe winter was put behind as the weather continued to warm and spring baling commenced. Taking a rest from making up the bales, he looked up at a hail from Theroux.

'Boundless!' The Frenchman crooked a finger in summons.

'What now?' asked Pinch.

'I do not know,' he said, as curious as Pinch at the summons.

To his surprise, Theroux led him towards Thibault's house, the *pilote* shrugging when questioned why.

The door opened and his perplexity increased as he saw Bannock standing there.

'Monsieur Thibault would speak with you,' said Bannock, giving Boundless a warning look.

Thibault sat at the table, a glass of brandy in hand. '*Asseyez-vous. Prenez un verre pour m'accompagner,*' he invited, motioning for Boundless to take a chair as he poured a glass of brandy.

Boundless looked around the room, it being the first time he had been invited inside Thibault's private domicile. The house was sparsely furnished with a table and chairs and a commode against the wall. A stone fireplace was set into the wall, the heaped logs crackling with smoke and flame. A woven Hidatsa mat hung on one wall, and a small painting on another. A lantern hung from a peg and a second candle lantern stood on the table. The door to what he presumed was the bedroom was closed. White Deer was nowhere to be seen. He took a seat, sitting alongside Bannock who had a half-drained glass in front of him.

Thibault handed him the glass of brandy. '*Votre santé!*'

'*Merci, Monsieur.*' He drank from the glass and set it down with a glance at Bannock. The other man gave a tiny shrug but said nothing.

Thibault made small talk for a few minutes, reminiscing on Boundless' first arrival at the post. 'We were certain you were a spy!' remarked Thibault as Bannock interpreted.

Thibault's voice grew serious as he questioned Boundless on his plans in the event that the owners decided to abandon the post.

'I have not thought much on it,' he admitted, feeling Bannock's eyes on him.

'Will you return to Pennsylvania?'

He shrugged, the colony seeming suddenly very far removed.

'I do not know. It's possible.'

'And you?' Thibault asked of Bannock.

'I will find another company, or maybe stay in Montreal for a while.'

Thibault nodded. 'It may all come to naught. We shall see.' He topped up the glasses. 'As you know, I am called back to Montreal to discuss with my partners the provisions of the peace treaty and how it may affect us.

What the outcome may be, I do not know. But I wish for you, Boundless, to again manage the post in my absence.'

'*Oui. Bien sur, Monsieur.*'

Thibault said nothing for a minute or so and appeared lost in thought. He glanced up. 'That is all, gentlemen.' As Boundless prepared to depart, the bourgeois regarded him with a rueful smile. 'Make no plans, my friend. Who knows but that I may return with good news?'

'He favours you, Boundless,' teased Bannock as they headed back towards the cabin. 'Of a certainty he has something in mind for you. Did I not say you were a capable man?'

Glancing around to make certain that they were alone, he guided Boundless to a halt. 'Thibault mentioned a figure of ninety bales for the season?' He looked to Boundless for confirmation before continuing. 'We—the Albany corporation—intend to take that much in the first year alone.' He paused to let the figure sink in. 'And to perhaps double that amount in the year thereafter. Think of it—Thibault's tally multiplied twice over. And then think of your own share in such a bounty!' He waited for a reply, his eyes intent on Boundless.

'It is no use.' Boundless shook his head. 'I am settled here. As before, your proposal holds no interest for me.'

Bannock groaned. 'And you will not change your mind—no matter the enticement?'

'I will not. I am content where I am.'

Bannock blew out a sigh, his face conceding defeat. 'Then let us speak of it no more. Only, remember my offer when next you are pinch-bellied and perishing from cold!'

Several times over the next few days, Thibault took Boundless aside to give last-minute instructions and advice, Bannock interpreting.

'Do not commence any new building in my absence. Reassure the Indians that business will carry on as before—they will have no need to seek other trade partners. A moment—' Thibault directed a sharp glance at where Pinch and another man had stopped to light pipes. 'Do you imagine that the furs will bale themselves?'

'Now, where was I?' He said, turning back to continue the conversation. 'Ah, yes. The Indians …'

In spite of his promise, Bannock made several more attempts over the days that followed to enlist Boundless into his venture, each time dangling the lure of partnership as bait.

'I had hoped,' he admitted finally, 'to recruit an experienced man such as yourself as part of this reconnaissance. Now I must return to Montreal with empty pockets.' He looked glum at the prospect.

'Henri is capable, and more experienced in the ways of the fur country than me.'

'True. But he has his allegiance elsewhere.' Bannock sighed in exasperation. 'Never mind. The new company I speak of shall prosper, exceedingly so—and I along with it. What?' he exclaimed, mistaking Boundless' silence for scepticism. 'You doubt I have the means?'

'I do not doubt it at all.'

'Youth, hard work and ambition are my capital—as good as money in the bank.' Bannock puffed out his chest, the muscular ambition resonant in his voice. 'Make no mistake, my friend, a great galleon stands ready to sail upon the tide of beaver riches. And I, Thomas Bannock, intend to stand squarely upon the foredeck!'

ALTHOUGH IMPATIENT TO BEGIN the long journey back to Montreal, Thibault was forced to wait a further two weeks until the ice broke up on the river.

'From Lake Superior he will take the express canoe to Montreal,' explained Pinch. 'He will have precious little time there before he must start back again. Always, it is a race against the ice.'

It was early May before the ice permitted travel. The canoes were dragged from storage and laid in the yard for inspection and repair. Pine pitch mixed with grease was caulked into the seams, worn cordage replaced, and fresh paddles cut from the trees along the shore.

On a cloudy morning, the canoes were carried down to the river and laid in the grass. A light rain began falling as the men carried down the heavy bales. When they had finished loading the canoes, Thibault appeared at the top of the bank, carrying the parfleche pouch containing the post ledger.

As the men bade their farewells, Bannock took Boundless' hand in a tight grip. 'Goodbye, my friend. May fortune smile upon you.'

'And you, Thomas,' he said, rueful at the departure.

'Pinch?' He whispered the word as Pinch came up to say goodbye. Bannock shook his head.

''Til September, or mayhap October, you Jesuit ne'er-do-well!' Pinch held out his hand.

'Aye. ''Til then, you Bostonian reprobate. Where is Bjorn?'

'He was here but a moment ago.'

'No matter. Bid him goodbye from me.'

Bannock nodded to Boundless. 'Remember everything I said.'

'What did he say?' asked Pinch as Bannock climbed into the canoe.

'Remarks about the winter and such. I scarcely recall.'

He raised a hand as the men readied the paddles and waited for Theroux's command. 'Godspeed!' He called as the canoes set out on the river.

Bannock turned and waved in response. 'Farewell!

## 18

## A Proposal

THE BUFFALO HAD RETURNED along with the blooming grass, and he busied himself with restocking the smoke house. In late summer, he caught his foot in a gopher hole and turned his ankle. For the next two weeks he hobbled about on a pair of makeshift crutches while cursing his misfortune.

'The brigade is late,' he remarked to Pinch as August ended and September began.

'They were late in leaving. They also have to wait on Guillaume's trip to Montreal. It would not surprise me if they didn't return until October.'

In the event, the brigade returned in late-September. Boundless had only just recovered full use of the leg when Pinch, up on the tool hut roof adding sod, scrambled down the ladder shouting for Bjornson to open the gate.

'They've returned!'

Waiting down by the river, Boundless heard a *'Bonjour!'* float across the water as the canoes drew closer. He spotted Thibault's felt hat amidst the woollen toques. Shortly thereafter, the *milieux* raised paddles as the lead canoe bumped up against the shore.

*'Mon Dieu! Quelle voyage!'* Thibault stepped gingerly onto the grass, wincing as the blood flowed back into his cramped limbs. *'Deux fois, je pensais que nous chavirerions!'*

After shaking hands with Boundless, he turned and beckoned to a slim, moustached youth who had just clambered out of the same canoe.

'Boundless, *rencontrez mon beau-fils.'*

The young man introduced himself in near-faultless English.

'Mathieu Simard, sir, at your service. I am, as Monsieur Thibault has said, his son-in-law.'

Simard was clean-shaven and wore a frock coat similar in cut to Thibault's own. His face was burned by the sun, the skin around his mouth dotted with tiny cuts, whether from shaving or insect bites. He studied Boundless through curious eyes, as if the two were already familiar.

Theroux's voice roared out as the men milled about on the shore, stiff from so much sitting and paddling. 'Get moving! Did you think to paddle all this way just to sit on your arse?'

'Where is Thomas?' asked Pinch as he surveyed the returned men. Spying a companion, he went off to investigate. The two held a short conversation before the Bostonian returned, a baffled look on his face.

'It seems Thomas has decided not to return. He bade farewell to the men at the *entrepôt* and then vanished along with some Frenchmen. Did he plan on not returning? And if so, why not mention it before leaving? Did he say anything to you?'

'He bade me farewell, the same as yourself.'

Pinch frowned, looking greatly put out.

As usual, a contingent of Indians had gathered to witness the return, the men reclining in the grass outside the stockade smoking pipes, the women nursing infants, and the older children tussling and shouting. Those Frenchmen with native wives exchanged affectionate greetings as they reunited with their country families.

Following disposal of the cargo, Thibault insisted on an inspection of the stockade. He seemed his usual sober self, his face or manner giving nothing away as he carefully noted the condition of the buildings and the log fence. Boundless checked his curiosity as to the outcome of the discussions in Montreal, explaining that repairs had been kept to a minimum as he pointed to the fresh sod on the bunkhouse roof.

'*Bien*,' murmured Thibault. Satisfied, he proceeded to the storehouse to check the quality of pelts and hides acquired during the summer trades. Selecting a beaver pelt for closer inspection, he rubbed it between his hands before passing it to Mathieu. '*Une belle pelure d'hiver.*'

The young man carefully examined the pelt, exclaiming at its softness as his father-in-law looked on. The two conferred briefly before Mathieu turned to Boundless. 'Monsieur Thibault asks that you join him for a walk before the meal.'

'Certainly.' He nodded at Thibault who smiled and held up a hand as if to say, '*In due course!*'

The late-afternoon sky was covered with a sheen of whitish haze, an early sign of approaching frost. Thibault inhaled deeply as they walked, savouring the smell of sage, earth and grass.

'*Mes jambes sont raides comme des pagaies!*' Stopping, he vigorously massaged his lower right limb.

'How well do you understand French, monsieur?' Mathieu's voice was courteous yet reserved.

'In equal parts salt and vinegar. I have Pinch and Bjornson for teachers.'

'*Qu'a-t-il dit?*' asked Thibault. At the reply he laughed heartily, his face crinkling with good humour.

They stepped across a gulley and headed up a small rise. At the top, Thibault stopped and sat down in the grass, motioning for his companions to do the same. '*Mon Dieu!*' he exclaimed, breathing heavily. He seemed content to linger for a few minutes, taking in the acres of blowing grass as Boundless waited, impatient to have his curiosity satisfied.

Turning to his son-in-law, Thibault broke the silence. '*Commençons.*'

Mathieu listened attentively as his father-in-law spoke, interrupting once to clarify a point. Despite concentrating, Boundless formed only an indistinct impression of what was being said, his toddling French unable to keep up with the rapid flow of words.

'*Oui. Bien.*' As Thibault finished, Mathieu turned to Boundless.

'As you know, *Monsieur,* the war went badly for France. Since the last brigade, the papers of surrender have been signed. The terms of the treaty have recently been made known to Monsieur Thibault—he has loyal friends in government—and he wishes to discuss the consequences for the company. A moment, if you will.'

Searching through the haversack he had brought with him, Mathieu pulled out a length of rolled oilskin. He unwrapped it to reveal a small map, which he carefully laid in the grass. Taking some objects from the haversack, he weighted down each corner. 'It was made a few years before the war,' he explained.

Boundless got up on his knees to better study the map, the first he had seen, of the New World and its colonies. To his surprise, the map was coloured—the different tints showing the respective French, Spanish, and English possessions. The dense lines and tiny, crabbed writing showed the Gulf of Mexico at the bottom, and Rupert's Land at the top.

Mathieu pointed to the portion coloured in a faint yellow tint. 'These are the English colonies. This is—*was*, New France.' His voice took on a mournful tone as he indicated the colony of Canada and the Gulf of Saint Lawrence. 'From here, the Great Lakes, and east and west of the Mississippi.' He pointed to the central portion of the map, coloured in green tint all the way down to the Gulf of Mexico. '*La Louisiane.*' His finger lingered on the trajectory. 'And there, New Spain.' He pointed to the orange-tinted portion of the map west of the Gulf.

Boundless stared at the map and the immense wedge of territory indicated by Mathieu, realising for the first time the full extent of the French possession.

'If Monsieur Thibault's friends in government are correct, it is all but certain that France will cede possession of Quebec. And, in addition, renounce all claims to the country east of the Mississippi.' Mathieu passed a hand over the map.'

'And west of the Mississippi?'

'Ceded to Spain, supposedly in return for her invaluable assistance during the war.' The Frenchman's tone was acidic.

'Do I understand you?' Boundless was unable to keep the shock from his voice, his mind reeling at the magnitude of the French surrender. 'That is the whole of New France, surely?'

'To the last acre. New France is no more.' Mathieu stopped, overcome by emotion. Thibault laid a consoling hand on his shoulder.

Plucking a blade of grass, Boundless rubbed it absently between his palms as he recalled the vast swathes of land he and Mose had crossed west of the mountains. *Now it is all England's.*

Mathieu sat silently, an anguished look on his face.

'*Continuez,*' prompted Thibault.

'*Pardon, Monsieur.*' The youth struggled to compose himself. 'As a consequence of the war, and English control of New France, the fur trade is in the grip of uncertainty. Many merchants are fearful of what may come— Monsieur Thibault's partners among them. They fear French companies will be disadvantaged through licensing and other restrictions.'

He looked at Boundless, seeking a sign that he understood.

Boundless nodded, still coming to grips with the greatly expanded English possessions. 'And the Indians? What of them?'

'They are now under the English Crown. But there is much resentment. The Ottawa are said to have started a campaign against the settlers, and there is great bloodshed, even as we speak. It is the way of things, is it not, that one war is parent to another?'

'*Assez avec la guerre!*' Thibault's voice was sharp.

A contrite Mathieu cleared his throat. '*Oui. Pardon, Monsieur.* As a consequence of the ... *uncertainty*, the company has been dissolved through the will of its owners.'

Even though prepared for the announcement, Boundless looked up in surprise. 'Dissolved?'

'*Oui. Dissous.* No more, like New France.' Mathieu halted, visibly overcome. His eyes misted with tears, and he took out a handkerchief to blow his nose.

'*Pourquoi t'arrêtes-tu? Ressaisis-toi!*' Thibault's voice was impatient.

'*Pardon*. Monsieur Thibault wishes you to understand that he has purchased the company and all of its assets from the owners. He wishes to make a proposal. Would you like to hear it?'

'TO SUM UP,' BOUNDLESS informed Bjornson as they walked in the yard before the *banquet des retrouvailles*. 'Monsieur Thibault proposes to make us junior partners in the new venture—to grow to full and equal shares once we have repaid our portion of the purchase price. I will stay on here as head man with yourself and Pinch. We will continue to supply furs as before. Monsieur Thibault will return to Montreal with next year's brigade to provide credit and goods and to sell the furs—the profits to be divided into three parts, minus the subtraction of our share of the purchase price.'

Bjornson's eyes widened. 'He proposed to make *me* a partner?'

'He did.'

'Why?'

'In truth, I made it a condition of my own acceptance.'

Bjornson said nothing, his mouth ludicrously open as he digested the news. His expression of incredulity was such that, for a moment, he put Boundless in mind of the absent Quoi.

'Well. What are your thoughts?'

'You said *two* partnerships?'

'Aye. In time to equal Thibault's own.'

'And Pinch?'

'He will carry on as before—as a hired man.' Boundless glanced at where Pinch stood on the storehouse steps engaged in bantering conversation with the returned voyageurs. 'He does not need to know the terms of our agreement. Monsieur Thibault agrees with this. Pinch is used to a … *daily* recompense. He has no thought for, or interest in, the niceties of ownership. Do you agree?'

'And what is your opinion?'

'As to the proposal? I am already decided to accept, provided you do the same.'

Bjornson said nothing for a moment, the wheels turning visibly in his pale, stubbled face.

Boundless waited with some anxiety, his companion's hesitancy bringing into sharp contrast his own instinctive acceptance of Thibault's offer. 'Well?'

Bjornson scratched behind one ear. 'What about Monsieur Lapointe? Is he not included?'

'He does not wish to be. Thibault offered, but he refused. He does not wish the responsibility. But he is content to stay on as my deputy for the time being.'

'It means we will stay on here for two, three, *four* more years?'

'Would you rather return to Delaware? Think on it, Bjorn. A *partnership!* You could return east a wealthy man.' The Swede's continuing slow deliberation provoked his impatience. 'Well?'

'I must think on it.'

'What in God's name is there to think on?'

'And what of White Deer?'

'What in blazes does she have to do with the price of fish?' Boundless saw Pinch look in their direction. 'Well?'

Bjornson squinted at the sky, a doubtful look on his face as if barely comprehending what Boundless had proposed.

'Think of the profits to be made! You could afford to build a mansion and to live in comfort all your days.'

His companion said nothing as he tugged at his chin.

Just as Boundless feared Bjornson was about to decline the offer, the Swede sighed. 'I owe you my safety, if not my life. If you stay, then I shall stay, also.'

'Then shake on it!' Delighted, he shook Bjornson's hand. 'And remember, not a word to Pinch!'

The following day, Thibault produced a contract, written in English and French. 'The new name of the business is the "Anglo-French Fur Company",' revealed Mathieu, pointing to the title. 'Monsieur Thibault estimates that the name will win favour from both sides, as well as with the Indians.'

Thibault produced a quill and each man signed, with Mathieu as witness.

'*Bien!*' Opening a bottle of wine, Thibault offered up a toast. '*Pour un avenir prospère!*'

A WEEK AFTER THE agreement, Boundless sat darning a shirt in the bunkhouse—in large part to avoid the incessant gossip provoked by Thibault's announcement of the new company during dinner a day earlier. The bourgeois had revealed Boundless' elevation to manager, while making no mention of the new partnership. As the company offered congratulations, Boundless caught Pinch observing him, a wondering look on his face.

The door opened and Bjornson stepped inside. He sat down on a crate, his elbows on his knees, his hands cradling his chin, a doleful expression on his face. He said nothing but sighed and heaved and shook his head as if in silent dialogue with himself.

'For pity's sake, man!' said Boundless, fearing the Swede had had second thoughts. 'You have a face as long as a donkey's!'

'The girl—White Deer.' Bjornson grimaced and scratched his head.

'What of her?'

'I just had a conversation with Monsieur Thibault.'

'And?'

'He asked if I would … take charge of her.'

'Take charge?' It took Boundless a moment to digest the remark. 'You sly dog!' He slapped the Swede on the shoulder. 'Pinch was right—you do have feelings for her!'

'I do,' Bjornson admitted. 'And Monsieur Thibault says that she has taken a fondness to me.' In spite of the Swede's perplexity, a bashful pride shone through the words.

'Then you will do this—take charge of her when Thibault leaves?'

Bjornson scratched his chin. 'If she will agree to it.'

'Then you intend to live with her, as Thibault does, as man and wife?'

Bjornson blushed, his broad features a study in discomfort.

'Not in that way.'

'What other way is there?'

'It must be within the laws of matrimony, as sanctioned by God.'

Boundless laughed. 'Why bother? The Indians do not place great store in such things. Look at Pinch!'

'I am not heathen—and not Pinch.'

'If you will not be bringing her back to Delaware, then what harm?'

Bjornson shot Boundless a horrified glance. 'The harm is to God's law!'

'Then marry her—according to the law.'

They were interrupted by a shout from outside. Bjornson got to his feet. 'I am needed.'

'Wait! What else—'

'Coming!' Bjornson pulled the door shut behind him.

Muttering, Boundless took a knife and cut the thread. He held up the shirt for inspection while ruefully acknowledging Pinch's prescience in the matter of White Deer. *The fellow has a sharper eye than me.*

He did not see his companion again until supper. The talk at table was all of the continuation of the post under the new arrangements. Several of the Frenchmen came up to shake Boundless' hand. Bjornson sat absently chewing his food, his mind clearly elsewhere. So noticeable was the Swede's air of preoccupation that it provoked an irritable *tut* from Pinch.

'Come, Bjorn. Has the Pope converted—or the gospels proved in error?'

Bjornson scraped back his chair. 'I must shit,' he said, a hand on his belly. He made hurriedly for the door. Pinch frowned after him. 'Does he have the gripe?'

'Leave him be. He has much on his mind.'

Pinch gave Boundless a shrewd glance. 'Speaking of which, you and Guillaume have been thick as two thieves since his return.'

'It is no secret. He trains me for when he leaves.'

'And you shall inhabit his quarters?'

'As post manager, yes.'

Pinch ruminated on this while taking out a deck of playing cards. 'An advancement you no doubt wished for?'

'Pardon?'

'The advancement—to head man. It suits you, no doubt?'

'Should it not?'

Pinch made no reply, shuffling the cards.

'It means the post continues,' said Boundless, softening his tone.

'Aye.' Pinch laid out the cards.

He waited for the other man to say more, but Pinch evidently considered the conversation closed as he studied the cards.

Boundless stood up. 'Good night. I must retire.'

The night air was cold, the scent of snow in the air. The dogs bayed and whined as he crossed the yard. He felt a stone in his shoe and stopped to remove it. The yelps and whimpers of the pack struck him as especially mournful in the sharp night air. *Perhaps they grieve for their dead companion.* He pictured the simple cross—twice replaced—in the grass behind the stockade. Lantern light gleamed from the window of Thibault's quarters, and he stared for a moment, his mind busy with idle thoughts.

The hall door opened behind him, and three men emerged, laughing at some jest. With another glance at Thibault's quarters, he continued towards the bunkhouse.

## 19

## The Distant Voice of the Kirk

As WINTER SET IN, he spent more and more time in Thibault's company, the bourgeois seeking to induct him into every aspect of post management, with Mathieu as interpreter.

'There is much to learn and little time,' said Thibault, waving off Boundless' concern that the time was better spent hunting before the snow came. 'A harsh winter is often followed by a mild one. Each day, the Indians bring in more food, so do not trouble yourself. I will send back an experienced hunter with the next brigade. Now, pay attention. This part is most important ...'

Although exacting in his demands, Thibault proved a patient mentor, flashes of humour leavening the instruction, as well as a fondness for expressing himself through apothegms. '*Order overmuch rather than too little,*' he advised when showing the list of food supplies from the previous year. '*Nuts ungathered in May cannot be eaten in December. Each trade is a coin in the pocket,*' he said when advising the importance of completing a trade on advantageous terms. '*What matter the weights do vary so long as the scale doth balance?*' he remarked, urging prudence in another matter. '*Measure judgement as you would add spice to a fish.*'

To the theoretical fish was added the practical salt, Thibault taking every opportunity to involve him in decisions affecting the post. '*What would you counsel?*' he asked when several of the men complained at a newly instituted ban on card games before five o' clock in the afternoon. He listened carefully to Boundless' reply before turning to Theroux. '*Tell the men the ban does not apply on days of foul weather. Better, let Boundless inform them. Let the flock know the voice of the shepherd.*'

The *bonbon* reflected the essence of the man himself, Boundless decided, his respect for the scope of the Frenchman's knowledge and the thoroughness with which he passed it on increasing by the day.

'Does Monsieur Thibault have many children?' he asked Mathieu, realising that he knew little of the bourgeois' domestic life.

'Two daughters and three sons. The eldest daughter being a few years older than myself. I am married to Camille, the youngest.'

'And his wife—she is well?'

'A fine woman. Devout. And as parsimonious as the *monsieur* himself,' Mathieu added with a smile.

'And, if you will pardon the curiosity, why does he not invite you to join the company?'

Mathieu chuckled. 'He has tried! But I have my own interests. My father owns a trading house and I follow him into the profession. Indeed, we purchase many pelts and export them to the overseas markets. We import them back as manufactured goods.'

'Why not manufacture the goods yourselves—in Montreal or Quebec?'

Mathieu shrugged. 'Before it was forbidden, but perhaps now … ' He left the sentence unfinished. 'I must go and talk to Theroux. Monsieur Thibault wishes you to attend his house, tomorrow after breakfast.'

Next morning, he joined Mathieu in *la maison du bourgeois*. A pile of ledgers sat on the table. He recognised the post journals, bills of lading, invoices and letters. Thibault was boiling a kettle over the fire. White Deer was nowhere to be seen.

'Monsieur Thibault wishes you to understand the business as a whole— which is why he brought the books back with him,' Mathieu began. He stopped as Thibault proceed to pour tea for both men. '*Merci, monsieur.*'

Thibault set down the teapot and took a place in front of the blazing fire, apparently content to let Mathieu explain the mysteries of proprietorship.

'You need not concern overmuch with the finer details,' Mathieu began. 'For the most part, you can allow Monsieur Lapointe and the junior clerks to take care of the books. But you are responsible for the honesty and faithfulness of the accounts and must therefore understand the principles.'

Mathieu fished a bound journal from the pile. 'The correspondence file,' he explained. He opened it to the first page. 'A report from our very first frontier post, by Lake Superior. The head man sends one back with every cargo. You will be expected to do the same. From reports such as these, a partner or managing clerk is able to form a faithful picture of each distant outpost or supply depot while sitting at his desk in Montreal. By studying the reports, he can tell with certainty if the manager is an honest man or a thriftless one, whether an outpost is in rude good health or stands on the brink of penury or starvation.'

'As we did, last winter?'

Mathieu looked surprised at the information. He glanced at Thibault and then back again at Boundless. 'Much depends on the author of the report,' he said. He selected another ledger. 'This is the Grand Journal—a record of all transactions on a daily and weekly basis. Do you remember that Mandan delegation two days ago—when they claimed two muskets on credit? And do you remember where Monsieur Thibault recorded the trades?'

He nodded. 'In the daily journal.'

'Good. Every transaction is recorded in the journal as it occurs, recording such information as the date, the value of the transaction and whether it is debt or credit. The daily entries are then copied to the Grand Journal—Monsieur Lapointe will do this. The Grand Journal summarises commercial activities for each month. The contents, once properly arranged, are then copied into the Grand Ledger.'

Mathieu picked up a heavy ledger bound in worn leather. 'Feel.' He gave the volume to Boundless, who hefted it in his hands.

'As heavy as a brick! Why is it called "grand"?'

'Because it contains all the different records from the various journals and other ledgers, and thus gives the truest and most comprehensive account of the business.'

Taking back the ledger, Mathieu opened it up. 'Here we find the complete record of expenses, revenues, monies payable, merchandise, cash loans, credits, company assets, and moneys owed.' He turned the pages, stopping every now and then to point to a heading. '… a record of assets and liabilities … and, there, a list of Montreal creditors and debtors … the value of furs sold last spring … the net credit or debit owing to particular merchants … the name of the merchant. Ah! Monsieur Blanc, I know him well … a list of transactions—. Pardon?' Mathieu bent an ear as Thibault interjected. '*Oui, Monsieur* … the credits and debits must balance, as evidence of good health.'

'Last year's accounts.' Mathieu turned the volume so that Boundless could see more easily. 'Eighty-four *pièces*. That equals to five thousand three hundred and seventy-six skins.' He pointed to the tally.

Boundless laid a finger on the column. 'Three thousand and thirty-nine of beaver? Yes?'

'Yes. Please continue.'

Boundless traced down the column of figures. 'One hundred and seventy-five buffalo robes?' At Mathieu's nod, he continued. 'Three hundred and ninety—racoon pelts? One hundred and eighteen bear. Ninety fox and three hundred and eighty muskrat. Two hundred and thirteen of …?'

'Squirrel.'

'Squirrel. One hundred and eighty-four … mink? Twenty-two—what is that word?'

'Wolverine.'

'Ah! And thirty … moose? Three hundred and ninety-five deer. One hundred and fourteen … fisher? Fourteen wild cat. Fifty-four wolf, and twenty-seven …?'

'Twenty-seven elk.'

Mathieu turned the page and pointed to a column of letters and figures. 'It is the estimated sum—at ten shillings per beaver pelt, average.'

'Why use English pounds?'

'For convenience. Much of the harvest was sold to English agents.'

At Boundless' questioning look, Mathieu tapped his nose. 'We fish where the trout will bite.'

Returning to the ledger, he pointed to a sub-total. 'Fifteen hundred and nineteen pounds and ten shillings for the beaver.'

Boundless let out an impressed breath. 'What is that word?'

'*Mixte*—referring to the remainder.'

Boundless studied the figures. 'Two thousand three hundred and thirty-seven remaining—at seven shillings per fur average?' He searched for the total on the page. 'Eight hundred and seventeen pounds and nineteen shillings?' He looked at Mathieu for confirmation.

Thibault, who had been following the route of the conversation, if not the stopping places, got up and pointed to a figure. '*La somme de tous les métiers.*'

'The sum of all trades,' explained Mathieu.

'Two thousand, three hundred and thirty-seven pounds and nineteen shillings!' Boundless read out the figure, murmuring in astonishment. Bannock's words came back to him as he imagined the sum doubling and tripling along the lengthy trade route to Europe.

Thibault poured more tea. '*Une entreprise rentable, vous êtes d'accord?*' He glanced at Mathieu for the interpretation.

'Tell him I do. Indeed.'

Thibault refilled Boundless' cup. 'And you now own a share of that business,' he said through Mathieu, his keen eyes regarding Boundless. 'But everything depends on the reliable supply of furs. Which, in turn, depends on our good relations with the Indians.'

'*Oui, Monsieur,*' said Boundless, judging the latter to be a question.

'He asks how your French is progressing,' said Mathieu as Thibault spoke again. 'French is the language of the fur trade and you must be able to speak to the men in their own language.'

'*Je le parle tous les jours, Monsieur,*' Boundless replied carefully. '*Mathieu est un excellent professeur.*'

'*Bien!*' Thibault's eyes twinkled with satisfaction.

BOUNDLESS RECOUNTED THE DISCUSSION to Bjornson as the two companions walked after supper. To his chagrin, the Swede seemed manifestly uninterested, his mind elsewhere.

'What in Jupiter makes you heave and sigh so?' demanded Boundless, vexed at his companion's preoccupied air.

'It is the girl!' Bjornson blurted out.

'Girl? You mean White Deer ? What of her?'

'Do I do right—by agreeing to take her on?'

'How the devil should *I* know? Do you have genuine affection for her, at least?'

Bjorn said nothing, a tormented look on his face.

'What has brought all of this on? I thought you had settled the question in your mind.'

'But she is a heathen!' The Swede looked distraught at the word.

'Is that how you see her?'

'I mean heathen to Christ, an unbeliever.' Bjornson gave a heavy sigh.

'I thought you were going to convert her—if it is so important to you.'

'Yes, yes.' Bjornson looked relieved. 'It is as you say. I shall instruct her,' he said, 'and bring her to the faith.'

'Unless *she* brings you over to the Indian camp!'

Bjornson looked so horror-struck at the prospect that Boundless broke out laughing. 'Nay, Bjorn. Have no fear. Your faith be as strong as a buffalo!'

'Such matters are not for jest.' Bjornson's mouth tightened with disapproval.

'No.' Boundless agreed, suddenly weary of the conversation. 'They are far more a cause for tears.'

AS THE WEEKS PASSED and Boundless became more deeply immersed in the accounts, his curiosity at the mechanisms of liability and credit increased. The wonders of double-entry in particular provoked his admiration.

"Tis the alchemy that transforms your friend Pinch into both burden and asset,' Mathieu joked. 'Each transaction has two faces: one that looks to the debit side of the account and one that looks to the credit side. As one figure changes so, too, does the other. If you give an Indian a musket on credit, then your goods inventory decreases by its value; but the Indian must repay the cost of that musket by supplying you, in time, with its equivalent value in pelts, which return balances the debt owed to the inventory. The debit of the musket is balanced by the credit of the requisite number of pelts. Do you see?'

*It is life itself*, marvelled Boundless, struck by the neatness of the equation. The distant voice of the Kirk came back to him as he pondered the ingenious calculus. *'A sin must be paid for by an act of Grace. A black mark cannot be erased except by an act of equivalent virtue. The ledger must balance or err on the credit side. Take stock, friends, I beseech you. Take stock.'*

He recalled the words, recognising for the first time the figure behind them. *I am taking moral instruction, again. Or was I ingesting, unbeknownst, the principles of bookkeeping whilst seated in the pew?*

He continued his study the next day, sitting by himself to leaf through the records while trying to deepen his understanding of the nature of his new role as manager and part-owner. The Grand Ledger, in particular, held his interest as he found himself immersed in pages that described the commercial quality of pelts or calculated tables of interest while charting the rise and fall of fur markets in France or London.

He murmured with recognition as he came across the bold hand of Thibault describing the material assets of the post. The entries carefully listed each building, noting the state of repair of each. One half-page detailed the extent of the post garden, comparing the harvest with that of the previous summer. Turning the page, he saw an inventory of the contents of the storeroom and cabin, down to the various pots and pans. Quantities of powder and shot were listed, the tubs of pork grease and sugar noted.

Taking the ledger to Mathieu for elucidation, he shook his head over a notation to the effect that the tool hut contained two ladders, one short, and one long, and that the roof had last been replaced on such and such a date. 'I recall doing that,' he said, his voice rueful. 'And did not think it worthy of record.'

Towards the middle of another ledger, he came across an entire section related to *les engagés*. The number of *hivernants* was recorded as well as the *mangeurs de lard* along with the terms of engagement for each. Among the names he found his own position, '*chasseur*', noted along with his contract start date and wages. Occasionally, a name was followed by a comment or warning, which Mathieu translated for his benefit: 'a great villain', read one; 'suspected thief', read another.

After several days spent immersed in letters, reports and accounts, his conception of the post had utterly transformed. From his initial impression of a chance collection of men drawn from God-alone-knew-where to traverse the snowy wastes in the hazardous pursuit of pelts, he now apprehended the post, and all of its occupants, as *agents* combined in a purposeful, collective *enterprise*. An enterprise that fed on supply lines and remitted profits in the form of greasy beaver pelts and hides, which in turn metamorphosed into exports, dividends and credits.

Bannock's figure of a 'chain of incremental supply' that stretched all the way from the wild frontier to the hat-makers of Paris and London came back to him with newly recognised truth. He sat at the supper table, his head swimming with figures and details. At times he stared, bemused, at his noisy dining companions. He no longer saw the tortured Bjornson, or the red-bearded Theroux, or the argumentative, pipe-smoking Pinch, but inked assets and notations in a cryptic drama played out across the lines and columns of leather-bound volumes.

'Not wealth, but capital,' Thibault impressed when the two sat down to review his understanding. The bourgeois nodded to Mathieu, who continued the theme.

'He wishes you to think beyond the annual return and consider the profits as an engine for future growth. Who knows? In time, the company may wish to issue stock in order to increase its capabilities.'

'He wishes us to expand—to other posts?'

'Why not?' Mathieu sat forward, his face earnest. 'The Indian lands— all the way from here to the Hudson Bay—represent a vast storehouse of minerals and furs. And gold too, perhaps. With sufficient resources of capital and, above all, *enterprise*, we may extract those riches and use them to further the growth of the company.'

When a group of Hidatsa arrived at the stockade bearing a supply of pelts and hides, Thibault invited him to oversee the exchange. 'Let us see how the lessons have sunk in,' said the bourgeois, motioning for Lapointe to step aside.

Self-consciously standing at the upright desk, Boundless carefully negotiated and recorded each transaction as Thibault hovered at his shoulder to offer words of instruction or advice. 'That hide is in poor condition. Demand an extra pelt for the large size hoe. Refuse that fellow credit—he has an outstanding debt from last spring. Calculate each muskrat pelt a shilling. Accept the hide in part-exchange—consider the goodwill a coin on deposit.'

Thibault elaborated on the latter sentiment during a lull in the trades. 'It can be accrued—and lost, both conditions affecting the value of trades.'

When the Indians had departed, leaving behind a sizeable heap of pelts, Thibault took command of the journal to view the results. Humming with satisfaction, he ran his finger ran down the list of trades as written by Boundless.

A white blanket, 2 beaver

A broad hoe, 4 pelts: 1 muskrat, 1 beaver, 2 wolf

A narrow hoe, 2 elk hides

4 measures of powder, 5 buckskins

A dozen of buttons, 2 squirrel pelts

2 yards of stroud, 1 buffalo robe

A small hatchet, 3 beaver

A musket, 10 beaver

A pound of shot, 12 skins (6 deer, 3 wolf, 1 racoon)

A bead necklace, 1 mink pelt

A large hatchet, 3 buckskins

A leather pouch, 1beaver

Brass kettle, 2 beaver

Small cooking pot, 3 beaver

A dozen of fishhooks, 1 mink

One yard of plain wool, 2 elk hides

A large knife, 1 robe

A dozen of beads, 2 beaver

'*Un matin profitable*,' declared Thibault, nodding at the figures.

'Monsieur Thibault wishes you to note the musket and its value,' added Mathieu. 'Do not hesitate to give the weapons on credit. The Indians must then return for flints, powder, and shot. Do you follow?'

He went to bed that night with his head reeling from the list of responsibilities imposed by his new position as owner-manager. The irony that he now stood, at last, in a position to reap some small portion of the fabled riches that Mose had promised, was not lost on him.

'But it is not as I had imagined,' he conceded before falling asleep.

## *Monsieur Bourgeois!*

HE WAS NOW UNIVERSALLY accepted as Thibault's deputy in all matters related to the operations of the post—the men working under his supervision to make repairs or cut firewood or go on trade missions. Thibault chose to issue pronouncements or instructions through Boundless, encouraging him to speak French as much as possible in spite of his uncertainty with the language.

'Do not invite questions,' he advised. 'Give the instruction simply and clearly and leave it at that.'

Indeed, he took Thibault himself as a model in this regard, the bourgeois issuing orders in a brusque economical manner that stood at odds with his penchant for elaboration in private discussion. 'Be a lion in command, an owl in conversation,' he counselled Boundless. 'Men prefer to be led as a fish prefers to swim.'

His engagement in each detail of post management was not lost on Pinch, who retained his relish for provocation as a diversion from winter boredom. 'Gadzooks if we don't have as many overseers as there are buffaloes,' he opined as he watched Boundless, Mathieu, Lapointe and Thibault emerge from the latter's private room.

Lighting up his pipe, he declared to all and sundry that the 'soft' days of Thibault were now a thing of yore and that he was fully reconciled to working in his sleep. 'It takes some practice,' he claimed, 'but works marvellously to save on food and lamp oil.'

THE WINTER CONTINUED EXCEEDINGLY mild, the snow barely deep enough to cover the prairie grass. As a result, Boundless rarely hunted—a constant flow of trade delegations from the Mandan, Arikara, Hidatsa and Cree supplying ample quantities of food. As he watched yet another party of Indians enter the post, he noted with satisfaction the comparative abundance compared with the privations of the previous winter.

'It is like that,' said Pinch when Boundless remarked upon the fact. 'The weather is so fickle as to be contrary from day to day. And yet, our lives depend upon it.'

One morning, a delegation of Mandan women turned up at the gates escorted by a small group of warriors, which included Shining Hair. The Indian stood in the yard smoking a pipe. He raised a hand in greeting as Boundless emerged from the cabin. *'Bonjour, mon ami!'* he grinned, showing stained teeth.

Inside the storehouse, Boundless stood with Mathieu and Lapointe at the front of the room as the women picked over the trade goods on the shelves. Pinch lounged nearby, pipe in mouth. Boundless' eye was caught by a slender young girl as she deliberated between a bolt of fustian and a wool blanket. Her coppery features were framed by glossy black hair separated into braids which fell about her shoulders. She wore an ankle-length deer hide tunic ornamented with a variety of bone and pewter buttons obtained from the post. Her countenance was, by turns, animated and grave, an air of pensive study instantly dissolving into laughter at some remark by one of the two companions who hovered by her side. She glanced up, having felt his gaze, and stared boldly back at him. The brief exchange did not go unnoticed by her companions, who broke into giggles and playful teasing, the girl obviously an object of great affection.

'Who is she?' he whispered to Mathieu, who in turn whispered to Lapointe. The senior clerk observed the girl before leaning in to confer with Boundless.

'I think I recognise her but cannot be certain. She is probably from the main village—the big one by the forks—but I do not know her father.'

At that moment, the girl approached, holding out the wool blanket. On it rested a brass thimble and six engraved pewter buttons. Her companion proffered a glossy beaver pelt in exchange. *'Dutse!'* The girl thrust the blanket at him, her lips pursed with determination.

Suddenly flustered, he turned to his companions for assistance.

*'Il est la* … What is the deuced word?'

Pinch offered no help, watching on with amusement as the girl awaited a reply. Her skin was smooth and unblemished, her brown eyes intent in the dim light of the storehouse. She pouted and gave a *tsk* of impatience at his hesitation.

'I do not know the value of the buttons,' he confessed.

'Perish the value! Make the trade!'

He reached out to accept the proffered pelt. The girl's eyes looked into his own for a moment. Next instant, she was gone, leaving him to gaze after her, the pelt in his hand.

Pinch guffawed. 'Your mouth hangs open like a trout for a fly!' He smacked his lips in a kissing noise. '*Mmch! mmch!* A lovelorn trout!'

'Balderdash!'

Later in the afternoon, he exited the bunkhouse to see Lapointe crossing the yard ahead of him. He hurried to catch up. 'Monsieur Lapointe! A moment!'

The Frenchman turned. 'Yes? Maurice, if it pleases,' he said, on recognizing Boundless. 'Since you are now—or soon will be—*patron*.'

'Then Maurice it is,' he said, pleased at the acknowledgement. 'The girl in the storehouse, would your wife know her name?'

Lapointe shrugged. 'Let us see,' he said, inviting Boundless to accompany him to his house

'You do not wish to be in charge?' asked Boundless as they walked, curious at the senior man's refusal of the position.

'I do not wish for the headaches! I am content to spend the winter at the post and summers with my wife's family. It is an arrangement that suits me well.'

'You enjoy living with the Indians?'

'Why not? They are a fine, hospitable people. And I have Jacques for company, when I wish for it.'

Boundless nodded, liking the older man's straightforward nature and unhurried confidence.

'*Voila!*' said Lapointe as they arrived at the clerk's house—second in size only to Thibault's—that he shared with Scattered Corn Woman. The latter was a bone-thin Mandan whose face was heavily marked with signs of the childhood pox. She wore a fine wool shawl over her buckskin tunic. The contrast between her dark, scarred complexion and the delicate shawl distracted him as he listened to Lapointe question her. Watching her face for any signs of recognition, he felt a pang of disappointment as she shook her head.

'*Elle aime* to, ah, sew *les boutons*.' Boundless swept a hand down the front of his shirt.

'*Boutons*,' her husband repeated, adding a few more sentences in French, and using his hands to indicate the girl's height.

Boundless saw recognition dawn upon the woman's face.

'*Ti'ka Owa*,' she said, her soft voice belying her ravaged features.

'*Répéter?*' Lapointe bent his head, straining to hear the soft words. '*Owa?*' He made a fluttering motion with his hand.

Scattered Corn Woman nodded. '*L'herbe*,' she said.

Comprehension struck Lapointe. 'You mean meadow—not grass?' Scattered Corn Woman frowned at the English. '*Oiseau des prairies?*' he added.

'*Oui.*' Scattered Corn Woman nodded. '*Oiseau des prairies.*'

Lapointe nodded and turned to Boundless. 'Your pretty young button is named "Meadow Bird."'

THE EXCEPTIONALLY MILD WEATHER lasted until after the turn of the year, when a fierce gale blew down from the north. The strong winds whipped up the snow into a powdery blizzard that made it impossible to see a yard ahead. Without the customary, if increasingly rare, escape into the physical release of the hunt, Boundless found the sheer *clericalism* of his new responsibilities increasingly burdensome. 'I grow tired of the wretched books,' he confessed as Mathieu arrived bearing a sheaf of correspondence. 'The figures begin to buzz in my head like angry wasps.'

'Then I have good news for you.' Mathieu smiled. 'Monsieur Thibault would like you to continue your education 'on the field of battle,' as the saying goes. He is sending a trade party to the Mandan village at the forks and wishes you to lead it. Monsieur Lapointe will accompany you to make the proper introductions.' Mathieu hesitated, an embarrassed look on his face.

'Yes?'

'Your pardon. Monsieur Thibault wishes me to add that no doubt you will be happy at the opportunity to see the young girl again.' Mathieu shrugged in apology.

'By the bones! Does the entire post know of my business?'

'I believe he learned of your interest from—'

'Pinch!'

ON A DAY OF gusting winds, he set out for the forks accompanied by Lapointe, Pinch, Henri and Mathieu, the latter keen to experience his first visit to an Indian village. They took with them a sledge laden with trade goods. Blowing snow made travel difficult at first, but within a mile, the wind dropped, and the sun came out, easing their progress. Boundless barely noticed the difficulties—his mind full of both apprehension and anticipation at heading the delegation and the prospect of seeing the girl again. *Will she remember me?* he wondered. *Perhaps she will remain in her lodge. Or mayhap she does remember and wishes to avoid me!* His trepidation increased as the village came into view and children raced out to meet them.

Inside Buffalo Hawk's lodge, they sat on mats eating the food offered them. The air inside the lodge was stiflingly warm, the pungent stench of grease and sweat causing Boundless to blink. From outside came the sounds of barking dogs and the shrill voices of children. He looked up each time someone entered. To his surprise, the headman, after a brief conversation with Lapointe, offered the customary pipe to him first. He glanced at Lapointe, who nodded.

Pinch nudged him in the ribs. 'See how your notoriety precedes you!'

After the smoke ceremony, the headman gestured to the door, and they rose to their feet. Outside, a crowd had gathered around the sledge. He looked among the faces for the girl, disappointed at not seeing her. She slipped from his thoughts as he became caught up in supervising the trades as Lapointe entered the transactions in the journal. Several times, he was called upon to settle disputes, Lapointe directing the parties his way for settlement. As he arbitrated, Thibault's precept echoed in his ears. *'Remember, we are here on sufferance. If the price of that sufferance be a few pelts here and there, so be it.'*

'The rascal cheats me!' Pinch protested as a haughty young warrior attempted to claim a prized musket for the cost of less than the required ten pelts. 'He offers but eight—and inferior quality at that.'

'Nevertheless, permit him the musket. Think of it as tribute.'

Pinch gave a sour look. 'You sound like Guillaume.'

'It is because the advice would be the same.'

With a yell of triumph, the youth grabbed the musket and held it high in the air to the admiration of his companions.

'May it misfire on the villain!'

Boundless had no sooner returned his attention to the bartering than he spied the girl. She was surrounded by four or five companions as she admired a bracelet of coloured beads. She wore the same fringed deerskin tunic that she wore at the post. His eye picked out the pewter buttons sewn to the tunic as decoration.

The girl was unaware of his gaze, so intent was she on the bracelet. A companion whispered in her ear, and she glanced in his direction. To his great disappointment, she seemed not to recognise him, turning her attention back to the bracelet. Her friends continued to dart glances at him, giggling to each other and prodding the girl. Finally, a pair of them physically turned her and, in spite of her laughing protests, steered her towards him. Prompted by her companions, she held up the wristlet for his attention, a bold look in her eye.

'A fine bracelet,' he said, aware of the barely concealed merriment of her entourage. One thrust a bag of pemmican upon the girl, and she held it up in exchange.

Glancing around to see if Pinch was within earshot, he made a motion ceding the wristlet. '*Rien. Un cadeau.*'

Her eyes widened as she took in his meaning. With deft grace, she slipped the bracelet over her hand and cocked her slim brown wrist for his approval.

'*Bon! Tres joli!*' he said as she stepped back and held up her wrist to admiring cries from her companions.

'A pretty pelt!'

Pinch's coarse jest fell on deaf ears as he was distracted by an importuning grandmother. When he turned again, the girl was gone. Searching, he glimpsed her just as she was about to vanish from sight around a lodge. At that instant she glanced back, her eyes holding his for a brief second before she disappeared.

The glance stayed with him all the way back to the fort, the brevity of the exchange only enhancing its import. He pictured again her slim, brown wrist as she held up the bracelet, her eyes dark and expressive in the winter sunlight. *She was pleased with the gift*, he told himself, mentally entering the exchange in the daybook: *Une fille—un bracelet.*

During supper, he listened with half an ear as Pinch and Henri argued some point or other, starting as from a dream when Pinch sought his adjudication.

'Are you off with your pretty young maiden?'

Before he could answer, the door opened, and White Deer entered. She paused on the threshold, balancing a stack of firewood in her arms as she closed the door with her body. As she struggled to balance the logs, Bjornson rushed to assist, taking the firewood in spite of her protests.

Pinch shook his head at the sight. 'Witness. Our love-sick Luther has no more thought for old Leviticus. Solomon, only, occupies him. The poor devil sinks deeper each day, whether he will or no.'

Henri had also turned to watch. Grinning, he said something to Pinch who laughed heartily. 'Henri claims that both you and Bjorn are becoming men of the country.'

The inference was lost on him until Pinch added the mischievous spice. 'And what does a country man need?'

'Out with it—what?'

'Nay, I but tease.' Pinch looked around. 'I miss the half-wit,' he said.

THOUGHTS OF THE GIRL continued to preoccupy him as February gave way to March. As the married men began to return for spring baling, he observed them with their families, the nonchalant relationships an object of ever-greater interest and curiosity. Seeing White Deer and Thibault together, he covertly observed the pair, noting the girl's attentive response to his words and gestures, and Thibault's own ease in her company. This affection continued in spite of her receptivity to the ardent glances cast by Bjornson. Indeed, Thibault seemed to encourage the prospective liaison, bidding the girl to remain behind while he retired early to his quarters. In his absence, the two exchanged brief, meaningful looks, Bjornson now smitten beyond recall.

Given hope by that fleeting backwards glance, Boundless approached Thibault for advice, his reluctance to publicly admit his infatuation pushed aside by his increasingly powerful desire for the girl.

Thibault listened carefully as Mathieu broached the subject on his behalf. The bourgeois cleared his throat, the habitual preliminary to a considered reply, and swirled the wine in the glass as Mathieu translated.

'Monsieur Thibault says that taking a Mandan as wife has great advantages. It would help bind the tribe to us in this uncertain time. And as a man, it has obvious advantages also. The winter is very long, and a cold bed makes it seem longer. He would counsel you to pursue your interest. A woman is a great delight in this unforgiving wilderness.'

They heard a sound from within the bedroom where White Deer had withdrawn.

'Pardon, *Monsieur*, but … White Deer ?' asked Boundless, hesitant to bring up the subject but feeling he must seek explication for the awkward and potentially fraught relationship between the girl and Bjornson. He looked to Mathieu for assistance. The latter spoke briefly to Thibault.

The question induced a fit of melancholy as Thibault cradled the wine glass. He glanced at the bedroom door before answering, his voice wistful.

'He says that he wishes he could bring her with him, back to Montreal, but that such a thing is not possible.' Mathieu glanced at Thibault before adding, 'in truth, he will miss her beyond words.'

Thibault gave a heavy sigh. Dabbing his eyes with a handkerchief, he complained of 'the damned smoke' issuing from the fireplace.

'If he could, he would stay here with her, but he says she will be in good hands with Bjornson, who is *un bon gars*, a decent fellow,' said Mathieu.

'*Un bon gars*,' Thibault repeated, his eyes damp as he stared into the fire.

BOUNDLESS AWOKE NEXT MORNING determined to ask for the young girl's hand. After breakfast, he sought out Lapointe for further advice, professing his ignorance of Mandan courting customs.

'Does the girl know of your intentions?' Lapointe asked. At a shake of the head from Boundless, he continued. 'Then you must first make her aware of your interest—to estimate your chances. Then you must approach the father with a gift. This will, ah, *illustrate* your intention toward the girl. The father will consult with her. If she approves, then the matter is concluded.'

'That is all?'

'The Mandan are a practical people, like most Indians. If the daughter agrees, the matter is concluded in a simple, straightforward manner. The father will accept the gift, and it is done.'

'What sort of gift would you recommend?'

Lapointe blew out his lips. 'Some blankets. A buffalo robe. A musket, certainly, with powder and shot.'

'Is this how you married your wife?'

Lapointe smiled. 'That was different. She had her own lodge and was divorced from her husband. I gave her a shawl and asked that she return to the post with me. She said yes.'

At Boundless' look of surprise, Lapointe chuckled. 'The Indians are very uncomplicated in these matters. They do not confuse sentiment with practicality.'

Pondering the advice, Boundless made his way back to the hall to fetch a mug of tea.

In spite of his attempts to focus on other matters, he was unable to keep the young girl from his thoughts. Now that he was in possession of her name, his preoccupation increased even as he reprimanded himself for his fond hopes. *She hardly knows that I exist.* He imagined her sitting by the fireside in Thibault's quarters, a shawl around her shoulders as he sat at the table making entries in the journal.

'What so occupies you?' asked Pinch as Boundless stared at his plate, his supper forgotten.

'I was thinking of you, Pinch, and your selfless devotion to work.'

The remark drew a choked laugh from Bjornson, bits of food spraying from his mouth.

'Indeed,' said Pinch, unruffled by the quip. White Deer appeared with a pot of beans and began ladling a portion onto each man's trencher.

'And double for you,' Pinch teased, eyeing the generous portion she ladled onto the Swede's plate.

Bjornson coloured and mumbled into his beans.

Finishing his supper, Pinch set aside his trencher and took a deck of cards from his pocket. 'And how goes your own amorous pursuit?' he asked Boundless, shuffling the pack. 'Does it sail upon smooth waters?'

'Again, you conjure fancies, or else mistake me.'

'So, there is no matter between you and the pretty fledge you fawned over at the Mandan?'

'In your head, Pinch—a most voluminous pot!'

Pinch spread the deck face down on the table. 'Take one. They say cards do reveal what is hidden.'

'You are as full of superstitions as a heathen with a forked stick!'

'Humour me, for the game of it.'

Muttering at the nonsense, Boundless nevertheless selected a tattered card and turned it over. 'There is your fortune!'

'Ha!' Pinch crowed with glee as the Queen of Hearts sat, face-up, on the table. 'Well?' He cocked his head at Boundless. 'Does she say true? Or do you deny her?'

'Who?'

'Zounds, there is more than one! The turtle dove that so besots you.'

'I have an interest. I do not deny it.'

'An interest! She is some share or stake, then?'

'Again, Pinch, you fish in barren waters.'

'There is no shame in it.'

'Did I impute there was?'

Pinch shuffled the deck again, his voice turning solemn. 'If you intend to make claim upon her, you cannot do better. There be no fitter helpmate or companion than an Indian maiden. I would not swap my Buffalo Bird for all the furs in the country.'

'Put away your hooks and lures, Pinch. I am sated on worms.'

'No hook, but the truth,' his companion protested.

'I have decided to ask the girl for her hand,' he confessed, suddenly blithely indifferent to the other man's opinion. Bjornson stared in astonishment, a spoonful of beans arrested halfway to his mouth.

Pinch grinned. 'The truth will out! She is a pretty young chuck. But what makes you think some Mandan buck does not have his eye on her?'

The unexpected remark rocked his new-found hopes—thoughts of a rival having never entered his head. Abandoning the unfinished supper, he left the cabin and paced the wet ground between the garden and the stockade fence. *Pinch is right,* he conceded, perturbed at the prospect.

*I was a fool to think she waited on my word alone.* On the spur, he made up his mind. *I shall approach her as soon as the brigade leaves.* Resolved upon this course, he rounded on his heel and made for the bunkhouse.

THE SOUND OF ICE cracking on the river was a constant reminder that departure day was looming. As the pelts were baled and roped, he held daily, and sometimes hourly, consultations with Thibault, the latter impressing upon him the need for careful auditing of the type and quality of pelt. 'Remember, you are a partner now, and must see to your return.'

On the eve of departure, he was invited to dine with Thibault and Mathieu. The table was set with china dishes, in stark contrast to the wooden trenchers of the hall. The bourgeois opened a bottle of wine and poured three glasses before raising a toast. '*Messieurs, à votre bonne santé!*'

They made small talk as White Deer served supper—an excellent affair of roasted rabbit, fish and wild rice. As they lingered over a pie made from maple syrup and dried berries, Thibault took out a pipe—something he rarely indulged in—and drew it to flame. 'This house is now yours,' he said, musing around the pipe stem as Mathieu interpreted. 'You have come a long way since your footsteps led you here across the wild plains five years past. You started a hired man, and now you are the master.'

'I am fortunate, and grateful, sir. I have learnt a great deal from your generous guidance.'

Thibault smiled. 'An apt pupil is the teacher's greatest reward.'

They talked late into the evening, Thibault fondly recounting his earliest days at the post—often using an anecdote as a pointed fable to impress upon Boundless the responsibilities of his new position. Finally, after a period of silence, he drained the last of the wine and set the empty glass back on the table.

Uncertain whether the evening was finished, Boundless was about to push back his chair when Thibault smacked his forehead. 'I almost forgot! I have a gift for you—to celebrate your new position.' Scolding his forgetfulness, he got up and withdrew a folded brown coat from the home-made commode. 'This is my spare, you might as well have it,' he said, holding it up. 'Try it on for size.'

The woollen coat had a wide collar and five brass buttons down the front. It had been cut so as to finish below the knee in the manner of a frock coat. Although shorter than Thibault, he was broader across the shoulders, and the coat constricted across the chest as he pulled it on.

Thibault laughed. 'Perhaps your Mandan sweetheart can loosen the stitching. A moment!'

From a peg, he took down a battered brown hat identical to the one he wore daily. Made from felted beaver, the hat balanced a round crown against a wide brim. He fitted it onto Boundless' head and stood back to appraise the effect.

'*Bien!*'

Pleased, but feeling a little foolish in the attire, Boundless mumbled thanks as Mathieu watched in approval. 'Monsieur Thibault says you must wear both tomorrow for the departure. The clothes will anoint you in the eyes of the men.'

Thibault laid a hand on his shoulder. 'Good night, my dear Boundless. We met as strangers and part as friends.' He regarded Boundless fondly, his eyes moist. 'I hope it is not too long before we dine again.'

SCARCELY TEN HOURS LATER, the two stood together again as the men placed the last of the bales on top of the poles laid across the bottom of the canoes. The water level was swollen with run-off, chunks of ice sliding by with the current. Boundless wore the newly bestowed hat and coat, self-consciously folding his arms before the amused glances of the Frenchmen. The hat felt odd and overheavy on his head.

The morning was mild, the sun climbing the sky as Thibault gave out last-minute instructions. Four of the five canoes were already in position, the voyageurs sitting in place, their paddles trailing in the clear, cold water. Pinch raised laughter with a ribald comment—leaping backwards to escape a splash of water from the paddles.

'I look forward to your first report next summer.' Thibault held out his hand.

'I shall not disappoint you, sir.' The two clasped hands in a firm, affectionate handshake.

Mathieu stepped forward, offering his hand. 'Goodbye, my dear Boundless. It has been a great pleasure making your acquaintance.'

'And I yours, Mathieu. Godspeed.'

Mathieu stepped into the congested canoe, perching on a bale as Theroux swept an arm through the air. '*En avant!*' The guide's voice rang out again as the *milieux* took up the stroke. The heavily loaded vessels moved slowly away from the shore, the men stroking in unison.

Thibault raised his hat in the air. '*Que la Fortune nous regarde avec bienveillance!*'

The companions stood watching until the last canoe had vanished around the bend. After Bjornson and Pinch had left, Boundless lingered for a few moments, his eyes on the silent river. He turned away, his new responsibilities suddenly weighing heavily upon him. The coat felt cumbersome and uncomfortably tight in the warm air. He took it off and draped it over his arm.

'Stride those legs!' Pinch hailed from the top of the rise. 'Hot tea awaits, Monsieur Bourgeois!'

# Meadow Bird

THE BRIGADE HAD BARELY departed before White Deer moved out of Thibault's house and into one of the smaller houses reserved for the clerks. Boundless watched her carry her few belongings across the yard assisted by the squat figure of Buffalo Bird Woman. A few hours later, he moved his possessions out of the bunkhouse and into the empty house. A vague feeling of trespass came over him as he looked around the bare walls. The commode stood empty. The fireplace had been swept out and fresh logs left stacked on the small hearth. A wall shelf contained the post ledgers as well as various daybooks, correspondence, and old invoices. He added his own journal to the shelf plus the new ones he had ordered from Montreal. A small, slim volume lying on its side caught his eye and he picked it up, smiling as he recognised the book of familiar tales Thibault had left him. On the flyleaf, Thibault had added an inscription. *A mon cher Boundless. Que ces petits contes réchauffent une nuit d'hiver.* Thibault had also left his barometer, a glass ink bottle, and a row of fresh quills in a pewter holder.

The bedroom was as sparsely appointed as the parlour: a chest of drawers and a wooden bed the sole furnishings. A candle lantern hung suspended from a metal hinge fixed to the wall beside the bed. The bed frame was laced with ropes and coarse sacking and topped by a large canvas bag stuffed with wool which formed the mattress.

The whole was covered by a sheet of Scotch linen and a blanket. Feather pillows and a fine bolster—imported from Montreal—lay atop the bed. 'White Deer will miss the pillows,' Thibault had remarked, his voice wistful. 'They belong to the bourgeois,' he said, dismissing Boundless' offer to give them up.

He had just folded his shirts and neckerchiefs into the chest of drawers when he heard a noise behind him. Pinch stood in the open doorway. 'It is smaller than I fancied,' he said as he peered around the interior. 'It is hard to credit that he is gone for good.

'Is White Deer settled in her new quarters?'

'Aye.'

'And Bjorn?'

'He hovers over her like a honeybee.'

'Collect him, and the two of you make a start on inspecting the store-house roof. Tell White Deer and Buffalo Bird Woman they can tend to the garden when ready.'

Pinch nodded, without moving. His gaze came to rest on the shelf of books while he absently played with the pipe sticking from his vest pocket.

'The roof, then?'

'My throat is parched.' Pinch wiped a hand across his mouth. 'It needs wetting first with tea.'

IN SPITE OF HIS eagerness to return to the Mandan village, he was fore-stalled by the need for repairs to the stockade buildings. When these were carried out to his satisfaction, he made several alterations to the storehouse. As an afterthought, he replaced the rusted shackle on the door. He kept the key on a thick cord which he carried in his pocket, carefully storing the spare in a drawer of the commode. Noting the diminished log pile in the woodhouse, he sent Pinch down to the river with an axe. Reconsidering, he sent Bjornson after him with a second axe. 'Else will he sleep and smoke until sunset,' he said, in a sour voice.

Feeling a new responsibility for the security of the post and its occupants, he made sure the gate was securely barred at all times. Summoning White Deer and Buffalo Bird Woman, he impressed upon them the necessity of keeping the heavy gate shut in the absence of the men. '*Fermé. Toujours*,' he said, tugging the bar for emphasis. '*Vous comprenez?*'

'*Fermé!*' Buffalo Bird Woman grinned, showing discoloured teeth as she repeated the word. She wore Pinch's straw hat, the brim secured with a bandana looped over the crown and tied under the chin. Her face, fleshy and wrinkled with laugh lines, beamed with good humour. White Deer stood beside her, her head unprotected from the sun. Her hair had been braided, and the two braids tied together with a blue ribbon. Always quiet in her demeanour, the girl seemed pale and distressed in the absence of Thibault.

He watched her walk back to the garden, her slight figure a contrast to the fat, waddling gait of her companion. *She has Buffalo Bird Woman for company*, he reflected, glad of the older woman's presence. *And soon, if Fortune wills, she may have a companion her own age.* He made a mental note to discuss the girl's future with Bjornson, the thought acting as a spur to his own desire to set out for the Mandan camp.

'Your Buffalo Bird Woman addressed me as Monsieur Bourgeois,' he remarked to Pinch. 'Can you explain to her that I am not a bourgeois—that title belongs to Thibault.'

'It is a title of respect, that is all,' said Pinch. 'She doesn't know shareholder from a canoe paddle. The brigade, when they return, will no doubt do the same. It is the title the men are used to.'

'But I am not Thibault.'

'Yet you wear his hat and coat!'

The spring weather alternated between sunshine and rain, strong winds blowing dust and dirt across the compound. When Pinch shouted that he had sighted buffalo on the horizon, the announcement came as a disruption to Boundless' busy schedule of tasks. On the brink of departure, he was further frustrated by an outbreak of distemper among the dogs. He shot three of the animals and bid Pinch keep close watch on the remainder until certain that the disease had run its course.

'Short-Tail is ready to whelp,' said Pinch, observing the swollen belly of a bitch acquired from the Hidatsa the summer before last.

On a day of light rain, he went out to the storehouse and pulled out two buffalo robes he had taken during the winter. He held each one up to the light, carefully checking for weevil damage or signs of mould. Satisfied that they remained in prime condition, he choose the better of the two, plying it between his hands. A fine specimen, he told himself. He folded and tied it with string. He then retrieved a musket he had previously set aside along with a quantity of powder and shot. Mulling over the items, he added an antler-handled knife and a stout hatchet.

He took down several boxes of beads, trinkets and buttons, and rummaged through each, stopping as he came across a necklace. The trinket consisted of glass beads, in alternating colours, threaded onto a chain above a silver, inverted rainbow. He held it up between his fingers. She will like it, he assured himself, putting the item to one side. He picked through the buttons and selected a dozen that struck him as somehow distinctive. Surveying the pile, he added a thimble and awl, and a number of coloured ribbons. He placed the items in the haversack, a quip from Theroux sounding in his head. *She who takes is already taken.*

He entered each of the gifts into the daybook—with a notation that the cost was to be deducted from his share of the profits. Returning to his quarters, he took down the new journal and the brass ink bottle together with several quills and added the items to the haversack.

'When will you leave?' asked Bjornson at supper. The cabin was almost empty. Pinch was elsewhere, and Lapointe had already departed along with Scattered Corn Woman to the Mandan village by the prairie creek. Abel remained, the blacksmith having fallen out with his Indian wife over his dalliance with another woman. Emile, the junior clerk, and Caron, the carpenter, completed the reduced company.

'Tomorrow. You will be in charge in my absence.'

'How long will you be gone?' Bjornson helped himself to another portion of fish.

He hesitated. 'I am not sure. If all goes well, a month, at least.'

At Bjornson's raised eyebrows, he added, 'If need be, send a message and I will return with all haste.' His eyes rested on White Deer as she poured water from a bucket into a cast iron pot suspended above the fire. 'And White Deer?'

Bjornson grimaced as he stared at the fish on his spoon. 'It is a time of great change for her. The new house … Monsieur Thibault …' The Swede's voice was glum.

'She is young and resilient. She will be herself again with time.'

'I hope so.' Bjornson glanced at the girl, his face miserable.

'Will you live with her?' asked Abel.

The question caused Bjornson to flush with embarrassment. 'These things must be done according to church law.'

'As you will.' Boundless cast another look at White Deer, who went about her tasks with a subdued, despondent posture. 'But do not wait overlong.' He gave a faint smile. 'On either the church or your own Swedish nature.'

That night he lay awake in Thibault's bed, a myriad of thoughts keeping him from sleep. The familiar night sounds of the post sounded differently from the unfamiliar vantage, his senses slowly adjusting to the new domicile. Eventually, he slipped into a half-dream of a pretty woman with a parasol ascending a steep climb, her dress blown back against her legs. 'This is the cargo,' a voice said as he fell asleep.

THE MORNING DAWNED BRIGHT and cool, a thin scattering of cloud promising a clear sky. Bjornson and Pinch farewelled him from the shore, shaking his hand and wishing him luck as he prepared to step into the small birch-bark. With their words of encouragement ringing in his ears, he set off, paddling strongly to take it away from the shore. He maintained a steady pace, enjoying the rhythm of the paddle and the freshening breeze. The water was calm, but he kept an eye out for floating logs or snags.

Halfway to the fork, he took off his hat, perspiring in spite of the cool breeze. Soon after, he sighted columns of smoke rising from the Mandan lodges. He slowed his pace, the optimism that had driven his paddle temporarily deflected by doubts. 'Fie!' he muttered. 'I go as a man of means, head man at the post.' Reassured of his worth, he resumed a steady stroke, the gift-laden haversack lying in the canoe. *Like a suitor of old*, he told himself.

Willing hands helped drag the canoe to shore. A cluster of Indians greeted him as he stepped out. '*Bonjour, Monsieur Bourgeois*,' one said respectfully, the salutation pleasing him and increasing his confidence. He walked up the bluff, returning greetings as he did so. Entering the village, he waved away several curious Indians who approached in the expectation of trade. Shining Hair, Wolf Tail and some other familiar faces looked up as he passed, surprised to see him.

'*Bonjour!*' he called out, stopping briefly to exchange pleasantries. They, too, addressed him as 'bourgeois'. He continued on, mulling at the speed at which Indians knew of goings-on at the post.

Continuing on past the outer lodges, he arrived at the one occupied by Jacques. Drawing aside the hide screen, he entered, calling out the Frenchman's name as he did so. He saw Jacques lounging by the fire idly conversing with another man. To his surprise, the other man was Lapointe, the latter having come by on a social call. They looked up as he entered.

'Boundless!' The grizzled Jacques beamed as he hailed him. 'You are here for the girl?'

A half-hour later, instructed in the ways of Mandan courtship by the two experienced men, he left the lodge and went in search of Meadow Bird. 'You must first approach her—to signify your intention,' advised Lapointe. 'Offer her the gifts you brought. If she accepts, you can then approach her father, Three Bears. The Mandan are strict about these things. There is a …' he hunted for the word. 'A behaviour—yes?—to follow. Remember, the girl will make up her own mind to accept or not. She may have other suitors.'

The unwelcome reminder echoed in his head as he scouted the busy plaza for the girl. Much to his exasperation, his search collected a retinue of inquisitive followers as he made his way past the fires. As he was beginning to despair of finding her, he spied where she knelt in the dust painting a staked buffalo hide. A plump, older woman knelt alongside her. She watched as Meadow Bird used a cottonwood brush, occasionally steering the girl's hand. The two were engrossed in the task. Approaching, he coughed to draw attention. The girl turned, a startled look on her face as she took in both himself and the knot of curious spectators clustered behind him.

'*Bonjour*, lassie,' he said, in his nervousness forgetting the formulaic Mandan phrase Jacques had been at pains to teach him.

The girl seemed taken aback at his presence and remained kneeling with the brush suspended in her hand. He licked his lips to say something but was forestalled by the older woman who urged the confused girl to stand up. '*Háu!*' she said.

The girl rose self-consciously to her feet. Her perplexity increased as one of the spectators called out something, the comment causing much merriment among the small crowd that had now collected.

'I have brought gifts for you.' He stepped forward to put some space between himself and the nosey onlookers. '*Quelques cadeaux*,' he said, uncertain whether she understood.

The girl's eyes widened as she comprehended the reason for his presence. She appeared nervous, twisting her mouth and fiddling with her tunic as she waited for him to speak. She seemed younger and slighter than he remembered—indeed, scarcely more than a child. Her skin was smooth and brown, a spot of ochre dye from the paintbrush on one cheek. She darted a glance at her older companion, who smiled and nodded encouragement.

The crowd had grown in size as others joined in to investigate the gathering. The onlookers began gossiping loudly among themselves in between offering advice to Meadow Bird. '*Haka'ta!*' her companion admonished, her cross looks drawing laughter.

He unslung the haversack and knelt to take out the gifts as the girl alternately looked away as if uninterested, and then returned her gaze, following his every movement.

'I hope these please you,' he said, forgetting the French in his own nervousness.

The onlookers pressed forward to see as he knelt to arrange the necklace, buttons, ribbons, and needle and thimble on a square of cloth. The girl regarded the objects, a quizzical look on her face. '*Pour toi!*' he said, gazing up at her.

Meadow Bird gave a long, appraising stare that took in his wind-blown hair, freshly shaved chin, linen shirt—soaked with nervous sweat—buckskin trousers and soiled moccasins. Some of the poise that had marked their earlier encounters seemed to return as she contemplated the gifts. She thrust her tongue in her cheek, contorting her mouth as she considered each item in turn. Someone in the crowd called out a humorous jibe that drew more laughter, but she appeared to not notice, so intent was her scrutiny. He said nothing, his eyes on her as he waited for a response.

A noise ran through the spectators as three of the young girls who normally companioned her rushed up to stand beside her, their faces alight with excitement as they laughed and whispered in her ears.

Confident now, bold even, in the presence of her companions, she bent to examine the gifts. A tiny frown puckered the corners of her mouth as she picked up a button to examine. Her action drew a gasp and murmurs from the crowd. He felt suddenly foolish, the necklace and buttons striking him as absurd trinkets, unworthy of a proposal, unworthy of a bourgeois. A gust of wind blew moisture in his face, and he glanced up at the grey, cloudy sky, suddenly doubtful of the entire enterprise.

The girl made as if to pick up the necklace and then suspended her hand, mid-motion, drawing murmurs from the onlookers. Her companions giggled and said something, but she ignored them. She put down the necklace, and then, changing her mind, picked it up again and held it against her, glancing at her companions for approval. One of the companions caught her by the arm and whispered in her ear. She turned and looked at Boundless, her gaze frank and grave. He felt he ought to say something, but his mouth had dried up, along with his brain. A hush filled the air, the spectators waiting in anticipation.

Meadow Bird stooped and, in one graceful gesture, scooped up the handful of buttons and deposited them, along with the necklace, in a hide pouch attached to her waist. The action brought ululating cries from the onlookers as her companions laughed in excitement and the older woman beamed.

Even as he struggled to understand the import of what had happened, several warriors pressed around to offer congratulations, grinning and slapping him on the back. Next moment, her companions had pushed and pulled Meadow Bird from his sight.

Back at the lodge, Jacques and Lapointe laughed as he recounted the details. 'It means she 'as to *accepter* your offer. *Félicitations, mon ami!*' Jacques grasped his hand.

'But she said nothing!'

'What do the English say? "Actions speak louder than words," yes?' said Lapointe, offering his hand.

'What happens now?' he asked.

'Now you must to ask her father for … *autorisation*—to permit,' said Jacques. 'He is a good fellow, and a respected 'unter. Bring,' he said, and pointed to the dowry gifts. Ducking under the lodge flap, he led the way outside.

The inside of her father's lodge was warm, the air fragrant with wood smoke. Meadow Bird sat among a group of women to one side of the firepit. She looked boldly at him as he entered. A thin woman with long, greying hair fussed over the girl's tunic and smoothed her hair. The woman glanced at him, and he fancied an air of expectation in her look, the notion reinforced by the knowing smiles of the women.

'*La mere,*' Jacque whispered.

'What is her name?'

'Devilish to say.' Jacques screwed up his eyes for a moment before replying. 'Stands Watching by the Creek,' he said, 'or some such.'

They were seated on a row of hide mats arranged to one side of the fire pit. Three Bears sat opposite. His face was dark and sanguine, one cheek marked with pinpricks of blue dye. His slumped and rounded shoulders seemed to belie his reputation as a clever and successful hunter.

A woman came forward bearing a long pipe decorated with a painted eagle feather and hanks of buffalo hair. Thumbing tobacco into the bowl, Three Bears proceeded to light the tobacco. After inhaling, he handed the pipe to Boundless. Accepting, Boundless lightly inhaled, suppressing the cough that invariably attended his attempts at smoking. The flap opened and a dozen or more males—ranging in age from boys to grandfathers—entered the lodge to sit cross-legged behind Three Bears. One leaned forward to speak in the latter's ear, drawing a grunt in reply. For some time, the Indians passed the pipe back and forth while regarding Boundless with impassive looks. To the side, the women made great ado over Meadow Bird, fussing over her hair and tunic and smiling at one another.

'What do we wait for?' Speaking softly, he addressed the question to Lapointe.

'You are an important man, Boundless, the bourgeois. Her father will milk the occasion all he can as it gives him great standing among the people.'

Jacques coughed. '*Washiteheresh,*' he began, addressing Three Bears as Boundless' representative. As he spoke, Three Bears listened, his face attentive but inscrutable. Boundless glanced at Meadow Bird. She sat with head bowed but appeared to be listening intently to the exchange.

Breaking off the conversation, Jacques turned to Boundless. '*Les cadeaux.*'

Unwrapping the dowry gifts, he laid them on the dirt floor in front of Three Bears. '*Pour vous, Monsieur,*' he murmured, uncertain of the protocol. The Indian grunted and picked up the musket, examining it with care as his kinfolk looked on. The powder horn and bone-handled knife were subjected to the same careful inspection, as was the buffalo robe in turn. Putting the gifts down, Three Bears looked at Boundless, his face showing neither refusal nor assent. No one spoke for what seemed, to Boundless, an eternity.

Three Bears turned and glanced at his daughter. An invisible communication seemed to pass between them. A similar communication took place between Three Bears and his wife. As if reaching a silent understanding, his wife disappeared for a moment. When she reappeared, she held in her hands a pale-coloured buffalo robe. To Boundless' surprise, she draped it across his shoulders. As if a spell had been broken, the solemn atmosphere abruptly gave way to smiles and animated speech.

Lapointe clapped him on the shoulder. 'Congratulations, my friend! You now 'ave a Mandan wife!'

He stared in surprise. 'He has agreed?'

Jacques shook his hand, a grin on his face. *'Bien sûr! C'est fait!'*

One of the women gave a shrill, ululating cry, joined immediately by the others. The hide curtain was thrust aside, and Meadow Bird's companions rushed in. Shrieking with excitement, they proceeded to drag her from the lodge.

The festive mood continued as the women came forward with dishes of corn balls, meat, dried fish and wild rice. A clay bowl of flavoured venison soup was thrust into his hands. Beside him, Jacques ate cheerfully, dipping his fingers into the soup to extract chunks of meat. Three Bears had taken out a different pipe and smoked peacefully amidst the feast. He gazed at Boundless, his eyes mild yet appraising over the pipe. He spoke in an aside to the Indian seated next to him, who chuckled in response.

Before too long, the hide drape was pushed aside, and Meadow Bird was escorted back in to cries of admiration from the women. Her face was heavily painted—her cheeks and chin dyed yellow, her brow coated with red pigment. Her black hair shone with freshly applied grease. The locks were separated into four long strands, each decorated with shells, feathers and porcupine quills. He noted with pleasure the beaded necklace around her throat. The buttons he had brought as gifts were already sewn into the front of the deer hide tunic. She stood bashfully proud for a moment as the elder women fussed and cooed over her appearance. A stout, elderly woman slowly approached and touched her face, speaking fondly in tones of great affection.

'The grandmother,' whispered Lapointe. 'A most formidable woman.'

To his mingled pleasure and embarrassment, his new bride came and knelt beside him, her gaze downcast, a tremble of excitement the only sign of nerves. He smelt the grease in her hair and felt the warmth of her closeness. He wondered if he should acknowledge her, but hesitated, aware of the Mandan's insistence on correct behaviour.

The feasting continued for the better part of an hour, Meadow Bird delicately placing morsels of food in his bowl whenever more was brought forward. Once, he attempted to reciprocate, closing her fingers around a sweetmeat. She refused the gesture, gently prying apart his fingers to place the portion back in his bowl. Only once did she look up to meet his eyes— her gaze reminding him of the wild, dark stare of a doe.

The rest of the day passed by in a blur as he and Meadow Bird were escorted around the village from lodge to lodge, the occupants pulling them inside for more food. Meadow Bird, closely attended by her coterie of companions, giggled and smiled, her girlish youth showing itself as she shrieked and ran in pretended terror from a large, bearish woman who attempted to fold a decorated hide around her shoulders. Her companions, shouting with laughter, rushed forward to rescue her.

As the long afternoon ended, the couple were led back to her father's lodge where they endured more feasting. He smoked another pipe, feeling dizzy from the effects. As it grew dark outside, a youth produced a bone flute and began to finger a thin, piping tune. The women began to sing in response, a rhythmic, repetitive melody. To murmurs of admiration, Meadow Bird stood gracefully to her feet. She lingered a moment, a shy, pleased smile on her face, as if to bask in the stares of the women. She then walked to one of the curtained beds around the walls of the lodge. She halted to glance back at him before drawing aside the hide screen.

He felt a touch on his arm. 'Go! She is waiting!' Lapointe urged him to his feet.

He got up, the buffalo robe still draped across his shoulders. He felt all eyes upon him, the mother and grandmother closely observing. Three Bears continued to puff on the pipe, his eyes also on Boundless.

'*Aller!*' hissed Jacques.

Taking a deep breath, he walked self-consciously towards the bed chamber. The fluting continued, as did the soft chants of the women. He ducked around the hide screen, glad for privacy and to escape the frank stares. Meadow Bird lay on the bed beneath a buffalo robe. Uncertain of how to proceed, he stood in place, the chants and noise from beyond the screen a distraction. She turned down one corner of the robe, her slim, naked body revealed in the flickering shadows. Her face was nervous but composed. Around her neck, she still wore the coloured necklace. He took off the buffalo robe and laid it to one side. Sitting on the edge of the bed, he tugged off his buckskin breeches. Still clad in his shirt, he joined her beneath the robe. The warmth of her body mingled with the smell of smoke and grease, and the sound of the flute.

With a murmur of disapproval, she tugged at the shirt.

'Pardon, lass.' Sitting up, he pulled the shirt over his head. Lying down, he pulled up the robe to cover his nakedness.

Neither said anything, both seeming to listen to the chants beyond the screen. Licking his dry lips, he turned to face her.

'Meadow Bird,' he said, his voice hoarse as he addressed her directly for the first time. The name drew a puckered frown. Tongue-tied, he tried to recall her Mandan name, but could not. 'Button,' he said, using the pet name he called her in his head.

'*Buu-ton!*' The name seemed to both please and amuse her.

'*Buu-ton!*' She touched a finger to her naked breast.

'Button, then, if it pleases thee.'

Another nervous silence fell during which he racked his brains for something to say. 'Boundless.' He pointed to himself.

'Bone-less.'

He laughed in relief, discharging some of the nervousness he felt. 'Close enough, lassie.'

The girl lifted the robe to better accommodate him. She tugged gently at his arm, entirely unembarrassed by her nakedness. Beyond the screen, the noise of the flute and singing had stopped. The sound of logs crackling in the fire pit came to his ears. The air was thick with wood smoke. The girl gazed at him, her face full of trembling anticipation. He touched her cheek, marvelling at its warm smoothness. She murmured something and fingered his bare arm, her eyes unreadable in the flickering light. He leaned forward to awkwardly place a kiss on her painted brow, tasting the flavour of pokeberry on his lips. *Wife*, he marvelled, the notion leaving him flummoxed. She gazed at him an expectant furrow on her brow. *Of all things!* He touched her warm belly, astonished to his soul.

FOR REASONS UNKNOWN TO him, the next day they moved out of her father's lodge and into the grandmother's house. The old woman received Meadow Bird with great affection, showering her with endearments while sparing Boundless barely a glance. Leading her granddaughter to a place by the fire, she began grooming her while clucking and murmuring.

He sat awkwardly by the fire under the curious gaze of the other occupants of the lodge. They were all female, of different ages, some nursing infants at the breast. None spoke, all studying him with the frank, unflinching stare of the Indian. He cleared his throat, at a loss how to behave in this *maison de femmes*. For distraction, he inspected the rafters and split-log walls, struck anew at the sturdy construction. The lodge seemed prosperous, numerous items of pottery, bone objects, and woven mats decorating the interior. The dressed hides screening the bedsteads were elaborately worked, some ornamented with quills and decorated with symbols. Meadow Bird and her doting grandmother seemed to have forgotten him. He got to his feet, offering his apologies. Exiting the lodge, he went in search of his companions for advice.

Over the next few days, he tried his best to fit into the life of the lodge, treading carefully to avoid giving offence, while yet drawing ireful glances from the grandmother at some accidental trespass. The old woman wielded considerable authority over the other females—issuing commands and barking instructions without hesitation. Once or twice, she caught him observing and looked at him crossly in a clear signal for him to go elsewhere. Privately, he gave her the name *'bourgeois'*, for her imperious manner and readiness to chastise all within reach of her tongue.

The sole ointment to her temper were the soothing ministrations of Meadow Bird, her granddaughter seeming to delight and enchant her. The two enjoyed a close and affectionate relationship, often seated side by side, chatting and smiling beside the fire as they completed a chore. He found that, respectful as he was to the old woman, she held him at arm's length, never addressing him directly, all the while fussing with great pride and warmth over her granddaughter.

At first confused by the many comings and goings within the lodge, he gradually identified the permanent occupants, privately giving each of the women a name linked to their physical features. Over time, he adjusted this nomenclature to accord with individual character traits, discovering the women to be as distinct and singular in this regard as their European counterparts. At least two of the women, he judged, were slaves, captured or traded from other tribes. Although dressed in the Mandan fashion, their features and bearing struck him as subtly different. Mostly well treated by the other women, they were tasked with many more duties, frequently despatched to fetch wood, wash clothes or assist with the children, all of which they did uncomplainingly. As he became more familiar with the village, he observed more of these slaves—almost always female. They seemed to him to have largely accepted their lot, adopting the manners and practices of the tribe, an observation confirmed by Jacques.

'*Oui.* They are mostly traded and will marry into the Mandan.'

'Are there many—slaves, I mean?'

'Yes. They are mostly traded from the Lakota.'

'Lakota?'

Jacques grimaced and spat in the dirt. 'Devils!' he said, without further explanation.

TO HIS SURPRISE, THE Mandan, *en famille*, were quick to laugh and enormously fond of a joke, an entire lodge at times dissolving into bouts of merriment. Indeed, as familiarity added depth to his gaze, he became aware of a rich vein of humour lurking beneath the grave, composed faces the Mandan presented to strangers. His clumsy efforts to learn the language proved a source of great amusement, the men pointing to objects and breaking into laughter at his efforts to enunciate the name. Even the children got in on the joke, pointing at a pot or mat and inventing absurd noises that drew an uproarious response from the adults as he pretended, gamely, to imitate the sound.

The women and children ate separately from the men. In the lodge, Meadow Bird served him first before eating with the other women. His attempt to coax her into sharing a meal drew a scowling glance from the eagle-eyed grandmother, the *major-domo* ever vigilant for breaches of propriety. While scrupulously attentive to his practical needs, Meadow Bird was nevertheless careful to observe tribal custom, remaining reserved and modest in her behaviour towards him while in public. At night, however, in the privacy of the bedchamber, she cast off the modesty of the day, becoming warm and pliable, and openly responsive to his caresses. Indeed, her forwardness in this manner caused him initial shock and discomfort, her disregard for propriety confounding him. Entirely comfortable with bodily functions, she seemed bemused at his own prudishness by comparison. *It is her natural way,* he reasoned. *It is I who am encumbered with false notions of modesty.*

When the mood took her, she fussed over him in front of her intimate companions, taking the opportunity to display the far greater liberality of relations available to her as wife to a *mashi*. Such liberality earned her, on occasion, the disapproval of her grandmother, the woman scolding her for some perceived breach of marital etiquette. She accepted such reprimands gracefully for the most part—although occasionally teasing the grandmother in return until the old woman burst into exasperated laughter. Her alterations in mood—between girlish high spirits and scolding maturity—frequently left him baffled and perplexed, his inexperience with the fairer sex compounding the differences of custom and tongue.

*I am a novice lover*, he conceded ruefully following a sharp reproach as he clumsily attempted to arrange the hair across her face. Once, mistaking her reluctance for playfulness, he bent to kiss her cheek only to meet with a rebuff, which he attributed to the watchful presence of the grandmother. On another occasion, he proudly addressed her as 'Ti'ka Owa' as she sat with the women, having practised the pronunciation with Jacques. The appellation drew amazed stares and, moments later, a furious response from Meadow Bird.

'*Buu-ton! Buut-on!*' She pointed angrily to herself, leaving him perplexed as to which taboo he had trespassed upon.

Pondering the matter, a jesting remark of Pinch's came back to his ears: "Tis not the tribal part that confounds but the womanly!'

His inexpert attempts to unpick the twined strands of sex and custom served only to irritate her while foundering on a rock of mutual incomprehension.

'Let be,' he chided himself. 'A castle is not built in a day.'

One morning while observing her decorate a hide with stick buffaloes, an image of the rock art chanced upon with Mose came back to him. Watching her deft hand movements, he conceited some distant, ancestral link between the primitive, unknown artisans and the Mandan, and thus Meadow Bird, and thus himself. Dwelling on the notion, he dismissed it with a sense of embarrassment, the conjuration striking him as ridiculous in its fanciful overreach. *I may as well join myself to the elephant bones!*

## *Fire!*

A S THE WEEKS PASSED and he grew more familiar with the life of the village, he looked on in amazement at the indolent behaviour of Mandan men. The women did all of the farming, food preservation, cooking, skinning, and tanning in addition to a great variety of other tasks, while the men contented themselves with hunting and male companionship. His own role seemed to be to provide meat for the occupants of the lodge—and little else. To pass the time, he joined the younger men in sporting contests, discovering the Mandan to be inveterate gamblers, willing to stake a horse or a prized knife on the outcome of a footrace or a game of chunkey. The latter contest, in particular, sometimes drew crowds of up to five hundred spectators, many from surrounding villages. The game—tossing spears at a rounded stone rolled across the grass—seemed to him unremarkable, but it attracted intense competitiveness, especially when clan loyalties were involved. On such occasions, gambling was especially profligate, some unfortunate individuals losing their entire worth on a single bet.

He became companions with two men from a neighbouring lodge—Spotted Eagle and Crooked Nose—joining them to hunt or fish. At times, they met up with hunting parties from outlying villages, the strangers regarding him with aloof curiosity. He was keenly aware that this aloofness could transfer, in an instant, to warm camaraderie or, equally, hostile suspicion—a changeability that left him ever vigilant lest some small error on his part be construed as an offence.

A month after his arrival, he received a message from Bjornson politely asking when he expected to return. After pondering the matter, he tore a page from the journal. *Before the brigade*, he wrote. He entrusted the missive to a Mandan youth, picturing Pinch's face as he received the news.

He had just eaten breakfast one morning when he was summoned by a hail from outside the lodge. Going outside, he found Jacques, Three Bears, Spotted Eagle, Crooked Nose, and Shining Hair, waiting for him along with another Indian. 'I present Buffalo Bull,' said Jacques, introducing the short, impassively-faced man whose long hair was wound up in a knot around his waist. '*Venez*,' said Jacques. 'We 'unt.'

They joined two more men waiting down by the river alongside four bullboats. Stepping gingerly into the nearest feather-light craft, he sat as still as possible while the Indians paddled skilfully upriver. They continued for two or three miles before turning into a creek and entering a densely wooded region where they pulled into shore. Abandoning the boats by the bank, they continued into the forest, walking in single file through the woods. Three Bears led the way, the others falling into the absorbed silence Indians adopted when preoccupied with hunting or travelling.

Thinking whitetail deer were the intended prey, he was surprised when the party stopped before a beaver dam situated at one end of a large pond. Following a brief discussion, Spotted Eagle and a few others set off toward the dam, striding purposefully toward the structure. Curious to observe their trapping methods, he watched as the Indians stood atop the dam, testing the soundness of the structure. Using hatchets, they began to hack at the sticks and branches that formed the roof. After some minutes of this, the structure began to break apart.

The others, meanwhile, tested the bank with their lances. Deciding on a spot, they began to stab at the earth, energetically digging through the bank to reveal a burrow or wash underneath. One man dropped flat on his belly to stick his bare arm into the wash. After less than a minute, he gave a yell of triumph and pulled forth a beaver, grasping the struggling animal by its tail. Before his companion could spear the creature, it turned viciously on its captor, raking the man's arm with its long incisors. With a shout, the Indian flung the beaver to the grass whereupon his companion promptly speared it with a lance. Undeterred by his wounds, the first Indian then plunged his other arm back into the dark water, seizing another of the creatures. The beaver was despatched in similar manner to the first.

Leaving the dead beavers in the grass, the men proceeded to a second spot along the bank, the one Indian ignoring the blood that dripped from his wound. Stopping, they proceeded in like manner, hacking furiously at the earth. As they uncovered another burrow, Boundless stepped forward. *'Moi!'* he said, dropping to his knees. Without hesitation, he plunged his arm into the cool, muddy water. Within moments, he felt the brush of fur. Grasping the beaver as it tried to wriggle from his grasp, he plucked it bodily from the water. Squirming and twisting, it tried to attack him with its teeth. He had hold of the creature's tail and used the appendage to slam the beaver to the ground where his companions swiftly impaled it. He heard a grunt of approval from Three Bears.

They returned to the village with a prize of six beaver carcasses. As they took the carcasses from the boats, Three Bears selected the one Boundless had captured and presented it to him. Grasping the beaver by the tail, he proceeded back to the lodge. He entered, proudly holding up the carcass as the women looked up.

'*Wárap!*' Meadow Bird came forward to take it from his grasp. She rubbed its glossy coat and then pulled her hand down over her hair to indicate a hat or headdress. The gesture made him laugh. She lightly touched his chest, her face smiling with pride.

TO HIS DISAPPOINTMENT, HIS new bride spent much of her time working alongside her mother or grandmother in the fields. When not farming, she was occupied with dressing hides, gathering and drying berries, or cooking or sewing, the many domestic chores leaving scant opportunity to develop deeper bonds of attachment. Occasionally, he prevailed upon her to abandon her duties to walk with him in the fresh spring pastures surrounding the village. Unused, or resistant—he was never entirely certain which—to the sociable intent of such walks, she took each one as an opportunity to collect wild herbs or search for bird eggs.

'Leave it, lassie,' he said, taking her by the hand as she bent to pick a patch of prairie turnips. To distract her, he resorted to pointing at birds and plants on the pretext of learning their Indian names. She listened critically, alternatively chiding him for mistakes or chortling with amusement at his missteps.

'And this?' He pointed at a heap of dried buffalo dung. She giggled at his thick-tongued imitation of the name, covering her mouth as she laughed.

'Then, shit it be,' he grunted—the pretended gruffness eliciting more giggles.

He stuck his fingers alongside his head. 'Buffalo!' he said, snorting and swinging his head to her considerable amusement.

'Boff-alo!' she called out. 'Boff-alo!'

'Well done, lassie.' Smiling, he touched a hand to her cheek in the Mandan manner of affection. The gesture seemed to please her, and she closed her eyes and lifted her face in preening fashion. 'Meadow Bird,' he said, fondly.

She pouted, whether in irritation or play-acting he could not tell. '*Buut-ton!*'

He laughed. 'Have it your way, then—Button!'

'*Bone-less!*' She surprised him by the use of his name.

Gently he held her mouth, shaping the sound. 'Bound-less.'

'Bone-less.'

'Aye, lassie. As you say.'

Just as often, his attempts to draw her into deeper intimacy left her confused and uncertain. "*I'll crown and deck thee all with bays. And love thee evermore,*" he teased, taking her fingers between his own.

She stared at him, her brow knitted in puzzlement. '*Watéwe'na?*'

'It is a poem. A Scottish poem.'

'*Warého'sh?*' She made the sign 'to eat,' placing her fingers to her mouth.

'No, not eat.' He sighed. 'No matter.'

'Are you content, lassie?' he asked one afternoon. They were sitting in the grass by the river in one of the rare interludes in which she was not busily engaged in work of some kind. Twining the stems of several golden-rods together he looped them around her neck. She seemed pleased with the gesture, fingering the stems with a smile. 'How will you like your new house at the post?' he wondered aloud.

She looked up. '*Nii-giguu!*' She pointed at where a hawk circled high overhead, its screeching cry faintly audible on the clear air.

'Aye. I see it.'

One particularly lush summer morning, he coaxed her away from her farming duties on the pretext of needing her services for a supposed hunt. He carried the musket while walking and made an elaborate show of scouting for game. Their perambulation eventually brought them within sight of the rock. As they came nearer the object, he motioned for her to sit amidst a patch of milkweed. Above them, the summer sky was a high blue dome threaded with sparse tendrils of cloud. The billowing grass lay empty on all sides, the wind rippling the stalks like waves upon the sea. The rock stood not a quarter-mile distant, the russet-coloured stone massive and unyielding in the strong light.

He opened the canteen and offered it. 'Drink, lassie.'

She drank thirstily, the smooth brown skin on her throat fluxing as she swallowed. She then sat contentedly, toying with a beetle she found clinging to a reed. He lay on one elbow, contemplating her as she took the beetle onto her finger and murmured to the insect. As he observed her carefully deposit it on a blade of grass, his profound curiosity with regard to aboriginality—never far from his mind, came to the fore once more. *What is the world through your eyes?* he mused, dimly recalling some long-distant conversation.

'There is a great division between us,' he said, the words at once affectionate and regretful. As if reading his thoughts, she turned her brown eyes on his, her brow puckered in a frown. She seemed to consider him for a moment before turning her head to gaze at the rock.

Plucking a blade of grass, he chewed the stem. He gestured to the rock. 'Buffalo,' he said idly.

'Boff-alo,' she repeated.

He sat upright, his heart suddenly beating faster. 'Buffalo!' He pointed directly to the great rock. 'Buffalo. *Oui?*'

She nodded, her eyes puzzled. '*Oui*. Boff-alo.'

HE JOINED SHINING HAIR and a dozen other men and youths as they prepared to chase after a group of buffalo spotted wallowing at a nearby creek. The group set out in high spirits, the expectation of fresh buffalo meat prompting laughter and jokes. He sat astride a borrowed pony, the unfamiliar sensation of riding atop a saddle consisting of a flat piece of wood covered with rawhide tempering his enthusiasm. The hard saddle rested atop a buffalo robe, the whole secured by a strip of rawhide tied around the belly. The halter consisted of plaited buffalo hair passed through the mouth of the horse, looped around the jaw and then roped around the horse's neck. Only one of the party—an older warrior, used stirrups, the wooden pieces sheathed in leather evoking amused disdain among the younger Indians. Twice, he almost tumbled to the ground, gripping the simple rope bridle so tightly the horse whinnied in protest. The Indians laughed uproariously at his clumsiness, themselves so adept at riding *sans* saddle and *sans* stirrups as to render him a novice by comparison.

He returned from the hunt determined to purchase two horses, one for Meadow Bird, and one for himself. Using Jacques as intermediary, he bargained for a mare and a gelding from Buffalo Hawk, owner of the largest herd in the village. At once, he taught Meadow Bird to ride, walking the mare around in a circle as she sat stiffly on its back. The sight of a woman riding, a first for the village, caused some consternation, the Mandan flocking around to observe while her grandmother alternately scolded and begged her to desist from the dangerous habit. But she persisted, pleasing him greatly by her determination. Soon, she was able to proceed, in halting fashion, by herself, her slow perambulations invariably shadowed by a gaggle of laughing children.

As the summer wore on, his responsibilities as bourgeois beckoned to disturb his placid existence in the village. One morning, he awoke before dawn, roused from sleep by some dream or other. Meadow Bird stirred in the crook of his arm, and he contemplated her face in the dim light. In repose, she seemed to him scarcely more than a child, her face smooth and trusting, her breathing soft and contented. He listened, eyes open to the sounds of the slumbering village. His ears picked out the whistle of a meadowlark and the distant, hooting moan of a prairie chicken. For a moment, he felt disoriented, as if this were his life, not the one that he experienced back at the stockade.

Several of the Frenchmen, he had learned, had refused to return home at the end of their contracted terms. They lived with their Indian families in the nearby villages, having deliberately abandoned their former lives and relations. In short space, they had, according to Jacques, lost their 'whiteness', forgoing the comforts of civilisation for a rudimentary existence in which they dressed, lived and spoke as Indians.

*I, too, am entered into that world of aboriginals*, he deceived himself. Briefly, the post seemed another, more demanding world. A woman's voice called from outside, the sound harsh and querulous in the half-light. Sighing at the improbability of things, he pulled his arm from under Meadow Bird's head. She stirred and moaned in protest. 'Good morning, lassie,' he said fondly.

She pulled a face and turned on her side. Laughing, he took her gently by the shoulder. 'Get up, sleepy head. It is time we returned to the post.'

He was collecting his few belongings when he heard shouts of alarm. Going outside, he saw a crowd had gathered. They gazed with great anxiety at the distance where the tinder-dry grass smouldered beneath a haze of black smoke. His concern quickly turned to alarm as he realised that the wind was blowing the fire in their direction.

As the smell of smoke grew stronger, the Mandan hurriedly prepared for a mass exodus of the village. Dozens had already gathered at the river, the women and children hastily ushered into bullboats and canoes. The younger men were driving the horse herd into the water, the frightened animals snorting and their nostrils flaring as they splashed and swam for the other shore. He pushed through the crowd of alarmed Indians, searching for Meadow Bird. He saw where she helped escort her grandmother down the bluff to the river, Meadow Bird holding one arm while her mother held the other.

He felt a gust of wind—the breeze hot against his face. The smell of smoke was now thick in the air. As he hurried towards Meadow Bird, she glanced at him, a frightened look on her face. All around them, men and women were hastening down to the water. The panicked cries of the smaller children filled the air as smoke drifted over the lodges. They were now at the water's edge, Meadow Bird calling out for one of the bullboats to draw up alongside.

Three Bears appeared, paddling furiously as he drove the birch-bark toward them. Meadow Bird assisted her grandmother into the craft as Boundless held the side. 'Get in!' he shouted above the clamour of voices. Three Bears signalled for him to climb in. He did so, feeling a hot blast of wind at his back. He snatched a paddle as Three Bears turned the boat and started to stroke for the opposite shore. At that point the river was barely a thousand yards across, and he wondered if the width was sufficient to defeat the leaping flames. Depositing the women on the shore, they turned back to fetch others across. All around the birch-bark, horses swam frantically, their eyes rolling with fear. Many of the younger Indians were also swimming across, some with infants clinging to their backs. A deafening noise of shouts and cries filled the air as the old and the infirm were carried to safety. Dogs barked and splashed into the river, only to retreat again to the bank, afraid of the deeper water.

Within the space of two hours, the entire village was relocated across the stream, the horses shaking water from their coats. The people stood gazing in horror at the conflagration that roared towards the village. Shrieks and moans went up as smoke rose above the lodges. Flames could be seen through the thick haze of dust and smoke. With a dry, cracking sound that carried across the water, a lodge caught fire, the flames engulfing it in an instant. A woman standing nearby cried out in terror as stray sparks ignited the grass nearby. He felt a hot cinder against his cheek and gripped Meadow Bird by the arm to pull her further away from the river. 'We must draw back from the smoke!' he yelled to Jacques.

As the men began to herd the people away from the river, the wind changed suddenly, a strong gust sending the smoke back upon itself. Cries of relief went up as the wind swept the choking black smoke away from the shore.

'*Through the mercy of Providence, the village was spared,*' he wrote when recording the event in the journal. '*But not before the conflagration had consumed the log palisade and burned several of the outer lodges. I paced the distance afterwards and judged the flames to have come within 200-yards of our own lodge. Indeed, the logs bear the singed evidence of the fire. In the afternoon, I and a party of Indians explored the territory around the village. The grass was scorched and blackened for miles in all directions. We came across dozens of carcasses of deer and antelope that were unable to escape the flames. The bodies were horribly burned even down to the hooves and antlers.*

*We found no buffalo carcasses, which led me to suppose the creatures were either wiser in the ways of fire or simply absent from that part of the plain where the conflagration was at its worse. The Mandan, although shaken by the narrowness of their escape, nevertheless quickly recovered their natural good spirits. Work parties began to immediately build lodges to replace those that were lost while bringing gifts of furnishings and food to the shaken survivors. The air remains full of the smell of smoke, and I have grave forebodings for the safety of the post.'*

Propelled by this fear, he hastened back to the post the next day, leaving Meadow Bird to follow on with her father and uncles as escort. The earth lay scorched and barren beneath him for the entire distance. When he at last came within sight of the stockade, he uttered a sigh of relief. It seemed unmarked, a band of green radiating out into the scorched grass showing it had escaped the flames by the narrowest of margins. 'Hup!' He kicked the pony, relief giving way to concern lest anyone had been caught out on the open grass by the fast-moving flames.

Pinch and Bjornson gave him an effusive welcome, expressing their fears that the Mandan village had been consumed by the conflagration. 'We barely 'scaped,' said Boundless, holding up a thumb and forefinger to indicate how close the village had come to calamity.

'Never have I seen such a fire,' said Bjornson, his eyes wide at the recollection. 'If was as if the last judgement was upon us.'

'He mumbled several rosaries,' said Pinch. 'Perish, if I didn't feel the urge to join in!'

Over glasses of rum punch, Boundless recounted in vivid detail the plight of the Mandan as they rushed down to the river in fear of their lives. 'The smoke was so choking I feared lest we all die of suffocation, never mind the flames.'

'And the wind shifted?'

'At the very last moment, else the village was lost.'

'A miracle,' declared Bjornson.

'A miracle wrought twice—by the evidence around the post.'

''Tis enough to convert a Turk,' agreed Pinch, his face solemn.

The next day, a distraught Lapointe showed up with harrowing tales of a burned village and numerous deaths among the inhabitants. 'We 'ad to escape our lives!' he reported in between gulps of scalding hot tea. The summer camp on the open prairie had been caught unawares by the swiftly moving fire, many of the Indians still asleep as the flames surrounded the tipis. 'We 'ad to jump, like fish, into the creek,' Lapointe recounted, his eyes recalling the horror of the scene. 'The smoke!' He drew a hand over his face, his expression telling the tale.

The smell of burnt grass lingered for days, the smouldering undergrowth threatening to burst into flame again as hot winds fanned the grass. Thus, there was general relief when a thunderstorm drenched the prairie, the rain churning the dusty compound into a quagmire before another change in the weather brought calm winds and dry, sunny days.

'We were saved through Providence,' Bjornson averred when the companions again discussed their narrow escape.

'Then why didn't your Providence prevent the fire in the first place?' objected Pinch.

Bjornson frowned, momentarily lost for an answer.

## The Great Confederation

FOUR DAYS AFTER HIS return, Meadow Bird arrived, riding the mare while her father and uncles rode alongside. As soon as she was deposited at the post, they left to return to the village, leaving her to inspect her new lodge.

'Mother Goose! So, this is the new bride?' said Pinch, gawking as Boundless proudly helped her down from the mare.

Bjornson took off his hat and held it to his chest. 'What shall I call her?'

'Ho! The artillery!' said Pinch before Boundless could reply. Buffalo Bird Woman and White Deer arrived from the garden to greet the newcomer, their faces streaked with dirt and sweat. The women looked at each other for a few moments while the men watched on.

'*Ni doosa!*' With a smile, Buffalo Bird Woman stepped forward and placed her hands on Meadow Bird's shoulders in the traditional welcome of her people.

'*Ni doosa,*' answered Meadow Bird, her eyes wide as she regarded the older woman.

'White Deer stepped forwards and repeated the welcome. '*Mihapnak,*' she said, her use of the Mandan drawing a pleased smile from Meadow Bird.

'*Mihapnak,*' she said in return.

'And all is done,' quipped Pinch.

The two women took charge of his bride as Boundless sat in the main cabin drinking tea and answering questions. He observed through the open door as they walked Meadow Bird across the yard, arms linked, to show her the married quarters. A feeling of pride coursed through him as he watched.

'What is her Indian name?' asked Bjornson, his eyes upon the girl.

'*Tik Ora*—or some such, as near as I can tell.' Boundless puffed the syllables in mimicry of the sounds taught to him by Jacques. 'It is the name by which her companions call her. But each time I repeat it she either laughs or frowns, so I am confounded as to the exact sound.'

'Their names be devilish hard to pronounce. "Meadow Bird" will do for me,' said Pinch.

It was on the tip of his tongue to tell of her pet name, "Button," but he reconsidered, keeping the endearment to himself. 'She is of an age to White Deer. I sincerely hope that they will become firm friends.'

'Of which,' Pinch gave a triumphant smile, 'Bjorn here has news of his own.'

'Indeed?'

Bjornson looked abashed as he cupped the tea cup in his big hands.

'I have taken her to wife,' he mumbled.

'So soon?' Boundless' eyes widened with astonishment.

'They lodge together in Laurent's old quarters,' said Pinch, referring to a departed clerk. 'Bjorn has not stopped grinning since you left.'

Bjorn reddened. 'He invents—as usual!'

'And does White Deer—'

'Hannah.'

'Pardon?'

'Hannah. Her name in Christ.'

Mystified, Boundless looked to Pinch for assistance.

'He dunked her in the river,' said Pinch, enjoying his surprise.

'Baptised her.' Bjornson cast a reproving look.

'And she took the name Hannah?'

'I gave it to her, to commemorate her rebirth in Christ.'

There was silence for some moments, Boundless not knowing what to say and Pinch relishing the moment.

'And she understood it—the baptism?'

Bjornson hawed and scratched his chin. 'In the French.'

Pinch guffawed in delight. ''Tis a certainty the mystery escaped her in the Indian!'

There was a noise from outside as the women returned. They seemed instantly familiar, standing in the dirt and conversing and signing with minimal difficulty.

'There stands the great confederation,' said Pinch, gazing at the scene. 'Hidatsa, Arikara, and now Mandan—to complete the pie. We be well-suited, Boundless, well-suited.'

The three watched in silence as Buffalo Bird Woman searched Meadow Bird's hair, as though for ticks. The latter maintained a modestly humble posture, accepting the grooming with bowed head.

'She will mother the girl—as she does White Deer,' predicted Pinch.

'Hannah,' corrected Bjornson.

'Hanged if I shall call her such!' Pinch glared fiercely at Bjornson, the subject evidently a bone of contention between them. 'Hanged!'

'You wish us to address her by that name?' asked Boundless

'For myself, Hannah shall be her name.' Bjornson stood up. 'It is a relief to have you safely back. But now I must feed the dogs. If I do not, they shall starve to death,' he said, with a disapproving glance at Pinch.

'The fellow is a dunce,' complained Pinch as he watched Bjornson leave. 'Hannah!' He snorted in derision. 'It is a pity he did not throw himself in the river!'

'All the same, we must respect his wish to—'

'Wish be damn'd! I have known her as White Deer these past six years—while the Swede was still making merry with the damsels of his congregation. It were good enough for Guillaume and it is good enough for me. I shall not abandon the name to appease his priestly conscience.' He took a splinter of wood and pricked the pipe bowl. 'Hanged!'

IN AN IMPERIOUS MANNER which recalled her grandmother, Meadow Bird took quick ownership of her new lodge, replacing the wool blanket on the bed with a buffalo robe and placing favoured possessions—a clay cup, a decorative deerskin, a lucky buffalo hoof, at strategic points around the cabin. The candle lanterns seemed to fascinate her, as did Thibault's barometer. Boundless tried to explain its use but gave up after several puzzled stares.

Although expecting some alteration in her behaviour away from her lodge and the gimlet scrutiny of her grandmother, he found her conduct, if anything, more Indian than when in the village. In spite of his attempts, she refused to allow him to serve himself at meals, taking such efforts as an infringement upon her prerogatives. In like manner, she firmly removed a garment from his hands as he attempted to repair a ripped seam. '*Maaru-wa shee taa*,' she scolded, tugging away the cloth.

Bored at first by the quietness of the post, she was quick to take up gardening, adopting the hoeing as her special task and assiduously uprooting weeds as soon as one appeared. She formed a deep attachment to Buffalo Bird Woman and seemed to blossom under the older woman's cheerful guidance. With Scattered Corn Woman, she was more reserved despite— or because of—both being Mandan. With White Deer , she developed a sisterly bond, the two chatting and laughing with such gusto that Bjornson was moved to remark upon the fact. 'All Hannah needed was another of her own kind, and age,' he said, as if astonished by the simple truth.

Between them, the four women took over responsibility for the cooking, mending, gardening and tanning. Indeed, so industrious were they that Boundless was forced to intervene to ensure that Pinch did his share of the work, taking the other man to task for his frequent bouts of idleness. 'The devils have taken a dislike to me,' Pinch protested as he leant against the fence to watch Buffalo Bird Woman feed the dogs.

'It is as well he is not a partner,' Boundless complained to Bjornson, 'else would his idleness soak up both our profits.'

WITH SUMMER DWINDLING, BOUNDLESS' thoughts turned to the brigade and his official assumption of the role of bourgeois. 'God forbid I should omit a single sack of beans,' he said to Lapointe as the two made an inventory of the remaining trade goods. 'Monsieur Thibault would jump into a canoe and paddle himself back!'

So many matters occupied his mind that he took to carrying a blank day book tucked into his pocket in order to write reminders as they occurred to him. *How did Thibault do it all so effortlessly?* he wondered, the multifarious tasks that required attention increasing his respect for the Frenchman.

At supper, he watched Bjornson compliment White Deer on the meal as she refilled the tea kettle. The girl smiled, clearly pleased, and appearing in much better spirits than at any time since the departure of Thibault.

'I envy that you can converse in French,' remarked Boundless. 'My Meadow Bird understands only a dozen words at best. For important matters, I must first converse with you in English. And then you—to Hannah, in French. And thus Hannah to herself in Hidatsa, and thence to Meadow Bird in Mandan. And back again! 'Tis an amazement we understand one another at all.'

'Have you not instructed her in the language?'

'I have tried. But her English be as authentic as my Mandan.'

Across the table, Pinch shifted to loosen his belly. 'What is it you would understand?'

'Why, her thoughts and feelings on matters. To bring us closer.'

"Fie! 'Tis the distance that is to be treasured.'

'Venerable Pinch is at an age where cherishment counts for naught,' said Bjornson. 'Is it not so?'

'What is intimacy but a foil of youth—a cause of endless squabbles and jealousy? Mature years bring ...' Pinch frowned for the word. 'Forbearance.'

'As much sense as your fortune cards!'

'Nay. 'Tis the right word, although I cannot explain why. It bridges both tongue and custom—being both ailment and cure.'

'As comprehensible as the double Dutch! For myself, I wish only that my Mandan were sufficient to hold a conversation.'

'You do press too hard. Your questions confuse and annoy her.'

'Whom do you speak of?'

'Meadow Bird, who else?'

Boundless frowned, nettled by the remark. 'Buffalo Bird told you this?'

'She did not need to. Such constant panning be a fester to the mind. I do believe you would harangue the buffalo itself if only it stood still long enough.'

'Sayeth Two-Tongues!'

Pinch shook his head. 'Can you not let things lie—be as they are?'

'Indeed, I think I do.'

Pinch raised an eyebrow but made no further comment.

## The Life of a Bourgeois

AS THE RETURN OF the brigade loomed, Boundless paced the yard, a look of frowning concentration on his face as he rehearsed the words of the welcoming speech. *They will measure me against Thibault.* He went over the speech with Bjornson, the Swede correcting his French while assuring him it was 'passable'.

The brigade returned on a sunny day in late September. Boundless resisted the urge to rush down to the shore with Pinch and Bjornson, nervously preferring instead a Guillaume-like adherence to the post. 'Let them come to me,' he told himself, having put on his bourgeois frock coat for the occasion.

From outside the gate, he heard shouts as the first bales were brought up from the shore. Moments later, the first group of voyageurs filed through the gates.

'*Bonjour, Monsieur!*' hailed Theroux as if not a whit surprised to observe Boundless waiting to greet him. The *pilote's* hearty greeting was repeated again and again as more of the Frenchmen entered the stockade, backs bent under the bales they carried.

Boundless took up position on the storehouse step, hands linked behind his back in the manner of Thibault, as the bales were deposited in the dirt. Lapointe, Emile, and the new junior clerk, Antoine, began the inventory as a sun-browned man clad in buckskins approached Boundless.

'Good day to you, Bourgeois,' he said, offering his hand in a firm grip. 'My name is Luc Bouchard. Monsieur Thibault has engaged me as a hunter,' he said, speaking fluent, French-accented, English. 'I understand you are partial to buffalo?' The man gave a confident grin. 'I shall endeavour to keep our bellies full all winter.'

The new post carpenter, Florent, also came up to introduce himself, solemnly addressing Boundless as 'Monsieur McLennan.'

Several other new faces gave added liveliness to the cheerful smoke and chatter of the traditional *fête de celebration*. For the occasion, Boundless again donned the overtight frock coat and took Thibault's accustomed place at the first table. Toward the end of the meal, he rose to his feet. He flexed his fingers as Theroux called for silence. Faces—some curious, others expectant—turned to him and he took a sip of rum punch. Clearing his throat, he congratulated the men on a successful return, and drew laughter by a brief reference to Pinch and his 'indefatigable enthusiasm for work.'

Folding and unfolding his hands, he finally thrust them into the pockets of his coat as he acknowledged the newest members of the brigade. He paid brief tribute to Thibault, praising his predecessor's soundness of judgement and years of leadership. The acknowledgement drew cheers and applause.

Following the pattern set by Thibault he then addressed the coming year, expressing confidence in the anticipation of a bountiful harvest of furs. At the conclusion, he sat down, gratified when the company raised their mugs in the traditional toast to '*Monsieur Bourgeois!*'

Near the conclusion of the feast, he excused himself and retired to his private room beside the hearth. Once inside the door, he listened for a few moments, filled with relief at the reception accorded his speech. He poured himself another glass of punch and then another as he sat down to read the letter Thibault had sent back in the parfleche pouch.

*April 1765*

*My dear Boundless, I trust in God that you are safe and well as are Bjornson, Pinch etc. And White Deer? Is she still at the post and content with her lot? Above all, I wonder at your own situation. Did you approach the Mandan girl—and if so, with what result? I await your letter with keen anticipation. I am once more settled in my own dear home on Rue Martin, just above the tree-lined promenade where Mathieu and I stroll on Sundays following breakfast. Mathieu, incidentally, is well and sends his fond wishes even as he transcribes this. [Hello, Boundless! M.]*

*You will note several new faces among the returnees, among them Luc Bouchard, an experienced hunter possessing what Mathieu assures me is excellent English. Antoine, the new junior clerk, also has a good grasp of the language. Florent not so much, but he has a reputation as a sterling carpenter. I trust you will find all the new recruits satisfactory. Each one has been vouched for by present members of the company. You will be pleased to learn that we realised an excellent return of over £2,000 on last spring's consignment. The details are listed on page 3 of this letter together with the disbursement of funds. You will note the subtraction, as agreed, to reimburse myself for the capital costs involved in the purchase of the company. Each expense is faithfully listed against recovery of the funds and will meet, I trust, with your approval and that of Mr Bjornson.*

*If you have questions relating to any part, please do not hesitate to inform me by return.*

*The condition and quality of the furs made a favourable impression upon buyers and assisted greatly in securing agreements with several reputable trading houses for future business. It is my intention to invite bids, one against the other, for next year's harvest. In addition, I have made representations to agents for buyers in London and Paris which I intend to turn to our advantage.*

*The price of fur remains constant and new ventures—and new rivalries—form daily. It was published last week that Quebec alone exported in excess of 100,000 pelts in the last 12 months! A remarkable number. Moreover, it was reported that a single beaver pelt fetched 13 shillings at auction in London. Competition for such reward is fierce on all fronts. 'The fray begins!' as the saying has it.*

*English merchants have established several new cooperatives in Albany and New York—all of which are anxious to secure a footing in the trade. You will remember a Mr Thomas Bannock, of prior acquaintance? He and several others have opened a small fur-trading business on Rue Saint-Paul. Thomas himself, I am given to understand, has opened a new route to the far north-west and forged several alliances among the Indian tribes resident in that vastness.*

*Every felt maker now relies heavily on carrotting to produce his hats, and parchment beaver is generally preferred to coat. There is growing discontent among the merchants at proposed licensing restrictions—said to manipulate the trade to the advantage of the Hudson Bay Company. Indeed, the glut of furs seems but to feed prices and increase the hunger for more. The clamour for beaver now extends to the Baltic countries as well as to Spain, Portugal and Germany. The English ports alone are reputed to ship in excess of hundreds of thousands of pelts and hats all over Europe. The pelts, 'tis said, go north, while the hats go south.*

*Lately there is much disquiet over the Royal Proclamation forbidding settlement of the territories west of the Appalachian Mountains. Proponents argue that the proposed law protects the Indians from rapacious settlers who would drive them from their lands, while opponents question the value of fighting the war if settlers are to be forbidden prime agricultural land. By such and such is one conflict ended and another begun. Doubtless these matters sound far away from you, as indeed they are. But the scramble for furs and the rush for profits will one day make itself felt even in your remote fastness, have no doubt.*

*The attached invoices list the goods sent by return. I trust you will find the quantity and quality to your satisfaction. I have added a dozen additional muskets and black powder as per your request. You will see, among the accompanying papers, a list of the personal supplies requested by yourself. The cost has been deducted from your returns. The supplies should prove ample, but husband the stocks carefully and trade for as much food as you can from the Indians. "To those who prepare, God sends reward." I look forward to another fine harvest next summer.*

*Until then, may God watch over you, my friend. My best to all, etc. Please convey my personal good wishes to White Deer. Tell her I think of our days together with great fondness.*

*Yours, Guillaume Thibault.*

Carefully folding the letter, he made several mental notes for a reply. He sat for a moment, gathering his thoughts. A burst of laughter sounded from beyond the door. Someone knocked and a merry voice called out, 'Come, join us, Monsieur!' He sighed to himself. Standing up, he composed himself and straightened his coat.

Stepping back out to the noisy hall, he caught the eye of Lapointe. 'Permit the men another keg of rum,' he said. He made his way through the festivities, stopping to shake hands with several of the *engagés*. He saved the youngest until last, waiting until the youth had scrambled to his feet to return his handshake. 'I hope you are not trying to keep pace with Henri,' he said in a mock-serious tone, drawing laughter from Henri himself and those around him.

'I do not dare, Monsieur!' the youth assured him.

Pleased with the success of his first *dîner de celebration*, he left the hall—again in the manner of Thibault, leaving the men to carouse in his absence.

Meadow Bird had waited up for him, sitting before the fire. For a moment, he held the fanciful notion that it was White Deer sitting there and that he was Guillaume returned from the supper.

Walking behind her, he placed his hands on her shoulders. 'I must make you a rocking chair, dearie. It will be more comfortable.' He kissed the top of her head. 'Let us go to bed.'

He carried the candle-lantern into the bedroom and hung it on the wall. Meadow Bird slipped under the covers and waited for him to join her. He sat on the bed for a while lost in thought until she reached out and tugged his hand. She snuggled to his side as he joined her beneath the robe—naked, having adopted her example. Within moments, she was asleep. He lay awake, staring into the shadows as he spectated the events of the day. Too wound up to sleep, he mentally catalogued the cares and duties of the morrow, reminding himself to order the construction of new steps for the storehouse and to oversee the conversion of an unused building into a stable for the additional Mandan ponies he had purchased. Still not sleepy, he reviewed the cargo, wondering if he ought to have requested more coloured blankets of the type favoured by the Indians. *They could perhaps fetch three pelts apiece.* Something the new junior clerk had remarked upon about the quality of the ordered cloth stuck in his mind, and he added it to his list of cares as his eyes grew heavy. *Such is the life of a bourgeois.*

THE WINTER PROVED BLESSEDLY mild, the gales of January and February muted and short-lived. The supply of pelts came thick and fast as Indians from the northern lakes joined the usual retinue of trade visits from the local tribes. To his immense satisfaction, a record ninety-eight *pièces* were sent back with the brigade. The day the voyageurs departed, he sat and poured himself a glass of wine, relieved that the year had passed.

As spring turned to summer, the horizon remained empty of buffalo, their non-appearance a major talking point among the companions. 'It is most unusual,' he agreed after Luc returned from a day spent scouring the ranges in search of the missing herds. 'The grass is plentiful, the weather mild, and yet the buffalo do not come. It is uncommon, this far into spring and summer.'

'The prairie seems strange without them, like summer lightning without thunder,' Boundless remarked to Bjornson.

'What thunder?' Pinch came to join them in the hall.

'We speak of the buffalo—or more properly, their absence.'

'The cause may be last summer's fire. The herbage may have been affected in some way. There is ash wherever you look.' Pinch thought about this for a moment. 'Mind, I have never seen so many prairie flowers as I do now. They seem to thrive, in spite of the ash.'

'Perhaps the fire drove the herds south,' said Bjornson. 'I should not miss the stinking beasts if they never returned.'

'Ha! Might as well wish for the grass to stop growing.' Pinch stretched, yawning. 'All this talk of buffaloes is making me thirsty. Is there tea on the boil?'

As the days grew longer and hotter, Meadow Bird expressed impatience to return to her village, reminding Boundless several times of his promise to do so.

'And so we will, lassie. But I have duties, first, that I must fulfil. At her sound of displeasure, he laid his hands on her shoulders. '*Iwahekosh*,' he soothed. 'Soon. I promise.'

In preparation for the visit, he took the journal begun in the Maryland woods. It was full, and he turned the pages, glancing at the entries. The last—made some six months previously—was a sketch of the interior of the bunkhouse. Placing the log back on the shelf, he took down the expensive new journal ordered from the east. Sitting down at the table, he opened the leather cover, pausing to admire the stitching. He dipped the quill, conscious of the moment. He began to write, scarcely conscious of where the quill—much less his thoughts, might take him. '*After a perilous journey across the plains, I came to this post, where I found employ as a hunter.*'

Dissatisfied with the continuance, he stared at the line. Does it conclude the first journal? he wondered. Or does it introduce the second? Is it a close or an opening?'

Fretting at the arbitrariness of things, he closed the journal and placed it in the haversack he would bring to the Mandan village, along with the quills and Thibault's ink bottle. He wrapped the latter in a shirt after first securing the top.

'There is plenty of food,' he said the next morning after breakfast. Bjorn, Pinch, and Luc sat at the table along with Abel, Florent, Emile and Antoine. 'The smokehouse is full, and more meat and fish arrive each day with the Indians. Bjorn will oversee the trades along with Emile and Antoine. Luc will hunt and help guard the post. Florent will draw up a list of repairs, and Pinch and Abel will help out where required. Questions, gentlemen?'

None being forthcoming, he dismissed them and made ready to return to his quarters. Pinch had lingered, the Bostonian clearly disgruntled at something.

'What is it Pinch? Your face is as long as my arm.'

Pinch stroked his grizzled jaw. 'It is unseemly for the bourgeois to quit the post for the length of summer. Guillaume would not do it.'

'I am not Guillaume. I leave tomorrow, and that is the end of it.'

Pinch grunted with displeasure but said nothing.

## The People

THE RETURN OF MEADOW Bird was greeted with great joy, the women flocking around to shower her with affection. She seemed transformed by the welcome, smiling and laughing as she was tugged from lodge to lodge to greet relatives and childhood friends. Boundless, meanwhile, was welcomed back as an honoured guest, strangers frequently interrupting his perambulations to drag him back to their lodges to join them in a meal. Indeed, so much food was pressed upon him that he feared he might swell up out of his breeches.

He quickly resettled into the rhythms of the village, rising with the lodge inhabitants shortly after sunrise and retiring to sleep while dusk still lightened the sky. With little to do other than hunt, he set up a spot for himself outside the lodge, sitting there for an hour or so each morning with his back against the wood frame to observe the life of the village.

It was not long before he started committing these observations to paper, placing a length of wood across his knees to support the journal. Turning to the first page, he wrote a general title: *Impressions of the Mandan: Their Habits and Customs*. Instantly regretting the choice, he drew a line through it and started again: *Life Amongst the Mandan*. He dithered for a moment, fiddling with ideas for a subhead. *Notes of a sojourn among the Indians … Impressions of a Fur Trader … Reflections of a Bourgeois*? Dissatisfied with each nomination, he simply drew a line under the original title.

Thinking how best to gather his myriad impressions into a coherent summation, he ruminated into the distance. Deciding to proceed from the general to the particular, he dipped the quill.

*The Mandan, or 'People' as they refer to themselves, are the foremost tribe amongst the upper Missouri Indians. They are closely allied to the Hidatsa, with whom they share peculiarities of dress and custom. They have a more fractious relationship with the Arikara Indians, who seem friends one moment, and enemies the next. The Mandan inhabit several large villages on both sides of the Heart River where it forms a junction with the Missouri. The chief village is set on a bluff above the forks. It is protected by a stout palisade which is, in turn, defended by a deep ditch* on the land side. The Mandan live in well-constructed earth-lodges which are sunk partly into the ground and offer excellent protection against the ravages of winter.

The houses in the 'Forks Village' number in excess of 100—more being added daily as the village is in a constant state of replenishment. I calculate the population of the village in excess of 1,000 people as each earth-lodge may house up to 15 occupants. The nearby villages are almost as large, raising the joint populations in the region to approx. 10,000. The women own the dwellings and, indeed, oversee construction of new ones. I have but lately witnessed one such 'lodge-raising' in which an old woman armed with a pointer stick gave detailed instructions to a group of men as they laid beams atop the cottonwood posts. The women appear to exercise considerable authority within the tribe, arbitrating quarrels or disputes, and presiding over the frequent ceremonies which distinguish Mandan society.

Due to its strategic location at the forks, the village is a thriving centre for trade—the extent of which would astonish those unfamiliar with Indian ingenuity in the matter of what may be called 'aboriginal commerce'. Since the widespread introduction of the horse, the traditional trading networks have expanded greatly. I have witnessed parties arrive bringing goods from as far south as the Spanish missions around San Antonio and as far east as Boston and Montreal. Delegations of Chippewa, Cree, Assiniboine and Crow are frequent visitors, bartering for corn, meat, pelts and painted hides. In exchange, they bring tobacco leaf from Virginia, oyster and clam shells from the Chesapeake, Spanish mustangs from the southern plains, and dyed cloth and decorative baskets from Mexico. Nations as far distant as the Comanche, Ute, and Apache send representatives to conduct treaty negotiations or broker trade relations.

Physically, the Mandan are strongly built and of a height similar to Europeans, it being not unusual to see individuals of six feet or more. Mandan males are inordinately proud of their long black hair which they grow to an extraordinary length. Indeed, it is a common sight to see a male walk past with his hair trailing the ground after him. The hair is often greased and separated into locks which are then adorned with shells, feathers, or porcupine quills. The men cover their torso with irregular lines of dye—whether to terrify an enemy or as a mark of distinction, I cannot tell. The Mandan love to feast and tell stories—the narrative often decorated with chants. Indeed, so fertile are they in this respect that I witnessed, one morning, a youth kill a bear using only a lance. Later that afternoon, a feast was held to celebrate the youth's fearless courage. Throughout the *feast, the epic tale of his encounter with the bear was recounted again and again—the telling embroidered with songs and dances. The passage of time from the incident to its rendition into story and song was a matter of hours—a facility of which the bard himself might be proud! The tribe are greatly skilled in the production of decorative hides and shields—the women favour geometric designs while the men prefer pictographic images. The Mandan rely on farming as a main source of food. Extensive areas of bottom land are cultivated for the production of corn, beans, wild rice and squash. The surplus is stored in earth pits for consumption in times of shortage. The women do the bulk of the work to maintain the village, whether dressing hides, cooking or tending the vegetable crops. The men scorn all domestic chores and fill their days with hunting or sporting contests, often wagering hides or goods on the outcome. Both men and women form intense bonds of friendship with others of their own sex.*

*The Mandan maintain strictly enforced relations between men and women and between adults and children. But more intimate observation shows a great deal of flux occurring within these relations. Even the natural boundaries arising from age and person are frequently crossed or ignored altogether, particularly given the great indulgence Mandan elders show to their young. On one occasion, I watched, mildly astonished, as a young girl roundly berated an older man who had committed some misconduct or other. The older man endured the chastisement with bowed head, much to the amusement of spectators.*

It did not take long for his daily jottings to draw the curiosity of the children. Each morning, a small group collected to observe him as he wrote. The group grew larger daily until an irritable Meadow Bird chased them off with yells and threats that brought shrieks of laughter from the recipients. The activity also proved of immense interest to the adult Mandan, who crowded around to witness. '*Waii-wis,*' one old woman muttered over and over again, a sour look on her face as she pointed to the ink marks.

He permitted the younger children to dip their fingers into the small brass inkwell, laughing when they inscribed their faces and bodies with the dye. 'Now I shall have to trouble Guillaume for more!' he joked and stroked his own forehead with a finger of ink.

One day, he saw a group of men, women and children clustered around something on the ground. Hearing strange, growling noises, he pushed through the spectators to see what held their interest. A man was writhing in the dirt, his body twitching and shaking in convulsive motions. A medicine man crouched and leapt around the prone figure, howling and screeching and shaking a gourd rattle. All at once, the stricken man sat up, looking around as though wondering how he came to be in such a place. He began to speak rapidly as though in a trance, ignoring the frantic shakes and rattles of the medicine man. His eyes rolled back in his head, and he gave a great yell—holding out a hand, whether in appeal or horror it was impossible to say. No sooner had he made the utterance than he fell back, lifeless, to the dirt. After some minutes several men, relatives or friends perhaps, dragged his insensible body from the scene.

Bewildered by what he had witnessed, he sought out the assistance of Jacques. The Frenchman listened to the account, shaking his head as though familiar with the details. 'His name is Ghost Wind In The Grass. He has these … spells—'ow do you say—*fits*? Three or four times a year. The Mandan regard him as—' Jacques smacked his forehead. 'By the gods, you know? They say he is a holy man.'

'He was gibbering like a madman. Whatever he said it seemed to terrify the Mandan.'

'He speaks always the same. Of some great disaster to come.'

'Of what sort?'

'Of the prairie grass burning. And the sky red with fire. And the buffalo. Pouf! Gone. Everything. Nothing left. *Rien!*'

'Gone—you mean the Mandan?'

Jacques shook his head. '*Non, mon ami*. All. Everyone.'

## The Great Buffalo Hunt

THE LONG, HOT SUMMER days passed slowly, each one bringing a glimpse into some subtle nuance of Mandan conduct or custom previously invisible to his eye. He found himself adopting Mandan habits as his own, addressing the older men as '*Itadu*,' or 'Uncle' and the women as '*Ihgash*' or 'Aunt', his mispronunciation of both provoking fits of laughter. Although still disliking the taste or smell of tobacco, he nonetheless fell into the Indian habit of quiet, reflective silence over the pipe as a prelude to speaking.

He learned from Jacques that extended ties among the Mandan were founded on clan relationships—the similarity to his native land bringing a gleam to his eyes. The Frenchman identified up to a dozen such clans, although professing uncertainty as to the exact number.

'It is *difficile*,' he said. 'And the names devilish 'ard.'

Jacques went on to reveal that the name of Meadow Bird's clan—now *his* clan—was the 'Speckled Eagle People'. Beguiled by the name, Boundless sketched a mock tartan embodying the colours of the bird. Beneath the sketch he wrote, '*Clan McSpekle!*'

On one occasion, he observed a group of visiting Arikara traders, his curiosity drawn by one member who was distinguished by a full beard. When approached, the man spoke in French—haltingly, as if it were a learned tongue rather than his native speech.

'Claude Grenier.' Jacques nodded knowingly at his inquiry into the man's history. ''Tis said he was captured by the Arikara and made a slave and then given his liberty for an act of courage.'

'And he has chosen to stay?'

'He has lost his speech to be *français*. He is now Arikara.'

'The fellow is distant—unfriendly.'

'He does not wish to be reminded of his other life, before the Arikara.'

'How did he come by his Indian name?'

'It is the Indian 'abit—to give a name that … *shows* to him—to something he do or say.'

'And do I have a name?'

Jacques grinned. '*Oui, mon ami.*'

'I do?' His eyes widened with curiosity. 'What is it?'

'In the Mandan? Too 'ard to say.'

'In English, then.'

Jacques scratched his grizzled cheek while studying the ground.

'Man who …?'

'What?' Boundless prompted.

'Make the, ah, sign. *Écrire.*' Jacques made a writing motion.

'Sign—as in ink marks?'

'*Oui!* Man Who Makes Sign.'

Pleased with the name, Boundless wandered past the lodges and into the open grass. *Man Who Makes Sign, of the Speckled Eagle Clan.*

He pondered the appellation. *I am not the same man I was in London, or even in the Maryland woods. Or am I?* It occurred to him that any faint notion he might have harboured of returning to his former life was now as impossible for him as it was for the bearded Arikara. *I could walk into the Cock and Bull and none should recognise me.* He pictured himself entering the tavern dressed in buckskin with Meadow Bird on his arm, the image so ludicrous he laughed out loud.

Three or four times a week, he accompanied Three Bears and Crooked Nose on extended hunting trips. At their urging, he tried his hand at the bow, provoking laughter with his wildly skewed attempts to bring down a deer.

'The musket for me,' he said, handing back the weapon.

He watched admiringly as Three Bears brought down a sage grouse in full flight. The Indian himself seemed proud of the feat, accepting the praise of his companions with smiling modesty while holding up the grouse with the shaft stuck through its body.

On these hunts, his companions kept a keen eye out for signs of buffalo. Accustomed to seeing the beasts everywhere to hand, even during winter, he was as baffled by their continuing absence as the Mandan themselves. *Mayhap the effects of the fire were greater than we witnessed,* he conjectured. *Or perhaps some other great natural event, of which we remain ignorant, has affected their passage.*

As June passed into July, the missing buffalo herds aroused feelings of alarm and apprehension among the normally phlegmatic Mandan. He witnessed a rare public display of anger as two men argued over a wager. He noted the incident in the journal, attributing it to the general feelings of anxiety over the absent herds.

*In spite of the presence of deer, elk, bear and other beasts in plentiful number, the buffalo remain their chief preoccupation, the continuing absence of the migratory herds a cause of great alarm. Each morning, scouts are sent out to look for the beasts—their return greeted with great expectancy. But each day, the dispiriting news is the same: the buffalo are nowhere to be seen. The reports cast a gloom over the whole village. Indeed, the prospect of a summer without the presence of the profligate buffalo is difficult even for myself to comprehend. How much worse then, for the Mandan, who prize the buffalo above all else? From their apprehension may be deduced their great material and spiritual dependence upon the animal.*

As summer reached its height, *sans bison*, the cheerfulness he had long associated with the Mandan gave way to nervousness and despondency. The men were short-tempered and abrupt, the women restrained and worried looking. Even the children seemed stilted and hushed in their play, as if unwilling to test the patience of their elders. The prevailing anxiety was reflected in numerous ceremonies, both large and small, designed to invoke the animal. He attended several, sitting cross-legged as the drumbeats sounded and the women chanted or held up painted buffalo skulls. '*Wei-aho*,' lamented one elderly singer, fluttering her fingers to indicate tears.

He was sitting in his accustomed spot when he noticed several men hurry past in the direction of the clearing. Thinking perhaps it was some news of the buffalo, he followed. He arrived in time to witness a party of horsemen enter the plaza. The newcomers were warlike in appearance, their demeanour arrogant and fierce as they sat their sweating ponies. Several had daubed their faces with paint, the streaked dyes adding to their martial appearance. Their presence aroused an air of antipathy among the watching Mandan. 'Who are they?' he asked Jacques.

'Teton!' Jacques spat the word. 'A cruel people notorious for to make war and torture their enemies.'

The strangers were dressed in loin cloths, their lower legs and upper torsos bare. Each warrior was armed with a bow and a lance. To a man, they were slight in stature, their wiry bodies baked almost black by the sun. Several of the horses towed captive slaves, their wrists bound with ropes of plaited buffalo hair. As the crowd of Mandan increased, three or four riders paraded back and forth to display the captives. To his surprise, one was a black woman, her face disfigured by scars. She fought to keep her feet as she was dragged through the dirt. The rider showed arrogant indifference to her suffering as he turned the pony and kicked its sides. The woman seemed on the point of exhaustion, her skin covered with a fine layer of dust and her bare feet bleeding and blistered. Leaping down, the rider untied the rope, jerking the woman after him with brutal disdain. He pushed roughly until she stood in a line with the other slaves.

Buffalo Hawk and White Buffalo Robe, chieftain of another Mandan village, arrived to commence the bargaining. After a smoked pipe, the trading began. The Tetons bargained loudly and disdainfully, occasionally turning to point out a particular feature of one of the captives.

When at last the Tetons left—still dragging two of the unfortunate captives—he felt an audible air of relief among the Mandan. The Tetons whooped and spurred their ponies as they rode through the palisade gates, the horses raising a cloud of dust. When he got back to the lodge, he mentioned the name of the Indians. The name drew an immediate response from Meadow Bird who stiffened, a look of hatred on her face. Her grandmother, noticing her reaction, asked the cause.

'Teton!'

A look of fright crossed the old woman's face and she muttered, casting a dire look in his direction as if he were personally to blame for the visitors.

When Lapointe and Scattered Corn Woman arrived for a visit, he mentioned to the Frenchman the disquiet aroused in the Mandan by the party of Teton Sioux.

Lapointe's eyes narrowed at mention of the name. 'Be wary of them. They be terrible cruel in war and notorious, even among Indians, for taking offence. The Sioux resent Mandan pre-eminence and attempt to assert themselves over both them and the Hidatsa. 'Tis rumoured they fought a big war some years ago and do fight it again at intervals. The Mandan give them no quarter and will rob or kill them whenever they raid into these parts—which they do now increasingly on account of the horse.'

'As may be, but they are striking fellows. And sit a horse better than I ever could, even without benefit of saddle and harness.' He chewed the jerky Lapointe had brough with him, remembering the arrogant look cast in his direction by one of the Sioux, a chieftain resplendent in a headdress of feathers and quills. The man had traded three female captives to the Mandan. The women, Ute or Shoshone, had been ill-used, each one bearing extensive marks of the lash or knife. It had seemed to him that the captives embraced the exchange, doubtless glad to have swapped the forbidding Tetons for the more peaceable Mandan.

'We may count ourselves fortunate that the Mandan stand between us and the Sioux,' continued Lapointe. 'Else would we be at hazard.'

'They do not know about the post?'

Lapointe shivered. 'No. And may the good Lord keep it that way!'

HE WAS CLEANING THE musket when he heard raised voices from outside the lodge. Going to investigate, he saw a youth race past followed by a flock of children, all shrieking at the top of their lungs. '*Mideegaadi! Mideegaadi!*'

The word leapt from mouth to mouth as a frenzy of excitement gripped the village. Meadow Bird came running back from the fields to pack pemmican and water as men, women and children rushed hither and thither. He hastened back to the lodge to pick up the musket, almost colliding with Wolf Tail as the Indian ran past with bow and arrows in hand.

Within a short time, what seemed the entire tribe had assembled in the central plaza. Many of the women carried infants in cradleboards. Others held the hands of young children, eagerly waiting for the exodus to begin. The men were mostly on horseback to track the buffalo and protect the tribe against possible enemies. Many of the horses dragged travoises loaded with lodge poles and skins, evidence that the Mandan were preparing to camp.

He decided to forgo the horse, searching instead for Meadow Bird among the hundreds of people milling around the plaza. A trilling cry went up from the warrior vanguard. In response, the throng slowly moved forward amidst the noise of barking dogs and crying children. He sighted Shining Hair and Spotted Eagle, on horseback as they rode alongside the column. The younger horsemen showed off their prowess by racing back and forth in the grass, raising clouds of dust as they did so.

To find the herd, the Mandan headed south in a long column, the mounted warriors staying pace to keep guard. By late afternoon, the tribe had travelled over four miles, the children falling quiet as heat and fatigue began to take a toll. Bothered by the hot sun, he marvelled at the fortitude of the women as, burdened by their young, they trudged along without complaint in the heat and dust. He caught sight of Meadow Bird where she walked with her mother and several companions, at one point carrying a child in her arms. As the day faded, the warriors signalled to make camp for the night. The women raised tipis as the children gathered sticks to make fire.

EARLY THE FOLLOWING MORNING, they set off again, the scouts leading them into a region of grassy bluffs punctuated by narrow defiles and gullies. Walking was arduous in the blazing sun and some of the older

Indians collapsed from heat stroke. Exhausted, the tribe made early camp by a creek, the water foul-tasting and cloudy with sediment.

On the third morning, scouts returned with reports that the buffalo were near. An air of jubilation lifted the spirits of the fatigued column. The day was hot and windy, the sun beating down fiercely on the parched grass. As he laboured in the heat, he heard sudden, eager cries from the head of the column. Straining his ears, he picked up a faint chorus of grunts and bellows carried on the wind. He hastened his steps, crossing a dusty creek bed to ascend a slope thickly carpeted with sagebrush. The rise was succeeded by another, and then another, as a loud, muttering thunder filled the air. He caught the odorous whiff of buffalo in his nostrils. To his left, the horses were being guarded by boys and youths—the hunters continuing on foot.

Surmounting a saddle-back ridge, he caught his breath. The prairie below was dotted with thousands of buffaloes. The sight brought ecstatic cries from the Mandan.

The hunters leaned on their lances as a respected hunter named Red Buffalo Cow stepped forward. Holding a stick, he pointed to a prominent nearby bluff and spoke commandingly restraining some of the younger men who were impatient to fall upon the grazing herd. The entire tribe then dispersed into several groups, each seemingly with a separate task. Signalling to the hunters, Boundless among them, Red Buffalo Cow led the way to the bluffs, keeping to a path that took them through the buffalo herd.

They followed a slope to the top of a rise, where the ground levelled out for a short distance before suddenly falling away—the sheer drop invisible until one was almost upon it. Proceeding to the edge, Boundless leaned over, peering down to a dry creek bed which he estimated to be at least fifty feet below. He kicked a stone over the side, watching as it fell without hindrance before bouncing off the cone-shaped rocks that littered the stony ground below the ridge.

Groups of women and children began to construct a fence of brushwood barricades that formed a line leading up to the rise. They then took up position behind the barricade. A group of hunters, draped in animal skins, meanwhile advanced on the grazing buffalo, picking out a large group foraging northwest of the bluff. Positioned behind the brushworks, he watched as the hunters spread out in a line behind the animals.

Expecting them to charge and stampede the buffalo, he was surprised to see, instead, the Indians set fire to the dry grass. As the smoke from the fires drifted over the herd, the Indians set up a great noise of shouting and banging of shields. The buffalo responded by slowly retreating towards the line of brushworks. The pursuing hunters drew closer, and the buffalo broke into a trot, beginning to panic from the noise and drifting smoke. As they approached the brushworks, the concealed women and children sprang from cover, shaking blankets and emitting hideous shrieks. The cleverness of the stratagem became instantly apparent as the animals wheeled away to seek escape up the side of the bluff.

Observing the scene with a mixture of anticipation and suspense, he watched as the Mandan herded the panicked herd towards the concealed drop, the scene obscured by clouds of dust and the drifting smoke of the fires.

'In their fright, the buffaloes milled in confusion before retreating up the slope,' he wrote later, describing the scene.

> The Mandan harried them with the most piercing shrieks while shaking blankets and banging hide shields so as to instil blind panic. Beset on all sides, the buffaloes lumbered up the ridge in a dense mass, unsuspecting of the peril that awaited. Finally, as if sensing the danger, the vanguard attempted to stop, but were swept onwards by the crush of buffaloes at their heels. Within the space of minutes, the entire herd of in excess of a thousand creatures had careened to their death amidst roars and bellows of terror. As the smoke and dust settled, I ascended the ridge, holding my breath as to what sight would greet my eyes. I came upon a scene ghastly to behold. Far below where we stood a great mass of buffalo lay strewn along the ravine bed. Many were already dead from the plunge, but others were still alive, as we could clearly see from our vantage atop the ridge. A terrible noise, as of lamentation, filled the air as those not killed outright by the fall bellowed and kicked helplessly, their backs broken on the sharp rocks or their limbs crushed beneath the weight of bodies. The piles of dead and dying buffaloes stood twenty feet deep in places, the topmost animals kicking and grunting piteously as they tried to stand upon the bodies of their dead companions. The women and children, who had retreated to the ravine for this purpose, now rushed forwards to commence butchering the stricken animals. Such was the abundance that the women selected only the fattest cows, clambering over the panting mounds to hack into the living flesh. I never before witnessed such unrestrained delight—a joy equalled only by the fervour and excitement with which they celebrated the slaughter at a joyous feast that continued long into the night.

The carnage extended for hundreds of feet along the foot of the bluffs, the jumbled mass of carcasses emitting unearthly sounds as surviving buffalo slowly suffocated under the press of bodies. The women filled basket after basket with meat—returning to the carcasses to remove the head, horns, tail and hooves. While they worked, the youths and children set up tipis and collected wood for a feast as the Indians set up a temporary camp to take full advantage of the harvest.

The butchery continued for three days, the women working tirelessly to skin and dismember the carcasses while others dried and smoked the meat. Flocks of buzzards circled above the gorge, waiting their turn to feast on the slaughter. At night, the men lit fires and patrolled the site to drive off the bears, wolves and wild cats that gathered in great numbers, drawn by the overpowering stench of blood and flesh.

Such was the tonnage of death that over a third of the buffalo remained unharvested when, on the fourth day, the warriors at last gave the command to depart. The travoises, each one heavily laden with meat or robes, carried the spoils back to the village. Those carcasses the Mandan left untouched were abandoned to rot amidst the suffocating heat and swarming black-flies. Buzzards alighted to feast on the bloody remains, the scavengers soon joined by wild cats that crept out of the rocks to feast. '*It was,*' Boundless recorded, '*the greatest slaughter I ever saw.*'

IT TOOK WEEKS FOR the great harvest to be processed—the clothes of the women clotted with blood and grease as the buffalo were rendered into the life of the tribe. Astonished at the multitude of uses to which every part of the animal was put, Boundless wandered among the fires collecting examples to write into his journal.

*Meat not immediately eaten is dried into jerky or pemmican. The rich deposits of fat are cooked into tallow to become soap. Bones cracked to extract the marrow or pounded to a fine, chalky powder for adding to pemmican or fashioned into farming and fleshing tools. Glue is extracted from the hooves. The woolly hair is used to stuff pillows or twisted into strands to make cord. The tendons are made into bow strings or thread for sewing. The skulls are boiled and painted for ceremonial use—the brains having been preserved for tanning. The horns are fashioned into cups, ladles, or headdresses. The softened hides are turned into bedding, breechclouts, robes, tunics and shirts. The rawhide is turned to moccasins, drums, shields, rattles and pouches. The tails form switches, fly brushes or decorations for shields and lodges. Drinking vessels are made from the stomach, and children's playthings from left-over bone and hide. So pervasive is the smell of drying meat and the stink of hides stretched on willow hoops that the air is heavy with the stench. Piles of dried dung, brought back by the small children, stand inside every lodge for addition to the fire. From morning until night nothing exists but is touched upon in some form by the buffalo. The cup I drink from, the meat I eat, the hide I sleep under, and the bone I use to pick my teeth are all farmed from the creature. Their clothes and food, their customs, the daily work and the preparations for winter, all are governed by their great dependence on the beast. 'Tis small wonder the Mandan venerate it as a god.*

He deliberated over the last sentence, half-poised to strike it out with the quill before letting it stand. *For they cannot live apart from the buffalo,* he reasoned. *The beast is their totem and their sacrifice, all at once.*

Amidst the songs and dances, a multitude of rituals and observances further impressed upon him the deep and reverent hold of the buffalo upon the lives of the people. On one occasion, he followed as a painted buffalo skull was carried ceremonially from lodge to lodge. The procession was attended by a file of chanting warriors and flute-playing women as sage grass and tobacco were burned in the plaza. Anxious to understand the ritual, he plied Meadow Bird with questions—his expanded store of words supplemented by gestures and grunts. She, however, proved a reluctant, if not outright contrary guide, taking umbrage at the questions until refusing to answer, her face scrunched in disapproval.

*The reverence in which the buffalo is held is something so natural to her as to be unremarkable. Indeed, my poor questions on the subject serve only to irritate and annoy. For the Mandan—as, undoubtedly also for the plains Indian tribes as a whole—the return of the buffalo is a matter of life or death, feast or famine. The people are as reliant on the buffalo as is the wolf or the bear. Nay, more so, inasmuch as the creature provides bodily and spiritual sustenance to the tribe, the great herds being both commissary and sacrament. Indeed, so enormous is the dependence that one wonders if, without the buffalo, the Indian might not perish altogether from the earth.*

TWO WEEKS AFTER THE great hunt, he noticed Meadow Bird conducting herself with unusual contentment. She laughed and hummed frequently and seemed the object of more than usual affection from the other women. Resorting to sign, he attempted to discern the reason for her happiness. Pointing to his face, he put on a gladsome expression. Meadow Bird looked on, giving no sign she understood.

'You are happy?' He touched her mouth, curving her lips upwards, an attempt which drew an instant frown as she pulled her head away. Exasperated, he took her by the shoulders. 'What is it?' he asked. 'What is the matter?'

A burst of laughter came from children playing outside the lodge. Meadow Bird took his chin between her fingers while regarding him with an intense expression. '*Wii-tah!*'

He stared, a perplexed look on his face.

She grasped his hand. '*Wii-tah!*'

'What?' he said, baffled. 'Wee-toh?'

'*Aiiee!*' Muttering in annoyance, she pressed his hand against her belly. 'Boff-a-loe!' she said. 'Boff-a-loe!'

## 27

## Deerskin Bundles

THE SNOW CAME EARLY, falling thick and fast throughout October. He was once again immersed in supervision of the post and the management of trades. Throughout the winter, he kept a vigilant eye on Meadow Bird—his over-protective efforts frequently rebuffed with an irritable *'hii!'* as she continued her chores, seemingly unhindered by the child she was carrying. She made plain her desire to return to her people for the birth and he assured her they would—making plans to leave the following spring, as soon as the brigade had departed. He kept an anxious eye on food stocks as the snow continued to accumulate. But Luc assured him there were plenty of buffalo wandering the plains. 'The snow is deep, but the air is mild,' he said.

The pelts continued to stack up in the storehouse as trading parties arrived throughout the winter. He had put into place a new business strategy of encouraging the Indians to visit the fort early and often, deliberately spreading tales of how recent delegations had stripped him of his most valuable trade goods. The strategy was rewarded by ever-increasing returns in the form of the glossy winter beaver prized by Guillaume. Twice a week, he sat down with Lapointe to review the accounts, taking satisfaction in the accumulation of pelts while keeping a sharp eye on the exchange of goods.

'One beaver pelt for a brass kettle?' He raised an eyebrow at Antoine.

The junior clerk blushed. 'Pardon, *Monsieur*. But it was a large pelt, or I would have insisted on two.'

'*Bien*. Better to err on the side of generosity. The Indians will remember such things.'

Antoine bowed his head. '*Merci, Monsieur.*'

In January, an experienced middle-aged voyageur named Pierre Desmarais collapsed and died suddenly from a heart attack in the midst of pulling on snowshoes. His unsettled comrades ascribed the unexpected death to the arduous strains of their profession.

'This was to be his last voyage before retirement to a farm outside Laval,' observed Theroux after they had interred the body in the same plot of grass that contained Quoi.

Boundless presided over the interment, reading aloud a passage from the Psalms:

*'As for man, his days are as grass: as a flower of the field, so he flourisheth.*

*For the wind passeth over it, and it is gone; and the place thereof shall know it no more.*

*But the mercy of the Lord is from everlasting to everlasting.'*

As he finished the men shovelled earth and snow over the corpse. He gazed around at the bleak landscape, the verse echoing in his head.

'Where did we bury Quoi?' he asked Pinch, the makeshift cross once again a victim of the weather.

'There.' Pinch gestured to a spot in the snow. 'Or over there, mayhap.'

Following the service, at the request of the dead man's comrades, he penned a letter to Desmarais' widow.

'But I hardly knew the fellow,' he complained to Bjornson.

'But you are the bourgeois. It is your duty.'

'Surely, she would rather hear from his comrades?'

'And so she shall, in time. But a letter from the bourgeois will help in her grief.'

As a result, he sat down and penned a letter in which he praised her husband's indefatigable spirits and pointed out the esteem in which he was held by his comrades.

''Tis somewhat of a fraud,' he confessed to Pinch as he entrusted the letter to the dead man's nearest companion.

''Tis all a fraud! Why, the sod upon which we stand is a fraud—as is this post and the heavens above.'

'Then why bother with anything at all?'

Pinch noisily cleared his throat but did not answer.

A few days later, Boundless passed by the burial spot. The only indication of the interment was the wooden cross, coated with snow and ice. A few feet away stood the new cross he had ordered to mark the approximate site of Quoi's resting place. *They lie there, together, neighbours who never met in life*, he reflected, *joint tenants of the same patch of grass*. Wind gusted against his face, and he pulled the hat more securely on his head. *As am I, who walk above*, he pondered, sobered by the thought.

IN SPITE OF HIS responsibilities and his preoccupation with Meadow Bird's health, he still found time for his nightly digestive with Bjornson. As usual, the Swede proved an original conversationalist, whatever the topic. But in contrast to Pinch, who took unalloyed pleasure in all things Indian, the Swede's granitic Lutheranism remained a point of contention whenever conversation wandered toward aboriginal beliefs and customs.

'Too sparing of the rod,' Bjornson opined on the Mandan habit of indulging young children.

'Too great a liberality!' The Swede frowned as a young Arikara maiden exchanged a frank caress with a besotted youth.

'Sinful and blasphemous!' he declared in no uncertain terms when told of a Hidatsa ceremony honouring the buffalo.

Boundless let out an exasperated breath. 'I see that Hannah has not softened you with regard to Indian ways.'

'I say only as I believe.'

'I hear from Pinch that you read to Hannah each night. He claims it is only a matter of time before she is able to repeat scripture word for word.'

Bjornson gave a rare smile. 'She likes the stories when I explain them. Genesis is her favourite. She says it reminds her of the stories of her people.'

Boundless thought about the remark later while lying next to the sleeping Meadow Bird. A passing wolf or coyote evoked a sudden chorus of howls from the dogs, and he listened until they fell silent. A cold draught blew in from under the door, and he pulled the buffalo robe up over his neck. He imagined Meadow Bird listening to the tales of Lot and Abraham and hearing in them the stories of her ancestors. Bemused by the notion, he drifted into sleep even as the rock pictographs across the Alleghenies came to mind—the stick patriarchs glimmering in the ancient stone.

IN SPRING, SHORTLY AFTER they returned to her village, Meadow Bird gave birth to twin sons, the births an occasion of great rejoicing among the occupants of the lodge. Peering down at the two infants, swathed in soft deerskin, he marvelled at the smallness of the tiny fingers that gripped his own. Meadow Bird beamed with joy, her brow glistening with sweat as she held them to her breast. Her mother and grandmother fussed over her, the latter leaving him in no doubt that he should remove himself from the vicinity.

'I am chased out,' he grumbled to Jacques, taking refugee with his father-in-law, who smoked phlegmatically, remaining aloof from what Jacques described as 'woman business'. Taking the Frenchman's advice that he should adopt the same posture, he went on a hunt with Spotted Eagle, bringing down a bull buffalo in honour of his sons.

'You are buffalo people, people of the buffalo,' he murmured as they slept in a wooden cradle covered with hide. He smoothed his finger gently over their warm brows. 'You are of the Speckled Eagle clan, beholden to no one, with neither sooty tenements nor bewigged peacocks to hinder you, only grass and sky and the freedom to live as you please. Hush,' he soothed as they cried out in sleep. 'One to venture, one to stay, and both to prosper at the end of day.'

'What names will you give them?' asked Jacques.

'Prospect,' he said, 'and Claim.'

Jacques looked nonplussed. 'English names?'

'Scottish. Old family names.'

'They will 'ave Indian names as well?'

He laughed, pleased at the notion. 'Aye. Whatever Meadow Bird decides.'

The duality of this New World extension to himself continued to please him throughout the days that followed as he amused himself by conceiting identities for his offspring. 'Mandan-McLennan', 'Highland-Prairie', and 'Scots-Indian' passed thought his mind until the resolute core of his nature rebelled at such hybridity. *They are but one thing: free-born sons of Boundless McLennan.*

THE FREQUENT CEREMONIES HE witnessed deepened his impressions of the Mandan as a highly religious people, governed from birth to death by ritual and belief. A remark of Theroux's—that the Mandan were a 'priestly tribe'—came back to him and he concluded that the Frenchman was right in his perception. *Indeed, I am among the most faithful people I have ever known* he wrote. That their faith was based on kinship with the natural world only increased his respect.

*Customs and Beliefs of the Mandan.*
*The people show a great fondness for the ritual ceremonies which govern the customary life of the tribe to an extraordinary extent. Not a day passes but some ceremony or other is taking place, either in the plaza or within the confines of the 'temple'—a decorative lodge set apart from the others and the sole purpose of which seems to be as a tabernacle for ceremonial purposes. The Mandan make no effort to exclude me from the many ceremonies, indeed seeming to welcome my attendance. One rite in particular stands out, if only for the great importance ascribed to it by the people. Extending over four days, the event features three dancers—the figures accorded especial veneration by the audience. The three are joined by others impersonating various incarnations of the natural world. I am able to distinguish representations of bears, wolves, snakes, beaver, birds,*

*buffalo and even the elements. I am told by a Frenchman long resident in the village that one dancer is the embodiment of a prairie thunderstorm while yet another represents either the sun setting or the moon rising, he was uncertain which. Holy women join with the dancers, who are accompanied by chants and the beating of turtle drums—the latter objects of particular reverence. I felt myself swept up in the fervour, much as I had been during the great buffalo dance. It is not uncommon to witness several dances or rituals within a single day—the seeming intent being to invoke or summon back the buffalo. In the long twilight following supper, the men beat drums and chant while dancers wearing painted robes whirl and step in imitation of the beast.*

*A sense of what might be characterised as Christian fellowship, at its deepest and most meaningful, pervades the entire tribe for the duration of the ceremonies. In this, as in many other respects, I am struck by the astonishing generosity of the people. Rather than hide or conceal the sacred mysteries (for such, they surely are) they are at all times eager to explain and share them, the spirit of brotherhood extending to include all who witness the rituals. I freely confess I was entirely ignorant of the extent and depth of what can only be termed religious feeling among the Indians. If the Mandan are any indication, then this impulse is as strong and striking among Indians, perhaps more so, than among Europeans in general. The indivisibility of belief and worship among the Mandan and the actions of their daily lives cannot help but make a deep and permanent impression upon the observer.*

*Within families or clans, certain objects—a buffalo girdle, an animal skull, or willow hoop—acquire great significance and are, I believe, passed between the generations. These objects, gathered into a 'sacred bundle', are considered of greatest importance to the wellbeing of the family— somewhat in the manner of the tutelary gods of the ancient Romans. Whether the Mandan believe the objects are imbued with magical powers, or whether they are held in esteem by virtue of antiquity or some other cause I cannot tell. Perhaps the bundles serve as family keepsakes or heirlooms. They are treated with the greatest respect, and the passing ceremony is considered of utmost significance and attended with feasting and singing. Such rituals testify to the deep spiritual beliefs of the Mandan and the place such beliefs occupy in the day-to-day life of the tribe. Crops and animals, particularly the buffalo, are also considered sacred—each pertaining to its own spirit; although, whether the multitude of spirits are united by a single figure or presiding deity I cannot tell.*

In an attempt to clarify the matter, he pointed to the fire one day. *'Dieu?'* he asked, drawing looks of such astonishment that he mumbled an apology for his foolishness and hastily vacated the lodge.

HE WOKE UP EARLY, lying under the robe while listening to the sounds of the village as it came to life. Meadow Bird slept beside him, the infants asleep in a wicker cradle next to the bed. The other occupants of the lodge were stirring as he opened the lodge flap and stepped out into the semi-darkness. The sun was rising in a haze of pink cloud as he made his way down to the river.

He came back to find the village humming with activity. He ate a breakfast of dried squirrel and roasted beaver tail. After eating, he stood outside the lodge, a buffalo robe around his shoulders against an unseasonal chill in the air. A flight of ducks chattered overhead. He watched them fly into the distance, his mind preoccupied with he knew not what. A party of men assembled for a hunt and a group of women set off for the fields. Still wearing the buffalo robe, he went for a walk in the prairie grass, nodding to several friends as he made his way to the gate. He stood for a time in the long grass, his mind full of thoughts. A party of hunters, led by Wolf Tail, rode up and he stood aside to let them pass, declining the invitation to join them.

He headed back into the village, meeting Meadow Bird as she returned from the fields. She carried the twins in a cradleboard strapped to her back. In her arms, she clutched a willow basket full of corn. He watched as she laughed and gossiped with her companions, stopping to allow them to coo and fuss over the babies. A smile lit up her face as she saw him. *'Mihapnak!'* she called out, her voice full of good humour.

*'Mee-hop-mok,'* he answered, hands stretched out to take the willow basket. She allowed him to take it, her face shining with pride as her companions looked on.

'We must return to the post,' he said, making up his mind on the instant. *'Demain.* Tomorrow.' He swept out a hand in the direction of the stockade. Amidst the merriment of her companions, she gave an imperceptible nod, her demeanour clouding with a reticence that he now recognised as sorrow.

## 28

## *Teton!*

THEY WERE WELCOMED BACK by Pinch and Bjornson, the former having spotted Boundless from the rampart where he had gone to smoke. He now came down to peer at the infants, who had awakened and began to cry. He exclaimed at seeing not one but two swaddled babes.

'A deuce, by God!'

'*Félicitations, Papa Bourgeois!*' Bjornson clasped his hand in a vigorous shake.

They heard shrieks of joy as Buffalo Bird Woman, White Deer and Scattered Corn Woman arrived to fuss over Meadow Bird and admire the babies. White Deer lifted one of the infants, cradling it to her breast. As she did so, she exchanged a glance with Bjornson.

Pinch nudged the Swede. 'Go on,' he jollied.

Bjornson rubbed his head, a look of bashful pride upon his face. 'Boundless, I … Hannah, that is—'

'Verily, verily, the angel has spoke!'

Bjornson scowled as Boundless looked on, baffled.

'Tongue-tied at the trumpet!' teased Pinch.

'What in Heaven's name are you gibbering about?' demanded a perplexed Boundless.

'Me? Why nothing at all. Him?' Pinch shook his head in pretended innocence before breaking into a grin. 'Boundless, shake hands with Father Bjornson.'

It took a moment for the quip to sink in. 'Is it true?' Boundless stared at Bjornson for confirmation.

In spite of his annoyance with Pinch, Bjornson gave a sheepish smile. 'Praise be to God, it is true. Hannah is with child. She found out just a week ago.'

'Well-a-day! I see you have been busy in my absence.' He grasped Bjornson's hand, smiling at the Swede's abashed pride.

Following their walk that night, the two stood by the fire in Boundless' quarters, having opened a bottle of wine to toast the news. United in paternal pride, they stood over the wicker cradle, watching the two infants sleep swaddled in sheepskin. Reaching down, Boundless took one of the miniature hands in his own, marvelling anew at the fragility and soft warmth of the flesh.

'Two bairns—and another on the way. We are raising our own tribe, Bjorn.'

'We bear a heavy responsibility for their welfare.'

Boundless smiled. 'Are you talking about their bellies or their souls?'

'Surely, you will raise them in the true faith?'

Gently, Boundless untangled the tiny hand from his finger. 'They are half-Indian, remember. And as deserving of Mandan grace as any other.'

As Bjornson opened his mouth to protest, Boundless laid a hand on the Swede's shoulder. 'They are unwritten pages, Bjorn. Let them author their own destiny. Come, another glass.'

Shortly after the turn of the year, word was received from the Mandan that Three Bears had taken ill and was not expected to survive the winter. Immediately, Boundless made plans for a quick visit to the forks, arranging for Buffalo Bird and White Deer, now a mother herself, to look after the children in their absence.

'We should be gone no more than two or three days,' he told Bjornson. 'If her father is not recovered, I shall leave her there and return by myself.'

They set out the next morning. In spite of the snow, the day was bright and sunny, and he hoped the weather would hold. Meadow Bird waited on the pony, swaddled in a buffalo robe against the cold air. Behind the pony was a travois bearing gifts for her family. With a few final instructions for Lapointe, Boundless set off at a walk, Meadow Bird riding just behind.

They had progressed no more than half the journey when they sighted a band of Indians in the distance. The Indians halted as they became aware of Boundless, appearing to consult with one another. His hopes that they might prove friendly and thus leave himself and Meadow Bird unmolested vanished as the unknown Indians suddenly broke trail and headed towards them. He shaded his eyes, trying to ascertain some detail that might identify the riders.

'*Nadouessioux!*'

He turned at the exclamation from Meadow Bird. 'Sioux? Are you certain?'

'*Nadouessioux!*' She had turned pale, her eyes wide as they fixed on the approaching Indians, their horses throwing up plumes of snow.

He pulled the musket from its sleeve, cocking the weapon. The Indians were now close. To his alarm, he saw that they were painted for war, their faces daubed with streaks of coloured dye. The riders reined to a halt in a spray of snow, their hardy ponies snorting and panting in the cold air. The party gave no sign of recognition or greeting. They were mostly bareheaded, save for the leader, who wore a feathered headdress. Fresh scalps hung from some of the lances. He saw Meadow Bird stiffen as she caught sight of the trophies.

'*Doosha!*' He held up his palm.

The Indians made no response, their expressions hostile beneath the daubs of paint. The ponies neighed and snuffled, a haze of frosty vapour issuing from their nostrils.

'*Tokiya la hwo?*' The Indian in the headdress addressed Boundless, his voice harsh and threatening. At that moment, Boundless recognised him as the Teton who had traded captives to the Mandan. The man's eyes were cruel and piercing, his eyes glittering with arrogance. '*Tokiya la hwo!*'

'What does he say?'

Meadow Bird whispered a reply, her posture a mixture of fear and defiance under the fierce gaze of the chieftain.

Unable to fathom her words, Boundless pointed in the direction of the Mandan village. '*Numakaki!*' he said, hoping to draw on their brief, prior acquaintance. The Teton gave a derisive snort that drew harsh laughter from his companions. Shifting his eyes to the direction from which they had come, the chieftain pointed his lance at the tracks in the snow. '*Tuktetanhan yau hwo?*'

'Arikara,' answered Boundless, hoping that the Sioux and Arikara were still on friendly terms.

The chieftain barked a command and one of the warriors climbed down from his pony. The buck's face was entirely covered in blue paint, his long hair twisted into plaits. Boundless tensed as the warrior prodded the bundles secured to the travois. He kept his eyes fastened on the Teton chieftain who returned his gaze, his eyes fierce and contemptuous.

'*Shíca!*' The dismounted Indian called out in a mocking voice as he hoisted an elk hide—brought as a gift for Three Bears—on the tip of the lance. He held it up for a moment before flicking it into the snow. Boundless sat unmoved, his eyes fixed on the chieftain.

The Teton chief pointed his feathered lance at Meadow Bird.

'*Wayanka!*'

The word brought jeers and laughter from his comrades. Boundless tightened his grip on the musket. The chieftain spoke again—gesturing to the ponies in a manner that drew more laughter from his companions. His eyes, cruel and scornful, flicked back to Boundless. He seemed to consider for a moment, his gaze taking in the tracks in the snow. His companions edged forward, their faces eager for the kill.

'*Hii!*' The chieftain held up a hand. The others hesitated, clearly reluctant to give up the prize. With a sharp command, the chieftain jerked the rope bridle and abruptly broke off the encounter. One of the young bucks, clad in buckskin and wearing a scalp fastened to his shirt, lingered, his face full of aggression. Uttering a piercing whoop, he shook his lance in defiance. Then, wheeling his pony, he set off after his companions in a cloud of snow.

Boundless watched their departure through narrowed eyes, itching to put a musket ball through the mocking chieftain.

'Button?' He turned to assure himself that she was safe. 'They are gone,' he said. He felt her tremble as he touched her thigh. 'It is alright, lassie. They shall not bother us again.'

She made no answer, nor gave any sign of having heard. Her eyes, full of hatred, were trained on the retreating Indians.

'It's alright,' he said again, trying to soothe her as he dismounted to pick up the elk skin from the snow. He shook powder from the hide and looked up at her. She nodded, her face pale—from distress, or anger, he could not tell which.

They hurried on toward the Mandan encampment, anxious lest the Tetons change their mind and return. *They judged us poor pickings, no doubt*, he told himself, wondering why the Tetons had not slaughtered them out of hand. *Mayhap the chieftain recognised myself or Meadow Bird.* His anger rose as he recalled the Teton's mocking voice and scornful glance. *That was Indian hair*, he reflected, seeing again the bloody scalps matted with blood. He turned to look at Meadow Bird who sat trembling atop the pony, her face drawn with emotion. *Mayhap I shall meet the fellow again, on more equal terms,* he told himself, the notion doing little to assuage his anger.

As soon as they arrived at the village, they told of the encounter. Immediately, a war party was despatched to pursue the raiders. Jacques approached, holding the bridle as Boundless dismounted. 'They will kill them if they catch them. They raided a Hidatsa village two days since.' He spat into the snow. 'Teton dogs!'

To Meadow Bird's relief, her father had made a partial recovery from his illness. She held his hand, tears in her eyes as he reassured her. He asked questions, his voice indicating his anxiety at the brush with the Tetons.

Later that afternoon, Boundless heard the sounds of the returning war party. A single glance at their disappointed faces was sufficient to reveal that they had failed to find the raiders. Returning to the warmth of the lodge, he adjusted the robe around Meadow Bird's shoulders, noting that her complexion had not lost its paleness.

'Let us go to bed.'

She clung to him under the robe as he held her, his mind recalling the chieftain's keen glance at the way they had come.

Upon his return to the post, he recounted the incident to his alarmed companions. 'Whether they are still in the area or not, I do not know. he said. 'But they seemed anxious to know from which direction I came. I suspect that they may be trying to discover our whereabouts.'

'Do they think we have horses worth stealing?' asked Pinch.

'Mayhap. Although more likely they are after goods and pelts.'

'Or scalps,' put in Bjornson, his voice grave.

'If they intend mischief, then doubtless they will seek to surprise us—if the Mandan do not discover them first. In the meantime, pass the word that no one leaves the post without my permission.'

'They would not dare attack us,' said Pinch. 'Our numbers are too strong.'

'Nevertheless, stay vigilant. And send an armed guard to watch over the men when they cut wood.'

THE AIR OF WATCHFULNESS continued until spring and the departure of the brigade, Lapointe with them. 'I must visit my dear wife,' said the clerk, without a trace of irony.

'What about your—Scattered Corn Woman?'

'She will go back to her village until I return.'

He mentioned the incident to Pinch, who shrugged. 'So it is for many of the men. A wife and family here, another there.'

'It must be a strain on the conscience.'

Pinch blinked in surprise. 'Only if you think it so.'

The canoes had hardly departed when news arrived of a pitched battle between the Mandan and a party of Tetons intent on stealing horses. The Sioux had been driven off but were believed to be still lurking somewhere west of the post. Each day the Mandan sent out war parties in search of the enemy, who remained elusive and threatening.

All was quiet at the post until a Mandan war party arrived with news that fresh tracks had been sighted nearby. With warnings to stay alert for danger, the Mandan party set off in pursuit.

When Luc returned from a hunt, he reported fresh Indian sign near the post. 'They know where we are,' he said. 'I do believe the devils have been watching us.'

'Keep your weapons close and ensure that the gate is shut and barred at all times,' warned Boundless.

He deliberated about sending word to the Mandan, but reasoned they were already in search of the raiders. The apprehension of the occupants increased as the steady stream of trade parties abruptly ceased. For several days, not a single visitor approached the post. The unusual cessation heightened nerves further, and he took to patrolling inside the stockade armed with the musket. He posted Bjornson, Luc, Abel, Florent, Emile, Antoine and Pinch as sentries, each man taking a turn around the clock.

'Fire the musket at the slightest alarm,' he ordered.

A tense few days followed. The melt water was rapidly drying and the prairie becoming firm and dry underfoot. *Good ground for horses,* he worried, training the glass on the distance.

An air of imminent danger—fancied or real—seemed to hang above the prairie grass, the tall reeds swishing with every gust of wind. A suspicion that they were, as Luc suggested, being watched, caused Boundless to remain up in the bastion for the better part of the morning. As he prepared to descend the ladder, he took one last, sweeping surveillance. A movement caught his eye, and he trained the glass on the spot. For long moments, he saw nothing. Then he glimpsed a brown form wriggling through the reeds. He kept his eyes fixed on the spot, but whatever he glimpsed had vanished, and he saw only the waving reeds. *Perhaps I imagined it,* he told himself.

After first discussing the matter with Pinch and Bjornson, he took the women out into the yard and instructed them in the loading and shooting of both musket and pistol. Meadow Bird, already familiar with the former, shrieked in delight when she sent a rawhide shield spinning to the dust. She proved the better shot of the three, both White Deer and Buffalo Bird Woman failing to strike the target after repeated attempts.

'No matter,' joked Pinch. 'The noise alone will suffice.'

In the event of a breach in the post defences, he instructed Pinch and Luc to fall back to the hall along with Emile and Antoine while he, Abel, Bjornson and Florent would take up position in the storeroom.

'We will be able to cover the entire yard and catch them in a crossfire. If they come, it will be at first light,' he warned.

'You speak as if it is a certainty that they will come,' objected Bjornson. 'God willing, they have left or been chased off already.'

'It depends,' said Pinch.

'On what?'

'On how many horses or scalps they have taken—or not taken.' Pinch lifted a hand to touch Bjornson's blond, unkempt hair. 'There be a prize to delight a Sioux maiden!'

Shocked, Bjornson pushed the hand away. 'Look to your own hair!'

THE DAYS GREW WARMER and longer, the additional light gentling the fearful caution that had gripped the post. *This cannot go on much longer*, reflected Boundless. *Either they will attack or flee before the Mandan catch them.* As the days passed, the occupants began to relax their vigilance, the warm air and mild breezes encouraging a sense of peacefulness and benevolence. He permitted the two clerks to visit an Arikara village upriver from the stockade, the clerks taking a canoe full of goods as an incentive for increased trade relations.

Thus, the assault, when it came, caught them by surprise. Shortly after dawn, he was awoken by the crack of a musket. Rushing outside in the grey light, he saw Bjornson up in the bastion. The Swede pointed urgently over the stockade fence before raising the musket to fire a second shot.

'They tried to open the gate!' Bjornson's face was white with shock as Boundless scrambled up the ladder to join him.

'How many?' he asked as Pinch and Luc arrived, their faces still dazed with sleep. A few minutes later, Abel joined them, the blacksmith hurriedly doing up his shirt. To Boundless' surprise, the blacksmith clutched a large hammer in his hand.

'My musket!' he said at Boundless' questioning look.

Meadow Bird, White Deer and Buffalo Bird emerged from their houses, frightened expressions on their faces.

'Go to the cabin and bar the door!' he pointed at the hall. The women hurried to comply as a series of hooting calls came from the grass. Boundless directed Pinch, Luc and the two clerks to the other bastion, urging them to pay attention to the rear wall of the stockade.

'If they overwhelm us, then retreat to your prepared positions,' he ordered.

'Can you see the devils?' Abel asked Bjornson, both men straining to see in the semi-darkness.

'It is too dark,' Bjornson said. 'But they know we are awake and ready for them.'

There followed an anxious quarter hour as the sun rose and spread light over the prairie. Boundless and Bjornson loaded the muskets, taking three apiece and priming the weapons before setting them against the stockade wall in readiness.

'There!'

Bjornson pointed at where a group of Indians and their ponies were gathered in the grass. How long they had been there in the dawn darkness, Boundless had no idea. But they made no attempt to conceal themselves as they finished a cold breakfast, unhurriedly making water or checking their mounts as they waited for full light. 'I count twenty-six. No, thirty,' he said, dismayed at the number.

'They are shameless devils,' said Bjornson as one Indian squatted to relieve himself. 'They care not to shit in plain view.'

'They know they have lost the surprise. The question is whether they will risk an open attack.'

The Indians mounted their horses and appeared to be in discussion, pointing their lances at the stockade as they argued among themselves. One trotted forward, halting almost within range of the muskets. He stared up at the defenders and pointed his lance towards them in silent threat. He then turned and rode slowly back to his comrades as if defying the watchful men to shoot.

'What are they doing?' Bjornson's voice was strained.

The question was answered almost immediately as the Indians ended their discussion. Half the party broke off and headed around the fort while the others spread out into a line facing the stockade. Boundless heard a shout from Luc in the second bastion. The hunter gestured toward the river.

'They will attack from behind as well,' he said, glad for the presence of the hunter, who was an excellent shot.

He peered through the spyglass at the Indians. One wore a feathered headdress. A shock ran through him as he recognised the cruel features.

'There is the brute who accosted myself and Meadow Bird!' He pointed to the figure, who seemed to be issuing commands. Two of the Tetons turned their ponies and spurred off into the grass.

'What in God's name is happening?' asked Bjornson. 'Are they sent to fetch more of the devils?'

'They are scouts. They are fearful the Mandan will hear the noise of the muskets and fall upon them.'

'Then let us hold them and pray that the Mandan ride to our rescue.'

The Teton war party trotted forward, maintaining an approximate line. Advancing to within three hundred yards, they suddenly whipped the sturdy ponies into a gallop as fierce whoops rent the air.

'Pick your targets! Hold fire until I give the command!'

The Indians milled beneath the stockade, letting fly with arrows as they uttered fearsome cries to unnerve the defenders.

'Fire!' shouted Boundless.

The three defenders opened fire as dust and smoke obscured the air. Through the haze, he saw two of the Indians spring onto the backs of their horses to throw loops of plaited hair onto the pointed ends of the stakes. The strategy became instantly clear as the Indians used the ropes to scramble up the stockade fence.

Already, one savage had reached the top. With a yell of triumph, the warrior jumped down inside the compound.

'They are inside!' Bjornson turned and fired down into the yard as another Indian joined the first, having scrambled over the side wall in like manner. Shrieking with bloodlust, several more Indians attempted to surmount the stockade as the defenders poured a volley of musket fire on their heads.

Searching through the drifting white smoke, Boundless looked for the Teton chieftain. He heard Abel shout out a warning as an Indian scrambled up the ladder to the bastion, a knife between his teeth. Before Boundless could react, Abel stepped forward and dashed out the man's brains with the hammer.

He heard a commotion from the yard and saw, to his horror, two Indians rush towards the hall where the women and infants had sought refuge. The Indians attacked the door with hatchets while uttering frenzied cries. Other Indians were now in the yard, making for the ramparts to access the bastions and slaughter the defenders.

'Retreat!' he hollered, thankful to see that Luc, Pinch and the two clerks had already abandoned the other bastion and were advancing across the compound towards the hall.

Six Indians were now inside the stockade. Some rushed at Pinch and his companions as they attempted to reach the hall, while others attempted to open the gates to admit their comrades. Boundless half-climbed, half-jumped down the ramparts to the ground. Seeing him, two of the Indians abandoned their attack on the stockade gates and raced towards him with murderous cries. He shot the nearer one and reversed the musket, gripping it like a club to receive the charge of the second. The Indian stopped suddenly abandoning the charge to feint and threaten with a hatchet. His painted face resembled a terrifying mask as he darted and menaced with the weapon. A shot rang out and the Indian groaned and slumped to the ground. Boundless turned to see Luc reloading, the hunter's face grim amidst the noise and confusion.

More Sioux were scrambling over the stockade fence, and he shouted a warning to Bjornson and Abel to retreat to the storehouse. 'Now!' He pointed urgently. Across the yard, the door to the hall opened as Luc and the others rushed inside, barely ahead of a group of Indians.

'Boundless!' Bjornson stood beside the open door of the storehouse, urgently summoning him.

Ahead, another Indian yelled in triumph as he rushed up the storehouse steps. Abel waited with his hammer, smashing the Indian's skull before he could stab with his lance.

Boundless raced up the steps as arrows thudded into the logs, Bjornson pulling the door shut behind him.

'There are too many!' the Swede shouted, his voice hoarse.

'Upstairs!' ordered Boundless.

From the second-floor window, they looked out over the yard. Several bodies lay in the dust. The Indians appeared to be regrouping, preparing to attack both fortified positions.

'We can hold out here and catch them in the crossfire,' Boundless reassured his desperate companions. 'They cannot bear many more losses.'

'You are the best shot, Boundless. You fire while we reload.' Bjornson handed him a musket. Abel was already reloading another. Cries of fury came from the yard as Luc and the others opened fire from the hall, dropping two Indians. Boundless killed a third as the Indians rushed to seek cover. He looked out over the deserted compound, counting six bodies lying in the dirt.

'Where have they gone to?' asked Bjornson, handing Boundless a reloaded musket.

'The are using the buildings as cover.' Boundless fired as he saw a head poke out from around the forge. A moment later, a shot came from across the yard, and he heard a cry of pain. *Thank God for Luc.*

For the next few minutes, there was silence, and he imagined the Indians creeping up on both positions. He risked leaning out the window to see if he could spot any movement.

In the lull from the musket fire, he heard sudden cries of alarm from beyond the stockade fence. The cries were mingled with shrieks of fury. The Indians inside the stockade heard the commotion as well, and stopped their attack, looking with concern at the ramparts. Abruptly abandoning the fight, they rushed back to the rampart steps to fight the new enemy.

The door to the hall opened and Luc stepped out, firing as the Indians scrambled back over the palisade.

Bjornson, his eyes red-rimmed with exhaustion, croaked out a cry of relief. 'It is the Mandan, surely! They are arrived!'

'Follow me!' Boundless shouted, rushing for the stairs.

Luc, Pinch and Florent were already up on the ramparts, firing over the wall. Hastening up the ladder, Boundless looked down at where Indian fought Indian, the dust and confusion making it difficult to distinguish friend from foe.

'Hold fire!' he commanded, afraid of shooting a Mandan. After several minutes of a fierce, hand-to-hand contest, the Tetons broke off the engagement and leapt onto their horses. Next moment they raced off into the grass, chased by the triumphant Mandan.

'Run, you dogs!' Pinch turned to his companions, his face jubilant. 'It's over! They're fled—with their tails between their legs!'

Only a handful of Sioux escaped the wrathful Mandan as they fled through the long prairie grass. The remainder had been killed or taken captive. Among the latter, he recognised the Teton chieftain.

The Indian fixed him a look of dull hatred as he sat slumped against the stockade wall, one arm dangling uselessly from its socket. The victorious Mandan trussed the captives with rawhide thongs while heaping taunts and blows on the defeated foe.

'What will happen to them?' asked Bjornson as the elated Mandan began to take the scalps of the dead Sioux.

'Tortured for a certainty. When death comes, it will be a mercy.'

He was on his way across the yard to speak to Shining Hair when he was halted by an agonised shriek. Turning, he was shocked to see Meadow Bird standing over the Teton chief, a skinning knife clutched in her hand. The Indian cried out in shock and pain as blood flowed from his stabbed eye socket. The jubilant Mandan ululated in triumph, shaking their weapons in approval.

'Good Lord, she has smote the savage!' Bjornson stared in horror.

The Teton lay groaning in the dust. A vengeful Meadow Bird stood over him, a look of burning hatred on her face. Striding towards her, Boundless took the knife from her hand. She seemed not to recognise him as she limply surrendered the weapon.

'Go inside, lassie. See to the bairns.' Gently, he steered her towards the cabin. She submitted without resistance, her shoulders slouched, her breathing shallow. The Teton was moaning, the gouged eyeball stringing from the bloody socket and sticking to his cheek.

Luc came up beside him. 'It was no less than he deserved, *mon ami*,' he said. 'Think what he might have done to us had they prevailed.'

The Mandan prepared to depart, the still-wet scalps of their Teton enemies hanging from their lances. The chieftain could barely stand, his ashen face hideous with blood. At a barked command from Spotted Eagle, the exultant Mandan set off, the defeated Tetons struggling to keep their feet as they were dragged behind the ponies by stout tethers.

'I do not envy their fate.' Bjornson watched the party leave, a sober look on his face.

'They would have done as much to us, and more,' said Pinch, repeating the words of Luc.

'The devils came within a hair of slaughtering us.' Bjornson was breathing heavily, close to exhaustion now that the battle was done.

Boundless stared at the closed door of the cabin. 'Within a hair,' he repeated, his mind fixed on the image of Meadow Bird standing over the fallen savage, her eyes wild, the vengeful knife raised aloft.

## 29

## *A Habitant of Grass*

A DECADE'S EXPERIENCE WITH THE harsh prairie winters, together with the careful husbandry of the Indian women, had transformed the post in the years following Guillaume's departure. The compound had been extended by the removal of a former munitions hut. Meadow Bird had promptly claimed the additional space for the garden, planting extra rows of corn, peas, potatoes, cabbages, rutabagas, onions, beans, beets and carrots. In the north-east corner, the women had dug an underground storage pit, lining it with grass and hides. Each summer, as a result, substantial quantities of corn and vegetables were dried and stored for the winter. The measures had greatly increased the food supply and largely eliminated the belly-pinching of previous winters.

Taking inspiration from the Mandan earth lodges, he had thickened the layers of sod covering the roofs of the living quarters, significantly adding to the warmth of each building. The division of labour, made possible by the industrious women, ensured that although autumn was still a month away, the smokehouse was full, the woodpile stocked, and the cabin walls freshly chinked with moss and clay. And grazing freely outside the post, a small herd of six Indian ponies cropped the summer grass.

Standing atop the rampart, Boundless surveyed the stockade, proud of what he saw. *Guillaume would be pleased.* He pictured the Frenchman pacing the yard, brow furrowed as he found fault with this split step or that badly hung door, while raising a finger to point out some imperfection in the roof.

A shout came from below where the four boys—Bjornson's and his own—bickered with each other, their shrill voices raised in accusation. Bjornson *père* passed by carrying a bucket of slops to the dog pen. Putting down the bucket, he admonished the elder of his sons, Anders, ordering the boy to follow him to the pen. *He walks like his father*, he thought, amused as he watched the chastened son trail Bjornson across the yard.

He shifted his gaze to the garden. Meadow Bird was on her knees nursing the plants on which she lavished so much care—her indisputable skills responsible for the fine crop produced the year before. White Deer worked alongside her, the two chatting happily as they weeded. Buffalo Bird

Woman sat in the shade, fanning herself while watching. Every now and then she raised a finger—how like Guillaume!—to point to some missed weed or plant.

Following the attack on the stockade three years previously, a peace treaty had been negotiated between the Mandan and the Tetons. The treaty, along with the resumption of trade between the warring tribes, had ushered in a period of mutual prosperity, the *Pax Mandana* cementing the sovereignty of the tribe over the region. 'We be sitting pretty,' Pinch had commented on more than one occasion, the protective Mandan embrace extending to the post and its occupants.

However, the reflection did little to cheer Boundless or to dispel the feeling of restlessness that niggled at his contentment, despite the fine summer morning. He sat down with his back against the log wall, folding his legs Indian fashion to accommodate the narrow rampart. Adjusting his position to put himself in the shade, he pulled Guillaume's letter from his pocket, rereading the missive for the third time since the previous autumn.

*Montreal, April 1769*

*My dear Boundless! A thousand felicitations to you and yours. May this letter find you as contented and secure as a dormouse in its burrow. I write with Mathieu by my side, industriously translating my thoughts as soon as quill touches paper. He sends his fondest wishes for your continued health and prosperity. In his spare time, he consents to teach me English—which tongue I grasp no better than the Chippewa! Here, all is flurry and purpose. The fur market booms as never before. Last year's cargo, in its entirety, was purchased by a Mr Hamilton on behalf of the famed London House. Even as I write, it sails on the high seas, bound for England. You will find an index of pelts and prices on the following pages—one which I trust will meet with your expectations. I am pleased to report that the cargo of 6,200 skins fetched the sum of £3285/10d. An excellent return and one which bodes well for the future. Each one-third share amounts to £1095, three pence and three farthings. I have reissued promissory notes for yourself and Mr Bjornson in the cumulative, and respective, amounts of £5,400, ten shillings and five pence. I keep the notes as securely protected as my own.*

*The Mr Hamilton I mentioned was most persuasive in importuning first refusal on next year's return. He is an agreeable fellow, pleasant in all respects, and I have given him assurances that he shall be given first inspection—with a bid to follow, he all but assures. His eagerness is matched throughout the city. Not a ship sails but is laden with furs of every quality and description. Beaver hats, both felt and wool, are everywhere the rage, with new markets, including Germany, Spain and Portugal, clamouring for more. Indeed, the harvest of pelts is so great that a Mr Robinson, a thoroughly knowledgeable Scottish clerk with whom I am acquainted, has privately expressed fears of an exhaustion in the supply. As evidence, he confides that the returns at the York Factory have fallen from an annual yield of 35,000 pelts to under 15,000 average in the last few years.*

*In the way of these things, the decline in supply has caused an answering increase in demand. Beaver which fetch an average of 12 shillings a skin in Montreal are resold in London for as much as seventeen shillings per pelt—an altogether astonishing price. In consequence, the fur companies are scrambling to find fresh supplies. Houses which hitherto restricted their activities to the East push out north and west in an attempt to find new and untapped riches. We have recently witnessed a great influx of your countrymen into the city, where they have taken over much of the French trade. The English companies are, for the moment, confined to Albany and New York but are reported to have great ambitions to expand. In particular, the Hudson's Bay continues to grow in wealth and influence. In its arrogance, it dismisses the 'Montreal pedlars' as it seeks to monopolise the supply.*

*As always, relations with the Indians are indispensable for access to the most valuable pelts. With the suspension of licenses, the trade is now unregulated, and much villainy occurs as a consequence. Bribery and corruption flourish as rival companies contest with one another for preferment among the tribes. "Each to his own malfeasance," as the saying goes. Whiskey and rum are shamelessly provided in return for pelts. The Indians express fears at the resulting spread of brutality and destitution—whole villages being impoverished through the desire for whisky. But the authorities turn a conveniently blind eye—so long as the profits continue to flow.*

*It is rumoured that the Province of Quebec may soon receive the powers of self-government from the Crown. But if rumour were coin, then would Quebec be equipped with its own mint! "If you wish to live happily, live hidden," as the adage has it. Meanwhile, the Colonial Assemblies continue to rail against the English Parliament over the question of taxation. 'Tis said the people brace for the imposition of fresh duties on tea, glass and paper—expected at any day. The new duties will, surely, cause much unhappiness and add to the growing calls for an embargo on imported goods in response.*

*You will be pleased to note that I was able to secure a grammar primer for the boys, as requested. In addition, I have despatched a supply of quills together with a quantity of powdered ink. You will find, also, a fine wool shawl for White Deer, a gift from Mme Thibault. Assure Pinch that his private stock of tobacco is included, along with a firkin of whisky and another of rum. See that he does not despatch both within the week! Mr Bjornson's requests are also included. If I may be permitted a tattle of private gossip … Whilst dining with a visiting clergyman from the Delaware Colony, I happened to mention the name Bjornson. The fellow racked his brains for a moment before recalling a great scandal among the Lutherans of that district. Thereafter, he plied me with questions over the whereabouts and circumstances of our Mr Bjornson. I smoothed over the question by assuring the fellow that the name was a common one among Swedish persons and that our own companion was a man of the most sterling character and reputation.*

*I mention the incident only to illustrate how astonishingly compact relations between the Colonies have become. The bird of rumour, 'tis said, hops from branch to branch! In other news, a most unfortunate incident was related in the newspaper whereby a young man of singular promise as a musician was struck on the head and killed by a falling chimney pot whilst walking along St Catherine Street. The mind trembles at such a contiguity—of the instant, pedestrian, and pot! And finally, White Deer, is she well? I remain anxious for her well-being and would welcome news by return. It remains to add—'*

His reading was interrupted by the sound of someone climbing the ladder to the rampart. The head of Pinch appeared above the platform. 'What ails?' The older man hauled himself onto the rampart, breathing heavily from the climb. His hair, now entirely grey, poked out from beneath a beaver cap sewn for him by Buffalo Bird Woman.

Boundless folded the letter and tucked it back into his pocket. 'I was thinking it is time to replace some of these logs.'

Pinch made a sour face. ''Twill be a chore. Can't it wait until the brigade returns?'

A shriek came from below where a squabble had erupted between Claim and Prospect. The twins began to fight, punching and kicking each other as they rolled in the dirt. Meadow Bird hurried to intervene, upbraiding the pair in Mandan. The two cast dire looks at each other as she scolded both while slapping the dust from their shirts.

He watched the boys trudge across the yard, keeping a distance between them. 'The rascals scrap at the drop of a hat.'

'They are fine boys—Bjorn's too.' Pinch sat down, dangling his legs over the rampart. 'Blasted flies!' He flapped at the air.

Buffalo Bird Woman had risen from her chair to jab at some roots with the sharpened deer bone she preferred to a hoe. Pinch watched her for some moments. 'Her ankle slows her down not a whit,' he said, pride in his voice.

Boundless blinked as the same fly that had pestered Pinch returned to buzz about his face. 'I am for a scout,' he said, making up his mind.

'Why bother? The day is half-done.'

'Then half yet remains.'

Resisting the pleas of the boys to join him, he saddled his favourite horse—Jack, a mustang purchased from Spotted Eagle—and left the stockade, telling himself that he intended to scout for game.

THE DAY WAS SULTRY, the prairie grass leaning first one way and then the next under a fitful breeze. Butterflies flew up at his approach, and his old friend, the prairie squirrel, rustled from sight amid the reeds. In the distance, a herd of antelope fed in the grass, their tails flicking. He allowed the horse its head, feeling lazy and disinclined.

Just over an hour after setting out, the great rock—the unrealised purpose of his expedition—rose up on the horizon.

Dismounting in its shade, he turned the mustang loose to graze. The sky overhead was clear, the afternoon heat fierce.

'What ails?' Pinch's question came back to tease as he sat against the stone and fanned himself with his hat. Hearing a distant rumble of thunder, he glanced up at the blue sky, concerned lest he be caught in the open by a sudden storm. He willed himself to return to the post, but a strange lethargy had taken hold of his limbs, and he lingered despite his concern, feeling at ease in the deep shade. The somnolent air hung heavily over the plain as another, fainter rumble sounded in the distance.

*Meadow Bird will fret*, he admonished himself. But still he lingered. He yawned, the mood of lassitude tightening its grip. Leaning back against the cool granite, he stared into the distance, preoccupied with he knew not what. He slid down to lie on his back in the grass. A remark in Guillaume's letter returned to niggle at his thoughts. A solitary white cloud drifted overhead, and he conceited he could fly up and rest along its length as it floated high above the grass. He laid a hand against the stone, drawing solace from its hard, unyielding mass. For a moment, he imagined that it rose and fell beneath his touch, as if respiring, before recognising it as the pulse of his own heart. Feeling drowsy beyond repair, he closed his eyes.

He awoke a short time later, something he had dreamt, or imagined, teasing his thoughts. He looked up at the towering rock wall and the fathomless sky. *What would it be like, to stand up there—on the height of the rock?* He clambered to his feet and tracked backwards out into the grass. Sunlight reflected off the granite, dazzling his eyes as he stood there, gazing up at the rock. The wind gusted and the grass rippled in lush, sibilant waves. High overhead, the cloud-flecked sky resembled an upended bowl, its vastness perfect fellow to the limitless, billowing grasslands.

'Good Lord!' he breathed, his mind suddenly ablaze with a marvellous conceit that held him rooted to the spot. He licked his lips, his mouth dry as the immensity of the thought, dream, delusion—he scarcely could put name to it—swept over him. He stood transfixed as the massive stone shimmered in the cloud-blown light. It was only when he felt repeated drops of rain that he came to himself and turned to look for the horse.

OVER THE NEXT FEW days, he alternated between elation and despondency, enthusiasm and dejection, as the fantastical conceit, by turns entranced and bedevilled his mind. *It would take a hundred years, and a tribe of masons*, he told himself, thrusting aside the absurd fancy. But still it lingered in his thoughts, the audacious seed—planted in the shade of the rock—arching and blossoming as it took root in every crevice of his soul.

His grimacing introspections did not escape the notice of Pinch, who studied him, a quizzical look on his face. 'What the devil perplexes you? Has the sun boiled your brains? For you seem spry as a lark one instant and grizzled as a wolf the next.'

'The brigade will return soon. I must ensure we are prepared to receive it.'

'What more could readiness call for?' Pinch turned to the passing Bjornson. 'How now, Bjorn! Are we ship-shape?' The question drew a blank look by return. 'His muteness doth testify more eloquently than words!'

'I shall not debate you today, Pinch. Have you fetched water, as I asked?'

For distraction, he embarked on a whirlwind of *doing*—edging and smoothing a cut log to refill a gap in the canoe shed and vigorously digging up a long-neglected stump in one corner of the stockade. Suddenly indefatigable in his energy, he earned the ire of Meadow Bird by taking the children up on his shoulders and parading up and down the compound after their bedtime, the boys squealing with delight as they whipped the 'horsey'. Their mother remonstrated with frowns and scolding remarks that eventually gave way to resignation and then laughter.

When a summer storm drenched the prairie, raising puddles in the dust of the yard, he sat at the table, the journal open before him. '*I have stumbled upon a grand project,*' he wrote, '*one that has been before me these past ten years but until now invisible to my eyes. It yet remains a phantasy, an impossible speculation, yet it has seized me with a sureness and urgency I cannot explain. It is the sort of mighty purpose, that one pursues in hopes of impressing oneself upon the curiosity of the world. As it is, I am like a parched soul thirsty for water or, better, like a man who stares at a mirage and wonders if it may be real. I try to put it from my thoughts, but each attempt merely redoubles its potent grip upon my senses.*'

Struggling to find purchase on the audacious scheme, he drew sketches on spare scraps of paper, willing the quill to reveal what his mind could not yet fully grasp.

'In summer. *Minaki,*' he said, showing the buffalo sketches to Meadow Bird. 'And, here, in snow. *Ma'pi.*'

Her gaze turned to the frayed collar of his shirt. 'Old!' she said and plucked at the worn fabric.

THE ASTOUNDING CONCEIT CONTINUED to consume his thoughts as July passed into August. He made frequent visits to the rock, finding inspiration as well as contentment in its presence. Bjornson and Pinch, both more than happy to remain at the post, watched as he rode off through the grass yet again.

'Pound to a snuff he heads for that rock,' said Pinch, lazily fanning himself with his hat. 'He sees something in it, don't you know?'

Bjornson snorted. 'It is in his head, not the rock!'

'Same thing, by Harry!' Pinch smoked on the notion, as struck by it as if he had turned over a nugget of ore.

## 30

## A Shaping Hand

THE BRIGADE RETURNED WITH the news that one of the more experienced voyageurs had drowned in a section of rapids. 'We never recovered his body,' reported Theroux.

The loss of their comrade cast a pall over the welcoming dinner, the customary reels and jigs suspended out of respect for the dead man. After several sombre toasts, the *chanteur* launched into a long and lachrymose ballad that left several of the brigade in tears.

Retiring to his quarters as soon as custom allowed, Boundless sat down to read Guillaume's letter with a distracted mind, his normal anticipation soured by the loss of the valuable *engagé*.

*Montreal, April 1770*

*'Since my last letter, the uncertainty in the Colonies has grown worse. Unrest in the streets of Boston is now a daily occurrence as feeling grows against England. The contagion—if that is the word, has spread to Quebec, also. We have our own factions busily agitating for this, that and the other, but they, too, are split. Some profess sympathy for the Colonists in their struggle with Parliament, whilst others insist it is time to chart our own course—independent of both our fractious neighbours and England. Just last week, the authorities here arrested a man on a charge of stirring up feelings against the Crown. He was conveyed through the streets in a prison cart. People stopped to stare as he was carried past yelling for rebellion through the bars!*

*News has but lately arrived of a dreadful massacre in the town of Boston, Massachusetts. The newspapers report a dispute between some Redcoats and a group of local townsmen. It is reported that the troops wantonly opened fire, killing dozens of the latter. The incident has caused enormous tension, as well as bringing to the boil long-simmering suspicions about English intentions. I fear that both sides are now descended on a slippery slope to God knows where. Patriots make hay from the episode and seek thereby to further draw the people to the cause of independence. How it will all fall out, I shudder to think. God's blessings upon you, my dear Boundless, and your wife and sons also. My fond remembrances, too, to Mr Bjornson and his. And not forsaking cantankerous old Pinch! Your faithful friend, Guillaume Thibault.*

*PS I trust that White Deer is well and happy? I have not heard.'*

He set down the letter, angered by the news. 'They are shooting the people,' he told Bjornson.

'The Indians?'

'The English!'

AS SEPTEMBER PASSED INTO October, reports filtered in of a smallpox outbreak to the south and the men exercised a nervous vigilance, scanning visitors for signs of the disease before admitting them to the post. He mentioned the rumour in the compendium of notes he maintained for inclusion in his own annual letter to Guillaume. Well aware of the Frenchman's avaricious desire for *les petits détails qui révèlent tous*, he made it a regular practice to note small, unusual incidents as they occurred.

Thus, he made reference to the appearance of a two-headed beaver which the superstitious Indians showed but refused to trade.

*To their mind it has great power and is treated as an object of veneration, as Catholics would a holy relic. The owner has refused all offers for the animal, believing it to be a powerful token or sign. According to reports, he has paraded the trophy around several villages, receiving great acclaim as a result. The depth of superstition, and its power over the Indian mind, is remarkable and is of such extent and catalogue—of meanings, omens and portents—as to constitute a religion of its own. Indeed, may not such credulous notions be the foundation of all religions?*

A day later, mindful of Guillaume's sobriety with regard to religion, he took out the letter to re-read the passage. After some thought, he folded the letter and placed it back in the drawer. *After all, reasonable men have long speculated on such matters.*

NOVEMBER CAUSED AMAZEMENT BY ushering in a week of temperate winds and clear blue skies, the unexpected warmth before the onslaught of winter delighting the men. Pinch declared that the seasons were turned upon their head and that Christmas would witness an unparalleled return of summer. 'Your miracle at last!' he said, nudging Bjornson and urging him to find scriptural precedent.

Glad of the opportunity to make one more visit to the rock before winter set in, Boundless saddled the mustang. 'I shall be back before supper,' he told Bjornson, signalling the men to open the gate.

He walked the mustang for part of the way, enjoying the glorious, late-autumn sunshine and the absence of flies. The grass was bone dry, and he kicked the willing horse into a canter, his heart relishing the bright day. *He, too, feels it!* Gripping the reins, he urged the mustang to a gallop while chanting its praises. The mustang responded gamely, its head bobbing.

The ground flew by as he felt the cares of the post slipping from his shoulders. After a mile, he drew rein, resuming a gentle gait once more. Soon, the rock hove into view. Opening the canteen, he took a swallow of water as the sweating stallion snorted for breath. The rock rose up massively before him, the stone a dull russet tint against the brilliant, autumnal sky. *It has no one true colour*, he reflected, *only that lent it by the light.*

He sat there for long minutes—absorbed in some vague familiarity as the stallion trembled beneath him. A powerful sense of nativity—to the rock, the grass, the pale autumn sky—surged through him as he sat atop the panting, snuffling horse. *This is home.* The simple truth struck him with the force of revelation. The narrow, wandering lanes of Edinburgh and London, the crowded tenements, the soot and dirt, the bustle of the busy streets, paraded before him as no more than distracting preludes to this vast, blustery solitude of grass and sky. *I inhabit here as surely as the Indian and the buffalo. And one day, this grass shall bleach my bones as it does theirs.*

The horse nickered, puzzled at the prolonged halt. He took up the reins but lingered still, unwilling to relinquish the mood or the spot. Faint stars gleamed through the gathering dusk. A bird screeched in the sky above him. He turned the stallion. 'Home,' he said.

Reaching the point where the rock all but disappeared from view, he drew rein, twisting in the saddle to glance back. The great stone seemed to soften and merge with the autumn dusk, its lines blurred and malleable in the gloom. *It awaits aught but the shaping hand.*

Seized by a sudden, exhilarating sense of destiny, he gave a loud whoop! and urged the mustang into full stride.

## 31

## A Most Excellent Third

AS THE FIRST WARM rays of spring sunlight melted the lingering snow patches in the yard, the men worked energetically to assemble and press the bales. He oversaw the activities, noting with satisfaction the growing piles inside the storehouse. In between, he sat down to finish his letter to Guillaume. After reporting on the number of bales and the quality of pelts, he included references to the condition of the post and the morale of the men following the loss of their companion.

*I have enclosed a letter to his widow. You may wish to add a few words. You will notice an increase in the figure of wool blankets and shot requested. Rest assured we shall undoubtedly dispose of both. Incidentally, your old friend Road Maker sends greetings—in the Indian fashion of solemnly enquiring whether you have tired of life in the city and wish to return to the post. He himself is getting older and had to be sent for to guide the brigade. I have urged him to train his son to take his place. He has taken this under consideration—again, in the slow, deliberate Indian fashion. Without him, as you know, the brigade could hardly find its way back—in spite of several of the older men boasting that they could navigate the route blindfolded. Florent, our carpenter, wishes to return for good with next year's brigade. We shall need an experienced replacement.*

From outside came the sounds of shouts and merriment as the canoes were dragged out of the shed for inspection and maintenance. He heard Theroux's voice rise over the hubbub, the men roaring with laughter at what was said, before returning to the letter.

*I conclude by attaching the requests of Bjornson and Pinch. For myself, I wish the following: a silver bracelet, as a gift for Meadow Bird. Whatever your wife recommends will prove suitable. In addition, 1lb powdered ink, as per previous order. A dozen good quality quills. For clothing: a pair of brown leggings, measurements as previously; two linen shirts; a pair of good-quality leather boots, again, as previously. For sundries, one tin, Mrs Godwin's biscuits; four bags of hard-boiled sweets; a fine-steel*

*razor; 4lb of tea; six bottles of wine; two of rum; a brass candleholder,
and a sketchbook.*

He set down the quill, listening for a moment at the raised voices
beyond the door. He picked up the quill again, addressing a separate note
to Mathieu.

*I have, of late, developed a curiosity about the rocks of this region—one,
in particular. I am sure you recall the big rock situated some four miles
southwest of the post. It set me to thinking about various stones and their
properties. This interest has led, in turn, to a consideration of the use of
such stones in carving. To indulge this diversion, I would be obliged if you
could purchase and forward to me a book on the properties and qualities of
commonly found rocks, in particular, granite. As well, any available books
on stonemasonry, particularly those by modern authors. Such books are
most desirable as observe the principles and methods of dressing or carving
the stone. In addition, a volume on statuary—particularly the antiquities of Egypt and Greece. All such works to be in English. Finally, and to
draw further upon your patience and goodwill, I am desirous of making
the acquaintance of a reputable and qualified stonemason to whom I may
address such questions as may arise from my studies. I have a project in
mind that requires a knowledge of carving stone, and such advice would
be most helpful.*

He re-read what he had written. *No doubt he will think me bored of the
long winters.*

After the customary wishes for good health, he concluded by noting
the passing of eleven years since his arrival at the post, the figure surprising
him.

*One third of my life has now been spent in this grassy wilderness. It has been
a most excellent third, and I should not wish to be anywhere else.*

Folding the letter, he sealed it with wax and added it to the pouch. He
walked back across the yard, absorbed in thought, hands crossed behind
his back in the classic manner of the bourgeois.

## 32

## Family Life

A SERIES OF GALES BROUGHT northerly winds and bouts of rain that swept the yard. Sequestered by a hailstorm, he got up and walked to the door, sticking out his head to check the sky. The hail poured down as a dull rumble of thunder sounded in the distance. Muttering imprecations, he returned to the hearth. But he had no sooner sat down than he stood up again. Taking down his capote from the peg, he pulled his hat down on his head.

'Where are you going, Father? Can I come?' Claim followed him to the door.

'No. You will drown in the rain. Go back inside.'

He hurried through the downpour to the storehouse and stayed there for the better part of the morning, checking sundry items against the list of goods. The hail was still persisting as he made his way back, passing Buffalo Bird as she walked past to feed the dogs, Pinch's capote covering her head. *The lackshift is no doubt fast asleep!*

He sat down before the fire, his head and shoulders soaking wet. Meadow Bird hung the wet capote over a chair, manoeuvring it in front of the flames. Ignoring his protests, she tugged at the damp linen shirt. Grumbling, he lifted his arms to allow her to pull the garment over his head.

'The shirt, woman. Not my arms!' He sat half-naked in the chair as she draped a blanket across his shoulders.

'Father! Look!'

'What is it?' He held out his hand as Claim deposited a coin in his palm. 'A *sou*? Monsieur Thibault must have dropped it.' He handed it back. 'For your savings,' he said.

'Let me see!' Prospect attempted to snatch the coin.

'Claim, allow your brother to examine it. Prospect, hand it back when finished. It is not yours to keep.'

An aggrieved look on his face, Claim handed over the coin. 'It's mine!' he said, his voice sullen.

Boundless watched for a moment and then looked up at the sound of rain on the roof. 'Fetch me the primer.'

The boys ran to fetch it—struggling for possession as Claim pulled it from the shelf.

'Prospect! Let go! You'll tear it.'

With a triumphant smirk at his brother, Claim handed the book to his father. He opened it on his lap as the boys sat down at his feet.

'Now then, let us see who can answer first. *Nightingales sing in time of spring.*' Holding his finger on the passage he eyed his sons.

'What is a nightingale?'

The boys looked at each other, vying for an answer. 'A bird!' guessed Claim.

'Aye, clever clogs! What kind of bird?'

'A big bird!' Prospect flung out his arms.

'Take the wool out of your ears and listen! Nightingales *sing.*' At their baffled looks he murmured in despair. 'My old school master would turn in his grave! A *singing* bird! Say it.'

'A singing bird!'

As the boys competed to make chirping noises, he glanced at where Meadow Bird was seated on a stool pricking holes in a patch of rawhide—for what purpose, he could not fathom. 'Will you not sit here and listen, lassie?'

Prospect abandoned his attempts at chirping to tug at her arm. '*Mihúus*? Please!'

Puffing her cheeks in surrender, she set down the rawhide patch. Boundless held the book in front of her, pointing at the illustration of a woodpecker. 'Bird,' he said, winking at the boys. 'Say it. *Bird.*'

'Burd.' She repeated the word, frowning at its ugliness. '*Máreksuk!*'

'What did she—'

'*Máreksuk!*' the boys repeated. She nodded and smiled.

'And what does this *máreksuk* do?' At their confused looks, he shook his head. 'Give me patience! *Time cuts down all, both great and small.* What does—thunderation, what now?'

Meadow Bird had leaned forward to finger a sewed patch in Claim's shirt. She tugged the shirt out of his breeches and felt the worn material between her hands, clucking as she did so. Holding the shirt with one hand, she pulled the sewing box in front of her with the other. She took out a small ball of thread and, in spite of Claim's protests, began to measure him, turning him this way and that.

'Father!'

'Good Lord, woman, will you not set aside the work for a moment?' With a sigh, he shut the primer. 'What claim has learning against the measure of a shirt?' He sat back, watching as Meadow Bird tied a knot in the thread to mark each measurement. 'My mother did much the same for me,' he reflected, suddenly melancholy as he pictured the remembered scene.

'*Ihapana!*' Meadow Bird prodded Claim to stretch out his arms. As he squirmed, she scolded in a way that caused both boys to snigger.

'What did she say?'

Prospect put a hand to his mouth, laughing. 'She called him a muskrat!'

Finding a bruise on her son's arm, she frowned as she examined the mark. The boy grumbled and said something in Mandan.

Boundless sighed, a grudging pride overtaking his exasperation. *I am raising a tribe of Indians.*

Sensing his gaze, Meadow Bird turned and pulled a face, causing instant hilarity among the boys. '*Xíh!*' She pointed at the damp capote and held her nose, causing further merriment.

'Mother said it is old—and stinky!'

'Aye. I remember the day Guillaume gave it to me.' Reaching out, he felt the damp wool between his fingers. 'Mayhap it is time to replace it.' He sat back for a moment, staring at the capote, an idea forming in his mind.

IN LATE DECEMBER, HE joined Luc in a buffalo hunt, shooting a prime bull as it struggled to escape through the snow. 'Wait!' he said as Luc bent down to hack off the meat. 'I want the robe.'

Upon returning to the post, he draped the heavy robe across a beam and began to scrape the gore. He scraped for hours, lighting a lantern and waving away Meadow Bird when she came to summon him for supper. It was past midnight before he smothered the robe in salt and set it aside. The post was silent as he made his way back across the yard, the lantern casting a yellow gleam across the snow. The northern fires flickered overhead, and he paused to observe them, holding up the lantern *as though to better see!* The notion amused him, and he chuckled as he continued back to the house.

## 33

## A New Coat

O N A W A R M S P R I N G day, he dragged a drying frame out from the tanning hut to a sunny corner of the yard. Lacing the fleshed buffalo robe to the frame, he began the arduous task of scraping and thinning, drawing a curious audience of the remaining Indian wives.

'They are not used to seeing the bourgeois work his own hides,' said Pinch as word passed around and the audience grew larger. 'Meadow Bird will not do it?'

'She would, but this is a project for myself—to keep my hands busy.'

'It puzzles them.'

'Then let them puzzle.'

Pinch scratched his chin. 'It is women's work,' he argued. 'They do not understand why the bourgeois would do it.'

'They should have left for their villages already. Tell them it is time to go home.'

Pinch lingered. 'Meadow Bird cannot be happy. It is the same as when Buffalo Bird sees me take up a hoe.'

'Ha! Has such ever happened?'

'Meadow Bird will feel—'

'Do not concern yourself with Meadow Bird! Look to your own affairs.'

Pinch made a grumbling sound and hawked in the dirt before walking off.

His irritation over the conversation was compounded when Meadow Bird did indeed attempt to interfere, openly remonstrating as she attempted to take the knife from his hand. 'Leave it, lassie,' he said firmly, steering her away. 'It is mine to do.' Turning, she held her head high as she pushed past the gossiping women.

Her umbrage continued over supper as she muttered to herself while directing a series of reproachful glances his way.

'I want to do it,' he said. She said nothing but grumbled again while ladling corn onto his plate.

'Stay indoors if it bothers you so to watch,' he said, his voice sharp with exasperation.

He scraped the robe of all vestige of tissue on the one side until he was left with only the smooth, white under. He then began to soften and stretch the cleaned robe. His sons and the Bjornson boys gathered to watch as he poked and prodded the hide. Pleading to take a turn, they quickly grew disenchanted and were glad to be called away. He left the robe to dry in the sun, returning periodically to prod and paddle.

A few days later, he repeated the washing and drying process, further tightening the robe on the frame. The following morning, he pinched the robe between his fingers to determine the thickness.

'What are you doing, Father?' asked Claim, as he and Prospect stopped to watch.

'I am getting ready for the next step. Do you know what that is?'

Prospect contorted his face. 'Scraping?'

Boundless sighed. 'Can you not see with your own eyes that it is already scraped? Do you not remember the deer hide you helped your mother prepare but a week ago?'

At their baffled looks, he shook his head. 'Mercy! We tan it! And what do we use for tanning?' He tapped

Claim on the head. 'What is in there?'

'Sawdust!' Prospect fell about with mirth.

'Sawdust yourself!' Claim flew at his brother.

'Mind the frame!'

He was kept busy with post matters for several days, overseeing construction of a new dog pen and installing a new roof over the blacksmith's forge. The days had grown warmer, and the prairie grass was quickly drying out under the influence of southerly gales.

On a fine morning, he took the stretched robe out of storage. Flies buzzed around the hide until he smoked it over a smouldering fire of rotted spruce and corn cobs.

'Look, Father!' Claim approached, cradling a new-born puppy in his arms. Prospect followed, leaning in to stroke the puppy as his brother turned to shield it.

'Let me see.' He lifted the puppy onto his knees, placing a finger in its mouth. The dog squealed and yawned before flopping its head and falling asleep. 'It is too soon to take him from his mother. Put him back with the litter.'

'Told you!'

'Can't I keep him?'

'He is a work dog. We need him to pull the sledge. But you may name him.' He glanced at Prospect. 'And you, the next one.'

He smoked the hide for the better part of the day, periodically restocking the fire. Once, he caught the younger Bjornson boy trying to pull apart the robe and chased him off with a stern reprimand.

Before supper, he took down the robe, smelling it and grasping the woolly fur in his hands. He carried it to a wooden frame, its soft heaviness over his arm reminding him of the long-ago greatcoat. 'Good Lord,' he muttered, recalling that hot Philadelphia day.

He dragged the frame outside and left the robe to air for the night. Inspecting it again the next morning, the heavy, pungent smell of smoke still clung to the wool. He left it in place to air for another day.

The next morning, he carried it into the storehouse. Laying it on the floor, he trimmed the length with scissors. The task was an arduous one due to the thickness of the robe. Finding a few overlooked holes, he sewed them with sinew. Wearing the robe, he marked the shoulders with pins. Spreading it out on the floor, he drew a circle around the marked spots, allowing eight inches for each arm. He began to pick at the hide with the point of his knife. He heard a clucking sound and turned to see Meadow Bird standing inside the door, a frowning look on her face.

'It is alright, lassie,' he said. 'It is how I like it.'

'What are you doing?' Luc stepped in to take a look.

'I am cutting out holes for arms.'

'Your wife does not seem too pleased.'

'She thinks of a robe the one way only. No doubt I am a severe disappointment to her.'

When the holes were cut, he returned to his quarters to fetch the walnut looking glass sent by Guillaume's wife as a gift for Meadow Bird. Angling the glass, he pulled the robe across his body and tied it with a red sash taken from the capote. He stared at the reflection, pleased at the fit. The coat felt thick and warm against his body, the soft hair giving him a ghostly, bearlike appearance in the dim light of the storeroom.

The door opened and Bjornson entered, carrying a mug of tea. He sipped while studying the picture that Boundless presented. 'Is it warm?' he asked.

'As a second skin.' Boundless tugged the coat against his body, enjoying the fit. Lifting it to his face, he sniffed the dark, thick hairs, smelling buffalo stink mingled with pungent smoke aromas. 'It is the finest coat I ever wore. It will keep out the coldest weather.' He studied himself in the glass, lost in thought.

They heard the sound of a curse as Pinch stubbed his toe while entering. 'Zounds!' he exclaimed on seeing Boundless in the robe. 'Methought for a moment I saw a bear stood on its hinds. Pray, allow a fellow Christian to try the garment.'

Boundless surrendered the coat, looking on irritably as Pinch admired himself in the glass. 'Why not make your own?' he said, holding out his hand to take it back.

'No fear! I look to my trusty capote. Wool suits me a treat. Deuce, but the thing be warm! But it is overlong for me.' Pinch took off the coat and handed it to Bjornson. 'Let us see a Swedish buffalo.'

Bjornson tried on the coat, frowning as he looked down at the fur. 'I feel like a savage. The arm holes look odd.'

'If I had the skill, I would fashion sleeves and sew them to it.'

Bjornson gave back the robe. 'Like Pinch, I prefer the capote.'

That night, when he went to bed, he reached out an arm for Meadow Bird. She turned against him, her nose buried in his neck. Sniffing, she uttered a shallow, grumbling sound.

'What is it?'

'*Mideegaadi!*' She wrinkled her nose as she burrowed closer to his side.

## 34

## *A Highland Fling*

THE SUMMER PROVED THE hottest in years—the long days filled with a scorching heat that withered the grass and brought a plague of mosquitoes. Meadow Bird smeared the children's faces with bear grease, and in spite of their protests, hung woven bunches of her namesake herbage around their necks. Unable to sleep in the airless cabin, Boundless made a bed for himself in the yard, pulling a wool blanket over his body in the cool of early morning. To everyone's relief, a succession of powerful thunderstorms broke the heat and ushered in a week of milder, albeit humid, weather.

The main buffalo herds had migrated further north, some mysterious alchemy imposing a collective instinct for cooler climes. Yet the grass abounded in deer, elk and antelope, along with wandering groups of buffalo that satisfied his taste for rib and Meadow Bird's desire for hump meat. On occasion, he witnessed groups of Mandan hunting on horseback, the Indians showing great skill at riding down the buffalo and despatching the beasts with arrow or lance. The transition from foot to horseback had greatly increased the hunting range of the various tribes and he sighted several bands of hunting Cree as well as small groups of Chippewa and Arapaho—the bands hunting with the permission of the Mandan. A few of the Indians carried muskets, the bare-back riders racing alongside a buffalo to discharge the weapon at point blank range, their nimble ponies quick to avoid the swinging horns of the beast.

He spent the mornings teaching the boys—his own and Bjornson's— grammar and arithmetic. The four pupils, perched on stools in the hall, recited letters and numbers as flies buzzed lazily in the air. The women sat outside the open door, suppling rawhide for moccasins while listening in. Sometimes, Pinch would linger nearby, smoking a pipe and nodding as the boys counted numbers or chanted the alphabet. 'I like to hear the letters,' he explained. 'It minds me of home and former days.'

Once, he interrupted the lesson to take the class outside to watch a great herd of antelope stream across the plain, their bodies shimmering in the heat. 'This, too, is schooling,' he said to Bjornson, who looked on, askance.

Thoughts of the great project, as he now conceived of it, were never far from his mind as he went about his duties. At times, the sheer scale of his ambition threatened to overwhelm his senses, and he took to riding or hunting for distraction. His evening digestives with Bjornson continued as before, both men welcoming the diurnal tramp through the long grass. On several occasions, it was on the tip of his tongue to confide his audacious scheme to his companion but held back each time. *No doubt he would think me a lunatic.*

To divert himself further, he embarked on a project to teach his sons to ride, in spite of Meadow Bird's remonstrances. 'The Indian boys learn at this age,' he said, leading one of the more docile ponies into the yard. He watched the excited boys as the pony plodded around in a circle, his mind wrestling with the problem of how or where to start. *At the beginning,* he prodded himself, wondering where that might be.

*How high is it?* The simple question took him aback as he adjusted Claim's hands on the rope bridle. 'Not too loose. You must keep control.'

*It offers a way of proceeding.* 'Prospect, use your knees to guide him. Think of them as a second set of reins.' *Measurements will also show the immensity of the task,* he reflected, sobered by the prospect.

He lifted down the boys, despite their protests, thankful for this foothold, however small, on his grand purpose. *It is not the voyage that bedevils, but the embarkation,* he ruminated, teasing out the conceit.

'Water them and brush their coats,' he instructed. He gave a heavy sigh as he watched the boys lead the ponies to the converted barn. *It is an immense task I have set myself. Is it a foolish one?*

As often as his post and familial duties allowed, he visited the rock, finding comfort in its aloof austerity amid the sun-drenched plain. He sketched the object from various angles, noting the effects of sunlight and cloud shade on the iridescent granite. Sometimes, he put the journal aside and simply sat in the grass to gaze, casting about for how best to embark on his great purpose. His eyes traced contours in the stone as he projected the removals and alterations necessary to wrest the buffalo from its adamantine tomb.

Following such excursions, he returned to the post both pacified and eager, the immense difficulties trumped by imagined success, the wild improbabilities balanced by an exultant sense of purpose.

The hardness of the granite was a continuing source of fascination and concern. He attempted to mark it with his knife and stood back, shaking his head. *It would need black powder to make an impression.*

Back at the post, he visited the tool shed and selected four chisels and two hammers of different weights. He placed them in the haversack and returned to the house for supper.

The following morning Prospect watched as he saddled the grey. 'Where are you going, Father? Can I go with you?'

'No.'

Seeing the disappointment on the boy's face, he relented. 'Next week, we shall go fishing in the river, and mayhap snare a whale—with old Jonah in his belly.'

He tutted at the boy's perplexed expression. 'You do not remember your primer reading of just two days ago? Never mind. Take both my canteens and fill them with water.'

'I shall be back before supper,' he informed Pinch who, ruminating on his thoughts, lifted his pipe in acknowledgement.

Hot, sweating, and bedevilled by flies, he arrived at the rock a little before noon. Taking advantage of the thin band of shade, he took out the hammers and chisels and knelt at the base. He placed the tip of the largest chisel against the granite and struck a forceful blow.

'Mother of God!' he exclaimed, as he felt the hardness tremor up his wrist. Angling the chisel, he flaked off a sliver of stone. He fingered the sliver before casting it aside.

After several minutes of hammering, he chipped off a larger piece, which he placed in his pocket. Uncorking the canteen, he took a long swallow of water, his throat fluxing as he drank. He sat against the rock and felt his wrist, grimacing at the soreness. *It is an impossible task, though I hammer for a hundred years. What is bone against granite?*

A coyote nosed the grass for jack rabbits as he pictured the looks of shock and amazement on the faces of his companions should they discover his ambition—a lunatic one as it now appeared to him. He gazed up at the summit as an image came to mind of an afternoon on the deck of the *Patience*—his face uplifted to the salt breeze as the sails flapped overhead and a sailor climbed the rigging to the topmost spar. *How would I even climb to the top, let alone shape the stone?*

He spent the following days absorbed in this new problem. He pictured a giant ladder propped up against the side, only to dismiss the absurdity as soon as it entered his head. The notion of a rope ladder, thrown across the top and secured on the far side, briefly appealed until replaced by doubts. '*Twould be the equivalent of climbing the rigging to the topmast and would prove slow and uncertain when carrying supplies.*

A memory of the steps cut into the side of the earth mounds encountered on the way to the Mississippi popped into his mind, and he twisted his mouth in rueful recollection.

THAT NIGHT, HE SLEPT in the yard to avoid the stifling heat inside the house. The boys and Meadow Bird slept soundly alongside. He awoke before dawn, as was his habit. Stars gleamed in the sky, the air mild before the heat of the day. He lay quietly, running the day's purpose through his mind while listening to the soft breathing of the boys. After some minutes, he got up, pulling the blanket up over his sons.

In the darkness of the cabin, he groped for the haversack, feeling the shapes of the journal and ink bottle within. He went to the stable and saddled the mustang before returning to the house. Picking up the musket, he went back outside and shook Meadow Bird gently by the shoulder. 'The gate,' he said softly.

She followed him, yawning sleepily as she watched him unbar the main gate. She said something, placing a hand to her mouth as if to chew. He nodded and tapped the haversack to indicate the jerked venison. Outside, he waited until he heard her bar the gate behind him.

He walked alongside the horse for five minutes to stir the blood, the grass crushing beneath his feet. He heard the hoot of an owl and the scuttling rustle of a creature in the reeds. A coyote yelped in the distance and a sage grouse whistled. The dawn air felt pleasantly cool against his face, and he frowned at the certain prospect of midges, mosquitoes and blackflies later in the day. Mounting the horse, he voyaged through the shadowy, bending pastures for the best part of an hour before sighting the rock projected against the pink, dawning sky.

BY THE TIME HE entered its shade, the summit was bathed in first light. The base was still in shadow, the grass cool and stiff underfoot. He unsaddled the mustang and turned him loose to graze. Choosing a point midway along the side, he set down the haversack and musket. He placed a hand against the rock, the stone hard and cold beneath his palm. Opening the canteen, he took a swallow of water. Bluebirds and waxwings swooped for insects in the dewy grass. In the distance, a herd of antelope foraged for their morning feed.

Opening the haversack, he took out the journal and ink case and placed them in the grass. Leaving the haversack as a marker, he set off along the base, adjusting his stride as he walked, and digging his heel to mark each step.

Crouching, he took out a strip of rawhide, which he had marked into feet and inches. He held the strip against the footprints, measuring the distance from the base of the heel of one foot to the base of the next. He repeated the process with a different set of impressions. 'Thirty inches,' he noted.

He paced back along the entire length, counting aloud with each step. Turning, he paced the distance back again, adjusting the count by two. Returning to where he had left the journal, he carefully opened the brass ink bottle and noted down the measurement: *south side approx. 190 feet.* He repeated the exercise on the north side, finding it a foot shorter. He retraced his steps, cursing as he lost count and was forced to start again. *North side, 189 ft,* he recorded. Walking to the front, he paced off fifty feet along the west face. He then paced off forty-one feet along the rear, exceedingly pleased at the near symmetry of the whole. *'Tis as if already primed.*

Sitting down, he chewed some jerky while mulling on the measurements. A low rumble sounded in the distance. He looked up to see a dust column rise up over the grass. Moments later, a group of buffalo appeared, the beasts galloping towards the horizon. He scanned the plain for any sign of what might have spooked them but saw nothing. Gradually, the noise subsided, and the dust drifted back into the grass. He took a drink of water and dozed for a quarter-hour.

When he awoke, the sun was directly overhead. He got up and walked along the base to a point he had marked beneath the highest elevation. From this reference, he paced outwards in a straight line to where the shade of the rock extended. 'Sixteen … seventeen … eighteen …' he said, measuring twenty-four paces to the line of shadow.

He then paced out from the 'head', counting twenty-two paces. He did the same for the lowest point at the rear of the rock, striding out to a count of nineteen.

A mounting sense of anticipation gripped him as he noted the various dimensions in the log. *Hump – approx. 60'. Head – 58'. Tail – 52'. Declination – 8'.* Sitting back, he stared at the figures, seized by a sense of elation, as though ambition and destiny intersected in the innocuous numbers. It took the yelp of a coyote to wake him from what—berating himself—he dismissed as a delirium. He took another drink of water and a bite of the jerked venison as he sat crossed-legged studying the figures. He sketched an irregular, geometric shape and lettered the four corners *a, b, c, d* before adding the number of feet for each side. Mulling this, he superimposed the outline of a buffalo upon the sketch, adding three dotted arcs to indicate the height at each point.

Contemplating the sketch, he mentally proportioned the head, forelegs, curving spine and sloped flanks into related quadrants. *This might form a trapezium*, he speculated of the prominent forepart, *and the remainder, a rectangle*. He drew a line bisecting the latter into two triangles. Taken with the problem of angles and proportions, he hunched over the sketch, lost in thought.

In part to convince himself that the entire audacious project was not a mere conceit, he took over an empty house and set his journals on the table along with a bottle of ink and several quills. He then collected several assorted sketches and fixed them to the wall. He stood at the door, looking around the single room. *If nothing else, I have a workshop.*

OVER THE COURSE OF the following weeks, he made several return visits, each time experimenting with various chisels and different methods of striking and flaking the stone. He found that, even after a short time, the effects on his hands and wrists were considerable, the soreness, and sometimes swelling, persisting for days afterwards.

His ventures did not go unnoticed, both Pinch and Bjornson expressing curiosity at his frequent absences. He waved off their questions and remarks with an affected air of impatience, as though surprised that the diurnal humdrum of riding and shooting should be cause for such inquiry.

'But you return empty-handed each day,' Pinch objected.

'I shoot for sport, not food.'

'Do you not have sufficient duties to occupy you here at the post?'

'Are you now bourgeois as well as scold?'

'I say only what is on my mind.'

He thought the matter laid to rest, yet suspicions lingered. Pinch, on one occasion, followed him outside the stockade, ostensibly to wave godspeed. 'I see you have packed your hammers,' he called out.

Surprised and mortified, Boundless turned, unable to conceal the anger from his voice. 'You have searched my bag?'

'Hefted it only—when I handed it to you.'

With an irritable grunt, he continued on his way.

'Do you practise the Highland fling?' The jibe hung in the air behind him.

He and Bjornson continued their nightly walks—on one occasion joined, much to their mutual surprise, by Pinch.

'I know the fellow!' Boundless said later to the Swede. 'He conjures up plots and conspiracies and would listen to satisfy himself of what we speak.'

'He wonders what you do in the clerk's old house—as do I,' his companion admitted.

Boundless hesitated, the words on his lips. 'In time, Bjorn, in time,' he promised.

'So, there is something?'

'In time.'

## 35

## 'You Must First Understand the Stone'

THE RETURNED BRIGADE BROUGHT some new faces and the absence of a few familiar ones. He learned that Gaston Theroux, the redoubtable *pilote*, had stayed behind in Montreal, having taken sick during the trip back. Henri was also missing, the Frenchman having decided to abandon the hardships of paddling—along with his Mandan wife and family—for the relative safety of employment as a nightwatchman in Quebec City. 'Safer, too, for the Mandan women,' joked Norman Dubois, an experienced *devant*, selected by Theroux to act as *pilote* in his stead.

Disappointed at the loss of two such dependable men, Boundless retired to his quarters as soon as the cargo had been inventoried and the goods and supplies transferred to the various buildings. Pouring himself a glass of wine, he propped his feet up on a stool and opened the pouch. Separating the various bills of lading, invoices and reports, he set them aside to take up the letter from Guillaume. *Well, old friend, what do you have to say?*

Following salutations to his health and family, the letter began with a summary of profits from the previous year's harvest. It continued in Guillaume's usual manner—a compendium of part-commerce, part-news, and part-gossip—the whole confection leavened with raisins of advice, reports of popular scandals, asides on the weather, and various reflections thrown up on the older man's daily walks. He sipped the wine as he read, enjoying the news of a world that seemed far distant.

*Montreal, May 1772*

*The division between the English authorities and the so-called Patriots runs deeper by the day. 'Tis rumoured that sentiment in favour of home rule grows with each passing minute. But in truth, we are beset by rumours—each one barely drawing breath before it is extinguished and replaced by another. Great import is attached to events of no significance in themselves, and minor differences quickly become raging disputes. I trust that goodwill and common sense may yet prevail. But in this I am a voice in the wilderness. Here, there is much natural sympathy for the Patriot cause and increasingly louder calls for Quebec to press its own claims for sovereignty. My own feeling is that we are so mired in English credit and commerce that disentanglement would prove difficult and costly. Many in the city hope fervently for war and a resounding victory for the colonials. Such an outcome, they finely calculate, is the best opportunity to negotiate a peaceful and separate destiny for Quebec. 'Native faith and native speech!' goes the new catchcry about the streets. Others express hopes for an English victory, fearing the American grasp. The Confederacy of Iroquois, meanwhile, stands on the margin to watch with increasing hostility.*

*What influence any conflict will exercise over trade and commerce remains a matter of speculation and despair. Suffice it to say that reports arrive daily of new fur companies opening up in the New York Colony. In addition, several companies formerly established in Quebec are now transferring their assets to Albany—whether through expediency or cunning foresight I do not know. 'Tis said also that some reputable enterprises now harvest the trade in the northern and far western regions, forsaking altogether the regions south and east of the Great Lakes. I fear that it cannot be too long before you encounter trading parties even as far distant as your location. My head aches from keeping abreast of the gossip and rumour! I find solace only in the index of furs and in matters related to prices and profits.*

*Attached, you will find a list of the bills of sale for last year's consignment and the profits incurred, with separate notations for the various kind and quality of pelt. I have redrawn the promissory notes of yourself and Mr Bjornson to reflect the year's dividend. The redoubtable Theroux has succumbed to illness and has recommended Norman Dubois, an experienced man, in his place. He hopes to have recovered to lead next year's brigade. You will notice a new face among the crew—that belonging to one Helmut Bauer, a former stonemason from Germany. He arrived with a letter of recommendation from a business acquaintance. He strikes me as a trustworthy fellow and will, I hope, form a worthy new addition to our little brigade. As an added bonus, he speaks English almost as well as Mathieu.*

*Stonemason!* Boundless set down the letter for a moment and stared into the fire, his heart beating faster at the coincidence. He got up and added a log to the fire, vowing to himself to interview the man as soon as trading permitted. 'Pot and pedestrian,' he remarked, contemplating the sparks. *How things do fall together when one is resolved upon a course!* He sat down again, elated at the news. He had returned to the letter when he was interrupted by a knock on the door. 'Come in.'

Emile poked his head around the door. 'Pardon, sir, but Monsieur Lapointe says that we appear to be one bale short.'

With a sigh, he set the letter aside and got to his feet. 'Then let us find it.'

WHEN THE POST WAS settled into its usual autumn activity of mending and repairing the buildings, he sent for Dubois to enquire about the newest member of the brigade.

'Helmut?' The *pilote* shrugged. 'He is a good fellow. German. Dependable. A little green in the ways of the canoe, but he caught on quickly. He gets along well with the other men and speaks passable French.'

'What was he before?'

Norman blew out his lips. 'I cannot think—wait! I believe he worked in a quarry, extracting stone.'

'Please send him to see me. I have some questions for the fellow.'

A short time later, he heard a tap at the door followed by a respectful, 'Monsieur McLennan?'

On opening, he found Helmut standing there, cap in hand, a hesitant look on his face at the unusual summons. The fellow appeared to be in his late twenties, with a slim and compact frame, the ideal physique for a voyageur. A growth of beard framed an apprehensive yet inquisitive face.

'Come in.' Boundless stood aside, glancing at the largely empty hall. It was after breakfast and most of the men were off on duties of one sort or another.

'Sit down.' He gestured to a chair. Helmut coughed and sat, his eyes darting to the door.

'Tea?'

Helmut looked greatly surprised at the offer. Clearing his throat, he was about to decline when Boundless poured him a cup from the steaming kettle he picked up from the fire. The two sipped in silence for a moment, the German mumbling, 'Thank you, Monsieur,' as he took a cautious sip.

'You speak English like a native. I was told you were German?'

'True, I was born there, sir, but raised in Rhode Island since I was five years of age. My father came from Germany to work in the quarries, as did I, after him.'

'So, it is true then—that you are a stonemason?'

Helmut's eyes widened. 'Stonemason? No. I was a quarryman, like my father.'

'Oh.' Boundless could not disguise the disappointment in his voice. 'And is that the sum of your experience—working with stone, I mean?'

Helmut gave a nervous laugh. 'If you do not count breaking rocks in New Hampshire!'

'Breaking rocks?'

'In the fields, to clear the land for farming.'

'What sort of rocks?'

'What sort?'

'Of what kind of stone, I mean.'

'Oh! Granite—for the most part.' Helmut took another sip of tea, evidently confused as to the direction of the conversation. He glanced covertly about the room, his eyes fastening on the kettle as it hissed in the fireplace.

'Could you teach me?'

'Pardon?'

'To break rocks. Could you teach me?'

Helmut pursed his lips as if to better grasp the question. 'Why?—if you will permit the question, sir.'

'I have a project in mind. Will you teach me?'

'Pardon, but to break rocks is easy—although hard. One simply uses a hammer.'

'No, I am the one that must beg pardon. I did not mean simply to break stone, but to shape it.'

Seeing the confusion on the other man's face, Boundless tried another tack. 'Why not begin by describing, in your experience, the difference between breaking up stones—loose stones, as you experienced in New Hampshire—and quarrying stone, as you also did in ...?'

'—Massachusetts.' Helmut knitted his brow to answer. 'To quarry you extract the stone from the surrounding rock.'

'Yes?'

'Yes?' Helmut repeated, growing more confused by the minute.

'The method?'

Helmut peered hard at the wall. 'For soft stone, such as sandstone or marble, we use hammers and pickaxes. For harder stones, such as granite, we drill holes and use iron wedges to break up the rock.' Sensing Boundless' wish for more, he continued. 'Another method is to heat the rock to break it up.'

'And if one wished to not split but shape the stone—in the interests of carving it?'

'Carving?' Helmut frowned. 'That be another matter altogether.'

'How so?' prompted Boundless, feeling as if he were at that moment extracting stone.

'I am not a mason, Monsieur.'

'But in your general experience?'

Helmut studied the tea leaves in the cup. 'For that you must rely on hammer and chisel—to remove the unwanted stone,' he added.

'Then you do not split it—as with quarry stone?'

Helmut scratched his ear. 'No.'

'Will you show me what you know—of splitting granite?'

Helmut considered for a moment. 'You have tools?'

'Only what is in the tool hut. Hammers, chisels, a pry bar and so on. Will that suffice?'

'The chisels, no.' Helmut shook his head. 'Wood chisels are too soft for stone. But I have some of my own that I take with me.' He tugged at his lip, his voice suddenly plaintive. 'One never knows where Fortune will land a man.'

'Indeed.' Boundless rose to his feet, Helmut scrambling after.

'Shall we start later this week, after breakfast? Oh, by the way,' said Boundless, opening the door, 'between us, yes?'

'Certainly, sir. As you wish.'

'Pinch in particular will ask questions. Do you know of whom I speak?'

'I do sir.' Helmut tapped the side of his nose. 'Never fear.'

A FEW DAYS LATER, Helmut presented himself after breakfast, a worn haversack over his shoulder. 'Shall we go, sir? I have found a suitable rock along the shore.'

Pleased at the fellow's initiative Boundless followed him outside the stockade, ignoring curious glances from the men. The day was cold, with contrary winds. He glanced up at the grey, leaden sky, estimating snow to be but a week away, at most.

The two trudged along the shore. Helmut hunched in the thick wool collar of the capote, Boundless clad in the buffalo robe. He was reminded of the missing sleeves as an icy gust blew from across the river.

Helmut bypassed several small rocks embedded in the cold mud at the edge of the Missouri. The river flowed in a turgid stream, as if conserving its energies for when spring returned. A gull landed on a floating log, screeching and flapping its wings as it paraded up and down.

'Here.' Helmut knelt and tugged at a boulder half-buried in the mud.

'This is granite?'

'Yes, sir. See the colour? And the grain?' Helmut tapped the stone. 'Hard as iron,' he said.

Boundless crouched down over the stone, placing his hands on the cold surface. 'And you broke up these?'

'I did. For six years, alongside my father.' Upending the haversack, Helmut shook loose the contents on top of the rock. A hammer, a grindstone, and several types of chisels of varying lengths lay on the stone along with a small wooden case.

'They all have distinctive uses?' asked Boundless, observing the different shapes.

'Yes.' Helmut held up a chisel which resembled a flattened nail-head at the strike end. The cutting end flared and then tapered to a pointed edge. 'A Cape Chisel. To bore holes into the rock.'

'Bore holes?' Boundless picked up the chisel, rubbing his finger over the end.

'Yes. It makes rectangular holes, the best for powder.'

'And the hammer?' He picked it up. It weighed about four pounds, with flat heads on either side.

'That is a hand hammer. We use it to make the holes.'

'And this?' He picked up an unusual-looking chisel with a scooped end.

'The spoon. We use it to remove stone dust from the holes.'

'Stone dust?'

'Yes. Caused by the hammering. It builds up and must be cleared. There is another way, which I will show you.'

Boundless set the chisel down, his mind going back to the sailing vessels he had voyaged on since coming to the New World. *There is a craft or skill to every trade*, he observed to himself, reminded of the great variety of knots associated with nautical ropes.

'And these others?' He picked up a small flat piece of iron with a tapered end.

'A wedge or plug, for splitting the stone. And these,' Helmut picked up one of a half-dozen objects with curved ends, 'these are irons, or feathers. We place them in the drilled holes and insert the plug between them.'

'And by this method you split the rock?'

'There are other ways. Sometimes we lay fire under the rock and douse it with water. It then splits under the hammer. Or there is the black powder.' Helmut wrinkled his face. 'It will … boom! Blow the rock to pieces.' He was distracted by the sound of a fish jumping in the river. He blew on his hands. 'It is cold,' he said.

'And getting colder.'

'Yes. Pardon.' Helmut brushed dirt from the top of the boulder. 'To begin, you must first understand the stone. We must look for the grain,' he said at Boundless' questioning look. 'The rock splits along the grain.' The young man spat on the stone and cleaned off the surface. 'Do you see the grains—where they run?'

'No,' said Boundless, squinting at the surface.

'It is hard sometimes, for the unpractised eye.' Helmut scuffed the surface. 'See? Tiny grains that run together in a line.'

Boundless shook his head. 'I shall have to take your word for it.'

Looking around, Helmut selected a small rock and struck it with the hammer, breaking off a small chunk. 'A moment, sir.' He picked up the small wooden case and extracted a magnifying glass. He handed the glass and the granite chunk to Boundless. 'Can you see the grains?'

Boundless peered at the chunk. 'Yes, I can. What are they?'

'They are minerals in the granite and give it its colour. The black-coloured ones are called *hornblende*, a German word. It means 'to deceive' as it is easily mistaken for other minerals.'

'And the pink grains?' asked Boundless, studying the granite through the glass.

'Potassium feldspar. And the other, smoke-coloured ones, quartz.'

Boundless set down the chunk. 'Even the stones have a story,' he mused, shaking his head. He turned his attention back to the boulder. 'The method—for breaking it up?'

'We drill holes along this line—not too close to the edge.' Helmut drew a line with his finger.

'The purpose?'

Helmut looked confused. 'What purpose?'

'To insert the plugs,' said Boundless, answering his own question.

'As I do not have any drills, we will use the Cape chisel.' Picking up the hammer, Helmut tapped the chisel across the rock, creating a shallow groove. 'We will make holes along this line,' he explained. 'The number and depth will depend on the size of the block. Four will suffice for this stone. Roughly three inches apart,' he continued, anticipating the next question. 'For smaller stones, you do not need to bore holes. Simply break them apart with the chisel. But for a stone this big, we need to bore.'

He struck the chisel with the hammer, rotating it a turn after each blow. He struck rapidly, with practised ease, holding the chisel perpendicular to the hole. Within the space of ten minutes, he had fashioned a rectangular slot approximately one and a half inches deep.

'That will do.' He inserted two 'feathers', tapping each one in place. He then lightly hammered the plug between them.

'Do you wish to take a turn, sir? The second hole, here,' he said, rubbing a mark three inches from the first.

Snowflakes drifted through the air as Boundless grasped the cold chisel. He struck it with the hammer, tentatively at first, and then with greater force.

'Thunder! It is devilish hard!' Shifting his grip on the chisel, he struck another blow.

'Hold it upright, if you please,' said Helmut, adjusting his wrist.

A half-hour later, his hands were sore, and his wrist ached, but a shallow slot had been chipped into the stone. He wiped his forehead, feeling warm in spite of the cold.

'It gets faster with practice.' Helmut took back the chisel. 'Shall I?' He created another slot in a quarter of the time it had taken Boundless.

'You said the chisels are soon blunted?' asked Boundless. 'How would you sharpen them?'

'A sandstone grinding wheel. You have one in the blacksmith's forge.'

'We do?' Pleased at the revelation, he watched as Helmut inserted plugs between the tapered shims.

'Perhaps three will do,' said the young man. 'Now, we hit each wedge in turn.' After lightly striking each wedge, he asked Boundless to listen. 'Can you hear the rock start to break?'

Cocking his head, Boundless heard a cracking sound as the stone split apart along the line of wedges.

'Use a pry bar if needs be to jar the two sides apart,' instructed Helmut as the granite broke off along the line of force.

Boundless picked up the white, cleaved rock. 'And how much stone can you split with this method?'

Helmut grimaced. 'The earth itself—with sufficient irons.'

A WEEK LATER, HE went out again with Helmut, the German showing him how to use powder to blow apart a rock. Selecting a small boulder, Helmut drilled a hole two inches deep and filled it with black powder. 'This is the fuse,' he said, showing a length of twisted hemp. He scattered some powder grains on the hemp. 'To help it burn,' he explained. He set spark to the fuse, and they stood back to watch.

The charge exploded, creating a V-shaped fissure in the stone. 'It is now easy to break along the cracked lines,' explained Helmut.

'But what if I wish to blow the rock apart, not simply break off sections?'

'Then you use more holes and more powder.'

'Let us try.'

Selecting another boulder, Boundless used the chisel to bore a hole approximately two inches deep. Helmut then took over, cutting two more holes. Boundless used his powder measure to fill the holes with black powder. Helmut showed how to cap the powder holes with dampened mud. He then threaded a fuse into each before joining all three fuses to a further length of hemp. 'They can explode singly, in turn,' he explained. 'Or together, like this.' He set light to the fuse.

They stood farther back as the flame ran along the main fuse and then into each separate fuse, igniting the powder. Pieces of rock flew into the air.

'The third hole never fired,' said Boundless, observing the spent fuse.

'Be careful. Sometimes a spark lingers and then ignites the powder,' cautioned Helmut.

'Just like hang fire in a musket,' remarked Boundless. He picked up the broken pieces. 'It is quicker and easier than the chisel.'

'But costly, and inexact.'

'The trick is to control the blast,' said Boundless, half to himself.

One day, he led Helmut to a particularly large rock further along the shore. 'I wish to remove a layer,' he said. 'But not so much as to destroy the entire rock.'

Helmut nodded. 'Like quarrying,' he said.

As they began boring a blast hole, Helmut peered at Boundless.

'Is it true you wish to blast a giant rock?'

'It is.'

Helmut mulled the information as he watched Boundless pour powder into the bored hole. 'The whole rock?'

Boundless grimaced at the powder. 'Not all. I wish to remove the superfluous rock. The rest is a matter of shaping,' he said, stating the fact for the first time. 'But this goes no further. Do you understand?'

'I do, sir.—The fuse needs to be longer. Sprinkle it with powder to make sure it catches. And use more mud to tamp it down. It will be a hard task, to shape the rock.'

'Very hard,' acknowledged Boundless.

'And you have no experience with carving stone?'

'None,' he admitted.

'You will need a great quantity of tools.'

'No doubt … Is this fuse long enough?'

They retreated several yards and watched as the fuse spluttered to the charge. The powder exploded with a muffled bang. A crack spread out in a v-formation from the blast hole.

'It didn't do much,' said Boundless, disappointed.

'Everything depends on the depth of the hole and the right quantity of powder. Often, you must make shallow blasts in several places and then remove the shattered stone with a pick. It is a laborious process. What is it you intend to carve?'

'Let us make another hole,' said Boundless.

He spent several more afternoons with Helmut, picking the other man's brain as to his knowledge of stone craft which, he grudgingly conceded, was not much beyond what had been demonstrated on the first day.

'How would I attach wood to granite?' he asked.

Helmut wrinkled up his face. 'You can't.'

'Might one not sink a wood plug first?'

'And attach a bolt to the plug?'

'Yes,' sighed, Boundless, feeling like the master instructing the apprentice.

Helmut considered the question as if he had been asked to adjudicate a theological dispute. 'I suppose,' he conceded, giving his verdict.

'I will take that "suppose",' said Boundless, 'and raise you "probably".'

'Eh?' Helmut grimaced, looking utterly confounded.

'I would like to buy your tools. I will give you five English pounds.'

'They were my father's before me.'

'Seven.'

'Done!'

They shook hands.

THE SHORE EXPEDITIONS DID not go unremarked by Pinch, who alluded to them one afternoon while moving stock in the storehouse. 'You spend much time with young Helmut,' he said, setting down a box of screws. 'Does he teach you the German?'

'He has many original opinions. Are you finished with the shelf? Then move on to the other one.'

He was passing the blacksmith's one afternoon when he heard the sound of a hammer striking iron. He stopped to look in. The interior was dim and warm. The sandstone grinding wheel stood in one corner. Abel stood over the anvil, striking a bar of hot iron with the sledgehammer. He glanced up, startled to see Boundless standing before him.

'Monsieur McLennan! Is there something you need?'

'No, carry on.'

Abel swung the twelve-pound hammer with ease, his practised arm striking the glowing bar each time. The heat from the fire in the brick forge was palpable from where Boundless stood in the doorway. After a few more blows, Abel stopped again, clearly uncomfortable at being observed.

'Are you certain that I cannot help, Monsieur?'

'What is it you are making?'

Abel brightened. 'An axe-head.' He picked up the glowing flattened iron with a pair of tongs. 'See?'

'And you made these bolts and nails?' asked Boundless, picking up a bolt from the bench.

'I did.'

'And the chisels, also?'

'Yes, and the hammers.'

Boundless hefted a chisel in his hand. 'It is, no doubt, a particular skill—to make?'

He spent the next several mornings in the smithy, observing how Abel heated and smote the iron tools. At his request, the blacksmith rehardened the tip of several of the post chisels. He watched closely as the blacksmith carefully heated his own acquired Cape chisel before 'dancing' the tip in cold water.

'By your leave?' Taking another chisel, he practised under Abel's watchful eye.

'How do you know when the iron is hot enough?'

'When the colour changes—not too much!'

Under Abel's tutelage he learned to operate the grinding wheel, sharpening each of the chisels to a fine edge.

'Has this grindstone always been here?'

'One of the old hands told me the army brought it with them. When they left Monsieur Thibault asked them to leave it behind, along with the anvil and supplies of iron bars and coal.'

Boundless smiled to himself. *Trust Guillaume!*

AS THE WEATHER SLOWLY improved, he took off by himself to test the sharpened chisels on the rocks along the Missouri shore. Finding a large boulder, he experimented with boring a hole in the hard granite. After a frustrating hour, he had bored just two holes, and the chisels were already blunted. Packing up the tools, he walked back along the shore to the fort wondering how he could secure Bjornson's assistance. *For without him, I fear it cannot be done.*

Back at the post, he massaged his left wrist and then flexed and re-flexed the fingers of his aching right hand while reflecting on the small return for so much effort. His thoughts turned to gloom as he pictured the massive rock. *It is impossible. A thousand men could not do it. Flesh and bone would wear out ere the stone. Best to abandon the mad notion.*

But he could not—the ambitious quartz too deeply lodged within his own stubborn grain.

Over the following days, his determination renewed as he pondered the rock sketches. *It could be done—with enough powder,* he told himself, recalling his conversation with Helmut.

*'And how much stone can you split with this method?'*

*'The earth itself—with sufficient irons.'*

## 36

## A Boundless Folly

ONE SULTRY AFTERNOON IN mid-summer, he returned from a visit to the rock, his head full of calculations. Following supper, he sat with his companions outside the dining hall, enjoying the warm twilight in spite of the plentiful mosquitoes. The other occupants were off playing cards, leaving the three companions to enjoy the evening hush by themselves. They sat in familial silence, Pinch smoking a pipe while Boundless and Bjornson sipped hot tea. Overhead, a pale, ghostly moon reflected the last rays of the setting sun.

Pinch glanced at Boundless. 'A penny for your thoughts?'

'Pardon?'

Pinch dashed tobacco from the pipe. 'You have been quiet all evening. Do you pine for the day just gone?'

'I intend to climb that rock,' he said, surprising himself with the blunt admission.

Pinch halted as he was about to cut a fresh plug of tobacco. 'What do you say?'

'The rock. I intend to stand atop it.'

'Stand on what?' Bjornson, jarred loose from his thoughts, glanced from Boundless to Pinch.

Pinch scratched his whiskery chin. 'Boundless here wishes to climb that rock.'

'Which rock? What do you prattle on about?'

'The big rock. I intend to climb it. I shall need your help, Bjorn—and yours, too, Pinch.'

'Climb it?' Bjornson's mouth dropped open in amazement. 'Why?'

'More to the point—why in blazes would we help in such a fool notion?'

'I wish to see the land as it is—from the height.'

Bjornson gaped in puzzlement. 'What is there to see but grass?' The remark brought a guffaw from Pinch.

'Nonetheless, I will climb it. Will you help me make a ladder?'

'A ladder? For what?'

'I cannot fly to the top! I must fashion a rope ladder.'

Silence followed. Bjornson scratched at a mosquito bite. From inside came the noise of the women as they cleaned up after the meal. Boundless heard an indignant protest and recognised the voice of Torsten, Bjornson's youngest.

Pinch broke the silence, fixing Boundless with a shrewd gaze. 'Madness, as spoke—unless there be a further notch to it. Truth, now!'

Boundless turned the empty cup in his hands. 'I concede that I do indeed harbour a further notion.'

'Knew it, by jingo!' Pinch slapped his knee.

'What do you know?' Thoroughly perplexed, Bjornson looked from one man to the other.

'You have not guessed? Why, he intends to shape it—the rock—into a buffalo! Do I say truly?' Pinch leaned forward as though daring Boundless to deny the fact.

'It is true,' he admitted.

Bjornson sat up, aghast. 'Shape it? What in God's name—'

Pinch hooted. 'Into a buffalo!'

Bjornson stared as if awaiting a rebuttal from Boundless. When none came, he sat back in the chair, a look of horrified amazement on his face. 'Such a thing!' He shook his head. 'Such a thing!'

'It cannot be done!' Pinch's voice was flat. 'And if it could be done, then it *oughtn't* be done. What in God's name would presume you to undertake such a folly?'

'Such a thing be vanity.' Bjornson's voice tightened with disapproval. 'More—it is blasphemy. The Bible forbids it.'

Boundless scowled. 'I do not propose it for worship!'

'For what, then?'

He paused. 'Why, but as a thing in itself—worthy of note.'

'A headstone!' Pinch hawed in triumph. 'A trump! Verily, verily!'

Ignoring the remark, he appealed to Bjornson. 'Can I at least count on your assistance? Say plainly, yes or no.'

'This madness of the buffalo? I cannot!'

'And you?' He looked at Pinch.

'I *will* not! 'Tis a foolish notion and I will not be party to it. You are the bourgeois and have your duties. The sun has boiled your brains to even think of it.'

'Such a thing I never heard of! You will tumble off and break your neck!' Bjornson flung out an arm to indicate the grasslands. 'There already be a plague of the stinking beasts. Why make another?' His eyes widened. 'And in stone!'

FOR THE NEXT FEW days, Boundless went about his duties in a prickly mood, answering brusquely when spoken to. On the fourth day after his confession to his two friends, Bjornson hurried after him as he crossed the yard and caught him by the arm.

'Come, Boundless, let us make peace. You have too many cares and responsibilities as bourgeois than to occupy your mind with wild schemes.'

'Wild schemes?' He bristled at the words. 'I had anticipated, nay expected, indifference from Pinch, but from yourself …?'

'But what point is there—even if such a thing were possible?'

Boundless frowned but made no reply as Bjornson continued. 'Monsieur Thibault, were he here, would surely condemn it, even as Pinch does. You are a sensible man, Boundless. Think. Such a task—to carve a rock as you propose—would take a hundred years, if it could be done at all. What skills have you for such a thing?'

'It is not skill I need, but dependable friends!' He stalked off, leaving Bjornson to stare after him.

In the middle of a rainy morning, a few days afterwards, Boundless entered the hall in search of hot tea. Bjornson, Luc, Abel and Antoine were gathered around Pinch, who held court over tea and a pipe. As he opened the door, he heard a roar of laughter at some 'Pinchism' or other. The laughter abruptly silenced as he entered.

'I must to my forge,' said Abel, rising so hastily he spilled his tea.

'And me to my guns,' said Luc, following suit. Bjornson promptly followed both men out the door.

Boundless poured himself a cup of tea. 'What the blazes was that about?'

Antoine, who had also risen to leave, glanced at Pinch, who drank blandly from his cup. 'Nothing, sir. Idle chatter to pass the time.'

Boundless narrowed his eyes, his suspicions further inflamed. 'And you, Pinch. You are well?' he asked.

Pinch nodded, emitting a cloud of smoke. 'As steady as a rock,' he said, drawing a suppressed giggle from the nervous clerk.

Later in the afternoon, Boundless saw Bjornson emerging from the storehouse and hailed him.

'What was that palaver in the hall this morning?' he demanded. 'And do not think me a fool to deny what I heard.'

Bjornson winced, his face a study in discomfort. 'It was nothing, really. One of Pinch's quips—you know how they fall out of his mouth like the stink from his pipe.'

'What quip?'

'What you said, about that rock.'

'Yes?' Boundless stopped, facing the Swede.

Bjornson cleared his throat. 'He, Pinch, called it the "Boundless Folly."'

'Did he indeed?' His mouth tightened at the jibe.

''Twas nothing. The jest of an idle moment, already forgotten.'

'By you—or those others who heard it?'

'It was nothing, I tell you. Where are you going? Leave it be!'

Ignoring Bjornson's plea, he went off at once in search of Pinch. He found him pushing a wheelbarrow from the garden.

'I hear you have been entertaining the post with your absurd quips,' he said, blocking the other man's path. 'What would you know of such a project, that sit only on the sidelines and mock?'

Pinch set down the wheelbarrow, a defiant look on his face. 'A man may think as he chooses,' he retorted. 'You are the bourgeois. You have responsibilities to the post—as well as to your wife and children. Suppose you slip and break your neck—what becomes of Meadow Bird and the boys?'

'And do you see me neglecting either? Or do you mistake your own bone idleness for the general condition?'

'Rebuke as will'—Pinch picked up the wheelbarrow—'but what will you do when winter comes? How then will you climb your precious rock?'

HE MADE ANOTHER ATTEMPT to persuade Bjornson to join in his endeavour, taking the Swede aside to press his case. 'Just for the summer,' he urged. 'To help me start.'

'For God's sake!' snapped Bjornson. 'Ask me no more!'

'But help with the preparation only? Surely, that cannot hurt your faith?'

'Do you not have ears?' Bjornson turned from him and walked away.

To his chagrin, Meadow Bird proved no more understanding of his great project. Attempting to explain his absence from the post each day, he sat her down at the table. Their sons stood beside his chair as he opened the journal and pointed to a sketch.

'Rock,' he said.

Protesting, she made to stand up, thinking this yet another language lesson.

'A moment!' Coaxing her back down he turned to another sketch. 'Buffalo. See?'

'Have eyes! Me see!'

'Patience, lass.' He turned the pages, finding the sketch he wanted. '*Voila!* Rock buffalo!'

She turned to Prospect and said something, her face cross.

'Tell her I am making the rock into a buffalo.'

'It is too hard!' The boy's face wrinkled in dismay.

'Never mind.' He pointed to the sketch and then to himself. 'Buffalo. Me make. At rock.' He pointed and made a shaping sign.

Meadow Bird ' eyes widened as she took in his meaning. 'Buff-alo?' She addressed the word to Prospect, who nodded, pleased that she had understood.

'Ai!' She stood up, her smooth face wrinkled with annoyance. 'Can eat rock? Can make robe from rock?'

'Good Lord, woman! Do you judge everything by what can be put into your mouth?'

Grumbling to herself, Meadow Bird picked up a wooden pail, which she carried to the door. Before exiting, she turned, her face tight with disapproval, to scold him in Mandan.

Exasperated, he turned to his sons for assistance. 'What did your mother say?'

Looking faintly shocked, Prospect laughed into his hand. 'It was rude!'

'Aye. I expect it was.'

From outside the door came the sound of a shout as Meadow Bird hailed Buffalo Bird. *No doubt to tell her what a great fool her husband is.* He closed the journal, greatly put out at the exchange. 'She does not understand.'

His sons were staring at him. 'Go!' he said, unable to think. 'Go do your chores.'

He muttered to himself as he watched the boys leave after their mother. *Bourgeois everywhere but in my own house!*

## 37

## A Question of Faith

ONE MORNING ABEL, THE blacksmith approached holding a two-foot-long iron bar, a pyramidal shape cut into its tip.

'What is it?' asked Boundless as the blacksmith presented the bar, a pleased smile upon his face.

'It is a star drill for boring holes.' The blacksmith held up the drill to show the cross-shaped tip. 'It will make drilling easier. Turn it a quarter-turn after every two or three strikes to keep the edge.'

The tool drew an exclamation from Boundless. 'Surely, this is Helmut's star drill?'

'It was Helmut who suggested it.'

Boundless was admiring the drill when Bjornson emerged from the hall. 'Are you off to the rock, again?'

'I am.' Boundless held up the drill, 'to practice this.'

To his surprise, Bjornson asked to accompany him.

'Why?" asked Boundless, his voice suspicious. 'Did Pinch put you up to this?'

Bjornson shook his head. 'It is a fine day. And I wish to understand for myself what claim this devilish rock has laid upon you.'

Stung by the comment, Boundless nevertheless held his peace as the two men rode through the tall grass. *Perhaps when he better understands my plans he might change his mind*, he counselled himself, holding onto this conceit as the rock loomed on the horizon.

RIDING INTO THE LEE of the great stone they turned loose the horses as Boundless rummaged in the haversack, pulling out the drill and a hammer. Bjornson watched on curiously as he placed the tip of the drill against the rock. Gripping the drill with one hand, he tentatively tapped the striking cap. Holding the drill to the perpendicular he struck again, harder. He rotated the tip and struck the cap three times before rotating it again.

I see only a scratch,' said Bjornson as Boundless paused to examine the drill tip.

'It takes patience.' Gaining confidence, he increased the power of his blows, creating a small indentation in the granite surface. After a quarter-hour of effort, he had bored a shallow hole in the rock.

'You try it.' Wiping the sweat from his brow he handed the drill to Bjornson.

'Surely, boring a hole is not blasphemy?' he said, seeing the hesitant look on the Swede's face.

After another moment's hesitation, Bjornson took the drill, hefting it in his hand. 'It is heavy,' he said.

'Hold it straight,' said Boundless, positioning the drill tip against the rock.

The Swede struck the cap, cautiously at first and then harder. 'God in Heaven!' he exclaimed at the hardness of the granite.

After persevering for some 10 minutes, he stopped and handed the drill back to Boundless. 'We still do not have a proper hole,' he said, peering at his efforts.

Boundless took another turn, blinking as chips flew up from the granite. After 20-minutes a hole a quarter inch deep had been bored into the rock. 'Let us take some refreshment,' he said.

Sitting in the grass they drank water and chewed on pemmican.

'How is your wrist?' asked Bjornson.

'Sore!'

They sat in silence, each man ruminating on his thoughts. The afternoon was bright and humid, a sultry southwester ruffling the swathes. Bjornson wiped a hand across his mouth and eyed Boundless, a look of genuine curiosity on his face. 'Do you really mean to do it—shape the rock?'

'I do.'

'Why?'

Boundless scratched at an insect bite. 'I have explained why,' he said, reluctant to reopen the debate.

'But you have no skill at it.'

'True. But I have a stout arm and a strong back. And I have sent east for advice. No doubt it will require much blasting.'

Chewing on the pemmican, Bjornson considered this. 'If, as you say, the rock already resembles a buffalo, then why not simply leave it at that?'

'Resemblance is in the eye of the beholder—as you and Pinch have already proven. The thing must look to the spectator exactly what it is—a buffalo. Such similitude can only arise from faithful detail.'

Bjornson pointed up at a drifting cloud. 'What does that suggest to you?'

Boundless followed his gaze. 'Nothing but itself. A cloud.'

'But as children we played guessing games, projecting shape or meaning into such airy masses. The merit was to tease out the forms—real or fancied—embodied within. The same is true of all Nature. Indeed, the bigger and more manifold the prospect, the greater and richer its power as an object of contemplation. By contrast, too definite a scene robs the beholder of his fanciful pleasure, do you not agree?'

'No.' Boundless put the cork back in his canteen. 'Faithful detail inspires resemblance between one thing and another.'

'So then, do you intend your buffalo to be free-standing—with legs and all? If so, it will take, I do not doubt, a hundred years or more—not to mention a thousand barrels of powder.'

'The legs will be scrimmed into the rock,' said Boundless, the solution coming to him for the first time. Pondering, he fleshed out the notion. 'The legs will be raised in relief. The head must be in the round, as it will be viewed from all sides. But the legs will be seen separately, on each side, and can therefore be inscribed into the stone.'

'And when will you start?' asked Bjornson. 'You have many duties as bourgeois,' he added.

'Not until I am furnished with the necessary advice and tools.'

Bjornson considered this for some time. 'It is arrogance,' he said finally, looking up at the rock, 'to think that you can impose upon what God has set here for all to marvel at.'

Boundless rubbed his hands over his eyes. 'Perhaps it is not arrogance but faith.'

Bjornson frowned. 'Faith in what? It is not faith but blasphemy to presume to subdue God's creation to your will.'

'One man's blasphemy is another man's faith,' argued Boundless, irritable at having to again defend his project.

'The scripture is plain on the question.' Bjornson's fingers took out the crucifix around his neck: "Ye shall make you no idols nor graven image, neither rear you up a standing image, neither shall ye set up any image of stone in your land, to bow down unto it: for I am the Lord your God."

'Good Lord, man!' Boundless snapped in frustration. 'How many times do I have to say it? I do not propose to build an idol for worship. I simply desire to bring out of the rock the creature that I see within it. Can I say it more plainly?'

Bjornson's tone was unyielding. 'It cannot be done in any case. It is folly to think otherwise.'

'You sound like Pinch!'

"Pinch is right, in this respect at least. Drilling a small hole is one thing. Carving the entire rock be another.' At Boundless' silence, Bjornson continued. 'I always took you for a reasonable man, Boundless.'

And am I not—reasonable?'

'Reason would not attempt such a phantasy.'

'Then perhaps it is something more than reason.'

'More? What is more than reason? Faith?'

Boundless cast about for an answer. 'Desire perhaps.'

'Is that not another word for vanity?' answered Bjornson, his voice flat. 'Our hearts worship that which we desire. And to create that desire absent God is vanity.' At Boundless' stubborn silence he sat forward, his voice grave. 'I urge you, as your friend, to abandon this foolish notion. You have your wife and your family and the post to care for. Remember, you are a partner and Thibault depends upon you for the success of the business. It is time to put a stop to this madness now before it begins.'

With a mutter of frustration, Boundless got to his feet. 'I see you are as obdurate in your opinion as the rock itself. Let us return to the post.'

THEY RODE FOR A half-mile before Boundless glanced back at where the massive rock stood aloof and undisturbed above the prairie grass as it had done so since the beginning of the world. He rubbed his sore wrist, annoyed at his own arrogance in supposing the rock would surrender so easily to his will. 'Perhaps Bjorn is right,' he conceded to himself. 'Perhaps the rock is not meant to be subdued.' The rueful acknowledgement lasted for all of another quarter mile before his mind hardened again. *But nevertheless, I shall do so.*

## A Certain M. Courtois

18 MONTHS AFTER HIS LETTER to Mathieu requesting assistance on stone masonry, a reply arrived with the returning brigade.

'The damn weather!' Dubois stomped to restore the circulation in his feet, his face exhausted. 'Everything was against us! The winds, the currents, the rain! Denis slipped on the rocks and cracked his leg. We had to lay up for a week for it to heal.' He shook his head at the bad luck. Around him, the weary paddlers took off their woollen toques and uttered sighs of relief at the conclusion of the trying journey.

Pausing to shake hands with Lapointe, who approached to commiserate, Dubois continued. 'Unbelievable, I tell you! On top of all, we ran into a surly bunch of Saulteaux and were forced to hand over two sacks of beans, another of flour, and a pound of tobacco to pass in peace. The devils stood all around us with arrows to bows! My God! Another voyage like that and I shall retire to my garden!' He handed over the parfleche pouch. 'We almost lost it, along with ourselves, in a storm, and survived only by God's mercy.'

'What news of Theroux?' asked Lapointe.

Dubois shrugged. 'I have not heard.'

Several new faces among the returnees required introduction, among them a fellow Scot. Another arrival, a German immigrant of the Lutheran faith, immediately took up with Bjornson. The nascent friendship foundered just as quickly with the German's discovery of White Deer and the children. Upon witnessing Bjornson's familial greeting, the German uttered a shocked exclamation and turned pale. From thenceforth, he studiously avoided his fellow congregant.

'The man is new to the country,' said Boundless as Bjornson seethed over the insult. 'He does not yet understand its ways.'

'The man is a dunce!' Bjornson clenched his fists. 'Does he not understand that she is a Christian, as faithful as himself!' He glared at the offender, who sat ostentatiously removed from his erstwhile companion. 'A dunce!' he repeated loudly.

AFTER HOSTING THE SUPPER and delivering his customary speech—by now no doubt already memorialised as a sermon, he wryly acknowledged to Lapointe—he departed as quickly as decorum and the frowns of Pinch would allow. Returning to his quarters, he poured himself a glass of brandy and opened the parfleche pouch. He rifled through the invoices, accounts, and bills of lading, before taking out not one but two letters. Setting aside the one from Guillaume, he opened the second letter, from Mathieu, marked *privé*, with anticipation.

> *Montreal, May 1773*
>
> *My dear Boundless, warm greetings to you and your family. I am exceedingly sorry to convey that the volumes you requested in your letter of last spring proved enormously difficult to obtain—there being very little information on, for example, stonemasonry. Volumes on statuary are equally scarce. Both M. Thibault and I have scoured the booksellers to no avail. It may be possible to order the volumes you requested from Boston or London. Let me know if this is your wish. I enclose, however (and for want of anything else), a single work purporting to describe the great sculptures of Greece and Rome. The book is written in English and was obtained, so the bookseller tells me, from New York. Of what value or honesty it may be is as unknown to me as the author's name and reputation.*
>
> *As for volumes on stones and the properties of thus, I am equally in despair. But rest assured, I shall leave no stone unturned(!) in my efforts to secure whatever may be available.*

Disappointed, he picked up the slim volume and glanced at the title: "The Mighty Antiquities of Greece and Rome." He opened the cover to read the sub-heading: "An Informed Guide to the Enduring Significance of Certain, Famous Sculptures, by Mr. S. J. Ransome, Esquire." He leafed through the densely written pages, dismayed at the scarcity of illustrations.

*Perhaps I can find some practical advice in the contents*, he consoled himself, setting it aside along with the business papers. Returning his attention to the letter, he continued reading.

> *In mitigation of this unwelcome news, I am pleased to introduce you to a certain M. Robert Courtois. It was through diligent pursuit of your enquiries that I made his acquaintance. M. Courtois descends from an old and distinguished line of stonemasons from a town famous for that craft on account of its magnificent cathedral and other works of stone. He was despatched to Montreal some twenty years ago to lend his expertise to the building of the church of Our Lady. Since then, he has stayed to*

open a branch of the family business and, in so doing, established himself as one of the city's foremost stonemasons. He is a decent enough fellow, although hardheaded, in the way of his profession. After hearing of your interest in his craft he agreed to share his knowledge, albeit at a price! He proposes one English pound per letter, setting a premium upon his advice. I attempted to bargain him down to half this amount, but the fellow is as obdurate as his stones and would not budge. But given his extensive experience and excellent reputation, I think you may find him the valuable and resourceful guide you seek.

Once we had agreed on a fee, M. Courtois invited me to visit him at his workshop, situated at a quarry outside the city. I did so, determined to extract whatever nuggets he was willing to provide. I began by inviting the good mason to provide a brief outline of the process whereby natural stone (i.e. granite) is transformed into a carving. It seemed to me the best and most useful way to discover that part of the process of most pertinent interest to yourself. The fellow agreed on condition of an initial payment of £5! When I questioned such an outrageous fee, he claimed that what I asked required 'a grand overview' and that such, in turn, subtracted from the 'dolings' (M. Courtois has a quaint turn of phrase) that a more regular correspondence would require. After some back and forth, we agreed on a price of £3, although not without some displeasure on his part. Loath as I am to admit it, he did indeed, 'dole forth' a considerable quantity of information, as you shall read for yourself. Mixed in with the disquisition, he mentioned sundry tools of his trade that were quite new to me. This being so, I asked him to provide a list of such that might be required by a project such as the one you hinted at in your letter. He agreed, but insisted on an additional fee for the same! He is a shrewd fellow and will insist on weighing out his advice by the shilling's worth! I kept copious notes of our discussion, which I afterwards transcribed. (See the following pages.)

M. Courtois speaks not a word of English and is blunt of speech, as no doubt suits his profession. He frequently interrupted his discourse on method to speak, most yearningly, of his native city and the many works of stone and statuary his family are associated with there. I have tried to capture something of his style or manner in the following record of our discussion. Of necessity, I have added my own words and interpretations where required in order to arrive at a comprehensible account. I have also rearranged his replies into some semblance of order and added the subheads to further impose regularity upon the details. I do hope that I

*have succeeded in delivering information useful to your needs. Monsieur
Courtois states his willingness to answer any other questions you may have
under the agreed arrangement of payment per letter.*

*With all good wishes, I remain your friend and humble correspondent,
Mathieu.*

Boundless cast his eye over the attached pages and, in spite of his curiosity nay, eagerness, to learn from the stone mason, got up to pour himself
another brandy before stepping out to check on proceedings in the hall.
After discussions with Dubois and Lapointe and observing several boisterous songs, he returned to his room and sat down, taking up the letter
with anticipation.

*Monsieur Courtois Speaks!*
*Mr McLennan. I shall get straight to the point, as I am a plain man and
plainly spoke. You ask about stone carving, and the methods and tools of
the stonemason in particular. I shall do my best to explain the rudiments
of both. I preface my remarks by advising you to abandon this indulgence,
interest, hobby or pastime, whichever it may be. You plainly lack experience or skill in working stone. Further, you are as far removed from
practical assistance as it is possible to be. And thirdly, you have chosen,
for your project, a stone of notorious difficulty. That be my advice.*

As if witnessing Boundless' raised eyebrows all the way from his home
in Montreal, Mathieu inserted an aside: *[NB: This is how he wished to begin!]*
'Did he, by God,' muttered Boundless before resuming the letter.

*However, since your M. Simard be sitting before me and pressing me
for method and procedure, I shall endeavour to supply the same, regardless
of my opinion as to the merits of your undertaking.*

*Introduction – The Properties of Granite. First, as to the stone itself
and its peculiar properties. From M. Simard I understand this to be a
considerable block of granite. Such stone is the hardest to work—hard
for an experienced mason, let alone a beginner. It is not the sort of stone
one would choose upon which to practise. Nevertheless, it is the stone you
have selected. (I take it upon faith that the stone is indeed granite and not
basalt or some other stone of like appearance?) In spite of its difficulty as
a material, it is a fine stone, firm and durable, although prone to cracking
or chipping. I am not entirely clear as to your intentions with respect to*

*the stone excepting that you wish to carve or dress it in some manner. The exercise will be exceedingly difficult, as you will no doubt discover—being hard on the tools, harder still on the poor body. Granite is, by its nature, resistant to close, or detailed carving. Such an ambition would be difficult even for an experienced mason or sculptor. The most you can hope for is a general likeness or reasonable facsimile of any model you may have in mind. With that caveat, let us then begin by describing the method to be followed.*

*Preparation. Most masons prefer to begin by making sketches and models (in wax or clay) of the desired figure. The model is scaled according to the size of the stonework. My cousin, a first-rate carver, casts a model of Paris plaster as his preferred method. Measurements are then transferred from this model to the block of stone. As you are, by M. Simard's account, an amateur in respect to this undertaking, I would advise you to have recourse to this method and to begin by constructing a model, whether it be in wax, clay, or plaster. The measurements are obtained through a 'pointing' system or, more simply, by a plumb bob, which indicates both vertical and horizontal points to be transferred to the stone.*

*Extracting the Stone. I know little of the placement of the granite— whether it be in a quarry or a 'found' block. But your M. Simard thinks that the figure you wish to carve is embedded in a larger mass of granite which requires removal in order to extract a definable shape. Proceeding on this assumption, it will first be necessary to evacuate the desired working surface (i.e. the rough shape of the desired form or figure) through splitting and breaking the surrounding rock. To do this, impress a series of shallow holes, using a chisel and hammer. The holes form a line along the desired plane. Iron wedges are then inserted into each hole and held in place between two shims [Note: being a thin piece of iron]. The wedges must first be coated with lubricant of grease or oil to smooth the insertion. You must then move along the line of wedges, tapping each in turn with the hammer. Tap the first wedge once only, and then the second and so forth, using equal force each time. In this manner, the wedges are driven deeper into the stone which then splits evenly along the line of holes. The result should be a smooth break.*

Boundless murmured to himself as he recognised the method taught to him by Helmut. A roar of laughter came from the hall, and he listened for a moment before resuming the letter.

'If the quantity of surrounding stone be great, as M. Simard attests, then you would do well to remove as much as possible by powder. This, again, is a process that properly requires knowledge and experience. In brief, it entails drilling a hole some 2 inches in diameter and from 12 to 20 inches deep, depending on the thickness of the granite. The hole is then filled with powder and plugged with wood or clay, through which a fuse is passed. If done properly, the granite will fracture in a 'v' pattern from the apex of the hole. Care must be taken not to blast too much rock and thus imperil the underlying 'figure'. By these methods, a working surface may be extracted.

Shaping. With your model prepared, and the surface extracted, you are now ready to commence roughing out the lines and planes of the desired form. The process is laborious and exhausting and requires great stores of energy and considerable industry for its achievement. I have appended a list of necessary tools commonly required for this purpose—most importantly, chisels of finest wrought iron. These will be subject to severe stress and will thus be in continual need of retempering if they are to retain their usefulness. [NB: Here followed a lengthy aside on the lamentable inadequacy of Montreal smiths!] The method is to 'point and chip': i.e. to clear away superfluous stone by using a point chisel and a smaller, mason's hammer. As you near, by degrees, the effect you wish to achieve, applied force must give way, perforce, to a more detailed mastery of approach. Here come into their own the toothed and flat chisels. These are used to give definition and 'finish' by refining and smoothing the stone. By following the above sequence, you will proceed from the general mass to the recognisable shape and, thus, to the particular form.

How much farther you intend to progress beyond this stage is dependent upon your skill as an artisan. Do not expect overmuch. Master craftsmen are able to work down even to the minute degree or picturesque detail. But this requires a lifetime of practice following an exacting apprenticeship under a skilled mason. [NB Here followed a sighing disquisition upon his own days as a 'prentice'] Given your limitations in both respects, along with the hardness of the stone, you must content yourself with a general likeness to the original form, as defined by planes and surfaces, rather than through representation founded on figurative detail. [NB The foregoing is my own transcription of the original dictum: 'Be happy if it suggests a duck rather than over-elaborate the feathers!']

That, in brief, is the method required to carve stone. The task is arduous, and care must be taken not to over-exercise the arm, particularly in the early stages. Much more could be said, but—given the circumstances *and distance, experience must be your mentor. Finally, if the block or working surface is of more than the height of a person, the first requirement is for a sound platform from which to work. Again, knowing nothing of your circumstances and experience in these matters—beyond that to which M. Simard can attest—and that portion being exceedingly small as he relates, I must end there or venture into pure speculation. I am willing to furnish such further information as you may require, or to answer your questions to the best of my knowledge. Yours cordially, etc.*

The inestimable M. Courtois then supplied the following list which, true to his word, he had delivered to me a week later by messenger.

*To work the stone you will require the following basics:*

*Hammers of suitable weight, including a 4lb mason's hammer*

*A pitching tool*

*A stone axe*

*Bow drill*

*Chisels—a variety: pointed, square, round, and flat; all to be of forged iron [M. Courtois points out—with exceeding regularity!—that each chisel will last but minutes before it must be resharpened]*

*Measuring instruments—square, spirit level, compass, straight edge and template, a plumb bob and line*

*Metal wedges and 'splints' [M. Courtois suggests two dozen of the former, to begin]*

*The same quantity of turned eye bolts—each of sufficient strength to bear the weight of a person*

*Pins and bolts [For the platform, I presume?]*

*Several hundred feet of stoutly twined rope, the ends tarred and bound [M. Courtois did not specify the use of such rope, but I am assuming it to be for climbing, suspending purposes etc? I observed several coils in the fort workshop]*

*30lb Plaster of Paris sufficient to construct a sizeable model [NB M. Courtois does not know the size of the carving you intend, but indicated a model 1/20$^{th}$ of the original as a rough guide. I asked him to err on the generous side as any remaining powder can be used to plaster walls throughout the stockade buildings]*

*Finally, there remains the question of gunpowder. M.Courtois was at pains to insist upon its importance. 'Gunpowder will prove the surest chisel,' he said, pointing out you will need a substantial amount if, as I suggested, you intend to carry out some project with respect to that huge rock nearby the fort. I recall that you possess a not inconsiderable quantity at the fort. If you could estimate your further needs in that respect, I will endeavour to supply the same.*

His reading was interrupted by the door opening. Meadow Bird entered, ushering Claim and Prospect before her.

'Father!' Prospect flew to his side, attempting to climb up on his lap.

'Your father is working. Quiet now until I finish reading this letter.'

He set the disappointed boy back down again. Returning to the letter, he mulled on the contents, sobered by the advice.

After some minutes, he emitted a sigh and opened the second letter. *Well, Guillaume, old friend, what do you have to say?*

*Montreal, April 22nd—May 3rd 1773*

*My dear Boundless, greetings!*

*This will reach you late as the ice is terrible on all the rivers and lakes. The winter here has been unusually harsh. Its severity was such that the administrators of the City ordered the churches to remain open to provide a sanctuary for the impoverished and homeless. A score of people froze to death in the streets of the city, some of the corpses not discovered until the spring. I myself discovered a poor wretch of a woman—I knew her from selling flowers on the street—a frozen corpse in the road not 10 yards from my own door. Even now that spring has crept in, my poor bones are froze! How it is with you, so far distant, I tremble to think. But, God willing, this finds you safe.*

*I am sad to inform you of the immense loss of the redoubtable Gaston Theroux. I learned of his passing quite by chance. A mutual acquaintance, a former clerk in the trade, happened to know of our association and remarked upon it in conversation. Upon confirming the friendship, the fellow baldly stated that Gaston had died! 'How?' I asked, shocked. The fellow merely shrugged. 'The heart, the constitution—who can say with death?' He then went on to praise the autumn weather. I only received full details when communicating with Theroux's widow. It seems the pilote succumbed to the same lingering disease he had contracted last spring—an organic ailment brought on, no doubt, by his years of hardship paddling the northern waters. He himself once remarked that he manned his first canoe at the tender age of 14 years. Since then, he had put in many thousands of miles at the paddle. He leaves behind his widow and nine surviving children—most of them grown, thank God. He was of sterling character, as you English say, and utterly reliable. He had but recently celebrated his fiftieth birthday. And now, too soon, has set forth on his last voyage. And who can that journey a breath postpone? He will be much missed by all who had the good fortune to receive his friendship. How our personal calamities do overshadow the great news of the world!*

*As if to further mock our hopes, the public news is all of discord and division. The Colonies now make common complaint against the Crown, a cause sparked by numerous outrages. If the English Parliament is not careful, it will provoke the very divorce it seeks to prevent through its heavy-handed governance and its refusal to heed justified complaints. Indeed, it does the work of the agitators for them. 'Tis rumoured that English warships are anchored in Boston Harbour. But rumours are the only currency in these fraught times. An astute observer and member of the Council, the estimable Mr Thomas Dunn, is said to have brilliantly summed up matters in a quip: 'The Colonies protest, the Crown rejects!' [The quip is rendered in the original English. M]*

*What influence any conflict will exercise over trade and commerce remains a matter of speculation and despair. Suffice it to say that reports arrive daily of new fur companies opening up in the New York Colony. If the evidence of dinner parties is anything to go by, all anyone seems to speak about is the race to tie up new sources of beaver before the animal is exhausted. Even grand ladies speak knowingly and knowledgeably of winter coats and parchment beaver. Meanwhile, my neighbour, Madame Cote—I mentioned her in a previous letter—has taken a tumble down the steps of her house and is admitted to the infirmary in great distress. We hold grave fears for her recovery. She has been our neighbour for over 30 years and is a woman of unblemished character and spotless reputation. Her two sons died in the recent war—patriots both. Madame Thibault and I have taken it upon ourselves to adopt the poor soul and visit her frequently. How our lives are governed by where we place our feet!*

*Attached, you will find a copy of the bills of sale for last year's consignment and the profits incurred, with separate notations for the various kind and quality of pelt. I have redrawn the promissory notes of yourself and Mr Bjornson to reflect the year's dividend. And that is all the news for another year. I hope to see you one day soon, my dear Boundless. You must return for a year and leave the post in Monsieur Bjornson's capable hands. Until such happy time, my fondest greetings, and Mathieu's also, to you and your family. And felicitations also to Mr Bjornson and irascible old Pinch himself. I trust that White Deer is well and happy? I have not heard—*

'Monsieur Bourgeois!' The sound of knocking was followed by an urgent voice. 'The Arikara and Cree are quarrelling! You must come!'

DESPITE A RESOLVE TO *put on Guillaume's coat* and pay renewed attention to his managerial duties, he was unable to push thoughts of the rock from his mind. Notions of how best to reach the summit teased and tormented him in equal measure amidst the good-humoured disorder of the returned brigade and the arrival of the Indian wives and their offspring.

Numerous trading parties turned up over the next few weeks, each eager to take first pick of the annual influx of goods. The idle days of summer quickly became a memory as he welcomed delegations of Chippewa and Blackfoot and supervised major repairs to the fence and main buildings before the arrival of winter. One of the younger *voyageurs* caused a minor sensation when he slipped from the post to liaise with a young Hidatsa squaw at her family's village. Boundless despatched Dubois to retrieve the wayward youth, who returned, chastened, out of love, and the butt of every quip and jest for the remainder of the year.

His frustration over his stalled ambition came to a boil when he chanced upon a group of men playing dice in a corner of the yard. Enraged, he threatened each with dismissal if caught malingering again.

News of the incident reached Bjornson, who urged him to patience. 'The men do not understand this urgency. You must be careful lest you alienate their affections.'

He brooded on the episode before conceding that Bjornson was right. *I must keep my emotions in check.* He retired early to his quarters, pouring himself a glass of wine and staring into the fire, his mind heavy with thoughts of the vexatious stone.

## 39

## Crossing the Ohio

THE WINTER PROVED LONG and particularly tiresome, his contrariness at being unable to start on his great project propelling his every mood as he fretted over the weather.

'Is it not colder than usual?' he grumbled to Bjornson.

The intuition was confirmed when Luc reported that the Missouri was thickly plated with ice. For the whole of January, they received no visitors at the post. In February, a heavy snowfall crushed the roof of the bunkhouse and the men struggled to repair the damage amidst blowing snow and freezing winds. Overseeing their efforts, he issued orders in a brusque, commanding voice, reminiscent of Guillaume at his sternest.

Frayed tempers among the company led to quarrels and factions. In late February, a brief remission in the freezing weather ended in a howling gale that confined the brigade indoors for the better part of the month. During that time, two of the men fell into a fierce quarrel over one of the Indian women. Before they could be separated, one of the disputants had pulled out a knife and wounded his rival. Further bloodshed was only averted by the timely intervention of Dubois, who threatened the adversaries with a drawn pistol.

After hearing from several witnesses to the affray, he summoned both antagonists to his private office in the hall. Dubois and Pinch attended as witnesses. He stared severely at the culprits, the wounded man angry, his assailant chastened. 'Well? What the devil do you have to say for yourselves?'

Immediately the men began to argue, each accusing the other of starting the fight.

'Enough!' He held up a hand. 'Do you suppose I have nothing better to do than arbitrate your petty squabbles?'

The men rounded on each other, both protesting at once. The wounded man was particularly aggrieved. In indignant tones, he denounced his rival while holding up his arm to show where his opponent's knife had ripped the shirt and caused a bloody gash to the flesh.

'Are you finished?' Boundless demanded, his voice harsh.

The men nodded, suddenly subdued and awaiting his judgement. 'You are both discharged—as soon as the brigade leaves. Go!'

'*Monsieur?*' Shocked, the wounded man looked from Boundless to Dubois. 'I did no more than defend myself!'

'It took two to make the quarrel.' Boundless waved a hand in dismissal. 'Are you still here? Go!'

Dubois ushered the men from the storehouse, the wounded man still vigorously protesting his innocence.

'It will go hard on Florette,' said Pinch, staying behind. 'It is only his second brigade. And he is a good fellow. He was severely provoked.'

'Let them continue their damn'd quarrel elsewhere.' He sat down in the chair, moody and out of sorts. 'What is it?' he said as Pinch lingered.

'Nothing.' With a shrug, Pinch followed the others out the door.

By mid-April, the river was largely free of floating ice. As the post rang with the sounds of baling and the shouts of work parties, he returned to his quarters to close off his annual letter. Dipping the quill, he resumed where he had left off.

*In the main, life goes on apace, although we have trials and grievances to endure—as one must, no matter one's station or whereabouts in this world. I have had to discharge two of the men for fighting to preserve order and harmony. Pinch has added to his store of grey hairs and mutters on occasion of returning east for a life of feasting and drinking, as he avers. But his heart remains here, along with Buffalo Bird Woman and the four boys to whom he is uncle, cousin-in-mischief and pillory post all at once. Mr Bjornson appears content with his lot although he presently carries a carbuncle on the neck which White Deer dresses with feminine skill. We look forward to a summer of respite from the insect swarms that plagued us last year. The buffalo already return in numbers. Mr Bjornson swears that they increase in quantity with each passing year, although Pinch argues that such is nigh on impossible given their staggering fecundity to begin with—'since the start of the good old world', as he put it. Last summer, we saw such an abundance of whitetail and antelope as has surely never before been witnessed. The mule deer, in particular, were so infestatious as to wander up to the very gates of the stockade and rub against the bark. Until you hear from me again next summer, may Fortune shield you from whatever vicissitudes these uncertain times may bring. Your devoted friend,*
*Boundless McLennan.*

He started a reply to Mathieu, thanking him for his efforts with Courtois and appending a list of questions for the mason. Setting down the quill, he got up from the chair and walked to the open door. In the yard, Bjorn and Lapointe were busily issuing instructions as the men dragged the canoes from their storage sheds. Pinch supervised the baling press, calling out jests and advice as the men compacted the pelts. Prospect and Anders tottered into view, struggling to drag a heavy bale between them. Claim and Torsten followed, straining and puffing to drag a second bale. He watched the four boys stagger across the yard.

Bjorn looked up and raised a hand. He nodded in acknowledgement. Overhead, the sky was blue with fluffs of white cloud that reminded him of something he couldn't put finger to. *Another similar day in the past? Perhaps one crossing the mountains?* He mused on the thought. *The world doth endlessly repeat, whether to buffalo or man or the grass itself.*

The idea made him melancholy as he leaned against the doorframe to look out at the bustling activity. A fragment of a *voyageur* song lodged in his head, and he mentally hummed the bars. Dubois cursed loudly as one of the men tripped over a bale, the other men bursting into laughter.

Turning away from the door, he sat back down at the desk and took up the quill.

*It is my wish that Monsieur Courtois shall immediately purchase those items listed in his original letter for consignment to me via the next available brigade. Please consider yourself my agent in this matter, with all necessary authority to make payments as required—all expenses to be subtracted from my account. I remain most grateful for your assistance in this as in all else.*

He re-read what he had written, feeling a momentous sense of occasion. *I have committed myself to it. There is no turning back. The die has been cast. The Ohio crossed.*

He sealed the letter, smoothing it flat. Sitting back, he gazed through the open door at the men as they laughed and joked while binding and lifting the bales. A memory of another day and a similar bout of high spirits played upon his mind, the two scenes clouding together so that he scarce could tell whether he observed the one or the other.

## 40

# A Person of Delaware

A MONTH AFTER THE DEPARTURE of the brigade, the weather turned hot, the mild spring breezes giving way to a furnace-like wind from the south. Around the stockade, the billowing grass rippled and swayed like a living thing. Luc returned from a hunt leading a horse travois laden with buffalo meat. 'Past the rock they are thick as flies,' he said.

Two days later, the buffalo appeared outside the stockade, their grunts and roars awakening him from sleep. Going outside, he climbed to the rampart, his ears deafened by the swelling crescendo. As always, the first sight of the astonishing plenitude of horns, tails and hooves took him by surprise. *I could walk across their backs all the way to the rock*, he marvelled, gazing out over the besieging host.

He took the opportunity to introduce his sons to the musket, the buffalo wandering up almost to within touching distance. Using a shot cow for instruction, he showed the spot to aim for. 'Just above the elbow,' he said. 'Wait until the foot is forward, out of the way of the vitals. Look carefully and you will see a patch of bare skin. Aim for that. Shoot only when you are sure of the target.'

Supporting the musket, he allowed both to aim at a spike bull. 'Watch,' he said. Taking back the weapon he shot the bull, dropping it in place. 'D'ye see?'

As both boys clamoured for the musket, he knelt behind Prospect. 'That one,' he said, guiding the boy's hands to a yearling calf. 'Ready yourself for the kick. Breathe!' He felt the boy tremble as he sighted the long barrel. 'Look at the buffalo, not the gun!' The boy's shoulder jerked as the weapon fired. The calf gave a bellow and sank to its knees.

'I kilt it!' Prospect turned to his brother, his face shining with triumph.

'It ain't dead!'

'Not yet!'

'Let me!' Claim begged for the gun. An indignant Prospect shoved him aside. 'It's mine!' The calf bellowed again as its mother trotted up to lick its face. 'I kilt it!'

'It is your brother's kill,' he said to Claim. 'He must finish it.'

He led Prospect closer to the stricken calf. 'Careful. It is not dead. Not too close—keep an eye on the mother. She will run you through in an instant.' Guiding the boy's aim, he finished off the calf. 'The mother!' he warned, retreating the boy as the cow trotted around in confusion.

Moving away from the dead calf, he reloaded the musket and handed it to the eager Claim. 'That one over there,' he said, picking out another calf. He knelt behind his son, helping to support the heavy musket. 'Hold steady. Take your time. Where are you aiming? Pick your spot.' He closed his fingers over the boy's hand. 'Ready?'

They shot two more buffalo in this manner, the boys hardly able to contain their excitement as he anointed them both with blood. ''Tis how the Indians do it,' he said, brushing his thumb across each forehead in turn. 'Now watch as your mother takes the meat.'

The women butchered the carcasses with blood-splattered efficiency, working quickly in the hot sun and attracting a swarm of flies.

''Tis a manufactory to them,' remarked Pinch, puffing clouds of tobacco smoke to keep at bay the midges and blackflies. 'Mark,' he said, indicating where Buffalo Bird Woman used a hatchet to sever an ankle joint. 'They say hungry Indians will consume even the bones.'

The buffaloes remained within sight of the stockade for two days, congesting the plain with more and more bodies until the lush summer grass was trampled and shorn down to the roots. The vast herd seemed at once both sedentary and in continual motion, the foremost animals replaced hourly as the tail caught up to the head.

By the third day, the plain was empty, the grass littered with voluminous piles of dung, much to Bjornson's disgust. 'Foul, loathsome beasts!' he protested loudly while scraping his shoes. 'They stink the very air.'

'Thank God I don't have to listen to that infernal bellowing one more hour,' agreed Pinch. 'It is as well you love them, Boundless, as their noise is deaf to your ears.'

A week after the buffalo had vacated the prairie around the fort, the musky stink still hung in the air. The smell was only displaced by a heavy rainstorm that soaked the grass

The rain was followed by another week of hot weather, the sultry heat bringing with it a fresh plague of mosquitoes. He applied grease to the boys, smearing it over their faces, much to their delight. 'Keep it off your clothes,' he said as they rubbed the grease into their skin.

HE WENT FOR A ride in the lush grass, reining in to observe the rock in the distance. *I shall be as old as Mose before I start.* The memory of his former comrade gave him pause as he sat contemplating the stone outcrop. *What would he make of it? Would he consider it a fool's task, as does Pinch, and Bjornson—and my wife—and no doubt everyone else at the post? Or would he understand? And if not, how would I explain it when I scarce understand it myself?*

He continued his ride, ruminating on the many different ways fate had charted his progress thus far. *A turn here, a rainstorm there, a stray arrow, all would have dictated a different life. Do we choose, or are we chosen?* He was pondering the question when he spotted something moving ahead. Shading his eyes, he saw a group of men walking through the long grass. To his surprise, he saw by their clothes and their muskets that they were white.

Riding to catch up, he hailed from a distance, unwilling to risk surprising the party and receiving a musket ball in consequence. 'Ahoy, friends!'

The men turned as he approached. One man led a mule carrying packs, filled—Boundless surmised—with trade goods. Their leader greeted him in an unmistakable Highlands brogue, the man immediately recognising his own Scottish provenance.

'Rab Duncan, friend.' The man, his face and clothes dusty from the trek through the grass, regarded Boundless, his expression friendly but cautious. His companions, five in all, eyed Boundless with a mix of surprise and curiosity.

'I thought we were the only white men in these parts,' said Duncan as Boundless dismounted. 'We are making our way north to a supposed Indian camp. Take a spell, boys,' he said.

'You are fur traders?' asked Boundless, draping the reins over the mustang.

'Aye. But first we must make contact with the Indians. We hear there is much fine beaver to be had in these parts.'

'How did you get here?'

'We floated up the Missouri most of the way and then walked the rest, as you see.' Duncan studied Boundless. 'It is passing strange to find a white man out here, alone.'

'Not alone. I have companions on the same Missouri, a few miles back.'

'A fur post?'

'A lodge. We are settled there.'

'Indeed?' The man considered this. 'Then you must be acquainted with the Mandan?'

'Only so much as to steer clear. They are suspicious of trespassers on their land.'

Duncan nodded at this. 'As you say,' he said. 'Would you take a pipe?'

As they sat in the grass, the men informed him that fighting had broken out between the colonies and England.

'You say?' He sat forward in surprise. 'I am starved for news.'

'Aye.' Duncan took a swig of water. 'Armies are gathering on both sides. They say George Washington will lead our boys into battle.'

Boundless furrowed his brow to place the name. 'The same Washington that fought against the French?'

'The very same. Do you know him?'

'I saw him once.'

'We are bound on trading with the Indians, but the boys here want only to join up with the militia to fight the redcoats. How about you?' Duncan eyed him. 'You look like you can shoot a gun.'

He shrugged. 'The war may be over in a week, or a month.'

'That is what I said!' Duncan twisted to look back at his companions. 'Hear that, boys? Why rush back when there are good beaver pelts for the taking?'

One of the men said something, to approving grunts from the others.

'Culloden again!' Duncan grimaced and shook his head.

'Are you in favour of colonial home rule?' asked Boundless.

'Why not? I have no love for England. And you?' He studied Boundless.

'A deer cannot yoke a buffalo.'

Duncan grinned. 'Well put!'

An hour later, they parted ways, the affable Duncan wishing him safe hunting. 'Whether of buffalo or beaver,' he said, a twinkle in his eye.

As Boundless watched them leave, a sudden nostalgia for the voices of his homeland prompted him to call out. 'Lang may yer lum reek!'

One of the men laughed, turning to raise a hand. 'Aye for a dreich day!'

'SCOTTISH, LIKE YOURSELF?' PINCH was bemused at the notion as Boundless relayed the encounter during tea in the main hall. They sat around talking as the boys played in the yard. The door was open to the warm air.

'And no French among them?' asked Bjornson

'Not that I could tell.'

'Then they will not have much luck with the Indians—unless they themselves speak French.'

'And they said that a war had started?'

'He mentioned only that fighting had broken out. But both sides are resolved on war as the only way to settle their differences. Guillaume suggested as much in his letter.'

Pinch frowned in dismay. 'I thought they might come to their senses at the last.'

'Who?'

'The Patriots, who else?'

'They call themselves Americans now.'

Pinch gave a snort. 'There be no such thing!'

'Since we are not gypsy fortune tellers, what, pray, do you mean?'

'Your American. No such animal exists.'

'Tell that to your countrymen in Boston, who now call themselves American.'

'Let others call themselves as they choose. I stand as a true Englishman. So was I born, and so shall I die.' Pinch glared around the room as though daring the bare walls to object.

'In truth, Pinch, you be the only Englishman among us, if indeed that is what you are,' Bjornson pointed out, 'since Boundless here was born in Scotland.'

'Pshaw!' Pinch roundly dismissed the notion. 'Look around. You will see nought but Indians. And—*And*,' he continued, defying Bjornson's attempt to interrupt, 'there is Abel—German. And Luc, Emile and Antoine—French. And what,' he argued as Bjornson opened his mouth again, 'is White Deer but Hidatsa?' He turned to Boundless. 'And your own Meadow Bird—is she not Mandan?'

'She is.'

'Ha! Then does she not stand contrary to your claim? And Buffalo Bird also, being Arikara? And you yourself, Bjorn—what in blazes are you?'

'Indeed,' said Bjornson, looking confused. 'Up until this very moment I had considered myself a person of Delaware—if I have given the matter any thought at all.'

'And therefore, subject to the Crown as any Englishman! Case proven!' Pinch drained his tea with a loud slurp.

'Hold fire.' Boundless raised a hand in protest. 'Could we not then—and with equal justice—claim that we are subject to the Mandan, since this is their land?'

'Zounds! You would no doubt have us happily subject to the buffalo?'

'Nevertheless, I am content to claim myself as American—as the colonists, the patriots anyway, describe themselves.'

'I must—on this rare occasion—agree with Pinch.' Bjornson ignored Pinch's feigned astonishment. 'Insofar as I am aware, the word lacks legal distinction since it denotes neither a flag nor a country nor a proper person, in law.'

'There you have it—as expounded by the learned theologian!'

'Then how else are we to understand the generality of colonists, as distinct from native Englishmen?'

'Why, as persons.'

'Persons of where?'

'By the bones! Persons—each of a locality and origin. Did you not hear Bjorn just now describe himself as a person of Delaware? It is as plain as the nose on your face.'

'Then take my sons—yours also, Bjorn—as a case in point. How must they describe themselves but as American, being native to this land of America, not England?'

'Fiddle! The word is empty, since there be no such country.'

'Suppose then that the Americans were to prevail. What then becomes of your argument?'

'Then, nothing. Your supposed Americans will tire of their own squawks long afore your "then" transpires.'

'The word is, as you say Boundless, original,' put in Bjornson, having given the matter thought.

Pinch hooted. 'Even to concede your point—which I do not—who then is your actual American?'

'A free-born man—'

'Then not a slave?'

'An abomination for another day. But, to continue … native to these parts—'

'Then you remove yourself?'

'Resident to these parts …'

'As are the Mandan. Do you miscall them American, too?'

'Resident to these parts. White—not Indian. Nor yet a buffalo.'

'And not French!'

'And not French. And in sympathy with the rights of the colonists.'

Pinch snorted. 'A long-winded declaration!'

'And yet, I so declare myself. From this point forth.'

'How so—since you fault your own prescription? Bjorn, here, has the greater claim.'

''Tis in the declaration,' suggested Bjorn.

'Nonsense! The claim be so windy as to blow down a tree.'

'A man may declare himself whatever he deems,' objected Bjornson. 'A Christian, for example. Or a non-conformist.'

'Fiddle! You play with words. I may as well declare myself a Turk.'

'That is to declare blood, as well as ancestry,' said Boundless

'Faith, also,' pointed out Bjornson. 'Your Turk being an Ottoman.'

'So, you admit! Your American lacks both parentage and birthright?'

'You speak to its benefit since, unlike the Old World, the word makes no claims as to either.'

'Hence its originality,' proposed Bjornson.

'Hence its originality. One might even say the term includes the invented man as well as the native one.'

'We have swelled to a term?' argued Pinch, professing astonishment. 'Indeed, your new-minted American does not lack for ambition.'

Invented?' Bjornson cast a confused look.

'As I sit here before you.'

'An invented American?'

'Invented and declared, both.'

'Truly, a creature altogether new to the world!' Pinch hawed with derision. 'Confounded on all sides! You have chased your American up and down the street and found him to 'scape you at every turn. You say what he is not, rather than what he is.'

'Specie to be determined.'

'Then it may be that force of arms will indeed settle the case,' suggested Bjornson.

The reminder gave pause to the debate. Pinch frowned and used a fingernail to pick his teeth. 'Your man was convinced—that this indeed be war? And not a local skirmish?'

'Aye. War, he said. And Bannock predicted the same long ago. It is unnatural to suppose that a small and distant island should rule a vast continent.'

'What will you do, Boundless?' asked Bjornson. 'Surely you do not contemplate abandoning all that you have here to join the fight?'

Boundless deliberated the answer, aware of Pinch's keen gaze. 'At one time, perhaps. But I see now that there is a …' he paused, searching for the word. 'A *hitherness* to things. Events that seem of great moment in themselves are less so when measured against—'

'Your buffalo, no doubt?'

'I know only that there are other things that matter equally if not more.'

Pinch nodded, his agreeableness coming as a surprise. 'A robust testament. And one that will stand in place of conscription. Do you agree, Bjorn?'

'I know only that such a war would be far from here, thanks be to God. Although it may drag in the Indians,' added the Swede.

Pinch shook his head. 'They are too sensible. They have learned their lesson from the last war. Whichever side wins, they shall suffer.'

The conversation fell silent, each man reflecting on his own thoughts. At length, Pinch yawned and got to his feet. 'I am off to sleep—a true Englishman, as I hope to wake each day.'

'Myself also—but for the English.' Bjornson pushed back the chair.

'Then I bid you both an American goodnight!' replied Boundless as he, too, stood up.

Returning to his quarters, he found the boys playing with wooden swords. 'Where is Mother?'

Prospect fended off a thrust. 'She has gone to visit Mrs Bjornson.'

'Stop playing. I have something to tell you. Come here, beside me.' He sat down by the fire. 'Do you know what you are?' he asked.

Prospect strained to answer. 'A boy?'

Smiling, he ruffled his son's hair. 'Aye. You are that all right. But what else? What sort of boy? Do you remember where your father was born? Claim! Stop waving that deuced stick. Come over here.'

'Scotland?'

'Aye. Are you a Scottish boy, for instance?'

Prospect scrunched his face. 'I don't know!'

'Ha!' Claim gloated at his brother.

'And you, master-know-it-all, what kind of a boy are you?' The look of triumph was exchanged for one of sullen dismay. 'Then try this. Where are you from?'

'Here!' said Claim.

Prospect looked ready to utter a scornful laugh, only to be forestalled by his father. 'Indeed, you are! Now, where is here? You too, Prospect.'

As the boys regarded each other for answer, he tapped each one on the forehead. 'You are American,' he said, 'since this is America. Say it, the pair of you.'

'Merri-can,' The boys mumbled the word.

'A-mer-ican. It is a most marvellous word. A word new to the world. It means that you are a free-born citizen of America.'

Prospect looked doubtful. 'And Mother?'

'She is Mandan.'

'Why?'

'Because she was born here. This is Mandan country.'

'But I was born here, too.' Prospect looked upset.

'And me!'

'Well, I suppose you were. But you are American, just the same.'

'And Mother?' echoed Claim.

'She is still Mandan.'

Seeing their distressed looks, he relented. 'Perhaps she could be American too, if she wishes.'

'Mother!'

Before he could stop them, the boys had raced off to tell their mother of her good fortune.

## 41

## A Jacob's Ladder

Two years after his letter of instruction to Mathieu, the brigade returned bringing the supplies and materials recommended by Monsieur Courtois. The many kegs, crates and sacks, all marked *Property of M. McLennan, Bourgeois*, drew questioning looks from Lapointe as the cargo was deposited in the yard. Ignoring the curious looks, he ordered all such marked containers be delivered to the workshop. 'Would you like them carried inside, sir?' asked one of the men.

'Yes. The door is unlocked.'

Later in the day, when all the post supplies had been sorted, itemised, and carried to the storehouse, he went to inspect the sizeable cargo. The kegs of powder had been stacked in a neat pile against the wall. The sacks of plaster sat in a corner. The heavy coils of rope were laid on top of the powder kegs. The wooden crates were lined up on the floor against the opposite wall. He dampened his eagerness to unpack the contents in order to return to his bourgeois duties and oversee the celebratory feast associated with the return. *Besides, they will no doubt be waiting on my speech,* he reminded himself with a rueful smile.

Following the supper, he retired to his quarters to read Mathieu's letter.

*Montreal, June 1776*

*My Dear Boundless,*

*It is with great pleasure that I at last despatch the tools and materials you requested the brigade before last. M. Courtois has been most diligent in his collection of the necessary items—including some he ordered from his native town, and others provided from his own private stock of materials. Everything, he assures me, is of the best workmanship. He gave effusive praise to the chisels, in particular, declaring them to be of the 'finest wrought iron'. He made only the suggestion of including a pair of callipers which, following your advice, I purchased on his recommendation. I could not recall whether or not we already possessed a pair at the post.*

*As you will see, the weight and quantity of the whole is considerable, and necessitated the expense of an additional canoe and four additional men to paddle it. M. Dubois assured me that such was required as the existing brigade was over-laden. He then worked miracles to accommodate all within the expanded fleet. The costs have been itemised on the attached page and the tally subtracted from your profits as per your instructions. You may rest assured that M. Courtois has been equally diligent in matters of the purse, finely calculating the cost of each item and weighing in the time and expense incurred in answering your additional questions! His letter is attached, translated by me. I jested that, surely, his thumb was on the balance! only to receive an admonishing look in return. He shows considerable curiosity as to your mysterious project, even to the extent of expressing a wish to travel to the wilderness to see it for himself. He is deterred only by the immense distance and the knowledge that it is not yet begun. If you have further needs, or questions for our redoubtable mason, do not hesitate to inform me.*

*I am pleased to act as your agent in this matter and in all else.*
*In deepest friendship, Mathieu.*

He murmured a heartfelt thanks to his distant friend before turning to Thibault's letter.

*Montreal, May 1776*

*The first faint signs of winter are on the air even though it is but*
*May. This morning, I caught such a cold blast as I ventured along St Catherine that I feared I might be whisked all the way back to the stockade! All the talk here is of the war and the progress each side is making. Rumour has it that the 2ⁿᵈ Continental Congress is preparing a declaration of independence. Is it not strange that allies in the recently concluded war should now be preparing to do battle with each other? Since I last wrote, the British have won a major victory in Quebec against an invading American force. Each day brings reports and rumours of fresh moves and countermoves. Like figures on a chess board, the pieces advance towards each other, probing for openings. A year or two ago, the odds would have been stacked heavily against colonial success in a war of rebellion. But the British, by their actions, are driving more and more of the colonials to the Patriot cause.*

*On to an altogether different and more salubrious matter. You are now a man of means, Boundless. I do not know the details of the mysterious project you hinted at in your letter, except that it follows your interest in natural stones and the stonemason's art. But that aside, it is surely time for you to consider taking up your gains to enjoy a prosperous retirement, especially given the fraught times. You are still a young man and with a family to raise. It is, as you have pointed out, sixteen years and more since your arrival at the post, and ten since your accession to bourgeois. Now is an opportune time to consider 'giving up the field' and retiring to the east, to either Montreal or Philadelphia. If the former, you would be welcomed as a senior partner, like myself, and help to advertise and sell the peltry. If the latter, you might act as our representative with the local merchants as we pursue new markets in that city. Your experience with all aspects of the trade would be unmatched.*

*I do not know what the future holds for Mr Bjornson, but a similar arrangement is open to him, also. M. Dubois would make a very capable bourgeois in your place. Please give every consideration to this proposal, as none may know what chance, or mischance, Fate has in store for us. I await your reply in fond hope and expectation.*

*Finally, I have engaged a new carpenter to replace the old. His name is Philip Bertrand. He is reputed to have first-class skills in his trade. Moreover, he is English, or American as he describes himself despite his name. He hails from the Connecticut colony, although he has been resident in Quebec these past few years.*

*God's blessings upon you, my dear Boundless, and your wife and sons also. My fond remembrances, too, to Mr Bjornson and his. And not forsaking cantankerous old Pinch! Your faithful friend, Guillaume Thibault.*

*PS Please pass on my fondest wishes to White Deer—if she has not forgotten me already!*

IT WAS NOT UNTIL the afternoon of the following day that he was able to attend to the supplies, after first assigning Lapointe to deal with the thousand and one questions arising from the return.

'But there are decisions to be made,' protested the head clerk. 'Who to assign to which lodging. The goods—some of them are damaged. The Indians are clamouring to begin trade—'

'You deal with it. Get Bjorn to help you. And Dubois, too, if necessary.' He held up a hand as Lapointe continued to protest. 'I will be along later. I need to attend to something first.'

Lapointe sighed, his disapproval evident. 'It is customary—'

'Take whatever decisions you think necessary. I will support you.'

He watched as Lapointe walked away shaking his head. *No doubt he is disappointed in me.* The thought vanished from his mind as he went to inspect the long-awaited supplies.

Taking a pry bar, he opened a crate marked *Chisels*. The implements were bundled in oil cloth and secured with string. The wrought-iron chisels were longer and heavier than the ones already at the post. He picked up a star drill. *Similar to Helmut's.* Struck by the thought, he opened the door and hailed a passing *engagé*. 'Find Helmut. Tell him he is wanted.'

While waiting, he pried the tops of another half-dozen crates. He was examining the contents when he was stopped by a knock at the half-open door.

'Sir. It is Helmut. You sent for me?'

'Come in, Helmut.' The ex-quarryman did so, after first exaggeratedly stamping his feet to clear them of dust.

Boundless pointed to the chisels. 'What do you make of these?'

He watched as Helmut picked up several chisels to inspect. 'They seem finely made, sir.'

Boundless picked up a short, heavy chisel. 'What is this one called, and what is it for?'

'That is a pointer. Useful for roughing away stone. As is this one.' Helmut set down the pointer and picked up a chisel with a broad, flat end. 'This is a pitcher. It is the first recourse for clearing away large amounts of unwanted rock. Both will become your best friends.'

'And these?' He pointed to a number of chisels bound by string.

Helmut ran his finger over the edges. 'The tooth chisel is useful for detail—although not usually on granite, the stone being too hard. The flat one, also.' He picked up a chisel with a bulbous end. 'This one is good for making rounded surfaces.' He peered at the other tools. 'He has sent you picks, I see. Useful for breaking up rock—like the pitcher. And rasps and files as well.'

Helmut whistled in surprise as he examined the contents of another crate. 'Rubbing stones as well! You use these to smooth the finish,' he said. 'The files and rasps won't be effective on granite.'

Boundless levered open another crate to reveal an assortment of rods, a protractor, a straight edge, a brass plumb bob together with lengths of twine, and a pair of callipers. Helmut's eyes were wide as he surveyed the trove. 'You certainly have all the tools you could ever wish for.' He glanced at Boundless as if to say something. 'You really wish to carve it—into a buffalo?'

'The buffalo is there already. I but plan to liberate it.' The words surprised even as he uttered them. *Is that what I am doing?*

'It will be difficult, *monsieur*.' Helmut's voice was sober. 'More difficult than you can imagine.'

FOR THE NEXT SEVERAL days, he was occupied with issues surrounding the returned brigade—confirming quarters for the married men, making copious notes on the state of the goods received, checking inventories and shipping lists, and overseeing the placement of supplies within the storehouse—undoing several decisions made by Lapointe in the process, despite his earlier assurances. He also dealt with a seemingly endless number of trade delegations, the various tribes anxious to have first pick of the new goods.

The delegations included a group of Lakota Sioux offering to exchange slaves for goods, a proposal that infuriated him. 'Do not approach me with any more such offers,' he warned the headman, a short, arrogant individual with a heavily painted face. 'And remove the paint if you wish to enter the fort again.' Clearly affronted, the Indian climbed back on his pony. With a barked command, he led his comrades out of the stockade, the hapless captives stumbling to keep up.

'Should we not have offered an exchange?' asked Pinch. 'The poor devils looked badly used.'

'If we do, they will keep taking more slaves and hostages.'

'That headman looked mighty put out.'

'To blazes with him. We don't need his kind around here.'

Amidst the many claims on his time, he endeavoured to maintain his schedule of educating the boys, his own and Bjornson's, setting an hour aside each morning for the purpose. By the time dusk fell, he was often so tired he went to bed without supper. To ease the burden, he handed Dubois the responsibility of managing all issues arising from the *engagés*. 'After all, you know them best,' he said. He turned over the supervision of trades to Lapointe, with Antoine or Emile responsible for copying the results into the ledger.

To Bjornson, he gave the task of mediating all disputes or questions of importance. 'Kindly do so before bringing them to me,' he said.

'And what will you do?' asked the Swede.

'Do you not see I have sufficient to occupy me the live-long day with letters, ledgers, bills, inventories and what nots?'

'You seem to have lost all interest in your duties,' remarked Pinch, who was listening from the storehouse doorway.

'As long as I have you to advise me, Pinch, then all is not lost.'

He mulled on Pinch's remark as he arranged the contents of the workshop. *It is true. The position no longer holds interest for me. But I need it. I need the resources of this post.* He experienced a twinge or guilt as he wondered what Guillaume would make of all the supplies despatched by Mathieu. *If he has questions, then let him ask, and I shall endeavour to answer them.*

His gaze strayed to the sketchbook drawings pinned to the wall. *Where to begin?* he wondered, the question seeming to repeat itself after each forward motion. His thoughts went to the advice offered by Courtois. *'Most masons prefer to begin by making sketches and models (in wax or clay) of the desired figure. The model is scaled according to the size of the stonework.'*

He hummed on the advice for a while, his mind cataloguing the tasks required. Opening his journal, he turned to the measurements he had made the summer before.

Highest point or 'hump': 60 feet
Height of 'tail': 52 feet
Height of head: 58 feet
Declination (from 'hump' to 'tail'), 8 feet
Length—190 feet
Front Width: 50 feet
Rear Width: 41 feet

With an eye on the length, he paced the room, frowning as he reached the wall. 'Too small,' he muttered. He thought for a moment before exiting the house.

'You want what?' Philip Bertrand, the new carpenter, a tall, muscular individual, blinked at the request.

'I wish the house I use as a workshop be extended by five feet. It is for a project I have in mind. Can you do it?'

'Sir, if it is room that you require, why not use the old guard house? That would give you ample space without needing to extend the workshop.'

'I thought the men were using it as a secondary bunkhouse?'

'They were, but the chimney became blocked, and they moved back to the main bunkhouse.'

'Can you unblock the chimney?'

'I can.'

'Come with me. Let us see this space.'

The guard house was bare apart from a table, two chairs and several stools. The bareness added to the impression of spaciousness as he paced the timber floor, measuring off 35 feet in length and 28 in width.

Pleased with the size, he turned to the watching Bertrand. 'A fine suggestion. How long have you been a carpenter?'

'Ever since I can remember, sir. I was apprenticed to my father, who was a master carpenter.'

'And you chose to join the brigade?'

'I enjoy the life. There is plenty of freedom and all the adventure a man could wish for.'

'I might have made the same answer myself. Do you have other skills, besides carpentry?'

'I can turn my hand to most things.'

'I need you to construct a wood mould, to these measurements,' he said, showing a diagram to Bertrand.

The carpenter studied the sketch. 'For the plaster?—I saw the sacks,' he explained at Boundless' surprised look.

Boundless smiled at the man's quick grasp. 'Aye. For the plaster. What?' he said at a questioning look from the other man.

'How do you propose to climb it, sir—the rock?'

Boundless raised a humorous eyebrow. 'You are well informed, friend.'

Bertrand shrugged. 'It is no secret, sir—that you intend to carve it into something.'

Boundless eyed the man thoughtfully. 'Do you have any suggestions— about climbing it?'

'There is but one way—if it be as high as I have heard rumoured—a rope ladder.'

'I had considered that, but fear it would be too fragile, and too unstable.'

'Not if it's made correctly, with wood rungs to make it easier to climb.'

The description twigged a memory. 'I may have seen such a ladder, as you describe—when boarding a schooner once a long time ago. I believe the deckhands referred to it as a Jacob's ladder. Is that what you propose?'

Bertrand nodded. 'It is. I have seen them on sailing vessels and once cut some replacement rungs for one.'

'And you could make such a ladder?'

'Yes. It is a simple matter of drilling the steps and securing each one with a knot. Danon Lacrosse was apprenticed as a ropemaker. I could consult with him as to the best ropes and knots and so forth.'

'It would need to be over 60 feet in length.'

Bertrand shrugged. 'Six feet or sixty. It is all the same.'

'Good man!' He clapped Bertrand on the shoulder, liking the man's unassuming confidence. 'You can work in the other workshop. I'll arrange to have the supplies moved to here, out of your way. Will that be sufficient room?'

At Bertrand's nod, he continued. 'You can use the ropes brought back by the brigade. And, if need be, you'll find more in the tool hut. Take whatever else you need. Tell Monsieur Lapointe I authorised it. Here's the key to the house. Keep it locked whenever you are not there and keep the key on your person. Do you understand?'

Buoyed by the conversation, he returned to his quarters feeling optimistic for the first time. *I shall have my steps,* he told himself, looking forward to a celebratory glass of wine.

IN THE DAYS BEFORE Christmas, the first permanent snow fell, collecting in nooks and crannies and whitening the grass around the post. Christmas Day itself was celebrated with the usual wild abandon shown by the brigade, who placed great store on both Christmas and New Year's Day. Drinking began with breakfast and continued all day long.

In spite of the cold, the men organised impromptu contests, venturing out into the snow to challenge each other to foot races and feats of dexterity. An elaborate feast, which the women had been preparing for days, saw the Christmas table groan under platters of venison, moose, beaver tails, dried fish and buffalo tongue.

*The men fell upon the feast like ravenous wolves,* he wrote in his journal, knowing that Guillaume would enjoy reading of the tradition that had started under his management.

*'Twas useless to try to get work out of them for days following, expectations turning immediately to the New Year festivities. There was a great dance—with fiddles and tambourines, drums and spoons. The men strove to outdo one another with kicks and spins and jumps. Songs were sung and bawdy tales told of former days and former comrades. There were two or three quarrels—including a wild fight between two of the Indian women, brought about by the intoxication and high spirits, but these were quickly broken up with no harm done.*

He made a brief appearance in the dining hall, during which he was roundly toasted by the ebullient Frenchmen—and toasted further when he authorised the opening of a second cask of rum.

As soon as he could, he escaped back to his quarters, where he entertained Bjornson and Lapointe to a dinner of roast buffalo hump and spiced duck. The women served the dishes, having refused to sit as guests along-side their husbands. The three men drank several bottles of wine as the noisy celebrations from the dining hall spilled out into the yard.

'It is a wonder they don't all freeze to death,' remarked Bjornson as shouts came from outside.

'It is why Dubois has arranged for two or three of the more sober men to patrol the buildings to prevent such a thing,' said Lapointe. He took out a pipe. 'May I?'

'I wonder how Monsieur Thibault is celebrating?' said Bjornson.

'Probably stuffed on goose,' puffed Lapointe. 'And no doubt missing a certain someone,' he added, with a pointed glance at White Deer. Although intended as a jest, the remark caused Bjornson to flush, the Swede clearly uncomfortable with the quip.

The jest came back to Boundless later as he made one final check of the dining hall festivities before retiring to bed. Bjornson was leaning against the wall, his face a study in melancholy as he observed two men engage in a drunken shuffle to the meanderings of an equally drunk fiddler. White Deer came up and said something to the Swede, rubbing his arm as she spoke. Bjornson's despondent features were quickly replaced by a smile as he said something in return, one hand laid across her back.

*Is she happier with Bjorn?* Boundless wondered, *or does she secretly pine for Guillaume?* He remembered the first time he had seen her, and her dark, startled glance as she caught sight of him. *Like a deer, indeed. Who can tell with Indians?* he mused, stepping out into the cold night air. The dogs howled as he crossed the yard. *Who can tell with anyone—myself most of all?* The thought briefly confounded him as he made his way back to his quarters.

AS SNOW BUILT UP on the plains around the fort, Bertrand sent word that the Jacob's ladder was finished. Eager to see the result, he immediately went to the workshop. Inside, he found Bertrand and Danon, standing beside a large wooden drum around which was coiled a thick mass of rope. A fire blazed in the grate.

'Good morning, sir.' Bertrand greeted him as he entered.

'And a cold one!' Shivering, he closed the door behind him.

'Here it is.' Bertrand indicated the drum, a proud look on his face.

Danon pulled on the ladder, extending it so that the rungs were visible. Each rung consisted of a pair of ropes passing through a drilled hole in the wood and tied off underneath with a knot.

'It looks very like the one I remember climbing,' said Boundless.

He tugged at a knot. 'Which knots are those?'

'A hitch,' said Danon.

'I am familiar with hitches but don't recognise this one. Will you teach me sometime?'

'I will be glad to, sir,' answered Danon, pleased with the compliment.

The ladder unfolded easily from the drum when Boundless pulled on it, extending it to its maximum length. 'What are those?' he asked, seeing canvas loops worked into the rope.

'To save your hands, sir,' answered Danon. 'The ropes will be rubbing against the rock and will strip your skin otherwise.'

'Well done.' Boundless smiled at the innovation. 'And these?' Two wood blocks were placed either side of the topmost rung.

'To brace against the rock and steady the ladder as you climb.'

'A thing of beauty!' He shook the hands of both men, pleased by the workmanship.

Danon picked up a crank handle and inserted it in the drum. 'To rewind the ladder,' he explained, demonstrating by winding in the unfolded rungs.

'How heavy is it?'

'It can be lifted by two men.' Grasping either side of the drum Bertrand and Danon lifted it onto the table with some exertion.

'Will it be used to anchor the ladder?'

'No, sir. The last rung detaches from the drum. It has iron rings attached that can be staked into the ground.'

'And the other end?'

'We suggest sinking two posts into the ground and using these to secure the hawsers with eyebolts.'

'Hawsers?'

Bertrand gestured to some ropes coiled in the corner. 'You will need to attach a throw line and hawser,' he said.

'Explain.'

At Boundless' question, Bertrand turned to Danon for elaboration.

'Sir. When I was an apprentice, we were often required to throw ropes over rooftops for building purposes. The method we used was to weight a light line as the lead rope. We tied the line to a hammer and spun it like this.' He whirled the end of the rope to illustrate. 'The hammer flies over the rooftop, taking the line with it. We then pull the line until it drags over the rope. In this case,' he indicated a sketch of the rock fixed to the wall, 'you will need to use the lightweight line to pull over a heavier cable, the hawser, which will in turn be used to drag up the ladder against the side of the rock.'

'And how do you propose I get the line up and over sixty feet of rock, with at least six additional yards of clearance required on top?'

'An arrow,' answered Bertrand, a smile on his face. 'We get one of the fort Indians to attach the light cord to an arrow and shoot it over the rock. We then pull on the cord to drag across the hawsers. And then use those to raise the ladder. And remember, sir, the ladder cannot be secured against the rock, it must be secured by the guide ropes on the other side of the rock.'

'Like raising a sail,' joked Boundless. 'Do you have any further counsel?'

'Yes, sir,' answered Bertrand. 'Try and put the weight into your arms rather than the steps. Also, to bring up supplies, it is better to haul them up separately. A block and tackle will be excellent for the purpose.' He halted at Boundless' grimace and then continued. 'There is a pulley in the tool hut. I can make another and show you how to combine them into a block and tackle. You will have to haul it up on the rock and secure it with bolts. But from then on everything becomes easier.'

He nodded, impressed at the carpenter's advice. 'And you?' he asked Danon.

'I have spent my share of summers working on hot, exposed roofs. I would recommend erecting a shade where you can take cover from the sun, or rainstorms. If a thunderstorm seems likely, I would climb down and take refuge.'

He was about to ask where when Bertrand spoke up again. 'We suggest you build a hut at the base of the rock. It will be indispensable for storing supplies and offering you protection against the weather.'

'Excellent work, gentlemen.' Immensely pleased with their contribution, he reached into his pocket and drew out two Spanish coins, pressing one into each of the men's hands, even as they demurred.

'Nonsense. Take them. They are well-earned, and your knowledge and skill have been of great service to me.' A thought struck him. 'How long do you think the ladder will last—before it needs to be replaced?'

Bertrand looked at Danon for the answer. 'It is manila rope, but like any rope it will shrink and expand in the elements. I would say no more than one summer, two if you are lucky. And you must take it down before the winter sets in.'

Boundless frowned. 'And raise it back up again each summer? That will be arduous.'

'It gets easier with experience.'

Boundless nodded. 'As do most things.'

He paused as another thought struck him. 'I will evidently need more than the one ladder. Can you draw up instructions for a ropemaker in Montreal?'

'I can.' Danon nodded. 'And can recommend my old master on Duvalle Street. He is highly skilled with a reputation for fine rope work.'

'Good. I will send the instructions back with the next brigade.'

BACK IN HIS QUARTERS, he noted the milestone in his journal alongside a sketch of the ladder.

> *I have finally received my means of ascending the rock. How difficulties do resolve themselves when broken down into parts and attacked with diligence and persistence! There be a method to all tasks. Only find the method.*

He stared at what he had written, his mind brimming with optimism. *The ladder was one part of the beginning, the plaster model shall be the other.* He dipped the quill and added a sentence.

> *In spring, I hope to embark on my grand project.*

## 42

## A Reasonable Facsimile

ONE COLD MORNING IN mid-December, he walked across the deserted yard to the new workshop, his mind busily conjuring the plaster buffalo from the fine powder.

'Father?'

He paused as he pulled open the door. Prospect and Claim had followed him, their footsteps flanking his own across the snowy compound.

'Come in laddies, before you freeze.' He held open the door. 'Stamp your feet.' They entered, their eyes wide as they took in all the supplies.

'What is that, Father?' asked Prospect. The wooden mould stood twenty-three feet in length, five feet wide and just over six feet high. The insides were lined with the smooth, polished rawhide he had requested.

'It's a form for holding plaster.' Blowing on his hands, he knelt to start the fire.

'What is this?' Claim held up a star drill chisel.

'That is for boring holes in rock.'

'Oh.' The boy looked doubtful at the information.

'And this?' asked Prospect

'That is a mason's hammer, or mallet. We use it to drive the chisel.' He added logs until the fire was blazing in the grate.

'What is this?' Prospect held up a rubbing stone.

'It is a stone, for polishing. Now go and occupy yourselves while I think.'

Sitting by the fire, he re-read Courtois' advice, knitting his brow as he memorised the instructions for mixing the plaster. Preoccupied with the advice, he didn't notice the boys leave as they wandered off in search of their companions. Opening a sack, he sifted the white powder through his fingers, a thoughtful look on his face.

For the next two hours, he experimented with different mixes, testing the consistency and setting times before settling on the recommended formula of two-parts powder to one-part water.

Opening the door, he saw a sleepy looking *engagé* pissing in the snow. 'Fetch four buckets of grease and bring them here,' he ordered the startled man.

In the days following the New Year, he was busy with his *bourgeois* duties as Indian trade parties arrived at the post with their snorting ponies. The various tribes took advantage of the occasion to parley—Cree, Arikara, Hidatsa, Sisseton and Mandan sitting around fires wrapped in buffalo robes as they smoked pipes and swapped gossip. A 'first-year man' cut himself severely while chopping firewood and two of the Indian women wrapped the affected limb as the wounded man groaned with pain. Two veterans and their country wives argued over possession of a row house—the dispute continuing until he arbitrated the matter, with severe warnings to keep the peace.

Despite his attempt to assign the duty, Lapointe insisted he sit down and go over the early trade figures. He had barely finished this when he was asked to authorise a trading party to the Mandan village. 'They expect it. It is customary to show we respect their sovereignty over the country,' said Lapointe when Boundless temporised over the task. 'The chieftain will take it as an insult to his authority if we don't go and pay our respects. In fact, it might be a good idea for you to lead the party. You could take your wife. I am sure she would appreciate the chance to see her family.'

'Send the party. Let Dubois lead it. And not a word to my wife.'

SUCH WAS THE GENERAL busyness of his days that it was February before he was able to return to the task that was uppermost in his mind.

'Bring your aprons,' he said, summoning the boys to the workshop. 'And no need to tell your mother.' He built up a blazing fire and placed the buckets of grease near the flames. He lifted each of his sons in turn to peer into the mould.

'I need your help to cover the insides with grease. Can you do that?'

'Why?'

'So that the plaster will not stick to the sides. Roll up your sleeves. Are you set?'

He lifted Claim and lowered him inside the crate, doing the same with Prospect. Standing on a stool to reach over the side, he handed down a bucket of grease. 'Take this. Smear it on the rawhide. Pretend you are tanning.'

The boys dipped their hands in the bucket and happily began to spread the grease.

'Do not stint,' he said, looking down. After a minute, he went and fetched the lantern, holding it up to better see inside. 'Over there,' he said, indicating with the lantern. He handed down another bucket as the twins coated both themselves and the rawhide in grease. They were almost finished when the door opened and Meadow Bird entered, looking for the boys. She screeched in alarm as she heard their voices coming from inside the crate. Hurrying over, she tried to peer inside.

'It's alright, lassie, they are—'

'Ai!' Stepping up on the stool, she motioned for him to fish out the boys—waiting until they were both safely deposited on the timber floor before berating him in a torrent of Mandan.

'Hold your tongue, woman! They are finished anyway. There. Good as new,' he said as their mother used a strip of linen to wipe the grease from their hands and faces. Still angry, she complained again as the boys sniggered. He caught the Mandan word for 'buffalo' and a curse word her grandmother often used.

'Come lassie,' he said. 'No harm done.' He linked his arms around her waist as she resisted, pretending to struggle to the delight of the boys.

With an 'Oomph!' she shook his arms off her. 'Sons come. Do cores.'

'What?' He looked blank for a moment before chuckling.

'*Chores*, lassie! *Chores*.'

She rounded on him again, scolding—whether real or in pretence he was unable to tell. He watched, his face rueful as she ushered the laughing boys out the door.

He mixed a bucket of plaster, slowly stirring the mixture—reminded, as he did so, of the slurry buckets inside Mose's tanning hut. When the mixture resembled a thick bowl of mush, he poured the bucket into the form. He did this for the next two hours, stirring each layer with a paddle before adding the next. By the time the plaster was level with the top of the form, he was down to his last two sacks of powder. He tested the top before blowing out the lantern. *A day or two to cure.*

Tired, he returned to his quarters to wash the bits of drying plaster from his face and hands.

'Will you read to us, Father?' asked Claim following supper.

'Not now. Read your grammars.'

Sitting in the rocker by the fire, he re-read Guillaume's letter, mulling the contents. A few moments later, he was fast asleep.

The next morning, he listened with barely restrained impatience as Dubois recounted details of the trade mission to the Mandan village. 'The headman was in good spirits although disappointed not to see you.'

'Did he appreciate the gifts?'

'He did, although he requested additional powder and balls for the musket.'

'Well done.' He stood up to indicate the meeting was over. 'Anything else?'

He proceeded at once to the workshop, acknowledging the respectful greetings of the men he passed on the way. Not bothering to light a fire, he used the mason's hammer to knock the sides and ends from the form. The solid plaster block stood pale and ghostly in the dim light. He took several rags to wipe away the grease clinging to the block and then walked around it—poking the sides, pleased at the way it had set. To test the finish, he took a hammer and chisel and chipped away at the foot of the block. The moist plaster crumbled and broke off causing him to stop. 'There are months of winter still to come,' he said, scolding himself for his impatience.

That evening, he re-read sections of Courtois' letter, making mental notes which he later jotted down in a journal he had acquisitioned for his own use. He made a list of questions to be answered by the mason, paring and refining the list—*to get my pound's worth!* He then made some notes for his annual letter to Guillaume. The boys kissed him and went to bed. It was on his mind to read to them, but he stretched his legs out before the fire instead. *Tomorrow night,* he promised, feeling tired.

The following day, after first greeting and conducting trades with a large party of northern Cree, he returned to the workshop, feeling curious eyes on him as he undid the padlock and entered. Lighting the fire, he sat down at the table, idly tapping his foot as he surveyed the plaster block. Getting up, he selected a hammer and chisel and made tentative chips, testing for hardness. Gaining in confidence, he began whittling along the corners. The size of the block made the work difficult, and he stood on a stool to cut with the chisel.

Over the next few hours, he removed several pounds of plaster, roughing out the shape of a head and hump. He stopped at one point to sweep the broken pieces of plaster from the floor. He continued in this fashion, chipping a declivity between the head and the hump, stopping every so often to stand back and inspect the result. Anxious not to ruin the model, he constantly referred to sketches in the notebook, sometimes stopping to jot down a note or take a measurement. Exchanging the square chisel for a pointed one, he turned attention to the tail, knocking off the end corners.

As the days passed, the dried plaster became harder to work with, the earlier pliability giving way to a substance that was more receptive to the chisel. He took the opportunity to learn more about the tools at his disposal, practising on sections of the plaster to observe the effects of the different chisels and the various rasps and files. He noted how the flat chisel took away the distinctive marks left by the claw variety and how each contributed in specific ways to removing or refining details. He discovered that angling the chisel allowed for greater control and refinement when removing plaster. As the superfluous plaster was removed, he used a stick of charcoal to draw lines on the model, chipping and shaving with greater delicacy as he observed the lines.

Becoming bolder—and more impatient—he took the point chisel and began chipping away larger sections. Overconfident, he struck a heavier blow and watched in dismay as a large chunk broke off from the plaster. Chastising himself, he stepped back to inspect the damage. *Luckily, there is still room for error.* The mishap proved a cautionary tale nevertheless. *If too much is removed, then the whole is ruined beyond repair.* From then on he proceeded more cautiously, taking lighter strokes with the hammer and chisel.

It took two weeks of shaving and paring before he had rendered a silhouette of the creature—snatching time away from his duties for the purpose. He had now fashioned the top into a distinct outline of a head, hump, rounded spine and tail. He turned his attention to subtracting plaster from the front, giving additional shape to the figure. The model was becoming recognisable as *something*, he told himself, although what sort of something remained in question.

Throughout the interminable evenings he made careful study of the slim volume on antiquities, hoping to find clues or suggestions that might guide his steps. At first clucking in annoyance at the florid style and paucity of detailed information, he gradually suspended his disapproval—deeper reading eliciting a series of useful nuggets which he made note of in the journal.

After spending one long, wintry day in the workshop, he took the lantern with him and locked the door. The dogs sent up mournful howls from the pen as he made his way through the cleared snow back to his quarters. Flakes drifted through the cold air and his mind went to Quoi—shuffling rapturously amidst the streaming snow. The image was succeeded by another—of the hapless wretch pinned to the stockade fence by a lance through his misshapen frame, his mouth froze open in agony.

IN HIS PREOCCUPATION WITH the plaster form, he turned an ever greater portion of his duties over to Lapointe and Bjornson. At the insistence of Lapointe, he attempted to lead the Swede deeper into the intricacies of capitalism via the general ledger only to meet with unexpected resistance. 'You are a partner and must see to your shares,' he admonished. 'Why the frown?'

'These entries be as particular as the index of sins!'

He composed letters to Mathieu and Guillaume while maintaining a separate list of questions to be answered by Courtois, paring and refining the latter. Tucking the list into the ledger for future continuance, he closed the book and went off in search of Bjornson.

As the snow began to melt in the yard, he returned to the model again and again, marking additional lines on the surface and making endless small cuts until arriving at what he considered a reasonable facsimile of a buffalo. Standing back, he pondered the result. *It looks blockish.* Using a length of twine as a measure, he rounded the hump, absorbed with the difficulty of reconciling the perspective between it and the head. The problem fixated his thoughts as he drew endless sketches, seeking to establish a harmony between the head and the hump. *Where none exists in nature,* he reminded himself, momentarily bemused by the idea.

Sitting down to peruse the rock measurements he had taken, he added a whimsical heading: 'Soundings.' *After all, I am embarked upon an unknown tide.*

Gazing at the sketchbook drawings pinned to the plastered wall, his eye was caught by a diagram of the rock, its dimensions marked. Nearby was a sketch of a buffalo, its head turned into the wind and rain. *I remember the day I made that sketch.* Liking the juxtaposition, he stood up and unpinned the latter, holding it briefly in front of the rock sketch before pinning the two side by side. He sat down again, lost in thought. After a while, he stood up and blew out the lantern. Locking the door behind him, he walked slowly back to the house, his mind preoccupied with an image of the rock and the buffalo folded in ecstatic embrace.

CROSSING THE YARD AFTER breakfast, he caught Pinch outside the workshop, bending to peer through a crack in the logs. He walked up behind the crouching figure. 'Have you lost something?'

Pinch straightened up to eye him, not the least abashed. 'What the blazes do you do in there?'

'Would you like to see?' Surprising himself and confounding Pinch, he unlocked the door and stood aside, holding it open. 'Look for yourself.'

Pinch pushed past him to gawk inside. 'Mother of God! What is it?'

'What does it look like?'

Walking up to the model, Pinch ran his hands over the smooth plaster. 'Is this what you intend?' He cocked his head with the question.

Boundless laughed. 'Always the sharp one! Indeed, it is. What is your opinion?'

Rather than answer, Pinch ventured around the walls, eyeing the ink and charcoal sketches. 'Rock is another matter, altogether,' he opined, staring at a sketch. 'It cannot be done—not by one man.'

'Are you offering to help?'

It was Pinch's turn to laugh. 'I had rather saw off my fingers!'

That same afternoon he invited Bjornson to witness the plaster casting.

'Have your honest say,' he said. 'Pinch already has.'

Bjornson hummed and hawed as he walked around the cast, a dubious look on his face.

'Well? Out with it, what do you think?'

Bjornson tugged at his ear. 'What is the point of it?'

'Point? To serve as a model. It was poured so as to scale one twentieth the size of the rock. There must be a declivity, like this—' He shaped a 'U' with his hands, 'separating the hump from the head. I intend to use powder to blow the rock apart. It is not so difficult as it seems. I estimate the removal of forty yards of rock, crosswise, and four yards in length, to a depth of, variously, eighteen to thirty-six inches.' He pointed to gouge marks in the plaster, hoping to encourage his companion's interest. 'The powder will remove most of it. It is then a matter of—'

'How do you know?' Bjornson scratched the offending ear.

'Know what?'

'That it is one-twentieth the original?'

'I have paced and measured it—the rock.'

He picked up a brass rod and a line with the lead bob attached. 'Hold this—upright,' he said, giving Bjornson the rod to hold. While Bjornson held the rod against the head, he stretched the line and lead weight to the tail end of the model.

'See? An ingenious method suggested by Monsieur Courtois. The weight hangs from the bar, allowing both vertical and horizontal measurements, which I then multiply by twenty and transfer to the rock.'

Walking back towards Bjornson, he dangled the weight over the face of the model. 'I can gauge the depth and position of each feature of the head and eyes by this method.'

'What method?'

Boundless grunted, wondering if his companion was being deliberately obtuse or perhaps baiting him with sly, Swedish humour.

'By erecting a sister mechanism on the rock itself.'

Bjornson digested this. 'And how will you carve the face?'

'I have thought of that, too. I intend to use a bosun chair—I saw one used on the ship that fetched me here. I bolt a frame to the rock, add an extension—like this,' he said, indicating the bob line, 'and hang suspended to carve the face.'

Bjornson deliberated on this as he studied the head. 'And how will you suspend yourself—or haul yourself up again?'

'I cannot—not by myself. I need someone to winch me up and down. I need you, Bjorn.'

His buoyancy at the Swede's apparent interest quickly deflated as a frown crossed the latter's face.

'No.' Bjornson's voice was blunt. 'I will have no part of this madness. And that is all.'

'Surely to God you have no objection to turning a winch?'

'I have given you my answer.' Bjornson walked to the door opened it, allowing a blast of cold air to enter. 'I must see to the trades.'

Boundless stared angrily at the closed door. *The fellow is a zealot! He would, no doubt, be happier chasing his lost tribe!*

He stood for some time, gazing at the plaster as he swallowed his disappointment. Finally, he picked up the journal, a determined look on his face. 'If needs must,' he grumbled and began noting measurements, stopping every now and then to vent his pique through scowls and muttered imprecations.

He used the two remaining sacks of powder to make a life-size head. At first, he worked with only the paring knife, carving as quickly as he dared while the fresh plaster was still moist and warm. He worked closely from his sketches and drew lines on the plaster to guide the knife. He took repeated measurements with the callipers, transferring the results to the notebook. He used a small, pointed chisel to delicately prick the nostrils, and a riffler to pick out the eyes. He attempted several methods of conveying the thick wool that coated the buffalo's face and jaws, finally settling on the tooth chisel, dragging it down and then crosswise to convey a sense of pattern and texture. He worked assiduously, often times bemoaning his inadequacy.

He used a flat chisel to suggest the beetling brow of the beast. Attempting to carve two small spurs into horns, he broke off the plaster on one side, roundly cursing himself for his carelessness. The plaster head resembled that of a buffalo, but it was bland and expressionless, he decided, stepping back to view the result.

*'It's all in the details, boyo.'* The truth of the long-ago remark came back to him and he worked with the fine-point chisel to try and lend some

particularity to the features. It was late into the night before he was finished. Positioning the head on the table, he sat back to inspect it in the glow cast by the lantern. *It looks like a buffalo. At least a reasonable facsimile of such. An honest spectator would surely agree.*

He had managed, he convinced himself, to capture the beast's fierce visage without, he readily conceded, rendering the eyes as he would have wished. He was still pondering the problem when his eyelids closed and he fell soundly asleep in the chair.

AS SPRING BALING COMMENCED, he reluctantly took himself away from the plaster model and turned his mind to the thousand and one details requiring his attention. He went over the pelts tally with Lapointe, pleased at the result. 'M. Thibault will rub his hands with delight,' he joked to Lapointe. 'How is the injured man?' he remembered to ask.

'His arm is too stiff to paddle. He must stay here for the summer.'

Boundless nodded. 'So be it.'

The following morning, he stood outside the stockade gates to farewell the men. Bertrand and Danon, now both *hivernants*, stood nearby. 'I depend on men as hardworking and sensible as yourself,' Boundless had said to Danon in delegating him a 'winterer' alongside Bertrand.

Danon nodded as if expecting the command. 'I shall not miss the paddling,' he said.

Dubois was less accommodating, grumbling that he was now two men short for both trips.

'The one trip only,' said Boundless. 'Hire two replacements for the return leg.'

From the hall steps, he watched as the Indian wives and children gathered to return to their villages, his thoughts full of the approaching summer. *All is in readiness. I have but to cast off.*

## 43

## A Mishap

APRIL WAS COOL WITH sudden gales and frequent showers that carried over into May. Eager to raise the rope ladder against the rock, he waited impatiently for the weather to settle and the ground to dry. 'The weather is your enemy,' remarked Bertrand, counselling patience. 'We must wait for dry, calm days.'

To distract himself he joined with Bertrand to replace a rotting log in the stockade fence. The two of them scouted the woods along the Missouri for a suitable tree. Selecting a mature cottonwood, they blazed a notch and prepared to fell the tree, taking turns with the axe. Boundless had just started, chopping in methodical fashion, when he heard a cracking sound.

'Look out!' shouted Bertrand.

Looking up, he barely had time to spring aside before a large branch crashed down through the lower limbs, striking him on the shoulder as it fell to the ground. The shock of the impact caused him to reel, clutching his arm as pain shot through it. Feeling faint, he sat down in the grass as Bertrand rushed to assist. After a while, he rose gingerly to his feet, cursing the misfortune as he leaned on Bertrand his thoughts full of the unladdered rock.

The shoulder was not broken, as he had at first feared, but severely wrenched. The injury caused a temporary paralysis, which healed to a painful stiffness that prohibited any but the least movement in the injured arm. Meadow Bird fashioned a sling, the boys watching wide-eyed as he walked around nursing the arm. The mishap drew scant sympathy from Pinch, who viewed it as vindication of the absurdity of the entire buffalo project.

'You have not even set foot on the rock and already you hobble like a wounded bird!'

'It had nothing to do with the rock. You might as well blame the stockade fence!'

Bjornson was similarly jaundiced, warning that the accident was a sign that it would be foolhardy to ignore.

'Sign? Sign of what?' he snapped, his crotchety mood worsened by a bout of inflammation that rendered every movement one of exquisite pain.

'A sign to abandon this foolishness.'

'Will you at least help me put up the ladder?'

'You know I cannot.'

'How in blazes is putting up a ladder blasphemy?' In his agitation, he jarred the injured limb. 'Christ!'

Frowning at the sacrilege, Bjornson stood up. 'I will not argue with you. The Cree are waiting.'

RESTRICTED TO EATING AND dressing with one arm, he roundly cursed himself for carelessness while gloomily conceding that the ladder must remain unraised until the following year. Cantankerous in his disappointment, he argued with Pinch and Antoine, berating the former for idleness and the latter for a perceived mistake in the accounts.

As the days grew warmer, he sat outside the cabin, the mild air beneficial to both the shoulder and his temper. Seated there, he watched the comings and goings as various trading parties arrived and departed. Not normally inclined to sit and watch, he privately marvelled at the insights gained through simple observation. Thus, he murmured in surprise at White Deer's industry, the young woman crossing his vision a dozen times a day as she fed the dogs, tended to the garden and fetched water or made leather. Buffalo Bird was similarly industrious, her stout bulk favouring her left ankle as she went back and forth carrying baskets of dried vegetables or sharpened the hoe or knelt to pound pemmican.

Meadow Bird seemed everywhere at once, her busyness astonishing him as she dressed a hide, shelled peas, or hung jerky to dry—all the while keeping an eye on the twins as they raced and tumbled with the Bjornson boys. *Without them, the post would fall down about our ears.* The notion was reinforced by the sight of Pinch coming outside the storehouse to scratch himself, gurgle and spit, tug absently at his ear and then retire to the storehouse again. *No doubt he has set aside a private bed for himself on which to doze.*

Slow and deliberate in his ways, the dependable Bjornson served as counterpoint to Pinch, whether cutting firewood, honing the axe or lending a hand to White Deer as she struggled to lift a basket of clothes for washing. *He, too, is a rock.* Of the other permanent occupants, Luc spent much of his time hunting or curing in the smokehouse, Bertrand carried out building repairs, and Abel worked tirelessly in the forge. Antoine and Emile supervised the trades and maintained the journals, bringing the ledgers to Boundless each afternoon for consultation.

AS THE SUMMER DAYS dragged slowly by and the stiffness in his shoulder began to ease, he spent more time with the boys, taking them down to the river to fish or watching as they played with the Indian children visiting the post. In July, he delighted Meadow Bird by taking her back to visit her family for a week.

Claim and Prospect were just as excited. No sooner were they settled in following a round of feasts than the two made immediate friends with boys from the neighbouring lodges. Over the following days, Boundless watched as they chased hoops or wrestled in the dust with their new companions. Dressed in deerskins, and as brown as rawhide, they were almost indistinguishable from their Mandan peers. He experienced a pang of envy as he watched them play a game of hoop, yelling in Mandan as they raced up and down in the dust. *They are as brown as Indians, and their mother's more than mine.* The thought sobered him as he reflected on his own childhood days navigating the rain-slicked cobblestones and winding streets of Edinburgh. *They know of no other life. And that is how I would have it.*

He went buffalo-hunting with his old friends Spotted Eagle and Shining Hair and tried teaching both the musket. After wasting several shots, Spotted Eagle uttered an exclamation and threw the weapon down. Taking up the bow, he crept close to a browsing bull and despatched it with an arrow to the heart and another to the lungs. He gave a trilling cry and held the bow aloft in triumph.

Shining Hair grinned and pointed to show that the other animals remained undisturbed by the kill. *'Bruyant!'* He pointed to the musket and covered his ears.

'Aye. You make your point. Perhaps it is I who should surrender the musket.'

One week turned into two, and then three, the cheerful bustle of the village and the obvious happiness of Meadow Bird tempering his desire to return to the post. *I should only fret over things undone,* he consoled himself.

Meadow Bird was unusually affectionate, snuggling up to him at night and importuning his attention as the lodge occupants slept. *What if I should abandon the post altogether and stay here?* The knowledge that at least two Frenchmen slept in nearby lodges with their Indian families played on his mind as Meadow Bird fell into a contented slumber. *It would be a life easy enough to fall into.*

As if to conspire with these thoughts, the formidable grandmother was unusually affable, doting on the children—whom she fondly referred to as *shót Núeta* or 'white Indians'. She even tolerated Boundless, her grimaces in his direction passing for smiles. Her greatest love was, as ever, reserved for Meadow Bird, the old woman fussing over her granddaughter with endless devotion as the latter teased and provoked her with the same unbounded affection. At times, he caught Meadow Bird gazing up at the sky, a yearning look on her face, as if willing the sun to stop in its advance. Other times, she glanced at him, a mute appeal in her eyes. *This is our home. The boys are happy here. It is a good life.*

He spent hours walking the tall grass or sitting outside the lodge in conversation with Jacques while watching delegations arrive to barter and trade. Once, recognising a party of Teton Sioux, he stiffened, drawing a laugh from Jacques.

'Relax, *mon ami*. They are peaceful—for the moment.'

He was now able to move his shoulder freely and his thoughts turned once more to the rock. *I shall be an old man before I start.* His growing anxiety at the thought reduced his pleasure in the Mandan sojourn. A few days later, he took Meadow Bird aside. 'It is time,' he said. 'Tomorrow, we go back to the post.'

'Tomorrow?' She spoke the word haltingly, her happiness visibly evaporating as she took in his meaning.

'Aye. Tomorrow. It is time. Think of how pleased White Deer and Buffalo Bird will be to see you.'

The following day, they loaded the ponies with jerky, pemmican, dried fish, and savoury balls of venison encased in fat. He waited in the saddle as Meadow Bird bade a lingering farewell to her parents and grandmother. The boys chatted cheerfully to their Mandan companions, who clustered around to watch them leave.

They set off, Meadow Bird trailing behind to cast frequent looks back over her shoulder. 'Don't dawdle, lassie!' He reined in to wait for her, then pointed towards the post. 'Home!'

THE MORNING AFTER THEIR return, he presided over the replacement log as it was hauled into place. Eager to assist, he threw himself into the task with such energy that he re-inflamed the injured limb. *I am cursed!*

Raging at himself for the injudicious haste, he took once more to the porch chair, gloomily predicting that it would be another summer at least before the ladder was put in place. *If then!* The irony that his grand project was stalled at its inception was not lost on him as he abandoned the porch for the workshop. Sitting on a stool, he pondered the sketches pinned to the wall, consumed with fresh doubts that the thing could be done at all.

*To carve a buffalo from stone!* The project seemed doubly foolish, given his present plight, the ambition breathtaking in its audacity. *How much stone must be removed? How am I to represent the hump? It will take a lifetime simply to carve out the head!*

Overwhelmed by the scale of the task, he seriously contemplated abandoning it altogether. *Pinch is right. It is no more than a mad folly!*

Cursing Fortune, the Fates, and whatever other deities presided over unwitting creatures such as himself, he got up from the stool and gingerly flexed his injured arm, wincing at a stab of pain.

**44**

## A Visitor and a Tall Tale

A DIVERSION FROM HIS SOUR mood arrived in the person of one Jeremiah Till, an itinerant hunter and trader who had found temporary refuge among a band of Hidatsa. When the Indians sent a party to trade, Till accompanied them, breezily introducing himself as 'friend to all and enemy to none, whether God-fearing or heathen.' The man was slight in stature, 'barely a lick over five feet' by his own estimate. His unkempt beard and tobacco-stained teeth were offset by a pair of keen brown eyes that took in the hall at a glance. 'Mighty fine,' he said, nodding. 'Solid as all get-out.'

As Bjornson poured from a kettle of tea, Boundless offered his hand to the stranger, wincing as the other man shook it with vigour.

'Ah! An injured bird, I see. I have suffered the same misfortune myself.' Till released his tight grip. 'Arrow?'

Pinch guffawed. 'A tree!'

'Well then, dangers everywhere.'

'Where are you from, Mr Till?' asked Bjornson.

'The places of the earth, friend, the places of the earth. And I go by Jeremiah to all and sundry.' The visitor gulped the hot tea and held out the cup for more.

'Is it not dangerous for a man to be alone—so far from other white men?' asked Boundless, suspicious lest the man be a scout for a rival fur company.

'Risky as perdition! But I have been on my own for so long I hardly speak anything but Indian and bear.'

With encouragement from Pinch, Till launched into a long and rambling soliloquy about his travels and the sights he had seen. 'Sufficient to astonish a saint!' he assured, giving a solemn nod.

'What sort of things?' challenged Pinch, enjoying the windy tale.

'Why, things to amaze the eyes and confound the brain!'

'Example?'

The man held out his cup for a refill, spying, as he did so, the cross around Bjornson's neck. 'Two year ago, give or take a month, I stumbled upon a tribe of Israelite Indians to the north of here who spoke in a strange tongue such as I had never heard—Hebrew, at a guess, and worshipped around a giant wooden cross set up in the middle of the lodges.'

Pinch chortled, slapping his thigh with glee.

Bjornson, however, sat as if transfixed. 'The lost tribe!' He turned to Boundless, his eyes wide. 'There are many stories of such.'

'I wouldn't know, friend, being a simple traveller,' said Till. 'All I say is what I saw, which was Indians worshipping before a cross, speaking in an unknown tongue and taking communion with one another.'

'Hold fire!' interjected Pinch. 'Are these mysterious Indians Hebrew or Christian?—being as you describe them as Israelites in one breath and Christian in the other.'

'No doubt, once the former, now the latter—through the miracle of divine Grace,' interjected Bjornson, drawing a surprised glance from Till.

'I ain't churched—regular, anyway—for as long as I care to remember, but they sure were a-worshipping and a-praying as all get out.'

'This tongue ...' Bjornson leaned forward, his voice eager. 'Can you recall any of the words?'

Tell stroked his jaw. 'I can hardly recollect. Oh! But one fellow was struck up like a priest—fancy fripperies and all.'

'A priest?' Bjornson leaned in further, hanging on every word.

Pinch gave a snort. 'Do you not feel a twitch when your leg is pulled?'

'Not so!' Till helped himself to more tea. 'Christian they were, for certain.'

'The tale hardens!' Shaking his head at the man's bland audacity, Pinch prodded for more detail. 'And where be this marvellous tribe?'

'Well now, that be the thing.' Till shook his head in sorrow. 'I hardly remember, so overcome was I—well, petrified, I guess some would call it by the Holy Spirit.' He dipped a finger in the empty cup to lick some of the tea leaves.

'And they worshipped a cross?' Bjornson had an ardent expression on his face.

'I ain't bible read. I say only what I saw.'

'But you said you saw a cross!'

'Did I?' Till looked mystified at his own account. 'Oh! So I did! By the hovering saints, I see it all now—as if 'twere before my eyes!' With stricken gaze, he stared upwards.

Pinch hooted with admiration and pounded the table, causing Bjornson to jump. 'If you ain't a card!'

Till looked at Pinch's tobacco pouch, which sat on the table. Tugging at a pocket in his breeches he produced a small, clay pipe.

'I sure could use a smoke,' he said.

Pinch pushed the pouch toward him. 'Help yourself.'

'Mighty appreciate, friend. Much obliged.' Till helped himself to a generous twist and put both the pipe and the tobacco back in his pocket. 'For later,' he said, a satisfied look on his face.

'And you could find them—the Indians, again?' Bjornson's voice held a fervent note that drew a worried look from Boundless.

Till scratched underneath his jaw. 'Me? No. It was a hard trip.' At Bjornson's crestfallen look, he relented. 'I guess I could point the way, if pressed to it.'

'Wait! I will fetch paper!' Bjornson scraped back the chair.

'Do not tease the poor fellow,' warned Boundless as Bjornson hurried from the cabin. 'He is credulous enough in matters of faith.'

'Every word the truth! Every dot and i certifiable and witnessed by these two eyes.'

'And now you travel—like a gospel Christian—to bear witness?' Pinch shook his head at such saintliness. He cocked an eyebrow at Boundless. 'Might we not send him north, with a party, to uncover these mysterious Indians?'

Boundless nodded. 'He could depart tomorrow morning—with an Indian escort.'

'Hold fire, now!' Till stared at the table, furiously scratching his face. ''Fore God if my poor memory don't fail me as to perticulars.'

'Surely, an approximation will do, the Holy Spirit will navigate the rest?' Pinch joined his hands, his face earnest.

'The Holy Spirit,' Boundless echoed, his eyes on Till.

Bjornson returned, bearing paper, ink and quill. 'A sketch!' he said, thrusting the materials at Till.

'I told you, my sun-addled brain ain't what it was.' Till glanced uneasily at Boundless and Pinch.

'As best you recollect!' Bjornson pushed the paper at the trapper.

'Do not fail him,' warned Pinch.

Till tugged at his chin. 'Well, I 'spect I might come by it, 'specially if I had some more of that fine tea.'

IN THE DAYS FOLLOWING Till's departure, an exultant Bjornson talked of nothing else but the mysterious tribe, the pinch of yeast the visitor had added to the simmering pot of faith bubbling and fermenting until it swelled into the loaf of conviction. 'It is a miracle,' he proclaimed, 'that a tribe so prophesised should exist on our very doorstep!'

Pinch sighed, weary both of the tale and Bjornson's single-minded recursion to the subject. 'The man played you the fool for his own amusement. You are too gullible, by half.' They were seated on the steps of the cabin, waiting for Boundless to join them.

'As you are too blind! I questioned him on various points for the best part of an hour. He averred the truth at each turn.' Bjornson produced a slip of paper. 'Judge for yourself—a map to the Christian village.'

Pinch glanced at it. 'I see dots and circles.'

'Till again?' Joining them, Boundless placed one foot up on the step. 'The man is a born braggart.'

'What reason had he to lie—given he claimed to be a Christian himself?' protested Bjornson.

'Ha! As well would he claim to be a Turk to give semblance to a story.'

'No doubt, if his tale has any grain of truth,' said Boundless, 'he stumbled upon some Jesuit converts.'

Bjornson carefully folded the paper and tucked it back in his pocket. 'Doubt as you will. There is God's hand at work here.'

'Do you not see the man was pulling both your legs at once?' argued Pinch.

Bjornson was unperturbed, his voice full of calm certainty. 'The Elders tell of a lost tribe that fled Israel for the wilderness. Some say they found their way here, seeking sanctuary among the Indians. I recall a book written by a Dutch rabbi in which he made such a claim. 'Tis said that the original tribe wandered here from Assyria—or maybe Ethiopia. I do not recall the particulars. They do not resemble your ordinary Indians. They are said to be lighter in appearance and to maintain beards.'

'Bjorn, for pity's sake—'

'William Penn himself believed in the tales.'

'He did?' Boundless stopped short at the mention.

'He himself said so!' Bjornson stared earnestly, his eyes fervent in their belief. 'Till may be a braggart, as you say, but he has stumbled upon something—something he himself does not recognise. The faithful believe that the discovery will usher in the coming of Christ, the return of the Messiah.'

'Preserve us!' Pinch hawked in disgust. 'Between the stone buffalo and the lost tribe, I am surrounded by lunatics! I will speak no more on the matter, since naysaying only fuels the madness.' Muttering, he got up from the step. 'Such imbecility!' With that, he stalked off.

The vow lasted less than a day before it was broken. Boundless and Bjornson were talking in the yard when Pinch turned the corner of the storehouse, a shrill Prospect seated on his shoulders. Claim followed at his heels, clamouring for a turn.

'No more! Be off with ye!' Puffing for breath, Pinch lifted the disappointed Prospect down to the ground. 'They grow longer each day,' he said, pulling a face.

'They could have come here by boat,' argued Bjornson, resuming his conversation with Boundless.

'Who could?' Pinch looked from one to the other. 'Still with the Israelites! He shook his head, muttering in exasperation. 'It is a fable! A trapper's yarn. Can ye not see it?'

'You do not know.' Bjornson's voice was stubbornly convinced.

'I do know! And so does Boundless. Jumping frogs, the entire world knows! If there were such a tribe, do you not think that they would have discovered themselves afore now?'

'Who to? Answer me that.'

Pinch threw up his hands in defeat. 'Go then! See for yourself.'

Bjornson gazed into the distance, a serene look on his face. 'I do hope to, God willing.'

A worried Pinch took Boundless aside that evening. 'I thought Luther laid to rest, but the fool hunter has raised him up again, and infected him with his own oddities. Speak to him, for pity's sake, lest he steal away in search of these phantasmic Indians!'

Concerned at the possibility, Boundless intervened as Bjornson returned to the subject the next morning. 'This has gone far enough,' he interrupted, his voice firm. 'It is a myth, a lie. Put it from your mind, I urge you.'

'I cannot.'

'Why not? Why does it mean so much to you?'

Bjornson sighed, a wistful look on his face. 'For the man who discovered such a tribe, brought their existence to the world—'

'Mother of God! Will you not get it through your thick head that there is no such tribe? To give such idiocy the least credence is sheer folly!'

'No more than your godless buffalo!' The Swede stomped off, an aggrieved look on his face.

Boundless stared after him, idly flexing his injured arm. He heard a faint shot in the distance followed by a shout. 'The brigade has returned!'

## 45

## Riding the Buffalo

THE ROPE LADDER LAY stretched out to its full length in the grass. The rock loomed above the wagon and the party of four men as they finished laying out the hawser lines. Spotted Eagle stood beside the wagon, attaching a lightweight cord to a small hook fastened to the side of an arrow. He had accepted the challenge with nonchalance, dismissing Boundless' concerns with a grunted assurance that shooting an arrow into the air was the simplest of matters.

'But will the line not interfere with the draw?' Boundless had persisted, demonstrating how the line might get caught up in the bowstring. Spotted Eagle made a dismissive noise at such an unlikely event.

'He has no doubts,' Boundless remarked to Danton. He watched as Spotted Eagle made a practice draw. He gazed around at the vistas of grass, consumed with impatience to finally begin and still fretting at the loss of the previous summer.

'Let us hope so,' said Danton, 'because it all depends on getting the line across.'

'Stay clear,' cautioned Boundless, stepping back himself to avoid getting his feet tangled up in the pilot line where it lay looped in the grass. An image of himself flying up into the air and over the rock made him grimace. *At least it would save climbing the ladder.*

Spotted Eagle planted his feet firmly in the grass and notched the arrow to the bow. *'Hii!'* he exclaimed, and let fly, the line snaking up into the air and over the rock. Moments later they heard a faint yell from Able, stationed on the far side.

'By God, but he did it,' said Luc, shaking his head.

Leaving Luc with the ladder, the others joined Able on the far side. With a triumphant exclamation Danton bent to pick up the arrow with the cord attached. 'Just like slinging a roof!' he whooped, a broad grin on his face.

Boundless patted Spotted Eagle on the shoulder. The Indian grunted as if the impressive shot were an everyday affair.

WORKING TOGETHER THE MEN hauled on the line, Boundless anxious lest it tear apart on the granite summit. A short time later they repeated the exercise, this time hauling across the much heavier guide ropes.

'Is it up?' hollered Boundless, unable to restrain his anxiety.

'It's up!' confirmed a faint shout from the far side.

'Now we must stake the guide ropes,' said Danton.

While he and Bertrand began to hammer four sharpened stakes into the grass, Boundless joined Luc on the other side, eager to see the longed-for result for himself. He stared up at the ladder as it snaked up to the summit—shaking in the breeze—scarcely able to believe the fact. *At last!*

Rejoining the others he saw where Bertrand and Danton had hammered the four anchor stakes deep into the grass so that they formed a square. Satisfied at the depth, they bored eye bolts into each stake.

'Are you sure they will hold?' asked Boundless as Danton began expertly threading the thick ropes to the bolts.

'They will pull against each other, not the bolts' replied a confident Danon. Boundless observed closely, noting the method, as Danton secured the ropes in an elaborate criss-cross fashion. It reminded him of a similar method he had seen aboard the Patience although he couldn't at the moment recall for what reason.

'Done!' After a quarter hour Danon stood up, slapping rope fibres from his hands.

The men proceeded around the rock to behold the rope ladder strung up against the granite, its ends secured in the grass by two eyebolts.

'Did you ever see such a thing!' Luc stood with his hands on his hips gazing up at the ladder where it reached up to the summit. He eyed Boundless. 'Are you sure you want to do this?'

'I am.' Now that the long-dreamed of moment was at hand, Boundless licked his dry lips and stepped up to the ladder, gripping the ropes, which felt dry and abrasive in his hands.

'It's a long distance up, but a short way down,' joked Luc as Boundless set foot on the bottom step, bouncing to test for safety.

'You will feel the wind as you climb,' advised Danton. 'Take rest breaks as you need them. Trust the ropes, you are quite secure.'

Taking a breath Boundless steeled himself for the climb, his limbs trembling in anticipation. The summit seemed far above him. He licked his dry lips and started to climb, clutching tightly to the ropes.

HE BRACED HIMSELF EACH time a gust of wind skittered the ladder sideways along the abrasive stone. Remembering Danton's advice, he endeavoured to place most of the weight on his arms, clinging to the canvas handholds each time wind shook the ropes. *Thank God for Danton's forethought, else I should have lost a yard of skin by now.* Looking down, he saw the men standing out in the grass, necks craned to observe his progress

Two-thirds of the way up, his legs started to shake uncontrollably. The wind roared in his ears, and he stopped his ascent, clinging tightly to the ropes. 'Thank God also for the wooden steps' he told himself, hanging on until the wind subsided. A memory of the crew aboard the Patience 'dancing' along the spar ropes as they attended the sails amidst the top masts flashed into his mind as he readied himself for the final ascent.

The summit was now only yards above his head. A crow flapped down from the rock, the harsh *caw!* startlingly loud in the clear air. The wind blasted again, and he froze in place as the ladder bounced beneath his feet. *If the hawsers should come undone!*

Reaching the topmost rung, he was dismayed to discover that the summit was still half a body length away. *We miscalculated in hauling it up, else we staked too much in the grass.* His muscles twitched with the strain, and he feared they might cramp. *I am so close.*

Precariously balanced, his legs trembling with exhaustion, he willed himself to make the effort that would propel him up to the top. Taking a deep breath, he scrambled upwards, his heart pumping madly as he pulled on the ropes and climbed against the bare rock. For a heart-stopping moment, he feared he had misjudged the distance. And then he was flopped on his belly like a fish, gasping for air, the granite cold and hard beneath him. He glanced back at the ladder, unable to see it. His hands—the knuckles scraped and bloody—gripped the hawser cables as they stretched beneath him and across the summit.

He picked himself away from the edge, crouching as he held onto the hawsers, the wind tugging at his clothes. He was halfway across the summit before daring to release his hold. Next moment, he was standing—on the very top of the great rock, his senses dazzled by the sunlight flashing through the clouds. The world seemed to drop away, leaving him as naked and exposed to the elements as if perched on the topmost spar of a ship at sea. On all sides, the buffalo grass billowed to the horizon in tremendous, wind-blown swells.

He turned in a half-circle to drink in the breathtaking prospect. He sighted the stockade in the distance and, beyond it, the broad Missouri glinting in the sunlight. To the north, he spotted a herd of mule deer browsing under the same bluff that he had visited with his sons. To the east, he spied a distant stretch of water that he recognised as an inland lake, home to a band of Arikara. As he took in the cloudy vastness, the rock seemed to tremble beneath his feet. *It is the turning of the earth!*

He heard a faint shout. Far below, Luc and the others stood out in the grass, the wind swirling the stalks in turbulent waves all around them. He called out and semaphored his arms, exulting in the dizzying height. The horses grazed near the stationary wagon. Cupping his hands to his mouth, he hollered at the top of his lungs. 'Ahoy, Jack!' The stallion raised its head, whinnying in puzzlement before dropping his neck to the grass once more.

THE SUMMIT WAS BROAD and smooth, and he proceeded towards the head in stooped fashion, braced for any sudden gust of wind that might swoop him up and over the side. He judged himself to have four or five yards of rock on either side, the smooth, even surface giving him the confidence to stand erect. The rock rose beneath him as he made his way up to the head, using his hands to scramble across the hump.

The pinnacle now loomed, the rock bulging outwards to culminate in the massive, vaulting head. Dropping to his hands and knees, he crawled to the edge of the windy precipice. Lying flat on his belly, he peered over the precipitous drop. Far below, the grass lay half in shadow. For a moment, he fondly deceived himself that it would prove soft and yielding should he tumble over the side. A gust of wind plucked at his shirt and he crawled back from the drop on hands and knees.

Returning to the ladder, he paused to survey the wind- smoothed granite. A flash of pride possessed him. *It has stood unspoiled since the beginning of the world.*

Lying flat on his belly and gripping the hawsers, he inched backwards to where the thick cables disappeared over the edge. He let himself down slowly, uttering a sigh of relief as his foot found the topmost rung.

Back on firm ground, he felt himself sway like a deckhand stepping from a gangway onto the wharf. The others came up to shake his hand, grinning in excitement at the success of the endeavour. 'By God, but you did it,' said Luc, pumping his hand. 'You climbed the rock.'

THEY WERE GREETED BY a small crowd back at the post. Bjornson stood alongside Pinch, a questioning look on his face. The children and the Indian wives were also there. Elated, Boundless stepped down from the wagon and strode up to Bjornson, animosity cast aside in his triumph.

'I have done it, Bjorn!' He gripped his companion by the arms, his voice hoarse with elation. 'I have ridden the buffalo!'

## 46

## A Thing Begun

HE PARKED THE WAGON alongside the tool hut. 'Are we set?' he asked Bertrand. Together with Danon they lifted the disassembled pulleys into the back of the wagon along with two coils of rope, a hammer and half-a-dozen iron bolts and a box of wood plugs. He went back into the hut and emerged with a roll of canvas and wicker basket belonging to Meadow Bird. The basket was filled with pots of paint, paint brushes, and sticks of chalk and charcoal.

Claim came to stand by Jack, who was tied to the rear of the wagon, 'Where are you going, Father?' he asked, stroking the mustang.

'Away to the rock. I shall be gone all day. Be good and take heed of your mother.'

'Can I come?' The boy's voice was wistful.

'One day, perhaps. But not now.'

'When?'

He held out an arm. 'When you are this high. Run along now. Find your brother. Stand!' He snapped at the yoked pony as it snorted and stepped sideways into its companion.

He climbed up on the seat and took the reins as Abel came out of the forge to watch. Antoine turned on the steps of the storehouse to observe. Pinch wandered out from the hall, holding a mug of tea in his hands.

'Remember the smokehouse door!' Boundless called out as Bertrand dragged open the gate. 'Hup!' He shook the reins, Bertrand clambering up onto the seat.

Pinch stared after the wagon as Bjornson came to join him 'Does he really intend to see this foolishness through—by himself?'

Bjornson glanced over to where Meadow Bird stood in the doorway, her eyes on the departing wagon. 'I fear so.'

'Then God help us!' Pinch tossed the tea grounds into the dirt.

PICKING UP A COIL of rope, Boundless began to climb with the coil slung over his shoulder. He was fatigued by the time he reached the top, thankful that the readjusted ladder meant he no longer had to scramble to bridge the distance between the top rung and the summit. Below, Bertrand waited for him to uncoil the rope and lower one end to the ground.

'Tie it off!' Boundless hollered as Danon tied the rope to the disassembled pulley. A short time later came an answering yell and he began to pull on the heavy rope. He was exhausted by the time he had hauled the load to the top. *Thank God for Bertrand's advice. I could never have climbed with that load on my back.* He pulled up several more bundles before descending the ladder to take coffee and confer with his companions.

A small hut stood near the base of the rock, the structure recommended by Danon as a supply shed and also as a shelter against bad weather. 'To be caught on a rooftop in the midst of a thunderstorm is a risky experience,' Danon had mentioned when proposing the idea of a hut. 'I shudder to think how much more dangerous it would be caught without shelter on the top of the buffalo,' he said.

'Wise words,' Boundless had replied, pleasingly noting that both men now referred to the rock in the same manner as himself.

An hour later, the pair watched him climb back up again before calling out farewell and driving the wagon back to the post.

'You are sure you do not wish us to stay?' Bertrand had asked. 'You may need our assistance.'

Boundless shook his head. 'I may as well get used to it.'

HE WAS SWEATING PROFUSELY, in spite of the breeze. But the pulley parts, the ropes, the canvas, and the basket of pots and brushes lay on the summit beside him. He removed his hat and wiped his brow with his arm, watching as the wagon disappeared in the swirling grass. He took a rest, eating some of the jerky and fried bread and swallowing a canteen of water before turning to the tasks at hand.

The sun was setting before he abandoned the assembled block and tackle and retreated to the ladder, rueful at how little he had accomplished. Just one corner of the tackle frame was secured to the granite—the work of drilling and sinking the two holes required and inserting bolts through the frame and into the rock taking him to late afternoon. Fretting at the expense of time and labour required for so little return, he tied the sack of paint pots and brushes to the frame before wedging one corner of the canvas beneath the wood.

Exhausted, he made his way back to the ladder. The prairie grass was already in shadow as he descended, his legs trembling with fatigue. He halted several times on the way down, afraid lest, in his tiredness, he miss a step. Luc's earlier quip about it being a short way down came back to him and he chuckled in spite of his tiredness.

THE NEXT MORNING, STIFF and sore, he arrived back at the rock in full daylight, driving the wagon and leaving Bertrand and Danon back at the post. 'You would get bored waiting for me,' he had said, waving off their protestations. 'And Pinch has complained of your absence,' he might have added, but didn't.

Something twigged in his mind, and he turned back. 'Could you describe how to make the ladder, including handholds?' he asked Danton.

'Of course, sir.'

'Good. I intend ordering ten more just like it from Montreal.'

'Then I will also give you the name of a rope maker on rue Catherine. My employer used him many times to make our roof ladders and he has a reputation for excellent workmanship.'

Boundless nodded, 'Draw up the instructions and I will send the order with the brigade.'

'Another obstacle overcome,' he told himself, pleased with the information.

HE DID HIS NOW customary bounce on the bottom rung, testing the ladder once more before climbing and experiencing the familiar disorientation as he left the grass and placed both feet on the swaying rungs.

It was afternoon and his back ached as he sank the last retaining bolt and secured the block and tackle in place. Wincing, he stood and tested the frame, satisfied that it would withstand all but the strongest gale. He tied the canvas over the frame as a cover and left his journal and quill and ink along with the paint and brushes in its shade. Too tired to do more, he returned to the ladder, a sense of satisfaction seizing him in spite of his fatigue. *''Tis all in the preparation, boyo.'* The long-ago voice sounded in his ear as he descended the steps.

He spent the next two days bolting a canvas sunshade into the rock, pleased to sit in its shelter as he took some refreshments. He flexed his 'chisel hand' noting its stiffness and wondering if it would ever adapt to the vibration of the mallet and chisel.

The next morning, he began charting the area to be excavated. Satisfied as to the general dimensions, he paced the bare granite, stopping to mark reference points with chalk. He repeated the process over and over, pacing from side to side, and up and down, while marking various spots and checking measurements in the journal. Once, to his alarm, he paced close to the edge in his absorption. Shocked, and cursing his inattentiveness, he hastily stepped back from the drop. *I must never forget where I am.*

Having laid out a grid, he took a pot of black paint and daubed over the chalk marks. He then laid out a length of twine and, using this as a guide, brushed thick paint strokes connecting the marks. Several times he stopped to refer to the journal, studying the plaster model measurements before returning to the task. A bird screeched overhead, causing him to look up.

He took a second pot of red paint, and brushed numbers representing various depth measurements—'36, 24, 16 and 12 inches,' he said, reading out the numbers. He paced back and forth over the finished grid, reassuring himself as to the accuracy of the lines.

*The hump starts here.* He studied the paint marks. *And the head, there. The rock in between must be removed.* For an instant, he doubted himself, wondering whether he should have erected the sister plumb bob mechanism he had mentioned to Bjornson. *'Twould be more precise,* he conceded. But a moment later, he dismissed the doubts, confident in the power of his unaided eye. *This is priming,* he reasoned. *The precise measurements can wait until the excavation is begun.*

He made more measurements near the tail, carefully pacing out distances before using the chalk, and then the paint, to mark the dimensions. The sun was beginning to sink before he had finished—the entire summit parcelled into a painted grid. He surveyed the squares, tired and sunburnt, but satisfied.

Before climbing back down the ladder, he rested for a moment, looking out over the grass. *'It will be harder than you can imagine.'* Helmut's words came back to him as he resumed the descent. A phrase from Courtois' letter echoed in his head, the imagined voice gruff and no-nonsense. *'Success lies in the preparation. If you stint on that, then you as good as guarantee failure.'*

'So many voices, so much advice,' he grumbled as he reached the ground. 'And only a single pair of hands.'

WHEN HE RETURNED THE next morning, he discovered a buffalo vigorously rubbing itself against the rope ladder. Furious, he reached for the musket and fired, aiming for the flank. With a loud bellow, the buffalo trotted off. The ladder was undamaged, although coated with wool. He went to the hut, finding it also coated with buffalo wool. 'Another worry,' he muttered.

On the summit, he took off his hat to allow the wind to dry his slicked hair. The now-familiar sensation, or wish, of being able to fly over the dizzying expanse around the rock gave him pause. *This height can play tricks on the mind. I have arms, not wings.* In spite of the clear blue sky, errant gusts of wind sprang up from nowhere, the occasional blast so robust he feared being whisked over the precipice. In the face of the strong gusts, he retreated to the block and tackle and knelt there with one arm around the supports as the wind gusted along the bare granite. A memory came to him of the sailors on the *Patience*—bodies braced as they strained to walk amidst the howling gale and pitching deck—*while secured by a safety line!* He frowned at his own obtuseness.

As soon as the wind permitted, he climbed back down the ladder and made his way to the hut. He filled a sack with eyebolts, a hammer, several chisels, and a coil of rope. Back on the summit, he winched up the supplies and laid them out on the rock. Next, he chalked a line equidistant from the sides, and marked at two-yard intervals. Taking the hammer and chisel, he laboriously sank four eyebolts, wedging them with wood plugs, before abandoning the task as his arm grew fatigued. He stored the rope and remaining eyebolts within the block and tackle tent before stretching his back and making his way back to the ladder. *Summer will be gone and I have yet to strike a meaningful blow*, he lamented, blinking as the wind drove dust into his eyes.

That afternoon, he consulted Abel before attaching an iron ring to a leather harness around his waist. 'It's to prevent me from being blown off the rock in a gale,' he explained to the curious blacksmith. He braced himself as the blacksmith tugged and pulled at the harness.

'There! Collared like a horse!' Abel pronounced when satisfied with its strength. He watched Boundless walk back to his quarters, still wearing the harness. Shaking his head, he returned to the forge, a smile on his face as Pinch's latest quip sounded in his ears. 'Indeed,' he chuckled, casting around for his favourite hammer.

IT TOOK HIM THE whole of the next day to finish staking out the eyebolts and then threading the rope through the line of ten bolts, doubling the rope over each eye. He used a sheet bend to secure a thinner line to the rope, the voice of the schooner deckhand who had taught him the knot instructing in his ear. He secured the line to the harness, experimenting with a hitch knot and then a bowline before deciding on a sliding figure of eight. Thus staked, he retreated slowly backwards, playing out the rope to a distance of ten feet. With the rope taut, he pulled against it, testing the line. Pleased with the result, he cupped his hands, hollering to the wind and sky.

'Blow thy cheeks!'

Tired from his exertions, he took off the harness. *Tomorrow,* he promised himself.

HE LEFT THE POST at first light, rousing a sleepy Meadow Bird Deer to open and close the gate behind him. The air was fresh and bracing. Streaks of gold illuminated the horizon as he drove the wagon across the grass.

By the time he reached the rock it was full light, mist rising from the long-stemmed grass. He turned the horse loose and watched for a moment as it neighed and shook its neck before bending to crop the dewy stalks. Now that all was in readiness, he was assailed by fresh doubts. Taking a deep breath, he looked up at the rock, suddenly daunted anew by the scale of his ambition. *Am I mad to proceed? Was Pinch—and Bjorn, right?* He rubbed his hands against his cheeks, a frown on his face. The horse whinnied and raised its head to look at him from the grass. *You, too, Jack?* With a wry expression, he proceeded toward the ladder.

Once on the summit, he walked up and down, eyeing the painted squares while feeling small and insignificant against the vast expanse of stone. *Like a gnat bothering a buffalo.* He knelt, wincing at the hardness beneath his knees. *I should have brought a pad to kneel on. Another omission!* Annoyed with the oversight, he sat back on his knees to gaze out over the plain, the grass resplendent in the full flush of morning. To his mind, the moment seemed as momentous as when he stood, astonished, atop the Alleghenies to gaze at the rich western promise. He gripped the chisel with his left hand, eyeing for a moment the unblemished stone. And with a single hammer stroke, he began.

He worked steadily all morning, boring a line of powder holes in the collar of fat that separated head from hump. He started in the middle, where the rock was thickest, planning to work his way back to the sides. He wore the safety line for less than an hour before taking it off, finding it cumbersome and restrictive. The sun had angled west of the rock. He sat down in the canvas shade to drink, feeling the smooth-hard granite through the buckskin breeches. He ate a few mouthfuls of jerky, indolent in the fierce heat.

By noon, he had drilled three six-inch holes and his 'bolt hand' was so numb he could no longer feel his fingers. Twice, granite chips flew into his eyes, forcing him to rinse them with water. Turning his head to avoid the flakes, he inadvertently struck his hand with the hammer. 'God's Blood!' He flung the offending instrument to one side to nurse his bruised fingers. The sun's intense heat was relentless. He wet the necktie and tied it around his neck. *I have prepared the rock, but not myself.*

His throat parched, he drained the second water bottle, critical of himself for not bringing a third. He stood to ease the strain in his back. His knees were bruised and sore from the hard granite. Both arms ached, and he was certain that, by the morrow, it would hurt to move them. Sweat irritated his eyes, already reddened from rock dust. Courtois' warnings about the exacting nature of the work came back to him as he stared ruefully at the meagre return on his labour. Kneeling down, he gripped the chisel, promising himself to spend no more than another hour.

The hour passed as he became absorbed in the task. Intent on what he was doing, he was unaware of the changing weather until a gust of wind sent the water bottle skittering along the top. He glanced up, surprised to see towering masses of white cloud directly overhead. Moments later, he heard a rumble of thunder as drops of rain splattered the rock. Hurriedly abandoning the tools, he made his way back to the ladder. As he descended, the wind made a muted roaring sound and shook the ropes like shrouds in a gale so that he was forced to stop and hang on.

He arrived back at the post tired, sore, frustrated, and soaking wet. Riding through the gate, he found Pinch and Abel admiring the newly hung smokehouse door.

Pinch waved him over. 'Come, Sir Bourgeois. Observe our very own buffalo!'

After a cursory examination, he proceeded to his quarters and changed into dry clothes. He warmed himself before the fire while Meadow Bird draped his wet shirt across a chair, clucking her tongue as she did so.

'Where are the boys?' he asked, irritated by her scolding glances.

'Play.'

'Play?' He cocked an eyebrow. 'Another word to your store, lassie?'

'Sky bad. Rain on lodge.' She sniffed as if such fluency was of no account.

He smiled, detecting her pride in spite of her grumpy manner.

'Tun-der,' she said, cocking a head to listen.

'*Th*-under.'

'Tah-under,' she repeated after him, her face perplexed at the stupidity of the word.

The rain stopped and he made his way across the wet yard to the hall. The door opened and Bjornson emerged. The Swede stopped short on seeing him.

'I expected you back sooner. The wind was strong.'

'Aye. And stronger up on the rock.'

They stood for a moment, stiff and awkward in each other's presence. To his disappointment, Bjornson showed no inclination to ask, however grudgingly, about his labours. Instead, the Swede motioned to the door. 'Pinch is inside, making tea.' With that, he continued past.

'Will you not take tea?'

'I have drunk a pot.' Bjornson long stepped to cross a puddle.

Rather than go inside, he wiped down one of the chairs on the porch and sat down with a sour look after the Swede. He heard a shout as his sons dashed from behind the storehouse towards him, the Bjornson boys close at their heels.

'Father! Can we go for a ride?'

'Not now. The grass is too wet. And it may rain again.'

'Where did you go? The rock?'

'Aye.' He mussed Claim's hair as the boy climbed up on his knee.

Pinch emerged from the cabin balancing a mug of tea. 'And did ye scale the beast?'

He winked at the boys. 'I did.'

'Can I climb it?'

He smiled at his son's eager face. 'The wind would sweep you up to the sky!'

'It strikes me,' said Pinch, sitting down, 'that you may claim credit as the first man to stand atop it since the history of the world.' The boys gaped as they took in the words.

He also was taken by the notion. 'Mayhap an Indian stood there before me?'

'How in blazes would an Indian get up there except by sprouting wings?' The possibility drew gasps from his sons.

Pinch took a sip of the hot tea, scrunching his face at the strong flavour. 'And you still intend to carve it—by yourself?'

'I do,' he said, braced for a quarrel.

'I see.' Pinch mused for a moment, his mood thoughtful rather than disputatious. 'It is a mighty project,' he conceded, the genuine note of reflection in his voice a rarity that drew a surprised glance from Boundless.

'You have come round to it?'

Pinch guffawed. 'Do you think me a fool? It is still madness. Boys—the first to fetch me a lighted taper wins a penny!'

'Me!' Prospect dashed inside as Claim jumped down and raced to follow. The Bjornson boys stayed where they were for a moment and then dashed after.

'Which, then, is your true opinion? A mighty project or a boundless folly?'

'I win!' Before Pinch could answer, Prospect returned, triumphantly holding a smouldering splint in one hand.

'Thank ye.' Pinch lit the pipe, savouring the draw.

'Well? Do not keep me in suspense.'

Pinch let out a puff of smoke. 'A thing may be both.' Pleased with the judiciousness of the statement, he reached into his pocket and produced a penny, which he handed to Prospect. 'Save it in a shoe,' he advised.

Boundless watched as the twins wandered off to bicker over the penny, followed by the Bjornsons. 'Perhaps you are growing wise, Pinch, along with your white hairs.'

'I have eyes. I see many things,' Pinch insisted, and drew on the pipe.

'Indeed,' he said, humouring the moment. 'And what else do you see—that we may benefit from your wisdom?' Pinch hummed on the pipe, considering. 'Well? Do you have no words?'

Pinch regarded him over the pipe. 'I see a spark, leaping to flame. And it shall scorch us all, ere done.'

The solemnity in the older man's tone—whether mocking or real—infuriated him. 'What balderdash is this? From sage to seer—in a breath!'

Unruffled, Pinch nodded over the pipe. 'As you say.'

'Is it your cards that tell you so? Like a savage casting bones!'

Pinch sucked on the stem, refusing to be drawn.

'Well? Speak our fortunes!'

'I have said what I said. Let the truth of it come out, or no.'

The exchange returned to prickle as he sat before the fire prior to bed. *The fellow will naysay the devil. It is in his nature.* Little consoled by the thought, he picked up the poker and broke up a smouldering log. *One day he will swallow that blessed pipe!*

## 47

## *God's Handiwork*

H E AWOKE TO A stiffness in his back and arms. His knees were bruised and the back of his neck tender from the sun. He grimaced at the chance of being both sunburnt and soaked to the skin within the same hour. *I must find some way to better preserve myself from the weather.* Mulling the problem, he pulled on his shirt and breeches and sat down again to tug on the worn leather shoes he preferred to wear while working on the rock. After breakfast, he took his time in the tool hut, humming to himself as he selected various items and set aside others.

It was late morning before he arrived at the rock, driving the wagon. Turning loose the horses, he hooked the bundle of supplies to the hanging tackle rope he had left wrapped around the ladder. Up on the summit, he hauled up a roll of sailcloth, a coil of rope, six iron spikes, a bundle of pre-cut lumber pieces, a keg of powder, and the buffalo robe he had brought with him from Mose's cabin, the hide now holed and threadbare with age.

Within the space of a few hours, he had fashioned a simple wooden platform roofed with canvas. The moveable platform provided a shade sufficient to protect him as the sun changed angle or as a shelter against a sudden burst of rain. *If the wind doesn't first blow it all to perdition!*

Pleased with the makeshift shade, he dragged it to where he had left off the previous day and weighed it down with the keg of powder. His mind marvelled at all the preparation required. *I was naïve to think it was a simple matter of hammering and chiselling.*

The sun beat down as he finished boring the last of the three powder holes started the day before. Pinch's remarks came back to sting and he muttered angrily. *What does that fool know?*

As he got to his feet, he was assailed by a wave of light-headedness. Taking a few purposeful breaths, he steadied himself before carrying a cup of powder and a hemp sack to the blasting holes. Scooping a handful of dried mud into a wooden bowl and pouring water over it, he mixed the two into a clay which he tamped on top of the powder in the first hole. He pushed a 'needle', fashioned from a wood splinter and threaded with fibres of hemp rope, through the plug and into the powder. The fuse extended two feet back from the hole. Sprinkling some grains of black powder over the rope, he worked them into the fibres.

After a few attempts, he ignited the char cloth and transferred the glowing threads to the fuse. As the hemp caught, he retreated several yards, bracing himself as he watched the spark run along the hemp. The muffled explosion was disappointing. He examined the small cracks radiating out from the hole. "Twill take much more than a pinch.' He chuckled at the notion. 'The real Pinch would surely cause a bigger disturbance.' He stuffed the second blast hole with as much powder as it would take. He counted to ten before the charges blew, throwing up dust and granite chips and fracturing a shallow fissure in the rock. The crack ran from the blast site to the next hole. The rock had fragmented, allowing him to pull out chunks of granite with his fingers.

Pleased with the result, he made a mental note to make the next holes deeper and wider, so as to hold more powder. He drilled three more holes that day, working with absorbed intent, a surge of energy rendering the usual tiring labour as of no account. He blew the charges, mining the granite to a depth of three inches in a constricted V pattern. Lumps of broken granite now marred the smooth surface of the rock. Standing back to survey the impact, he took in the wide expanse of rock still to be excavated. *It is no more than a scratch.*

He walked to the side of the rock, monitoring himself for dizziness. The plain below was thickly dotted with antelope, hundreds of calves gambolling among the mature bucks and does. He stared at some commotion on the fringes of the herd, regretting that he had not thought to bring the spyglass. *I must make a list.*

He rode back to the post, tired and dusty, but pleased with himself in spite of the minute progress. *After all, it is begun.*

THE LONG, HOT DAYS turned to weeks as he continued his determined assault on the rock. He grew more confident in his handling of the blasting powder, increasing the charge and correctly predicting the depth and direction of each blast. Preoccupied with the measurements, he referred constantly to the figures jotted in the notebook, going out to the workshop model after supper to make revisions.

The variable summer weather posed a constant, and dangerous, challenge. Twice, he hurriedly evacuated the rock at the sudden onset of a lightning storm. At other times, absorbed in the work, he glanced up in dismay as drenching rain swept the exposed rock, soaking him before he could retreat to the ladder. He learned to keep a wary eye on the clouds as he laboured—on one occasion hurrying down the steps as threatening rumbles echoed across the plain.

Worse, to his mind, than the wind and rain, were the long, hot days when the sun beat down on the bare stone with punishing effect, the granite itself becoming hot to the touch. In spite of the moveable shade he had constructed, his face and neck were burned to the colour of rawhide. Allied to the scorching heat and scouring gales was the discomfort and sheer exhaustion wrought by the constant kneeling and hammering. His hands were roughened and callused from the constant blows of the hammer against the resistant stone. His back, he decided, was permanently bent from bending his spine as he walked up and down the rock. A fleeting memory came back to him and he grinned, in spite of his discomfort.

Driven by a fierce desire to make observable progress, he overexerted himself in the first few weeks, ignoring the mental and muscular fatigue exacted by the long days, the hot sun and the physical toil. The strain on his body was so profound that he was forced to abandon the rock for three days to recover—Meadow Bird clucking and grumbling as she applied a poultice to his sore muscles. *She doesn't understand what I'm trying to do. Or perhaps she does and still thinks it a foolish waste of time.*

He was obliged to curb his impatience and to pace himself—climbing down from the rock during the hottest part of the day to rest in the shade. He took to riding back to the stockade for dinner or a nap, returning to the rock in the late afternoon, and working into the long summer twilight. The one reward, as he remarked to Bjornson, was the freedom from flies and mites afforded by the high elevation. 'The wind blows them all to hell,' he declared.

Occasionally, he halted what he was doing to stare at some drama unfolding in the distance—whether an Indian hunting party or a wolf attack on some hapless deer or buffalo. Unseen, he stood and looked out over the plain in godlike aloofness, the high perch conferring a sense of detachment from the world that lingered as he rode home through the swells and bluffs.

Bjornson remained unmoved by such accounts, nodding or uttering a gruff 'aye' at each rendition but refusing to be drawn into a discussion. Frustrated, Boundless tried another tack. On a day when both Bertrand and Danon were absent from the post, he persuaded Bjornson to ride out to the rock on the pretext of re-securing the ladder to its anchor bolts. Bjornson grudgingly agreed, after first reiterating his refusal to have anything to do with the 'devil rock' itself.

After re-securing the ladder, they sat against the stone to drink water and rest. The day was humid and they were grateful for the shade. A herd of white-tails grazed the rippling pastures, their tails twitching as they bent to graze the parched grass. Above, wisps of cloud threaded the sky. The only sound came from the gusting wind as it swept across the grass in long, curving swathes.

'It has its own beauty, I suppose,' Bjornson conceded, leaning back against the rock to gaze at the fertile plain.

Surprised at the remark, Boundless nevertheless seized on it.

'Is it not an equal sin—of self-pride—to deny oneself the chance to admire God's handiwork from an even higher vantage?'

Bjornson grunted, closing his eyes. 'Jehovah did not create trees so that we must climb them.'

'But if we did, where then is the fault?'

'You mislead one thing into another. Trees are one thing, graven images, another.'

He scowled at the words.

'And you are short-sighted—to see nothing but that which your faith tells you. There are other things—even grander things. The buffalo in their numbers. This land. The grass itself … this great vastness that surrounds us.' He swept out a hand to indicate the sun-baked plain. 'Do you not feel something grand in all of it?'

'It is God's handiwork.' Bjornson's voice was stubborn.

'Then perhaps God will not mind a monument to his works?'

'The rock is already a monument. As is the buffalo, and we ourselves most of all. He does not need another.' Bjornson studied him, the skin around his eyes crinkling. 'But you do not do it for the glory of God.'

Boundless tugged a blade of grass and put it in his mouth and made no answer.

## 48

## A Night Full of Stars

T OWARD THE END OF summer, he estimated that he had removed more than three hundred pounds of rock. A cut—two feet deep at its deepest point, eight feet long and a yard wide—marred the smooth granite. From the rock, if not yet from the grass, the declivity between the head and hump was now more pronounced. He had endured sun, rain, hail and wind, and twice almost crushed his chisel-holding left hand. He fancied that his right, hammering arm had grown larger than his left. Progress was still incrementally slow, but he had learned to strike the rock with measured blows that married force with efficiency and had learned to read the granite bed and anticipate where it would split and how far apart to bore the holes. Above all, he was now proficient in the matter of explosives, having relied on the black powder to blast all of the removed granite.

The loose stones themselves he had swept to the earth, later collecting and carrying them in the wagon to dispose of along the Missouri shore. The removal was unnecessary, he acknowledged to himself, but hauling away the broken rocks at the end of each day was a measure of his efforts. Indeed, the growing pile of removed rubble along the Missouri was itself testament to his progress. He stacked the pieces of broken granite stones into a mound, telling himself he was twice engaged—in birthing a buffalo while at the same time building a pyramid of bones.

Any fleeting guilt he felt at the continuing delegation of his *bourgeois* duties was assuaged by a conviction that he was embarked on a mission of far greater import than mere bartering. *After all, Maurice, when here, enjoys the responsibility of overseeing the summer trades, and Bjorn is at last taking his full share of partnership duties.* The boys also seemed content, seeing him off in the morning and waiting by the gate to be the first to spot him on his return. Meadow Bird, however, remained baffled and annoyed whenever he attempted to explain the project.

'Already have plenty buffalo,' she said, her voice stubborn. 'Have two sons. Two!' She held up her fingers.

Confined to the post by a late-August storm, he spent the day going through the ledgers and general accounts. His sons sat beside him at the table, working through the exercises in their arithmetic primer in between making rude faces at one another. After supper, he read to them from *Robinson Crusoe* before despatching them off to bed. Meadow Bird followed an hour later, but not before placing a log on the fire and wrapping a blanket around his shoulders.

'May the Indian gods bless you, lassie.' He kissed her forehead as she wrinkled her brow into a mock-impertinent frown. Relieved that the tension between them seemed to be over, he watched her enter the bedroom. *I should take her out there. Show her what it is I am trying to do. But she wouldn't understand.* The thought saddened him.

His shoulder ached and he absently rubbed it while mulling on the hardness of the rock. Picking up the book on antiquities, he turned to a passage he had marked earlier: *Granite is hard, and impervious to weather. It is the stuff of pyramids and cathedrals.* Looking at one of the few illustrations, of a Greek statue on a plinth, he pictured his buffalo—granitic and iron-horned—staring out over the plain a hundred—a thousand—years hence.

Turning his thoughts back to his *bourgeois* duties, he opened the compendium of notes he had made for inclusion in his annual letter to Guillaume. Taking the numbered and dated pages to the table, he moved the lantern and opened the large glass ink bottle bequeathed to him by his mentor.

After making additional and sundry notes on the weather, the condition of the post, and the unexpected arrival of a party of Blackfoot bearing a plentiful supply of prime coat beaver, he predicted a record number of fur bales to be despatched the following spring.

'*Our reputation as fair and honest dealers is the surest guarantee of continued patronage in the event of rival companies advancing this far north. Since the turn of the year, we have received trade parties from the Arapaho, Crow, Chippewa, Dakota, Cheyenne and Cree from the northern lakes as well, of course, as those from the Mandan, Hidatsa and Arikara. I believe that we are now firmly established as a vital part of the Indian trade alliance that stretches from south of the Brazos to east of the Mississippi and north to the Yellowstone and all the nations encompassed therein.*'

He set down the quill, his thoughts drifting back to the Patapsco and the slow-drifting barges laden with tobacco and hogs and slaves that trafficked back and forth between the farms and plantations. Pinch's figure of an 'invisible thread' that connected the beavers taken from remote northern streams to the milliners of London and Paris returned to him, and he pictured a spider's web—suspended from all points of the compass—the filmy tendrils delicate yet firm, anchoring the post to the furthermost cities of the earth, the spider spinning in spite of war, drought and pestilence.

Taken by the image, he dipped the quill. '*Surely, trade is the great engine of the world. The primitive Indians that arrive here to barter pelts for goods are engaged in the same enterprise as the powdered merchants of Philadelphia or London.*'

He sat back in the chair. 'And against this ceaseless trafficking to-and-fro stood the rock, his rock, immovable, rooted in the earth, imperviously disdainful of all such webs and conveyances.' He placed the top back on the ink bottle, pleasuring in the thought. A draught blew under the door and the lantern flickered. He blew it out, rising from the chair.

The ruminative mood followed him to bed, beguiling his thoughts as he curled against Meadow Bird for warmth, his mind drowsy with images of canoes and shallops, and great sea-going ships. Meadow Bird muttered in sleep and he tugged the robe up over her neck. *Perhaps it directed my steps*, he mused, his thoughts roaming once again to the rock. *Who knows but it pulled me here—all the way from the Maryland woods, mayhap from Scotland itself?* The notion of destiny inherent in such a conceit suddenly cast what had hitherto passed for chance, aimless wandering into a revealed fate, charged with purpose. He murmured to hold onto the notion, his mind heavy with slumber. "*Get thee out of thy country, and from thy kindred, and from thy father's house unto a land that I will shew thee.*"

STANDING ATOP THE ROCK the next day, he gazed at the fragments of stone lying scattered on the surface. Cracks and channels marred the smooth granite where he had blown chunks from the rock face. He surveyed the expanse of granite that yet remained, struck forcibly by the truth of Courtois' dictum: '*The entirety of the carver's art lies in the reduction or elimination of superfluous stone.*' The knowledge that such reduction was, in effect, freeing and shaping the beast he saw within the stone offered little consolation at those moments when he doubted his ability to complete the audacious project. *If there were two of us, the work would go that much faster.* Resentment at Bjornson's intransigence swelled into a sense of betrayal as he started to bore holes in the secondary layer of granite. *I saved him from the half-breed, and this is how he repays me!* He hammered the star drill against the stone.

But, in the way of such things, he acknowledged on reflection that the resentment was leavened by a sense of satisfaction at his own unaided efforts in tackling the mighty project. '*Things of worth are seldom gained without great effort, and thereby their worth increases.*' The words of Guillaume sounded in his thoughts as he gazed out at the horizon. He had stayed later than was his custom, and he reproached himself for not noticing the passage of time. The sun was sinking in reddish glory, the resplendent rays illuminating the prairie grass.

The brigade was due to return any day, and work would have to cease. He despaired as he pictured the cold, unrelenting winter. The thought of interrupting the work to accommodate both winter and the demands of business—a business he had grown increasingly tired of—tormented him. *So much wasted time! But what is to be done?* He stood there, lost in thought. As he turned and walked to the ladder, his eye was caught by the setting sun as it illuminated the horizon in a final burst of light.

He was about to descend, with one foot on the rungs, when a notion struck him. He halted, gripping the handholds as the idea rushed through his brain. He hurried down, almost missing a step in his haste.

'WHAT?' BJORNSON LOOKED HORRIFIED when told of his intention, his expression so thunderstruck that Boundless could not help but laugh.

'It will be for just the one night,' he said. 'I need you to return the horse and bring it back again in the morning. I cannot tether it for fear of wolves.'

Pinch shook his head when told—grunting as if entirely unsurprised by such madness. 'Now he sleeps with the creature!' Sighing, he smoked a pipe on such folly.

Suspecting Meadow Bird might prove harder to convince, he merely told her of his intention to spend the night sleeping out on the prairie. This drew a single quizzical glance in return. She went away and returned holding his buffalo robe.

'*Iktáh!*' she declared, wrapping the robe around his shoulders in demonstration.

He kissed her cheek. 'I had thought of the same thing myself, lassie.'

The next morning, he drove the wagon out to the rock, provisioned with additional water, jerky and pemmican, and with the buffalo robe in the back along with a blanket to serve as a pillow. After much persuasion, Bjornson had agreed to accompany him. The Swede sat on the seat beside him, his face dour, although he held his peace—at least until they reached their destination.

'You still intend to sleep up there?' he asked as Boundless readied to climb the Jacob's Ladder.

'Yes, come join me!' said Boundless, brimming with cheer at the prospect of spending a night atop the rock.

'I am not a lunatic!' With a shake of his head to signal the idiocy of the plan, Bjornson set off while promising to return in the morning. 'If you have not been blown off!' he called over his shoulder.

As the sun sank in the sky, he spread Mose's buffalo robe beneath him and the newer one on top. Rolling up the blanket, he placed it beneath his head. The night was warm and cloudless, although he felt a distinct chill not long after sunset. Pulling the buffalo robe higher, he shifted against the hard stone, staring upwards at the bright diorama of stars. Again, he felt the curious sensation as of the earth turning and experienced a dizziness—whether due to real or fancied motion, he was unsure.

The stars shone with a brilliance that took his breath. A shooting star streaked through the firmament, the sight evoking an entranced gasp. He saw other bodies that seemed to move more slowly—amidst a constellation of sparks and vivid lights. The breeze was cool on his face and Bjornson's warning echoed in his mind. But so captivated was he by the blaze of stars that he stood up to see better and further. All around, the prairie was swathed in dark night, the only sound the occasional yip of a coyote.

A fancy took him—the notion absurd yet irresistible as he lifted his arms above his head. 'I am Boundless McLennan!' His voice was immediately swallowed in the darkness. Undeterred, he hollered to the stars. 'I am master of this rock—creator of the buffalo!' The boast echoed in the night. 'Hear me, ye distant heavens! Heed my voice!' He dropped his arms, trembling with the sensation of starry vastness beyond comprehension. The endless leagues across the Atlantic, the head-scratching span of the Chesapeake, the thousand-mile passage across the grassy plains, the surging tempest that was the join of the Mississippi and Missouri rivers, the countless buffalo themselves—all shrank to insignificance against the cosmic immensity at play just above his head.

He sat down, vertigo and fancy combining to induce a state of breathless wonder that drew a long *'ahhh!'* from his lips as he gazed up at the bright, sprawling heavens. He shivered, suddenly conscious of the cold night air. Tugging the robe about him, he closed his eyes—only to open them again—staring up as if spellbound by the spiralling stars. It was well after midnight before he slipped into a fitful sleep rocked with dreams of stars, darkness and the buffalo upon which he lay—still standing, still insistent, after all but the stars had perished.

A WEEK LATER, HE had just climbed down from the rock when he noticed a horse and rider spurring through the grass towards him. *The brigade must have returned.* The Indian youth drew rein and motioned to him with some urgency, pointing towards the post before heading back out into the grass.

He followed slowly, trying to tear his thoughts away from the rock and back to his duties as *bourgeois*. As the post came into view, he saw that the brigade had indeed returned—a line of men filing in through the gate with bundles on their backs. *Maurice will be annoyed I was not there to greet them.*

He was within a few hundred yards of the post when Bjornson stepped through the gate, waving an arm to urge him on. The Swede appeared agitated and Boundless kicked the horse into a canter, concerned that something was amiss with the brigade.

'What is it?' He reined in the horse as Bjornson advanced to meet him. 'Did something happen to the brigade?'

Bjornson clutched the bridle, his face distraught. 'Guillaume is dead!'

## 49

# A Bargain Struck

ONCE MORE THE FUTURE of the post was the subject of fervid speculation as the men awaited some indication of his intentions. He read and re-read Mathieu's letter, absorbing his account of Thibault's death and his hopes for the future of the post. Distressed by the shocking event and consumed by anxiety over the implications for his grand project, he fended off persistent enquiries from those few *engagés* who dared approach him directly on the matter.

'In good time,' he snapped, his vexed expression discouraging further enquiries.

Norman Dubois fell alongside as he crossed the yard one afternoon. 'Will there be a brigade next year? The men need to know,' the *pilote* asked, ignoring his frown.

'Mayhap. I must think on it.'

'And beyond?'

'Beyond what? Who the devil knows what lies beyond tomorrow, let alone next year! Tell them they will have an answer when the matter has been fully discussed.'

He continued to the storehouse as Dubois stared after him, frustration written on the *pilote's* face.

Pushing open the storehouse door, he found Bjornson inside, idly chatting with Antoine. Both men looked up as he entered.

Antoine stood up, offering a courteous, 'Good morning, sir.'

'Tea, Antoine, if you please,' he said, despatching the clerk to the hall. He waited until the door closed behind the clerk before turning to Bjornson. 'There is no peace on the matter of the cursed brigade,' he complained.

'The men are anxious about the future. You must reassure them, else there will be no one to paddle the canoes back.'

He grumbled at the reminder. 'And what about you, Bjorn? You have kept close counsel on the matter.'

Bjornson rested his hands on his knees as he considered his answer. 'For myself, I am tired of snow and pelts and this forsaken wilderness.' He scratched his jaw, his pale face a study in hesitancy. 'It has been on my mind for some time to return to the east.'

Rocked by the announcement, Boundless could only gape, momentarily at a loss for words. The door opened and Antoine re-entered, balancing three mugs upon a wood board.

'You may drink yours in the hall,' he said as Antoine distributed the mugs and prepared to sit down.

Taken aback, Antoine stood up again. 'Of course, sir.'

The clerk had barely shut the door behind him before Boundless rounded on the Swede. 'What the devil do you mean—return east?'

Bjornson picked up the mug of tea and nursed it between his big hands. 'I intend to leave the post and take my family to Boston, or perhaps Montreal.'

'Now you tell me!' Boundless stared accusingly.

Bjornson's voice was soft, almost apologetic. 'As I said, it has been on my mind for some time. Monsieur Thibault's death has …' He left the sentence unfinished.

'But I need you! What if I decide the post is to continue as before?'

Bjornson gave a deep sigh. 'Whatever decision you make, I am resolved to leave.'

'But you cannot! Your life is here, as is mine and Pinch's.'

'Pinch may do as he likes. I wish my sons to grow up in society and to enter a profession. They cannot do that here.'

'Why now?'

'There is no better time. Monsieur Thibault has … departed, and you, yourself, I suspect, have made up your mind to disband the company. You are sick of the business, as am I. Is that not so?' He sipped the tea, eyeing Boundless over the mug.

'I had thought to have your support at least.' Boundless could not keep the bitterness from his voice.

'And you have it. But that does not alter the fact that I will leave.' Bjornson stood up, holding the mug. 'I must go and speak with Hannah.'

'Do not let me prevent you,' said Boundless, his voice prickly with betrayal.

Bjornson paused in the doorway. 'You could come too … We could go together.' Not receiving an answer, he closed the door behind him.

Bjornson made his way across the yard, his mind full of the conversation. So absorbed was he that he almost bumped into Pinch. 'What hails, Bjorn? Has our gracious master made up his mind on our future?' Pinch was carrying a bucket of feed which he set down as he waited for a response.

Bjorn grimaced. 'He hasn't said so, but I believe he himself will stay, no matter the fate of the brigade.'

'Did you try to enlighten him at least?'

'It is useless.' Bjorn shook his head. 'He is bound to that rock. He will not leave it.'

Pinch grunted as he picked up the bucket. 'And what binds him—beyond folly?'

Bjornson sighed, weary with the topic. 'I suspect that he himself does not know.'

AFTER BJORNSON LEFT, BOUNDLESS sat motionless in the cold storehouse, greatly put out at his failure to conscript Bjornson into his scheme. After a while, he muttered and stood up, tossing the cold tea from the mug.

During supper, he was morose and preoccupied, grunting in answer to questions from his sons. After, he poured himself a glass of rum and sat before the fire. The boys played quietly on the floor, darting glances in his direction. He poured himself another glass of rum, his frustration spilling over as he gulped it down.

'Father?' Prospect stood beside him.

'What is it now?' he snapped.

His son's eyes brimmed with tears 'I want to say goodnight.'

Contrite, he kissed the boy's brow. 'Pardon, laddie, my mind is elsewhere.'

Bestowing a second kiss on Claim, he attempted some playful humour, holding up a pretend stick to measure each boy. 'Ye both are sprouting up like grass!' He mussed Prospect's hair. 'Now off to bed—both!'

Meadow Bird soon joined the boys, leaving him to his thoughts as he brooded into the flames, a sick feeling in his gut. *Why now—when I am just barely started?* He contemplated himself alone in the deserted post with a wife and two children to care for—all hopes for his grand project dashed to pieces as surely as if they had been flung from off the top of the rock itself. His thoughts turned spitefully to the Swede. *He has betrayed me. He knows how much I count on his support. The fellow is as stubborn as a Pennsylvania mule!*

But even as he mentally voiced the accusation, he gloomily acknowledged his own weariness—the business of furs, trades, and accounts a constant diversion from his single-minded preoccupation with the sinuous vine that wrapped and twisted his insides—the creeping plant sprouted in the granite shade now lodged so deeply in every crevice of his being that to uproot it was to tear out his soul itself. He sat brooding long into the night, his hopes, like the greying coals, crumbling to ash.

He avoided Bjornson, and most of the company, for the next few days, remaining shut up in his quarters as he deliberated on the future. Lapointe came to see him, ostensibly to discuss some trade discrepancy or other, and was sent on his way, as was Dubois a quarter-hour later.

Pinch was next to stop by the Bostonian bluntly accusing him of neglecting his duties and the welfare of the men. 'Abel and Luc deserve to know if they should make plans to leave.'

'And so they shall! Close the door as you leave. It is cold enough in here.'

Pinch lingered in the doorway. 'Is it the post or your rock that you worry for?'

'The door!'

Emerging from his quarters the following morning, he beckoned to Danon. 'Tell the men to remain in the hall following breakfast. Tell them I have an announcement to make.' After downing a second cup of sugary tea, he made his way across the yard. The day was cold and depressing, snow flurries sweeping across the compound. Mounting the steps to the hall, he heard a hum of anticipation from within. The noise fell away as he entered.

Bidding a brusque 'Good morning!' he took up position at the front of the hall, feeling curious eyes upon him. Lapointe and Antoine sat at the end of the table closest to him, the former reserving a chair for Bjornson, who took it as Boundless prepared to speak. Pinch leaned against the wall to observe proceedings.

'Friends,' he began, his voice sounding hoarse in his ears. 'The news of Monsieur Thibault's death has hit us all hard.' Murmurs arose from the assembled men. 'He was a fine man, and an excellent *bourgeois* of the company that he himself founded.' It flashed into his mind to recount the legend of 'Guillaume's Luck' as told to him by Pinch, but he dismissed the notion.

'It is because of him that all of us are here. Without him, there would be no post, no company, no brigade.'

He paused to let the words sink in. The men were silent, their eyes fixed upon him.

'As his lawful business partner, and his successor as *bourgeois*, it falls to me to make an announcement as to the future of the company in the wake of his death. In doing so, I take heed of Monsieur Thibault's own wishes, and also the advice of his son-in-law, Monsieur Simard, to whom he confided his intentions.' He paused, acutely aware of the tension in the audience. 'With these considerations in mind, and as his lawful partner and successor, and with a heavy heart, I regret to announce the dissolution of the company he founded.'

The decision was met with stunned silence. He glanced at Lapointe who shrugged. All at once everyone started talking together—whether in objection or agreement he could not tell.

'And the brigade, *Monsieur*?' a voice asked.

'I have decided that the spring brigade will be the last. There will be no return. I see no reason to have another.'

The revelation provoked a burst of protest, the men talking over each other as they argued, the air filling with aggrieved voices.

'*Monsieur McLennan*?' A hush fell as Jean Provencher, a veteran of ten years with the company, stood up and respectfully touched his forehead. 'Could not we—the men of the brigade'—he indicated the crowded tables— 'could we not purchase the stock and continue the company ourselves? I have heard of such a thing.'

The suggestion met with a chorus of approval. Waiting until the noise died down, he spoke again. 'Monsieur Thibault was our founder. Without him, there is no company.'

'But sir, with yourself as *bourgeois* and Monsieur Simard in Montreal?'

'Monsieur Simard has already declined to take over from his father-in-law. He has his own business interests to attend to. The decision has been made.' He glanced at where Pinch stood in the corner, pipe in mouth, following the exchange.

'Surely, Monsieur Thibault would wish us to continue!' a voice protested.

'I am ready to pledge!' declared another man. 'Who is with me?' Cheers and applause met the announcement.

As more of the men seized on the suggestion, he took out Mathieu's letter from his waistcoat. 'Hear it from Monsieur Simard in his own words!' A hush fell as he began to read.

'Monsieur Thibault left extensive instructions for the disposal of the enterprise which I convey to you now. Regretfully, the company he founded is legally dissolved by his death. In his last conversations with me, he expressed the wish to conclude matters as expeditiously as possible for the sake of his family.'

In the dismayed silence that followed, he held up the letter. 'There you have it. Moreover, it is only a matter of time before rival fur companies set up in the upper Missouri in competition with us. It is foolish to suppose that we can continue on as before.'

He motioned to Lapointe, who in turn signalled three of the younger men to begin serving from the keg of rum he had ordered breached beforehand. Waiting until the mugs were filled, he held up his cup. 'A toast! To the memory of Guillaume Thibault!'

'Guillaume Thibault!'

OCTOBER GAVE WAY TO November as Bjornson made plans for departure in the spring. 'So soon?' Boundless protested. 'There is much to consider.'

They were standing outside in the snow, watching a party of Hidatsa as they prepared to depart, laden with goods.

'Have you decided where you will you go?' he continued as Bjornson made no answer.

'Montreal first, to collect my savings. Then, who knows? I may stay there and open a business. Or else …' Bjornson left the sentence unfinished.

'Or else what? Return to Delaware?'

The question brought a peevish frown. 'No matter, so long as I am rid of here.'

'Have you thought of Hannah—how she will cope in the city, amidst all the fine ladies in their hats and cloaks?'

'I shall buy her a hat. And a cloak too, if that makes her happy.'

'And the boys? Have you given thought to how they will miss my own sons and the wild, free air?'

'They are young. And I wish to enrol them to a profession. Perhaps they will become lawyers or apothecaries.' Scratching his jaw, Bjornson regarded Boundless, a quizzical look on his face. 'It is you who ought to reconsider. Why would a man toil to build a fortune for his family only to throw it all aside in order to hammer a useless rock?'

'The money will still be there in a year or two.'

'Year or two!' Bjornson laughed, his voice incredulous. 'A decade or two, more like.' His voice grew serious. 'Come with me, Boundless. We may enter business together. Or buy a farm.'

'Farm? I had rather blow my brains out with a pistol!'

'As you say.' Bjornson's mouth set stubbornly. 'But I shall not change my mind.'

'Pinch is staying on. He told me so.'

'Pinch may do as he likes, as may you.'

'Have you tried speaking to him?' he asked Pinch the next day as they discussed life at the post sans the brigade.

'Who?'

'Bjorn. Who the devil else?'

'Why would I? What Bjorn does is up to him.'

'He is a fool to leave all he has here for some uncertain future in the east. What about his boys? And White Deer—how will she be received as his wife? You ought to reason with the fellow.'

'Is it for White Deer's welfare you concern yourself—or do you inveigle for some other reason?' Pinch cocked an eyebrow.

He scowled at the other man's knowing look. 'What do you care the reason—so long as he stays? Besides, Buffalo Bird would greatly miss White Deer's company. She is like a mother to the girl.'

Pinch considered this. 'True, but she will have Meadow Bird for company, will she not?'

'Nevertheless, you would oblige me by speaking to him. He needs to hear a voice other than mine.'

Pinch snorted. 'Do you involve me in your stratagems!'

Vexed beyond measure, he stalked off, colliding with an *engagé* who stepped aside and uttered a hasty apology at the angry frown on his face.

The conversation deepened his anxiety as he contemplated splitting his responsibilities between the rock, maintenance of the post, and the welfare of his family. *I cannot do it. Not alone. Not with just Pinch for support. Damn you, Bjorn!*

Supressing his disquiet, he composed a letter to Mathieu, expressing condolences for the loss of Guillaume.

*He was among the finest men I ever knew, and I shall miss him greatly. It may be of some comfort to his spirit to know that White Deer grieved his death most piteously. The loving affection between the two was a model for my own relations with my wife. After much deliberation and consultation, Mr Bjornson and I have concluded that we have no desire to continue the company in Monsieur Thibault's absence.*

He broke off the letter, anxiety over the future consuming his thoughts.

He spent much of the days that followed shut up in the workshop or brooding in his quarters. At night, he tossed restlessly, his dreams a muttering drama of disappointed hopes that drew sharp pokes from an irritable Meadow Bird.

In search of diversion from his increasingly desperate thoughts, he went on a hunt with Luc, trudging through the deep powder in pursuit of game. After searching the chill landscape for three hours, they came across a moose frozen to death in a drift. A wolf howl floated on the wintry air as they hacked off parts to load onto the sledge. They stopped to rest, their breath rising like smoke in the winter light. A raven flapped up from the snow, something in its beak.

'What was that?' He glanced at Luc, aware the other man had said something.

'I said spring will be upon us afore we know it.'

'What will you do—now that the company will go out of business?'

Luc slapped his hands against the cold. 'What I have done all my life, I suppose—hunt.'

'For some other company?'

'For myself. I have a cabin on the Lachine River. I shall retire there and farm—until it bores me and I run off into the woods!' The Frenchman laughed, breath streaming out of his mouth. 'And yourself?' He studied Boundless, his face curious. 'The men gossip you will retire to Montreal and live in a fine mansion.'

He made a rueful face. 'I should be as bored as yourself. But what do they say of Bjornson?'

'That he will take his family and return east.'

'To also live in a fine mansion, no doubt?'

'Maybe. Denis overheard him say he wished to rejoin the Lutheran church as an elder.' Luc smiled. 'Although Pinch has him opening a tavern within a month of leaving—and imbibing his own stock out of boredom.'

Boundless laughed in spite of himself. 'He may yet confound us all!'

Luc cocked his head as another wolf howl sounded on the air. 'The devils are close. Shall we start back?'

The wintry landscape was glowing with dusk by the time they arrived back at the stockade. Retiring to the workshop with a bottle of brandy, he built a fire and poured himself a glass while staring at the plaster model. He threw back the drink, suddenly enraged—at capricious fate, at the rock itself, at the recalcitrant Swede. *An elder! If his religion so concerns him, then why does he not stay here and convert the blessed Indians?* He briefly considered urging the notion on his companion before abandoning the idea. *I cannot entice him. His mind is set.* He poured himself another drink. *The fellow is as hard-headed as a rock.* He drained the brandy in a gulp. *Damn him and his church! No doubt he plots to use his new-found means to win back favour.* He closed his eyes, his mind drenched with gloom. A moment later he sat up, startled, his eyes wide. 'Ye Gods!'

'I WILL DO IT—IN exchange for your solemn promise.'

He had summoned the Swede to his quarters immediately after breakfast the following morning. Bjornson frowned and retreated slightly as Boundless leaned forward, his voice and manner intense. '—Your solemn promise to help me finish what I have begun.'

Bjornson licked his lips, clearly intrigued by the offer, yet suspicious. 'Do you truly—'

'Yes!'

'Permit me to finish! Do you truly believe the tales of the lost tribe? Truth now!' His eyes bored into Boundless, his honest, open face keen with scrutiny.

'I believe the trapper fellow—that he saw them with his own eyes.'

Bjornson raised an eyebrow. 'Indeed? Before, you were not so convinced. You declared the man a liar and a braggart.'

'It is in my nature to be suspicious of such claims. But suspicion is not proof. At least this way you will know for certain. Think—if you return to the east you will go to your deathbed wondering if the claim was true. And consider this also ...' he added, his voice gaining urgency as he saw Bjornson waver. '—Think if some other man were to discover what is rightfully yours to claim. How then would you feel? Could you live with yourself?'

'But perhaps it is as you say—'

'Fiddle to what I said! And Pinch! What do we know of such things? Think of what it would mean—to be the man that discovered the lost Christian tribe and brought them to the attention of the world! Think how much would be forgiven—of any man—for such a miracle?' He leaned forward again, his voice insistent. 'Why, such a personage could demand a bishopric and a parish of his choosing. He would be lauded as a Christian hero. Your chance, Bjorn, to win the acclaim of the entire Lutheran church. Seize it and return to the east with the staggering news—and an Indian to accompany you as proof! I shall not argue, you have my word,' he urged, dangling the lure before the increasingly torn Swede.

'And should the claim prove to be false?'

'Then you must pledge to me in return. You know what it is I require.'

'Why raise this now—at the last minute?'

'Because it *is* the last minute. Once you leave, the chance is lost forever. Is it not your Christian duty to at least investigate the claim?'

Bjornson tugged his jaw, his face clouded by indecision. 'I shall think on it, and give you my answer.'

'When?'

'When I am ready!' Bjornson made to get up, only to be detained by Boundless' hand on his arm.

'Remember, we must leave this winter. The brigade departs in spring, and Mathieu must have an answer.'

'I said I would think on it!' His voice testy, Bjornson tugged his arm away.

'So you would help him find the misbegotten tribe?' Pinch shook his head as Boundless relayed Bjornson's acceptance of his proposal the following day.

'We leave as soon as the weather improves.'

Pinch snorted. 'Is he so foolish? Does he not spy a certain buffalo rising up behind this compact?'

'He understands my condition and agrees to it.'

'And does he really think to find this wretched tribe?'

'Christian tribe, Pinch. Christian.'

'And yet this thing you propose is most unchristian, is it not?' Pinch raised an eyebrow.

'You are staying; why begrudge him the same?'

'Do I say that I do?' Pinch grunted with annoyance.

'Then am I mistaken?'

Refusing to answer for a moment, Pinch eventually conceded. 'I am settled here, and too old to change. And I would not subject my Buffalo Bird to the gossip and stares of the city for all the pelts in the world. But Bjorn has a family, and a future. What you propose is a fool's errand—as well you know. You do shamelessly take advantage of his credulity for your own ends.' He eyed Boundless, daring him to deny the accusation.

'No matter. He has agreed. And I pray you—do not disturb his thinking with your doubts.' Boundless stood up. 'You have your own future to consider.' With this warning, he left off the conversation.

## 50

## In Search of the Lost Tribe

THEY DEPARTED FOR THE northern lakes on a cold, clear January day, leaving Lapointe in charge in their absence. The flimsy route described by the trapper, Jeremiah Till, indicated that the alleged camp of the elusive tribe lay a good two hundred miles to the north on the shores of a small lake. They took a sledge hauled by twelve of the strongest dogs, and carried sacks of tobacco, sugar and flour as gifts.

They travelled ten miles the first day, taking time to condition the dogs to the distance, and themselves to the exertion. They took rest breaks, sitting in the snow on reed mats as they chewed on strips of pemmican. Toward sunset, the wind kicked up, and they built a snow wall in open country to camp and shelter the traineau. Just before dawn, the dogs began to snarl, waking Boundless. His hand instinctively reached for the musket. The moon was full, the stars blazed overhead. Bjornson slept soundly next to the fire using a sack of flour as a pillow.

Boundless listened, but heard nothing. Getting up, he hushed the dogs and patrolled the perimeter of the camp. In the bright moonlight, the snow glowed with a pale radiance. Nothing moved. The dogs were still restless and he quieted them again. *It is wolves, mayhap, or a bear that has them spooked.* He sat up for a while, the musket across his lap. As tiredness began to close in on him, he glanced at the now-sleeping dogs before lying down, feeling warm in the heavy buffalo robe. The fire glowed and sparked as he fell asleep.

THEY STARTED AGAIN SHORTLY after full light. Neither man spoke, each full of his own thoughts.

'The dogs were restless last night,' he said at a rest break. Bjornson nodded, his mind clearly elsewhere. *Is he thinking of his lost tribe—or regretting the promise he made to me?*

At a second rest break, he sounded out his companion, curious to know what he was thinking. 'Have you any notion of what you might say to them—the Indians—once we find them?'

'Indians?' Bjornson shook his head. 'I was thinking of Monsieur Thibault, and of how I miss him.'

'Indeed. We are minus a friend in the world, Bjorn. A most upright and dependable companion.' After a moment, he said, 'But have you no thoughts of your Indians?'

Bjornson grimaced. 'I am more concerned to find them. So far, I have seen no sign, of any sort.'

Boundless looked around at the paper birch forest. The sun was shining in a blue sky, the snowbound woods silent and desolate. Taking a breath, he got to his feet. 'Are you able?'

They covered twenty miles that day, the dogs pulling eagerly in the traces and the snow firm underfoot. The forest stretched ahead and on either side. The few open areas were barren with snow and showed no signs of human passage. A doubt began to gnaw at him. *What if we don't discover any Indians? Will Bjorn take that as an indication that our agreement is voided?* He put the troubling thought out of his mind as they continued.

After travelling for four days, they came across snowshoe tracks and followed these, hopeful they might lead to a village, only for the tracks to disappear across a frozen stream. Bjornson insisted on scouring the stream for a mile in either direction before abandoning the search. Boundless watched the Swede pace up and down in the snow, a preoccupied expression on his face. *It is hopeless. Surely, he must see that Till was a fool and a liar?* But he held his tongue, content to let Bjornson come to his senses in his own time.

Late in the afternoon, they made camp in a small clearing between the trees. Collecting strips of dry bark, they used the fuel as kindling to light a fire. When the fire was blazing, they heated a pan of dried venison stirred with beans and hung a pot of water over the flames. After eating, they reclined on the reed mats and sipped tea while listening to the chorusing howls of a wolf pack. Although only afternoon, the landscape was already steeped in gloom, the moon looming large in the sky. The dogs lay on their bellies in the snow, their ears pricking at each new round of wolf calls.

'They are noisy devils.' Bjornson tilted his head, listening to the howls. Pulling out his Bible, he studied a passage by the leaping flames.

Boundless watched as the Swede moved his lips, intent on the words. 'Which passage are you reading?'

Bjornson glanced up, his face full of the verse. 'What?'

'Which passage do you read?'

'Exodus.'

'And which verse?'

'You wish me to read it?'

'Aye.'

Bjornson cleared his throat. "They looked toward the wilderness, and behold, the glory of the Lord appeared in the cloud."

'Do you suppose that He is here—in this wilderness?'

Bjornson looked up, distracted. 'Who?'

'God.'

'He is everywhere.'

He watched his companion squint to see the text, his face intent in the gloom.

'And is He up there, too?' Boundless gestured at the blaze of stars.

'You make mockery.'

'Not at all. It is a question I have often asked myself.'

'Why—since you do not believe?'

"Then not God, but man. Are there beings like us—up there?' Boundless lay on his back to stare up at the bright, twinkling stars.

'No.'

'No?' The abrupt rebuttal irritated him. 'How can you be so certain?'

'I do not waste my time in thinking about it.' Bjornson immersed himself once again in the text.

Boundless made himself comfortable, drawing the robe tighter around him. *He avoids me. Is he anxious about his Indians—lest they truly be no more than a drunken fancy of that braggart, Till?*

He woke around midnight, his senses pricked. The dogs were on their feet, growling and snarling at the darkness. Sitting up, he reached for the musket.

'Bjorn!' he hissed and shook his sleeping companion.

'What is it?' Bjorn startled awake.

'Something is out there.' He strained to see into the dark woods. As Bjorn armed himself, Boundless got to his feet, staring at where the dogs growled. He glimpsed a form—darker than the surrounding shadows—move to conceal itself behind a tree. He levelled the musket as other forms suddenly materialised from the darkness. 'Make ready!' he called to Bjornson.

A blood curdling shriek shattered the silence and an arrow whizzed out of the darkness. He saw something move in the trees and fired. He grabbed for the second musket. The dogs were now snarling and snapping in a frenzy, straining at the picket that held them. Bjornson fired as the intruders suddenly melted back into the night.

There was no sleep for the rest of the night, both men mounting guard until daybreak. As streaks of light lit up the sky, they made ready to break camp, silently agreeing to skip breakfast. With Bjornson ready to mush the dogs, Boundless signalled a halt and went to investigate a dark form lying in the snow beneath the birches.

'Bjorn!'

Bjorn hurried over, catching his breath as he caught sight of the crumpled figure.

'By all the saints!' The Swede crossed himself. The figure was that of a man, wrapped in wolf skins. The face was entirely blackened with dye, the eyes wide open.

'He minds me of the ones Pinch and I saw six or seven winters back. Only this one has iron weapons.' Boundless indicated the tomahawk lying next to the man's outstretched hand.

'Half-man, half-wolf,' breathed Bjornson. He took Boundless' arm. 'Come. Let us quit this spot lest the demons return.'

They put the place behind them, travelling until noon before halting to rest and eat. Bjornson, clearly shaken by the incident, was suddenly voluble, breaking his silence to expatiate on 'wild men', 'half-human beasts', and 'wood demons', until Boundless interjected, holding up a hand.

'Enough! They were men, the same as you and me.' The thought occurred to him that perhaps they were members of the same lost tribe that Till had bragged on, but he held his tongue, concerned not to cause his rattled companion any further anxiety.

Shortly after resuming, they came upon a frozen lake and spotted smoke in the distance. 'It is them!' Bjornson cried out with excitement, the words pouring out like steam in the cold air.

'Hang tight. They may be the same ones who attacked us last night.' Boundless took out the spyglass. A dozen lodges were clustered along the lake shore. He studied the village, looking for any indication that the inhabitants might be hostile.

'Is your musket primed?'

At Bjornson's nod, they set off across the ice. As they neared the lodges, several figures emerged to observe them. Raising arms in the air, they hailed the watching figures. To their relief the hails were met with waves, beckoning them on.

'It cannot be them. The village is miserable—just a few sticks,' said Bjornson as they drew closer.

One of the Indians ventured forwards to meet them as they approached, calling out '*Monsieur Bourgeois!*'

The man was friendly, and obviously pleased at the unexpected encounter with Boundless so far from the stockade. He escorted them to the village, speaking in a mixture of French, Hidatsa and Mandan. Proud to act as host to the *bourgeois,* he took them to a lodge, offering food and drink as his companions crowded inside, their faces curious. 'Ask him,' urged Bjornson as they finished eating.

Doing his best to make himself clear, Boundless asked a series of questions, straining to understand the replies.

After consulting with a companion, their host replied in the same smattering of tongues and sign.

'Well?' Bjornson's voice betrayed his impatience.

'As far as I can tell, it seems the tribe we're after have moved to their winter camp, closer to the Missouri. The fellow indicated they are about three days' journey to the northwest. They are neither Mandan nor Hidatsa, it seems, but some other tribe. Cree, maybe. The Indian was uncertain as they speak an unknown tongue and keep to themselves.'

'An unknown tongue!' Bjornson's face lit up.

'He said something else, too.'

'What?'

'They may be dangerous.'

After spending the night at the Hidatsa village, they started out again the next morning, Bjornson driving the dogs with a look on his face that caused Boundless fresh concern. *His doubts are disappeared. He believes with all his heart.*

Following the Indian's directions, they travelled along a trail through the birch forest, Bjornson whipping the dogs in spite of Boundless' words of caution. 'For God's sake, Bjorn, you are tiring the dogs.'

They travelled a considerable distance before Bjornson relented to Boundless' urging and agreed to make camp as the sun declined in the sky. Over supper, the Swede was voluble and excited, even praising Till as 'an unknowing prophet, guided by Jehovah.' 'God has decided that now is the time to reveal the existence of his lost sheep to the world,' he declared, almost giddy with anticipation at the closeness of the long-rumoured tribe.

Boundless did his best to rein in his companion's excitement, increasingly worried at how Bjornson would react to the dashing of his hopes. 'We do not know that they are the same tribe that Till spoke of,' he warned.

'Did you not hear the Indian! He said a tribe that spoke an unknown tongue and that kept to themselves. Who else could it be?' Bjornson's face was feverish with certainty in the firelight.

After adding wood to the fire, Boundless lay down to sleep, his mind full of foreboding.

The next day was much the same as the previous, Bjornson urging the team forwards as Boundless insisted on breaks to rest the dogs. 'Patience, Bjorn. They will still be there on the morrow.'

The forest thinned out, the trees giving way to snowfields, frozen creeks, and snow-covered bluffs. Towards noon, they came across horse tracks and snowshoe traces.

'*Mush!*' Bjornson whipped the dogs, his excitement growing as the tracks became more numerous. Boundless hurried to keep pace, half-caught up in his companion's fervour. *If by some miracle they are of the faith, then surely they are Jesuit Indians.*

A half-mile onward, Bjornson uttered a cry and pointed to where smoke rose in the air. They soon sighted a goodly number of lodges nestled in the shelter of a line of bluffs. A horse herd was picketed along the frozen lake.

'Wait, man, for pity's sake!' Boundless seized Bjornson's arm and dragged him to a halt. He saw a flurry of activity among the inhabitants. 'They have seen us.'

They watched as five or six Indians sprang onto horseback and headed out to intercept them. He gripped the pistol thrust into his belt. 'Be on guard,' he said, remembering the warning given at the Hidatsa camp.

Bjornson took no heed of the caution, his companion gazing at the approaching Indians with a rapturous look on his face.

'Bjorn!'

The Indians rode up in a flurry of snow, their wild cries piercing the air. Forming a half-circle, they sat the snorting horses, their looks hostile and arrows notched to their bows. Their faces and naked upper bodies were caked with white clay, creating a sinister, ghostly effect.

'*Dosha!*' Boundless gestured to himself and Bjornson. '*Dosha!*'

The Indians gave no sign of having understood, and neither did they lower their weapons.

'*Níorootre!*' he said, switching to Mandan.

'The crucifix!' Bjornson stabbed a finger in the direction of a large silver crucifix hanging around the neck of one Indian. 'Praise be, we have found them!'

Before Boundless could prevent him, his excited companion had advanced upon the surprised Indians, his face exultant. 'Greetings! We are brother Christians, like yourselves! *Gloria in excelsis Deo!*'

The Indians recoiled in alarm.

'*Hie!*' The Indian wearing the crucifix raised an arrow, the tip pointed directly at Bjornson's chest.

'*Ne tirez pas!*' Boundless stepped forward, his hands raised in the air. '*Les amis!*' He pointed to the sled. '*Nous sommes commerçants!*'

'Ny-yah!'

At the barked command, the arrow was slowly lowered. The Indian who had spoken nudged his horse forward. Leaning down, he used his lance to turn back a corner of the hide cover.

'*Le sucre!*' Holding up a palm so as not to incite an arrow, Boundless stooped to pick up a sack of sugar. He handed it to the Indian. '*Pour vous!*'

The Indian opened it, scooping out a handful of sugar, which he poured into his mouth. The gesture brought laughter from his companions. Pleased—whether with the sugar or the reaction—the Indian passed the sack to the rider next to him. He turned back to eye Boundless, his lean face threatening and suspicious under the clay mask. After a long stare, he grunted and turned his horse, motioning for them to follow.

They set off, escorted by the Indians, who joked among themselves while taunting the one with the crucifix, much to his displeasure.

'You damn fool! You almost got us killed!' He rounded on Bjornson, his blood up.

'Did you not see the crucifix?' The Swede laughed, giddy to the point of ecstasy.

'Aye. And it was nearly the very last thing I saw!' He breathed hard, his heart still racing. 'Likely he traded for it or took it off some poor Frenchman he has slaughtered.'

'No! It is as Till promised!' Bjornson gripped his arm as if to infuse him with his own, jubilant faith.

As they approached the encampment, others advanced to meet them. Like their companions, they were half-naked in spite of the cold, their faces and bodies caked with the same white clay.

'I see no signs of a cross.' Bjornson's voice was subdued as he surveyed the snow-covered lodges. 'Till claimed it stood out in the open.'

More Indians surrounded them as they were shepherded to a clearing where several large fires burned. Near the largest fire, a crowd of Indians were clustered around a dog sledge. They turned to stare at the commotion caused by the arrival.

'*Qu'avons-nous là?*' To their surprise, a white man dressed in a red capote thrust his way through the curious onlookers. He stopped short on seeing Boundless, his face showing astonishment. '*Qui es-tu? Qu'est-ce que tu fais ici?*'

Behind the man, Boundless glimpsed a sledge piled high with pelts.

A blanket, spread on the snow, contained pots and kettles, several small casks, assorted bottles, muskets, and bags of powder.

The Frenchman studied him, his eyes sharp. '*Je ne m'attendais pas à voir un autre homme blanc dans ces parties.*'

'*Pas plus que nous-mêmes. Nous sommes des commerçants, comme vous. Mon nom est Boundless McLennan. Et voici mon compagnon*, Bjorn Bjornson.'

'*Ah, les Anglais!*' The Frenchman switched easily to fluent English. 'Claude Levesque,' he said, thrusting out his hand. 'And these are my companions.' He turned and gestured to three other white men standing among the Indians. They nodded, their eyes watchful.

'You are traders? Here?'

Levesque laughed. 'Why not? We are from further north, from Fort Rouge.'

The Frenchman stood no more than five-and-a-half feet tall, his lively features framed by a short brown beard. He wore a red toque to match his capote. His manner was animated, and full of *joie de vivre*, as he gestured to the sledge and its cargo of pelts. 'We have taken the best, friend, but there are plenty left, do not doubt. These Indians—'

'Are they Christian?' interrupted Bjornson, who had been staring at the Indians.

'Christian?' Levesque stared at Bjornson. 'Why, in the name of God would—'

'One has a crucifix around his neck!'

Levesque grimaced. 'I saw that. No doubt he scalped the owner and kept it as a bauble or trinket to impress his squaw. I doubt that—'

'You did not see a large cross—or observe them in prayer?'

'Prayer?' Levesque stared, dumbfounded, as if doubting Bjornson's sanity.

'We heard rumours,' interjected Boundless, 'of a missionary tribe up this way.'

Levesque took off the wool toque and scratched his head.

'These Indians are no more Christian than yonder dogs.'

'No matter. It was merely a rumour.' Boundless gave a concerned glance at Bjornson, who appeared deflated, his fervour evaporated into the cold air.

'Claude! We should go.' A youth pushed through the Indians to accost Levesque. 'Now!' he urged in English.

'In time!' Levesque threw off the youth's hand. 'There are still pickings to be had.'

'We must leave quickly before—'

'Hush now!' The Frenchman gave the youth a stern look. 'We go when we are ready.' Turning to Boundless, he shrugged. 'These damn chickens! *Bonjour, mon ami!*' Levesque broke off to address an Indian, not much taller than himself, who approached, wrapped in a buffalo robe that trailed in the snow. Two other Indians followed at his side.

'Habisich! Chief of these rascals!' Levesque gestured at Boundless. '*Un commerçant venir vous harceler avec des pots et des casseroles!*'

The Indian's face was impassive beneath the clay mask. His heavily greased black hair contrasted with the white clay on his face. His stare was unflinching as Levesque introduced him to Boundless in a mixture of French and pidgin Indian.

'He is a hard fellow! But you won't find finer beaver pelts … *Mère de Dieu!* ' Levesque turned in exasperation as the youth tugged urgently at his sleeve. 'Will you let be! In time!'

'Are there no other Indians nearby?' asked Bjornson, a distressed look on his face.

Levesque grimaced. 'None, friend. I assure you.'

'Hold yourself together, Bjorn,' said Boundless, increasingly concerned at his companion's agitated manner. 'Let us deal with what we have before us. Agreed?'

With one eye on Bjornson, he made great play of gifting the chieftain small sacks of flour, sugar and tobacco.

The Indian's face showed disappointment under the clay mask and he muttered the word 'firewater'.

Levesque chuckled at Boundless' surprise. 'He is the very devil for whisky and prizes it above all else!'

Boundless looked closely at the bottles lying on the trader's blanket. 'You trade whisky?'

'And muskets. They are greedy for both. Jean!' He shouted to one of his party. '*Montre au chef un mousquet!*'

As the Indians turned their attention back to the trades, the Frenchman glanced at Bjornson. The Swede stood as if in a trance, his face ghostly pale. 'Your companion, *mon ami*, he is sick?'

'Just disappointed, that is all. He had expected to find missionary Indians. What tribe are these? I do not recognise the tongue.'

'These are the A'ananin or White Clay People. This is their winter camp. Come summer they move back out to the grasslands.'

Boundless glanced again at Bjornson. But the Swede showed no sign of interest in the conversation, his manner distant as though detached from those about him. 'And you are certain that they are not Christian?'

'That word again!' Levesque looked exasperated at the question. 'These rascals be as far from Christian as it is possible to be. Ask the band of Nakoda whom they slaughtered last spring for the fun of it.' He turned to chide his companions. '*Dépêche-toi! Avant que les diables rentre dans le whisky!*'.

Boundless frowned at Levesque. 'Are we safe?'

The Frenchman nodded. '*Oui.* They are fierce, and not to be trifled with, but hospitality is sacred to them. As long as you are in their charge you need have no fear.'

'Is it not dangerous—to provide them with both guns and whisky?'

Levesque appeared not to have heard, his attention on the trades. '*Dépêchez-vous, les gars. Allons-y!*'

The Frenchman seemed suddenly eager to depart. As the chief examined the musket, sighting along the barrel, the Frenchman's companions tied down the pelts. The English-speaking youth began to collect the remaining goods. 'Leave the rest!' Levesque shouted.

'Will you not stay for a visit?' he asked, perplexed at the Frenchman's sudden haste. 'How far must you travel?'

'A distance, friend! A distance!' Levesque bent down to check the knots on the cargo of pelts. He ran his fingers through the topmost fur. 'Fine as a Spanish whore! A fair day's trading, boys. What do you say, Joseph—your first trade?'

'We must go!' The named youth stared nervously at the Indians as they admired each other's trades.

'Never fear, your topknot is safe this day.' Levesque made as if to scalp the youth while winking to his two older companions. Laughing, they joshed the discomforted youth, good-naturedly pushing him back and forth. Levesque looked around as if to check that all was well before farewelling Boundless. 'We must start if we are to finish!'

He was about to mush the dogs when the chieftain called out to him. With a glance at his companions, Levesque followed the Indian to one side where they carried on a conversation.

A woman approached and summoned Boundless and Bjornson to follow. They followed her to a small lodge. Pulling back the deerskin flap, she motioned for them to enter. A small fire burned inside.

Boundless paused and turned to Bjornson. 'They intend for us to stay the night. But maybe we should go. The Frenchman seems in a great hurry to leave.'

'Go or stay, what matter?' With a strained face, Bjornson pushed past him into the lodge.

Boundless followed, searching for words to cheer up his companion. 'At least you found them—Till's mysterious tribe. You have that satisfaction at least—as well as knowing the fellow for a shameless liar.'

The words made no impression, Bjornson remaining sunk in a profound malaise.

Boundless heard shouts and a musket shot. Pushing back the flap, he saw the trading party about to depart.

'*Adieu, mon ami!*' Levesque's cheerful voice rang out as the Frenchman waved before cracking the whip over the dogs.

It was on the tip of his tongue to call the Frenchman back. With a worried glance at Bjornson, he sat down cross-legged by the fire, concerned at his companion's haunted expression as he stared into the flames. *Does he consider himself now indentured to me?*

## 51

## *A Narrow Escape*

T HE SAME WOMAN BROUGHT them food, handing it to them without a word and then leaving. They had just finished eating when they heard shots from outside followed by cries of alarm.

Stepping out from the lodge, Boundless saw a group of Indians gathered around a man who lay moaning in the snow. Blood issued from a wound in his chest. Barely had he taken in the sight, when there came another musket shot followed by more cries.

'What is it?' Bjornson, joined him, the Swede seemingly jolted out of his lethargic state by the commotion.

An Indian tottered towards them, a shocked look on his face. The sleeve of his tunic was bloodied, the blood dripping into the snow.

Habisich came from his lodge to investigate the disturbance, quickly gathering a crowd of observers. A warrior with blood despoiling the white clay on his face, rushed up to the chieftain, a musket in his hands. Angrily, he thrust the weapon forward. The chieftain inspected the musket as Boundless and Bjornson joined the onlookers.

'The muskets are defective,' opined Boundless as he watched the warrior gesticulate and complain. 'The muzzle charge probably ignited on the poor devil.'

Hearing them speak, Habisich turned and pressed the musket into Boundless' hands. *'Regardez!'* His voice was cold.

As the Indians watched, Boundless inspected the weapon. Keenly aware of the hostile stares, he made an elaborate show of examining the barrel and firing mechanism. He pulled back the hammer only for it to stick at half-cock.

''Tis badly kept,' he said to Bjornson, who hovered at his shoulder. 'The bore hole is fouled. It is what caused the misfire.' He muttered as he examined the flint. 'Dull as a ditch!'

He repeated the demonstration for the benefit of Habisich, rubbing his finger over the edge to show the lack of sharpness. *'Mal!'* He used his pick to unplug the clogged grease and powder from the borehole. He showed the grease plug in the palm of his hand, the sight drawing cries of outrage. *'Est-ce que tu vois?'* Shaking his head, he handed back the musket. *'Pas bien!'*

Other A'ananin stepped forward, examining their muskets in the same manner as Boundless and with the same results. Cries of outrage arose at each new demonstration.

'The weapons are doubtless all of the same poor quality,' he remarked to Bjornson. 'Now we know why Levesque was in such haste to leave.'

'Let us hope they did not dawdle, and are far from here,' said Bjornson, increasingly alive to the danger presented by the aggrieved looks cast in their direction.

Habisich began to speak amidst shouts of anger from the assembled warriors.

'We should go!' Bjornson urged in his ear.

'We cannot. We would only bring suspicion upon ourselves.'

After several minutes of heated debate, the chieftain spoke again, his voice harsh. The words brought an ululating cry that was quickly taken up by the gathered crowd. Several warriors rushed back to the lodges for weapons while others raced to where the horses were picketed. Within minutes, an armed force had assembled on horseback. Habisich took out a tomahawk and pointed it in the direction the trading party had taken. With loud whoops, the war party set off in pursuit.

'What will happen to them?'

'They will be forced to hand back the pelts and make reparations for the injured men—that is if they do not attempt to resist or put up a fight.'

They returned to the lodge, sitting in apprehensive silence for the better part of four hours. Dusk was falling, and Boundless was about to remark on the possibility that the Frenchmen had escaped or evaded their pursuers when loud shrieks and yells erupted from outside.

Bjornson crossed himself. 'Wait!' he remonstrated as Boundless made to exit. 'They may turn on us as well.'

'Remember what Levesque said—about the hospitality? They will not harm us.' He pushed back the flap. An uneasy Bjornson followed.

Outside, all was in uproar. The entire tribe had turned out to greet the returning war party, raising knives and sticks and shrieking in approval as the warriors rode triumphantly into the village. One held a fresh scalp aloft on the point of a lance, the bloody pelt drawing whoops of joy. Three figures staggered through the snow behind the horses. He recognised the red capote of Levesque, as well as the face of the anxious youth—the latter petrified with fear as he slipped and stumbled on the rope leash.

A scream went up from one of the squaws as a warrior, lying prone across his horse, was lifted down by his companions and laid in the snow.

The woman rushed to the motionless figure with wails of grief. Grasping a knife from her waist, she chopped at her fingers, severing two as blood spurted from the stumps. Wailing and weeping, she was supported by several relatives as she tried to amputate more of her fingers.

In response, the enraged A'ananin rushed forward to rain kicks and blows on the helpless captives. The three were dragged up and down before the vengeful mob who beat them mercilessly with sticks and clubs.

Habisich stepped forward, his hand raised in command. The murderous cries fell away as he orated in a severe, threatening voice. As he spoke, a dazed and bloody Levesque surveyed the angry crowd, his hands bound tightly before him. His gaze alighted on Boundless where he stood helplessly amidst the crowd. To his amazement, the Frenchman gave a ghastly grin, a wry shrug seeming to say, *The game is up!*

The panicked youth displayed no such fortitude. Spying Boundless, he held up his bound hands in wailing supplication. 'For pity's sake, help us!'

*I cannot!* he mouthed while shaking his head. He saw Levesque say something to the blubbering boy, perhaps attempting to console him, but to no avail. The third man remained silent, his head sunk in despair.

Habisich uttered a command and one of the Indians stepped forwards. Standing over the kneeling Levesque, he brandished a hatchet. The Frenchman bowed his head, stoically accepting his fate. Cries of bloodlust erupted from the frenzied watchers as the hatchet swept down, hacking the Frenchman's neck. Levesque made a gurgling sound before the hatchet descended a second and a third time, severing the head. The executioner snatched the grisly trophy by the hair and held it aloft to triumphant shrieks. Above the cries and whoops, Boundless heard Bjornson gasp with horror.

A pair of Indians dragged the third captive to where a long stake had been driven into the ground. The unresisting man was bound with rawhide thongs, his arms pinned tightly to his sides. His face was battered and bruised, the skin bloody with knife cuts.

The tribe broke into cries of merriment as a squaw stepped forward to lift the bowed head of the Frenchman. Wielding a knife, she severed an ear from the captive, the action drawing a dreadful shriek from the bound man. Grabbing a fistful of hair, she turned his head for several seconds to display the bloody wound, drawing exclamations of delight. Other females flocked around the Frenchman to inflict further cuts, drawing agonised cries in response. The sport continued for some time, the bound man lapsing into babbling delirium as the clothes were stripped from him and his nose and privies progressively hacked from his naked body, each grisly trophy held aloft to joyous shouts and trills of acclaim.

Several warriors now came forward bearing sticks and branches, which they heaped at the foot of the captive. They poured pitch on the wood and set it alight. As smoke drifted up into the air, an old man seized the moaning captive by the hair, jerking back the head. He sliced away the scalp with a tomahawk, leaving behind a bloody mass of flesh and pulp. Gleeful at his prize, he held the dripping scalp high in the air, the sight greeted with frenzied approval. As the flames grew higher and licked at his calves and thighs, the bound captive gave out terrible shrieks—the agonised cries eliciting jeers and mocking laughter from his tormentors. Sickened by the torture, Boundless looked away, the screams of the burning captive ringing in his ears.

An Indian stepped behind the ashen-faced youth, who was convulsed with terror as he waited his turn. As the tribe yelled for vengeance, he cried out for mercy, sobbing and pleading as he held up his bound hands.

A voice rang out and Habisch stepped forward. As the cries subsided, the chieftain pointed to a lodge where the grieving squaw and the dead warrior had been taken. He spoke with a commanding voice, stilling the exultant Indians to silence. The stricken youth stared around in a daze, as if he might be dreaming after all.

'What will happen to him?'

'He is young. They may spare his life to keep him as a slave.'

'We must do something!'

'Wait until they settle. Perhaps we can bargain for him.'

A huge fire had been lit and the A'ananin began to chant and shuffle back and forth. Boundless saw bottles of whisky appear as the jubilant Indians passed them around.

'Come.' He nudged Bjornson, who seemed rooted to the spot, his face pale with horror at what they had witnessed. 'Let us return to the lodge. We are safer out of sight.'

For hours, they sat in fraught apprehension as the Indians danced and celebrated with whisky. They heard shouts and arguments and occasional cries as the triumph continued far into the night. Boundless kept the musket primed, concerned lest the general bloodlust overwhelm the A'ananin duty of hospitality. In spite of Bjornson's protests, he briefly exited the lodge after midnight to ascertain if they were in danger.

The air was freezing cold. A dwindling crowd of Indians were still assembled around the campfire, which roared with flames. In the firelight, men shuffled and stumbled, clearly affected by the potent whisky. Others, both men and women, lay insensible in the snow. He heard cries and saw a man atop a barely struggling woman as another man watched. He passed a shirtless Indian snoring against one of the lodges, an emptied whisky bottle by his side. Another Indian lay face down, arms outstretched—whether alive or dead, he could not tell. A man and woman coupled clumsily in the snow, oblivious to his presence. The woman stared up at him as he passed, a vacant look on her face. He continued, coming upon a bloodied body. Scrawny dogs licked at the dead flesh. Another man sat slumped in a pool of vomit, drool escaping his mouth as he sucked mindlessly at an empty bottle.

He returned to the lodge, greatly disturbed by what he had seen and more than ever concerned for their safety.

'What did you see?' Bjornson looked up in fright as he stepped back into the lodge.

'It is bad. The whisky …' Boundless shook his head. 'Try and get some sleep. We must leave at first light.'

In spite of the occasional shouts coming from the darkness outside the lodge, they fell asleep, exhaustion combining with apprehension to induce a brief and troubled slumber.

Towards dawn, Boundless awoke. He listened carefully, but other than the occasional bark, could hear nothing from outside. 'Bjorn, wake up!'

'What is it?' Bjornson sat up, his eyes wide with alarm.

'We must leave now. While they are still asleep.'

'But will they not pursue us—as they did the Frenchmen?'

'Why should they? We have not wronged them. We may be in worse danger if we stay.'

Outside, the air was fresh and sharp. Breaking daylight illuminated the camp. Boundless shivered in the cold. The village was silent, the A'ananin seemingly spent from their frenzied debauchery. Several bodies lay recumbent in the snow. He bent over the figure of a woman. She was half-naked and frozen to death, ice crystals clinging to her face. He quickly checked two of the other figures, finding them similarly frozen.

Shocked at the sight, Bjornson urged him to hurry. 'They will awaken soon and perhaps blame us.'

The dogs were already on their feet, whining with eagerness to start out. They were preparing to depart when Bjornson tugged at Boundless' capote. 'Over there!'

The charred and blackened corpse of the tortured Frenchman lay atop a pile of burned sticks. A few yards from the corpse a figure was slumped in the snow. It took Boundless a moment to recognise the captive youth, the unfortunate wretch bound firmly to a stake.

'He looks dead.' Bjornson's voice was hushed.

'Leave him be. We can do nothing for him.'

'He may be alive,' said Bjornson.

'Wait! Bjorn!' he hissed as his companion went to check on the youth 'Leave him, for God's sake!'

Bjornson knelt in the snow before the captive youth and shook him by the shoulder. Boundless reluctantly joined him, glancing around to check that they were unobserved.

The boy gasped as he awoke. A wild look came to his eyes as the fear and horror of the previous night flooded back to his senses. His mouth opened in an abortive cry as he saw Bjornson.

'Hush!' Bjornson laid a hand across the boy's mouth. 'We are friends. Do you not remember us?'

The youth seemed to then recognise the Swede. 'Friend, you have come to save me!' His voice was hoarse, his eyes wide with fear.

'Hush!'

Boundless bent to speak to the terrified youth. 'We can do nothing. But they will not kill you. They will give you to the woman whose man was killed.'

'Friend, I beseech you, as a fellow Christian! Cut me free!' The youth stared wild-eyed at Boundless as he squirmed desperately against the ropes. 'I beg you, save me!'

'I cannot, laddie. We put our own lives at risk.'

'Then trade for me! They will accept whisky, guns or powder.'

'We cannot. We have nothing left to trade. We came with gifts only.'

'Then I am lost!' The youth began to sob, his face wretched in its anguish.

'They will not trade for you. But neither will they kill or torture you—or they would have done so already. Do you understand?' He looked into the youth's eyes, seeing only shock and incomprehension at his fate. 'We will return in spring to see if we may offer a ransom in exchange for your freedom. Do you hear me?' He spoke soothingly, trying to calm the frantic boy.

'For pity's sake, help me—as a Christian! I beg you!' cried the youth as if he hadn't heard.

'What is your name?' asked Bjornson.

'Joseph Willox. My father will reward you for your trouble. Please, friends, I pray you.' He looked beseechingly from one to the other. Bjornson glanced at Boundless, who shook his head.

'I am sorry. We cannot.' Bjornson's voice was heavy.

'Then you would abandon me to these savages!' The youth shuddered with horror.

Boundless laid a hand on the boy's shoulder. 'We cannot help you now. But we will return for you in the spring. I give you my word. Do you understand?'

'Do not abandon me, for pity's sake!' The youth burst into fresh tears.

They turned away as the youth called after them in wailing supplication.

'Hurry!' Boundless pulled Bjornson toward the sledge. 'The fool will wake the entire village!'

They drove the dogs out of the encampment, stumbling alongside the team to quicken the pace. The risen sun illuminated the frozen wastes as they hurried to put the sobbing youth and the sleeping village behind them.

## 52

## *Adieu!*

SPRING CREPT IN SLOWLY, the frozen ground yielding to the miracle of fresh grass as ducks quacked overhead and chunks of ice floated down the Missouri. The men made ready to depart, an air of regret hanging over the post as the fur bales were compacted and roped. Taking Bertrand and Danon aside, Boundless questioned them as to their future, complimenting their diligence and assuring them that they would find other employers willing to take them on.

'At least you have a good supply of ladders,' said Danton, referring to the six brought back by the brigade.

'I do, and thanks to you.'

The days seemed to fly by. A near-record number of bales stood stacked in the yard. ''Tis a great pity we are abandoning the post,' said Lapointe as he showed Boundless the figures. 'It is an abundant storehouse of furs. Monsieur Thibault would be full of regret.' He eyed Boundless. 'Do you not think so?'

'He was always the most practical of men. He would recognise the inevitability.'

'But still ...' Lapointe tugged his jaw. 'This post—this business—was his legacy.'

'And still is. Where is Dubois?'

As the men waited for the *pilote's* signal to drag the canoes from storage, Boundless set a date for the departure and announced a farewell banquet.

The dinner was marked by numerous lachrymose toasts to former comrades. Pinch stood up and called for quiet as he made a solemn and heartfelt tribute to Quoi, describing the fellow's 'excellence of heart, gladness of spirit, and innocence of soul.' The description evoked tears from the veteran *engagés* and a heartfelt sigh from Pinch as he raised his cup in a toast.

Boundless made a farewell speech praising Thibault and acknowledging the lamentable loss of the redoubtable Theroux. He expressed sorrow at the demise of the 'splendid company' and thanked the men for their faithful efforts. He singled out Bjornson, Pinch, Lapointe, Luc, Emile, Antoine and Abel for special praise as dedicated *hivernants*. He concluded by recalling his own early days at the post. 'Everyone thought me a spy,' he said to laughter, 'and could scarcely believe I was simply lost!'

To his surprise, Dubois stood up at the conclusion of his remarks and made a brief speech thanking Boundless for his 'fair and honest management.'

'To the *bourgeois!*' he said, raising his cup.

'Huzzah!' a man shouted, the entire brigade joining in the cheer.

In spite of the decision by the married men not to inform their country wives, news slipped out that they would not be returning. This led to several quarrelsome confrontations as fathers knelt to give a final embrace to their children.

'I shall return!' insisted one man to his wife, who stood before him holding an infant in her arms. 'No matter what you have heard!'

He motioned angrily as his wife remonstrated in broken French and Indian.

'Have it your own way, then!' he shouted, and walked off.

The day following the feast, Lapointe approached Boundless to inform him that he had decided not to join the general exodus back to Montreal and Quebec.

'You won't?' he asked, taken aback.

The clerk smoothed the beard he had grown over the winter. 'I have decided to return to Scattered Corn Woman's village and live there, with her family. It suits me.'

'But do you not have a wife, and children, back in Montreal?'

Lapointe cleared his throat. 'I have given Dubois a letter for her. Now, if you will excuse me, I have much to do.'

'So, he abandons one wife for another?' Pinch took the pipe from his mouth when he heard the news.

'And you, yourself, have no second thoughts on staying?' he asked.

Pinch gazed fondly at where Buffalo Bird Woman stood gossiping and laughing with a group of women. He blew out a cloud of smoke, his face wreathed in satisfaction. 'Where would I go? Perhaps I could go live with her people. But I am settled here, as is she. Meadow Bird and White Deer are like daughters to her now. It would grieve her to leave them, and I am too old to go adventuring.'

'Will you not miss your supply of rum and whiskey?'

Pinch gave a rueful shrug. 'That will be hardest of all. But alas, it does not justify a brigade.' He was silent for a moment as he watched the men drag out the canoes for inspection. 'How is Bjorn taking it? Surely, he must regret his agreement with you?'

'He has some regrets, naturally. As do all men when something comes to an end.'

Pinch nodded, his face sombre. 'Regrets that he did not find his lost tribe or that his life is now forfeit to your mad scheme?'

Boundless scowled, stung by the remark. 'Had he found the Indians I would have stood by my word.'

'Found? Ha! Better chance of finding a white cat in a snowstorm.'

'It is done now, and I'll thank you not to bother him with hindsight.'

Pinch scratched his ear, his face thoughtful. 'In truth, I am glad he is staying.'

Returning to his quarters, Boundless took out his letter to Mathieu, reading it over before adding additional lines.

*I have assigned all post ledgers and records to you for safekeeping. Thank you for overseeing the liquidation of the company. In a separate document, you have my full authorisation—as well as Bjornson's—to act on our behalf. Both he and I have the utmost confidence that our returns are secure in your safekeeping. There is no need to send even a limited brigade next summer, as we are overstocked with necessities. Please convey my gratitude to M. Courtois for his assistance in so greatly advancing my little project. Tell him that the kegs of black powder will be used to full advantage, as will the masonry tools when the time arrives that I may use them. And finally, my profoundest appreciation to yourself, dear Mathieu, for your friendship, assistance and ever fruitful endeavours on my behalf. It is my deepest wish that we may one day shake hands again and swap tales and remembrances of our remarkable friend and patron.*

*I remain—even in absentia—your most affectionate friend and well-wisher.*

*Boundless McLennan.'*

Wrapping all the post ledgers, records and correspondence in oilskin, he placed them in a box and handed it to Dubois, who assured him of their safe delivery to Mathieu.

'I shall place the box in his hand myself,' Dubois promised. He thrust out his hand, his weathered face solemn. 'Goodbye, Monsieur McLennan. It has been an honour to serve as your *pilote.*'

Boundless was surprised to see a tear in the other man's eye. 'I am in debt to you for your faithful service and loyal support,' he said as they shook hands.

In the days before departure, he bade farewell to each of the men in turn, reserving special acknowledgement and appreciation for Helmut.

The latter listened, a faintly embarrassed smile on his face. 'Keep your tools sharp, *Monsieur*,' he said, his brow furrowed as though making a note to himself.

He summoned Bertrand and Danon to share a glass of wine, praising their workmanship and the excellence of the completed ladder. 'It is a great relief to know that I have six more reliable ones in store.'

He walked with Luc in the grass outside the stockade, the two men reminiscing over the Sioux attack on the post.

'I remember that painted savage crawling over the wall,' said Luc, glancing up at the stockade. 'I blew his brains out afore he could think to remove the knife from between his teeth.'

'It was a close-run thing.' Boundless frowned to himself at an image of Meadow Bird shrieking in triumph, the bloody knife upraised.

He spent an hour with Abel, going over various points of tool maintenance and confirming the operation of the forge and bellows. 'There is plenty of spare iron,' said the smith, indicating the bars ranged along the wall. 'Remember, keep the coals hot.'

HE STOOD ON THE shore as the brigade made ready to depart for the last time. The day was bright and mild, the sun glinting on crystallised snow clumped in patches along the shore. Meadow Bird , White Deer and Buffalo Bird Woman watched from the top of the bank. The four boys joined their fathers to bid farewell to their favourite *voyageurs*. After the bales were laid on poles along the floor of the canoes, the brigade lined up to wish himself, Pinch and Bjornson fond and heartfelt farewells. One of the younger members—bashful until now—shook Boundless' hand with enthusiasm. 'Thank you, sir, and goodbye!'

'Let's go, boys, before the ice comes!' Dubois shepherded the men into the canoes before stepping in after them. Abel, Luc and the two clerks sat uncomfortably among the paddlers. Dubois took one last look around before tipping the brim of his felt hat to Boundless. 'Stroke away, boys! The lakes within a month!' Pinch cupped his hands in a holler as the canoes drew away. 'Remember me to your wives and sweethearts. Give them a kiss from their darling Pinch!'

The quip was met with laughter. '*Au revoir, mes amis!*' he called out.

'*Au revoir mes amis!*' The boys chorused after him, waving as the canoes dipped and bounced in the water.

They watched the canoes as they battled against the stream, a final, faint '*Adieu!*' reaching their ears.

As the brigade reached the bend that would take it from sight, Boundless felt a melancholy pang, reminded of another river and another day.

"Twill be awful lonesome without them.' Pinch stared at the empty river, his face wan.

The sun was growing warm and mites swarmed around them as the three men walked back to the stockade. They sat down for a glass of wine, each preoccupied with his own thoughts. The hall seemed quieter than ever, the air filled with the unspoken knowledge that its silences now belonged to themselves alone.

## *Joseph*

ON THE DAY FOLLOWING the departure, Boundless took Bjornson aside, the Swede having largely avoided him since their return from the abortive expedition to find the lost tribe. 'It is time to get to work,' he said lightly, uncertain of the other man's mood. 'We will take it in stages. Tomorrow it will be sufficient for you merely to stand atop the rock and see what needs to be done.'

'Have you forgotten?' Bjornson's voice was testy.

'Forgotten what?'

'The boy, Joseph? We must return for him, as promised.'

'Patience. It is still too wet further north.'

'You gave your word!' Bjornson regarded him accusingly.

'As did you—to help me! We start to tomorrow,' he said, his voice sharp, and walked away.

The next day, he reached down to assist his companion up onto the rock. A trembling Bjornson stood tentatively erect, terrified of being blown from the summit and dashed to the ground below.

'I have been frightened of high places ever since I was a boy,' he said, his voice strained.

'Fasten this to your waist.' He handed the safety line to his companion who was wearing the leather harness Abel had designed..

Clinging tightly to the line—and with frequent checks to ensure it was securely attached, Bjornson allowed Boundless to shepherd him towards the head, a look of panic flashing across his face at the increased exposure to the gusting wind.

'Heavenly Father!' Bjornson repeated the words over and over, his face sick with fright.

Around and below them was a dizzying patchwork of sky, cloud and grasslands—all linked by the warm, blustery wind.

'Look!' Elated to be back on the summit, Boundless pointed to the distance where the sun glinted on the Missouri. 'The post!' He turned the terrified Bjornson in a half-circle, his voice jubilant above the hum of the wind. 'The Hidatsa settlement!' He pointed south-west. 'The Mandan village at the fork!'

He coaxed his fearful workmate into standing with him on the very edge of the dizzying precipice. 'See, it all lies before you!' He gestured to the herds of buffalo dotting the plain into the distance. 'Do you not feel like an eagle surveying the world?'

'I do not!' Aghast at the head-spinning height, Bjornson retreated backwards from the edge, a petrified look on his face.

'You find nothing in it to enjoy?'

'Nothing! I fear only lest this damnable wind blow me to perdition! Let us go down, for pity's sake!' Bjornson hastened back towards the ladder, playing out the safety rope as he did so. In his eagerness to quit the windy summit, he flopped on his belly and squirreled backwards, one leg dipping in the air as he sought the sanctuary of the steps.

'Take your time!' Kneeling, Boundless helped his companion over the side. 'Let go of the rope!'

The frightened Swede released his grip on the safety rope and clung to the ladder handholds with a deathlike grip, too terrified to begin the descent.

'Don't look down. Just let your feet find the next step.'

Safely back on the ground, Bjornson paced up and down as though to reassure himself of the earth beneath his feet. 'Blood of the Saviour!' His complexion was deathly pale, his limbs still trembling from the heights.

Boundless placed a hand on his shoulder. 'Now you, too, have felt the buffalo.'

'I felt nought but the heart jumping out of my chest!'

It took all his powers of persuasion to coax the reluctant Bjornson back up onto the rock the following day. Himself inured to the dizzying height, he watched with baffled impatience as the Swede secured himself to the safety rope, refusing to advance a step without the line fastened to his waist. The southerly breeze was calm and temperate. Even so, it was all Boundless could do to keep his companion's attention as he explained the painted lines and the area of rock to be removed.

'The number indicates the depth. We blow the rock to within an inch or so of the required mark and—Bjorn! Are you with me?'

'Pardon.' Bjornson mumbled an apology. 'My head reels from the thin air.'

'This section needs to be quarried to a depth—Bjorn!'

Bjornson listened with a faintly shocked expression as though only this minute coming to comprehend the full dimensions of the project. Turning, he swept out a hand to indicate the extent of rock to be removed and shaped, a horrified look on his face. 'It is impossible! It cannot be done—not by two men alone.' He slapped his head as though to knock the outlandish venture from his brain.

'You swore on oath to assist me,' Boundless reminded, his anxiety rising at this last-minute resistance.

'As did you—to rescue Joseph!'

'My oath was to find your Israelite Indians. Whatever I said to the boy had nothing to do with that. Come, drink.' He offered Bjornson the water bottle, his voice conciliatory. 'This is your first impression only. I myself was daunted at the start.'

Bjornson brushed aside the bottle. 'Pinch is right! What you propose is madness!'

'In a week you will think it no different than walking about on the grass,' he said, keeping his voice calm.

'You think to have an answer for everything!'

'A week is all I ask, before you form an opinion. Now, if you will not drink, let us make a start.' He picked up a chisel and handed it to his disgruntled companion. 'Let us see how you drill.'

Progress over the next few days was slow and laborious, Bjornson making no attempt to disguise his unhappiness as Boundless re-inducted him into methods of turning the drill and striking with the hammer. The Swede went about his assigned tasks with an air of sullen, aggrieved sufferance that made Boundless grit his teeth. *Is it the supposed blasphemy that alarms him or resentment to what he has pledged himself?*

The unsettled spring weather twice drenched them with rain as they scurried to reach the ladder, the incidents further unsettling Bjornson.

On a day of gusting winds, he flatly refused to climb the ladder, remaining stubbornly below as Boundless worked on the summit alone. When, the following day, he finally ventured back up to the summit, he clutched tightly to the safety rope, his body braced in anticipation of the next wind blast.

'I am a man, not a crow!' he snapped when Boundless tutted at his fearful reliance on the line.

The following day, the winds had died down and they proceeded to drill a series of blast holes. Bjornson flinched as he held the chisel while voicing apprehension at the flying stones that threatened 'to fish out his eye'.

'Then turn your head a degree. Do not look directly at it.'

'It is the Devil's stone! We shall break our bones ere this rock.'

'You will accustom to it by and by. It is but a matter of time.'

They stopped to eat, sharing portions of peppered hare as they sat on the exposed granite. Bjornson chewed slowly, staring moodily at the horizon, his digestions leavened by loud, heaving sighs.

Boundless eyed the recalcitrant Swede, concerned lest he take it into his head to get up and abandon the project. *He has given his word. Surely he will not break it, in spite of his misgivings?*

They studiously avoided eye contact while packing the blasting holes with powder and then standing back to blow the rock. After six or seven charges, they halted to sweep the rubble over the side, watching it tumble silently to the grass below.

THE WEATHER GREW WARMER and the days longer. They laboured until four or five o'clock each afternoon—each day a repetition of the one before as they drilled and blasted. Before leaving, they collected the loose rubble to bring back with them to the Missouri—in spite of Bjornson's arguments to leave it where it lay. 'What difference if it be here or at the river?' he protested as he helped Boundless load the broken pieces of granite onto the wagon.

'It is a measure of our progress. Besides, if we do not collect it, we risk stepping on it every time we walk.'

Bjornson grimaced at the explanation, muttering to himself in Swedish as he lifted a chunk into the wagon.

They remained at the post on Sundays, the Swede adamantly refusing to break the Sabbath. 'Even God rested,' he said, astonished that Boundless would even consider riding out to the rock 'merely for a peek'. Pinch, meanwhile, continued to take delight in poking fun at the venture. 'A hundred years from now, a passing savage will stop and scratch his greasy head to wonder at the misshapen lump that towers o'er him.'

'Aye. While you sit and scratch your greasy arse,' Boundless retorted, unable to think of a better riposte.

'With a chisel!' Pinch guffawed so loudly it brought the boys running in to stare.

Vexed at Bjornson's continued refusal to embrace—nay, consider, even—the scale and ambition of the great enterprise, Boundless turned back from the ladder one morning.

'Let us take a turn around the grass,' he said, surprising the Swede.

The day was cloudless, the grass beneath the rock still in partial shadow. He set off at an agreeable pace that resembled their evening rambles—deferred since their labours on the rock.

'It is a mere lump of stone at present,' he ventured, unconsciously using Pinch's word. He gestured up at the towering rock sides. 'But think ahead to when it is finished. Picture in your mind what a feat it will represent.' He stopped to face his companion. 'You once said that we would be here until Judgement Day. Do you remember?' At Bjornson's surly nod, he continued.

'Not us, Bjorn, but this rock will stand so long—to the end of the world! And if all goes well, it will carry our handprint through all of that time. Think on it. A thousand—two thousand, years from now—and time beyond that. It will make our names remembered by all who look upon it.'

'Fie!' Bjornson waved off the claim as he would a bothersome fly. 'I do not trouble my head with such fancies. The life of man is but threescore and ten. Long enough for me.' He started walking again.

'It will stand as a monument to faith,' Boundless argued, catching up, '—faith that such a thing was possible in this empty wilderness.'

Bjornson stopped, incredulous. 'Faith? Will they not think it equally a monument to vanity?' He eyed Boundless closely. 'But perhaps you see no difference between the two?'

AS SPRING RIPENED INTO summer, the fate of the captive boy remained a bone of contention between them, Bjornson daily reminding Boundless of his promise. 'You swore you would return for him in spring,' he accused.

'Be reasonable. They will have moved to their summer camp. Who knows where that may be?'

'You gave your solemn promise!'

'Aye. And I intend to keep it. Just be patient a while longer.'

'I cannot!' Bjornson grimaced in distress. 'I am haunted by thoughts of him.'

'If he has been adopted into the tribe, they will treat him well. Have we not seen that often enough with Mandan captives?'

'They are not Mandan. Do you forget what they did to the Frenchmen? And who is to say he has been adopted? More likely a slave. The notion torments me—as it should you.' He gazed at Boundless, waiting for a response.

'I will ask among the Indians. They may have heard something. Now let us get back to work.'

'But each day we delay—'

'Work, I pray you.' He picked up the hammer.

That evening, Pinch took out his pipe following supper. Drawing the tobacco to flame, he regarded Boundless. 'So, do you not intend to go back for him—the boy, Joseph?'

Boundless shot an irate glance at Bjornson, who sat quietly picking at a blister on his hand. 'The time is not right.'

'Indeed?' Pinch puffed out a cloud of smoke. 'Did you not swear an oath to return for him?'

'An oath is it now? How do you know what was promised? Were you there?'

'No, but I was,' interrupted Bjornson, moodily picking at the scab.

'He would have woken the whole village and got us scalped. Or did you neglect to mention that?'

'You have a Christian obligation.' Pinch eyed Boundless over the pipe.

'Who knows if he is still alive? Or that he has not been ransomed by his friends or family?'

'More likely that he is still a slave and waiting for the succour you promised him.'

'They are a nomadic people. They could be anywhere.'

'Like as not they are near where you left them.'

'The weather is too hot to travel. The flies and mosquitoes will be the very devil. Wait until it cools.'

'Cools? First it is too cold and then too warm! Which is it?' interjected Bjornson.

'Good God, man! Do you imagine the Indians will welcome us with open arms? Remember what happened to the Frenchmen!'

'Let us start tomorrow, with horses.' Bjornson's voice was stubborn. 'We will be back within the month.'

'And you know for certain where he is? Or would you have us wander the wilderness like your Israelites!'

Bjornson flushed. 'I kept my word—do you keep yours?'

In the silence that followed, Boundless felt Pinch's eyes on him, waiting for a response.

'The boy is dead—or ransomed. And if not, I am not responsible for him. He should not have cheated the Indians.'

'Do you then sacrifice him to your buffalo?' Pinch puffed out the accusation in a stream of tobacco smoke.

'The two of you may chase off on a wild goose hunt if you wish.' He scraped back the chair. 'But be prepared to lose your hair. Goodnight!'

Back in his quarters, he acceded to his sons' request to read to them before bed. He did so, barely able to keep the irritation from his voice. Later, sitting before the fire, he grumbled in protest as Meadow Bird insisted on measuring him for a pair of buckskin trousers.

'Still!' She scolded, much as she would talk to the boys.

When she went to bed, he sat there, brooding on his argument with Bjornson and Pinch. His eye fell on Guillaume's final letter sitting on the shelf alongside the one from Mathieu. He reached for the letters and sat down to re-read their contents. In the lantern's glow, he smoothed Guillaume's letter, trying to catch in the words, the sound of the once-familiar voice.

*Montreal, April 1777*

*My dear Boundless. A springtime hail to you and yours! I am gratified to convey news of an excellent return on last year's cargo. Prices on beaver hold steady on fears of a diminishment in supply—whether to the war between the Colonies and England, Indian hostility, or simple exhaustion of Nature's ample larder, I cannot tell. The price of parchment beaver remains high, at 18 shillings per skin, an increase of sixpence on last year's figures. It is reported that a new company has established headquarters at the head of Lake Superior—from whence they hope to control the fur trade in the north-west. For the moment, their attention is concentrated on the routes west provided by the Pigeon River. I fret daily, nay, hourly, lest they stumble upon our own water road to the Missouri. I resign myself that it is but a matter of time before our secret is discovered. Indeed, Mathieu claims he overhead a conversation between two merchants in a tavern in which such a route was remarked upon. [NB The word used was 'speculated upon'—as to the possibility of such. Mathieu.] I note, with comical alarm! your correspondence with Mathieu and the redoubtable M. Courtois and the resulting fleet of canoes! Are you secretly planning, I wonder, a stone palace for yourself and the splendid Meadow Bird? I know you to be a man of admirable abilities and quite capable, therefore, of fulfilling your duties as bourgeois as well as accommodating this interest in carving stone. All the same, I beg you to consider my earlier suggestion that you bring yourself and your wife and children back east—whether to Montreal or Philadelphia. You have already been occupant at the post longer than any man of my acquaintance. Of what use is a fortune if one is unable to enjoy it?*

*My own health continues variable, the ague one day, stiffness in the joints the next. What creatures we are! A mere breath and then no more. I had a dear friend of some forty years' standing who, just three days ago, when reaching out to take the salt, uttered a surprised word and fell dead at his own table! We attended the Collège Jésuite together and were married within one month of each other. Barely two weeks past I bumped into him on the street. He was on the opposite side and rushed across to greet me, narrowly avoiding a trampling under the wheels of a calèche. 'Careful!' I cried. And now, alas, from calèche to the salt pot! He was a man pre-eminent among those merchants who supply cloth and sewing necessities to Quebec and the Colonies. "Plead grandeur with him, or renown, Unblushing Death shall all strike down." But now, my bones do creak—Mathieu glances up at the sound! And my dear wife petitions me to rest.*

*Once again, I urge you to consider my advice to retire back east, notwithstanding this late fashion for things of stone. Dubois would make a trusted replacement, or perhaps M. Bjornson, if he wishes to stay on. Give my warmest regards to Bjorn and the venerable Pinch. I expect the rascal to return with each brigade and thenceforth to devote himself to a life of pipes and ale! Please convey my affectionate regards to White Deer. Does she ever speak of me, I wonder? And to you, my old friend—a mild winter, an abundance of pelts, and an early spring. Yours in fondest good wishes, Guillaume Thibault.*

*Tuesday afternoon. I pick up the pen a few days later—after I had thought to seal the letter. The cause is yet another onset of that malady which has troubled me these past few months. The enemy besieges from within, and I fear my defences must soon crumble and fall. If such indeed prove the case, I have no complaints, and few regrets—save only that we do not get to meet again and toast times gone by like true comrades. Perhaps it is a good time to leave—while the world shakes with war and one order gives way to another? The entire city is under curfew, and news comes daily of more arrests as the authorities seek out American sympathisers. Suspicion abounds, and 'mistrust is the mother of safety'. Just this morning, I heard of the arrest of a M. Cote who had the misfortune to be found in possession of a letter full of Patriot sentiments. By such high-handed actions, the authorities foolishly alienate the populace—many of whom supported the Loyalist cause prior to these arbitrary arrests. Not out of loyalty to England, I hasten to add, but through fear of American ambition should the Colonists prove successful.*

*But soon, perhaps, such mighty events will be as murmurs carried on the wind to one who no longer has ears to listen or eyes to observe. How all things do crumble to dust under the auspices of eternity! But truth be told, I shall miss seeing what mighty events may unfold and what marvels of science may yet be to come. But soft! My physician, the venerable M. Provencher, attends with long face and grave murmurings, to bid me rest. 'As prelude to what condition?' I protest, but my wit falls upon deaf ears.*

*If, indeed, life's road has come to an end, then I have arranged with Mathieu for you and Mr Bjornson to continue the partnership without me, if that be your wish—which I hope it is. If not, he has my instructions regarding disposal of the assets, and the safe keeping of your own and Mr Bjornson's promissory notes. No more remains to be said, except—lest this be my final letter—goodbye, dear friend. And goodbye also to Mr Bjornson and old Pinch. Does he still shirk wood-cutting duties, I wonder? I have sent a small keepsake for White Deer. Please assure her that my days with her were among the happiest of my life and that I thought of her often. 'Goodbye', as the English say, and 'Atque vale atque', in the style of the Romans. Remember me. Your faithful friend Guillaume Thibault.*

*PS I add this note the next (Wednesday) morning, as I awoke feeling refreshed after a sound night's sleep. Perhaps I shall wrestle this pleurisy to the ground, after all! It is a glorious spring day. Just five minutes ago, I bade farewell to a M. Jean Roubelard, whom I may have spoken of previously. He came by unexpectedly on the rumour that I was at death's door! Such is the power of expectation that he looked shocked when ushered into the parlour—where I received him with sombre, reclining courtesy, whispering in a faint voice as if in extremis. After a few minutes, I could hold the joke no longer and popped up and burst out laughing. Thankfully, M. Roubelard saw the humour and joined in—heartily relived, no doubt, that he sat in company with a man and not a ghost!*

*How my mind wanders this bright morning—fondly, I assure you! I think of my early days and the great expedition up the Missouri. What fortune—to meet Road Maker and to discover the water-road to the east. How our lives are shaped by such accidents. I think also of White Deer and of how she looked when I first met her. How young! Does she ever*

*[The letter finishes here. The same day, M. Thibault took to his bed and, shortly after, passed away. Mathieu]*

Boundless stared into the fire as he recalled his arrival at the post and the spontaneous offer of employment, which had changed his life. *How indeed, are our lives shaped by chance. But for a thunderstorm I should never have arrived at this spot.*

A log crackled, throwing up sparks. He took up Mathieu's letter.

Montreal, May 1777

*My dear Boundless. It is with deepest regret that I convey the sad news that our venerable friend, guide, and patron, Guillaume Thibault is no longer with us, having perished from the pleurisy. He passed away in the first week of May, leaving behind his distraught wife, his grieving daughters, and his many distressed friends. He will be grievously missed by all who knew him. To me, he was like a wise father, steady, compassionate, and ever ready to give counsel or advice. I write this in his study with tears in my eyes and surrounded by his possessions. I have enclosed his final, unfinished letter to you as a fond remembrance of the solicitousness and attentiveness to detail with which he discharged all his earthly duties. He remained in good spirits until the end—his vigour and wits seemingly unaffected. He spoke often and fondly of you, and of his days in the Indian wilderness. They were, I think, the happiest of his life. At times, he expressed regret at having left so early to return to Quebec. But duty and family called to him and, as ever, he answered.*

*He left extensive instructions for the disposal of the partnership which I convey to you now. By condition of the agreement, the partnership is annulled by his death—although leaving it open to yourself and Mr Bjornson to revive it as a joint stockholding. Shortly before his final illness, Monsieur Thibault expressed fond hopes that the company he founded might continue with yourself at the head. He had also hoped that I might join the partnership in his place. Alas, however, I am fully immersed in my own legal and financial affairs, which demand all of my energies. Certainly, there is no reason why the company cannot continue to operate as prosperously as before, with Mr Bjornson and yourself as managing partners. In any event, Monsieur Thibault wished that matters be resolved as expeditiously as possible for the sake of his family and also to remove any legal obstacles for yourself and M. Bjornson should you decide to continue the company.*

*If you do wish to continue, I can forward the necessary papers. I will witness them myself as legal representative for Monsieur Thibault's estate. I can also recommend several experienced and reliable traders to act as your agent in Montreal. There is a glut of fur on the market, but despite the present uncertainty, still the world clamours for more. Situated as you are, conditions are greatly to your advantage. I have no doubt but that you could expect each annual harvest to be received with open arms—and purses! The venture could be revived under the same name or a different one, as you wish.*

*Due to the war, a new and nervous fear of bankruptcy haunts the merchant class and has even the most prosperous on edge. Some acquaintances of mine, who once invested eagerly in ships and cargos, now invest their wealth in agriculture, claiming it offers the better prospect for security. But you and M. Bjornson sit handsomely on a well-established enterprise that promises to provide wealth and security well into the future.*

*Meanwhile, I look forward to receipt of your letter and instructions. Until then, may God keep us all in the palm of his hand.*

*Yours in warmest friendship, Mathieu.*

He sat back in the chair, sipping the wine as he reflected on the contents. After a while, he leaned down and placed both letters on the glowing logs. He watched the edges blacken and curl before bursting into flame. Wind gusted against the door, and he cocked his head as rain began to lash the roof. *Goodbye, old friend.*

## 54

# This Madness Will Cost You Everything!

SEVERAL DAYS OF THUNDERY, unsettled weather had confined them to the post. After supper one evening, he returned early to his quarters. He sat before the fire nursing a cup of tea, his thoughts idly roaming from his latest *contretemps* with Pinch to the departed brigade and from thence to wondering on the progress of the war. *I am starved for news since the end of the brigade.* He stared into the flames, rueful at the thought great things were happening in the world, all unbeknownst to him. *It might be over already, the Americans crushed and England in command.* The thought jarred him.

The children had gone to bed, protesting that it was still light outside. Meadow Bird sat on a stool sewing squares of buckskin together. Sunk in rumination, he only gradually became aware of her glances. He looked up to meet her gaze, even as she turned her head away.

'What is it?'

She shook her head and bent over the buckskin, a faint smile upon her face.

After several more covert glances, he clucked in exasperation. Kneeling beside her, he stopped her hand as she made to add a thread. 'What?'

Her eyes studied him for a moment, as if seeking something in his face. She made a pretence of scolding as she took up the buckskin again.

'What is it, lassie? *Watéwena?*' Amused at her pouting reticence, he coaxed her into putting down the cloth.

Satisfied she had his full attention, she placed his hand on her belly and looked at him, her eyes bright.

'What?'

'*Hie!*' She gave a hum of displeasure and pressed his hand.

His eyes widened as he comprehended. 'By the bones! After all this time? Are you sure? A baby?'

She smiled. '*Ba-be,*' she repeated, and resumed sewing the cloth, a look of serene happiness on her face.

Stunned by the news, he shared it with his companions over breakfast. The morning was blessedly dry, adding to his celebratory mood.

Pinch was the first to react, his face crinkling with pleasure. 'The Lord be praised! 'Tis indeed gladsome news.' He pumped Boundless' hand. 'Most welcome news indeed!'

Bjornson's scratched his cheek, a bemused look on his face.

'That is why Hannah has been so cheery of late.'

'She knew?'

Pinch laughed. 'She is a woman!'

'And Buffalo Bird?'

'Mayhap—now that I come to think upon it.'

'Meadow Bird swears it is a girl.'

'What name will you give to her?'

He stopped, taken aback by the question. 'I have not considered. No doubt Meadow Bird will give her a name when she is ready.'

'But she must have a Christian name—in addition to the Indian one.' Bjornson raised an eyebrow with the question.

Boundless considered the matter. 'Fiona was my mother's name.'

'Fiona McLennan.' Pinch nodded in approval. 'It sounds properly Christian—what say you, Bjorn? Do you now consider an increase in your own tribe?'

'Is it not ten years since the boys were born?' asked Bjornson, his face chasing the figure as he ignored Pinch's question.

'Twelve. Meadow Bird can hardly contain herself.'

'Then it truly is a miracle.'

The three sat in contemplation for a moment.

'Are you set to go?' Draining the tea, he stood up.

'Hark! The buffalo calls!'

'Bjorn?'

The Swede gave a sigh of sufferance and got to his feet.

THE WET SPRING WAS followed by a hot, humid summer, which taxed their endurance as they laboured on the exposed summit. By late August, they had removed an estimated one ton of rock, the rubble forming a pile two feet high and ten feet long on the banks of the Missouri. 'Do we build a storm wall or a buffalo?' remarked Bjornson, an exasperated note in his voice, as they contemplated the growing pile.

In spite of the excavated granite, the rock remained much as before, the unyielding stone defying all their attempts to impose a definable shape or form on the granite mass. Boundless became concerned at how much remained to be done before they could even begin to show observable progress. *Bjorn is right. At this rate, we shall be up here until our dotage.* His thoughts were interrupted by an exclamation from Bjornson, who was drilling a few yards further up the rock.

He found his workmate nursing his eye and grimacing in distress.

'What is it?'

'The godforsaken stone. I am blinded!'

'Let me see.' He peered at the reddened eye. 'There is a fragment lodged there.'

They returned to the post where White Deer flushed out the stone, clucking and remonstrating with her husband as she did so.

'She is no admirer of your buffalo,' remarked Pinch as White Deer applied a poultice to the injured eye, now puffed and swollen.

'It is but a chip. By tomorrow, it will be healed.'

His vexation at the delay was compounded over supper when Meadow Bird scolded him for allowing the meat supplies to run down. 'Shoot buffalo, not make!' she said.

'Tomorrow,' he promised, preoccupied with searching for a way to make the work go faster.

It was three days before he remembered his promise, and then only when a small herd of buffalo turned up to forage the grass a mere hundred yards from the post. Taking the boys with him, he shot a cow with a young calf, firing another shot to chase off a curious bull. As the distressed calf licked the shot cow, he handed Prospect the special, short-barrelled musket he had ordered from the east. 'The heart!' he said, guiding the boy's arm. 'Brace yourself for the recoil. Claim. Stand back. Yours is the next shot.'

The women came out from the post to butcher the carcasses on the spot. He guided his sons into position to observe. 'Watch how they take off the robe. They keep it as whole as possible.' He looked on as the boys practised skinning the calf, taking it in turns to kneel on the splayed animal and push the knife down the spine. 'Mind yourselves, the blade is sharp. Watch your mother, how she does it. By the end of summer, you shall each skin a deer,' he promised. 'Stay and learn. I have work to do.'

'Can we come?'

'No. Stay here with your mother. Help her carry the meat into the post.'

Meadow Bird stopped butchering as she watched him ride off, grumbling as she complained to White Deer.

She was still in a mood when he returned, rebuking him over some trivial offence and pointedly ignoring his attempts to coax her back into a good humour.

'She is cross with me without cause,' he complained to Pinch as they sat on the hall porch to observe the sunset before retiring. 'Has Buffalo Bird mentioned anything?'

Pinch snorted. 'She cannot understand why you waste so much time on that fool rock when you could be hunting or doing something useful.'

He tutted in frustration. 'She is Indian. She measures usefulness by other means.'

'The means of the world?' Pinch raised an eyebrow.

'What do you mean?'

'By means?' Pinch chuckled. 'Nay,' he said, seeing the annoyance on Boundless' face. 'I but jest.' His face grew serious as he smoked the pipe. 'Do you intend your boys to follow you up onto the rock when they come of age?'

'I do. What of it?'

'And you wonder why she is cross?'

'What else would she have them do? Chase buffalo and make sport with girls all the day long, like the Mandan?'

Pinch grunted. 'And which would you, as a young man, prefer?'

THEY RETURNED TO THE post early—driven from the summit by the threatening growls of a summer storm. In the event, the storm did not materialise, and he took the opportunity to fix a loose board on the wagon. Returning from the forge, he noticed the stockade gate standing ajar. He went to close it but halted, his hand on the bar. A few hundred yards from the gate, Meadow Bird sat in the summer grass darning a pair of breeches. The boys knelt alongside, playing jackstraws. Dressed in buckskin, their faces browned by the sun, they seemed to him, in that instant, wholly Indian, as indigenous to the prairie surrounds as their mother. Immense white clouds threw shadows across the bluffs, the wind shaking ripples in the grass.

Meadow Bird, now showing signs of her maternity, glanced up and saw him. Smiling, she beckoned him to join them. He did so, feeling a sense of trespass as he was welcomed into the circle. Meadow Bird sang softly to herself as she sewed. The boys joined in, unselfconsciously inflecting their voices with hers as they played.

'Sing, Father!' Claim's hand pushed into his own as the boy urged him to join in. His tentative, clumsy attempts to do so quickly reduced mother and sons to fits of laughter.

'I know not the words, nor the tune,' he said, chagrined at their amusement.

'Like this!' Prospect began to chant, his childish voice raised in inflections so natural and spontaneous as to reduce his father to gaping idiocy.

'Do you understand what you are singing?'

'Of course! I'm singing to the buffalo.'

'When did you learn this song?'

'Uh!' Prospect blinked, looking confused and unhappy at the question. He looked to his mother, who stroked his cheek while murmuring in Mandan.

Boundless got to his feet. 'Continue,' he muttered. 'I must get back to work.'

He walked back to the stockade, feeling distinctly out of joint. Pinch was standing at the open gate, observing the scene. He gestured with the pipe. 'A fine family,' he said. 'You are to be congratulated, Boundless.'

'Aye.' He turned to look. Meadow Bird and the boys were happily singing once more, their voices joined in unison amidst the rustling grass and the restless, swooping wind.

OCTOBER BROUGHT A WELCOME interlude of balmier days, the lucent air prompting him to delay taking down the rope ladder. Meadow Bird was now heavily with child, her happiness manifest as she leaned on White Deer's arm for support, or sat in the rocker, singing and talking to the unborn child whom she fondly referred to as *shópka* or 'squirrel'.

'*Shópka*,' she murmured, chanting softly before cocking her head as if to listen for a reply. '*Bientôt*,' she said, employing the French word.

In his spare time, he built a cot, carving the outline of a squirrel into the headboard which drew a pleased smile from his wife. But just as constantly as his thoughts turned to the unborn child, they were drawn away again by some problem or preoccupation with the rock. *I shall soon have four children*, he mused, *two still in labour*. The comparison amused him as he pictured a mewling calf squirreling free of the bellied stone, its cries mingling with that of his flesh-child as it, too, squirmed free of its living tomb.

Taking advantage of the fine weather, he rode out alone one morning. Bjornson remained behind, insisting the time was set aside for his fatherhood duties.

Scaling the summit, he went about his tasks with a determination that hardly paused for refreshment. After a day spent boring and blasting, he climbed back down the ladder, wishing for the long light of summer.

Returning to the post, he drew rein to look back at the rock. And the longer and harder he looked, the easier it was to imagine the iron stone conforming to his buffalo vision. As he saw, or imagined he saw, form emerging from the granite mass, he was transported by renewed feelings of attachment—to the rock, the grass, the sky. *I am of this earth*, he told himself, looking around the desolate grass-blown prairie. *A part of it all*. He sat the horse, pondering the fact that the granite buffalo was the umbilical cord to such nativity. *Being both mother and child*, he told himself.

As the fine weather continued, so too did his rebirthed enthusiasm for his project. He ate the rock, dreamed the rock, brooded on the rock—pushing aside the pleas of his sons to abandon the fireside and join them in some pursuit or other. 'Not now; I am busy,' he said , staring into the rock-flames. And as he pored over his sketches, the great vine arched and bloomed and insinuated ever deeper into his entrails, driving from sight his family obligations, his duty to the post, and his all-but-forgotten promise to the captive Joseph.

NOVEMBER ARRIVED WITH EERIE calmness, the short autumn days bathed in cold sunlight, the grass dry and brittle under frost-blue skies. One day, he returned early to the post to find Pinch stationed at the gate, awaiting his arrival.

'Has something happened?' he asked, fetched short by the sombre look on Pinch's face.

'It is your wife. She has need of you.'

Alarmed, he rushed for the house. Throwing open the door, he found Bjornson and the boys inside. They were staring at the closed door of the bedroom, anxious looks on their faces.

'What is it?' he demanded. 'Is it the bairn?'

'In there.' Coming in behind him, Pinch motioned him toward the door. 'The women are inside.'

Fearful of what he might find, he opened the bedroom door. White Deer and Buffalo Bird were inside. Both women turned anguished faces to him as he entered. Meadow Bird sat in the rocking chair he had made for her, her features illuminated by the fire blazing in the grate. She had a woollen shawl around her shoulders and his old buffalo robe across her lap.

'Lassie, what is it?' He knelt down beside her, placing a hand on her arm. 'What is it? Are you poorly?'

She stared into the fire, a distant look on her face, as if she hadn't heard.

'What the devil is going on?' He turned to the women, his voice harsh in his demand for an answer.

Meadow Bird gave a distressed moan and laid his hand on her belly. He gazed at her, his face worried. 'Is it the bairn?'

Her lips began to move and, imperceptibly at first, she began to croon, her voice rising to a chant.

'My dear, what—?' Suddenly, he realised the belly beneath his hand was different, the growing roundness somehow changed. He stared at his wife in horror. She continued to chant as she rocked gently in the chair, her voice rising and falling. He sat back on his knees, a look of despair on his face.

'My poor, wee lassie!' Tenderly, he kissed her hair, his throat choked with grief.

Meadow Bird mourned for three days, remaining pent-up in the room while the women tended to her. Feeling helpless, he went about his chores with his mind elsewhere, his thoughts constantly returning to the small room. At night, he lay beside her, humbly clutching her hand while she remained silent and sleepless, her eyes open.

A week later, he was eating breakfast with the boys when the door to the bedroom opened and Meadow Bird stepped out, wrapped in the buffalo robe, her face pale and drawn.

'Mother!' Prospect ran to embrace her, resting his head on her arm. Gently but firmly, she set him aside. Buffalo Bird Woman and White Deer entered and stood beside her, as though anticipating this moment.

At a loss, he laid a hand on Prospect's shoulder as the boy stared wide-eyed at his mother. A burst of bright winter sunshine dazzled his eyes as the women opened the door of the cabin and stepped outside into the yard.

'Father! We must help her!' Prospect looked up, his lip trembling. Claim stood transfixed, a panicked look on his face.

'Leave her be for the moment. It is the Indian way,' he said, bereft of consolation.

After some minutes of strained silence, he went outside. 'Wait there!' he commanded as the boys made to follow. The women were gathered in a corner of the compound next to the fallow garden. Meadow Bird stood with her hands half-raised, as though to implore the wind and sky. Behind her, Buffalo Bird Woman and White Deer began to chant, their voices tremulous in the cold air. Meadow Bird reached down to tug up the hem of her tunic and he saw, with horror, that she held a knife in her hand. Before he could utter a protest, she had slashed at her legs with the knife, first one and then the other. She then stood erect, blood dripping from her legs as the other women continued to chant. This continued for almost an hour as he stood watching, powerless to intervene. Suddenly, his wife collapsed into the arms of her companions.

Murmuring and consoling, they half-carried, half-assisted her back to the cabin. She was led past him, her face almost unrecognisable with grief. He stared after her, his heart sorely rent.

For that day and the next, he stayed at the post, comforting the boys while Meadow Bird remained cocooned in her grief. He tended to her wordlessly, imitating the consoling silence of the Indian women as he covered her at night and brought her food—which remained untouched in the morning.

On the third day, unable to endure the heavy silence in the house a moment longer, he saddled the mustang and led it to the stockade gate.

'Where are you going?' Pinch blocked his path.

'Out of my way!' he snapped, his mood foul. 'I have no time for your games.'

'Game, is it?' Pinch's voice was edged. 'Your wife lies stricken, and you ride off to peck at your godforsaken buffalo!'

'She wishes to be left alone. The women are in attendance. Now out of my way!'

Pinch remained where he was, refusing to step aside. 'Good God, can it not wait a day or two more? Your boys need comforting. They have taken their mother's condition hard.'

'Damn you!' Boiling with pent-up grief and frustration, he shoved Pinch hard in the chest.

The older man stumbled backwards and lost his footing, ending up on his backside in the dirt. He glared as Boundless led the horse past him towards the gate.

'What man puts a lump of rock afore his wife and children? Answer me that! What man?' Pinch stood shakily to his feet. 'This madness will cost you everything!'

Boundless looked back as if he might say something, but mounted the horse instead and rode off.

'Are we all Joseph to you now?' The accusation followed him out into the grass.

IT WAS NOT UNTIL the following spring that Meadow Bird's spirits revived sufficiently for her to listlessly scold him for dragging mud into the cabin. He bore the reproof gladly, smiling at the boys as they looked eagerly at their mother. The wounds on her legs had scarred over, although a lingering distress seemed permanently etched into her features. Occasionally, he caught her fingering the scars, a brooding sadness on her face. Overnight, so it seemed to him, her movements became slower and less vigorous, her face lapsing into sorrow whenever she sat warming herself by the fire. To divert the attention of the boys, he plied them with extra lessons, testing them for grammar and arithmetic and hectoring any mistake.

The episode opened a rift between himself and Pinch, the latter's disapproval expressing itself with unconcealed disdain whenever the subject of the rock buffalo was raised.

'Off he goes again, on his fool's errand,' Pinch muttered as he watched Boundless ride off. 'You will not go?' he asked as Bjornson made to close the gate.

'Not today. I made a promise to the boys.'

'You are not so driven by pride.' Pinch hawked in the grass.

Bjornson set the bar back over the gate. He glanced sheepishly at Pinch. 'Perhaps it is as he claims—a desire to leave a mark upon the world.'

'And what is that, but pride?'

TO FURTHER DRAW OUT his wife's affections, he proposed a summer visit to the Mandan camp to see her family. She agreed, albeit to his disappointment, without her usual enthusiasm. The boys, in contrast, whooped with glee at the prospect of reuniting with old friends amidst the freedom of the Indian camp. Their excitement drew a distracted smile from their mother as they chatted merrily in Mandan.

'It will be like an adventure,' he promised. 'We shall visit the rock, on the way, to show your mother,' he added, provoking further excitement.

'I shall be gone a week or so,' he announced to Bjornson, who seemed as pleased as the boys at the unexpected reprieve.

'Take two!' he answered, drawing a guffaw from Pinch.

The day was cool and dry, gusts of wind scudding the long grass as they proceeded at a walking pace. Several times, he had to reprimand the boys as they challenged each other each shrieking that they 'bid the buffalo' as soon as the rock came into sight.

He pulled rein at a distance, pointing out the parts. 'Do you see the hump?' he asked, pleased as both boys shouted 'Yes!'

'And that big protruding part is—or will be, the head.'

He turned to Meadow Bird, who sat stony-faced regarding the object. 'Do you remember the buffalo? Behold!' He swept out an arm.

Their faces flushed with gaiety, the boys rattled off in Mandan as they importuned their mother for a response.

'Mother?' Prospect prompted. 'Do you see the buffalo?'

'Not buffalo!' She jerked the bridle, drawing a whinny from the mare. 'Buffalo gone!'

## 55

# A Quarrel

IN THE SCORCHING HEAT of midsummer, the two workmates toiled to finish excavating the caul of surplus 'fat' between the head and hump. Progress had slowed as fatigue and repetition combined with the increasingly hot weather to impose a limit to their labours. Frustration at the lack of progress caused Boundless to urge that they work longer hours each day, the demand driving both men to the breaking point.

'Take a spell, Bjorn.' Taking off his hat, Boundless fanned himself with the brim as he surveyed the squares of marked granite yet to be blasted. Sweat dampened his hair and forehead where the hat had been.

'What now?' Bjornson's voice was testy in the suffocating heat.

'There is a yard or two that still needs removing, but the quarrying up here is largely done. We are ready to proceed to the spine and tail.'

'Why not leave it as it is?' Bjornson shook the water bottle, grimacing as he realised it was empty. 'We have the hump,' he said, gesturing with the bottle at the bulge of rock. 'And there is the head. What else remains to be done?'

'What else?' Boundless eyed his companion, wondering if the sun had softened his brain. 'We have hardly begun!' He instantly regretted the words as a scowl crossed Bjornson's face. The Swede's shirt was stained with sweat, his every movement slow and fatigued. A warm, blustery gale added to their discomfort.

'You said the rock already suggests a buffalo—why not leave it at that?' Bjornson wiped an arm across his brow. 'Others may also see the resemblance without further tinkering.' He took out the patch of linen he used as a handkerchief.

'Tinkering!'

'You claim to see the buffalo? Then leave it so that others may see it also.' Bjornson held the neckerchief against the side of his face, as if tending to a toothache. 'Between your endless scribbles and sketches we will be stuck on this godforsaken rock until the crack of doom.'

'We have only begun to block out the parts. We have not yet begun to carve.'

Bjornson grimaced. 'You speak of carving as easily as if it were a turkey.'

'What has gotten into you? You're like a bear with a sore head!'

'When do you intend that we finish?' Bjornson removed his straw hat to run his hand through his sweat-slicked hair. 'Ten years? … Twenty?'

'It will take time,' he said, noticing how tired his workmate looked. Bjornson's face was etched with lines and grimy with dust and sweat. It occurred to Boundless that he must look much the same.

'How much time?' Bjornson persisted.

Boundless looked into the distance while trying to come up with an answer that would not further rile his disgruntled companion. 'We measure things in buffalo time,' he said, attempting to lighten the conversation.

'What in blazes does that mean?' Bjornson spat out some rock dust.

'The buffalo do not think in months or years. They come and they go with the return of the grass.'

'Confound the buffalo! What riddling is this?'

'Only that it is a mistake to apportion months or years to each step. It will be done when it is finished.'

'What the devil are you saying?' Bjornson's voice was pitched with exasperation.

'Patience, Bjorn. I only counsel patience.'

They stood in strained silence for long moments. A cloud passed over the sun to throw some fleeting shade. Bjornson mopped his flushed brow. 'Let us escape this hellish sun!'

They climbed down, glad to rest in the rock shadow. Bjornson looked around, a tetchy look on his face. 'My brains are boiled! Where in the name of God are the horses?'

They rode back to the post in silence. When they arrived, Bjornson gave a cursory nod before walking off to his quarters, leaving his sons to wipe down and water the horse. He passed Pinch on the way, brushing off an attempt at conversation and leaving a surprised Pinch to stare after him.

The next morning, Boundless joined Bjornson in the hall, hoping his companion's mood had improved overnight. But there was no sign of reconciliation. The Swede's voice was blunt as he stated his intention to rest from the rock for several days, no amount of argument on Boundless' part able to change his mind.

'Tomorrow, I take my boys fishing. And the next day, too!' Bjornson got up from the table, muttering a curt greeting to Pinch as the latter arrived bearing mug of tea.

'What's got Bjorn's goat? He nearly bit my head off yesterday, and now today!' said Pinch, sitting down.

'It's this heat. It's hard on a body.'

'You push too hard. Remember, he was tricked into this.'

'It was his own decision,' said Boundless, pushing back his chair.

'Aye. And one he no doubt regrets. You work him to the bone. It is your buffalo, not his.'

The words stung as he headed to the workshop.

In the days following the quarrel, he and Bjornson were studiously polite to each other, their distant manner drawing several barbed comments from Pinch as he tried to stir the conversational pot after a rare supper together.

'When do you plan on giving up the fishing pole for the chisel?' he asked Bjornson, barely concealing the mischief in his voice.

'When I am ready.'

Boundless listened to the response while contriving to give the impression it mattered little to him. Pinch was not fooled as he turned his musket on Boundless. 'So, you must work sans Swede for the nonce?'

'Bjorn will return when he feels it is the right time,' he said, careful not to offend and thus revive the quarrel.

'Come now, friends, cards on the table. Something be amiss between ye. And my guess is that the confounded buffalo is at the root of it. Do I speak truly?' Pinch looked from one to the other.

'It is not a matter I wish to discuss,' he said, frowning at Pinch's proclivity for mischief-making.

'But I do!' Bjornson's forceful exclamation took both Boundless and Pinch by surprise.

Boundless sat back in his chair. 'Spew forth then!'

'When will this labour ever end? You seem intent on achieving a buffalo down to the last detail.' Bjornson's expression was as vexed as his voice was sour.

'Not so,' protested Boundless.

'Then tell me plainly—when will you be satisfied?'

'He means,' chimed in Pinch, 'at what point will you call a halt to the foolish business?'

'I do not need you, Pinch, to explain—'

'Pinch is right! When will it be good enough for you?'

Startled at the vehemence in Bjornson's voice, he attempted to mollify the Swede. 'We are still removing excess rock. The carving stage is yet to come. You know this, Bjorn.'

'And do you presume to carve the head like the decapitation in your workshop?' asked Pinch, reaching for his pipe. 'In such fine detail? For if so, I fear this lifetime is not sufficient.'

'I do not intend an exact copy. The model and drawings are for guidance only—'

'Not true! You intend a faithful copy—a portrait!'

He stared, too flummoxed at the Swede's combative mood to respond.

'Do you forget you have a grieving wife?' put forward Pinch.

The remark angered him. 'I forget nothing!' He stood up. 'I will leave you two to gossip and invent as you may. I have work to do.'

'Come now, Boundless!' Pinch called after him as he strode for the door. 'We do but debate the merits of the question. Surely, there is no need to put yourself so out of joint?'

'Good night!'

Instead of returning to his quarters, he went to the workshop. Cursing the lantern for being out of oil, he lit a candle instead. Placing it on the table next to the plaster head, he sat down, his thoughts savagely despondent. As his anger began to subside, his thoughts turned to Bjornson as he stood atop the rock—his face pale with exhaustion in the hot sun. *Surely, he will not abandon me?* The prospect caused his heart to flutter with anxiety. *Might he not consider himself to be discharged of his obligation? Mayhap Pinch is right and I do push too hard.* The candle spluttered, the smell of tallow in his nose.

He stared broodingly at the detailed head he had fashioned. The features shone with a dull light that seemed to mock his hopes. *Bjorn is right. I must rethink. The stone is too hard.* He rubbed his sore wrists, plagued with anxiety at the prospect of having to abandon his great project, leaving it merely a disfigured rock. The notion was so fearful that it affected a paralysis of mind, one that quickly turned to gloomy doubts and self-recrimination. *I overestimated my abilities. It was all for nought. Mayhap I should leave it as it is.*

The candle extinguished and he sat in darkness, contemplating the ruination of all his hopes, the grand project eroding to a paltry nothingness before his eyes. An overpowering fatigue claimed him and his chin sunk to his chest.

He awoke with a start. The room was cold, and he shivered. He got to his feet, grimacing at the stiffness in his limbs. He stepped outside, shutting the door behind him. The night sky blazed with stars and he stopped to gaze up, briefly distracted by the vast galactic steppes.

Lying in bed alongside Meadow Bird, he remained restlessly awake, his head a whirl of divergent thoughts. He turned heavily on his side, drawing a murmured protest from his bed mate. A dread of failure kept sleep at bay no matter how he longed for its forgetful balm. Muttering and sighing, he stared into the darkness, seeing his buffalo vision turn to vapour like breath on a winter's day. He stifled a groan, fearful that Bjornson would renege on his promise before the summer was out. A small, whispering voice pursued him into sleep. *For the living know that they shall die, but the dead know not any thing, neither have they any more a reward; neither have they any more a portion for ever in any thing that is done under the sun; for the memory of them is forgotten.*

He awoke to the sounds of Meadow Bird talking to the boys in the outer room. He stared up at the roof, his thoughts leaping back to the previous day as summer light invaded the small room. He racked his brain for a way to bring the Swede back onside, convinced that Bjornson's cooperation was key to achieving his goal.

He brooded on the problem, aware they had reached a fork in the road. Either we repair our differences or go our separate ways. Is this what Bjorn wants? Is he forcing a quarrel in order to release himself from perceived bondage?

The rock titan loomed in his mind, bursting forth from the captive granite in all its bellowing glory. He lingered on the image—so real he could almost reach out and touch the unbound creature. But slowly, a stark realism seeped into his thoughts, tempering his grand vision like a heated chisel bronzing and blueing from the flames. The more he tried to summon the vivid particularity he saw in his mind, the more his grasp gave way to a sobering, resigned acceptance. *Pinch is right. Plaster is one thing, stone another.*

He gazed at the fretwork of shadows on the plastered wall, seeing his creation chipped away bit by bit. And the longer he wrestled with the imperfectability imposed by the unyielding stone, the more a reduced projection of his hopes seemed inevitable—ambition perforce yielding to the constraints of time and flesh. But still he clung stubbornly to the visionary ideal, loath to let go in the warm morning light.

He heard the boys squabble and White Deer issue a sharp rebuke. He rubbed his stubbled cheeks, mulling regretfully over Bjornson's furious charge. *'You intend a portrait!'* He was fixed on the accusation when something flickered in his thoughts, the notion causing him to catch breath. What was it? He scrambled to seize hold of the conceit, which seemed to float just out of eyesight. *Not portrait, but landscape!* The simple insight rocked him to the core. All at once, the bluntness of feature he had long feared now struck him as not only right but the true face of the buffalo. *After all, it is part of the earth. It must look … natural. A representation, not a faithful copy. The skill is to subtract, not to filigree!*

In excited fancy, he lashed out an arm, sweeping the intricate models and sketches to the workshop floor. *Nature, not artifice!*

'Father!' The door opened and Claim stuck his head inside. 'Are you sick?'

His hopes revived, he sat with Bjornson after breakfast. Using a sheet of paper and ink, he illustrated how they might proceed by diagramming the rock into three sections—the head, the hump, and the tail. 'It is a matter of patience,' he said, doing his best to inspire confidence in his obdurate workmate. 'And working one section at a time—so as not to be overwhelmed by the whole. We are not after particularity of detail, as in the sketches, but broad impression only—as suggested by the stone itself. Do you agree?'

With held breath, he studied his companion, willing the Swede to assent. 'Bjorn?'

Something of his renewed faith miraculously transmitted itself to the phlegmatic Bjornson, who also seemed contrite following their quarrel. He opened his mouth to speak when Pinch approached with a mug of tea.

'How are the two lovebirds this fine morning?'

Boundless waited for Bjornson to reply, unwilling to risk what appeared to be a handful of restorative earth in the breach between them.

'Boundless is telling how we may proceed,' answered Bjornson, his voice strained yet conciliatory.

'Proceed with what?' Pinch sipped his tea.

'With the carving.'

'Carving what?' Pinch set down his tea mug, a bland look on his face. 'Oh, the buffalo!'

'Not carve, remove,' Boundless risked correcting. 'It is as Monsieur Courtois said: you take away to reveal what is there.'

Ignoring Boundless' frown, Pinch reached over and picked up the sketch. 'Like skinning a deer—to reveal the innards,' he suggested, eyeing the sketch.

Uncertain if this was intended as jest, reproof or simply as *aperçu*, Boundless took back the sketch and stood up. 'As it happens, yes,' he replied. 'Bjorn, let us take a holiday today.' He smiled at Bjornson's started glance. 'The rock will still be there on the morrow. What say you?'

Bjornson nodded, an air of affability returning to his expression as he mumbled agreement, Pinch watched the door close behind Boundless before turning to Bjornson. 'Your acquiescence fuels his madness. Do you now commit yourself to another twenty years of hard labour? You know he will not quit until one or both of you are dead?'

Bjornson sipped his tea but made no reply.

'You have White Deer and your sons to consider,' pressed Pinch.

'And my oath to Boundless,' said Bjornson, the words uttered so quietly that Pinch strained to hear.

## 56

## A Savage Winter

THE WINTER OF 1783 was of a severity not seen since the 'famine winter' of two decades before. The first hint came in late September as the nacreous skies of autumn disappeared behind a solid bank of grey cloud. In the first week of January, a bitterly cold wind swept down from the north, ushering in a blizzard that buried the buildings beneath a mass of soft white snow.

Boundless awoke one freezing morning to feel Meadow Bird burrowed into his side beneath the covers. The air felt icy cold and he briefly ducked back into the warmth of the robe. He shivered while dressing, pulling on the buffalo robe for warmth. Hurrying across the snow-filled yard, he entered the hall to find White Deer piling wood on the fire while Buffalo Bird Woman heated a pan of fried bread and beans.

'Ye Gods!' Pinch entered, stomping his feet, a blanket pulled over his head. 'The snow be as thick as a peddler's yarn!' His cheeks were pink, the hairs on his chin white with hoar frost.

He was followed in by Bjornson, the Swede pushing his companion in his haste to shut the door behind him. 'Mercy!' He gasped, his cheeks pale and trembling. 'My hands are froze!'

'Is there any tea?' Pinch glanced at the boiling kettle. 'Thank God!'

The door opened again and a cold blast swept the room—drawing a curse from Pinch. 'Zounds! Close the door, for pity's sake!'

Prospect kicked shut the door behind him. 'The wind is fierce!' He blew on his cupped hands. At seventeen, and rangy in build, he stood half-a-head taller than his father. An expert and insatiable hunter, he was forever riding off with his Mandan cousins to wreak havoc on the returning buffalo herds.

'Where is your brother?'

Prospect crouched before the fire, holding out his hands over the flames. 'With Anders and Torsten, seeing to the dogs. I wish spring were here.' He gazed moodily into the fire.

Boundless watched his son grimace and fidget. *He has the same impatience as myself.*

The door opened again—eliciting more protests from Pinch. Claim, Anders and Torsten tumbled in, their faces mottled with cold. 'Old Rufus is dead—froze stiff!' Claim stamped the snow from his feet.

'And half-ate!' chimed in Anders, hurrying to the fire.

Following breakfast, they sat warming themselves before the flames. 'We need to replenish the pile,' said Bjornson, placing another log on the blaze. He glanced pointedly at Pinch, who returned the look with a bland stare.

'I wonder how the war is going,' said Boundless, thinking aloud.

'What makes you mention that?' asked Bjornson. 'Have you heard something?'

'No. I was just thinking about those poor soldier boys freezing in the snow and getting shot at. I would give my teeth for reliable information. I miss Guillaume's letters.'

A month earlier, on a visit to the Knife River Mandan encampment he had learned, to his sorrow, that Jacques, his prime interlocutor during his early days at the post, had passed away. And so it was to another Frenchman, one Ambroise Cloutier, formerly a member of the brigade but long since married into the Mandan, that he had turned to for information. 'What news of the war?' he had asked as he sat with Cloutier in the latter's lodge.

'It is no different than before,' he complained to Bjornson on returning to the post. 'Rumour upon rumour. One report contradicts another. One minute we are victorious, the next on the brink of defeat.'

A passing band of Assiniboia hunters brought more confusing news— the accounts so mixed up that he was at a loss to understand whether the Americans or the English were in the ascendancy

'It is all gossip and folktale!' he grumbled to Pinch. 'What I would not give for some reliable reports.'

Pinch puffed on his pipe, unperturbed. 'Cocked hat or crown, it be all the same in the end.'

Boundless took more comfort from a 'trustworthy' account, passed along by Cloutier just two weeks previously, of a great American victory six months before at Yorktown where the Americans, aided by the French, had forced the surrender of a large English army.

'The alliance with France will prove crucial,' he ruminated, sitting forwards to warm his hands.

Pinch, absorbed in drinking tea, made a slurping noise over the cup.

'What?' asked Boundless. 'You doubt it?'

Tossing the tea leaves into the fire, Pinch gave a dismissive grunt. 'Let your Americans beware lest their ally gobble them up in turn.'

'Not so long ago, we were fighting the French. How the world doth turn!' Boundless cocked an ear to the blasting wind. 'I wonder what became of him?' he said, voicing his thoughts.

'Who?' Pinch took up the kettle to pour more tea. He offered some to Boundless who shook his head.

'No one. A French soldier I met once, long ago.'

'Do you think they will win?'

Jarred from his thoughts he looked at Bjornson as the Swede bent forward to place another log on the fire. 'Who are *they*?'

'Your Americans.'

'*My* Americans? Are they not equally yours?'

Bjornson took some time to consider, knitting his brow while poking the log.

'Well?'

'His tribe are Lutherans, only,' suggested Pinch.

Bjornson threw back his head and laughed heartily as Pinch looked on in bemusement.

'Well?' Boundless repeated.

'I suppose so,' said Bjornson, still chuckling.

'You suppose so?'

'Come now, Boundless,' chided Pinch. 'We do not all share equally your enthusiasm for all things American.'

Prospect stood up. 'I'm going to the house,' he said, a restless look on his face.

'Me too.' Claim got up to follow his brother, followed in turn by the Bjornson boys.

'Close the door after you!' called Pinch as a blast of weather blew into the hall.

'This forced idleness is hard on them,' said Bjornson.

'At least they avoid the war,' said Pinch. 'Thank God it is so far away.'

'They are the only true Americans among us,' remarked Boundless, 'being born here.'

'As was I,' protested Pinch.

'And me, also,' added Bjornson.

'In a different time,' Boundless added weakly.

Back in his quarters, huddled before the roaring fire, he marvelled that anything could still be alive outside on the frozen plain. His mind roamed to the earth lodges of the Mandan and the warm smoky gloom illuminated by the hearth fires. *They have endured these winters for how long no man may tell*, he ruminated. *They be as hardy as the wolf or the buffalo.*

He opened the logbook—the duty of making daily entries as *bourgeois* now an ingrained habit.

> *The air crackles with cold, searing the lungs of anyone unfortunate enough to be caught outdoors. The mercury in the barometer fell to minus 44 degrees. I rose one night for the express purpose of observing the glass and found the liquid suspended at mark minus 47 degrees. Such monstrous cold is a deathly hazard to even the beasts of the field. For days at a time, we have been confined to our quarters or the hall, venturing out only to feed the dogs and horses or to fetch logs from the woodshed. A bucket of water left outside froze solid within the hour—the air so bitterly chill that Pinch declares it the coldest winter he has ever known—a claim he makes every year or so.*

Meadow Bird, swathed in a blanket, came over to where he sat and knelt beside him. He extended the heavy robe across her body while drawing her to his side. To his delight, she did not resist. 'We must tell the boys to cut more wood,' he said. She nodded, caught up in her own fire thoughts.

The boys had joined him on the rock the summer before, showing the same fearless indifference to heights as their father. Bjornson's sons promptly followed suit, despite the objections of their mother and father. 'What else are we to do, Father?' Torsten had asked, momentarily stumping the Swede.

Before entrusting the four boys to the project, Boundless insisted that they observe and assist Bjornson and himself in an apprenticeship while they learned the proper use of the various tools. 'First, we need to rough away the excess rock,' he said. 'For that, you will need to use this.' He held up a pick. 'Or this.' He showed a pitching chisel. He demonstrated with the pitcher before giving each of the boys a turn. 'Mind your eyes,' he cautioned as the boys began to practise with the tools on chunks of removed granite. 'Blink or look away to avoid the chips. Torsten, your father got a chip in his eye one time. He won't thank you to do the same. Prospect, slow down! Control your strikes.'

Further fuelling their impatience to begin, he made them study the plaster model as he explained what he wanted done in exacting detail.

Finally, he painted fresh grid marks on the rock hinds and assigned each a small square—the only section they were permitted to work. He watched critically as the four went about the task with enthusiasm, Claim and Prospect competing with each other until a sharp word from him ended the contest.

Their initial enthusiasm soon faded as the arduous and repetitive nature of the work sunk in over the following days and weeks. 'Is this all we do all day?' grumbled Prospect. 'I had rather tan hides!'

'What did you expect—that it would carve itself?' snorted Claim.

'You are sick of it, too!'

'Not so!'

'Then go back to work, why don't you!'

'You first!'

'Perhaps we can go fishing after supper,' said Anders, putting an arm around Prospect to calm him down.

'He dislikes it as much as me but is too square-headed to admit it!' Prospect cast a dire glance in the direction of his brother.

To solve the growing problem of navigating the extensive work site, he devised an ingenious method whereby stout lengths of rope were suspended over both sides, the ends securely staked in the earth below. Using these as anchors, he oversaw the construction of a rope scaffold or rigging by connecting the vertical stays with up to twenty horizontal 'sheets' on either side of the hinds. The boys each wore a simple safety harness he had designed, one end of the safety line attached to the harness, the other end to the rigging.

'Make certain you are hooked to the line at all times,' he said, showing the boys how to secure the line to the rope scaffolding by the use of a sheet bend knot.

'Hold to the rope!' Arms on hips, he stared upwards as first Claim and then Prospect climbed the rigging to demonstrate its utility. Claim leaned out from the rock, holding one arm out in the air. Not to be outdone, Prospect did the same, wrapping his leg around the rope and raising both arms. 'They compete like monkeys!' he complained.

The Bjornson boys went up next, climbing cautiously and flattening themselves against the rock at each gust of wind.

'Check the line!' Bjornson shouted up. He craned his neck, a worried look on his face.

'The rope gets in the way,' complained Anders on climbing back down as his father scolded the omission.

'I get caught up on it,' agreed Torsten, aware of the scornful looks cast their way by Claim and Prospect.

'Ye will long for it when tumbling through the air!'

Boundless assigned all four boys the task of smoothing the hind section so as to mimic the natural fall from the hump to the tail. He gave Bjornson the duty of overseeing their efforts, anxious lest they inadvertently disfigure the shape. He was adamant in his refusal to allow the boys any blasting privileges, adding further to the restless boredom of both his sons. 'Hammer, hammer, hammer, that's all we do the whole day long,' complained a frustrated Prospect. 'I guess I wish I was dead!'

Impatient at the long halt dictated by the brutal winter, Boundless surprised Bjornson by announcing his intention to finally start work on the centrepiece of his creation, the massive frontispiece, once the weather allowed.

'It is time,' he said. 'After all, I have served my apprenticeship, as have you, my friend. We may both legitimately call ourselves stonemasons, if nothing else.'

He prepared by drawing a cross-section of the plaster buffalo head, making minute calculations to ensure the correct size and proximity of the nostrils, jaw and horns. *It is as much surveying and engineering as carving,* he reflected, not for the first time. *Add to which, dangling from a hoist.* The project kept him busy for the remainder of the winter as he spent hours alone in the draughty workshop inspecting and refining his plans while reminding himself of his decision to forgo detail in favour of broad perspective. The eyes, he decided, were the critical features and he worried for days on how best to incorporate them into the giant head. *They should be looking,* he told himself. He filled dozens of pages in the notebook with sketches, unhappy with each one. He modelled the eyes in the plaster head but was left equally dissatisfied with the result. *They can wait until last,* he consoled himself. *Perhaps when the head is finished, they will suggest themselves.* Buoyed with this hope, he set aside the sketches, pondering instead on how best to carve the face.

THE TERRIBLE WINTER DRAGGED on into April before finally easing its grip. On the Missouri, thick plates of ice lingered in the shadow of the trees as spring slowly softened the earth. Flocks of ducks and geese flew overhead, and he looked daily for the return of the buffalo. The mud within the stockade turned to dirt as the days grew longer and the lakes of water dried in the prairie grass. To his disappointment, neither of his sons showed the least interest in returning to the rock.

One morning, Prospect stole away to the Mandan camp, despite being ordered to remain at the post. It was a week before the youth returned, by which time Boundless, Claim and the Bjornsons had already resumed work on the project.

'Where the blazes have you been?' he demanded upon his son's return, knowing the answer.

Prospect shrugged and stared up at the rock. 'Hunting, I guess.'

'Hunting what? Girls?' Claim thrust his face at his brother. 'You know they can't stand you—the stink!' He held his nose in comical fashion

The gesture infuriatedProspect. 'And what do you know—lunkhead!'

Next moment, they were stood eyeball to eyeball, fists clenched.

'Enough, for God's sake!' Boundless dragged them apart, berating both as they glared at each other. 'Ye muckle like a pair of rutting elk! Claim, go back to work. You!' He looked crossly at Prospect. 'Go around to the other side. Now!'

Exasperated, he watched them go. Anders and Torsten followed, the two brothers shaking their heads and smiling at this latest altercation.

*How are they so dutiful and my own so contrary?* Something Pinch had said came back to him and he mumbled under his breath as he walked around to the ladder.

In late spring, both sons sneaked away from their duties to team up with their Mandan cousins and massacre a buffalo herd. 'We kilt over a hundred!' they exulted in a rare show of unity as they described the grand feast lasting three days at the Mandan camp.

'Never mind the deuced buffalo—you have responsibilities here.' He rebuked the boys for the better part of five minutes before throwing up his hands in frustration. 'Go! Your mother has supper waiting.' He watched them trudge sheepishly to the house. 'And no more running off!'

They had returned to the post following a long day atop the summit when an Indian arrived bearing a scribbled note from Ambroise Cloutier. Pinch and Bjornson looked on as Boundless read, his eyes widening as he took in the contents.

'What is it?'

He stared in disbelief. 'The war is over! We have won!' 'Who are *we*?' demanded Pinch.

Bjornson gaped. 'You mean—'

'We are victorious!' Grasping Bjornson's hand, he pumped it vigorously. 'The English are defeated!'

Stunned at the news, Pinch stood with mouth open. 'When?'

'Sometime late last year. A treaty was signed. Cloutier heard of it from a French trapper who had word directly from the east. Cloutier said we can trust the report, as he knows the man.'

Bjornson shook his head in wonderment. 'Well, you have your America,' he said.

'For better or worse,' noted Pinch, his face glum.

The news sparked a celebratory supper in which he and Bjornson took turns raising toasts to the astonishing victory.

'To the republic!' He raised a glass of rum—having hidden two bottles from the avaricious Pinch in hopes of just such an occasion. Pinch sat in uncharacteristic silence as Boundless toasted a new age of progress and liberty. Bjornson then took a turn, raising his glass to 'Christian prosperity and the advancement of faith.'

Irritable at the indifference exhibited by his sons during the celebration, Boundless took Prospect aside. 'Do you not understand what this means?' Still jubilant at the glorious news, he looked into his son's eyes. 'No longer are we to be subjected to the tyranny of a distant monarch. You are a free-born American, subject to no authority other than that to which you subscribe as a lawful citizen.'

Prospect shrugged, puzzled at his father's excitement. 'I never was before,' he said.

Later, Boundless sat in his quarters sipping the last glass of rum as he exulted in the staggering triumph. The timing of the news—coinciding so closely with his decision to start carving the massive head—struck him as so propitious as to suggest the hand of Providence at work—the miraculous congruity of rock and event lighting a blaze in his mind that burned fiercely all night.

'It will stand as a monument to the new republic,' he announced the next morning, his voice hoarse from lack of sleep.

Bjornson knitted his brow. 'A republican buffalo?'

'For a buffalo republic!' He gripped his companion's arm. 'You were looking for a reason—do you not now see the one that Providence has provided?'

Bjornson exhaled a long-suffering sigh. 'I do not, as you, see the hand of fate in such matters. It is akin to divination, and therefore—'

'No matter,' Boundless declared giddily, his vision bubbling to the fore. 'It will stand imperishable!'

Whipped on by an image of the nascent republic arising, Phoenix-like from the Promethean rock, he drove himself to exhaustion over the next few weeks, working long, hot hours under the burning sun and demanding the same from his workmates.

'It needs shape, prominence, above all, life!' he insisted, as Bjornson urged him to rest and take water.

One morning, he was fine chipping a section of rock when he heard a shout. Looking up, he saw a dark cloud in the distance. He stood up, exasperated at the thought of a thunderstorm.

The others stared at the horizon, perplexed looks on their faces. 'That ain't thunder,' insisted Prospect.

'Well, it ain't snow either!' scoffed his brother.

Puzzled, they stared at the dark mass—the cloud seemingly touching the tops of the grass.

'It moves!' Anders exclaimed.

The sky above was blue and clear, the grass waving back and forth in the breeze. Boundless shaded his eyes, wishing he had remembered to bring the glass. The cloud glittered like silver. A dull rushing noise, like the rustle of wind in the grass, reached his ears.

'It's smoke!' Bjornson shouted in alarm. 'The grass is on fire!'

A moment later, the truth struck Boundless. 'Locusts! It is not smoke, but grasshoppers!'

They hurried back to the post, arriving barely ahead of the ominous cloud. Pinch and the women were standing outside the gates to stare at the great host as it drew nearer. They had no sooner secured the horses than the storm engulfed them, grasshoppers falling from the air like autumn leaves. The great mass darkened the sky as the noise of countless whirring bodies produced a crackling, sibilant thunder that deafened the ears. Mouths masked with neckerchiefs, they raised arms to protect themselves as the locusts descended *en masse*, the insects overwhelming the post in a rushing, chittering storm.

'Merciful Jesus!' His voice muffled by the neckerchief, Pinch rushed to bar the gate, as if attempting to keep at bay the darkening blizzard. Boundless helped lift the bar into place as grasshoppers rained about their ears and eyes, the locusts catching in hair and clothes. The air was now choked with the winged insects, the ground littered with their bodies. He heard the dogs howl and snap furiously at the teeming wings. He hastened to join the others inside the hall, groping his way through the insect storm. The women were frantically stuffing every crack and aperture with hides or cloth as the men stomped hundreds of the crawling insects underfoot. The great torrent of locusts had reached such proportions that the grasshopper cloud blotted out the sun, leaving the stockade in a sinister twilight that resonated with the sibilant hiss of countless wings.

When, towards evening, Boundless ventured outside, he found the ground buried beneath a moving carpet of crawling pests. Holding the neckerchief to his mouth, he made his way across the yard to check on the dogs, crunching locusts underfoot. The animals lay on their bellies, heads buried beneath their paws, as grasshoppers clung to the hairs on their bodies and crawled over their ears and nostrils.

'The Egyptian Plague', as Pinch coined it, persisted for several days, the sheer mass of insects threatening to suffocate the post and all therein. The garden was stripped of every ounce of vegetation, the grasshoppers leaving only a few dried stalks to wither in the sun. The plague only eased when a strong north-westerly gale swept the cloud away from the post. The inexhaustible host departed leaving behind a multitude of dead as the pestilent storm moved westwards. Boundless muttered in disbelief at the sight of the prairie seemingly stripped bare of grass. The tall buffalo reeds were laid waste as if swept by a giant scythe. He heard a noise and turned to see the women scooping up masses of the grasshoppers into pots and pans.

'What are they doing?' asked Prospect.

'They will fry them up and eat them,' he said. 'An Indian will never let a meal go to waste.'

'They've devoured everything!' Bjornson stared out over the shredded grass, a horrified look on his face.

Pinch grunted. 'Mayhap they've chawed the deuced buffalo as well.'

## 57

## Those That Toil Under The Sun

THE FOLLOWING SPRING, HE and Bjornson unbolted the block and tackle and moved the apparatus up onto the head. They bolted the frame to the granite, sinking each of the six bolts four inches into the rock. He then ran a thick rope from the winch up and over the pulley wheel. He finished by tying a hook to the end of the rope. This done, he inserted the hand crank, testing the iron gear wheel designed by the ingenious Bertrand.

'It will work,' he said, confident in the carpenter's skill.

Bjornson watched, a doubtful look on his face.

Tying a bucket full of rock pieces to the hoist, they practised lowering and raising it over the edge, satisfied that one man could winch two hundred pounds of rock.

'Thank God for the gear wheel,' said Bjornson, puffing as he cranked the rocks back up to the top.

'Do not forget to brake the wheel before you let go,' said Boundless, inserting the iron rod into the gear teeth. 'You will need the boys to help. Boys, over here!'

He attached the leather sling seat—designed by Bertrand in the style of the bosun chair seen by Boundless onboard the *Patience*—to the hook and sat in it, testing it by swinging back and forth. He then put on the harness and secured the safety line as the others watched. Satisfied that all was in readiness, he produced two whistles attached to cord neckties and gave one to Bjornson. 'It is how they do it aboard ship,' he explained. 'One blast means lower; two means raise up. Repeat each blast after me to confirm the signal.'

Bjornson gave the winch a practice turn, slotting the brake rod into place. Positioning the bosun chair beneath him, Boundless stood on the precipice and glanced at the grass far below. 'Are you set?' he asked.

'Let us hope that the rope does not break.'

'More Swedish cheer!' he laughed, jubilant at embarking on the final stage of his great project. The day was fine with a mild breeze from the south. Backing cautiously over the edge, he held on tightly to the rope slings.

'Good luck, Father!'

'Hold on to the line!'

'Let me down. Slowly!'

Carefully, Bjornson let out the rope as the boys lay on their bellies to watch.

A moment later, he was hanging freely from the sling. He experienced a brief bout of vertigo as the chair swung in a half circle. The wind, so mild atop the summit, tugged at him and he tightened his grip on the rope harness either side of the seat.

'Lower!' Remembering the whistle around his neck, he released one hand to blast the signal.

'Lower!' echoed the boys peering down.

Slowly, the chair was let down as he used his legs to kick himself out from the rock face.

He blew another three blasts as a signal to stop, berating himself for forgetting this elementary instruction.

'Mr Bjornson asks what three whistles mean!' hollered Claim.

'It means stop until I signal!'

Dangling from the sling, he stared at the sprawling plain, his heart leaping at the dizzying prospect. *I am looking out from the rock—seeing as does the rock itself!* A wind gust rocked the chair and he checked his breath, reaching out a hand to steady himself. He experienced the now-familiar sensation that, if he fell, the wind would buffet his fall, depositing him unharmed onto the grass far below.

'What do you see, Father?' Prospect yelled down, his hands cupped to his mouth.

'The world!' he shouted.

He tried propelling himself across the rock face by scooting his feet against the granite—dragging them to brake his progress.

At one point, he kicked too hard, overbalancing. His heart skipped a beat as the chair dipped to one side. He held fiercely to the rope sling for safety.

'Are you alright, Father?'

The boys seemed far above him, although only twenty feet or so away, their heads poking over as they peered down. From his present vantage, the rock bulge he had designated the head seemed vaster, smoother, and far more formidable a challenge.

'Winch me up!' he shouted and then, remembering the whistle, blew two sharp blasts.

Winched back to the top, he slipped out of the chair, elated at the success of his first foray to survey the rock face. 'Tomorrow, we can mark off the points.'

But first, he was forced to acquiesce to the urgent pleas of his sons to try out the bosun chair. 'If I give in, will you quit your pestering?'

As Bjornson worked the winch, he looked over the edge to watch as first Prospect, and then Claim, dangled over the precipice. The boys shouted in excitement as they kicked and scooted along the granite, oblivious to his fears for their safety.

'I can see the Missouri!' shouted Prospect.

'I can see the wind!' cried Claim when his turn came.

Flushed with excitement, both boys urged their companions to take a turn. Anders and Torsten shook their heads.

'Are you scared?' mocked Claim.

Torsten fidgeted and seemed about to agree, however reluctantly, to go over the side when his father intervened. 'Torsten! I forbid it!'

Boundless took both boys aside 'Not a word to your mother. She would scalp me if she knew.'

Over supper that night, the elated boys teased and tormented their mother with tales of their father hanging suspended from the summit.

'You'd think he was a bird, mother!'

'An eagle—*máare!*' echoed Claim. 'Father, tell her!'

Their mother said something in Mandan, causing the boys to snicker.

'What does your mother say?'

'She says the rock is stupid!'

Wounded by the remark, he grumbled to Bjornson as they relaxed in the hall. 'She judges it a foolish waste of time.'

'Hannah says the same.'

He frowned. 'And your Buffalo Bird?' he asked Pinch, who pored over a hand of cards.

'She is of the same, womanly opinion. As am I—of the manly kind.'

'No doubt you would sing a different tune if a card game were held atop!'

'Whistle,' Pinch said, peering at the cards.

'What?'

'Surely the proverb, if it be such, is to "whistle a different tune", is it not?'

'Sing or whistle, what care I?'

'No matter, then.' Pinch returned to the cards, humming to himself.

The following day, he went over the side again to begin marking the rock face. The plumb-bob method recommended by Courtois proved invaluable for the purpose, the markings made on the plaster template transferring easily and accurately to the sister apparatus he had erected on the rock. He carefully marked the eyes, the nostrils, the mouth and jaw, taking the entire day to do so.

'When will you start carving, Father?' asked Prospect.

'When all is in readiness. You must first shoot the buffalo before you take the robe.'

Prospect grimaced, his expression saying, *Sufferation, I knew that!*

The following day Boundless had worked his way across to the right-hand side of the granite face when a distant movement caught his eye. 'Buffalo ahoy!' He blew a piercing blast on the whistle.

Throughout the following week, the great spring migration continued as the sea of brown washed ever closer. Dangling high above the grass, he watched the buffalo swell in numbers so great that the rock seemed in danger of submersion by the noisy, bellowing multitudes.

'Secure the horses!' he shouted as the musky stink of buffalo befouled the air.

He watched Prospect scurry to calm the stock as the boys fired muskets and waved blankets to ward off the encroaching mass. He blew the whistle. 'Winch me up!'

Islanded on the rock, they watched as the buffalo swarmed around the base, spooking the horses where Prospect had tethered them to the wagon.

'By hookery, but they are thick!' Prospect paced back and forth, agitated in his eagerness to shoot a dozen or so. The cacophony of grunts and roars was deafening on the air, the great buffalo tide washing over the entire plain for as far as they could see.

In spite of his reluctance, they were forced to abandon the rock and 'part the seas' to navigate through the mass as they made their way back to the post.

'They have come to worship!' quipped Pinch when told of the great immersion.

He resigned himself to several days of forced rest until the great herd moved on. In the meantime, he acceded to the pleas of his sons to join them on a buffalo hunt. 'Although it is stretching the truth to call it a hunt,' he admitted to Bjornson. 'Since the beasts are so plentiful one could close his eyes and point the gun in any direction to bring down a fine specimen.'

Despite his attempts to keep an eye on Prospect, the boy managed to steal away to join up with the Mandan, returning two weeks later with a travois loaded with dried buffalo jerky, pemmican, and several fine robes.

'Did I not tell you to stay here?' Irate at his son's wilful disobedience he berated him out in the yard.

Prospect's face fell as his pride in the trove of meat dissipated before his father's displeasure.

'Heck, I wasn't gone long,' he protested, sliding down from the horse in the Indian manner.

'You missed a week of work!'

He was about to admonish further when jubilant cries rent the air as the women rushed up to examine the bounty. Meadow Bird took her son's hand, her eyes bright with pride and pleasure.

Acknowledging her happiness, Prospect flashed a triumphant look at his father, as if to say, *see!*

Frustrated, Boundless turned away, catching a glimpse of Pinch leaning against the hall steps observing, a frown on his face.

The summer heat continued to build, the warm air smothering the plain like a heavy blanket. On certain days, they were forced to abandon the summit altogether when the furnace-like heat made it too dangerous to work. He persuaded his companions to toil for a few hours in the late afternoon and into twilight, the tired workmates sometimes not returning to the post until darkness had set in.

Bjornson remonstrated with him over the dangers of such a practice, protesting that the lengthening shadows made it difficult to determine where the precipice lay. 'One missed foot and we perish!' he exclaimed, forbidding his sons to move about without wearing a safety line.

While Boundless worked the face and Bjornson manned the pulley, Claim and Anders used the pickaxes to remove a layer of granite to enhance the natural fall of the spine. Prospect and Torsten attended to the tail and flanks. Whenever powder was required to blast a stubborn section of rock, Bjornson took over, much to the disappointment of the boys. 'You will blow up half the rock, if not yourselves,' the Swede said, rejecting their pleas to manage the blasting.

Hunting parties of Mandan or Hidatsa stopped by to look on as they worked on the summit or clung to the sides. Once, as they sat resting in the shade, a party of Chippewa from Turtle Lake rode up. The Indians sat their horses while glancing up at the summit, pointing and gesturing.

'Keep the muskets visible,' Boundless cautioned, suspicious of the interlopers. 'Look to the horses.'

The Chippewa chieftain, a scowling fellow with half his face painted in one colour and half in another, watched these precautions, seemingly in two minds. He glanced at the horses, and up at the rock, a glowering look on his face.

'The devil means business,' muttered Bjornson, licking his lips.

'*Voulez-vous monter?*' Doing his best to appear indifferent to the watchful braves, Boundless gestured to the summit. The invitation provoked a surprised silence as the Indian took in his meaning.

'You have challenged him,' cautioned Bjornson.

The Indian gave Boundless a haughty look. Then, with a barked command, he turned the horse and set off back into the grass.

'He was afeared to fall off!' Prospect shaded his eyes to watch as the party rode off into the distance.

'Yellow as anything!'

'Or perhaps he took offence.'

'Offence at what?' Boundless looked at Bjornson

The Swede shrugged. 'Who knows?'

'Chippewa can't shoot for toffee!' declared Claim.

'He was painted the same colour as the woodshed!' said Anders, all four youths collapsing with laughter.

EVEN THOUGH HE HAD carefully calculated the amount of rock to be removed in order to sculpt the features, the sheer difficulty of the undertaking was overwhelming. He abandoned the notion of removing the surplus rock by hand, realising the enormity of the task. Instead, he resorted to the drill-and-blow method that had proven so successful in excavating the summit. Frustrated at first, as every blow of the hammer against the chisel swung the chair off balance, he gradually learned to compensate for the motion by bracing his feet against the rock. But the effort was considerable and placed an unnatural strain on his back and spine.

He quickly shed his earlier, optimistic projections for the length of time required to carve the face. *Not years, but a decade*, he admitted to himself. *If my back doesn't break first or my arms fall off.* At times, as he dangled in a half-circle, memories of his days oaring the shallop came to mind. *What would Thompson, or Cass, make of this?* he wondered, marvelling at the tales he could tell his former comrades. *And what of …?* He frowned to think, knitting his brow. 'Theo! How could I forget?'

One afternoon, he drilled two shallow blasting holes for where the nostrils would be. Packing the holes with powder, he inserted a long fuse, taking the end up with him to the top. Lighting it, he let it drop, hoping the wind would not snuff it out. He watched on his belly as the smoulder crept up the fuse and ignited the powder with a faint bang.

Lowering himself, he muttered in despair at how little impact the explosion had made. Over the following days, he honeycombed the rock with holes as he blew twenty charges in succession in an attempt to transform the face. The boys pestered to take a turn but he refused, adamant in his decision that he, alone, would work the face.

'We are consigned to the arse!' complained Prospect. 'Like buffalo shit!'

One punishingly hot day, they had taken refuge beneath the canvas shelter they had erected at the base of the rock when Anders gave a loud groan. He got to his feet and staggered about like a drunk, his face pale and distressed. As his brother shouted in alarm he collapsed to the grass in a dead faint.

'Anders!' Rushing to his son's aid, Bjornson screamed at his other son to fetch water. As the others gathered around, he dampened a cloth and laid it across his son's brow. Holding the bottle, he tipped water onto the youth's lips. 'Drink!'

Anders mumbled, his eyes glassy, his sunburnt face now dreadfully pale. Suddenly, he vomited, his body gripped by violent spasms. 'Merciful Jesus!' Cradling his son's head, Bjornson looked up at Boundless, his eyes wild. 'We must get him back to the post!'

'Perhaps it were better to leave him in the shade?' Kneeling, Boundless laid a hand against the youth's chest. The heart felt erratic, fluttering wildly.

'Now!' Bjornson stared about him like a man possessed. 'Torsten! Bring the wagon.'

Back at the post, the distressed youth was lifted down as White Deer hovered, beside herself with anxiety. Buffalo Bird Woman took charge, ordering the boys to fill a tub with well water. They immersed the stricken youth, White Deer scooping water onto his brow. Bjornson muttered and railed, alternately blaming himself, 'the cursed rock!' and 'the devil sun!'

Pinch watched grim-faced, shaking his head while eyeing Boundless with a wordless, accusing stare, its import clear.

It was two days before Anders was recovered sufficiently to walk about unaided, his movements slow and careful, his face drawn with exhaustion. The heat stroke sparked furious recriminations from Bjornson, the Swede blaming Boundless and his 'sinful mania' as the cause.

'I did not raise two sons to sacrifice them on your devilish rock!' he snapped as Boundless expressed his regret over the incident.

To appease his companion, Boundless contritely pledged restricted hours, longer rest periods, abundant drinking water, and work cessation at noon on hot days. Bjornson listened to the proposals with a taut indifference that barely acknowledged the concession.

Scorning such limitation for himself or his sons, Boundless resumed the schedule of long, physically arduous days—ignoring the boys' constant complaints and bickering.

Prospect kicked at a chisel, his face rebellious. 'I may as well be a slave!'

'Then go. Be a slave—to the Sioux!' jeered his brother.

'Go yourself!'

'Enough! Prospect, fetch some water. You'—he frowned at Claim—'work over there—away from your brother!'

Pinch, meanwhile, puffed sagaciously, observing matters with a jaundiced eye. 'By Joseph!' he took to saying, varying the expression to 'St Joseph!' and 'Josephus!' whenever Claim or Prospect complained about the unending toil. He trumped himself by declaring Saint Joseph of the Buffalo to be the patron saint of the project.

'Should it not be St Francis?' remarked Bjornson, in a rare moment of amity as Anders continued his recovery. 'Since he is the patron of animals?'

'But the rock is not a creature, as such, despite what Boundless may think.' Pinch deliberated for a few moments. 'St Joseph the Martyr,' he declared, satisfaction in his voice. He looked to Bjornson for understanding. 'What? You do not remember the captive boy? What does Boundless say—a monument?' He frowned over the word. 'A headstone, more like!' He gazed soberly. 'One that shall be inscribed with all our names ere it is done.'

A week after the incident, neither Bjornson nor his sons had returned to the rock, the Swede brushing aside all of Boundless' hints. 'He bible-talks at the boy's bedside,' reported Pinch after a visit. 'The boys will hunt and do work around the fort,' said Bjornson, his ears deaf to argument. 'I will help, as I promised. But my sons?' He shook his head. 'Never again.'

'It was exhaustion from the heat,' Boundless objected. 'It might have happened to anyone of us. What?' he demanded at Pinch's sceptical look.

'That makes two.'

'Two what? What the devil are you talking about?' Pinch shook his head but did not answer.

Prospect and Claim expressed envy at their companions' good fortune, Prospect in particular lamenting his servitude. 'Why didn't I get sick from the heat?' he moaned. 'It sure would beat climbing that pernickity old rock every day!'

## 58

## The Great Devastation

ONE HUMID AND THUNDERY day, they abandoned the rock early and returned to the post under cloud-laden skies. As they approached, they were hailed by an agitated Pinch.

'What is it?' asked Boundless as Pinch advanced to meet them.

'Smallpox!' Pinch cried out.

The word aroused instant alarm. Dismounting, they clustered around to listen as a disturbed Pinch expostulated on 'the great pox' afflicting the Hidatsa and Arikara. 'It has now spread to the Mandan,' he announced breathlessly, his eyes bulging with the news 'Whole villages are wiped out!'

'How do you know?' interrupted Boundless.

'That trapper fellow, the Frenchman, passed by—he didn't come in! He shouted through the gate that the Indians were dying like flies and that he himself was headed upriver to escape the pestilence. Here, see for yourself.' He thrust a note at Boundless. 'The Frenchman delivered this from Ambroise Cloutier.'

Boundless read the note aloud, his voice conveying his dismay as the hastily scribbled contents told of panic and death in the Mandan villages. *The agony is great. Dozens die every day. The afflicted jump into the river or simply lie moaning feverishly until they perish. Do not venture here!*

'Christ preserve us!' Bjornson crossed himself.

'Bar the gate,' said Boundless, his face grim. 'Let no one enter. No one!' he commanded, posting Claim as guard above the gate.

For the next three days, they remained shut up in the post, refusing to admit a party of Cree who demanded to be let in—for what purpose no one was clear.

'Be off! Go away!' shouted Boundless from the rampart. His alarm increased when he noticed one of the party wrapped in a blanket in spite of the heat, the man's face entirely covered. He turned to Prospect. 'Shoot if they attempt to enter!'

'Why do they come here?' asked a worried Anders.

'They seek refuge. Or perhaps, being white men, they imagine we have a cure.'

Meadow Bird and White Deer were beside themselves with worry over the fate of their families in the villages and it was all he and Bjornson could do to restrain the women from riding off to investigate. 'Not now!' he dissuaded a frantic Meadow Bird as she tried to saddle the mare.

'Danger!' he said, taking her hands from the bridle. He pointed to the boys, who had followed him to the stable, their faces drawn with alarm. *'Áakana!* Sick!' he remonstrated, undoing the bridle.

'Mother. You mustn't go.' Prospect spoke to the anxious Meadow Bird in Mandan, rubbing her arm as he did so. The words seemed to reassure, or at least calm her, as she reluctantly allowed Prospect to escort her back to the house, his arm around her waist.

They remained closeted inside the post for the whole of summer, subsisting on their plentiful supplies of food and venturing out only to turn the horses loose to graze. On halfa-dozen occasions, they turned importuning Indians away from the gates, threatening one insistent party with muskets before they would depart.

It was September before the weather cooled and he finally gave in to his wife's insistent pleas to check up on her family.

'Why risk it?' protested Pinch. 'You could get contaged and bring the pox back here with you.'

'I will be careful. I won't touch anyone or anything.'

Bjornson also objected, pointing out that White Deer was just as concerned but understood the risk of venturing into the Indian villages. 'It is foolhardy and puts us all in danger,' he argued.

'I must go, or else Meadow Bird will take off by herself.' He resisted the demands of the boys to accompany them on the visit. 'The danger is too great. I cannot risk it.'

The next day, he sat atop the mustang, an anxious Meadow Bird by his side on the sorrel mare.

'Remember,' he warned, as the others gathered to watch them leave. 'Bar the gate after us. Admit no one until we return.'

The day was mild, the cloud-flecked sky reminding him of his earliest days on the prairie. He glanced at Meadow Bird, who sat the mare without a word, the fear of what they might find rendering her mute with panic.

THE SCENE AT THE main Mandan village was one of utter devastation. The normally thriving settlement was semi-deserted, frightened Indians disappearing back into their lodges as soon as they sighted the visitors. Dozens of bodies lay out in the open, the infected carcasses gnawed by dogs or coyotes. Many of the lodges were smouldering ruins—whether fired deliberately in an attempt to contain the infection or through inattention, he could only guess. A fearful Meadow Bird hurried to her parents' lodge as he attempted to hold her back. The lodge was empty, the fire burned out on the hearth. Before he could prevent her, she had rushed off to her grandmother's lodge.

Abandoning the horses, he hastened after, shouting for her to stop. Ignoring his cries, she entered the lodge. He heard her scream as he followed. Nine or ten bodies lay dead on the ground. Among them he recognised the grandmother, her face swollen with pus-filled abscesses. Her father lay on his back a few feet away next to a blanket-covered body he guessed to be that of her mother.

'Wait!' He grabbed Meadow Bird as she attempted to touch the bodies. 'You can do nothing! We must leave!' He pulled her, struggling and crying, out the door.

A few people had gathered to watch, their faces drawn and fearful. He recognised Shining Hair, his friend's face deathly pale and pock-marked with sores. The Indian said nothing, a dazed expression on his face as if he did not recognise Boundless.

Pulling and pushing the wailing Meadow Bird, he dragged her back to the horses. 'Come, lassie! There is nothing to be done.'

He led off through the wide plaza—once noisy with shrieks and laughter, but now deserted save for dogs wandering among the dozens of dead bodies. They rode along the top of the bluff towards the river. A distraught Meadow Deer moaned in terror at the sight of bloated bodies floating in the water or washed up on the shore. The canoes and bullboats were all missing.

The villages that had stood along the east shore were abandoned, the occupants either dead or having fled—the detritus showing that they had done so in great haste. Taking out the spyglass, he surveyed the empty lodges. To his mind, the devastation on that side seemed even greater, the fire-blackened lodges and unburied corpses mute testimony to the ravages wrought by the plague. He put away the glass. 'We must leave here.'

Meadow Bird, dazed and exhausted, made no protest as he turned the horses for home.

Back at the post, the occupants listened with horrified expressions as he recounted the details of their grim excursion. 'The head village is no more. There is only death to be found there.'

'Cloutier?' asked Pinch.

'I did not see him. But ...' Boundless shook his head, not finishing the sentence.

'It would have struck the other tribes equally hard,' said Bjornson, concerned about White Deer.

'We must stay away from any Indians until this business is done,' ordered Boundless.

'When will that be, Father?' asked Prospect, returned from comforting his mother.

'Who knows? But we must keep to ourselves until we can be sure. Do not worry, your friends are young and capable,' he reassured Claim. 'I am sure they fled ahead of the disease.'

Anders and Torsten said nothing, their faces pale with anxiety.

'Remember. Stay inside the post. Here, we are safe. Out there ...?' He left the sentence hanging.

THE EFFECTS OF THE devastating plague lingered for years afterwards. Throughout the ensuing winter, entire villages perished from starvation as the crops lay ungathered in the fields or buried beneath the snow. The men were too sick or decimated to hunt, the burning of corpses becoming a daily event. Word arrived from Ambroise Cloutier—who had miraculously survived a bout of the disease—that the main Mandan village above the forks had now been abandoned entirely, along with most of the remaining group of villages clustered along the Heart River. The survivors had fled north along the Missouri to form new settlements along the Knife River with their allies, the Hidatsa.

The toll exacted by the pox manifested itself even in the wolves who had feasted on the diseased carcasses. For several winters after, the fur on their bodies was so thin that the pelts were not worth taking. Paradoxically, the buffalo swelled to numbers never before seen, the greatly diminished population of Indians contributing to the increase.

The occupants of the post were not immune, either, to the effects of the outbreak. One morning, Boundless and Pinch were just finishing breakfast when Bjornson entered the hall. Declining Boundless' invitation to sit and take tea, Bjornson remained standing, his expression sombre as he cleared his throat. 'Hannah and I have decided,' he said. 'Our boys are leaving.'

'Leaving? For where?' asked a perplexed Pinch.

'For Montreal.'

'Montreal?' A befuddled Pinch exchanged glances with Boundless. Bjornson remained in place, his stance formal as if delivering a report.

'How will they get there?' asked Boundless.

'We will follow the Missouri to the Mississippi, and from thence across to the Lakes.'

'We?' Boundless could not keep the alarm from his voice.

'Their mother and I will guide them.'

'But you are coming back?'

Bjornson grimaced, his face a study in confliction. 'Yes.' With that, he exited the hall, leaving a dumbfounded Boundless and Pinch in his wake.

Rocked by the announcement, Boundless tried every means over the next few days to dissuade Bjornson but found him immovable on the question. 'What will your boys do?' he asked, appealing to the Swede's paternal instincts. 'They have no knowledge or experience of the world beyond the fort?'

'Which is why they must go,' Bjornson replied, his voice calmer, more reasonable now that he had made his decision. 'I will entrust their care to Mathieu. I will ask him to find them suitable lodgings and an apprentice-ship in a merchant company. In time, they will use my savings to start a business and set up house for themselves. Mathieu will guide and advise them. And in time, also, Hannah and I will join them.'

The reply heightened Boundless' alarm at the unsettling prospect.

'But have you asked your sons if they want to go? Anders is only of an age to my own boys, barely eighteen—and Torsten, younger still.'

'They will be well cared for by Mathieu and will benefit from his com-mercial knowledge and circle of acquaintances.'

'Can you blame him?' asked Pinch, in a rare moment of amity between himself and Boundless. 'Bjorn has never forgiven you for inducing his sons to climb the rock and then almost causing Anders' death through overwork.' He held up a hand as Boundless opened his mouth to protest.

'His words, not mine. Between your buffalo and the pox, he calculates they are safer making the journey back east. But I have no doubt he himself will return. The poor sould considers himself indentured to you and that godforsaken rock.'

Indentured? The word stung, and Boundless spent the morning mood-ily ingesting it as he walked down to the Missouri to collect wood for the fireplace. *He freely gave his oath in exchange for my own. I did not force it from him.* He scooped up an armful of fallen branches, his mind railing against the circumstances that conspired to confound him at every turn. *Perhaps they do not wish me to finish.* If questioned as to the mysterious 'they,' he might have replied the fates, the buffalo spirits, or the sky gods of the Indians. Perhaps he might even have included his own wilful nature, had he but eyes enough to see.

A few days later, the remaining occupants of the stockade gathered on the shore to farewell the family. The canoe was loaded with supplies. Anders and Torsten were already seated, paddles in hand, their faces uncertain as they accepted the good wishes of Prospect and Claim.

Meadow Bird and Buffalo Bird Woman were in conversation with White Deer, the three women exchanging tearful and affectionate farewells.

Boundless shook hands with Bjornson. 'You are certain that I will see you next summer—like the brigade?' he added in an awkward attempt at levity.

'I have said so.' Bjornson's voice was stiffly formal as he stepped into the canoe.

'You look like a *pilote*,' joked Pinch.

White Deer sat beside her husband, picking up a paddle in readiness to depart.

Claim and Prospect waved farewell to their boyhood companions, swearing eternal friendship and vowing to meet up again one day for a 'fine old reunion'.

'Godspeed your journey,' called out Pinch as the canoe drew away from shore.

'Don't get hitched!' Prospect yelled after the dejected Anders.

'Or drowned!'

'Or scalped!' hooted Claim.

For the next several days, Boundles kept a close eye on both his sons, concerned that the loss of their childhood playmates might unsettle them. Prospect seemed especially downcast, oftentimes speculating on where the brothers might be at that moment and what might lie ahead for them. 'I sure do miss Anders,' he said wistfully one evening at the supper table.

His mother gently rubbed his neck, calling him *psáka* or 'frog', her pet name for him in childhood, while offering consoling words in Mandan.

'I guess so.' Prospect, answered. He glanced at his father and continued in Mandan as Boundless tried to pick out the words.

It was the following spring before he felt confident enough to freely greet any Indians they chanced upon while riding to the rock or out hunting, which they did whenever the weather was too wet or too windy to permit scaling the buffalo. The few Indians that they encountered he nevertheless scanned vigilantly for signs of the pox, aware that they were doing the same. The occasional Mandan hunting party gave witness to the severity of the calamity that had befallen the tribe, the hunters being hardly more than boys.

'They are finished—as overlords of the Missouri,' Boundless remarked on his return to the stockade one afternoon. 'My fear is of who will replace them.'

'The Sioux?' guessed Pinch, pushing closed the gate.

'Aye. Unless they have been as badly hit as the Mandan.'

'Is it over?' asked Prospect. 'The pox, I mean?'

'God willing.'

'Do you think the plague runs all the way to the east, Father?'

'I don't know. Maybe.'

Prospect looked towards the Missouri, his face anxious. 'I hope the Bjornsons are safe.'

One damp chilly day in late April, his sons assisted him as he took the rope ladder out of storage and prepared to shoot it over the rock. He examined the ropes carefully, noting the frayed tendrils and a pair of cracked steps.

'It is time to replace it,' he said to the boys. 'Only two left,' he noted.

After taking the morning to stake the new ladder, he paced back and forth in the grass beneath the giant head, shading his eyes as he picked out the nascent nostrils, lips and roughed-out beard. *They need greater prominence*, he noted, hoping he could rely on Bjornson to keep his promise and return. *But mayhap White Deer will convince him to stay in Montreal with the boys.* The thought troubled him as he stepped foot on the ladder.

Up on the summit, he drilled the boys on the operation of the pulley, despite their protestations that they had assisted, indeed, taken over the duty from Bjornson in the past.

'Which one of you shall wear the whistle?' he asked, holding it out.

'I will!' Claim snatched the string.

'Work together, for God's sake!' he warned as they lowered him over the side. The bosun chair abruptly halted and then started again. He kicked against the rock face, positioning himself alongside the jaws before blowing the whistle. The chair came to a stop as he gazed out over the plain.

'Father?' Prospect was on his belly, looking down from above.

'Hold it there!' The chair turned in the breeze and he looked into the distance for a moment. He then returned his gaze to the paint marks indicating the facial features, mentally joining the marks into a distinctive face. He took up the mallet and chisel to drill small bore holes. *I miss his companionship, his steadiness.* Carefully placing the point of the chisel, he tapped the head, pinpointing the blast hole.

Within minutes, he was lost in the work.

In the absence of their boyhood companions, and with only the stultifying tedium of the pulley to operate, his sons quickly became bored, squabbling endlessly and complaining about the 'wasted hours' atop the rock. His efforts to invest them in the project by asking their advice—and even permitting them to dangle over the precipice and remove some marked rock—did nothing to assuage their increasing resentment at being forced to spend the long summer days marooned high above the prairie grass with its tempting abundance of game.

Prospect, in particular, was unwilling to sacrifice buffalo hunting with his Mandan companions and one day stole away before first light to join up with his friends at their new village on the Knife River.

'Do you think to come and go at your pleasure?' Boundless remonstrated upon his son's return from the extended visit. 'We labour and sweat while you go off merrily chasing buffalo!'

'I guess I'm fed up to the teeth with that pernickerty old rock!'

'You will do as you are told!' He glared at his son, ignoring remonstrances from Meadow Bird who had come out to investigate the row. 'No more running off to hunt—not for the rest of the summer? Do you hear?'

Meadow Bird said something and he held up his hand to silence her as he confronted his rebellious son. 'Do you understand? Answer me!'

'I hear you.' Prospect went over to unhitch the travois, muttering under his breath.

'What do you say?' He rounded on the boy.

'I guess it's your rock, not mine!' Prospect's voice was tight with defiance.

'No matter! Do as I say—no more running off to please yourself.' He turned away, only to encounter the hovering Meadow Bird. 'Do you yet stand there?' He pushed past her and into the cabin.

Prospect's face was suffused with anger, tears falling as he struggled to undo the travois poles. Meadow Bird bent to assist. 'It is alright, Mother. I can do it.' Gently, he took her hand away from the pole. 'I hate that blamed rock!'

'*Psáka,*' she said softly, taking his hand in her own.

He sniffled and wiped his eyes. '*Psáka,* Mother.'

With a grave smile, Meadow Bird touched his cheek. She regarded him for a long moment, her brown eyes soft with affection. As she turned to go back indoors, he called out after her. '*Mihúus.*' He touched a hand to his breast. She looked back fondly before stepping inside.

The next morning, Boundless waited for Prospect to join him out in the yard. He sat the horse, irritable that Prospect was nowhere to be seen. Indeed, the youth had missed breakfast, something unusual in itself—unless he had stolen away again to hunt. Half suspecting this to be the case, he despatched Claim in search of his brother. 'Shake him if he's still asleep!'

Minutes later, Claim returned, breathless. 'He's gone!'

'Gone? Gone where?'

'His things, too.' Claim held up a scrap of paper, an agitated look on his face. 'He left this.'

Boundless' brow furrowed as he scanned the three-sentence note: 'Have gone east south—to St Louis. Do not follow—my mind is made up. Say sorry to mother and father. Signed, Prospect.'

He sat for a long moment, staring at the words. 'Did you know of this?'

Claim shook his head, increasingly agitated. 'No. But he went, by golly!'

With a heavy sigh, Boundless climbed down from the saddle. 'I must tell your mother. Turn the horses out to graze. There will be no work this morning.'

He halted before entering the quarters, his hand on the door. Taking a deep breath, he pushed it open.

## 59

## A Smiter of Rock

I N THE YEARS FOLLOWING Prospect's departure, news of his son reached him just twice: a vague report passed along from mouth-to-mouth via fur trappers; and a creased, water-stained letter carried by a trapper and dated a year earlier:

*Dear Father and Mother. I am in St. Louis. I shoot buffalo for a bunch of Spanish. The pay is good. Tell Claim I am married now. Her name is Annabelle. I am in good health. Mother, I hope you are keeping warm in the winter. Father, are you done with that rock yet? Your loving son, Prospect.*

Meadow Deer cherished the meagre words, insisting he read them again and again. She then tenderly folded the faded paper and tucked it inside her tunic.

'*Psáka,*' she murmured, her voice filled with longing.

In the lantern light, her face was warm and smooth, her skin unscrimmed by age. Only her eyes and a certain tiredness around her mouth betrayed the passage of years. Her movements were slower, more studied, and she took rest more often. Her hair, once glossy black, was now threaded with grey. She spent most of her time in the company of White Deer—herself of matronly proportions, the slim girlish figure now rounded and fleshed out. If the two resembled sisters in their closeness, Buffalo Bird Woman represented the beloved and giggling matriarch, teased and showered with affection in equal measure.

The three women formed the beating heart of the post, their union the vine that nurtured and bound its occupants in tendrils of familial duty, sureness and recognition. The men, by contrast, had grown increasingly isolated from each other and themselves, as if baffled by their own silences and uncertain purchase on the passing days. During supper, they sat chewing on their own slow cognitions, acknowledging each other with nods and perfunctory conversation. At times, they engaged in animated differences, as if such oppositional friction was the only way out of a profound and engulfing silence. Of the three, Pinch seemed most willing to emerge spontaneously from his cocoon, the gadfly spirit provoking and pricking his companions from lethargic slumber.

Visitors were rare, the post long since closed to trade. The decimation of the Mandan and the absence of the brigade belied the bustling activity of a time when the post was a thriving hub for Indian trade parties. The occasional itinerant hunter or trapper provided what news there was of the greater world, although that, too, seemed more distant and irrelevant with each passing year.

The garden supplied most of their needs, the harvest supplemented by fish and the fresh meat delivered by Claim once each week. Shortly after the departure of his brother, and the return of Bjornson, the remaining son quit the rock, professing to be 'heartily sick' of climbing it each morning. He since spent most of his time in the Mandan camps, becoming more Indian with each passing year. Boundless had argued the decision, insisting that his son's labour was indispensable. But the youth was adamant. 'It's about done, anyway,' he said.

'Not so! The details remain. There are a thousand things—' Boundless paused, recognising the stubborn look on the youth's face. *He minds me of myself. He will not alter.* 'Remember to visit,' he said, his voice grudging. 'Your mother will miss you.'

The only matters to trouble their isolation were occasional rumours of fresh outbreaks of the pox, or the occasional, yet ominous, reports of continuing Sioux depredations as the Lakota established hegemony over the region. The tribes fought several pitched battles, the desperate Mandan and their Hidatsa allies combining to deter the relentless Sioux advance. But the toil taken by smallpox and unremitting warfare had fatally weakened the former overlords. An uneasy peace treaty, brokered by the Arikara, was punctuated by the incursion of Sioux war parties as the Lakota continued to seek dominance.

Safe in their grassy remoteness, the inhabitants of the post felt little cause for alarm, the Sioux seemingly unaware of their existence. The stockade itself was increasingly derelict, the unused buildings long since fallen into disrepair. He no longer bothered to replace worn sections of the palisade, restricting his efforts to the maintenance of the living quarters and the smithy. The storehouse roof had fallen in three winters before, the wrecked timbers stark testament to its former importance. The bunkhouse and the row houses were similarly neglected, the wind blowing through holes in the walls and rain falling through the broken roofs. The dog pen was no longer in use, the few surviving dogs kept as watch dogs and quasi pets.

*If Guillaume should see it now.* The thought crossed his mind as he idly surveyed the stockade from the open doorway of his quarters on a late February morning. The weather was cool and grey, the air flecked with snow. He saw the hall door open and Pinch emerge onto the steps, pipe in hand, a blanket around his shoulders. He watched as the other man, now increasingly frail and irascible, dragged the rocker up behind him and sank into it. The two maintained civil but frosty relations, the rift opened by their constant disagreements now an unbridgeable distance between them. On occasion, he made half hearted attempts to mend the quarrel, the latest being an invitation for Pinch to come and view the much-changed rock in the summer. The offer was vehemently rejected.

'Why the blazes would I?' Pinch stabbed the air with his pipe, his voice testy at the notion. 'It's still the same, blamed-fool rock, isn't it? Or has it changed into a buffalo and galloped off?'

As he watched, the door opened again and Bjornson ventured out to join Pinch. The two sat side by side, with only the occasional word passing between them. The Swede was thin and grizzled, and increasingly plagued by stiffness of the joints, which he blamed on the years spent climbing and kneeling on the hard granite.

Boundless knitted his brow at the thought. *It has taken a toll—on all of us.* Hearing Meadow Bird call, he went back indoors, mentally tallying the weeks before the weather permitted work to resume once more.

SPRING ARRIVED IN A great bloom of grass. The days grew warmer and longer as swooping gales chased giant shadows across the bluffs. He felt the winter lethargy drain from his bones as he saddled the horse. Whistling for his favourite dog, he set off at a brisk pace, relishing the fresh spring morning. Quail whirred up at his approach. A fluttering of butterflies rose up from the purple coneflowers. The dog loped alongside, racing off to chase a ground squirrel or bark at a prairie chicken. A herd of antelope took fright and bounded off through the grass, their short tails flicking. He passed a fresh wallow and saw wisps of buffalo wool clinging to the grass.

A few miles from the post, he drew rein on a hillock. A fierce elemental pride overtook him as he feasted his eyes on the stone colossus that was the object of his excursion. The Vitruvian rock rose stubbornly above the rippling, grassy sea. The majestic head faced imperiously west, indomitable in its solitary grandeur. Amidst the blustery amphitheatre of grass and sky, the stone gleamed with a vermilion splendour that caused his heart to leap. *Surely, even Pinch would crumble before such a sight!*

Walking the horse, he rode about the buffalo in a great circle, viewing it critically from every angle. The forequarters, meticulously contoured into the granite ribs, stood out in striated relief against the rock. He rounded the tail—coming back into view of the bulbous overhanging head. Riding into its shadow, he looked up at the intricately fashioned brow. The giant features were framed in a wiry bundle of nocks and ridges, which, softened by the blowing sunlight, resembled nothing more than the woolly coat they were painstakingly etched to evoke.

He acknowledged to himself that extracting the buffalo from his thoughts had been as troublesome as dredging it out of the rock, the idea-buffalo as elusive as its rock counterpart. *I saw it so plainly once—before it was begun. And now it is almost finished.* Even as the thought occurred, he recognised its falsity. *Not so that it lives and breathes!* He sat for long minutes drinking in the bestriding beast before turning the horse and heading back to the post.

He had dangled over the face all morning, attempting to flare each nostril with the stone drill. He stopped for lunch, after which he and Bjornson had taken a stroll around the rock. The June air was pleasingly warm, fanned by a breeze that kept away midges and mosquitoes. They had rounded the head again when they saw dust rise up in the distance. As they stared, they observed a party of Indians headed in their direction.

'Sioux!' Bjornson uttered a cry of alarm and made to rush back to where they had left the muskets at the foot of the ladder on the far side of the rock.

'Wait! There is no time.' Boundless reached out a hand to restrain his companion as shrill cries sounded above the noise of pounding hooves. 'Show no fear! They have no cause to harm us.'

The Indians drew rein in a shower of mud and dust, their horses panting and snorting. The braves appeared in a state of excitement as they milled about on their sweaty, snuffling mounts. They were clad only in breech-clouts, their bodies glistening in the sun. To his surprise, they showed little or no interest in either himself or Bjornson, seeming to have eyes only for the rock. Talking volubly among themselves, they stared up at the buffalo, looks of amazement on their faces.

'Are they Sioux?' Bjornson was pale with nerves as the fierce riders shifted and stepped around them.

'Cheyenne, I suspect. Be calm. They intend us no harm.'

One of the warriors nudged his horse towards them. '*Hotóá'e,*' he said, addressing Boundless.

He shook his head. *'Ia.* I do not understand.'

The Cheyenne regarded him closely. *'Né-tónésevéhe?'*

Even though the look was piercing, the voice was curious rather than hostile. The Indian was burned almost to the colour of bark, his body rank with dirt and sweat. After a long moment, he turned and gestured to his companions, who slid down from the horses. To Boundless surprise, the chieftain offered him a hide pouch filled with warm water. *'Hahó!'*

He accepted the drink—aware that he was the object of intense scrutiny by the Indian.

The Cheyenne lingered, wandering up and down the rock and poking the granite as if to satisfy themselves of its solidity. One made an exaggerated spearing motion that drew boisterous laughter from his companions. Another pretended to scoop the side of the rock, placing his hand to his mouth. The chieftain and another warrior stood back in the grass, conferring in solemn tones as they gazed up at the giant head.

'What the devil do they want?' whispered Bjornson in his ear.

He shook his head, as baffled as his companion. 'You know how superstitious Indians are. Perhaps they see it as …'

'As what?' Bjornson eyed him. 'As what?' he demanded.

'Nothing. Just a buffalo. A totem, perhaps.'

After much gossiping among themselves, the Indians made ready to depart. Before leaving, the chieftain looked up one more time at the buffalo, an expression of mingled puzzlement and—something else, on his face. He seemed as if about to say something, but instead turned his horse. *'Aiii!'* With a trilling cry, he led the Cheyenne back into the grass.

'Thank God!' Bjornson heaved a sigh of relief.

'Did they ride here especially to see it?' Boundless asked, wondering if the buffalo's existence was now common knowledge among the tribes.

'More like they were passing and happened to see its shape.'

Over supper, they mentioned the incident to Pinch. 'Cheyenne?' Pinch grimaced and fished a piece of gristle from his teeth. 'They are allied to the Sioux. Let us pray that *those* gentlemen do not come calling.'

Back in his quarters, Boundless stared into the fire, recalling each detail of the encounter. They saw something—something Bjornson refuses to see. The chieftain … what was it he wanted to say?

He saw the Indian's face as he looked up at the buffalo, an aspect almost of reverence shading the savage countenance. It reminded him of something—his own response when viewing the ancient rock figures on the canyon walls all those years ago as he rode through the narrow defile with

Mose. The pale, ghostly etchings had evoked the same speechless amazement that confounded the Cheyenne!

He took in a sharp breath at the realisation, humbled and prideful at the same moment. The original artisans were nameless, their authorship lost to time, swept away by the dust of centuries. He pondered the fact, perturbed at the thought. A log cracked on the fire, sending up a shower of sparks. He sat absorbed in thought until brought back to himself by Meadow Bird calling him to bed. Getting up, he poked at the glowing embers, mentally inscribing his name upon the ashes. *A headstone, Pinch had said. Well then, let it be so!*

As winter snows once again closed in around the post, a letter—a full eighteen months in conveyance—arrived from Torsten and Anders. The missive, carried by Cree hunters paid with muskets for their trouble, described marriages, children, and a thriving grain business jointly managed by the brothers. It also included compliments to Boundless from Mathieu, now the head of Montreal's largest export house.

> *M. Courtois passed away four years ago. I met him occasionally on the street, and each time he enquired to as the progress of your 'buffalo', as Anders describes it. He showed the greatest interest in the project and lamented the impossible distance that kept him from examining it with his own eyes.*

He ruminated on the words as he snowshoed back and forth between the buildings after supper. Bjornson no longer accompanied him on these rambles, his erstwhile walking companion preferring to sit before the fire with White Deer while reading aloud from Genesis—the book she preferred above all others, declared a proud Bjornson. He pulled the robe tighter around him as he passed the canoe shed. The building was as rundown as the others. Inside, the last norther lay in waterlogged decay.

Returning to the warmth of his quarters, he blew on his frozen hands. Meadow Bird sat before the fire wrapped in a blanket, fast asleep. Wishing he had a glass of brandy, he sat down at the table and took out the quill case, intending to write a reply to Mathieu. After considering the contents, he set down the quill. *Who knows but we are all dead ere the reply?*

In January, a raging storm blew down a section of the palisade facing the river. Long since rotted, the timbers tore away with a loud groaning noise that sent his rudely awakened senses reeling back to the almost-forgotten *Patience*. The next day, he and his two companions investigated the damage. Through the blown-down portion of the stockade they could see the Missouri, little more than a stone's throw away.

'The place is falling down about our ears.' Pinch pulled the blanket tighter around his body, shivering in the cold.

'We cannot replace it, at least not until summer.' Boundless surveyed the fallen timbers, rueful at the thought of the cost in time and labour to repair the damage.

'To hell with it.' Pinch turned away. 'My innards are frozen.'

He followed, walking alongside Bjornson. 'We are knocked down, too,' said the Swede. 'Like that fence.'

That night, he tossed restlessly, beset by a vivid dream. He was clinging to the shrouds, witnessing the turbulent waters in the aftermath of the near disaster at sea. In his ears, a voice—stormy with the wrath of prophecy—trumpeted from the roiling deep. He strained to hear as the sounding echo splashed up over the Chesapeake and across the woods and endless grasslands to wash around where he stood beneath the great buffalo, dressed in leggings and wrapped in a robe. He looked on helplessly as the sea, the grass and the rock itself spumed up great gouts of mud and stone as the sky dazzled with fire. He gasped for breath, choking sounds coming from his throat.

'*Nitéwena?*' Meadow Bird was shaking him by the shoulder, urging him awake. He opened his eyes, his lungs gulping for air. She peered at him, a frightened look on her face. '*Nitéwena?*' she repeated, her eyes wide.

'I am me. It's me. Go back to sleep.' He pulled the robe up over her and lay back, breathing heavily as the wind gusted and the timbers groaned.

LONG SMITTEN WITH THE splendour of the grasslands in summer, he had but lately awakened to a stark beauty in the monochrome landscape that dominated the long months between October and March. '*Tis plainsong to the polyphony of summer,* he wrote. As the weather improved, he went on solitary snowshoe walks along the Missouri, stopping every so often to sit down on a log, his breath wreathing in the cold air. *I am old.* The awareness perplexed and frightened him. He stared at the chunks of ice carried on the Missouri stream, his mind counting up the years since his arrival at the post. A wave of restlessness, or longing, swept over him.

An image came to his mind—of Mose gazing down the Valley turnpike, the trapper's eyes misted over with contemplation of his youthful self venturing up the same pike decades before. A gust of wind swept the trees along the river and he shivered. Seized by a manic urge, he stood up and shuffled the steps of a clumsy reel, stumbling and almost falling over in the snowshoes. Wheezing and spluttering, he bent over for breath. 'Jinks!' Abashed at his own foolishness, he started off back to the post, bedeviled by the erratic impulse to jig.

He accompanied Claim on a hunt, watching ruefully as a misfire sent an unsuspecting elk bounding away through the snow. 'I am back to the beginning,' he said, drawing a mystified look from his son.

'Come, Father. Let us follow the tracks. He cannot get far in this snow.'

He followed, ruminating on past and present lives.

WINTER GRUDGINGLY GAVE WAY to spring. Eager to stand back up on the rock, he harried Bjornson into joining him even while hard snow still glimmered in the shade.

'What is the hurry?' Bjornson protested, grumpy at the resumption of toil and the end of his winter peace.

'Do you not feel the lively day?' He tugged at his friend's arm. 'Come. The ride alone will do us the world of good!'

The repaired rope ladder, the last of the supply ordered from Montreal, had been left up over the winter—the effort of taking it down and setting it up again judged too laborious in the absence of Claim. He mounted the wood rungs with growing anticipation, checking the rope supports along the way. Hauling himself up onto the rock, he was grateful for the additional step Claim had added. He turned to lend Bjornson a hand up, noting the other man's laboured breaths. *We creak, both of us, like these steps.*

They trudged up the spine together, each man toting a haversack containing food and water. Bjornson had dispensed with the safety line some years before. 'If it has not blown me off by now, then perhaps it has given up trying,' he had said with stoic fatalism.

The hump rose up before them and they scrambled up the incline. A small rock spire protruded just above the granite on the right side of the head, and it was to this that he turned his attention. He frowned at memory of the Herculean labours required to wrest from the implacable granite this crowning glory of the head. He had spent one entire summer painstakingly chipping away the background stone to raise the horn in a manner illustrated in his single text. Although the bulk of the horn had been carved in relief, he had taken advantage of a small natural spur to form a projecting tip, which rose mere inches above the head.

Exhausted and grimy with dust and sweat, they descended the ladder and stood in the grass to look up at the result. 'Can you see it?' he asked Bjornson, anxious for a favourable verdict.

Bjornson nodded, staring up while shading his eyes. 'It stands out against the stone.'

'And you see the tip?'

'Barely.' Sensing Boundless dismay, he added, 'But yes, I see it.'

The left-hand side of the head had proven more problematic, the absence of a second fortuitous spur rendering the goal of symmetry impossible to attain. To achieve a free-standing tip or point, parallel to its twin on the right, he was forced to gouge into the top of the head, risking a lop-sided effect and ruining the lines he had been so careful to achieve.

'If only I could sew the pieces together like hides,' he grumbled, rueful of the fact.

As the head slowly took final shape, he was frustrated by several critical deficiencies in the stone—a defiantly stubborn outcrop, an inconvenient crack, a chunk of 'wool' that broke off under a blow from the hammer. The forced adjustments to his design gave him several sleepless nights as he digested each new reminder of imperfectability. *It's the buffalo*, he concluded, *asserting itself.* His frustration reached new heights when a section of the brow split off and he was forced, cursing and raging, to reshape the entire forehead.

'You will kill yourself,' Bjornson warned, concerned at his exhausted state.

'I am as a blade of grass against this rock!'

Surrender came in a pre-dawn revelation that roused him from a tormented sleep—the faint light flickering an awakening in his drowsy soul. *Mayhap I am but a hand—an instrument within some greater design.*

The tantalising notion confounded him for days as he wrestled with the import. *Does the buffalo reside in the stone—or within my own soul?* He dismissed such fanciful notions as a product of his feverish race to finish. Nevertheless, he continued toiling with a new humility, grudgingly accepting that the stubborn irregularities in the granitic beast were as organic to its physical being as the lumps, bruises and scars of his own body.

He had reserved the eyes for last, aware that they were key to the success of his creation. 'They must *look*,' he repeatedly told himself, beset by indecision as to how to achieve this. He made numerous models from tallow and Missouri clay, etching and gouging—and finally breaking the copies in frustration. He shot a buffalo for the purpose of close study of the eyes and cranium. *How the deuce do they see?* he wondered, cutting away the matted hair to better observe the black orbs. Using the skinning knife, he pared away the flesh to reveal the bones and eye socket, mopping up the blood to better see the hollow that held the glassy ball.

'You concern yourself with what can hardly be seen!' To make the point, Bjornson squinted up from where they stood in the grass.

'Why waste time on something that only the birds will notice?'

'They must see,' answered Boundless, stubborn in his conviction.

'Merciful Jesus! See what?' Scolding and grumbling, Bjornson strode off into the grass.

Consulting his sole reference work, he studied the tiny illustration of a Greek head. Liking the far-seeing gaze imparted by the blind eyeballs, he decided there and then on the solution.

To achieve the desired effect, he laboured incessantly throughout a long, scorching summer, suspended high above the grass. He chiselled a rounded surface to represent the eyeball using lumps of sandstone to polish the granite to as smooth a finish as the stone would permit. In spite of the hat tied under his chin and a dampened neckerchief to protect his neck, he endured burning heat each day as the sun moved out of the shadow of the rock. For the hottest part of the day, he had Bjornson winch him up so that they could drink water and rest in the shade. Later, as the sun moved west of the rock, Bjornson let him down again to continue.

After weeks of arduous toil, cramped hands and sore muscles plagued him as much as the heat. On a particularly unbearable afternoon, he signalled for Bjornson to winch him back up to the top earlier than expected.

'Let us see the result from the ground,' he said, wiping the sweat from his brow. 'I have done all that I can.'

After several rounds of the head, viewing it critically from different angles, he deferred to the judgement of Bjornson that the effect was, indeed, striking.

'It will do,' he conceded, noting where the light reflected on the polished eyeball. He flexed his cramped hands, secretly pleased at the effect. The buffalo stared blindly into the distance, the gaze lending a presence that elevated the creature out of the rock tomb.

'Why spend so much time on them?' asked Bjornson, both irritable and curious. 'They were sufficient a week ago.'

'It was for me,' he said, uncertain himself of what he meant.

Thus, chaperoned by doubt, fostered by indecision, he slowly and painstakingly completed the head and, in so doing, finally exorcised the fabulous beast that had stalked his thoughts since the second day of his landing in the New World over three decades earlier.

On a suffocatingly hot day, twenty years after first charting the woolly behemoth, he stood back in the grass, hands sore and blistered, eyes reddened by dust, to survey the sum of his immense labours. He sank to his knees, his limbs trembling. *It is done.* Overcome with sensations, he lay flat on his back in the grass, arms spread out, his mind too exhausted for triumph. *It was stone, and now is made flesh.* He looked up at the high, steepling clouds. Do they notice anything different as they look down—a strange beast where none was before? He indulged the fantasy for several minutes, picturing himself a bird eyeing the fantastical creature from the heavens. *It will outlast the birds, myself—perhaps even the grass.* Bjornson called to him and he got to his feet, his eyes full of the buffalo where it rose up in imperishable splendour against the cloud-turreted sky. *A monument not to faith, but to reason*, he fondly imagined. *A symbol of the republic, hewn from rock as America was hewn from battle.*

The following morning, he had Bjornson lower him over the face for one last time. He scooted over to the right to survey the granite eye. He then kicked his way across to its companion. *They are finished. Leave them be.*

Blasting the whistle, he waited as Bjornson winched him back up to the top.

'Well?' Bjornson looked at him expectantly as he took off the leather harness.

'Let us move down to the flanks.'

'It is getting hot. Let us rest for a while.'

He wiped an arm across his brow, suddenly fatigued. 'As you say,' he agreed.

'Is it finished?'

The question surprised him. 'Aye,' he admitted. 'But for some smoothing and polishing.'

'Let the weather smooth and polish it. It will do a better job than we can. And it can take as long as it likes.'

He mulled the thought, his mind projecting to the future. *Bjorn is right*, he conceded, both elated and depressed as he contemplated the buffalo, *his* buffalo. *It will gaze into the sunset a thousand years hence. When I am dust as if I had never been.*

## 60

## And the Trumpet shall Sound

THEY WERE RETURNING TO the post when they spotted smoke in the distance. Alarmed, they spurred the horses—arriving to find several buildings on fire. Flames rose up from the burning logs as thick billowing smoke drifted across the yard. Leaping down from the horse, Boundless grabbed the musket and raced for his quarters while shouting out Meadow Bird's name. Bjornson followed, calling urgently for White Deer. Both quarters were empty. They checked Pinch's house and found the door open and chairs turned over as if the occupants had abandoned it in a hurry.

'The hall!' He ran for the burning building, Bjornson at his heels.

The rear of the hall was as yet untouched by flames and they made entry there. Coughing at the smoke, they made out two bodies lying on the floor, one a woman.

'Meadow Bird!' He ran forward in a panic.

The body was that of Buffalo Bird Woman, her tunic drenched in blood. She had been scalped, the hair and skin peeled back from her forehead. Pinch lay a short distance away, a shocked look on his face. He too had been scalped and the ears hacked from his head. His breeches were pulled down—the gruesome wound testifying to the attackers' savage intent.

Pulling the mutilated bodies from the burning cabin, they left them lying in the grass while they went in search of Meadow Bird and White Deer. They searched from building to building, dreading each moment that they would come across the mutilated remains. But there was no sign of the women, or the attackers. They came across the corpses of several of the dogs. Wolf, his favourite, lay with lips drawn back in a snarl, an arrow through his neck.

Calling and shouting, they continued the search.

'The Sioux have taken them!' Bjornson cast about frantically. 'We must go after them!'

Suddenly they heard a shout. Both women hurried towards them, their faces harrowed with fear. He embraced his wife, his voice breaking with relief. 'Thank God you are safe!'

From the frightened women they learned details of the murderous attack. Meadow Bird and White Deer had been tending the garden. Unusually, the stockade gates had been left open, the fact that the rear portion of the palisade had collapsed contributing to the negligence. The women heard shouts and then a scream. They were about to hasten back to the yard to investigate when they heard the shrill whoops of a war party. Terrified, they took refuge behind a building. From there they watched in terror as Pinch and Buffalo Bird Woman—caught out in the open—ran desperately for the shelter of the main cabin as Sioux warriors roamed about the yard. The women watched in horror as the shrieking Sioux set fire to the hall before rushing inside. They heard a shot followed by furious shouts and a bloodcurdling scream.

Fearful for their lives, the two women abandoned their hiding place even as the Sioux wandered through the stockade, searching for other occupants. Fleeing via the collapsed back fence, they took refuge among the trees along the river. From this hiding place they watched as the Sioux showed sudden signs of alarm before hurriedly abandoning the attack.

*They must have seen us coming.* A sombre glance from Bjornson confirmed his suspicion.

The smell of smoke and burned wood filled the air as Meadow Bird and White Deer wept bitter tears over the body of their 'mother'. They dressed the body in fresh clothes, after which they sat by it, wailing and cutting themselves. They continued thus for the remainder of the day and the whole of the next, refusing to eat, and chopping off locks of hair in their grief.

Finally, Boundless intervened. 'We must bury them,' he insisted, worried lest the Sioux return.

Arming themselves with muskets, he and Bjornson carried both bodies outside the stockade and laid them in the grass. He turned to look at Meadow Bird, afraid she would insist on erecting a burial scaffold for Buffalo Bird, in the manner of her people. Rather to his surprise, she made no protest in her grief.

Scratching his chin, he tried estimating where Quoi and the departed *voyageur* might lie. *It was foolish not to blaze a notch in the wall.* Agreeing on a spot with Bjornson, he took turns digging a grave while the other stood watch. The entire time, the two women knelt by Buffalo Bird, wailing and chanting in lamentation. Before lowering the bodies into the joint grave, he laid a square of cloth over each face—wincing at the frozen expressions. The women stooped to pluck handfuls of prairie crocus and knots of grass, which they tenderly scattered over the bodies. Sweating in the sun, he began to spade earth over the corpses.

Throwing the last spadeful of earth, he glanced at Bjornson. 'Will you read a verse? I think Pinch might have liked it.'

Bjornson took out his Bible and turned the pages. Stopping at a passage, he cleared his throat and read aloud in a sombre voice: '*For the trumpet shall sound, and the dead shall be raised, imperishable.*' The words lingered on the wind as both men stood with bowed heads. The women's faces were etched with grief as they clutched each other for support. They maintained a vigil until sunset while he and Bjornson sat waiting in the grass, muskets by their side.

In the wake of the assault, the post was deathly silent. The one surviving dog wandered forlornly from spot to spot, sniffing for his lost companions. The smell of smoke and charred wood hung heavily in the air—the wreckage of the burned-out hall continuing to smoulder for days. Boundless made several scouts of the surrounding grass, searching for any signs that the Sioux had returned. But he found no trace, the war party apparently content, for the moment, with the scalps they had taken.

A few days after the attack, Claim galloped up to investigate, having heard of the incident from some Arikara allies of the Sioux. Relieved to find both his parents alive, he urged Boundless to abandon the post altogether and move, along with Bjornson and White Deer, to the safety of the Mandan camp on the Knife River.

'At least there you will have protection,' he argued, baffled and upset at his father's refusal. 'Is it that cursed rock that keeps you here?'

Boundless grimaced at the remark. 'We are used to our home. Besides, I doubt that the Sioux will return. They must have richer pickings elsewhere.'

'They are savages. They will not hesitate to murder you and Mother should they come back.'

He touched the musket stock. 'If they return, they will find us waiting.'

'It is Mother you must think of.'

'I do.' He frowned. 'And she is better off here. She has Bjorn and I to protect her.'

Claim sat the horse, his face showing his unhappiness. 'Be it on you, then,' he said.

Meadow Bird came forth to bid her son farewell. He leaned down from the saddle to touch her cheek. '*Mihúus,*' he said softly. Clasping his hand, she gazed up at him with anguished affection.

Gently, Claim disentangled her grasp. 'I must go, Mother.' Turning the horse, he glanced at his father. 'Remember, she is dependent on you for protection.'

The death of Pinch, for so long his *bête noire,* affected him greatly. Several times a day, he glanced towards the burned-out cabin, half expecting the Bostonian to exit, look around, scratch vigorously, and pull up a rocker—there to sit, puffing and observing, his face crinkled with scepticism at whatever caught his eye. *He was a decent enough fellow. I am sorry we fell out.*

He felt Buffalo Bird Woman's absence just as keenly. Her ready smile, quickly devolving into giggles, and serenely accomplished stewardship of all within the post, left a vacuum that afflicted his wife and White Deer profoundly. In their grief, they became closer than ever, the two forming an indissoluble bond as they darned, tanned or cooked, each taking consolation from the nearness of the other. Watching with envy this instinctive comfort, he grew slowly to resent it, feeling himself an intruder upon their sorrow. *I am of no use to her.*

Bjornson helped him reinforce their separate quarters until they resembled blockhouses. They now took all of their meals together in one of the houses, leaving the one surviving dog roped outside.

'Our brave fort has reduced to this,' he lamented as they stood outside in the dusk before retiring.

Bjornson stared at the horizon, his face gaunt in the twilight. 'We should have left while we had the chance. Now our bones will bleach this wilderness, like poor Pinch.' He went back inside while Boundless was still searching for a reply.

His attempts over the following days to rouse his dejected companion were met with resentful glances or grim-faced silences.

'We should go back to the rock,' he ventured one morning, a week after the attack.

Bjornson stared, horrified. 'Are you mad? The damnable rock is the last thing on my mind. We are needed here.'

'The women will be in no danger. I have scouted for miles. There is no sign of the Sioux. We need only refine a spot here and there. Nothing too arduous.'

'Then go by yourself! I am done with it.' Bjornson stared accusingly. 'If we hadn't been on that perditious rock, we would have been here when the Sioux came.'

The accusation stung, and he went about glum-faced the remainder of that day whilst inwardly protesting his innocence. *Who is to say the Sioux might not have come while we were out for a hunt, or fetching firewood?*

To his astonishment, Bjornson approached a few days later to indicate that he was prepared to return to the rock. 'Maybe we could go back, just to get out of their hair,' he allowed grudgingly.

Boundless stared in amazement at this turnabout. 'What about Hannah?'

Bjornson shook his head. 'She wants me out of her way as she grieves. She has gone back Indian.' He walked away, a tortured look on his face.

The first day back on the rock was a subdued affair, each man keeping his own counsel. They sat in the shade to eat dried venison and cold fried bread. He glanced at the Swede from time to time, but the latter remained sunk in gloom, his thoughts clearly elsewhere.

'What is it that concerns you, Bjorn?' he asked, breaking the silence. 'Is it Hannah?'

Bjornson mumbled a reply.

'Do you think of your boys?'

'Always.' The Swede chewed listlessly.

Casting about for some means to cheer his companion, he gestured up at the stone flanks. 'See how far we have come? What was a rock is now a buffalo. Flesh, carved from stone.'

Bjornson showed no response to the claim. Indeed, Boundless wondered if the other man had even given ear to it. 'Perhaps we can finish early today,' he said. 'What say you to a fish in the river? A plump sturgeon might please the women.'

Bjornson noisily cleared his throat. 'This summer will be my last,' he announced. 'Next spring Hannah and I will leave to join the boys back east.'

Boundless stared, too taken aback to respond.

'You could come too,' continued Bjornson. 'I know that Meadow Bird wants this. We have discussed it.'

'She has discussed it with you?'

'Not with me. With Hannah. Do not blame her. She has worried for years about you slipping and falling off the rock or injuring yourself in some way. She blames it for Prospect running away.'

The words stung with truth, leaving him unable to reply.

'It is not only the rock, it is the Sioux too, and what happened to Buffalo Bird and Pinch. Women feel these things deeply.'

'She should have said something.'

Bjornson huffed in exasperation. 'You do not see what is in front of you. You have eyes only for your buffalo.'

Flummoxed by the conversation, he brooded on it all afternoon, glancing up to stare at the distance. *If it bothered her that much, then why in blazes didn't she say?* He struck angrily at the chisel. *She blames 'it', he said. Does that mean me? What else does she blame me for?*

As the day wore on, however, and Bjornson's words bored deeper into his conscience, a sense of guilt began to steal over him, displacing the anger he felt. *Am I so blind?* Recalling the look Meadow Bird had given when told of Prospect's departure, he muttered to himself. *Nothing could have kept him here. It was in his nature.*

His mind awash with doubt, he stared at the ochre-coloured stone beneath his hand. *What else could I have done?* The agonies of creation and contrition, arrogance and remorse, coloured one another until, like the specks in granite, all were subsumed into the rock whose dust stung his eyes and parched his throat.

That evening, he took Meadow Bird by the elbow as she went to replenish the fire.

'Lassie,' he began, his voice conciliatory. 'In a year or so—two at the most—it, the buffalo, will be finished.'

'Do you understand?' He signed the meaning. 'Speak to White Deer. Ask her to wait until—' He stopped, shocked at the bitter look on his wife's face.

Several times in the succeeding days, he attempted to revisit the matter, only for Meadow Bird to turn aside, an air of grievance in her manner that stirred up his feelings of guilt and remorse. When he tried to coax her into visiting the rock to view the finished buffalo for herself, she refused as vehemently as Pinch had before her.

'Me have seen many times buffalo!' Her eyes flashed with temper. 'Rock not buffalo!'

'Then have it your own way, woman!' Scowling in frustration, he walked away. It took a quarter-hour of pacing up and down the compound before he calmed himself sufficiently to re-enter the cabin.

The next morning, he rose early, saddling the horse and leaving before she was awake—although he felt sure she watched him leave. He had climbed the rock and was stood on the brow before he saw the thin dust cloud in the distance that signalled Bjornson was following to join him. *At least I may still count on him—for the moment.*

Having announced his decision to quit the buffalo the following spring, the Swede wore a new air of contentment that riled and provoked Boundless in equal measure. The two worked largely in silence except when stopping to confer over some troublesome detail. During a rest spell, Bjornson tried again to persuade him to depart. 'It is past time,' he urged. 'We could go together, if you wish.' He eyed Boundless, a hopeful tone in his voice.

When he did not reply, Bjornson sighed, but did not press the point.

Unsettled by all that had happened, he developed a peevish dissatisfaction with certain sections of the rock—sections long since considered finished. Irascible and indecisive, he went over the carving foot by foot, finding a detail here or a feature there that fell short of his expectations. Displeased with the hump, he insisted on reshaping it, ignoring Bjornson's vehement objections.

'We must shave it down,' he argued. 'It is too pointed. Stand further down the rock and you will see for yourself.'

'But it will be seen from the ground—not from up here!' Bjornson scratched his neck in agitation. 'Did we not measure it a thousand times already?'

An injury to his wrist prevented the contentious reshaping and further depressed his mood. He retreated to the run-down workshop, taking advantage of the forced respite to pore over the original sketches. Comparing them unfavourably to the realised buffalo, he fell deeper into misery. 'It is too … squarish!' he muttered, studying one sketch. 'Too grotesque!' he complained, eyeing another. His mind returned to the shimmering archetypes he had seen etched into the canyon wall so many years before. The contrast with his own amateurish effort drew a despairing groan. Seizing on one particular sketch, he took it to show Bjornson, startling the Swede as he banged impatiently on the door.

'Is it the Sioux?' Bjornson had grabbed the musket in his alarm. White Deer hovered in the background, her face terrified.

'I wanted … spirit, breath, like this.' He thrust the sketch under the confused Bjornson's nose. 'Not to make—' he fumbled for the words, 'a damn cow!'

'Good Lord, man! I thought the Sioux were upon us! And you bring me this!' With a furious stare, Bjornson slammed shut the door.

His dissatisfaction increased when he returned to the rock after a week's absence. 'It is too dull,' he complained, looking up at the edifice. 'The head droops. The eyes are …' his voice choked with disappointment.

'You see only faults.' Bjornson stood next to him, looking up. 'It is like a great cathedral. Men will see the perfect whole, not the imperfect parts. It will make you remembered forever—if that is your wish.'

Humbled and gratified by the words, he turned to his companion. 'As it will you, Bjorn.'

Bjornson pressed his lips, a sombre expression on his face. 'I do not bother my head with such notions. I am content to wither with the grass and to bloom again in Paradise.'

The strained relations between himself and Meadow Bird hardly improved with the onset of autumn. Following supper, he sat before the fire, reading, while she busied herself with domestic chores. His awkward attempts to break the silences that had grown between them were met by a puckered brow or grunts. Rain beating against the window compounded the insularity of the small cabin, so that soon he, too, lapsed into silence, spending as much of the day outdoors as he could.

'I do not know what will make it better,' he confessed to Bjornson. 'Or why she has taken on so.'

'Did you talk to her about what I suggested? I am sure that would raise her spirits.'

'We will not be going with you. At least not for another year or so.' He eyed his companion. 'You and Hannah should stay. That would cheer her up.'

'No.' Bjornson's voice was firm.

'At least until the end of autumn.'

'No!'

'A month or so—at the most! You owe me that!'

'Owe you!' Bjornson turned on him, his face outraged.

'Owe you?'

'I am sorry, Bjorn. That was the wrong word. Forgive me.'

Contrite, he searched desperately for some way to persuade his companion. 'It is your buffalo as much as it is mine. It is so close to being finished. Surely, another summer—the last, I promise you. It is not too much to ask. For our friendship,' he pleaded. 'And the years we have spent together.'

'I thought you said it was finished?'

'And so it is—but for a polish here, a smoothing there.'

Bjornson stared at the snow-covered ground. 'I will give you until the end of May, no more,' he said, his face grim. 'The first day of June, we leave. Not one more day!' With that, he turned and walked away.

As soon as the wet spring allowed, he threw himself into the task with renewed vigour. Throughout the next few weeks, he worked feverishly, driven by a new and fearful sense of mortality. With a feverish thirst to finish, he drove himself—and the exhausted Bjornson—with an energy that recalled his first days on the rock.

'I see it now, in every detail!' he claimed on a day of frantic activity, exhorting his companion to still greater effort.

'For God's sake, let it be!' Irritated beyond endurance, Bjornson threw down the chisel, his face flushed and angry. 'The devil take it!' He turned suddenly and stomped off towards the steps. 'Let me be!' he repeated, his voice shaking with anger as Boundless attempted to follow.

Instantly remorseful, Boundless called out. 'We will take a rest—I promise! Shortly. I will join you! It is just this one last thing.' He gestured to the section he was working on. 'In no more than—' He turned to see Bjornson's head disappear below the rock.

At supper, a still visibly upset Bjornson avoided his gaze. Dining on fresh venison delivered by Claim, the four sat mostly in silence, the women exchanging glances as Boundless made awkward attempts to lift the mood. Following supper, he lingered in his seat as the women sat outside to talk and darn. Bjornson moved his chair nearer the fire and sat there, Bible in hand.

He watched the Swede recite a passage to himself, his mouth working as he read. With the passing years, Bjornson's finely chiselled features, his strong jaw and sharp cheek bones, had softened into something less determinate, less convinced. His blond hair had silvered to grey, the wispy stubble beneath his chin now a full beard.

*What are we but a knot of flesh and bones?* The thought, bitter and oppressive, seared him as he observed Bjornson's head begin to drop. *Would that I could find consolation, as he does.* He watched enviously as Bjornson startled himself back to attention and resumed reading. *I have placed my faith not in words, but in stone.*

The knowledge that even that was insufficient haunted him as June beckoned. The buffalo returned in greater numbers than ever before, the multitudes dotting the bluffs and turning the uplands dark with their numbers. He watched from the rock as Indian hunters moved through the herds on foot, shooting dozens of the beasts at a time, the forays making no impression upon the inexhaustible throng.

The days ticked down as he worked frantically to detail a foreleg into the rock. White Deer began packing items in the cabin and Bjornson spoke eagerly of his desire to see his sons again. 'You should come,' he said, trying once more to lure Boundless into accompanying him.

He muttered in reply, the subject greatly annoying to him—the more so when he caught sight of Meadow Bird tugging White Deer's arm as if pleading with her to stay.

'One more week,' Bjornson reminded him as they made plans to chisel a recalcitrant bulge of rock.

'Fetch the powder,' he said, beginning to drill another hole. 'We must remove this one last piece.' But following the blast, he discovered another 'must', while hectoring his companion to match his efforts. 'The tail lacks detail,' he argued, keeping them up on the rock until sunset. *But one week to June.*

Kneeling back to relieve the strain on his limbs, he stared at his roughened, stone-calloused hands. *They were soft once, and black with ink.* An air of unreality stole over him. He turned his head to see Bjornson labouring over a loose eyebolt. The day was still and cool. In the distance, a herd of buffalo foraged the grass and massed cloud overshadowed the bluffs and uplands. *How am I here?*

To his intense dismay, the next morning dawned damp and blustery. It had rained all night, but he insisted that they climb the rock, anxious to finish a section he had started the day before. 'Else you must subtract this day,' he argued.

When Bjornson refused, he pressed him to reconsider. 'You promised me until June,' he said. 'That is still three days away. The sun and wind will dry the granite in no time,' he assured the hesitant Bjornson. 'Harness yourself, if you doubt.'

He worked all morning at a feverish pace, groaning to himself as more imperfections caught his eye. *One more month. He owes me that.*

He was leaning over the brow, carefully chipping a fragment of rock when he heard a cry. He looked up. His companion was nowhere in sight. 'Bjorn?' He walked over to where the Swede had been working on a part of the hump. 'Bjorn?' *Did he go back down?*

He peered over the edge. Bjornson lay sprawled in the grass far below. He stared at his friend for some moments, his mind refusing to acknowledge what he saw. Then he rushed for the steps.

THE WOMEN STOOD IN stricken silence as he heaped the last mounds of grass and earth onto the grave. The day was humid from the recent rain and when he finished, he leaned on the spade, breathing heavily. White Deer had remained stoic and relatively composed during the internment, but now she sank to her knees with a wretched, keening cry. An anguished Meadow Bird placed an arm around her. He was about to read Bjornson's favourite verse, lettered in English on the inside cover of the worn Bible, when White Deer began a sorrowful chant. Her voice, at first low and tremulous, like the soughing of wind in the grass, gained in strength as she farewelled her husband in the timeless manner of her people. He stood listening, his mind drained of emotion.

In the days following the burial, Meadow Bird spent much of her time consoling White Deer , a deep, unspoken sympathy binding the two women ever more closely together. Once, returning from a hunt, he grew unreasonably angry when he found the cabin deserted. Searching for his wife, he forced himself to bite his tongue as he found her suppling a hide alongside White Deer.

'You have a husband to attend to,' he said, his voice sharp.

To escape his thoughts, he busied himself about the derelict stockade—reminded at every turn of the stoic, dependable Swede. He pictured him carrying slop buckets across the yard—Quoi hobbling alongside!—or working steadily with a crew of Frenchmen to re-sod the storehouse roof. He saw him slowly chew his supper, his face pale and serious as he contemplated a remark by Pinch. He saw him look up from repairing a harness or escort a young and blushful White Deer across the yard, Guillaume watching from the steps. And he saw him hesitate, reluctant to climb the wet steps to the top. 'It is too dangerous. Let us come back tomorrow.'

'Ah!' With a loud cry, he struck his fist against the tool shed door.

At his wife's insistence, the grieving White Deer moved into their quarters. The three barely spoke, the women communicating by touch or gesture while occasionally talking softly in Hidatsa or Mandan. Together they prepared the meals and sewed or mended—Meadow Bird all the while maintaining an aloof forbearance that reminded him of her grandmother. He made clumsy efforts to restore the bond between them—praising the venison stew while awkwardly touching her arm or stroking her cheek. She greeted these overtures with a grave compliance while offering no encouragement in return. Indeed, she seemed irritated by his presence in the cabin—once asking why he didn't return to the rock.

He did so, saddling the horse one morning, bitterly contemplating the look of relief he saw cross her face as he agreed to go. He climbed the ladder like a man ascending the scaffold. The summit, bare and windswept, seemed naked and indifferent minus the presence of the faithful, industrious Swede—sometimes whistling, sometimes mumbling to himself, always busy. *You should have been buried here, beneath the buffalo.* 'It is where he belongs,' he had argued, reluctantly yielding to White Deer's insistence that her husband be laid alongside Buffalo Bird and Pinch.

He lost the heart to pick up where his loyal workmate had left off—the chisel still lying in place where Bjornson had dropped it. *Did he slip? Was he preoccupied—taking a careless, backward step?* The mystery haunted him. He sat for hours looking out over the prairie, thoughts churning in his head. Once or twice, he picked up the hammer or a lump of sandstone, half-heartedly smoothing a detail. He even contemplated lowering himself over the towering face, anchoring the pulley and letting the bosun seat down four or five feet. But a fear of being left in suspension, unable to pull himself up again, led him to abandon the notion. Disconsolate, he climbed back down the steps, each one a reminder of shared toil.

'I thought we might go for a walk,' he said to Meadow Bird. 'Will you come with me—along the river?' It was October and the days were pale and hazy with the glow of winter. *'Niir?'* He made the walking sign. She pretended to be busy with the fire and not to hear him.

The door opened and White Deer entered, bearing a bowl of shucked corn, and he stood aside to let her pass. He watched as Meadow Bird reached to take the bowl, saying something that drew a smile from the other woman. The two sat together by the fire, preparing the dried vegetables. He stood and watched for a moment, jealous of their intimacy.

'I am going to check on the horses,' he said, and shut the door behind him.

A few days later, he went down to the Missouri to replenish the log pile. He spent the morning chopping and stripping branches, relishing the cleansing labour. He rested the axe on a branch to catch his breath while looking out across the turbulent flowing river. *I have lost her, too.*

Resentment, driven by guilt and remorse, coursed through him as he attacked the branch, splitting the wood and then splitting it again. Exhausted, he sat down on the shore, reluctant to return to the cabin. A flight of geese flapped overhead, their calls echoing through the translucent autumn skies. Something stirred in the nearby brush and he reached for the musket. Next moment a fox emerged, regarding him with a quizzical look.

'Come!' Acting on impulse, he took some jerky from his pocket and held out his hand, tempting the fox forward. It watched him, its eyes bright and inquisitive, yet wary, its bristles stiffly erect. 'Come!' He leaned forward, hand extended, coaxing it like a domestic pet. The fox took a step back, its gaze wild and impenetrable. Next moment, it was gone, only a rustle in the undergrowth betraying its brief presence.

Bundling the cut logs, he roped them to the sledge and set off back to the post, pulling the sledge behind him. He detected a fleck of snow on the breeze. *It will be hard without Bjorn.*

Entering the stockade, he stopped short in surprise. Meadow Bird and White Deer sat double atop Bjornson's horse as if waiting for him. He set down the axe, perplexed at the sight.

'What is the meaning of this?'

'We go.' Meadow Bird pointed through the open gate. 'Home.'

'But you are home!' Even as he said it, he noticed the stuffed packs on the horse.

'Home. To People.'

White Deer said nothing, her face pale as she sat with arms linked around White Deer.

'I don't understand.' He blinked in the bright, cold sunlight.

'Home. You follow, if want.' With that, White Deer nudged the horse forward.

'Wait?' He seized the rope bridle. 'Are you coming back?'

'*Hii!*' She kicked the mare.

He watched helplessly as the horse plodded off through the gate. Looking straight ahead, the women ventured deeper into the grass, swaying atop the horse. He gazed after them, one hand shielding his eyes until they were no more than shimmering specks in the grassy, wind-swept sea.

## 61

## *And In Thy Labour That Thou Givest*

MEADOW BIRD NEVER RETURNED. He learned from Claim that she had joined White Deer's relatives at a village on the Knife River, moving two or three times in the intervening years.

'She knows where I am,' he insisted, stubbornly rejecting Claim's offers to accompany him to her latest reported camp. Just as stubbornly, he refused his son's pleas to abandon the increasingly derelict post to join him and his family at their lodge on Bear Creek.

'You are here by yourself. The Sioux may come and find you.' Claim sat his favourite, spotted gelding as he made ready to return to his family. He was clad in a simple buckskin shirt and leggings in spite of the cold. A quiver of arrows was tied across his back, and he carried a bow in addition to the musket. His face was lean and brown. Two eagle feathers were stuck through his long flowing hair.

'What is it?' he asked, irritable at the old man's obduracy.

Boundless squinted up at his son. 'You look more like a Mandan with each passing year.'

'I am Mandan. White Bear!' Claim struck his breast, uttering the Mandan name he had adopted.

Boundless sighed. 'Yes, you are. Your mother's image. Now go, Rain Woman will be waiting for you.'

'See sense! You will be warm and well-fed.'

'I am warm now. Aye, and with a full belly, thanks to you.'

'Have it your way, then—you always do!' With a scowl, Claim kicked the gelding into stride.

He watched his son leave, bemused that the fine strapping figure atop the horse had sprung from his loins. *Another buffalo!* With a glance up at the sky, he returned to the run-down house. Psáka, the puppy Claim had brought as a gift, leapt and licked as he bent to fondle it. 'Hello, little frog,' he said. 'It is just you and me now.' He built up the fire and, taking the dog on his lap, sat on the rocker, wrapped in the robe.

He woke to find the puppy growling over a scrap of rawhide. The fire glowed in the grate. Wincing with stiffness, he stood up and placed a log on the embers. He had a dead leg and walked up and down to rid himself of it. He lit the lantern and lay down on the bed as the puppy whined and whimpered on the floor.

'Hush now,' he said. Getting up, he lifted the puppy and brought it into the bed with him, pulling up the robe to cover them both. He lay awake in the candlelit darkness, listening to the prairie wind as it shook and tormented the log walls.

The ensuing winter was as severe as he could remember. Fierce gales blew down what remained of the rear palisade, and a blizzard collapsed the main cabin roof. The same blizzard tore a gap in the roof above his bed, forcing him to abandon the exposed corner and sleep next to the hearth. Shivering with the cold, he made up his mind to forsake the post altogether.

'It is all blown to perdition, anyway,' he said to Claim on the latter's next visit. 'In spring, I intend to build a cabin out near the rock.'

'Why build when you have a warm lodge waiting for you? Perhaps if you came to live with us, then mother might—'

'Might what?' His voice was sharp. 'She has made her choice. In the end, she loved White Deer more than she loved me.' He sat down on the rocker, his face full of resentment.

'You are as hard-headed as that rock!'

The old man chose, or pretended, not to hear. 'In spring,' he said, settling into the chair.

Bored and fretful throughout the winter, he dug through the brass-tipped chest to find his stored logs and journals. The ink in the earliest journals had faded and was hard to read—some parts indecipherable from water damage. He turned the pages, marvelling aloud at each barely recalled incident.

'That is the day we crossed the mountains,' he told the pup snuggled into his lap. 'Mose near drowned! As did I,' he said of another page. Lost in the almost-forgotten raft crossing, he sat and stared into the fire.

'Well-a-day,' he muttered. 'I am old now, older than poor Mose ever was.'

The thought confounded him. He furrowed his brow as another memory tugged.

'What was that Frenchman called?' He stroked the puppy, frowning to recall.

'Perish!' he grumbled. 'It has all gone out of—Louis!' Gleeful at this small triumph, he leaned down to scrabble through the half-a-dozen journals on the floor. Finding the one he wanted, he turned the pages, staring in perplexed wonder at the details of another life.

That night, he dreamed of his days ferrying up and down the Patapsco. So vivid was the dream that he awoke at one point, convinced that he slept on the deck of the shallop. He raised his head to look around for his companions. 'Theo?' he asked of the darkness. The embers glowed in the grate as he listened. After a while, he fell back on the stuffed hide pillow, ruminating if old age was a dream within a dream.

DUCKS SQUAWKED OVERHEAD AND the prairie crocus poked its pale mauve flowers through the melting snow. Claim arrived one wet and windy morning to help him look for a suitable spot for the new cabin. After a day searching out possible sites, they chose a location under a bluff, a half mile from the rock.

'There is a creek,' Claim pointed out. 'And plenty of wood.'

As the days grew milder and longer, they constructed a small, sturdy cabin in the shade of a birch tree grove. He built it to face the rock-buffalo where it stood in the distance. When the cabin was finished, they furnished it with the contents of his quarters, piling everything onto the buckboard of the wagon. Taking the rocker, he set it down just inside the doorway so that it faced the rock. 'It pleases me to look on it,' he said.

Spring turned to summer and he dug a small vegetable patch, using the skills Meadow Bird had taught him. 'Next year, mayhap, this will help fill our bellies,' he said to Psáka as he knelt beside a furrow. He set trap lines in the trees and snared a hare, which he kept for himself, and a squirrel, which he fed to the dog.

One morning, returning from the traps, he spotted a party of Indians in the distance. Hurrying back to the cabin, he fetched the eyeglass and returned to the top of the bluff. The Indians were closer, with no apparent destination in sight as they walked their ponies through the long grass.

'Sioux!' he muttered, scrutinising the lances and war shields. The party stopped to observe the rock, sitting their ponies to stare. 'Keep going, you painted fiends!'

The Indians appeared animated, gesturing and arguing with each other. Finally, one pointed his lance and headed his pony towards the rock. After a short delay, the others followed. He held his breath as they approached, their path sure to take them perilously close to the cabin. His alarm increased as one glanced toward the bluff where he lay hidden.

All at once, the Indians stopped short, their attention turned to some disturbance in the distance. He scanned the horizon but could see nothing beyond the grassy bluffs. The riders appeared agitated and argued briefly, gesturing with their lances. And then the leader suddenly spurred his pony towards whatever had spooked them. The others galloped off in pursuit uttering faint, shrill yelps. *Let us pray they are fleeing the Mandan and have not discovered some poor devil minding his own business.* He shut the glass.

He slept fitfully at night, taking time to adjust to the new cabin. Occasionally, he awoke to some troubling thought or image that pricked or perplexed him as he lay under the robe. Once or twice, he got up to make water or replenish the glowing logs in the fireplace—the dog raising its head to whimper and follow his every move.

One night, awakening from a restless sleep, he opened the cabin door at an hour well past midnight. Wrapped in the buffalo robe, he gazed at the dark form where it slumbered in the distance, silhouetted by starlight. That it was the work of his hands seemed of no consequence as he gazed. That it was his life's work, too, seemed incidental against the great wash of stars. Shivering, he turned away. Returning to the narrow bed, he stared into the darkness, anguish keeping him from sleep as figments of his life nagged at him. 'I had no choice!' he protested. He woke again before dawn, staring into the grey light, his fingers flexing on the heavy robe.

That summer, for the first time in memory, he did not labour on the rock—climbing it just the once to walk cautiously up and down the spine as the wind gusted and birds shrieked overhead.

One fine spring afternoon, a year after abandoning the post, he was outside hoeing the garden when the faint smell of smoke drifted on the air. He walked back and forth to determine the source.

The next day, Claim turned up to announce that a Lakota war party had discovered the stockade. 'They have ransacked it and burned it to the ground,' he said, his voice sober. He waited, hopeful that the news would at last persuade the old man to give up his hermitage and move in with himself and his family.

'Ransacked? What was there left to find but wood and nails?'

'Nevertheless, it cannot be too long before they discover your whereabouts.'

'Let them come! I am too old to move. And I like it here.'

'Stay, then! I expect one day to see your hair hanging from a Sioux lance!'

For the next several nights, he slept with the door stoutly barred and the musket primed and close to hand. In the mornings, he peeped cautiously through cracks in the logs before exiting the cabin to make water. 'Keep watch,' he told Psáka. 'And bark to raise the devil if you smell grease!'

On his way back from the creek one morning, he stumbled and turned his ankle. He limped back to the cabin, his ankle on fire with every step. He eased into the rocker and raised the swollen ankle on a stool, furious at the infirmity. The afternoon shadows lengthened, and the fire burned out. He laid on some more logs and sat in the semi-darkness, too tired to bother lighting the lantern. In spite of the leaping flames, he felt cold. Getting painfully to his feet, he hobbled to the bed to retrieve the buffalo robe. Breathless, he sank back into the chair, the robe pulled around his shoulders. His stomach growled, but he ignored it. The dog chewed noisily on an old bone. 'That is buffalo rib,' he said, causing the dog to stop and stare. 'Mose preferred it above all else.'

He was still hobbling on makeshift crutches a month later when Claim turned up with a sack full of dried jerky and pemmican. 'The winter will be bad, Father. I feel it in my bones. Come home with me. You can return again in the spring. The cabin will still be here.'

'No need. I am well-provisioned.' He pointed to a fresh doe draped across the skinning log. 'I shot her from the door!' he said, his voice triumphant. 'She came down to the creek to drink.'

His leg had recovered sufficiently by autumn to permit him to chop down two saplings and build a considerable wood pile. But the effort exhausted him, and he sat down frequently to catch his breath and rest his ankle.

'I remember old Mose and I chopping a giant tree on the Shenandoah,' he said to the dog. 'Or was it on the Ohio?' He laid the axe across his knees while trying to recall. 'The Shendo!'

That evening, he felt a chill in the air and wrapped himself in the buffalo robe, tightening the sash around him. *I never did learn to sew arms.*

He spent much of the early winter sitting before the blazing fire as the wind raged and deep snow built up around the walls of the cabin. The cramped cabin contained a bed, a small table, two chairs, the rocker he sat in, and the stool beneath his ankle. The floor space was taken up with hides, snares, guns, spare lanterns and bric-a-brac. He had acquired a painted deerskin from Claim and tacked it to the wall above the fireplace. In the dim light, he fancied the painted images to move, a figure on horseback gesturing with a lance. 'My single portrait!' he had said when Claim presented it.

He sat before the fire, idly stroking the dog as he stared into the flames. Something struck him and he got up and rummaged in a corner. 'Where in tar is it?' he muttered. On his knees, he poked among the dried pelts and bundled hides, pushing aside tallow candles, snares and fishhooks.

'Found!' He limped back to the rocker holding a battered volume in hand.

Settled once more, he turned the pages, squinting and frowning his way through the dense, well-thumbed text. To his surprise, the style, once so thorny and impenetrable, now seemed less of an effort. *It limps along, like me!* Turning a page, he lingered over a small drawing of a Greek statue. *My buffalo would trample it!* Prideful at the thought, he put down the book to gaze into the fire.

A fierce blizzard dumped a half-foot of snow around the tiny cabin. The storm howled for the best part of two days. When the shrieking winds subsided, he found himself unable to push open the door, so deeply was the snow piled around the cabin. *Claim will have to burrow to find me.*

Cocooned within the white, suffocating mass, he used a bucket for a toilet while keeping a roaring fire—throwing on additional logs before retiring at night. The reek of smoke from the fire and tallow from the lamp produced a powerful stench that made his eyes water and his head spin. He tried pushing open the door a crack to let in fresh air, but the effort exhausted him and he gave up. The air grew icy cold and he spent much of the day in bed, wrapped in the buffalo robe. The dog lay alongside for additional warmth. He fell into a waking dream during which he fancied himself back in the hold of the *Patience*. He awoke drowning and gasping for breath. The dog licked his hand, whimpering and whining.

During the hours out of bed, he busied himself as best he could—greasing the muskets and sitting before the fire to darn his worn shirts and socks. 'That boy—what in thunder was his name?' He put down the sock to think. Unable to remember, he ruminated on the question as he pushed the awl through the buckskin. 'And that other one—Joseph! What became of him?'

Suddenly furious, he glared at the logs. 'Go yourself! You always were a lazy bones!' In his agitation, he pricked himself with the awl. 'Tarnation!' He sucked his thumb, grimacing and cursing as he picked up another sock. 'He was not my responsibility!' he protested. A log spluttered and sparks flew up. 'I am not to blame!' He set aside the sock, grumbling to himself. He was still protesting at the injustice when his head sunk to his chest and snores disturbed the cabin silence.

A THAW ALLOWED HIM to crack open the cabin door a few inches to let in fresh, cold air. The snow had melted sufficiently for him to hollow a tunnel to the creek, but the effort was so tiring that he took to his bed, falling into a fatigued sleep. When he awoke, it was to find the heaped snow walls had collapsed and the path was blocked again.

A warm southerly allowed him to re-clear the path over the next two days, his heart pounding with the strain.

'By hooky!' Leaning on the shovel, he gasped for breath, his exhalations steaming into the air. Tiny icicles had formed on the hairs of his chin as he looked around at the snow-bound pastures. Panting and huffing, he resumed, shovelling the snow to one side, his eyes misting with the strain.

He had fallen into the habit of talking aloud—querulous and argumentative with himself—as he heated a pan of venison or sat, half-dozing before the fire. 'Come friend, a glass. She will gallop all the way to Balty! Such a villain!' He glared at the burning logs. 'I did it to please her,' he complained on awakening from another doze. 'Mayhap if I had paid more heed, they might not have left,' he conceded. His throat was constricted with phlegm and he gobbed noisily into the fire. *In the end, I disappointed them both.*

A coughing fit awoke him during the night and he lay wheezing under the robe, his breath coming in gasps. Shapes, real or fancied, rose up before him in the darkness. 'Theo!' he cried. 'And Cassidy—Cass! I see you!' He reached out as if to shake hands. Tears filled his eyes. Sterling fellows! Who would know of their fate—of their stoic forbearance and simple good fellowship? Or their trek through the woods—dancing with glee beneath the pigeon cloud?

Grief filled him. What Providence should govern so scrupulously that a glance, a flicked mote from a shirt sleeve, a fish dangling from a line should all pass register as of no more account than particles of grass or leaves floating down from the heights above them as they sailed beneath? The notion infuriated him. 'I remember!' he cried out. 'I am still here!'

At daybreak, he lay in bed until driven to get up by the smouldering fire and the hungry whimpers of the dog. He sat back in the rocker, dozing and waking. Sorrow, mixed with guilt and thickened by self-pity, consumed him with a sudden loathing for his own failures. 'Was it a careless misstep that made him fall?' *"Not a rock but a sacrificial altar!"* Pinch's jibe came back to torment him. A notion possessed him and he got up and went to the door. In the distance, the buffalo rose above the white plain in bleak, solitary splendour. He stared as if seeing it for the first time. *It is a thing made. It has no relation to me.*

And thus, in his confusion and despair, he stumbled upon a truth that divorced him forever from his creation whilst, in the tricksome nature of things, reaffirming his dependence upon it.

IN THE END, IT was the rock that saved him. He had thought himself finished with it—but that summer he returned, drawn by a desire to correct some small deficiencies in the carved stone. As always, the first few days after the winter interregnum left him quickly exhausted, his body needing time to accustom once more to the bending and kneeling. But as the days and weeks passed, the familiar rhythm of climbing, chiselling, smoothing and polishing reasserted itself, directing his body and giving purpose to his hands. And slowly, gradually, his mind reshaped itself to the motions of his limbs, the original vision glowing back to life at the feel of the warm, compact stone. *I am an old man, but a late child of this rock.* Coming upon some imperfection, he passed over the flaw with a sanguine eye. *Bjorn was right. Men will look upon the whole, not the part.*

Claim looked in on him once a week, bringing food and what news there was of the world. 'They had the yellow fever, in Philadelphia,' he said. It was early autumn and he had arrived bearing the gift of a pound of tea secured from a French fur trader in exchange for two prime beaver pelts.

Boundless boiled the tea in a pot over the fire and they sat at the table drinking the brew. Through the open door, the buffalo rose in the distance, sunlight glinting on its sides.

'By thunder!' Boundless smacked his lips in appreciation. 'I had almost forgotten the taste!' He blew on the hot tea. 'I wonder how Prospect is doing?'

'Probably fat and bald by now.' Claim looked around the one-room makeshift dwelling. 'I wonder how you do not get lonesome here.'

A flock of birds flew past the rock, and Boundless shielded his eyes to watch. 'I saw a flock of pigeons once, many years ago, that were so numerous they blotted out the sun. Their numbers were greater even than the buffalo.'

Claim snorted. 'Nothing is greater than the buffalo!'

They sat in silence until Claim spoke again. 'The French trapper—the one who traded for the tea—reckons that the government has passed a law giving slave owners the right to chase runaways wherever they go.'

'When?'

'When what?'

'When did they pass the deuced law?'

'Blamed if I know. A while back. But it's causing a ruckus in the free states. Heck, there's even talk of fighting—of the states going their own way. Ain't it a thing? The country is hardly rid of the British and already the states squabble among themselves.'

He ruminated on this. 'Do you see that?' He motioned to the rock buffalo in the distance.

'I could not help but see it.'

'That is the republic.'

Claim waited for some further elucidation, but none was forthcoming. He wondered if the old man's mind was beginning to drift.

'You ought not climb that rock anymore. What if you slipped, or fell, like Bjornson?'

His father was sitting with his head tilted back, his eyes closed. The thick grey beard, which he no longer bothered to trim, flowed down onto his chest.

'You are too old for it,' added Claim. 'Leave it now. It's done.'

Just when he thought his father had not heard—or had chosen to ignore—the remark, he answered. 'Mayhap it is done, with me. I was only the hand.'

'Sometimes … the way you talk!' Claim drained the last of the tea. 'You've spent half your life atop that fool rock. It's past time—'

'I did not make the buffalo.'

'What? Then who in blazes did?'

'It made me.' He opened his eyes in sudden understanding.

Claim shook his head, defeated. 'You almost broke your ankle that last time.'

'It is a ship.' His father chuckled, a mischievous note in his voice. 'A rock and a ship!'

'How in perdition can a rock be a ship?' Claim grunted in exasperation, certain now that the old man was losing his wits. 'What happens if you fall into the damn creek?'

'It is a riddle,' his father said, provoking.

With a sigh, Claim gave in. 'How? How in tarnation is it a ship?'

'Because it carries me.'

'Carries you? Where?'

'Wherever it goes!' His father cackled and slapped his knee. 'By hooky!'

'I don't have time for such blather! I must be getting back.' Claim got up, irritable at such foolishness. 'I will come by in a week,' he said. 'And I hope not to find you scalped!'

After watching his son ride off, he returned to the cabin. *It is true*, he told himself.

What exactly it was that was true, or the nature such a truth might take, however, escaped him. 'Mercy!' he said, longing to see.

## 62

## A Graven Thing

THE OLD MAN CLIMBED the rock. Every fifth or sixth step, he paused, his breath frail and rasping. Reaching the top step, he halted again, legs trembling from the climb. He lunged upwards, panting and wheezing as he hauled himself up on to the smooth granite. He lay there for a while, catching his breath. The wind gusted as he climbed to his feet, the blast threatening to sweep his scant flesh over the side. Before advancing up the rock, he carefully secured himself to the once-despised safety rope. Thus tethered, he walked slowly up towards the head, his body bent against the wind. He paused before attempting the hump, picking his way up on hands and knees, his body tensed for unexpected gusts.

Once atop the summit, he rarely did much beyond walk up and down, his eye seeking out imperfections in the surface. The hammer and chisels lay in a jute sack, tied to an eyebolt. Every now and then, he took the point chisel to flatten some small protrusion. The effect was hardly noticeable, but he persisted out of habit, finding solace in the repetitive rhythms, and relief from the doubts that tormented him in the bracing prospect.

His favourite pastime was to sit and watch the great herds of buffalo as they returned from their winter feeding grounds. Cackling with glee, he watched as the brown tide washed up against the overhanging rock.

'You cannot shake it!' he hooted, his legs dangling as he looked down on the noisy, bellowing mass.

His eyesight was still sharp and he sat for hours at a time, shielding his gaze to murmur at every disturbance to the undulating swells. When it grew too hot, or when he felt fatigued by the bareness of the empty granite, he made his way back to the steps, forgetting to undo the safety line until brought up with a jerk. He climbed down cautiously, holding fast to the rope sides while noting with dismay the worn fibres and the loose and rotting steps. *They are as rickety as me.*

Once safely back on the grass, he leaned against the rock to catch a breath, his legs shaking with the strain. Looking down, he saw that the seams of one moccasin had split. He studied where his toe poked through the worn and grass-stained leather. *She would scold!* He mulled the thought as he walked through the grass with his dog at his heels.

One task yet remained—to inscribe his name and the names of all who had worked and suffered alongside him. He gave much thought to the undertaking, writing down the names of himself, Bjornson, and their sons. Thinking over the list, he added the names of Meadow Bird, White Deer and Buffalo Bird Woman. *They had a hand in it, too.*

The next day, he added the name of Pinch, chuckling as he pictured the latter's irate scowl at the inclusion.

He ruminated on an inscription, ransacking his memory for a suitable line or verse. *It will be seen in time to come.* The notion pleased him. But try as he might, nothing suitable came to mind. Hoping for inspiration, he moved the rocker outside, enduring the mosquitoes to sit and observe the buffalo as the sun set. He debated with himself whether he preferred to see it at daybreak—rising up out of the mist—or at sunset, when it stood molten-red against the fiery dusk.

In late autumn, he risked climbing it at night to better observe the green, flashing sheets which shimmered over the plains. The coruscating drama made him dizzy and he felt the rock tremble in harmony with the heavenly fires. He imagined himself a speck upon a speck, lost against the vastness of the starry sea. He reached up a hand as though to touch the bright stars, his face etched with yearning. Climbing back down as he grew cold, he sat shivering before the cabin fire, a tortured look in his eyes.

He slept badly, waking often to stare up at the roof, his mind in turmoil as remembered scenes stalked his thoughts. One night, he awoke from a dream of Mose and pictured the grassy mound where he had buried his comrade, wondering if the wooden cross still marked the spot. *Of course it was blown down by the wind ages ago!* He chided himself at his own foolishness. His thoughts roamed to where Pinch and Bjornson and Buffalo Bird lay buried beneath the prairie sod, along with Quoi and one other whose name or face he could not now recall. Troubled by the fact, he lamented to himself in the darkness. 'And when I am gone, who will remember their names?'

Following a restless slumber, he got up before dawn, fumbling for the journal in the semi-darkness. Sitting down at the table, he wrote by the light of the glowing embers—dipping the quill and writing quickly so as to capture the dream-inspired epitaph: 'For those that sleep in the dust.'

'We shall all be joined in the endless grass,' he thought, pondering what he had written. The notion comforted him as he put away the ink. Returning to bed, he slept soundly until late morning. After a breakfast of jerky, he walked out to the rock and picked out a spot just above eye level where the stone was smooth and polished by wind and time. But the day was cold and gusty, a norther blowing through the grass. *Tomorrow*, he told himself.

But before he could put hand to the task, winter rode in on an avalanche of snow. *It will wait until next spring.* But when spring returned, he put the inscription on hold in favour of long, meandering walks through the fresh prairie grass. He stopped every now and then to look up at the buffalo-likeness, as if confounded to find it standing there.

Once, Claim rode up to find him holding out a bunch of grass shoots before a suspicious buffalo cow, encouraging her to feed from his hands.

'Are you mad?' Claim berated his father while angrily shooing off the buffalo. 'That cow could have spiked you clean through! She had a calf with her.'

'I thought I might feed her.' His father's voice was mild with disappointment.

'Rain Woman made you some pemmican and smoked fish.' Claim took down the sack from the horse. 'That buff might have run you clean through!' he said, angry again. He took his father by the arm, shocked at how thin it felt. The old man's flesh had been pared down to the bone.

'I don't want you living out here by yourself anymore,' he scolded. 'Mother would have a fit.'

'Mother?' The word perplexed him for a moment. 'Ah! Your mother?'

Claim stared, perplexed. 'Whose mother did you think I meant?'

Boundless chuckled. 'The mother of us all.' He was looking up at the buffalo. 'Did you see Maurice?' he asked.

'Who?'

'Maurice, the head clerk?'

His son looked at him strangely. 'You do not remember? He died some fifteen years back.'

'He did?' Tears sprang to his eyes. 'How?' He clutched his son's arm as though it were important.

'How? Old age, I guess.'

'He didn't have a buffalo to suckle him, to keep him young.' He resumed walking, leaning on his son's arm.

'You must promise me, Father—never to go up there again.'

He made a sound in his throat that could have been such a promise.

But he did climb it again, one last time in early summer. The day was warm and mild, a beguiling breeze rustling the stalks. A fierce pride gripped him as he gazed up at the great beast: emblem of the republic, guardian of its future, benign overseer of the grass and the world itself. He climbed the worn ladder, wheezing for breath as the rungs swayed dangerously beneath him.

He stood on the summit, a serene look on his face as he turned in a circle to survey the blooming grasslands. An ache, part gladness, part sorrow, clutched at his heart. *One day I will not be here and still you will bloom again in spring. But not I.* The thought both pained and comforted him. In the great turn of the world, he would be dust, part of the grass. In that sense he, too, would bloom again. He thought of Bjornson and smiled. *You did not need to go to Paradise, Bjorn. It is right here, where we are.*

Great white thunderheads drifted across the sky, their towering heights shadowed in the bluffs and uplands. Wind rippled the bounteous grass; birds shrieked and squabbled as they wheeled in the sky.

'Ah!' He gazed longingly at the splendid prospect as the voice within that had prompted, whispered and insisted ever since childhood fell silent, as if at last heard.

THE WINTER WAS THE worst in years. Icy winds whipped the plain, freezing exposed flesh in minutes. Howling blizzards dumped two feet of snow on the grasslands, perishing those animals that had neglected to flee south. For two weeks, Claim was unable to leave the lodge to check on his father's welfare. Increasingly anxious about the old man, he risked setting out on a day of blustery winds, sub-zero temperatures and blowing snow.

He travelled along the frozen Missouri, using the dog team to drag a sledge of provisions. The snow blew into his eyes and the cold knifed through his clothes, the foul weather making him determined to bring his father with him on the return journey. Leaving the Missouri, he trekked inland, whipping the dogs in his haste. When the snowbound cabin finally met his eyes, he exclaimed in alarm. No smoke issued from the roof pipe and the door stood partly open. 'Git!' He urged the dogs onward.

'Father!' He shoved the door open against the pile of drifted snow within. 'Father!'

The old man was lying on the bed, wrapped in the robe, his face pale, his arm dropped to one side. 'Father!' He bent over, listening for breath or any signs of life. He felt for the pulse, feeling it weak and erratic beneath his fingers. The skin was cold, but a faint warmth signalled that life yet flowed. 'Father! Can you hear me?'

The old man opened his eyes, seeming to take a moment to recognise him. 'Claim?' The voice was weak and uncertain.

'I'm taking you home with me. Can you get up?'

'Wait! I meant …' He wheezed for breath, his chest heaving. 'The buffalo! I meant to carve—'

'You did! You carved the buffalo!'

Swaddling his father in the tattered robe, he carried him out to the sled. The old man's hair was long and unkempt, the bushy beard flowing over the robe. Swathed in fur, he seemed as much animal as human. *He has become the thing he worshipped.* The thought surprised him yet gratified with its aptness. He tied a rope to secure his father to the boards. He watched closely for signs that he still breathed, relieved when he saw the chest rise and fall beneath the robe. He was trying to say something, struggling feebly against the rope restraint.

'What is it?' Claim knelt by the sledge, pressing his ear close. He felt his father's hand clutch his arm, the fingers that had once split rock now weak and grasping.

The old man's voice was feeble, the words the merest puff in Claim's ear. Tears were in his eyes. 'It was—' he gasped for breath. 'It was shining!'

'What was? Father! What was?'

But the old man appeared exhausted from the effort of speaking. His eyes closed and his head slumped against the boards.

Claim stood up, determined to get them back to the lodge as quickly as the weather would allow. The wind had whipped up again and he briefly worried whether to risk travel. *It will be easier once we reach the ice.* He cracked the whip. 'Git!' The sled jerked forward as the dogs strained to pull, noses to the snow. The wind gusted and the sled bounced as it got underway. He glanced behind him. The old man appeared to be sleeping, his fur-wrapped limbs passive under the restraints.

They passed under the lee of the great beast as it looked stonily westwards, the muscled foreparts braced against the blustery, temporal elements. A blast of wind blew snow from the icy brow, the powder swirling around the frozen nostrils.

'Git!' He flicked the whip as the dogs panted and yelped. The trail they had cut from the river had already vanished. He bent his head to the gale, anxious to reach the surety of the river ice. Soon they were swallowed up in the dense, swirling whiteness. In their wake, the immense, bestriding beast loomed through the blizzard before it, too, vanished in the tempest of blinding snow.

*The Fur Post* concludes the second part of *Monuments of Grass*, a five-book series charting the creation story of one man's epic vision and its unfolding over time. The five books in the series are *Exile*, *The Fur Post*, *The Claim*, *New France*, and *Voyages of Discovery*. Print copies can be ordered online through bookstores, libraries, and online retailers such as Amazon. The series is also available in eBook format.